KISUMU

Okang's Ooko was born in Rusinga Island, Lake Victoria in Kenya and grew up in the seventies and eighties in Kisumu. He is the author of Kisumu, *When You Sing To The Fishe*s and *Tandawuoya*. *Businesswoman's Fault* is a collection of seven stories.

Find out more about Okang'a Ooko by looking at his own author website
www.okangaooko.com

Also by Okang'a Ooko

Businesswoman's Fault

When You Sing To The Fishes

Tandawuoya

KISUMU

Okang'a Ooko

oba kunta octopus

AUTHOR'S NOTE

This book is a work of fiction. All names and characters are either invented or used fictitiously. Because some of the stories play against the historical backdrop of the last three decades, the reader may recognize certain actual figures that played their parts in the 1970s and 1980s. It is my hope that none of these figures have been misrepresented. The historical events and accounts based on real occurrences are merely used to enrich the plot. Any resemblance to actual events or locales or persons, living or dead, is entirely coincidental.

Typeset in Nairobi by Mikozaba (Mikono Za Baraka – Gifted Hands) Cover design by 'Ondiek Marach' Kwach Rakido Okang'a Kwach Rakido © www.obakunta.co.ke

ISBN: 978-9966-093-52-3
KDP ISBN: 9781521902578

This paperback edition is printed and bound in Kenya by Oba Kunta Octopus

For further information regarding special discounts for bulk purchases, please contact Okang'a Ooko Special Sales at +254 733 826 811 email address: **info@okangaooko.com**

For my fellow Kisumuans.
For the life we live here.
Living for the next day.
For childhood and fun and growing up.
Here in Kisumu We're old men today
After all these years.

Kisumuans still we are.

For Dr. Stephen Mogere.
A Good Man.

Contents

PANDPIERI

RUSSIA. You are probably thinking of Russia, that old and cold country up there somewhere in the map: you're wrong; it's not the one. It's our very own Russia down here in Kisumu. Well, it's our biggest hospital and my father says the Russians made it.

The year was coming to an end; it was now October, the 25th day. The year hadn't gone unabashed, er—Tom Mboya's recent killing in Nairobi two months ago felt like yesterday and hearts were still heavy. I couldn't wait to step into 1970 and go to class 6 and forget. We were singing *Kenya Nchi Yetu Tunaipenda Sana* on the side of the big *lam* road near Kibuye and waving. Our President was here in Kisumu this day to open Russia. The former vice president Jaramogi Oginga Odinga was in Russia too. We were singing but with these two mighty men, things were still and tense. There was a sound. Suddenly. A sound bigger than one thousand voices singing. An ugly sound. A sound which broke the harmony of ten thousand singing voices and broke hell loose.

Bang!

Then another bang. And more bangs.

Magak grabbed me by the shirt collar and sent me flying. 'Run!' He then grabbed Oliver and did him likewise.

I ran. We ran.

A scream there was suddenly leashing out loudly, propelling me to bolt faster just as a gray cloud of confusion closed up the roadside to Russia. I saw Magak's *afuong'o* swirl as he dived

1

through a small opening in the *ojuok*, his shoulder hitting/ skidding on the ground. He came up with a stout tree limb and bashed the first higher vertebrate he landed into. He spun around, got on his feet and scurried away.

I followed, Oliver followed me.

Bang! Bang! Bang!

And suddenly everyone was running for their lives. People were running as fast as they could with the air filled with swishing sounds over their heads. I saw two fellow Std 4 pupils fall onto the ground but I couldn't stop to find out what had happened to them. The sound of blasting terror was getting nearer and nearer. I looked back and saw a long convoy of fast moving cars and army lorries rushing towards Ahero on the great Nairobi highway. Pupils, some hurt and bleeding, kept falling down as we continued to run through the town towards our school.

Chaos ruled Kisumu. Confusion set in rudely... lots and lots and lots (and lots!) of confusion and movements and crying and groaning and wailing and running. In the sky there were planes. Military planes. *Ndeke jolweny*, the kind we normally saw at Kandege. Pupils were wailing and screaming and running amok. Dogs were barking and cows were mooing and goats were bleating. The skies, too, had taken on a strange color. The sun looked down and got so scared it hid behind the clouds.

Turning around, I dashed my foot over a tree limb which snagged me, spraining my ankle somewhat as well as pinning me. Suddenly, a major disturbance erupted—an ugly noise of something coming. Oliver shouted at me. I barely had time enough to duck out of the way, seriously wrenching my ankle as I did so. I rolled over and pressed my back against Magak and Oliver. It came close! It was a truck! A big truck, not one of those big yellow MOW trucks, no. This one was a huge over-sized army truck. And watch out! It was going to run us down. I struggled wildly like an animal in a snare, pulled my foot lose and rolled double.

2

The behemoth Mercedes Benz truck roared past with its rack blaring fire and belching smoke and dust. In it were men in army uniform with guns, firing. The men shrieked and made horrible hissing sounds. Along with the shrieks, they sprayed bullets at us school children.

Magak picked up a piece of Kimbo tin and hurled it at the firing men as the truck drew away.

'Who are those? What are those things?' asked Oliver in an excited girlish voice after the vehicle has passed.

'Guns. Soldiers,' Magak decreed. 'And they kill people. Run.'

As we took to, something suddenly fell in front of me with a plop. It was a black plastic can. It fell with a warbling sound and started fizzling and producing a lot of smoke.

'Tear gas!' Magak shouted, 'Tear gas!'

More cans landed. They were burbling and spitting real bad. They were covered with a reddish funky slime; they were gross and speckled with dark specks and smelled horrendous and a lot like those burst MCK sewers near Anderson. The air begun to stifle and become unbearable. There was a lot of coughing and sputtering, gagging and choking. I'd heard of tear gas before, had seen them in mobile *filims* at Nyalenda Railway open grounds. Didn't ever dream I'd have these terrifying things thrown at me. We were wiping our eyes and coughing our lungs out. Men were on their hands and knees sputtering, cursing and coughing and hurling and trying their best to get their senses back. We kids coughed our lungs out. Afterwards we were trembling and frightened out of our wits.

When finally the truck had gone and the sounds of guns had died and calm had returned, we came back to our senses and begun to inquire excitedly about what had happened. Many pupils had been shot, many of them badly.

How did this happen? I remember education officers having brought miniature *'Kenya Nchi Yetu'* paper flags which were given to every upper primary school pupils who were requested to go and line by the roadside to wave at President who had come around to Kisumu to open Russia.

My father had been unhappy about the President's coming here. You see, it was barely three months since *they* shot and killed Mboya on a Nairobi street like a dog. People were still angry and groggy and sad. Mboya's body was still fresh in the ground in Rusinga. We were still mourning here in Kisumu. My father had a bad feeling the President's coming. 'There will be bloodshed,' he had said. *'Yawa ji biro tho yawa.'* He was right.

On my way back home I met many injured people who appeared to be lost and dazed. People were talking and asking questions. 'Call it official opening of Russia by the President,' one man said

His colleague answered. 'For sure there is to be a story about it in the newspapers and on the radio. But Oginga...'

'Is he killed?'

'I don't know, *yawa*, I don't know. *Ma masira mangongo.'*

I hurried home to find my brothers looking for me. They hastily grabbed me and hushed me up.

2.

But just before midnight—

It was no better.

Terror had always reigned here in Nyalenda and Pandpieri. Tonight it was horror. Mama had a horrible headache. It took a few minutes to gain some semblance of her senses. Then she sat up and started praying. Fear held its grip. The night was accompanied with occasional ugly sounds and wailing. We could hear sounds of doors being kicked and crashed and heart-rending screams of women and children. Our father was not home and with her eyes shut, our mother prayed with great emotion, all blame heaped on the good deed our father had committed himself to as one of Oginga's men. But there was no denying the fear that was hanging over Kisumu like a wet blanket, no denying the feeling or the compulsion to pray.

My mouth was dry, sticky, and downright icky. The only sound was of the whining gnats and mosquitoes playing havoc on us. A slight feeling of nausea begun to surge and the pesky need to go pee began to pressure me, but I dared not get up.

Where was our father? This was the question my brothers kept asking. Ouru was weeping, Odingo tried to comfort him. Keya kept clicking his tongue against the roof of his mouth. A slight ringing in my ear confounded me, my eyes were itching, and my body was on fire. Nothing concrete came to me about what had happened and why I was lucky just to remember how I had come to be alive.

As the webs of cob became untangled, I realized Mama was scared (and it horrified me). Had the men with guns tracked our father down? Was he killed? Arrested?

Too many questions, too little answers.

After a time, Mama got up, checked on us (as if to reconfirm all her children were still alive) then left to go sit in the dark in the sitting room and resume her silent but intense prayers. Our family attended church now and then every once in a while; we were SDAs but not devote. I knew how bad death was, today I had seen it. It was an unfortunate thing to have happened, but the other results would have been more disastrous had Magak not been available—like getting arrested, getting shot on spot near Ofafa etc. Now the unpleasant chilled my blood, the thought that our father may have been killed. I knew that wherever my father was, he was alive—and of course, he wouldn't dare die and leave us. Fathers don't die... our father was such a strong man with six lower front teeth removed in *our* ritual of manhood. He was a man his family honoured and was proud to boast about. Not one to be the cause of family strife. Somehow over the years he had entered into many abhorred occupations, first as Tom Mboya's youth winger and later as Oginga's operative in KPU (Oginga's party). *Wuora* loved politics. He was tough and rough and he loved to take active part in things politics.

The death of many people I had seen today was upsetting, but I couldn't understand what it was.

But right now I had bigger worries: *was our father safe?* Something was wrong. My heart pounded and my mind thought up all sorts of things. Surely, though, if something serious had happened to our father then we will be in serious danger.

Mama had stopped her prayers for a breathing spell. She came to the dark room where we boys lay wide-eyed. She talked to us softly, told us to pray. I didn't want to pray. I wanted to be mad.

Then we heard something. Suddenly we all froze. We all crept into the living room.

Fading moonlight drenched the room in just enough light to allow us to see the time on the grandfather clock on the wall: it was now 1pm.

'I hear something,' Ouru whispered.

Then footsteps. Then nothing.

Pausing for a *long* while we listened intently.

Nothing. Then footsteps again, loud enough.

We knew it was our father and Mama hastily got up to open the front door. My father entered huffing and sweating, he hastily told us all not to fear.

Mama was shaking. Shaking real bad, not crying; just shaking as if in a trance. '*Wuon Keya,*' she kept saying. 'God is merciful.' The cobwebs of deadly fear still inundated her creating a blind spot (literally) blocking her peripheral vision allowing her to only see directly ahead in a hazy shape kind of view. As in her mind and in her faith with God, it was; therefore, dark everywhere else.

Our father tried to get a grip on the situation. Trying to gather himself was difficult. He failed. He tried to hold Mama but she wouldn't let him. She was too confused; she could scarcely move—scarcely think.

Then we knew what was to follow: *Ogwang and his men.* Senior Chief Ogwang was everyone's pet peeve here in Pandpieri, in Nyalenda and other parts of rural Kisumu. I remember seeing him once when he came for my father in a *sirkal* Land Rover. He was a stout man with large arms and hawk eyes and he carried a two-headed *boka rao* (hippo skin whip). It was widely known with terror that if he caned you once he would have caned you twice. We had grown up under the terrifying spell of the great chief. My father's association with *Kapu* had made him Ogwang's favourite fiend. At this time, Oginga was the most awesome being that lived. Oginga was big and enormous and he had a new name: Jaramogi. He was legendary and mystical and larger than our world. According to our father, Oginga was bigger than *sirkal* (the Government).

Ogwang was the great fearsome chief and on the side of the Government. To us, he was the enemy.

As expected, Ogwang and his men made their visit to our house that night. There were two Land Rovers, one belonging to the *kanga*, administration police; the other was Ogwang's. We were shocked beyond disbelief to see Ogwang himself alighting from the Landy. I saw him. I saw his big arms and his two-headed *boka rao* whip and his evil grin.

In the darkness, the great Senior Chief swept the haphazard throng of people thronging outside aside like *odundu* reeds as panic begun to surge due to his appearance. The policemen accompanying him made a search, conducted an 'investigation' which was chasing away the onlookers and scaring our barking dogs. Then my father was ordered to lie down. My father did so—but not first taking in Ogwang, giving him a look full of hate.

Ogwang spoke. *'Ne akweri, wuod Nyangao K'Odundo ni iweri gi siasa Oginga Ajuma Ja-Kang'o. Siasa mar kech.'* He spoke softly and kindly, but we could all see the devil. His very presence evoked diabolical fear. This night, as we watched, us boys screaming at the top of our voices and Mama wailing, and our dogs barking, Ogwang made my father, Odundo son of Mbaja, lie down and severely caned him with his *boka rao*. Twenty strokes. I counted. I saw my father, a strong man who worked long nights in the lake... a real *onagi* Luo male with six missing lower front

7

teeth totally humiliated. We saw him wailing like a woman.

Ogwang was a land-dwelling monster. I was convinced. I hated him. We all hated him. Everybody in Nyalenda and Pandpieri hated him. But I never hated him the way I hated him now.

They took my father away and locked him in Kodiaga, the dreaded prison. Two nights later, Ogwang returned. He returned to tell my mother to warn my father to keep off Oginga's politics.

My father was released two weeks later and Mama praised God. You see, my mother was pregnant and there were horrible rumours and whispers about what they did to political prisoners at Kodiaga that freaked everybody here in Kisumu. Mama's fear had swelled (to new heights) with the fear that her husband's proper lack of faith was surely leading him down a path of darkness and indignity among other things. She had a duty to save him, to save her children, her family as a whole. Well, our father returned and Mama made him sit down. We saw Mama with tears streaming down her face screaming at my father to stop all his associations with *Kapu*; she had given him five boys to take care of, hadn't she? And now there was a sixth child coming: this one in her belly. What did he want from this life creating danger for himself and putting his family in danger engaging in Oginga's *siasa ma onge tich* (useless politics)? Being picked up by Ogwang's men all the time and locked up? What was this politics thing with Oginga taking him? She wanted him to stop all political associations with *Kapu* and she wanted him to swear to her that he won't go back into discreet night meetings with *Kapu's* men. And she wanted him to start keeping Sabbath like he used to. Failure to which she will leave him. Yes, she will take her five boys and go back to Kanyakwar, to her parents. On and on my mother ranted, her voice pitching higher and higher amid tears and she terrified us to death. My father said not a word, he sat there on his favourite sofa, head down, and shoulder slouched, elbows on his knees.

And each time I saw my mother quarrel my father like this, I felt rotten.

Kisumu, days later.

Things returned to normal and we returned to school with many stories about Kenyatta, the Russia shooting and about Mboya assassination and about Oginga. In our school, many stories were swapped about the Russia fracas. One boy had a bullet shot through his buttocks, the other was shot across the mouth while shouting and two others got shot on the arms. Others had suffered injuries ranging from sprained ankles, cuts from barbed wires etc. Many pupils had gotten lost with the fleeing crowds. We heard it said the day following massacre people saw the largest pile of shoes never before seen here in Kisumu. The nightmare continued as much as the confusion and absurdity. Curfew was imposed on our town, and with it came police brutality. Everything was scary: the large contingent of GSU camping at the Kisumu Stadium after the President's departure was scary. There were horrifying tales told about these *majoni* men; about what they did to men and women in their houses. We heard blood chilling tales of what the *majonis* did to women *in front of their children!*

There was a very sad story told of a man who had run to his home several kilometers away only to collapse and die on reaching home due to exhaustion. Indians had been watching the fracas from their balconies, they got shot too. But those shot most were school children who had turned out to welcome the president. Most of them had refused to go away from the road when the ministry of education personnel, on realising that all was not well, drove along Nairobi road asking the children to go home.

Stories come, spewed forth. We heard many weird stories about how Oginga turned himself into a bird and flew when the shooters wanted to shoot him. Other boys said he turned into a housefly. Earlier on in the year when they had shot and killed Tom Mboya, we heard many stories about how it happened and who did it and why they did it.

Well, Kisumuans soon put it behind. Mama went back to her

9

routine of walking twelve kilometers each day to work at our family shop, Rusinga Island General Store, on the corner of Kendu Lane and Odera Street and my father went back to riding his bicycle to Ogongo, to work as fishing net artisan and going to watch football matches between Kisumu Hot Stars and Black Stars at the Kisumu Municipal Stadium during Saturday afternoons. He never stopped his activities with *Kapu* either, he never stopped meeting Oginga's men.

3.

One year rolled by but it was the same world here in Kisumu. Life was the same, people continued to milk fear out of their recovery and Kisumuans tried hard to move on with their problems. The town was not much the same—lame. It was swelling, more people, more buildings, more businesses, more people. This tidy town of ours was named Port Florence in 1900 when Florence Preston the wife of the engineer drove the last nail in the last sleeper. Since then, this tidy town of ours didn't see itself "advancing" or backtracking further into history. 1970 Kisumu town, Kenya was a nice place to be. Many people were moving in from the rural areas. There was a Jamhuri Day we went to Kandege to see the World War II vintage airfield staging air shows and old aircraft acrobatics over the lake. The event was also a big boon because the few white men who were still remaining in town after Independence were the ones who performed those acrobatic air shows. We delighted in seeing the old noisy Beechcraft airplanes landing in the lake.

Once in a while we loved to venture out of Pandpieri to go into Kisumu town and it was a nice, the streets were clean and rolled up early. There were big Indian *dukas* with nice things in them. Hotels, bars with music, two cinemas, the Post Office, huge buildings, churches and such as the likes that there was—so much for a town. Kisumu tried to maintain its small town appeal, keeping out the riffraff and maintaining the 'family orientated' atmosphere. Many folk were indifferent to the growing-town appeal, except of; course, us kids. And there were new things to gape at. There was a new television at Kisumu Social Centre— *Sosial*. There were new cars we loved to stand at the roadside gaping at—Cortinas, Citroens, Peugeot 404! And Mercedes Benz! They were mostly driven by rich *wahindis* and some *wazungu* although *wazungus* mostly drove Land Rovers.

Africans rode bicycles or walked on foot and it was normal.

Our family was a growing family in Pandpieri as were some other families—we had cousins and many, many relatives staying with us. We had friends in school. We loved to gatecrash nice weekly Indian parties and got to eat some of the nicest foods we'd ever eaten, full of spices but tasting like heaven.

One bright morning, our little brother was born in Russia and our father named him Tom. He was named so to remind us of the horrific and vile, vile, vile, poignant torture we went through after *they* killed Mboya in Nairobi *on the street!* Tom Mboya's death had brought blessings. Mama said that judging by the baby boy boom in Nyanza this year, our Mboya had not really died. He had returned to us in many forms. Many of the children were boys; all were Tom Mboyas by default. Nearly every household had a Tom Mboya. For many it was just Tom, for others it was Thomas Joseph Mboya while for others it was Tom Mboya Odhiambo. We even had T.J. Mboyas.

Another boy was named Russia and he reminded us of how school kids were shot here in Kisumu during the opening of our hospital.

We heard it in the news that *Kapu* had been banned because of the Russia riots. Our father took it badly. When they had the chance, my father and his colleague Dimba got their friends and they attended *Kapu's* meetings where they badmouthed the Government and Kanu all day. Nobody could come to terms with the fact that what happened in Russia that day last year really happened. It riled our father, but his mind was clearing and so maybe he could accept it— fake being normal. Mama used to advise him to decide whether he was going walk the pipe dream to escort Oginga to be president or be a realist and go to church and repent, forget politics. Then he'll be on the right footing as a father and a husband.

Anyway, growing up on the outskirts of Kisumu, I was your typical bad boy. Maybe even too typical. I was just another wee-wee bare foot, horny-toed boy growing up with my dusty feet and bare chest here in Pandpieri. Days of our lives were made up of going to the lake to swim or fish, throwing stones at crocs and jeering at hippos, chasing wild ducks and geese the whole day and watching naked women bathing (as long as it wasn't our mother!) It was cool to hide with the boys in the bushes near Dunga shores watching women as they bathed in the lake, getting excited seeing all the naked female bodies. Of course I loved going hunting in the bush with our dogs, then coming back home for a beating. I got many of Mama's harsh scolding and cheek slaps those days.

Mama did not call me dense, stubborn and hard-headed for nothing. She claimed they were my father' traits and I seemed to have gotten them in greater quantities than the rest of my brothers and sisters. I never understood Mama all the time. Mama was the most philandering lady of the house: she was mean, ornery and cantankerous. My mother was from Kanyakwar, the place where strong women of Kano were made. Kano people had fought battles with the Kipsigis and were warlike. Mama was particularly harsh on me and my brothers Ouru and Agwenge. The three of us were a pack and seemed to cause most trouble. My two older brothers, Keya and Odingo were the first pair. They were much older than us... there was a five year gap between me (the third born) and Odingo (the second born). Keya and Odingo had manners, they were reserved and, being teenagers, they had the respect of my parents. The one who was respected most was Odingo and it was decided that he had good brains. But Odingo and Keya were close, independent and had their freedom. They had their own room and they never ate with us, they ate together on their own. The second pack (me, Ouru and Agwenge) were always watched. Hardly a day passed without one of us causing trouble and Keya and Odingo had been given permission by Mama to punish us in case we caused trouble both inside and outside the home.

We lived in this rumbling relic we called 'Fort Jesus'. It was our home, really... the only home we knew. My father's family had long moved from Rusinga Island in South Nyanza, down to Pandpieri here in Kisumu, or, in the vernacular of old sailors of wind and water, up to Pandpieri—(as the Dunga shores more or less favoured the prevailing South Nyanza winds). Until the post-Colonial dawn of the new era, one didn't have to go down into the depths of South Nyanza unless they were nuts and wanted to die. South Nyanza was a deep, wild and primitive land teeming with diseases and epidemics and wild animals.

Life was modest; it was like we were faced with a lifetime of genteel penury. We still preserved fire (because Mama said match sticks were expensive). Our night visitors were night runners and mosquitoes. We still had to trek many miles to *Sosial* to watch television; we had no electricity! And there were rats; there indeed were these pesky rodents in Fort Jesus. Hundreds. We had a rat trap and our cat, but it didn't help. The rats keep breeding. And there are bugs. They were loud and unseen and just a little spooky—along with being annoying. Mosquitoes and other insects loved to make their presence known along with assorted pesky pests. *Chwarni, olwenda....* you know them. Rats, roaches and bugs.

Kimbo was the only cooking fat we knew and there were many things we couldn't make with the tin once the cooking fat in it was used up. We could turn into a drinking cup, we could flatten the tin and cut it into pieces and make Safari Rally cars. Or we could sell it to Njoroge the scrap metal dealer of Kamas.

Growing up here in Pandpieri, really, singled out the joy of living very close to Lake Victoria and more experiences came in

13

form of many bizarre stories our parents told us. The favourite one was the tale of my grandfather Nyangao and our house in Pandpieri.

Parts of Mama's fantastic story began to resurface. As fresh air unlocked doors, as dark night skies opened for us to see the stars, darker stories came from the lips of our father about our house to haunt us for years. My father, Odundo son of Mbaja was a fishing net artisan at the big Indian fishing company down at Dunga. We called him *Wuora*, as any Luo kid calls their father. It was the most common and respectful way of addressing him. He worked with Ogongo Fishing. He got the job because he was an excellent swimmer and he did not fear the dreaded lake. Here's how he got the job: he had this story we loved to hear of how he rescued Mr. Khan's son from drowning when their vessel *MV Kisumu* hit the rocks near Hippo Point and ripped it's bottoms and started sinking. My father and some Dunga young men were there swimming or fishing. He single-handedly saved the six crew members of the vessel, including Mr. Khan's son and he was later employed Mr. Khan. Mr. Khan, himself, was an old merchant fisherman who made his wealth from Lake Victoria mainly as a transporter of goods to Tanganyika. My father took me to Mr. Khan's office once. It was all in the motif of all things 'nautical'; rigging rope, nets, life vest, life rings, spears, and portholes. Out in his backyard he had a small scale fishing trawler that served as a playhouse for his grandchildren.

Coming from Dunga you passed Nyamedha Centre as you headed to a small bushland on the bosom of Nanga. Up on a lofty hilltop you saw a white house that stood tall. That was Fort Jesus. Many found Dunga wastelands incorrigible. But you'd be something of a fool to judge an apparent wasteland by its narrow, humpy bridge. For all most people knew, the white house on the hill with its trimmest dooryards sheltered the darkest secrets because for the many years a lonely Whiteman lived there. Take it as an article of faith that the house on the hill, indeed, harboured deep dark secrets. I'm about to tell you about Fort Jesus, our

14

house.

Odundo son of Mbaja had inherited this house from his father, Nyangao K'Odundo, who had fought in the Second World War. When he came back after the war, my grandfather was not very right in the head and he didn't live long. When I was born in Old Nyanza General in 1960, my grandfather was already on the brink of retirement from the same hospital and, by the time I was old enough to communicate with him, we both had shocks of weak thin hair: mine burgeoning, sun-bleached and vibrant; his weary, washed-out yet worldly and wise.

According to my father, my grandfather Nyangao was a very strong man, well-built and muscular during his youth. He had been born here and lived his entire life in the town of Port Florence, eventually seeing its name changed from Port Florence to Kisumu. He had extraordinary powers that baffled the *wazungu* who had only a few years ago reached Kisumu with the completion of the Uganda Railway line. He was also known as Nyangao Magere, a name he gave to himself after the legendary Lwanda Magere. He claimed he had been a very tough warrior in Lwanda Magere's army and would boast of the many *jolang'o* people he had killed during the Luo-Kipsigis wars. Indians who had been used by the British to build the railway had settled in the small town of Port Florence by then and had set up shops where they were selling sugar, salt, flour, grains and textiles to Africans.

When Nyangao's first wife gave birth to her first born Okal Bongo, it was said my grandfather went to one of the Indian shops and carried one sack of sugar and a sack of *unga* which he brought to my grandmother who had just given birth. Nyangao then went to a herd of cattle kept by the white men for dairy products and chose a huge bull which he strangled and carried on his head to my grandmother. Then came Nyangao's time to marry his second wife. He was escorted to his in-laws by a few of his age mates where they were to sleep overnight. It was said that the following day Nyangao could not be seen anywhere and the granary was also missing. Nyangao had disappeared with the granary and the marriage had to be called off. Nyangao continued to steal thereafter from the Indian shops until one day he was arrested by the white and Indian police. He was given his wish to sleep with his second wife and my father was conceived.

For his punishment, my grandfather Nyangao was forced to join the British army. Nyangao fought in Egypt, Burma, India and some countries whose names I have forgotten. Like many others who had fought the British wars, my grandfather was mentally unstable right from the time I knew him when I was a small child. When my grandfather returned, he went to work for a wealthy Englishman known as Mr. Patterson as a cook. Mr. Patterson was himself a Second World War veteran and was very fond of my grandfather. He had acquired many acres of land near Lake Victoria and built his home in Pandpieri.

When Mr. Patterson died, he was survived by his younger brother, Mark who did not live long after the death of his brother. My grandpa inherited large tracts of land which were later grabbed by his first son, my uncle Okal Bongo. His second wife (my real grandmother) Mbaja Nyar Ogam had run away to go and live with her brother Okech Ominde when my grandfather became mad and his sons became hostile to her since she had only one child (my father) who was very young. Our aunt Binda and her husband also had inherited a large part of grandpa's land which they later sold to the Kisiis and that's the reason for the large number of Kisiis in our village. Okal also did the same. The two later migrated to Kabondo and Kajulu respectively after disposing of my grandfather's land for as cheap as 600 Shillings for an acre. Okal migrated after his home was struck by lightning killing several of his children. He later died in Kajulu where by the time of his death he had no land.

By the time my father Odundo son of Mbaja of had come of age, the only thing he got was the ten acre parcel upon which our house stands. The house and the land upon which it stands survived because my grandfather was still alive and was said to be a lunatic. I remember as young boys we used to provoke my grandfather into outbursts by calling his name loud. Calling him Magere was something that would rile my grandfather. He never forgot and would give chase whenever he met you in the village path. He lived for a long time until his death in 1966. Unfortunately my grandfather's grave cannot be traced now because his cousins sold the grave along with the land where the Kisiis later built the low-income tenement dwellings of Pandpieri. Those who sold my grandfather Nyangao's land to the Kisiis with abandon have since all died mysterious deaths. Was it a curse?

Well, we got the house.

Patterson's house on hill overlooking the shores became the family gaff. We called it Fort Jesus because it resembled something we had seen in history books. The huge fortress sat on a nice lot with lots of room for our animals. On one side was a large corral enclosure while the other had mostly black cotton soil and some lawn, a few fruit trees, a cactus garden, and a lot of openness. One of our bulls, Jowi, was a big beast who won the best prize at ASK in 1967, handsome and gallant. Two other bulls, one a *dichol*, were just as nice-big BIG animals who fathered many calves. There, too, were sheep and a lots chickens and roosters. My father hated goats, found them messy and hard to control.

We had now accommodated the new arrival into our family of seven; Tom the little, noisy infant. Tom Mboya Odhiambo became the eighth member and the sixth child. Another boy! All over Pandpieri, people whispered and wondered after Odundo son of Mbaja's virility. To keep on getting boys year after year! The family was growing, many of our cousins and aunts had come to stay with us, so babysitting Tom was not a problem and Mama had no need for a *japidi*.

4.
And it came to pass—

Schools were closed for long December holidays and whenever schools closed, it was time to play. With school finally a done deal, it was time to frolic. Not like we hadn't been frolicking already, but. There were family issues and romping with the family for that togetherness bullshit, then, as the parents returned to their jobs, the kids romped on their own.

As it happened, a few things happened.

The gang was made of Magak, Tut, Oliver, Opoko Kiguru (who was a disabled moron), Joginder, Onyango Shika Dame, Anton Othwele, Gonzaga, Otieno 'Kachweya', my kid bro Ouru, Rose Bonyo and Okello Mariko. These were not just school friends; they were not just Pandpieri kids. They were Kisumu normal kids. Otieno 'Kachweya' came from Makasembo, Gonzaga lived in Pembe Tatu near Kibuye and Onyango Shika Dame came all the way from Nairobi Area in Kondele.

But Pandpieri was the center of action. All the boys down here were troublemakers or got into trouble in various assorted ways; stone throwing; window breaking; raiding the homes of Indians and stealing fruits—with real *umbwa kali* dogs in hot pursuit (I mean very fierce big dogs); bike riding—also not their own but borrowed for the use of their joyriding; watching bathing women at Dunga; pushing freaky little kids in the water and laughing as we watched them drink *adila* and then saving them from near-death experiences (I didn't know how to swim myself); scavenging for edibles at *kataka*; fighting; transporting liquor; shoplifting. None of the previous offenses were outlandish, just 'good ole boys' in the back-country trying to have some fun.

Magak was from the village. He was a stout boy with pug face and bad teeth. He was aggressive in nature, a bully, no nonsense, a sneak, a liar, talk smacker, sassy, and a whole line of extras to follow. He was from far and had no relatives besides his parents. He actually hailed from South Nyanza and had only moved with his parents to Kisumu at an early age just prior to his teen years.

All but me, Anton and Rose Bonyo were eight year old *totos*. Rose Bonyo was nine and could pass for eight. She was the skinniest and tallest. Magak was the so-so leader of the group, although Gonza tried to assert himself as the boss one time. Got one hell of a wallop. Magak and Onyango Shika Dame were cousins. Oliver and his sister Achi were twins. Joginder, who most often went by 'Poker Joker' unless in trouble with his parents or teachers, was the whiner of the group—over cautious. He also delved into being a bit of a rebel, ran away from school to catch wild ducks at the nearby lake, etc. Did a short spell at the Children's Remand Home near Rotary.

Oliver and Achi. Oliver was older by two minutes. He was a bit bossy at times, but deeply cared for his sister. He and sister Achi got into some hellacious arguments—but always made up—usually by a food fight. Achienge (full name) was beginning to admire fashions and sensible shoes at Kashmir next to Nyanza Cinema.

There were nicknames and then there were kiddy names—some were cute, some were curt, some were HORRIBLE!? Some names were descriptive; like, Magak 'Lwanda'—'cause the kid was built like The Incredible Hulk. Or Joginder, because the kid from Makasembo liked mimicking Safari Rally cars, imagined he was a Rally driver. One moment he was Bjorn Waldergard, the next he was Vic Preston Jnr. We called him Joginder. We used nicknames to fool our teachers and parents. Other names were forms of affection or derogatory in nature. For instance do you know how Panyako Onyango became known as Onyango Shika Dame? Orchestra Lipua Lipua from Zaïre had a hit song called 'Nouvelle Generation' which had a sweet dance sequence in its *sebene* and an animation chant that went like: *Koyaka pamba te, sukuma ha!* We didn't know what that word meant, so we twisted it in our own language and now it went like this: *Onyango shika dame, kamata ha! Ae Mama!* Other names were associated to the owner's physique. Omondi 'Wiye Duong' belonged to that large headed kid from Upper Railway; 'Kachweya' meant 'Fatso' and was for Otieno who, apart from being overweight, was a boy of 'weighty' issues. We also called him 'Fat and Furious' because he was easily

19

flared up. Nyadundo was for any person who was height challenged.

OTC—his given name by fact, encountered a young lad who was unaware his nickname referred to something most of us here in Kisumu found disgusting. OTC. It was actually the initials of his three names, Owen Timothy Chacha. He was part Kuria part Luo; a happy kid of eleven, seriously into soccer, liked adventure, and was just starting to 'notice' girls. OTC, ha! To us his name meant Onyango Twende Choo. OTC was the serious one of the team; jolly mannered, easy to get along with. Both parents were Kuria-Luos with his grandparents being directly from Kuria land and living with their children, OTC's parents. He spoke the language of both lands, played soccer like Pele, and was keenly interested in music; strumming imaginary guitar and whistling with his eyes closed... stuff like that.

Magak 'Lwanda' was a happy-go-lucky kid, hard as a nail, a fighter—liked to bully kids—and ate as many *gobits* as grownups. A rough kid, he volunteered to help out others wherever there was any beating to be done and food to be grabbed or some cents to be made. Yeah. He liked to use us to make the extra shilling. Nearly killed my brother Ouru once.

Dorothy 'Dorry' Adhiambo was a nice looking girl who had beautiful features; supple beginning titties, a very pretty face, a curious girl who was going to be a beautiful woman one day. Her cousin Okello Mariko, tall, slim, bighead, ten, was the oldest boy in the pack. He looked like a Somali; actually he could have been a Somali who was raised as one of us. Thick-headed and nearly always at the bottom of the class, he repeated class four every successive year. We found him in class four and by the time we moved to class five this year, he luckily came with us. Okello was a troubled kid, a quasi-orphan. His father, Otieno Ja Yien, was a renowned tree cutter from Nanga and Nyalenda. Otieno was a buddy of our father. He worked in entire logs, focusing so exquisitely on the twines and twists of wood grain and you wondered how anyone had the temerity to cut down such huge

20

tress and dismember them, sort out the stuff, much less the snarled-up birds, snakes, squirrels and bugs that came down with the falling trees. He normally carried the dismembered pieces in his *othiwi* to Kibuye where he had a big yard. He was a good humuored man who told us great stories about old Kisumu. And he knew all the places: Nyalenda, Pandpieri, Kabakran, Kasale, Kamas, Obaria, Kichinjio, Dho Chiro, Otonglo, Nyawita, Mamboleo, Kodiaga, Obunga, Pap Ndege, Kibuye, Dunga, Dho Nam, Kamakoha and Manyatta Gonda... these were the newest features and names in Kisumu town and these were the places we loved to plod over in the midday sun.

Thick headed as he was, Okello was the perfect host whenever we visited him at their 'home' and not only set his father's watch dogs at ease with his witty chatter and charming ways, but his cheerful step mother cooked *ogira* for us, too. His family lived in the perfect human habitation, a ramshackle *mabati* house in Nyalenda that managed to bore a visitor off the face of the earth ten seconds after stepping through the front door. It was clean enough and neat enough to assure the guest that all personal belongings were kept out of doors due to lack of space, and, if the housekeeping could otherwise be called low-key, the reason seemed to be that the home was furnished with wooden furniture and wooden beds and wooden coffee table. Everything was made of wood. Obviously the family was more into making its living from wood, which was a good thing because selling *omena* (which everyone was doing) was a young fisherman's occupation and one really didn't want to do something else they weren't good in as a life's vocation, if possible. That was why Okello's step mother sold charcoal in Nyalenda. Okello's older brother, Olwande, was a carpenter. You see, this was a pretty woody family.

Now with schools nearly opening, December holidays were seeping away past Christmas and a new year was around the corner. We had no time. We hated the idea of school again. Soon all the fun was going to disappear and there would be homework to be done and mean-gutted teachers to obey. These last days of freedom were good... outings were good with clear skies, a light breeze, and a flat out landscape to trudge out to in the outer boundary.

When we didn't want to go to the lake, we found ourselves going down to the Kachok playground and generally doing things kids everywhere do. Trips across Nyalenda Railway flats to the *kataka* dumping ground near Kisumu Municipal Stadium to scavenge were a special treat for us.

Today it was Oliver's idea that we 'adventure' across the Nanga meadow to some nearby hills and forest searching for Nanga EAR on new year's eve.

Magak squinted his eyes and made rude facial expressions, nodding that the idea did sound appealing. In this company of best friends were Tut, me, OTC, Otieno 'Kachweya', Anton, Oliver, Gonza, Rose, and Akoth. Plus some special girls—Susy Anyango and Dorry among them. Normally, usually, girls of any age, just didn't 'go off' adventuring. Normally, usually, things didn't turn out well for those who did. But this was the Dunga country, not the town of Kisumu. Most 'bad things' didn't happen in Dunga. Sure, bad elements were just about everywhere but in the countryside it was deemed 'safe enough.' So, we ventured off across a huge well overgrown meadow to seek fortune. We ventured off looking for some hidden or abandoned train depot called Nanga EAR.

The landscape out from the Fort Jesus hill was mostly flat, a few dips and small-small hills; large tracts of meadows with multiple vegetation in various forms, including shrubs and small diameter trees. The lake was out that way, out past Nanga Canyon—another 50 kilometres or so. A colonial military base was still here, a small 'town', a rinky-dink Leyland truck nestled up against the lake land (sound odd?) and not much else. A new direction was needed. The derelict military base was a no-go zone. We could miss the cabin by the creepy bush land. There was that abandoned mine, too. It was certain there was a story there, a mystery to solve.

A few boulders, too, dotted the landscape within the distance surrounding the entire sector rolling lush hills on three sides with an incredible dense forest in the fourth position. It was to the forest that Magak was leading us, each time out he wanted to go a little further, if only one or two hours further.

Reaching the forest took some hours, more with Otieno Kachweya's intermittent breaks. Once reaching the forest for the first time, Magak took a moment or two to give it a good look-see. He then got Tut and Gonza to hold position while he took a brief trek inside.

There was some degree of raised alertness as traipsing off alone usually meant more adventuring than wanted. A few steps inside the forest and Magak looked back. Behind me, Gonza sat on a small boulder with Tut nervously watching and waiting for Magak to 'disappear.'

The forest was, for all intents and purposes, spooky. Dense, deep, and not too fresh. A lingering odor indiscernible filled the still sullen air. Not a sound there was, either. Thick layers of moss clung to the massive trees; the trees were nothing like we kids have ever seen, but closely resembled abomination along with giant things. A deep ancient forest it was, we all assumed. Untouched with many of the trees and shrubs unknown to man. After a few minutes the air was noticeably cool. There were birds chirping, far up in the great height of the trees. Squirrels and monkeys fluttered about the bark of the trees. Somewhere deeper a branch fell to the moss covered forest floor. It made very little sound as it hit.

The near silence unnerved Magak. He closed his eyes, wrenched his fist tight and held his breath. Was it the footstep of an ogre? A personal encounter with an ogre brought on by his foolish antics in the other world, worlds? A sort of punishment? The silence was deafening, if that made sense.

There was nothing.

He dared not move from where he had come in,

wandering away from the 'entry point' could be unwise.

Presently, a creature appeared. A creature that was hairy and stood on its hind legs like a human.

'It's an ogre,' whispered Oliver.

'No, it's just a baboon,' said Joginder who had a book on animals.

'*Bim nyajuola.*'

'*Nyasadi?*'

'*Nyasadi?*'

'*Nyasachiel.*'

It was the first time I had seen a baboon. It opened its mouth and you can imagine the sound that came forth.

We ran. Run, ran and ran. Till we got out of breath and just walked. We didn't know where we were. Oliver led the group out of the bramble bush field. Once done so Oliver checked over who was hurt and how badly damaged they were. Mostly it was sprains and scratches. There was a significant amount of itching going on, the spores from the bushes.

'I think we need to get to water.' Gonza said. '*Wadhi uru nam.*'

'This way!' Anton spoke up. And again, Oliver led the way. Till we saw the lake. A gulf there was, lined with soft moss and clover. The gulf spanned six feet wide and some three feet deep. It wasn't powerfully rushing like the lake it extended from. Small and medium sizes trees there were, chirping birds and warm sunshine.

'We've got to get out of our clothes.' Magak told the group.

The girls and boys of the group looked at one another. They were covered in gunk that was turning brown and something like burnt sienna. It was sticky and was becoming difficult to peel off.

There didn't seem to be a lot of willingness to jump to the suggestion.

Magak did, though. He was naked in seconds and in the

creek in no time. The girls were awed. Oliver stripped down and got into the creek himself, sitting down and scrubbing off the goo.

The girls and boys on the shore continued to look at one another, I decided to shirk modesty as the itching was too much. I stripped off my clothes and basically fell into the creek. My companions on the shore giggled at my antics. Akoth refused to look. Dorry's eyes fluttered, someone farted—someone giggled.

Something to think about...

The others, after their giggling, looked to one another again, bit their lips and decided to put the modesty issue to one side— long enough to wash off their bodies anyways.

Otieno "Fatso" needed help, undressing and getting into the water. Tut helped him. The girls were busy with themselves. Oliver emerged from the water in all his nudity. The girls were growing a little frightened eyeing his little dangling thing. Susy closed her eyes, shaking her head. Gonza and Tut were next in the water watched— and watched. Susy gulped, blinked her eyes and shook her head.

Akoth, too, shook her head and looked highly confused.

'Easy—relax.' OTC cooed to the girls. He looked to the others to see how they would react. They waited, virtually clinging to the ground.

Magak walked towards Dorry. She eyed his thing and traveled her eyes up to lock on his face—then back to his naked thing. Dorry had never seen such a thing, she had seen little boys and boys her age, but seeing this one so close held her. Her mouth hung open. Tut watched with his eyes wide, Magak didn't seem to care one way or the other and gave a mere bemused look as Dorry turned away and started undressing.

Akoth was awed at the nude likes of the others, Rose and Sussy the same—and she instantly knew that she and her friends were in the company of depraved kids.

When the preteen girls stood up (and gave the 'don't look at us' command, no one took them seriously. In fact, OTC smiled and gingerly helped the girls out of their clothes, taking care not to frighten them (too much) and not 'touching' any of their personal parts. All the boys were curious and took sneaking peeks at the nude girls in the water. I was most curious about the girl's clothes—their 'underwear' specifically. I could see no underwear.

Like us boys, none of the girls had underwear.

Afterwards the girls were helped into the creek—Gonza and Oliver quickly averting their eyes. Akoth was his *good* friend.

Dorry and Rose surreptitiously came out of their clothes and eased themselves into the water. We were all eyes! I blinked my eyes and felt suddenly ill—a huge wave of warmth kissed my young body all over and then—THEN I felt like something was pulling me—pushing me to go stand up behind the naked girls. Dorry was blessed pretty breasts. It was the first time I had seen a girl's naked breasts. The water was cold and quickly caused the girls to shriek.

I gulped, shrugged, and begun to sweat. I was confused, and embarrassed. It was awkward—way clumsy, but having the girls naked was steaming the boys. No one looked to one another as they bathed—the cold water very much eased our pesky scratching from the bush spores.

The four girls huddled near together bathing and trying to be inconspicuous. The boys, though, were shy and, on the sly, stealing furtive glances at the girls. Magak and Anton were to themselves, but close at hand just the same.

Dorry maintained a confused state of being aware and not aware complicated by thoughts that were not hers but then again, her 'don't look at me please' and 'you shouldn't see us naked, it's not right' warnings along with 'you boys promise not to tell anyone in school next term please' were ignored by all.

Then there was the little matter of their clothes.

They needed washing, too.

Oliver sat on the sandy shore. OTC had come out—the water was getting a bit much overbearing. He collected his clothes and gave them a few dunks to wash off the dirt. A good wringing out, another dunk and rinse and then laid them out to hopefully dry in the sun. The girls gave him subtle quick looks and giggled.

'Come on out,' OTC spoke to the girls. 'Get your clothes washed off so they'll dry in the sun.' Logic and presence of commanding/ demanding voice in a tone of authority. It could be done the easy way with the girls acting on their own— or the hard way with the girls NOT acting on their own. Either way suited OTC.

Rosey found that her sprained ankle was no longer sprained. Gonza offered her a hand out of the water. She avoided direct eye-to-eye contact with the boy-man. Sitting down somewhat shielding herself she gathered her clothes.

There was a goodly amount of vegetation at the shore; typical plants along with plants that thrived in water. The shoreline was shallow but enough to immerse oneself in and be refreshed. Along with the freshness of the water there, too, was the aroma of fish. Specifically the *omena*. Of course, there was a fish landing beach nearby so it went without saying (that the air was sullen with the scent of fresh fish).

It didn't bother Magak. He loved water, he normally stayed longer in the water, long after we had finished swimming and lay on the sand to warm ourselves; long after the warming sun on our skins and the sand became hot prompting us to put our clothes on. He relaxed nakedly in the water until hearing one of the girls whining fairly close by. It was a tiring and trying thing to manipulate the girls and get them naked but it was a done deal. I knew Magak and Gonza still wanted to be naughty-naughty-naughty together. But I knew he won't try something stupid likely 'seducing' Dorry or Susy or Akoth. Magak was proud of his accomplishment.

'Let's go home,' Otieno called out.

Magak's heart, though, was still holding firm for them— he wasn't ready to part with the girls. Their time was coming, though, that was sure. But in the meantime—

'What about the mines?' Oliver asked.

'Another day, *wuod Abandu*. I don't want your mother to cane you again today. Let's go.'

We all laughed at Oliver

'Where do we go from here?' asked Tut.

'*Jamna*,' answered Magak. '*Jamna* or *kataka*. I'm hungry.'

We knew with dread what he meant. *Jamna* meant going to Milimani to steal mangoes. Indians were wonderful people with great wealth and even though they lived in Milimani near Pandpieri, their homes were enclosed with very high fences. They planted all types of fruits: dates, *jamna*, mangoes, *zambarau* and others which were very sweet. The Indians also kept very fierce dogs that were a deterrent to mango thieves but once in a while when hunger took hold of our bellies, we could be daring enough to climb the high fences to steal mangoes. It was Magak's favourite dangerous adventure. Last time we did it, Otieno Kachweya was nearly mauled by a dog. On another of the escapades I and a group of children managed to steal as many unripe mangoes as we could from one of the homes. Afraid that older boys would take them from us by force, we decided to sit under a tree to eat our stolen loot. We ate our fill and left for home with distended stomachs. That night my stomach grew so big and tight I could hardly breathe. Fearing that I was going to die, my mother went for my grandmother who came with her tobacco pipe which she used to tap my stomach several times. When she finally left, I was exhausted and soon fell asleep. When I woke up the following day the stomach had come back to its normal size but I had to a new problem. I spent many hours in the toilet 'diarrhearing' my *nyimbich* out.

Blinking sweat out of my eyes, I said, '*Kataka*.'

5.

It was January again. Schools were going to open in three days and we are sad. Couldn't believe I was in class six now.

Pandpieri Primary School was the factory where my young brain was constantly fed with all sorts of things. But, alas! School was the slaughterhouse ruled by the lordly tyrannical masters: the teachers. Caning was the order of the day, one you could not escape in a single day. It started with lateness: gate was locked at 8.00am and prefects were always there to round up all the late pupils who will be caned by the master on duty. If you escaped that, you had more shocks in the real slaughter house: the classroom. The first trap was always homework, and all those who didn't complete their homework were required to lie down for *kiboko* to land on their buttocks. Okay, maybe you had done your homework, yes. But still you still weren't safe: chances were very high that you'd gotten some answers wrong. What then? Punishment, of course. Then of your name was found on the noisemaker list. Or your hair wasn't well combed or your teeth weren't brushed. Or your school shirt was torn. Or you didn't know an answer to a question when asked to raise your hands and say them during lessons. Or the class monitor had some grudge against you.

Caning was something we got used to. Some subjects were too difficult. But mathematics, Lord Have Mercy. Maths made me a little woozy. It was only obvious that something was amiss with me. Whatever it was I was keeping it to himself. I was not good at all in mathematics. As a matter of fact I hated maths. In fact maths lessons were dreaded dangerous episodes. Everything had been good with addition and subtraction. Then we got in std 4 and now had this very horrible teacher, Mr. Omolo, who started us on multiplication and division and I knew I will go no further from here. Every morning before he started his lessons, Mr. Omolo came up with what he referred to as mental arithmetic. Unfortunately the desk I shared with Oliver and another kid was in the front row and I was normally expected to answer the first mental sum. Man, I hated multiplication. Man, it scared the living daylights out of me. I normally got it wrong attracting several school rule hits on my clean shaven head.

Oliver looked panicky at me that I didn't know the answer to 7x7. 49, someone whispered and I began to be more calm. Mr. Omolo debated his next move—he had to check on the kids not to help me out. So he asked me to stand up.

'9x9?'

I knew I was done for. More gulping, sweating, hesitating, trying not to answer but ultimately revealing the fact that he'd very much exposed to the whole class how stupid I was. I knew I wasn't stupid. I was good in English and History. But that didn't stop the laughter from the whole class. I was humiliated to death.

'81,' someone whispered.

I was about to smile when it happened. Mr. Omolo went ballistic and I had a fit.

A few scant years and we were in class six. I was in *upper primary* and I was certainly well 'schooled'. I felt I had been in school for so long. We knew all the rules than ran our school. For instance, if you didn't sing 'Mungu yu mwema' in RE class, then it was not RE. Everything we found absurd could be made into fun. The fattest boy in our class this year was a Kikuyu kid called Kibira. *Kimbo Cowboy Kibira kachweya,* came the new song.

Our accents, our experiences in school, our fumbling attempts in the social scene, the teachers that caned us from time to time – politicians, our friends' parents, TV programs... you name it.

Hahahaha. Hohohoho. Hehehehe.

I wished our teachers knew the dangerous gossip we swapped about them. 100% per cent of the stuff we traded about our teachers was BAD, of course. NASTY. It was designed to get back at them for punishing us.

Every day when morning sessions ended and hunger bit our bellies, we sang rude silly songs. *Naskia sauti, sauti ya mama... sasa ni saa sita, mwalimu kwa herii* was the lunch time melody.

But perhaps the funniest stuff was the 'kuchanukaring' that happened to us when were kids trying to feel much more sophisticated than we were. We developed monstrous imaginations in lip expression! We could turn every song and every word to mean what we wanted. And this was more than fun, it was an indulgence. We found a word, any word. Then we gave it a new meaning, or we turned it into an acronym and cooked up what stood for. We wrote it down in our exercise books and passed it around and set it on fire, cast it into the wind and crammed it onto every kid's lips. For instance, in Magak's books, you could you guess what the word KENYA stood for? I won't tell you this one, it's too loaded. We could only whisper it. This was a time we had just left the '60s, remember and we could get as wild as we could because we were now in the 1970! The '70s brought exciting newness. We knew we were getting into a tougher world. Tougher than going to see Joghinder Sigh and Safari Rally at Sikh Union. My brother, Ouru, had softer versions for what Kenya stands for. This we could say without fear as long the teachers didn't get to know. Here goes: *Kiss Everybody Near Your Area.* Hohohoho. Kenya. Alice Wamboi the clever Number One Girl had this one: *Keep Everything Nice Yet Arousing.* I wondered where she got that one. She was a clever girl, clever and demure.

The 'baddest' boys, remember were Magak, Tut, Oliver, Gonza and Onyango Shika Dame who had silly, contaminated brains.

All we could think about was sex... sex that was far away in reality and which only existed in our dreams and in our fantasies. We were young and bursting with youth and knowledge and imagination far beyond. Look at what Gonza had to say about sex and love:

Love without sex is like tea without sugar.

We believed this, imagine.

We were not even in adolescence, yet we knew more... much more. We; thus, had invented crazy coined-word stuff. Our schools badge depicted a wild boar with its tusks showing. Wild boars or pigs, if you like, used to roam the fields of Pandpieri and we used it see them when I was in class two. We used to hunt them which, really, was not to kill them; just to chase them into the bushes with our dogs. Later on they disappeared. They were either pushed further by encroaching human population or eaten into extinction. These beasts had tusks, and those tusks found their way into our school's emblem. We called our badge Tusker because it had an image of two protruding tusks. Tusker now had other meanings *T....teachers U...union S....should K...keep E...education R....running.* Kisumu Municipality Council was abbreviated as MCK. We turned it to mean *Mon Chodo Kaloleni* (Women prostituting in Kaloleni) Kaloleni was that old slum place near Lumumba and Shauri Moyo famous for *chang'aa,* busaa *and* prostitution. There, too, were other assorted images of the naughty kind filling our young mind; such as:

Tusker: Teenager Under Sixteen Kiss Even Rats
SMILE: Sweet Memories In Lip Expression.
BYE: Beside You Every time.
KISS: Kenya Industry of Sex Services!
KISUMU: Kisses In Sex Undermine Men's Urge
MATHS: Mental abuse to healthy students

Know who made most of these? Gonza. Apart from Magak and Oliver, Gonzaga Gonza was the other kid who had most influence on us this year. He was smarter, funnier, worldlier and bolder. His lofty sense of humour got me mesmerized all the time. So funny he was he could make a dog laugh. He knew everything that had to be known about anything. Every kid wanted to stick with Gonza. When you went to soccer, girls he was there, in Safari Rally he was there, in cinemas he was there. He was in everything. If you plotted anything with Gonza, it all went according to plan. I normally hung out with Gonza and I'd come out with really bad education and brain mutilation, and I was anything but compliant. Gonza didn't come from a strict household like ours, his parents had given him so much freedom.

Well, look at the latest from Gonza's filthy mind. To him L.O.V.E stood for *Lies Of Various Entries*. And LUST? *Lies Upon Something Terrible*. Gonza had more sleazy stuff in his book. Some were too gross I won't tell. But sample these:

KIMBO: Kiss Is My Best Occupation
SUSAN : Sex Usually Starts At Night
AGNES : African Girls Never Enjoy Sex
OTC: Onyango Twende Choo
BOMBAY: Both of My Breasts Are Yours
FANTA : Foolish Africans Never Take Alcohol!

6.

On Friday afternoons I was normally sent to Dunga to get fish and stuff from our father for Sabbath preparation. Once in a while, I got bike rides from Rose Bonyo's father who was always going to Pandpieri SDA to prepare the church for Sabbath. At the church, the haven of heavenly activity, Mama had encountered Rosey's mother, Nyaimbo or Min Rosey. I liked Nyaimbo, she was different—a modern woman, looked older than Mama. Looked refined and spoke a few English words. I found her more beautiful than my mother. The woman was friendly and was always chatty. She wanted to get my father involved in the church, in the capacity of working for God; to have him involved in lesson studies, utilize his skills as a craftsman to help refurbish some cabins up in a nook of the hills where the church could retreat to for camp meetings or so—for couples, for married, and of course for children. Rosey was their eldest child and they lived about two kilometers from our home. Rosey's father was a deacon and ran a marriage counseling class at the church and worked as a *ja on kitepe*, selling SDA books door to door.

I loved Rosey's pa's bicycle rides. Once around the bend of the rough looking shoreline land, there was a downgrade; he never got as far as the dusty Kochola corner. He dropped me off somewhere close to Kochola, gave me a ten cent to buy sugarcane from the women traders. Then he hoped on his bike, took a right and continued on towards Pandpieri SDA.

There were dirt roads about the flat land area leading to different places, one leading to one place or another—somewhere. There were two 'splits' on the road, the first one sent drivers and walkers on a roundabout traverse back to the main dusty road—it was a big circle for no particular reason. There were many off-roads to the various fish landing beaches in the area to Nanga and Casablanca and the open world out there but mostly Junction Kochola made a 10 kilometer round trip on itself.

The other split from the junction ran off along the shoreline to Milimani and Hippo Point and to Kisumu town. It was confusing. Only the locals knew the differences of the 'splits'.

I was a local.

The sun scorched the land and did doubly on the cracked paved road. On the right Nyabende farmlands stretched and dipped toward the faraway lake; craggy, chipped, and formidable. To the other side stood up smaller hills casting off more heat like from Okello Mariko's father's charcoal oven. The heat of the day was just about unbearable. Just about—and traipsing about the long dirt road was no fun. I walked in the hot sun sweating and chewing sugarcane until I could smell the lake. It was a long walk but I was used to it. I reached Dunga with rivers of sweat cascading down my neck.

A stiff breeze brought a myriad fishy smells and odors. Dunga normally smelled that way; it was a fish center and a strong smell of fish was overbearing. There were gulls swooping with the wind, and hawks, crows and *onyinjo* birds scavenging for *omena* spread on white fishing nets next to the lake. Little boys were always chasing the birds while women fish traders haggled endlessly with fishermen. Then there was the sound of the lake with waves breaking and crashing, and sights of boys swimming and shouting. There were great many canoes pulled up on the beach, and Okoth the artist was always at work painting and decorating new canoes. My father had taught him. My father was an artist on the side and took contracts to paint and decorate new canoes. He got many of such contracts during his youth painting canoes and decorating them with owners' portraits and helping the owners come up with names for their boats. But now after getting employment at Ogongo, he had left it all to Okoth.

The road to my father's workplace went out to 'nowhere.' It seemed to swoop right into the lake. To the right was flat land with small rolling hills that segued to larger hills and large groves of trees. To the left was Lake Victoria. It was possible that a better road was near at hand. Not likely, but possible.

A large open space there was right on the shore. One lone tree stood right on the edge of the lake behind a couple of boulders and a fire pit where Indians families came to party by day and witches and night runners meet to plan and strategise by night, and that was it. Soon afterwards, I spotted the hand-painted sheet metal decorating the perimeter of the place where my father worked. But a fence I could see, an enclosed place with huge neat buildings. A chain link fence topped with razor wire surrounded the place. The large signboard reads 'Lake Victoria Ogongo Fish Processing Ltd.' There were lots of *wazungus* and *Wahindi* here in wonderful cars. This was also the research centre where they were breeding *mbuta* (Nile perch) to be introduced into Lake Victoria, my father had told us.

I found my father and Dimba in a blue Chevy truck that was parked by the gate. Today something was wrong. My father Odundo son of Mbaja was in a foul mood.

'You're late, boy!' he bleated in his gruff voice.

Dimba the driver shined him on, smiling and showing very white large teeth. 'Go easy on the boy,' he told my father. 'Can't you see? He walked all the way from Pandpieri and—'

'Go with him.' And the gruff burly son of Mbaja got off the truck and stomped off. 'Yard.'

'Get in kid,' Dimba said. He opened the passenger door and I climbed in. The yard was a large-large gravel/dirt speck with warehouses, a parking lot here, a loading dock there, an outdoor grading and sorting belt.

'Wait here, *ojana*,' Dimba said, jumped off the truck and went away. I sat in the truck watching people moving about for close to two hours, till darkness seeped in. Presently my father and Dimba came, got into the truck and fired it up and moved it to another bay and, after opening the rear doors, returned to the front seat to let the dock workers unload as he had been instructed by my father.

'Let's go,' my father ordered Dimba. 'Drive, *wuod Gem*.'

It wasn't a far stretch of the mind to believe that something 'funny' was going on. In the floorboard of the passenger seat, two packages lay, wrapping in sisal gunnies. It was covered up by a tarpaulin and other assorted cargo van crap to conceal it. My father sneered—as long as he didn't get busted for it—whatever it was.

My father was always smuggling things from Ogongo. The unloading took just a few minutes. Then Dimba eased the truck out of the premises, past the gates and down the natty road into Dunga. Afterwards, my father slapped Dimba's chest with one of the gunny wrappings.

'This is for your wife,' chipped my father. 'Go!' he snarled.

But Dimba wasn't fooled. My father was obviously trying to dump him.

'I'm taking you home, *omera* son of Mbaja,' he said.

'*Aya!* Let me drive then, *wuod Gem*,' my father said. He grabbed the van keys from Dimba and pushes him away. 'Get out. Go around. Get in.'

Dimba gave my father a God-awful look, went round and got into the passenger seat. I squeezed myself in between them. And soon we were bouncing down a dusty dirty poof dirt rain rutted lakeside road. The big suspension in truck lessened the effects of being bounced to death. It looked like we had taken a different road, but I was not sure.

Not until making a long turn and coming up on a small hill; then, a few kilometers out there was the great outcropping of boulders— the only prominent object in view was the lake, the magnificent 'city of lights' created by omena fishermen across the end of the lake and the enveloping darkness.

My father floored the truck and literally flew off the road into a field and the van tumbled over the rugged and broken earth. With no 'road' to speak off he plunged ahead slip-sliding along, the wheels of the old truck spinning sending the truck smashing against trees and bushes as it tried reverently to negotiate the woods.

My heart was pounding as we cut through a maize field. As the truck rushed over the rugged earth, the knot in my stomach increased in seemingly tensile strength. My mind swam with horrendous thoughts, none of them very good—about my father's crazy driving and wondering where we were going in such a great hurry. I knew all this had to do with me.

At length there was a reprieve as the truck lumbered over a hill that slopped down. Below was a shore. It was a woodsy road, dirty and rocky but a road nonetheless. It was also soaked with the recent rains.

The truck slid sideways down onto a clearing in the bushes and Dimba clicked his tongue against the roof of his mouth with distress. We made it as far as the end of where the earth met the water. There was a great boulder surrounded by huge deciduous trees and bushes. Finally the truck stopped. It was dark but I knew the place: it was Lela, the dreaded rocky beach. Waves were pounding and the wind was harsh.

My father and Dimba got out of the truck and moved to one side. A conversation there was between the two, it took a while for me to get it but the gist seemed to be of a slight rift between the two— Dimba stood back by the lakes' edge against the a boulder, he seemed nervous somewhat, arms folded across his chest, shifting his weight.

'My son needs an education,' I heard my father say. He

turned and walked towards me. His eyes narrowed the way they normally did when he was about to pass judgment. 'I understand your testicles have filled your hand,' he said in an aggravated huff. 'That you're now a man. Let's find out. In the water! Go!'

Dimba once more tried to help but was shoved.

One shove too many. I was in the water! With clothes on! *And I didn't know how to swim!*

The water was foul, but not too awfully bad. And, I couldn't find a footing with my legs. I didn't know how, I knew there must have been some sort of rock down there in the water to support my weight, but I couldn't find anything. Not very clearly or the exactness of all things about me, but...

'Swim, boy, swim!' my father kept shouting.

I screamed. I was going under.

I screamed and I got in.

Naturally.

I was rolling and going under several times, popping up like a wooden cork. I thrust about in the water fighting hard to reach a rock precipice I could see about two meters away, finding the water depth not deep but swift. Quickly I was swept to the bottom and I was very much drowning.

Somehow, though, I managed to surface and grab hold of the solid edging. Abruptly I shook my head to clear it. A bit of water surged into my throat and a huge knot twisted dramatically in my stomach. Tossing my head around, I caught a glimpse of my father, swimming powerfully towards me. With confusion, my hands grabbed the solid rock; I felt hands grabbing me, pulling me away. I was disorientated—instead of aiming 'downwards' from the dive, I was going upwards! It didn't make sense!

I swam up regardless, finding nothing of which to grab onto but dire determination propelling me up. I was weighed down and being a young boy with no swimming experience was a bit of problem, the lack of air, the inability to see, all that put a bit of panic in me. Hands grabbed me, from above. My screams of panic and fear filled the air; they were mostly dull to me as my ears were filled with gunk. Laboriously I kept pushing, kept fighting. Twice my father managed to catch me, twice the rushing water forced him to lose his grip. My weight took me down and I was surprised to see that I could see!

Underwater!

In brackish/greenish/putrid water near Kisumu Sewage! Not too clearly and just a bit in all directions about me. I found myself rolling along the bottom and then I was pinned to some rocks. I was being swept with the waves offshore. I swam with all my might reaching the rocks, grabbed and climbed virtually up the sides of the curved rock surface (which was actually slippery). I knew I had to make for the shore. At least now I could attack the water and stay afloat.

I tossed myself into the water and pushed myself for the shore. The swiftness of the water was too powerful and there was nothing more to grab onto. Then a wave rolled over me and pushed me forward. The water seemed to subside—both in depth and swiftness. It allowed me time to breathe; vomit up the goo I had swallowed, and to press my body against the wave.

I felt my hands and feet scrap onto the lake bottom. The shore was broken, slick, and nowhere to hoist myself to safety. I attempted to get on my hands and knees and another wave crashed over me. I opened my eyes just in time to feel my father's hands grabbing me. The gunky Lake Victoria water had easily cleaned me up, soaked into my bones. Soiled and dirty as I felt, I experienced happiness. I had lost my fear of water.

I heard my father's voice. 'Your first test of being a man. Rule one; learn to conquer water like a Luo. No fear.'

Dimba smiled and continued to shine the unruly man on.

Then my father turned his red eyes on me. 'Don't tell this to your mother.'

I nodded and washed mud off my feet. Then I made to get into the truck. I was wet and cold and I was shivering.

'Wait,' my father said.

I turned.

He held his nostrils, blew mucous fiercly into his cupped had and hurled the snort on the ground.

'You did well. Better than Odingo. It's Ouru's turn next year. Maybe in the next two years. If he's not ready.'

7.

The following day I plodded the dust and dared the sun to Nyalenda Railway to see Magak. I told him about the swimming lesson with my father. What my father had said about my balls filling my hands and making me into a man disturbed my young mind.

I had come to Magak for help. 'What do you want to know?' he asked me.

'Is it true? About the balls filling your hands and making you a man?

Magak stared back at me. Then he laughed. Laughed so hard and long till his eyes were streaming with tears. 'What? *Ni ang'o?*' It was like he couldn't believe what he was hearing. He sat on his family's rinky-dink handmade sofa hunching over some as kids did. I plopped down by his side waiting.

'Your *father* told you?'

I nodded. 'Is it true?'

A slight pause, then he nodded his head. 'Yes.'

I gulped. I needed a moment to think; he stared a second at me. *'Nyasadi?'*

Magak crossed his heart the way Catholics do. 'You've to obey him, he's your father.'

I didn't know quite what to think, it wasn't exactly as I thought it would be; my father was always right, much as he was so crude. That was something to be concerned about.

I closed his eyes and hoped my father wasn't going to elevate me to the high rank where he had placed Keya and Odingo. Being a kid had advantages and disadvantages—being schooled at home allowed for a broader explanation of taboo subjects in the norm school setting. But still, though I knew somewhat what 'sex' entailed, absoluteness remained unknown. In other words I didn't want to believe that by my father saying my balls were big meant I could start engaging in sex. I didn't want to even think about it. I knew a thing or two about rites of passage in our community like removing six lower teeth. But my father had his own queer ways. By forcing me to learn to swim, he has pushed me across the line. My father had made this clear when he said, *'Your first test of being a man. Rule one; learn to conquer water like a Luo. No fear.'*

Magak and I later found some things to occupy ourselves with. We had too much time on their hands. We planned our day. We will go to Upper Railway to look up Oliver, Gonza, Onyango Shika Dame and other boys. Then we were going to Kaburini near Joyland to either hunt *tunda* or we would go to *kataka*. Magak had turned us into a gang and a football team and we even saved coins to buy little brown *abisidi* footballs. He also taught us karate and we had to save coins for him to watch Bruce Lee movies at Nyanza to learn karate skills to coach us.

Little thought was given to Tut and OTC; they were no longer worthy of thought since they had repeated class five and were now behind us. We had new friends as we were now in class six. Dan Odago, was worthy of thought; as were the others Magak had already brought in: Opiyo and Odongo the twins; Alice Wamboi, Chicky Ochieng, and Jack, and other boys. Dorry, too, had failed to get the marks needed for her to proceed to class six with us, so her parents took her to another school. Dorry was a snob, snooty, and only so-so bright (in school). When she didn't do well on a test she whined and complained blaming some boy for breaking wind or some excuse enabling her to re-take the test. She usually cheated. She got her way on most occasions; for school punishments, she got her way by sniveling and having parents who operated the school kiosk which would inevitably provide our break time edibles—*uji* for twenty cents, *gobit* for *otonglo* (ten cents) and even *mandas* for *otonglo* (ten cents) and *nguru* for *nduru* (five cents).

Dorry had now transferred to Kibuye Girls.

Quite a cute girl to suddenly miss in our class, wasn't it? Anyway, we needed new boys and girls in the gang. Magak thought about that—thought about that—that about thought it. He needed more kids in the gang. From the Catholic Church near Kibuye he had seen some perfect boys. We pulled them into the gang and many of them were interesting. For instance, Odago filled the top notch and was already as steady resident at Magak's gang. Odago had introduced us to Kisumu Area Library where we loved to go read *Sinbad the Sailor* and *Hardy Boys*. We also had *Foolish Abdul*, *Tintin* and *Asterix*. And many more: *Dennis The Menace, Rodger The Dodger*.

Disabled Opoko was awed by Magak's leadership abilities— more so about how he managed to keep rug tags such as Gonza, Oliver, Okello Mariko and Onyango Shika Dame in check. He wasn't aghast, just awed—there's a difference. What were the benefits of sticking in with Magak in his gang anyway? Good question. Mostly it was fear that falling out of Magak's gang would leave one exposed and vulnerable. Something would happen to one of the kids if we didn't stick together. We had lots and lots of fun being together. We helped each other. Helped each other with maths homework, swapped stories and laughed all day long, listened to steamy stuff about girls and sex told to us. We shared things and kept secrets. Yeah, you know: cigarettes, *Playboy* etc. When one of us was in trouble we all moved in and sorted things. When one of us was attacked by ruffians from Nyalenda or Kaloleni or Manyatta, we retaliated and fought back.

What benefits did Magak get for leading the gang?

Magak didn't care—so we didn't care too.

Magak was too busy having fun of his life leading the pack. He loved to get us kids fighting. But he didn't like fighting himself. He was always provoking us into fights; saying things about other kids, about what such and such a boy had said about so-and-so and inciting us. He organized the wrestling matches and got us to fight for his own amusement. And since we didn't want to be left out of Magak's circle, we fought. He made us believe we were men, so we fought. While fighting the sun roasted our bare backs. Dust, grass and dirt, got into our eyes. Sticks and bugs get into legs; our knees dug into the hard ground and biting insects took pleasures onto our burning and sweating bodies. We fought a lot, those days and created laughter for Magak. We fought, we ran, we found adventure and mostly tried to stay out of trouble (with little success).

Magak was speaking. 'We go to Upper. Then we get Onyango Shika Dame, Gonza and Oliver. Then we go wrestling at *kataka*.'

An image popped into my mind—it was one of all the nice things at *kataka*.

I smiled and said, 'Okay.' Magak beamed, he was okay with that—very cool. You see, a few days ago Magak had fooled me into believing I could be a good wrestler, a footballer, a goal keeper. I didn't believe him. Knew deep down I could never become any of these. But what the heck! There were too many wrestling matches taking place between young boys from different villages these days.

Magak quickly rounded up the other kids and told us his plan. There was a reward of one shilling for the boy who beat Oduwo Nyang from Kasagam. Now that was a name that sent shivers every kid: Oduwo Nyang! The dreaded Kasagam champ. But Magak and Gonza had everything worked out. Little did I know that by accompanying the team I was automatically a competitor. The wrestling ground was near Kachok.

We passed through several villages, crossed the Auji River and found ourselves in the sisal plantations of Kachok. My uncle Odima worked here as foreman, worked for that damned white haired *mzungu* we called Achok. (The sisal processing factory's name, Kachok, was actually adopted from this damned mean *mzungu* people nicknamed Achok). He had dogs like lions. According to my father, Achok and his friend, Mandeville, who people used to call Mand Afil, had, in the '50s, settled on this land and set up their ventures. Mand Afil became the man in charge of Kisumu Stadium and was in the business of rescuing lost children. Children simply ran away from home to be part of the Mand Afil family. They were later on to be employed by the municipality.

We passed the huge towering cypress and eucalyptus trees of Kachok, crossed the highway and reached the wrestling ground at *kataka*. We found it teaming with lots of kids. The dumping ground was unkempt and rundown ratty, infested with *mineme* varmints and big rats. I was smiling but I soon lost my smile when Magak ordered that I was the one chosen to challenge Oduwo Nyang and win the one shilling. The boys arranged themselves on opposite sides of the pitch and started singing and cheering. It was common that the youngest competitors be the curtain raisers, so I thought this was Magak's gaff. How could I be chosen to compete to win one shilling in place of heavyweights such as Oliver, Gonza and the unbeatable Onyango Shika Dame? Well, I was released from our side. Oduwo was a head shorter, VERY muscular, had thick arms, and was stronger than Onyango Shika Dame. Magak knew his plan well—I knew he deliberately want Oduwo Nyang to win this game! That's why I was chosen. I had my secret plan, I wanted to hit his balls! Surprise everyone. From my vantage point, slinking in the alley behind garbage cans and other assorted discarded household refuse, I watched the boys as they baked in the waning hours of the afternoon sun; the *kataka* property was fenced in by a tall six foot fence, several old trees occupied space on the unkempt grassy landscape inundated with weeds, misbegotten shrubs, broken cutlery, abandoned cars, old buses, stacks of tyres, old *mabatis*, boards, bones, hides of cows and goats, broken bottles, cartons and cartons of this and that—lots of places to 'hide' from a pissed off parent or throng of bullies. Unused foodstuff, solid rocks of sweets, canned meat, stale bread, sacks of rotten biscuits, Tree Top, biscuits and loads of debris and edibles and many more. Not one, not two, but ten grounded motor cars were in the place and we used to 'drive' them. There, too, was a Pepsi Cola kiosk that was so-so used. A mix of broken furniture, wood, brick, cinder block, and shrubs.

Cheered on by my team mates from Pandpieri, I walked majestically into the field towards the middle of the pitch, the same happened with Kasagam side who also released Oduwo Nyang. We both moved towards the middle. Oduwo was stark naked and from the look on his face, it suddenly occur to me that I was no match to him. In the blink of an eye he engaged me in a fierce combat in which he lifted me into the air above his head. I swear I saw blue sky before he hit me so hard onto the ground and then stood astride my limp body which lay still on the ground. I lost my breath on the impact and for a few minutes I couldn't move or stand up. When I stood up, I broke into sobs and ran off without waiting to watch the rest of the matches. I never went back to the wrestling.

Oh, here... more drama. More prequel. That's just how it was. Even in a prequel there could be enigma, paradox and trifling little sub stories. For example, I just remembered the little superstitions we had... back in the day. When playing football; to keep a clean sheet or to win a match, the goalkeeper would take a small strand of grass, make a note and place it under the 'goal post' (read a stone). This ritual would, sometimes fail ...badly! Especially when playing bigger boys; then, like 'Brother aka Bra' of 'Mosko Ma Malo' estate. I remember once—after all the rituals—we lost a match 15—0! My bro Ouru was the goal keeper. Afterwards we provoked a fight by uprooting grass and putting on the opponents head to show that we were still tough and could beat them thoroughly even if they pulled a surprise on our team by beating us 15 nil! I still remember the football incident that prevented me from being a footballer and goalkeeper.

In one football match, I was the goalkeeper for my side then one of the opposing team members hit the ball so hard towards me, I attempted to get hold of the ball but missed. The ball hit me so hard on the chest that I fell to ground on impact. The shot left me in so much pain and writhing on the ground. After that incident I never participated again in any football match to date. Am not a football fan either. Talk about Luo United, Gor Mahia or Abaluhya Football Club, it doesn't impress me.

8.

The year was now wearing out, and as the end drew near, I was growing up to the world. I was going to be in class seven next year, then I will do my CPE and go to form one. Like all the boys, I wanted to go to Kisumu Boys. That was always my dream. Still this was a fine year. I was growing... growing well and maturing. It was just weeks before my 10th birthday. My brother, Ouru, actually, was eight years old.

Ouru and I were about as different as brothers can be. Mama was right: sometimes Ouru wasn't a brat; sometimes he could be a snitch and often got his bros (mostly me) in trouble for some infraction or another. But Ouru was my little brother, a little too 'mature' despite the fact that I was supposed to be more mature than him.

In my spare time I dabbled in books, actually spending some time in Kisumu Area Library reading up on what I could (and could understand). After reading King Richard's desire for a horse and a kingdom to rule over, I think those days I had grown up to be a definitely a 'good boy', always trying to please adults and wanting to be tough like King Richard the Lionheart, while Ouru was still a free-spirited little devil. The more I grew up, I become introverted and dorky, unattractive, and not very athletic. Think I was even growing to be shy. I spent much more time reading *Robin Hood, King Arthur, King Treasure Island* etc in my bedroom than playing outside. Ouru, on the other hand, was outgoing and self-confident, good looking and a natural at sports. He was popular and had a wide circle of friends... even among boys who were my age and older. Despite me being the older bro, Ouru was more powerful. He was athletic and a sort of bully, but he had a way about him (blind fury) and pelted me with surprises. We never got along very well, and he had a talent for teasing me and for getting his way when we had disputes. One thing he could always hold over me was that I had been a bed-wetter, and he nicknamed me *odudu*. I didn't tell you that, I guess. I don't want to talk about it. It had started when I was three and it hadn't ended. It had leaked in school and pretty much wrecked my self-esteem. I didn't dare join Scouts, because I might be in a camp and during a sleep-over my 'terrible secret' will be revealed. Even as puberty set in, I was pretty clueless about sex. I had had some wet dreams in the months before 1973 begun, but they were just the strange 'wet dreams' referred to in my school's teenage boyhood gossip. Boy-girl sex-play bypassed me entirely, until a few days ago.

I was in the boys' room in the afternoon reading and fantasizing about living in historical times of the great English kings and the Vikings and being someone other than my nerdy self when Ouru busted up laughing. Behind him was Dorothy. I hadn't seen her for close to a year since her parents took her to Kibuye Girls and I was surprised at how much she had transformed. When I last saw her, she was a skinny girl, all elbows and knees. Now she was tall, long limbs, and so virtually looking fine. Her eleventh birthday was months away; her breasts were bigger; she was a little shy but eager to please.

Ouru plowed into me and announced he had brought Dorothy to be my girlfriend, adding to my terror. Dorothy was a wild girl. Too much for her age. She knew things about sex and kissing and more.

Ouru said, 'Owiro, you like her, don't you?'

I automatically without hesitation nodded and confirmed so.

'Owiro, do you have a girl?' asked Dorry.

Unfortunately that would be an unconfirmed Yes. Of course it was a lie. I shook my head my head.

'Would you like to be my boyfriend?'

That would be a fortunate wholeheartedly confirmed Yes.

'Yes,' I said.

She smiled.

Then Ouru left us and we just sat there awkwardly silent. Outside the house dogs barked and goats bleated and the wind shook the trees. Inside there was nothing good; there were *chwarni* bugs in our furniture—not to mention it was more than just a little warm. The room (boys' room) was jammed with crap that did not fit nicely. Hardly a place to seduce a girl in according to me. Too creepy, dark, and dank.

Dorry smiled a quirky smile—one of the traits I liked about her. Taking my hand, she put it on her small titties. I was scared of her directness, terrified even . . . the feeling of terror was to be the single note that rung in my head throughout that afternoon. To begin with she demanded that I show her my thing and you guess that made my fantasies boil over.

'Owiro, have you ever kissed a girl?'

I shook my head. She gave me a hard questioning look. Then she laughed. 'Stand up,' she said.

I got on my feet. There was no holding back, no fear, no trepidation.

'Remove your *siruari*.'

No hesitation, I unfastened my buttons, then (on continuation of input from the voice of the Devil) pushed the school khaki shorts down to my ankles.

'*Ai yawa!*' blurted Dorry as I did. Then it is her turn. She lifted her dress, peeled back the flaps, and showed her thing to my gasp of wonder. I stared at it wide-eyed. It was small and pretty and Dorothy told me to touch. To feel it. She was bold, this eleven year old skinny girl. Bold and not afraid! I had the same feelings; it was a rush as I was brought to the brink of sexual pleasure—the ultimate pleasure all boys sought from girls. I found myself engulfed with sensations I did not understand.

That this was the beginning of my journey into the wonderful world of sex is probably an understatement. The following months, Dorry socialized me into kissing and touching.

Dorothy, oh Dorry. This girl. No matter what—my mind was filled with her. Was it love? Was it passion? A little of both? No longer did it matter that she was a year older than me—she was a girl, a lovely girl, and the nights of passion in the moonlight were during the hot December of this year 1973!

Dorry was my girl, she was my girl everywhere; in school, in the neighborhood, in church. She was in my dreams and in my thoughts. Jesus, I felt love for this girl . . . felt it in my heart. Honest.

We carried on with the wonderful affair until we were caught by Dorry's older brother, Mika, and severely punished us. Mika lit a big fire over the issue and took it to our church. Dorry and I were punished for committing sin. In Sabbath School, we were called up to stand in front of the other kids and asked to repent our sins and confess that the Devil had deceived us. It was the worst moment of my life, I wanted to die of shame and guilt. From then on we were watched and never allowed to be together. But Dorry remained to be the girl of my dreams for many years afterwards. I missed her touches, her kisses and the way she always fondled me then lay back for me to play with her priv... parts. Oops! Call it growing up.

9.

We had gone to Kaloleni to see a dead dog. It was one of Magak's dogs, Sibuor. Sib was a disciplined dog, so we were all shocked at how and why he had wondered to Kaloleni to be run over by Muspal's *otonglo pipa* rubbish truck. Magak was now twelve and he was a rascal; vandalism was just one of his casual pranks. His other pranks were knocking over wooden crosses in the *Kaburini* cemetery, killing cats by stoning them, putting glue in teacher's seats, spitting on teacher's teas, urinating on the walls of the church, stealing story books from the Kisumu Area Library, throwing stones at police during football matches at Kenyatta Sports Ground, jeering at Indians and bashing their gates with stones. He had become a bad boy since repeating class six. He hated school, adults, maths and figures, and then everything else. He was short statured, missing front teeth, kept his hair shaggy, folded up his short shirt sleeves and left the two top buttons of his shirt unbuttoned. He cursed a lot, made bad friends, seldom went to school, never went to church and was at the scene of several crimes but never got caught.

Magak will forever be twelve.

The image of the boy filled our minds—more so to Gonza as he had had the same problem not so long ago; getting his foot stuck in the underwater rocks when he took a hard dive. It was said Magak was high on bhang. Apparently he was hanging with some rude boys from Hindocha Secondary School who introduced him to *njaga*.

Whether or not he had been with the Hindocha boys at Hippo Point, though, was not known. Surely he hadn't been; he was always—always with his buddies, Gonza and Oliver.

'I know they were there.' Gonza surmised.

'But I don't understand.' Oliver replied, the image of our drowned leader consuming his thoughts. *'Ati njaga?'*

'How did he die?' I asked.

'He dove down at Hippo Point.'

'But how could he? He didn't know how to swim?' I protested.

Oliver nodded. 'His foot got stuck in the rocks.'

I didn't get it. 'Magak feared water. How do you dive with your feet first on a deep end? You dive hands first, its basic rule for swimming.'

'He was not a swimmer,' Oliver said.

'Of course he wasn't. How could he dive yet he couldn't swim?'

'Unless maybe he was pushed?' Opoko suggested sneaking in on our private conversation.

'Yes!' Gonza said excitedly as he came to a realization.

Oliver stood up. 'Yes. They pushed him.'

'They freaked and left him there!?' Onyango Shika dame said more than asked.

'*Yawa*, and CPE is just one month away,' whispered Rose Bonyo.

Otieno Kachweya whined, he had never seen anything like that. What he saw at Hippo Point he regarded as horrific. He had been there when my father was called by the police to dive and retrieve the body. He hadn't told Onyango Shika Dame and Odago to save them from the horror of seeing the body of our Magak pulled from fifteen feet underwater where his foot had jammed between rocks.

It was an image that refused to go away.

And we remembered Magak fondly; how he used us... to raid for him Indians homes for mangoes. And *jamna* and *zambarau*.

'He was a bully,' Otieno Kachweya started to say.

'Don't be stupid, Kachweya!' shouted back Oliver. 'He was our leader.'

The outburst caught the fat boy off-guard. He realized he should have shut his mouth or at least not involved himself with the rescue team.

'Why did you hate him?' I asked.

'Owish!' Kachweya shouted.

'His sister,' said Oliver. 'But what could you do, Otii? She loved Magak, hey *bwana*.'

Otieno Kachweya fumed. He opened his mouth to say something. The look on Oliver's face made him change his mind.

'It's funny how his dog was killed on the same day he disappeared,' I wondered aloud.

Opoko stared out to the gloomy skies. He sighed and limped about on his stick but the mood was solemn so he did not giggle about the way he loved to. He had hated Magak, just like Kachweya—but unlike Kachweya, Opoko didn't have his sister as

Magak's chick. Magak had turned Akinyi down. She was an ugly girl... the ugliest in Pandpieri and Nyalenda. She was ugly but she was bold like Dorry. As I watched Opoko, I observed an emotion suddenly sweeping over him and he quickly turned around on his stick then limped his way from us into the bush.

'Let's do it then,' said Oliver. 'I need to go.'

Onyango Shika Dame lifted Sibuor's carcass in his arms and struggles with its weight over to the hole that we had dug in the bush land in Magak's favourite spot. Oliver helped, took one leg and Gonza grabbed the tail, and very gently, they lowered the carcass into its shallow grave.

Gonza wiped his hands on a *nyabende winy* plant. Curiously, he said, 'So, do we say prayers?'

'For a dog?' asked Onyango Shika Dame. He spat. *'Guok aguoka ni, yawa.'*

Nobody said a word, nobody wanted to. Then Oliver turned. 'I'm going.'

I didn't believe him. 'We leave him here like this? Uncovered?'

'We'll come back,' said Oliver. 'We can't cover him with soil while Magak is still lying in Russia in the mortuary. Let him be buried first then we will come back for Sibuor. Come on, let's go.'

Suddenly we heard voices

The voices that we couldn't make out but clearly they were boys. We all slipped into the bushes for cover and were mostly concealed by the foliage. Four boys came down the hillside, one was shirtless.

I asked, 'Do you know them?'

Oliver shook his head, 'High school thugs,' he said. I squinted hard to make out who they were: Obat John, Nelson Ochieng I recognized and could identify—they were from Hindocha, the *Wahindi* harambee secondary school in Kibuye Estate near Robert Ouko Estate which my brother Odingo hated. They were four in total, the other two boys I didn't know.

By their talk and demeanour, I determined that the boys

were 'not nice.' Bully-like if not fully bully; bad mouths; crass; and muscled. They came down the hill pushing and shoving one another. The leader, Obat John, was most muscled, shirtless. He made a quick look to the lake then made for under the trestle and up inside. The others followed pushing and shoving one another.

The voices could hardly be heard but we caught something like, 'He shouldn't have smoked too much *njaga* if he was not man enough,'

'Police can't prove anything!' one of them says.

'You didn't have to push him.'

'*Ei yawa*, it was an accident.'

'He was a good kid.'

Other statements were made but we couldn't make them out. The four big boys went down the hill kicking the dirt and howling with laughter.

Suddenly Gonza lit a fire. 'They are talking about Magak! They killed him!' And he was pissed.

'What?' Opoko gulped.

Gonza shot him a sneering look. He looked a fright.

Then,

'Hey!' shouted Oliver, 'Let's go to Ogwang!'

'Oh, shut up,' I warned. 'Keep off. Ogwang? Please shut up.'

'We all know those *Hindocha* boys,' Odago says. He was furious and looked around madly, 'Obat and Ochieng are bad boys. Let's get away from here before they come back.'

So we left Magak's ground. I hoped it wasn't going to rain on poor Sibuor. Magak was due to be taken to his father's home in South Nyanza to be interred by the weekend.

Days and weeks passed. Magak slowly ceased to exist in our thoughts and in our talks. We soon had other things to worry about: CPE. We studied hard and eventually did The Exam. Then December came dragged on and on and on. I was a little miffed that my girl, Dorry, was going to bug out by the end of long school holidays and the start of her secondary education in a boarding school. I wanted her to go to Kisumu Girls. She went to spend the holiday with her grandparents.

December, however, was a long month. Full of events.

10.

With school over and done with (for three months anyways) kids all over took to new adventures. Some got holiday jobs. Some got lazy (lazy-er). Some went to Nairobi to visit relatives. Some traveled to *oshago* to build their *simbas*. Then came the day—

'Let's go for adventure.'

Oliver loved dangerous adventures. Gonza was game for it.

'So any word about your folks?' Gonza asked Oliver, 'Remember the way your mama caned you recently.' We all laughed.

Oliver rolled his eyes—sometimes Gonza could be so crude. 'You think I'm a *standadi one* or what? I'm twelve years old and I did my CPE!'

Everyone gave him a knowing look—we tried hard to keep our smiles down.

I was not much in the way of a talkative mood; mainly losing Magak had left an indelible gap. The kids were trying their best to forget. Dorry was also making me feel lousy. I was missing her. Living in Pandpieri was nipping away so much so that her grandma cut her some slack being raised a town girl. But with CPE results just around the corner, I thought she had started to get used to the idea of soon parting ways with me and go to another life in form one. She wanted to live with her grandma in Siaya. That truly sucked. But we had two bold girls in our ring who were real tomboys: Oliver's Susy and the very beautiful Alice Wamboi.

'This will probably be my last adventure.' Oliver said sadly.

'How come?'

'My father wants me to go to Kakamega.' Then, 'He wants me to go to KK High and I should stay closer to home during school hols.' Then, 'She's a pain.'

He meant Susy who was his chick. 'She's just trying to keep you prepared.' Onyango Shika Dame replied. 'When you go to form one you'll forget her. She fears losing you.'

Oliver shrugged, 'I guess.'

'My aunt's been on my case, too.' Otieno Kachweya chimed in.

Onyango Shika Dame said, 'Haha, my folks been yapping at me, but as long as I do some chores and avoid running into Ogwang's youth then they cut me some slack.'

'Don't ask about mine!' Gonza giggled.

We kids laughed and bopped our hands together in some sort of union cementing our union.

'We need a name for ourselves.' Oliver shouted. 'This is our last December. Next year: form one!'

'Yeah!' Gonza agreed enthusiastically.

'Kisumu Boys Club!' Otieno Kachweya shouted excitedly.

'KBC,' supplied Oliver.

Odago laughed. 'Yah. We already heard that one.'

'It was Magak's idea,' said Onyango Shika Dame

'Please let's go if we're going,' said the brave and beautiful Alice Wamboi who was a Kikuyu but spoke DhoLuo like any of us.

We gathered ourselves and slipped off through the grassland and bush making for nice sandy shore somewhere between Hippo Point and Yatch Club. The day was hot, muggy, and virtually unpleasant—a nice swim was just the thing to crave for. Strange that in an area where it was scorching hot through and through except April and July, there were such nice looking vegetation and abundant water nearby.

'But it's damned hot!' exclaimed Susy boldly. *'Piny liet dem.'* She fanned herself and even had her button top open fanning her chest.

'We're almost there,' said Otieno Kachweya haggardly.

'We're lost!' exclaimed Alice Wamboi exhaustedly.

'No we're not!' Gonza said almost angrily.

Onyango Shika Dame nodded to Gonza 'Yes we are.'

We followed each other along a very narrow pathway that, after what seemed an hour, came to a crossing path. We stopped, we had never come to a path crossing our path to the lake.

'We're lost!' Alice whispered again.

'I think it's this way,' Odago suggested pointing through the tall grassy meadow. The boys and girls looked to him and then to each other.

'How do you know?' Gonza asked almost sarcastically.

'Because it's that flat ground near Hippo Point after we cross the road and we can walk along *Aora* Wigwa.' (River Wigwa was the only blot on the otherwise flat meadow landscape.)

Oliver wrinkled his nose, shunned the sun with one hand and looked to the direction Odago indicated.

'We haven't crossed the road,' Alice complained. 'How far are we?'

'It has to be close because we're just in line with that power transformer,' said Otieno Kachweya. On the right was one of those huge power transformers with a piece of sheet metal marked 'Danger Hatari' nailed onto it. The boys and girls hung loose debating with themselves. Alice sighed exasperatedly and pushed her way between them heading straight through the shoulder high grass and weeds. Susy followed quickly turning to the boys.

'*Wadhi uru!*'

The boys looked to one another—

'No way! To be shown the way by a girl! No way!' was our shared sentiment as we started after the girls 'Hey! *Nyinyi, ngojeni!*'

Minutes later and we were at the sunken swimming shore. We were so hot the girls were naked and in the water in seconds, smiling big. The boys were dejected but stripped off their clothes and let it be. The girls could win one once in a while. Once.

Alice and Susy still weren't too comfortable with swimming

out into the middle of the fresh water *or* swimming down to where River Wigwa poured its brown filth into the fresh water. The current brought in by the surging river made the water thick and repulsive and swimming outshore was a big risk. The undercurrent was tenacious. Gonza and I had no fear. We were excellent swimmers. Suddenly, though, Gonza came shooting up from the depths in a dire panic.

'What?' The crippled Opoko, who was also an excellent swimmer, asked not knowing the cause of our friend's panic.

Gonza tried to conceal his fright; he did not want to alarm the girls.

'Someone's down there.' he said in a hoarse whisper.

'Say what!?'

Gonza tugged on my arm and pulled me down. 'Someone or something.'

'What are you up to?' Oliver asked aloud and made a backstroke.

'I have a feeling. I saw something.' Gonza replied.

'You Luhyas, the way you fear water.'

'I swim as good as any Luo.'

'I have to be home soon,' said Alice wading on the sandy depth , her hand covering her dark patch. 'Don't peek.'

Susy too swam up and wobbled onto her feet shaking water out of her ear. 'Me, too; my mama's been suspicious. Kind of been on my case a bit—mostly bitching about me hanging with the boys too much.'

'Parents can be bitchy,' Oliver said holding out a hand for her.

Otieno Kachweya agreed and languished by the shore facing the girls; Alice kept vigil on her feet—not trusting the boys and anticipating that they will try to sneak up on them from underwater and try to drag her down or something.

Suddenly Odago and Opoko who had swum outshore shot up to the surface and looked seriously panicked.

'What is it?' Oliver demanded.

Neither boy answered but swam to the shore and clung there

looking very panicky.

'What is it?' Oliver persisted.

'We need to get out.' Odago said trying to be calm.

'Why? What is it?'

Neither boy wanted to say but we all got it that the two boys who were super swimmers weren't playing, something had spooked them.

After gathering our clothes, we headed for the tracks. Odago said, 'Crocs. Two of them. Let's run to the train shack and put on our clothes there.'

We walked in haste and silence a little ahead of the girls. The girls were worried, concerned, and peeved about walking naked.

At the train shack we boys slumped down inside to be out of the immediate heat and put on our shirts. The girls had, somehow, put on their clothes while we ran.

'School's going to open soon,' Oliver said panting and leaning his weight on the cracked wall of the shack, 'This is our last day together as boys before we turn into men.'

'So?' Susy asked.

'I've always wanted to visit the old train station at Nanga.'

I sighed. 'The train station. What about the girls?'

Susy laughed. 'I guess I'm a country girl at heart.'

The boys remained quiet.

'How far is it to the train station?' Gonza asked.

'Very far.' Odago said standing up scratching his butt off.

'We couldn't make it?' Otieno Kachweya asked curiously.

Oliver regarded the fat boy as if seeing him for the first time. 'To the train station? We might. We follow the *reru* tracks. The *reru* tracks will lead us to the mines. Let's go.'

I had second thoughts as we hoofed down the track to the first trestle, the one over the dusty road. It was quite a weary walk and the great behemoth locomotive, *Gach Jo Reru*, was due. On the left were thick brambles and bushes and not a lot of space between the tracks and them; on the right was the marshy part of the meadow and not pleasant to walk in.

When the trestle over the dry river came into view, the ground beneath our feet began to tremble.

'Hey!' yelled Gonza.

We were tired and way hot but— 'Look out!' shouted Oliver grabbing Susy's hand. I grabbed Alice and held her. Smoke could be seen darkening the skies around the great sun, cinders were already in the air and the mighty mightiness of the magnificent locomotive was ominous at best.

Scarcely and did we reach the bridge and down the embankment to get safely (safely?) underneath. The massive iron beast roared across the tracks but noticeably not as charging as it usually did. Still, though, it was threatening and fearful.

The massive East African Railways thing lumbered along coming almost to a complete stop.

'It's never done that before.' Odago, whose father was once an engine driver with EAR, stated. We scrambled back up the embankment and watched as the last train car barely crept along.

'What's going on?' Otieno asked aloud.

No one had an answer. I was miffed. I was the only one who noticed the engine driver climb down and hide himself behind a *nyabend winy* bush to piss.

'Maybe it's waiting for me!' I said to cover for the poor fellow taking his call of nature.

'Waiting for you?'

Gonza shrugged. 'Yeah, I've always wanted to ride this thing,'

'Serious?' Oliver asked.

I shrugged. 'I guess, just to get me across the lake to Kandege to see the airplanes.'

'This thing doesn't go to Kandege,' Oliver said, 'it goes to Nairobi.'

'Yeah,' interrupted Otieno, 'but it slows down or stops once over the Kisat River, that's as near to Kandege as you can get!'

'No problem,' said Oliver shirking off the threat, 'that's nearer to the Bandani mines—that's our next adventure destination. Today, Nanga.'

Just then the train couplers banged and the wheels begun to turn faster.

'It's taking off.' Onyango Shika Dame stated the obvious.

'We should, too,' said Oliver, 'this heat is killing me, *bwana*.'

Everything was suddenly offensive. The smell of the great locomotive and its *bogies* rumbled on steel rails and out of sight. I was repulsed. Suddenly repulsed by the smelly odour of the creosote ties, the stench of the nearby swamp, the oppressive heat drove us to traipse into the woods and to seek shade, the ghostly ranting of *agak*, the thick-billed corvus crow. All repulsed me.

'Let's find a short cut, 'Oliver declared.

'We ought to have had our Boy Scout camps out,' I said in an attempt to fill in the silence. A thick layer of grassy moss made up the forest floor, a natural canopy was high overhead from the forest on either side of the expanse.

'This is getting scary.' Gonza murmured. Another glance back at Oliver dragging Susy and Alice and he continued trekking.

The girls were more repulsed than me, each held onto their boyfriend and seemed to wear faces that sought to know whether or not their 'men' were going to hold for long in the woods and in the heat. We boys seemed to be a little 'lighter' and jostled one another as we made our way into and through the thicket. We paused to pee and plucked at some wild fruit. The girls shook their heads at the 'boys' and withdrew away until they were out of sight then they parted their legs and pissed while standing. Something had spooked them and they weren't comfortable at all.

We trudged onward along the tracks going the opposite direction from the trestle over the river. We had passed some villages and the trail into the woods to Oliver's favourite ground—we were off to a new direction, a new exploration way past Dunga towards hell-knows-where.

After getting messed in mud holes in the remote woods, we sloshed around exiting at the other end. A great grassy field awaited us but with the recent rains, Gonza, who was leading, knew better than to make a trek across. To the right was flat land with small farmlands that segued to larger farms and large groves of trees. To the left were bushes and trees. The lake was nowhere to be seen though we could smell more than feel it. But a fence we could see, an enclosed meadow. It was possible that a better road was near at hand. Not likely, but possible.

We trudged on. Suddenly the lake came into view. Suddenly, too, there seemed to be a road, right from where we entered the open ground as we left the woods. There was a space some hundred feet wide. The entire landscape was of flatland racing fast towards the lake. Grazing lands and farmlands made up the flat land, there were the two rivers—one with water and one without. Farmland and vacant empty land—it all made for a hot—hot/humid—stifling existence and not particularly nifty for sprinting through.

'I'm Kimaru Songok!' shouted Onyango Shika Dame as he broke into a run.

'No!' we all shouted in unison.

'Joginder Singh!' piped in Gonza picking up a good speed.

'STOP!' shouted the girls.

We watched them run across the grazing land. They ran until they got tired and stopped. We soon caught up with them.

'Kisumu Boys!' Oliver chirped.

No one even responded to that one.

'AR Khan Brothers!' Opoko cheered. 'Safari Rally.'

'I think we need a better name,' said Oliver flatly. 'Kisumu Boys.'

We soon got tired of it, fell silent and shuffled our paces and continued the hoofing.

'I'm tired' Alice said in a low quivering voice. 'I'm hot.'

Oh it was hot. Hot and stifling. We were on the railroad again. The mix of the oil-soaked railroad ties didn't stop us.

Alice stopped walking. 'Just how far is this place?'

'Not far.' Oliver observed.

Alice gave him a knowing look, 'I think you will soon have to carry me.'

'Hey,' he said defensively, 'It's not very far now.'

'I've heard my father talk about it,' I told him, 'all the EAR trains stopped there way back when he was a kid.'

'We go past that village and that's it!' said a getting-angry Oliver.

Though Oliver wanted to get to the old train station supposedly somewhere on the line, he was getting tired, too. Our last weekend before New Year 1975 was getting eaten up by just walking.

'Could be worse,' I chirped.

'How?' Alice asked a little peeved at all the walking.

'Could be another hill if I'm not wrong,' I joked.

Alice stood still and made an ugly face. If it weren't for the heat zapping all her energy, she would have slapped me. I was lucky she liked me and held herself together. I took her hand and dragged her along. We rounded the next long sweeping corner and there it was.

'*Yawa, yawa, yawa,*' Susy sang uncharacteristically. The heat was really getting to her for her to swear so. She shielded her eyes like the rest of us and stared up to a well-weathered piece of rotting steel sign board some feet above our heads. Some letters were missing.

'East African Railways?' Gonza quipped. 'Nanga Mines Depot.'

We all stared and stared and finally the intense heat drove us to our next find—

'Aren't we trespassing?' blurted Opoko. '*Kanyaga.*'

'What's *kanyaga,*' Oliver retorted, 'that ended with Colonialism. This place ceased to function in 1958. Let's go in.'

It was the remains of a large train station, one wall remained and part of a porch. Something of another building could be seen across the tracks and there were foundations of other buildings all retaken by weed and decay and the lake.

Oliver blurted, 'My father used to work here. With EAR.'

He seemed to know his way around the place. He led us

through it until we came to where a set of tracks came off from the main line and turn heading into the new woods—young saplings and trees more than fifty years old. Buried mostly into the earth sunken down some several feet was a locomotive. Not a big fire spitting serpent like the one we had seen earlier but a regular engine from about the Colonial age, judging from the writings on its side, *British East Africa,* and no less thunderous than the new engines that we had seen going to Kandege that were fed with timber and coal and looked so powerful when they thundered by, you could hear the ground and the trees shaking. Of course there was that mark of the owner: OHMS.

'What does that mean?' asked Odago pointing.

I wondered how stupid he was. Did he ever read history. I helped out. 'OHMS means On Her Majesty's Service.'

'Her majesty means the Queen,' said Alice.

'Queen Victoria or Elizabeth,' I added.

'Look at that,' said Oliver. The engine looked like it had burrowed itself into the landscape and had been there a long time; the entire boiler section was into the earth clear up to the cab!

'It must have run hard and hit a dead end!' supplied Onyango Shika Dame.

'No, they grounded it,' said Oliver.

Alice and Susy looked at one another, not impressed. We boys babbled on about engines and cars and this and that. I sweated and couldn't believe—didn't know what Oliver was up to. We had walked twenty miles—for this? He'd been talking about this place since we were in class four.

I watched him and the boys as they scrambled all over the remains of the old locomotive. Oliver and Gonza were occupied gawking over the sunken engine. Most boys liked to play *Kalasinga* and Cowboys. And Lwanda Magere and Safari Rally, KAR, or Arab pirates like Sinbad the Sailor and Alibaba. Oliver and Gonza? They played engine drivers. The girls sought shelter from the heat by exploring the interior of the woods by the remains of the train station. Foundations were everywhere and at length the pair found another sign giving them insight to where they were. *Workshop*: so said a sign that was barely readable. Old benches, pails, lanterns, clipboards, and so on were found all over the place. Alice squatted to pee; Susy noted the boys crawling all over the locomotive engine; she shook her head sadly but was smiling.

I continued to follow the girls on their own exploration when suddenly—

Susy prowled around outside the foundation of what was once a large structure, possibly a warehouse. There was an old water pump that took the girl's attention, she worked the handle that was stuck and required some umph. Suddenly the wooden floor she stood on gave way and down she went.

'Susy!' screamed Alice.

The boys came running, 'What happened?' Oliver asked.

'She fell,' cried Alice, 'down there.'

I knelt down and peered. 'Are you alright?' I asked.

'I don't think so,' she said in a small voice. 'Think I'm hurt.'

And it was a good fall, too; about fifteen feet. Luckily for Susy, though, she fell onto something like weed or rotting chipboard. It still hurt despite the thickness of the misplaced decaying chips strewn about the depths of the subterranean level. In a flash, Gonza, Oliver and I were all down there. We had taken the 'leap of faith' and jumped down to Susy. Jumped down through the hole in the flooring Susy had broken. She didn't need our help. The olding chips and debris was old but thick. Oliver knelt down by Susy checking if there were any bones poking through the skin (fracture.) There wasn't and he was glad of that.

'That was some fall!' Gonza said enthusiastically.

'Not so,' I said. 'It was soft landing.' I didn't want to spread panic.

'I wondered what this is.' Gonza stood and looked around but couldn't see much due to the darkness.

'Is everything alright?' shouted Alice from above. Peering

down the hole with her were Odago, Opoko, Otieno and Onyango Shika Dame.

'Oh, yes, we're having a doing well.' Susy bitched back.

'Can you climb out or should we go for help?' shouted Odago.

'We will be in so much trouble if we don't get out of here.' Gonza reasoned. 'We could get stuck here and one of us could get hurt. We need to go.'

'Come up then,' Odago replied, 'You can't just stay down there.'

'Ssh, listen!' Susy said sharply. 'I hear water running.'

Blathering around in the near darkness and I found an old rusted lantern, some huge rope, an iron wheel from a mining cart, and then the cart. As my eyes adjusted I discovered that we were in some sort of basement; it's exact dimensions I couldn't really know—it was dark!

But I heard water, too. Determining exactly where the water was running was another matter. The closer I got to the end of the cavern where it was darkest the more I heard the running water which begun to sound like waves. It was colder at the back of the cave-aka mining staging area; damp, too.

'Owiro,' called Gonza musing, 'this looks odd.'

'What?' Oliver asked still not moving from the huge pile of decaying debris where he was holding Susy.

'Well, there's this wall, what's' this?'

Oliver joined us and ran his hand over the wall. 'Look like moss.'

'It's strange,' said Gonza.

I wondered what was strange. 'Why strange? This place is old and it's like a cave.'

'Not really, well, maybe, I don't know but...,' Oliver tried to explain that his sister Achi had a book that said moss didn't grow on walls of caves unless there was air. 'There shouldn't be moss or any vegetation on the walls.' He looked around suddenly. 'Unless...'

'Oliver, what are you trying to say?' Susy said getting a grip of herself.

'Wait,' I told Oliver.

I ran my hands through the moss. It was thick, coarse, and filled with small critters that fluttered away—some were luminous! The stirring up of moss-dust made me and wheeze. My nose got irritated and a cough bursts through causing me to panic. I lost my balance and my weight crashed into the moss covered wall. Into something soft. I felt through with my hand and discovered unknowingly that the moss was a curtain—or a makeshift doorway concealing an adjoining wall opening into a new room. Oliver pushed me aside and felt through the mass of green matter. Then he went in. We heard a horrible gargled scream and a crash that jarred us.

'Oliver!' screamed Susy.

'What's going on?' Odago asked from above.

'It's Oliver,' Susy said with a sob.

Gonza peered through the doorway.

'What happened?' asked Alice.

'Oliver fell through this doorway,' Gonza said. 'He's down there but I can't see him. It's dark.'

'We're coming down.' Odago said flatly.

We peered through the doorway. Couldn't see a thing. It was even more queasy with Oliver not talking. Susy sighed and tried to relax—it wasn't easy. I peered into the darkness, any minute the adventurerous Luhya kid was going to come busting thru the door—more pissed off than ever. We took turns and called for Oliver but got no answer. That frightened Susy and motivated the slightly injured girl to move. The chips and debris had cushioned her fall but the fall was fifteen feet! It still hurt!

'Oliver!' Susy called. 'Oliver!'

The others had joined us. 'I better go down,' suggested Onyango Shika Dame. I thought it over and agreed, tugging on Gonza. We looked around and found a sisal rope. The rope was firmly secured. Onyango Shika Dame grabbed the rope and serpentine-like swished his way down. After some time, Onyango called us from below to pull him up. So we pulled the rope and got him up. We all looked at him as he struggled to breathe. He looked to me, glanced at Susy, slumped down on his hands and knees and burst into tears. Dirt and grime coated his eyes and choked his throat.

'What will we tell his father!' he sputtered. And cried.

All the others burst into tears too. I quickly took the rope Onyango had used, made sure it was well secured then I lowered myself in through the doorway. Chances were that Oliver was hurt and unconscious.

I was wrong.

The grit in my eyes remained but there was enough light to make me see in the darkness. Oliver had hit his head on piece of rotting rail bar. I saw blood and white things. His skull had broken on impact. My foot stepped on something that felt like a tomato. It squirted, sprung up and hit me smack-dab on the middle of my forehead. It fell on the ground. I peered down to take look. It was one of Oliver's eyes that had been knocked off his socket.

I shook and trembled.

The air was heavily laden with mixed scents of the lake, wild weed, blossoming sage, blood, and brain matter. The boy's and girls's eyes were wide.

Susy stared blankly but she was calm. She sighed and slumped on the wall thinking. Her thinking was disrupted by a sound.

11.

Days, weeks later it becomes apparent that I was *not* unable to handle this because it was not my first death. Magak wasn't my first death either. The Russia massacre wasn't my first encounter with death. My first death had been my grandfather Nyangao in

1966. We all find it hard to come to terms with the 'firsts' of life. First girlfriend, first kiss, first sexual intercourse... don't they all terrify? First time you try to smoke... first time you taste beer. First time you see your father cry, first police brutality... first death. All these things terrify.

I felt bad.

I was going to die too someday.

But my place in Heaven or Hell was already made. Where were the kids shot dead in Russia massacre? Some were in hell, some in Heaven.

Magak and Oliver filled my mind. Magak, definitely, was in hell. Oliver, I didn't know. It dawned on me that Oliver, really, had been my only friend. We'd been together in Pandpieri from class one till we did our CPE. We'd played as kids making models, racing cars made out of Cowboy and Kimbo and Blue Band cans and rolling old tyres on the road and twanging guitars made from wood. We'd conducted scientific experiments with dead dogs and cats and frogs, raced our Safari Rally cars, flown kites and shot at targets in the gardens with our *feya* catapults and killed weaver birds.

Well, like Magak, Oliver will forever be twelve.

1975

SAKAYO looked funny. He looked like a dork, a geek, and a nerd all rolled into one. A longish face like Scooby Doo, bowl-shaped head like Frankenstein and a hooked nose like Captain Haddock. And, though he was thirteen years old, he looked twenty years old. He was another regular Kisumu horndog teen with a tiny brain, a big mouth, a rude smile, a terrible attitude and an eye for girls.

A small gathering of girls milled about, giggling and laughing and chewing gum, pointing and making small talk. The teens were assembled at Kisumu Social Center. We called the place *Sosial* or just *Sosi*. It was our warming zone and meeting point. The talk was of the recent record 'Fever' by Ishmael Jingo, the football game Kisumu Day lost to Kisumu Boys, the recent Bruce Lee action in a Factual open air movie near Nyalenda, the new Peugeot and girls. I was one of the boys and we milled about continuing our efforts to instill that we should get a chance to 'tune' the girls. Sakayo, the main character in this spin, pointed at the cutest of the girls and ordered me to go over and call her for him. Her name was Angelina, she had a cute face, nice *matuta* hair, large eyes, and a nice body. I went over and explained my mission. The other girls took puzzled looks at Sakayo, got ruffled up and left leaving only two of their friends behind.

Angelina and her friend Christine agreed to come and Sakayo got all nervous as he chatted with them. All boys set their eyes on Angelina, she was a hottie. Sakayo asked her to be his chick. She thought it over. Then she suggested to Sakayo to 'tune' her friend because she was 'already taken'. She moved away,

71

got herself a soda. As she returned to rejoin Christine, she winked at me. Sakayo was sweating like a rat. It was clear that he didn't have much experience with girls and most likely he was a virgin. I knew Angelina, though, was no virgin. Both girls were from Kisumu Girls. Angelina was Gonza's chick and Christine was her friend. Gonza had made it to Kisumu Day like me.

Pretty soon Gonza showed up. 'Angeline, Christine, come here.' The gathering crowd grew somewhat quiet but a slight chant had begun (Fight! Fight! Fight!) The girls gulped, pursed lips, and looked to one another. They moved to him, leaving Sakayo drooling. Gonza and the two girls slipped away from us, passed through Arms Bar and walked up the sidewalk to Wananchi Shopping Centre within where they made a purchase of other treats not available at Sosial. Big G, 7-Up, Toffee and stuff like that. Then they walked up to the sidewalk to the opposite end of the shopping block and were chatting and noshing on their treats all the way towards Rotary.

Some kid with a tiny voice crackled up some noise. '*Ei bwana*, look. How can a form one grab a chick from you, heh? *Ei, omera*. A form one!'

'*Yawa!*'

"Form one *awana ni, yawa.*'

To wit there came an uproarious chuckle from me which cascaded down to the gathering. Laughter billowed in the hot sun. Sakayo made a sudden jab-flinch, fumed and followed Gonza and the girls. He followed them around the building to the back of the shopping area to the cinder block fence diving Wananchi and Rotary where he got nice crotch shots as Angelina and Christine straddled the six foot fence and swung their legs over. The girls made the jump down to the dirt ground beyond while Gonza clumsily fell and rolled. Sakayo was mad—more than embarrassed.

We continued to watch. Sakayo reached the fence and fumed. He watched helplessly as Gonza and the two girls slung their school backpacks to their shoulders and continued on their way into Rotary.

2.

Our town of Kisumu was going through some changes; growing, expanding, and so forth. In schools, teachers were making the most changes, busy bodies making changes no one else cared for. Their intentions were good and all, it was just that it was upsetting to most secondary school students of the town, especially those of Kisumu Boys, Kisumu Day, Muslim, Hindochar and Siri Guru Singh Saba Secondary School. Form ones were slaughterhouses and there was nothing the teachers could do about it.

Being a 'mono' at Kisumu Day put me into a world I couldn't understand—it was too confusing, I tell you. I had encountered some of the baddest boys I had ever seen since Magak. Boy, that Sakayo, the ugly form two kid, was a first class nincompoop. He picked on me right from the day he lost Angelina to Gonza. He ordered me to replace her with my sister. I told him I had none. But he laughed me down, said I go home and get my sister to write him a love letter. I hated him but I let it go because I needed to get away from him. Thought that was the end of that.

One morning, exactly one week after the *Sosial* drama, he cornered me and asked for the letter from my sister. I looked at him like I thought he was nuts. And that's how the bullying drama begun. He terrified me. His beef with me? That I had refused to give him my sister. I thought that was a bluff; he wanted to hang something on me to make me a good target, a soft pad for his darts. Being a bit smaller in size, I was no match to him. That's why I suffered most... form twos easily picked on me as their favourite 'mono'. Well, I was taking it all in and badly too. I got bullied every day. They took my money and roughed me up... made me polish their stinking shoes, copy notes for them, and other nasty things. But Gonza didn't think Sakayo was a tough kid. Usually he cornered us in the company of other kids, mostly form twos and one or two form threes. Nearly like a whole battalion. And they normally warned us not to tell the teachers. In primary, I never got bullied. I was one of the most popular

73

kids and I never used my physical strength on lower primary kids. But now here in secondary I was being humiliated (surprisingly). I put up with it for almost four months and it was just getting worse. I got nasty nicknames too: the brown ugly kid (I don't call it an insult). I got pushed down the steps and whenever I opened my mouth to talk they'd yell 'Shut up Form! You are a *Miindi!*'

Suffice to say I was entering the hardest period of my life. I hated this year. In fact I hated 1975. It was meant to be a fine year for me as I entered teenage and into secondary school.

But now...

I hated school. Can you imagine a few days ago one the bullies took my *mandazi* from me during break time saying, 'Form zeros don't eat where we form two are!' I got pissed and had no choice but to hand it to him.

Well, day by day it got worse. Every morning I woke up to go to school, I just wanted to die. In the thick of it all, I had made some friends in D stream who had big bones to pick with Sakayo too. We knew the massive-headed bully was a jerk who delighted in picking on little form ones to make himself feel better and we knew that the more times we let him have whatever he and his buddies asked for, the more likely it was for him to get stronger and the more they'll continue doing it.

We had to do something.

Towards the end of the first term, a form one kid from D stream rounded us up. His name was Zulu. 'You know what I would do if those stupid form twos pick on you again, I will put them in Russia (hospital) and they'll put me in Kodiaga (prison) but again later when I come out of Kodiaga I will put them in the grave where they belong.'

Nerve? You can say so.

No kidding this made me smile. You guess, I was having really bad days so thanks for that boy, Zulu. I really hoped he was not like Gonza; that he was going to put his words into action. Thanks for giving me hope, bro! Those form two kids deserved to get kicked in their freaking faces. I was happy. In days, Zulu became my friend and replaced Gonza (whose parents had transferred to Kisumu Boys). Afterwards it was so stressful when he and I had to make a decision to carry on with our plan without Gonza.

Slowly, we refined the plan; a trap. Poor Sakayo and a few form twos never knew how they got into it, they got caught in the middle us form ones. Seeing Zulu tackle Sakayo and ground him and pound him was priceless. Zulu hauled off and smacked the head monkey in the jaw followed by a pummel to the stomach. It was unexpected and Sakayo doubled over. Zulu brought his knee up and smacked the youth in the nose. There was blood everywhere. The jock went to his knees and Zulu glared at the others: 'Anyone else?' the jocks retreated.

'You broke my nose!' shouted in a terrified shocked Sakayo. '*Tumbafu* you're going to die!'

'Wrong words, *chieth gweno*.' Zulu chirped and turned to walk away.

Sakayo naturally made a lunge. It was expected. I pummeled him with his elbow into the form two's without even turning about. All the form ones descended on him like bees. And as he got pounded, as he begged us, we saw one piece of a scared and ugly bully. I grabbed him by his waistline, suplexed him on the concrete and followed it with pounding punches. I punched him till my fists ached. Then we set him free. Sakayo fell away to curl up and retch on the ground. He got up and ran like a sissy.

The "incident" was taking place under the covered breezeway between Science Lab and D Block. The breezeway was with waist high cement fencing--painted school color lime green. Zulu swung his legs over and walked out into the grassy area between the buildings, no direction at all--just away from the "incident."

He could still see the gathered teens at the breezeway; he saw, too, Mr. Munda and Mrs. Kamasya racing to the scene and some pointing fingers in Zulu's direction. Senior prefects came lopping across the quad and making their way to the scene as well.

Zulu and I held our hands together and made a dash for it.

Passed English Hall, the Library, Student Lounge, Music Lab. Across from the cafeteria then the great choir/drama building. Boys Gym and then the Chapel. Up on the walkway leading down to the general offices the odd-shaped high school icon stood with its newly painted surface and polished emblem, Kisumu Day High: Swift and Sure.

I mulled this over, licking my lips and being most curious. I ran as swiftly and surely as I could. 'Otieno Owiro!' the tall history teacher called. I ignored him. The prefects caught up with me, grabbed me. Zulu quickened his steps but another teacher, a Mr. Odongo, was in hot pursuit. He could hear the man's jingling keys and rustling clothes.

'Suleiman stop!'

Zulu shook his head, not looking back, and continued his forward destination, the Tree garden beyond the tree line and across the basketball gym towards the open football field.

Mr. Odongo raced up and grabbed Zulu by the shoulder.

Zulu whirled on him with glare and disdain.

Punished we were, heavily.

But it worked. Nobody picked on me again.

Life in Day took more colour. I liked to think I was so smart but I was struggling a lot with identity. My classmates found me weird. I was the one who always screwed up the grading curve because I was poor in maths. I was also excluded more so because of where I came from: the ugly Fort Jesus in Pandpieri. In Day, it mattered where you lived. It was a day school and we had kids from Ondiek, Makasembo, Lumumba, Arina, Shauri Yako, Pembe Tatu... even Milimani. Kids from Nyalenda, Manyatta, Kaloleni and Pandpieri (ouch) were considered weird. Added to the fact that I had a funny name: Owiro. I quickly become known as the skinny kid with a funny name. I very quickly got a nickname: Owaya or O-Weird. It seemed like every kid in the school treated me like I was a weirdo and I was already having drama going on at home because Mama wanted my father to take me to another school and my father would have none of it. Home

76

in Fort Jesus, I was different because I read all of the time and kept mostly to myself. I couldn't help it. I had this insatiable curiosity about the world around me. Whenever I had a question about anything, my father faithfully directed me to the set of Britannica encyclopedias that my grandfather had inherited from Mr. Patterson together with the house. I had read each one from cover to cover. I was the only kid in my family that really enjoyed books. The rest of my family took a lot of pride in that. That I was the bright brother who read story books. In primary I had read *The Beano, Dennis the Menace, Enid Blyton* and *Secret 7* and *Tintin.* Now I knew about *Sinbad The sailor, Robison Crusoe, Treasure Island, Alibaba And The Forty Thieves, Robin Hood, King Arthur's Sword* and *Hardy Boys.* And a whole lot more. I was also reading *Big Ben of London* and *Spear* magazines. And Lance Spear Man and The Big Ben crime busters shaped my macho thought. There were more heroes like 'Fearless Fang' (an African Tarzan) and The Son of Samson (an African Superman in a wrestler's body suit).

I was a dreamy kid. I was really shy and had not many friends except for my four good buddies: Zulu, Pascal, Opash and Odhis. The five of us first hooked up in the Music Club. I was not a group person but the equipment that they had at the school were amazing and I couldn't resist playing with the piano. After the meetings in the club, we just gravitated together whenever we saw each other.

Zulu was thirteen; football and hockey were good games of sport for him, but he excelled in football. He was big for soccer. He was one of those admirable players but did not go out of his way to display his talents—only when with his football buddies.

Pascal was a geek. He liked cars, comic books, fantasy books and movies, and liked to talk about airplanes. He wore glasses and looked almost frail but was a typical average youth of fourteen. He had a funny-looking head, almost box-shaped.

Opash was always music crazy. A pudgy fella, not seriously overweight, just pudgy. He was swaggeredly in his step and stance.

He came off as a junior-jock wanna-be at his junior high school and a self-proclaimed lady-killer though he was mostly lame in both departments. A lover of basketball and music, the boy wasn't inclined to follow in his father's footsteps, instead the boy sought for a life of adventure and sports. His taste in music was so eclectic it was insane. He loved music. Soul, Afrobeat, Kelly Brown, Earth Wind & Fire, The Temptations, Kool & The Gang, Bonny M, Jackson 5... the like. I loved Zaïrean rumba.

Odhis was in his own little world. He was a math, physics and chemistry guy and he had big dreams...spent most of his time reading Abott and plotting to make his scientific inventions come true. He could have been a really popular guy in school if he gave a try. I never really figured out why he chose to hang out with Zulu, Pascal, Opash and me. You could tell he fascinated the other kids. They were always trying to get to know him better. Always trying to include him in while Zulu and I stood on the sidelines. For some reason, he stayed on the sidelines with us when things could be different for him.

Being a congenial fellow, Zulu generally got along well with everyone; he was not a prankster, but goose pranked along just the same. He was the Magak of this new age. He was funny, humorous and half likeable—save for his upper class bullies. Yeah. Zulu had friends in high places... form twos and from threes, prefects and even teachers. His comedic abilities helped him in avoiding some fracases but not all. There were some bullies who just refused to laugh at his jokes and bashed him.

And he had nasty surprises. Like the time he got some SM cigarettes and we hid away at Kaburini and smoked a few illicit fags. We'd smoked untold spliffs there at Kaburini, too, swapping stories with kids from other estates.

We also pored through back issues of *Playboy* some guilt-ridden Indian pervert had discarded in *kataka* (and all boys and girls my age did here in Kisumu). We had our dream of seeing the outlandish in living colour, over the top sexual shenanigans that each page contained. We kept the *Playboys* a secret, supplanting ourselves into them. We became the strapping lads who suddenly knew more wonderful sexual reality than our parents ever knew. Well, *Playboy* put in me the habit of wanking.

Pascal never went through the awkward adolescent stage that most boys go through. His very black skin always remained smooth and creamy. His rich black hair was thick and long. He was tall and slender but wasn't clumsy and awkward like most teenage boys. He moved deliberately, like he had all the time in the world. He was just chill like that. Cool and easy. It was probably obvious that I idolized him. He was different from anyone else I had ever known. Why he took a weird little kid like me under his wing, I'll never know.

Not to say I ever had the type of looks that really made somebody stand out; I was used to being told that I was good looking. Personally I just didn't see it. This was me. I wanted desperately to look like Pascal. I thought he had a strong manly physique. I wanted to be the *guy* girls drooled over, and while I was not bad looking, I never seemed to extract any drool from any girl's mouth. On the outside I pretended to be fine with that, but on the inside I was dying for some more attention than what I was getting.

But do you imagine being told you are cute and you hate it? Even my cousins and other girls said that I was cute like a girl. *Jaber ka nyako*, my friends said. I hated it. I hated anything that was going to make me be the center of attraction. My fellow students said I didn't like sports because I thought I was too cute, too special. I knew it was my shyness... I hated sports and athletic and spent a great deal many hours reading James Hadley Chase and singing Lingala songs.

My father, Odundo son of Mbaja was Scrooge himself. If we asked him for *smon* (fifty cents), he'd give us *otonglo* (ten cents). Twenty if he was in a good mood. That's why we were so surprised when he brought home one of those new-fangled gramophones, one that played 45s and long play vinyl albums. In terms of today's shillings, this player was expensive, and so were the vinyl records, which our father bought.

He said he bought it for us... the family. But nobody was fooled. *Wuora* loved music... the way he loved himself. He bought the thing for his own pleasure. And family we surely were: there were six of us at home: big bro Keya, older bro Odingo, I, Ouru, Agwenge, Tom and sister Akong'o, who was an infant in its second year. Like the dutiful father he was, Odundo son of Mbaja taught the four of us boys to operate the machine, so that we wouldn't meddle with it in his absence and damage the needle causing it make awful scratches on the vinyl. It was his pride and joy, and woe be unto anyone who messed with it. He kept it in a corner of the living room, next to his favourite sofa seat. Our guess was that it was there so that if any of his friends came over, they would see it. He had it, he was proud of it, and he didn't mind letting other people know. This gramophone was instrumental in realizing my journey into music. It brought into my young life the likes of Fela Kuti, Franco, Dr. Nico, Kallé, Rochereau, Miriam Makeba, Boney M, Elvis, Otis Redding and many more. It brought music into my life and music stuck in me for the rest of my life. Franco was our father's greatest idol. Fela Kuti was our greatest idol. When he stated the philosophy: *I don't want to be a gentleman at all*, we all agreed and adopted it. My brothers and I used to say: *an African is not a gentleman.*

3.

The day was not unlike any other August day in Pandpieri: hot-humid-and-muggy. It was fifteen minutes past noon judging from the *Wimbo wa Taifa* on radio. The news had just been read. It was a good hump to the beach at Hippo Point; it was further and in the heat it was a bitch—but no one wanted to go the beach swimming anymore. Unless there was a band playing and the bands only played in the evenings when it was cool. The place was deserted in the cool of the day. Zulu suggested an early 'get together' at Sosial to beat the heat and then we would walk all the way to Hippo Point in the evening and dance and sweat to death to the music of this fresh new Zaïrean band called Bana Ngenge.

I had come to Hippo Point early in the day with one mission: to look at the musical equipment and talk to the musicians.

1975 was going to be a fine new year. I was going to be a musician. This is the choice I made in this new year. I was fourteen and spent the days gaping at people's bizarre clothing, ridiculously ugly faces, funny hairstyles, listening mostly to my father's atrocious Zaïrean music and wondering why I struggled so much to fit in.

I was going to be a musician. I was in form two and I was wearing in-style preppy clothes. I was going to be a guitarist. I had practiced singing in the bathroom and when alone walking in the open fields in Pandpieri, I sang aloud. Just thought I hated my singing voice. I sounded so bad... so bad the *ochongorio* birds in the trees flew. Maybe I was a hopeless musical snob... maybe I could fool myself with this singing. But I knew I would never make it as singer. But guitar... I knew I had a chance there. I was going to work hard at it. I was going to play like Franco. Like Dr. Nico. Or better.

Yes. Music was dazzling. Music was good. It gripped me. I was going to create music here in Kisumu that had never been heard of in Africa. I knew it, I could feel it deep down. I told no one, I kept it in my heart. I kept it close because if I told it to people, no one was going to believe me. Either they wouldn't believe me or they would try to talk it out of me and rubbish it.

What triggered this dream? I don't know. I think I was made this way. Last year I had gone with my brothers to the 1974 Kisumu ASK Show and saw this spectacular Zaïrean band playing. It was the most awesome thing I saw. They were something out of this world to me, the way they sang in this dazzling language called Lingala. Talk about love; to them the word was *bolingo*. It's was a freaking romantic word: *bolingo na ngai*. Lingala was more than beautiful; it was mesmerizing. It flew by very fast and had a lot of nice syllables and catchy phrases. I felt it go deep in me. My brothers and other kids watched them passively. I, on the other hand, was taken by it; was possessed. I seemed to reel. I felt a sensation of falling; and, looking round... these guys were singing and dancing and playing their instruments with passion. They were dressed in amazing bell bottoms, tie'n'shirts, bell tassels on crouched sweaters and platforms. Great big afros, beards and bushy sideburns. Their dancing girls wore mini-skirts and tightish shirts and black knee-length boots. Totally unlike any-thing I ever saw.

It took us a good one hour to get to Hippo Point.

It was half-term and the biggest endorsement a school kid like me with limited money could offer was buy tickets worth 20 Shillings. We got there in good time and I indulged in the glory of the equipment. I talked to the musicians. I had, in the way of dogmatic and foolish adolescence, dismissed them as 'hippies'. After all, they had bushy afros like all musicians. They appeared to be 'deep'. My mind was changed by actually hearing them practice, at which point I realized the preconceptions I'd built up based on stories I heard from Zulu and on the fact that Fataki Lokassa was not the actual leader were way, way wide off the mark.

By the time Bana Ngenge (or, as their records suggested it was called, Bana Moja) came out I was pumped and primed, ready to immerse myself in this backwoods Zaïrean fairytale-world they created through music and lyrics.

The lights were set up at the side of the stage, rather than above, flickering across the band, shedding light and casting shadow in equal measure. Whoever did the lighting had done an amazing job. Seeing an actual band on an actual show was something of a revelation. Djo Djo Ikomo and Moreno whirled around the stage, throwing vocal hooks unashamedly. I was seeing live band action for the time, so the gig was just amazing, the musicians tended towards mesmerizing goodness.

The star, of course, was Fataki. His hair was blown up in a

gigantic afro. Pinned to his jacket were dazzling things. His belt was large and had shiny metallic studs on them. I was inclined to roll my eyes. I thought he was a riddle wrapped inside an enigma all bundled up in mystery, which was surely what I was supposed to think. And their dancing style was energetic and hard. Until then, I was used to seeing this slow dance where you held your partner close and whispered all the magic gibberish into each other's ears and when the rhythm changed and *sebene* took over, you showed what stuff you were made of by your feet and waist movements.

Bana Ngenge was different. They were the rockers, the enigma to me. They knew how to hold a crowd. Their playing was, was...guitars were... it was like three descending notes, unresolved and repeated. A little scratchy riff, again ending on an unresolved chord. Then into the strangest, uneasiest 'climax' with Fataki flashing in and out of focus as the lights flickered around the band. Bell bottom jeans clinging hard and high on tiny waist, love beads and a fringed vest rounded out the perfect image a showman. Ah, fashionable.

I wanted to be like them; was going to be like them. Have you had one of those defining moments in your life when suddenly you understand everything? That was it for me. Falling in love with a group is usually a gradual process: you hear, you like, you hear more, you listen closely, you start to love. A few times it happens in an instant. My dream was kept alive and fueled when I heard Ishmael Jingo's *Fever* and Air Fiesta Matata's, *Africa* featuring Steele Beauttah on the VOK radio. I liked Ishmael Jingo. In fact the first single I bought was 'Fever' and then I bought *Africa* (which was actually awesome and, fashion apart, more groovy and well talked about). I bought *Africa* on a trip to Nyanza Supermarket, just outside Standard Bank. I clearly remember the iconic cover of the 45 and Zulu approving of the fact I was getting into music. I'm not sure he would have been so impressed if he'd heard this, mind you. That I had dreams to become a musician, myself.

4.

In my mind I was trying to figure it out, you know...trying to put all my ducks in a row, getting ready to take on my life, whatever may come my way.

In music.

A guitar came into my possession through a quirky circumstance. This is the story of how I got my first guitar: I bought it using scrap money. Being fourteen, I was a little young to be contemplating a career in anything. Nevertheless, when our world seemed too wide and wonderful and the days long and sunny, when our only fear was waking up one morning to find Idi Amin had sent his troops to cross over the border to shoot us and bang our heads at will, you can find you don't have much time. So I was a little impatient.

A great part of my year in form two, in Kisumu Day, was spent out of school because Odundo son of Mbaja had problems paying my fees. With many mouths to feed, souls to clothe, a house to keep up, this and that and that and this—sometimes there were unforeseen events and problems that made our family life a little more difficult. And though try as our parents might, life's problems had increased since the '70s. In the '60s things were easier, but the '70s brought in hard times and often led us down a path Mama attributed to signs of the End Time. The family was growing, for sure. Over extension, uncertainty, contemplation, wishy-washy, and a host of other assorted adjectives applied to my parents.

Mama loved her life of constant prayer despite life's near constant problems. There was always something and usually that 'something' cost money. She made some money. Our father made money. But with the school fees, food and etc. etc., Mama often found herself over extended at the general store.

The burden of paying school fees was squarely on our father, who was earning 150 Shilling per month. There were three of us in secondary school: Keya, Odingo and I. Ouru was set to join form one next year. So I was out of school, wandering with my dusty feet around in downtown Kisumu town center day dreaming about the action I had recently seen in *The Wilby Conspiracy* at Nyanza Cinema and singing things inside my head and picking my nose. I wandered by Ojal's store in a back corner of downtown. Ojal's general store was a throw-back to those old general stores of the modern day 1950s. It was a small store (the kind that sold used electric appliances, second hand furniture, fridges, sports kits, household utensils, old books, fishing gear... you know the type). Ice chests filled with various sodas, old fashioned odds and ends, antiques, aquariums, picture frames, collectibles, and general stuff from that era, but stuff for the modern day times, too.

Ojal was a nice old *mzee*, a devoted Adventist, very nice to everyone—putting himself in a bind by extending credit to virtually everyone. Eventually, though, some people paid their debt. Eventually.

Well today I had wandered here and saw it. In the window was a pristine Yasuma acoustic guitar.

It was worth a look-see.

My music teacher had exactly the same type. No, his was a Yamaha. I'd fooled around with strumming and plucking. I walked into the shop and asked Ojal the price. 120 Shillings, I was told. I thought the old geezer was nuts. Now in 1975, things had suddenly become expensive but I wondered: 120 shilling!? I could get a VW beetle in running condition for that amount. Not as good a deal as the 50 Shillings electric guitar me and my friend Zulu had seen at Victoria Music store. The thing was so little used, I had to have it. Just had to.

I said I could pay 100 shillings and Ojal frowned because he didn't want me to steal to raise the money. He cleared his voice. 'Son,' he said, 'do you know the eighth commandment and what it says? It says *Thou shalt not steal.*'

Turning around, I glared at Ojal for all its worth. 'I'm not a thief,' I told him. I looked up Pascal, Zulu, Opash and Odhis and we went to Dunga, fell into the sun-warmed lake to cool ourselves. Zulu and I had spent the day together, supposedly hunting wild hare, but our hearts hadn't been in killing the little lovely mammals, so we'd digressed, spending much of our hunter/gatherer time telling the kind of stories young teen boys enjoy. We swapped lies about the number of girls we had kissed, each one of us trying to pretend he had been more frightened by the experience. It had been fulfilling, helping Zulu master his wanting swimming skills, because even in this new age after use of life jackets had gained notoriety there was such a thing as real men skin dipping, and I had to be especially careful of making sure my friends didn't drown due to the insular nature of the lakeside community. So it was some relief that we left the water, pretty clean, and found our clothes and were on the way.

As we dressed, I told them my problem.

I told them about it and we came up with ideas on how to raise the money: sell scrap metal.

The only scrap metal dealer I knew in Kisumu was Njoroge operating three shops: one in Manyatta Flamingo, another in Manyatta Arab and a third in downtown Obote Road near Baharia Estate at the Railway quarters. Prices of scrap metal had recently shot up and were now in the following categories *1.* Aluminum, 40cts paid for 1 pound of scrap aluminum. *2.* 15cts for iron and steel, *3.* 50cts for a pound of brass or bronze *4.* 65cts for a pound of scrap copper wire which was the most expensive.

I focused on buying the guitar and set about working at it. I slaved for six months collecting scrap metal and selling them and saving the money in a Cocoa tin can. I saved for the instrument of my dreams, got the Yasuma acoustic in its mint condition for 80 shillings. It was like Ojal never imagined I could raise the money. He hastily packed the Yasuma in a tweed case propped against the corner and pushed it across the counter at me.

At home, I carefully studied the instrument. It was made (label stated handcrafted) in Japan probably in late '50s or early '60s.

I hadn't had my guitar for very long and I was playing.

Starting out seemed a bit overwhelming. Without much instruction, because I wanted to teach myself, knowing what to do was difficult. I decided to just start strumming. After all, I couldn't really play anything, but at least I was faking it pretty good. It was a confidence booster.

My father became my greatest fan. I knew why: I could play something close to 'Africa Mokili Mobimba.' My brothers and the relatives staying in our house at the time were simply enthralled that I had talent. My other support group included Ajuma, an older neighbor who worked as part time butcher and part time guitarist with a little known benga band; he taught me all I needed to know about chords. He had a trusty dog-eared guide to playing the guitar. With this information by my side, it was easy getting started strumming and creating some music. Mama, on the other hand, was against it all, didn't want to see me playing the guitar. Good thing is she worked at Rusinga Island General Store shop many hours a day the whole week except Saturday which was Sabbath and a day for worship and service to God.

Mama hated to see the guitar...embroiled me with long lectures of vices of being a musician. It was like Mama knew I was on the road to becoming a musician and was doing all she could to stop it. Call it parental instinct. She was, really, a paranoid hard ruler who read my every move towards independence as a rejection of her. I explained it was just a hobby and my father and brothers supported me. I think the fact that my father and my brothers appeared to support my guitar playing stopped Mama from either giving my guitar away or destroying it. My father, by now, was a withering figure who was cobbling together a life trying to work hard to pay school fees for his sons and get them on their own. To him, my finding my own path at such an early age was a big relief.

The first day I only practiced for about ten minutes, the second day probably less. I know that probably did not speak volumes of success, but at least I strummed for a while. Not to mention I actually held the guitar much longer; but I guess it depended on Ajuma's definition of practicing. I would soon find out practicing was actually doing something purposeful that pushed me closer to success. I was just strumming. I even went to Kisumu Area Library and looked at some of the guitar books. I saw one that was *Easy Blues Guitar Songs* and dreamed of a day I could play one of those songs.

I struggled with the chords. I never knew true pain until I realized that two out of the five fingers on my left hand were completely numb. They felt as if they had blisters on the tips (and they just did not go away!) It was painful and I'm not going to lie about it. But it kind of made playing a little difficult. I soon learned that this was the formation of calluses. And Ajuma the butcher had told me be prepared for them; I guess he wanted to say I was meant to be playing guitar.

Numb fingers? I had been warned. Pressing down on a little metal string that felt like it was going to cut through your finger was not normal... at least not for a person who hadn't played guitar. Yet I knew that if I wanted to one day play a song on the guitar, I had to eventually do more than just strum. So I started to tackle some chords. I started to pick. I quickly mastered the C chord and the D chord. The E chord and the A cord followed. I didn't know if it really mattered, that you learned one cord first before you could learn another. I guess I was impatient and burning to master it all in one gulp. But Ajuma the butcher told me this was a journey and that I needed to take it slow and practice, really practice, going step by step. So based on his teaching, these were the chords I practiced switching between. Pretty soon I picked up a floating E, or whatever actual guitar players refer to it. I guess it gives it a jazzy effect.

Then I took weeks and weeks working through the dreaded chord of all: The F.

Nursing my numb fingers most of the time, I could only imagine myself plucking away at some easy Franco or Dr. Nico. I was pretty sure I was one day going to play better than Franco. I was going to start my own band. My friends, my family... all were going to enjoy my guitar talents. So, while I could only imagine, the day was coming when I was going to be able to enjoy playing a song that adults were going to listen to as well, especially since the itch to practice my guitar was still very strong, even with the numb fingers!

My father said to me, 'Son, you have a talent. Use it to make money and get rich and famous.'

I held these words close to my heart for the rest of my life.

5.

Suffice to say I felt at odds about my new ability. It bugged me, greatly. In some respects it was familiar, but in others it was new. Was I yet again evolving? In some respects I felt as though the guitar was a curse. A bane. In some respects I wished solely that I had never laid hands on it; in that I wondered how my life would be had I not discovered the instrument at Ojal's. There was no way of knowing, not for sure. There were probably choices.

Kisumu was a different place now. The mid '70s had brought in urbanization that bolstered my fascination. I was a young man awakening to the world and chasing dreams. There were new things... new Bud Spencer and Amitah Bacchan movies at Tivoli, new lifestyles, new music like The Mighty Cavaliers' new funky hit called 'Dunia Ina Mambo.' At first we had been a Dholuo-speaking community, but now new families were arriving from Nairobi and Mombasa and Kisii and Kakamega and Kampala and came to with new the new urban language: they influenced us with their Kiswahili. They made us feel embarrassed with our Dholuo. And since they were so admirable, we wanted to be like them. Sheng was another urban language that had emerged from Nairobi and was spreading very fast and connecting young people. It involved mixing of English words with Kiswahili. In Kisumu we had our own version. For example to say terror, we said *otero*.

Names had been shortened. Onyango was Onyi, Otieno was Otii or Otis. Odhiambo was Odhis... all in that manner. *Kusosi* for eating, *mathee* for mother, *fathee* for father, *siste* for sister, *brathee* for brother, *kutia dame dira* for seducing a girl... were some Sheng words that formed our vocabulary.

We were growing up, just a bit and finding our way. It was suddenly okay to like what you liked in terms of being trendy and talking Sheng was an advantage. Our parents loathed this new distasteful language but we were so eager to learn it. Sheng soon changed our lives and we renamed everything. Our identities changed and our names changed for better, I think. From Owiro, my name was sweetened to Owish or Owaya or Owinye.

I couldn't stop listening to new music and Mangelepa had just appeared from the woodwork and now were firmly in command. They ruled on radio and in bars. Great band! They had just broken up with Baba Gaston and were recording a lot. At one time I only knew 'Aoko' and 'Sakina'. Then suddenly one day in early 1978, the VOK radio announced the arrival of 'Embakasi'. Before the year ended, they had two albums that took people's breath away: *Walter* and *Embakasi*. One after another. Nobody could describe the feeling inside me each time 'Nyako Konya was played on radio: Freedom. 'Walter,' 'Embakasi,' 'Maindusa,' 'Mimba,' 'Nyako Konya,' soon became the greatest chart busters of our times! Great lyrics, great sound... excellent rhythms, excellent talking and walking bass. Mangelepa was surely a veritable charm that threw my imagination into a tizzy. 'Kasuku' also came in 1978, a sequel to the chart bursting 'Embakasi'! I attended their concert at '78 Kisumu Show. They had huge afros, swanky bell bottoms and platform shoes and they danced their tiny waists till dawn. I was torn between crying for joy and mimicking their songs. Boy, oh boy. Those wind instruments were breathtaking.

With Mangelepa came fashion. We had no money, so we wore *omboto* checked shirts, polyester bell bottoms as well as some kind of jumpers.

Then the unthinkable thing happened.

It must have been August 1978, and there I was home from a tea party buried under the blanket late one morning, listening to radio and wishing for a Mangelepa song while my dad stomped up and down outside the room in a huff because I wasn't 'reading' like a 'normal' form four student.

The presenter at VOK interrupted the music. In came the announcement that President Kenyatta had just died.

I didn't believe it.

I was a big VOK fan and could have sworn it was Norbert Okare on the radio, although it appears he wasn't doing a morning slot then—but let's say it was him because that was part of his work and he was the finest of the finest at VOK. Anyway, this announcement came in as if from another planet and drifted in under the blanket; hitting like a punch in the face segueing into an eerie, almost mechanical beat; and then a bizarre, baffling disbelief. After it finished, there was dead silence.

Of course nobody believed it; nobody ever believed Mzee Kenyatta would ever die. Then there was commotion. Ouru was sitting under the *jamna* tree in the garden his feet on the *orindi* stool, reading *After 4.30*. Suddenly he shrieked, '*Kenyatta otho, otho Mumbasa!*' He and other family members all ran into the house to listen to the radio. Mzee Kenyatta's death swooped down like a dark ominous cloud. It disrupted our lives and put an end to normalcy. I was in form four and a candidate for 'O' Level exams, so the one month mourning period for the head of state somewhat interfered with our learning. It was in the newspapers, in the radio and on every lip. Funny thing: nobody ever imagined Kenyatta could die.

'*Kinda piny, thu! Owewa,*' my father said finally.

'I think we should all pray for his soul.' Mama said. And she did. I recall my father saying that Kenya was not going to be the same without Kenyatta. It was like saying Kenya was Kenyatta. Mzee Kenyatta was the only president we knew and he was a mighty man. I remembered seeing him occasionally on TV at

Sosial giving his tough speeches. I remember catching a glimpse of him when he came to open Russia Hospital in 1969 when I was in primary and the fracas that followed.

Pretty soon, life returned to normal and Kenyatta took a quiet retreat into in our memories. Moi was our new president and everyone seemed to love him because he promised to follow Kenyatta's *nyayo*. Then at the end of that year, war broke out in Uganda. Amin was finally being forced out. You guess we could only breathe a sigh of relief. You guess we could only wish they would get rid of him quicker.

One evening in December 1979, at the time Tanzanian soldiers and Ugandan rebels were pounding the President of Uganda Idi Amin Dada and the combined force of Libyan soldiers out of Uganda, my career appeared to take off. I was just turning eighteen in two days and with pubescent developing face and my soft palms and crackling adolescent voice and skyscraping height, I knew I had my whole life ahead of me. My mind was feverish as I walked around Kisumu looking for a job and singing things in my head and dreaming. I had passed my O'level (barely made it with school-fees-problem tag sticking on my back), got a strong third division which was enough to take me to form five, but I couldn't proceed. My father was having problems with his job at Ogongo and I had to step aside for Ouru to go to secondary as well. I made the realization that no amount of good grades or college certificates could fill up a certain bottomless hole. I had 'baggage,' as I was fighting to get a conviction that my life was now firmly in the hands of God.

I came to the realization then and made the decision to begin my journey.

For me, it was bye-bye to formal education and I started scuffing around for something to do on the road to nowhere. That's how it felt. I went into 'survival' and familiarised myself with that road; working for a year in a radio repair shop. Lengthy spells on the dole followed and a short miserable spell in Rusinga Island General Store helping my mother.

You have to admire my guts. As the 1970s folded over, I had only one pair of trousers, a green shirt and sandals. Nothing in hindsight, and certainly not a poor fashion decision. Man, I was poor. I knew I was made for great things but Kisumu yobs had no time for the dreamers like me, so my father's decision to take me to go earn 15 bob per day kneading dough at Koywa Superior Bread bakery with my distinctive haircut—all hot-comb-blown-up and hippy—seemed to me to be brave in the extreme.

That job was going to be my first. If I got it. If I liked it.

Kisumu had grown. But it was still a small town burg, small town Africana. A typical post-Colonial type town, virtually everyone in town knew everyone. There were get-togethers, socials; women selling things on the roadside, big market days every Sunday at Kibuye. Little league football matches at *Stadi*, Saturday night movies at Nyanza and Tivoli, disco at Action Centre, Beograda, Dark room and Octopus w/o violence or sex— just the suggestion of it. Africans were beginning to start enterprises. Koywa was the first African-owned bakery in town and a focal point for the center of bread supply and served multiple outlets including Kericho, South Nyanza and Western Province.

Well, my father ordered me to report to the mill, near Kibuye. The area was called Koywa, anyway... just somewhere along Ramogi Road.

A short swarthy man with a typical Maragoli face was washing a ton of dishes and cursing. Benga music blared out of a radio nearby. There was yet more activity. Another big burly dumpy man in serious need of a bath, a shave, a haircut, was fussing about checking a huge pot of something bubbling within.

'*Ei*! Oloo son of Oywa *yawa!*' bitched the man washing the dishes.

'Aa? *Eei, stupid ther nyang* Oloo son of Oywa *yayee!*' amended the burly beefy fellow in need of bath.

'Marrying a third wife while we work ourselves dead with no overtime!' said the man still washing the dishes.

'Stuck here while he goes to Nairobi to have a good time!' added the second man. He stirred the huge vat of bubbling Devil-knows-what.

'Making bread to meet deadlines with no raise!' he sparked.

'Man, I'd be glad the day he dies!'

'Ha! Then you won't have a job.'

'Hey!'

'Hey what?'

'We can *make* him close! Then *we* take over.'

'*We?* How?'

'His wife trusts that thieving accountant from my village.'

'Aha.'

'He'd probably blame himself if this bakery goes down. Imagine earning two hundred a month and we are now in 1980!'

'Yeah, and we break our backs while he changes cars and girls all the time. Ouma said this business won't last the next year.'

'Whatever. Serves him *kuma-ya-mamake* right for making us stay here and do these *kuma-ya-mamake* dishes and watch over his precious *kuma-ya-mamake* bakery!'

The men seemed upset. I hung lose for a moment, there was a black cat nearby noshing on something under the huge boilers. There was more of a conversation from the two men, I missed some of it.

'Next year I'll be in Mayfair. My sister's husband is working to get me there' said the beefy pudgy fella.

'Add a dash of this—!' smirked the tall goofy hunk. In his hand he had some packet with powdery stuff in it. He poured a smidgen of whatever into the precious batch of Devil-knows-what. Then he dumped the whole thing and tossed the packet into the trash.

The pudgy man roared with laughter.

'What else?'

'What?'

'What else to add to the perfect prize winning Koywa Loaf seven years in a row that would spoil it for sure...'

The swarthy man perused a rack and through the various other accouterments. Suddenly, the pudgy man cringed and got the look of a woman in labour, *'Ei yawa!'* he cried out, 'my stomach!' and he grabbed a piece of newspaper and dashed off into the darkness down a hall.

The swarthy Luhya man shook his head, and made a selection. He dumped an entire sack of whatever stuff into the batch of boiling stuff, gave it a rough-around, then spat on the floor.

His companion returned, smiling sheepishly. *'Thu yawa iya!'* he exclaimed, *'Don't* go in there!' he warned.

'Omunyololo!' bitched his friend fanning the air, *'Kwani* what did nyar Nyahera cook for you last night!' as the noxious odour wafted from the toilet—and quite possibly from the pudgy man himself.

'*Mbuta.*'

'Omunyololo!' coughed-sputtered the swarthy man. He shook his head and returned to the dishes. 'Go to Russia they check your stomach, *bwana.*'

'What about Oywa's loafs?'

'Weri gi mkati nyieni!' scoffed the swarthy man. 'You will die.'

'Well, I'm fine. Let's get this shift done with!'

I rolled my eyes, so did the swarthy man washing the dishes.

'Are you going to mop the messy floor or do I do *that,* too!?'

'Alright, alright!'

The pudgy man grabbed a nearby mop, and then—his eyes bulged and he gritted his jaws, gnashed his teeth. 'My stomach!'

'*Si* you go to Russia, *bwana,*' bitched the dish washing man. 'How will we finish this shift and go home if you keep bugging out to dump *wen* in the *choo* every five minutes!'

'I told you it's no use!' added the pudgy got-the-shits-man.

'*Kwenda.*'

'The way I keep piling *wen* there and coming back, Oywa would shit bricks golden if people ate his precious loafs and got the shits!' added the man in the bathroom down the short hall.

95

More noxious odor came wafting down and filled the small back room. Dish Washing Man coughed and sputtered, '*Eei!* close the door, *omera!* Close the door!' he shouted, fumbled about in the near darkness and flung open the screen door, propping it open. The cat noshing on its evening meal hissed at the man. The Dish Washing Man stomped his feet and scattered the kitty.

'Did you hear what I said?' Pudgy Man said coming back to the room, sweating and zipping up his ill-fitting jeans.

Then they all saw me.

'What do you want, kid?' the swarthy dish washer asked.

I said nothing. I walked out.

6.

I felt I was now a man. I was talented and fully engaged in working my head off to excel and to succeed in the many challenges life was putting on my path. I was tall and angular, six feet four and weighing about 70 kgs and just awakening to thoughts of girls, feminine beauty and possibilities. Ok, I admit it. Compared against my peers, I came out a little, hell a lot! My good looks had attracted many girls: there was Dorry while I was in primary, then again Achi (Oliver's sis) when I was in class seven. During my secondary at Kisumu Day, I had Nancy, Ruth and Redempta. Nancy and I had become sort-of-friends. I helped her study, and she let me take walks with her around Makasembo, Nubian and Joyland, and that was the end of it. We never went out, never hugged or kissed, never visited each other at home. She was in Rang'ala Girls and all we did was write each other romantic letters. I was vaguely aware that Nancy was a staunch CU member and a Catholic, but since Catholics never appealed to me, I made no attempt to seduce her. (I later found out that she planned to become a nun).

Then Ruth came...I just wish... (sigh). Folks, let me tell you a story. I was in form three when Ruth happened. Every Kisumu guy has a Ruth in his past, somewhere. That first love that floored you ten nil. I loved her more than I ever had anybody else in my life. She didn't even know I was alive, though, and it hurt. I would have done anything for her, and she knew that, and took advantage of it. I did her homework, usually when she was out on a date boogieing with another guy. I didn't care, figured that eventually she'd wise up and realize that I was the only guy for her. That didn't happen, and she's gone now... but I always wanted... I always wished... this girl I loved would love me just as much. That's what I was hoping for, that I wished Ruth loved me as much as I loved her. I'd had my head split and my heart ruined on the only date I was to have in that year; Ruth Adhiambo, warm for an instant, then forever cold; that was that, no appeal.

Other chicks came along, fantasy miracles who I never spoke to; other blips in the haze, but no contact with the targets. Soon I was hitting them. But these were just plutonic stupidities of writing each other letters on foolscaps and on pages of exercise books, walking and talking in secret places to steal kisses and hugs, exchanging novels, saying too much I-love-yous... such things. They were real enough to make my heart stop beating. I felt the love, it was too strong, I felt it. Too strong and dangerous to hurt my ego. I could kill a guy for just looking at my girl. The problem was I was shy in many ways, so they had never blossomed into full contact sexual relationships.

Redempta was a Tree Top girl. She had nice legs and in 1980 people no longer fancied girls with slender legs. People had now come to glorify girls with fat legs and we called them Tree Top legs. Redempta, especially, was a goddess, that Banyala girl from Busia. There was this burning electricity between us. Her presence filled my senses and my soul. I talked with her often and finally got up enough courage to ask her to attend a cinema on the week-end. We dated several times, and I would always walk her back to Okore where she lived with her aunt, and shake her hand as we said goodnight... very warmly. After about three dates, we progressed into kissing and the like. It was quite clear something was going to happen between us. It was the way she behaved when we were alone, the way she looked at me, the way she touched me looking deep into my eyes. It was not solely my pubescent developing faces, nor my soft palms eager to grip her tenuous flesh, nor my distinctively spermy, pollen-filled scents that made her swoon as I held me so tight. Nor was it her soft fleshy body, smelly armpits, developing tits, delicious lips and softly-downed limbs that gave me a churning burning need deep at my core. Nor was it the sweet crackling tone of her adolescent voice, the inhuman cry of a virgin girl in the throes of laughter, anguish or ecstasy, the deep penetrating stare from young sexy eyes, the pent-up libido, the flaring temper, the quest for satiation of curiosity. NO. Something about the mysterious combination of these forces drew me and her to race towards seventh heaven, and to the pleasures that lay therein.

She is the one who... who... er, um... took away my virginity. No, I took hers. Yeah. It was real.

After doing her O'Level at Kisumu Girls, soon, too painfully soon, Redempta had to relocate to Busia. It tore us to pieces. Letters we wrote, passionate and full of anguish at the distance. Time passed. They say time is the greatest healer of human anguish.

I was always wandering around checking out the latest chick crop and had focused on another Maragoli girl. The new vocabulary for girls was chick, so she was my chick. Her name was Riana Adisa and she was now turning to become the first true love of my life.

Aarrggh!

Riana was different. She knew on some private mental plane that I was hopelessly in love with her, but didn't make me feel bad about it, didn't ridicule me about it. She rejected my affections without making me feel bad, and in my own private hell, that earned her high marks. So we remained friends, good friends, the kind of friend you will take long walks with... just to talk. We had private jokes, inside little comments that we threw back and forth like a personal, private code that only we could understand. If it were possible to have a love affair without the sex, Riana and I did. We were closer than most boyfriends and girlfriends, and we reveled in it.

7.

The odd relationship, kismet, between Riana and I, flourished. She was, oh, so churchy and deep into her faith and Bible study. But she was kinky and naughty on the side! She liked me. I saw Riana on the average of about once every week. Usually for lunch after church service, or in Kisumu Area Library. We would stop and talk and laugh and catch up on things. One time I spotted Riana in the library with a guy. I knew him from Ondiek Estate; he was popular, a jock and big in the fraternity Kisumu scene. He was also an Adventist and a regular church-goer, and was very popular in church. His name was Erick, nice modern name it was. Watching them together, it wasn't hard to surmise that they were dating. Riana was all smiles, and she took every opportunity to touch him, running her hands up and down his arms, across his back.

I didn't want Riana's boyfried to misintepret my intentions towards her, so I stayed away. She sensed what I was doing, and the smiles she gave me made it all worthwhile. You see, at our age, friends (true 'friends' of the opposite sex) were hard to explain to your significant other. Riana and I had never talked specifically about it, but we both knew that we were, somehow, more than 'just friends,' yet less than boyfriend-and-girlfriend. It was something not easy to explain and define but it existed. It was valid and true and one-of-a-kind. I'd tell her how pretty she was and she'd ask me coquettishly if I truly thought she was pretty. We were comfortable with it, as it was, and didn't want to jeopardize it by exploring it any further.

Seeing her with her boyfriend made me realize something too. Somewhere along the line, I'd fallen in love with Riana.

Quietly, desperately in love with a girl that I could never have. And it became a problem. It wasn't the burning hormonal passion that marked 'love' at our youthful age. I'd be lying if I said I never thought of making love with Riana. But that wasn't all of it. The feelings I had for her ran true and long and very, very deep. I knew, even then, I'd have a special place in my heart for that woman for the rest of my life. Everyone has a person like Riana in their life.

One day Riana came to me after the church service. 'Otis, join Gloryland,' she said. 'Play guitar for us.' Gloryland was this dynamic youth choir.

I gave it a thought, playing with a church choir and performing as an acoustic guitar player. Wasn't a bad idea. So I joined the SDA youth, I joined Gloryland Choir. For six months I played steadily with them, pleased Mama and earned a special place for myself in church. In Gloryland, I sat with another acoustic guitar player/singer occasionally. His name was Bob. He was quite a bit older than me, in his 20s I'd guess, and he was full of stories. We hit it off pretty well, and we soon realized we were both interested in getting paid to play in a cover band at the time. We'd do some acoustic duo stuff, some solo-and-rhythm stuff— very chill. I was in it for the new experience, he for money. He wanted to produce a gospel album. He was friends with famous record producers and musicians in Nairobi, blah blah. Me, being a big greenhorn, I wanted to believe him. He mesmerized me and I hung on to his every word. We started playing music together, with me backing him up on guitar during some solo sets he'd play during church events and even private parties.

It sounds insane, but the guy did have a lot of charm; he played well and could sing too. However, my experiences with him got weirder. I sensed there was something unreal and ominous. He was a little too fast and complicated. The guy had no fixed abode, in the first place. He was staying with this person, then that person. He was staying at church— it was odd.

I was hanging on his shirt like a sore thumb and was

beginning to wonder where this was leading to when he came up with this idea on how to make money from music. He knew a singer and guitarist and said that they just needed a solo guitar player, so I was down for it. Or so I thought! That's when the worst freaky experience of my entire life began to unfold... remember here I am a shy kid who was very vulnerable to the inward turning of the real world. He starts telling me that real money from music business was 'out there'. Not in church. He had a few connections and wanted me and him to follow them through. And hey, would I like to come with him, back him up?

Sure, I said. But first I would have to ask my father.

Yeah, he said. He already knew my Dad loved my guitar playing. No biggie. All we needed to do was meet the record company guy and audition for him. If lucky, he will connect us with a band.

Oh, and we were to pay sixty bob each.

I paid, got the money from Riana. Lied to her about a church trip.

We packed up the guitars and went to Sosial Centre for the big audition gig. He took me to an empty room, asked me to give him the sixty bob and wait. I gave him the three crumpled blue Moi notes. I waited. No record company guy showed up. I saw Bob pacing in the front looking concerned. Then I saw him making a call at the dial-up payphone at the entrance. So I left him to it, crossed over to the main hall and kept myself busy watching cartoons on the black and white TV.

After a while I went looking for Bob and couldn't find him. I waited for three hours. Neither Bob nor the record company guy was anywhere.

I'm still waiting getting twitchy but hanging on shreds of hope. Then some wiry boy I remembered seeing in church shows up. His name was Ojuku, I think. 'You waiting for Bob? he asks.

Yeah.

He laughs. 'I saw him heading to Makasembo.'

What?

He nods. 'To see Monica.'

Monica?

'The girl he met in church choir and made pregnant.'

Oh my. While I am staring, Ojuku continues. 'That guy is a phony. He's not who he says he is. *Weri kode.*'

Point taken. On my way back home I decided to drop Bob's hat off my squat and never hang out with the guy again. If it sounds too good to be true, it isn't. Life is not easy. This was my experience with phony characters, my first nasty experience in life. I am eighteen and this is how I am welcomed into adulthood, into the world of men. I draw one rule: never trust anyone with your talent. It makes me know the value of my talent... life is full of fishy characters who come to you in sheep's clothing. I didn't need my father or anyone to tell me that there are always people who come close to you with the sole purpose of exploiting your talent, I saw it.

It made me more determined. What I found hilarious was it seemed Bob was going to all the trouble of stringing me along for weeks on end so he would use me to solder on with his own ambition to get into the recording world only to rob me. How cheap? Sixty bob! He went to church to get a good kid to use since he was already rotten. I couldn't see any other reason, beyond delusional insanity.

I remained active in church but I decided that Bob had given me an idea. He had taken my innocence away and given me an idea. I was going to meet other guys in future and we were all going to hit it off and life was peachy. I played guitar for Gloryland which led to many of the people at our church wanting me to play (and sing) at their weddings (and funerals) and such. I did, alright. For money. I insisted I get paid. I was nobody's fool no more, I was an adult. I didn't need my father to tell me I had talent and that I should use it to make money. I knew it. I made money and bought myself nice trousers and *mocassin* shoes and shirts and string ties and nice t-shirts.

Well at one wedding the bride and groom had a particular

song that I had never heard before. They supplied a cassette of the song and I became somewhat proficient at performing it in our bedroom. On the day of the wedding, I arrived about thirty minutes early to warm up and be ready for the service.

Now this was a Catholic wedding and the bride would come in from the outside of the church. Well about ten minutes before the wedding, I realized that I had a mental block and just could not remember the melody line for the song (I had three or four songs to do at this wedding). I ran (yes ran in the hot sun with my borrowed white polyester leisure suit) to the shopping center at Kibuye, found a phone booth and called the number of the house Riana lived with her aunt. Luckily she was in and I asked her to call my sister Akong'o. I instructed Akong'o on what to do and she got the cassette of the song (that was in our bedroom) and played for me the song over the phone! She did and I immediately remembered the song and ran back to the church where by this time the bride was outside sweating... waiting for the soloist (me!) to begin. I sheepishly smiled and said sorry and ran up to the balcony to sing the song while sweating like a rat.

All was well, and the bride seemed to forgive me!

I was thankful for that! But the groom was pissed off. So he pissed on me. 'Why don't you go to Kondele and play with Nicholas Opija in that damned band of losers called Delta Force if you are so incompetent. *Chiedhni!*'

I thanked him too. He gave me another idea. I had to face the real world, stop hiding in churches. The real world was out there. Of course by now I had learned to use each and every opportunity. Life was giving me very little opportunities, each was golden. The next day I must be in Kondele to see this band called Delta Force. I must succeed in the real world; the world of men.

8.

Even though I was a natural bone-deep Kisumuan, born and bred,

I could sometimes be the 'new guy' when it came to Kondele. I had my haunts which were Pandperi and Nyalenda and Milimani and its Dunga surroundings. Kondele was another world altogether, a dark gray world of strange people and strange things I was lost in. One that chocked me and I felt uncomfortable in. But my love for adventure was also something I'd grown very passionate about as well and rediscovering my own love for music which by now was quite compulsive.

Kondele lies in the middle of three roads: Jomo Kenyatta Highway (racing towards Kisumu town center), Kakamega Road (racing towards Western province) and Kibos Road. So no matter what direction you approached it from, you eat dust. Today it was just as dusty and brown as I knew it. I had come in one of the old Peugeot 404 station wagons that were usually, frail and rattling but sturdy enough, somehow, to carry a dozen people. I alighted and looked around: here I was in this mess of dusty potholed roads clogged by a lake of humanity. I found my way about like a lost goat past street preachers and hawkers and idlers. Today there was a crusade on the huge open field next Russian Quarters and Medical Training College and a Pentecostal preacher was screaming his head off at a pocket of nonchalant flock. His message was poignant: the drought and famine affecting parts of this country was due to Kenyans' disobedience of God's commands for a revival. True, we were experiencing famine to the extent the United States of America had recently stepped in to provide famine relief. That was the explanation for the *bando mar onding* (yellow maize) we were now eating because the country had recorded bad harvest. But famine or not, Kondele, this was. Seeing mad men like this screaming preacher was normal. Why take advantage of hunger? Rains were going to fall again and yellow maize was going to go out of our plates soon. To me, this was just another crazy loud mouth that would, at the end of his ranting and raving, demand *sadaka* from the miserable flock.

I plodded in the dust and found my way around and about Kondele and wondered after the awful weather here. During the day, it was hot and dusty and windy with gusts that blew dust on people and on the shops and speakers from record shops along the dusty streets and men and women going about their businesses. Everything including trees and green leaves were caked with thick layers of brown dust. At night, it was fully awake, its hot spots teeming, its discos throbbing. Kondele had had many popular 'watering holes' since the 1960s. It had so many bars and clubs and cheap prostitutes.

Some of the bars had live music. I was here for such.

I asked a bored-looking, dust covered cobbler where I could find this band called Delta Force. 'Olindas Bar,' he said. I didn't know my way around Kondele, so I looked around for someone to give me directions. Some carpenters sat looking nonchalantly at passersby from an open air workshop next to a posho mill. Their products, displayed on the dusty pavement and caked with dust, included coffee tables, beds, coffins and side boards. They knew where Olindas Bar was, near the Post Office. One of them, an Amin of a youth (chewing sugarcane), stood up and volunteered to take me there.

On the way as we went, he told me his name was Thwaka. Morris Thwaka, but people called him Mo. He was a tall, gangly man-boy, dark-skinned with thick lips and a tiny voice. He was high as well as broad; he towered over me and I'm a shade over six feet. He went further to tell me he came from Kobura in Kano and he called me *Jayadha*. I outrightly knew the kind of Luo he was: the village Luo. He was talkative and loud and mostly said unnecessary things. He was uncouth and unpolished; you know that kind of Luo... the one who verbalizes and vocalizes each and everything he sees. The kind who makes you hate talkers. He wanted to know what I wanted to do in that bar, a young boy like me and I told him I wanted to see a Mr. Nicholas Opija who had a band that was playing here. 'Kisumu Delta Force?' he asked. I nodded at him. He appeared to know Opija and warned me that Opija was not a straightforward man. When I told him I was going to see the band (and not Opija) because I was hoping to play guitar with the band, he told me he was a singer. Thought he had a singing voice and wouldn't mind joining too. I wondered after his carpentry work and he said it was his uncle's place. I had summed him up within four minutes. I didn't want to listen to him anymore for who he was: a *ja keto kore*. A hanger-on, a freeloader.

Olindas Bar was well-known. It was located in an increasingly upscale section of Kondele, behind the Post Office near Arina Scrap Metal Yard where it was vying with other bars offering beer specials nightly and live music. The club was housed in a building marked Mzee Obunga & Sons (Since 1935) and had an unlit sign along its side entrance, and the only branding in its outer brick wall was a lone neon light advertising Pilsner.

It was a few minutes close to midday, but the bar room was deserted. It was a fairly large bar that had seen far better days. The interior was a bit like your typical Kisumu boarding & lodging bar room, with a single bar on one far end, about thirty feet of lonely empty space that would've been much happier with some customers to occupy it. There were eight big wooden posts, about 12 feet high, rising from the middle of the floor and holding up the ceiling. The four people at the bar could have been wooden Kamba carvings considering how little they reacted to us. The room was warm and comfortably Kisumuan. Tables, booths and stools were empty, the single dartboard corner unemployed. The jukebox was silent. What caught my attention most was the instruments. The stage was not raised, it was a cleared floor area between the side door and restrooms with lights mounted from the ceiling and monitors in front. I had always been fascinated by band instruments: everything looked magical. An oversized double set of clear blue drums, three mics, huge speakers, a couple of tumba drums, three guitar stands told me this was a 4 or 5 piece band. The instruments looked new and the way the cabling was done, I was afraid if a drunk danced too close one of the mic cords would wrap around his leg. Other than the four zombies at the bar, there were two men and two women who were yapping away and giggling at a far corner.

A middle-aged bored looking man who would be the bartender was hunched over a pile of papers on the dusty countertop with the concentration of someone working on his month-end budget. As Mo Thwaka and I entered the bar from the stinging sun outside, he looked up and squinted at us.

Tapping the sharp end of a Bic ballpoint pen against his teeth, he asked *'Ojende, amiu ang'o?* Get you something, boys?'

Mo seemed to know him. 'Musa, *ber*,' he said in greeting.

'Ber ahinya, mita un.'

'We are here to see Opija,' Mo said, sitting on the nearest stool. He rested his forearms on the padded edge of the counter and sighed. 'Give me a cold Coke. And one for my friend here. Is Opija here?'

'Yes he is,' the bartender said, putting down his pen. 'There he is over there, the one in white shirt.'

While the bartender fetched our Cokes, Mo looked around and set his eyes on the two men and two women sitting *kijebres* at the corner. Mo was beginning to irritate me. I was still trying to figure him out, trying to size him up. True, he was helping me. But I didn't like the way he was taking over. He had gone ahead and bought me soda. That meant he had invested in this quest. Technically I now owed him. I didn't know what was in this for him. I was getting rankled. I had to find a way to shake him off. My dislike was evident in the cold manner in which I answered him. But something told me to be patient; he was my ammunition for now and his aggressiveness gave me an advantage, and I knew enough to wait. Suddenly I knew. I wanted him to initiate the discussion of how we should approach discussions with Opija. He wanted to be part of this, fine. I wanted to use him.

Mo pulled me close to him. He lowered his voice confidentially and pointed. 'That man there in white shirt is Opija. The other one is Sam Olindas, the owner of this bar.'

Involuntarily I looked at the group sitting in the corner.

The men were casual in appearance and manner. The one who would be Opija had his eyes glued to the pages of a newspaper. The two women were rather on the hefty and broad side, with *wenge ma okorore* hungry eyes of regular Kondele harlots.

So much for the effort and ingenuity of Mo. I could see he was stubborn like a jackass and as ignorant as the village idiot. A sixty-kilogram mouth attached to a one-gram brain, that's all he was. He looked at me and said, 'Let's join them.' To the bartender, he said, 'Bring our drinks over there.'

I followed him. The man who would be Sam Olindas lifted his head and watched us come. He was about thirty-five, big, fat, soft and good to look at. The typical Luo mobility of his face was sobered by the warmth in his eyes.

'How are you boys?' he asked.

'Fine,' answered Mo flippantly. Me and him had our eyes on Opija, encountering only a single pair of eyes that fluttered up from a newspaper for a quarter of a second to peer at us then went back to scanning the pages of newsprint.

We settled ourselves, ours drinks were brought. The bartender yanked the bottle tops off the bottles with an opener, whispered something in Olindas' ear and went away.

Olindas fed us with warm eyes. Cheap lager and lovely cocktails couldn't be as warm as his friendly style. I liked him, he looked to me a nice guy. Suddenly he extended a handshake. Mo beat me to it. Olindas' big, meaty paw covered Mo's hand, and I wondered if they were going to get into one of those insane hand-squeezing tests. Perhaps I should add that although Mo was over 80kgs, Sam Olindas made him look like a dwarf. He was six foot six, and weighed close to one hundred and thirty kilos. And not an ounce of it, a single ounce of it...was muscle. He was a huge blob of a man, with swinging jowls that reminded me of those things on roosters or turkeys. (What do you call those things, anyway?)

So, here we were. Olindas welcomed us to his bar and said that as the owner he must make this small bar a must-see and it certainly seemed popular with locals and visitors alike. I liked that. He told us of his plans on simplifying the food menu to the good quality pub grub served beside lager and other drinks. I liked that too. I immediately had a name for him: the Friendly Son of Africa.

His audacity was for a specific purpose. But after a moment, seeing a faint restiveness in Mo's eye, he changed the subject.

'I hear you boys want to see Opija. Are you boys musicians?'

I wondered how he knew. Mo Thwaka looked at me, so I said, 'Yes.' All eyes including the two sultry pairs belonging to the two harlots turned on me.

'How old are you, boy?' Opija asked. I looked at him then, the tactlessness of my youth and recent entry into adulthood betraying my polite instincts. And, folks, I almost had to take a knee. His breath was so revolting; he nearly made me pass out. His look unsettled me a bit, yes, but his breath... *Weeh!* And he was also ugly. He was the ugliest man I had ever seen, with hair jutting out of his ears and nostrils. My elder bro, Keya (who loved to make soft jokes about how people looked) would describe him of being as ugly as seven ugly men. But despite his ugliness, he looked self-assured, dashing, intimidating. I found fault with his stammering too: he was the kind of Luo who spoke in short choppy sentences like a *dodo* singer.

I refused to lose all the willpower and composure; I refused to blush under pressure. I looked at him back. Mo looked at me. Olindas looked at me with a frown. The harlots looked at me. But I held my look. My direct look must have unnerved Opija somewhat. He told the two half drunk, giddy, laughing harlots to excuse him.

'What's your name?' he asked me as soon as the two whores had moved away.

I bit my lower lip. 'Owiro Odundo.'

'That's your name?'

I nodded. (The name comes from my moniker in adolescence. I had recently dropped Otieno and Dinosus.) 'My other name is Otieno. People also call me Otis.'

'You want to join Delta Force, you need a new name. A name that sells you. How about Otis Dundos? I will personally call you Abonyo, you have an Indian nose, you're also brown like those Kamas Indians.'

There was an outburst of laughter from Olindas and Mo. Olindas laughed pretty much constantly, rumbling belly laughs, all through. The way he laughed alone could make you laugh.

Meanwhile, I remained mute, recovering from the shock of meeting a star quality figure with a revolting breath and electrifying personality. I was saved from further embarrassment when the officious band leader announced, 'Sit down and tell me about yourself.'

After being seated, Opija's amiable questions permitted me to find my voice. Overcoming my shyness, I responded to the man's genuine interest in my life and career aspirations. Opija was an excellent listener and did little more than ask questions and listen. I was impressed his queries revealed a real curiosity and interest—not at all like my father's cross-examination or Mama's hard questions that were designed to entrap.

'Do you have your own guitar?'

No.

'Problem here, boy, is guitar. Benz!'

A short guy appeared dressed in an outdated 1960's *katera* shirt and with a lazy-looking persona. He looked almost like a lifeless scarecrow. Being an artist, I loved form. I judged people by the first impression and I read body language. I didn't like bad looking people; I was good looking myself. I didn't like floppy dressers. Mama usually scolded me about this. She told me that she hated my attitude about people, that in my heart, I am fastidious and conceited. I didn't like this guy due to his outdated dress code and his lazy persona. He was somebody who was not serious about himself, and cared less about how he looked. An amiable man like this couldn't be taken seriously.

Opija spoke to me, 'This is Benz Benji Obat, our *chief*

guitarist. Solo guitar!' To the solo player, he said, 'Benz *yo*, this Abonyo is called Otis Dundos. Give him your guitar and watch him play. Whatever he wants to play. I want to see if he has talent in benga.'

Talent. Of course.

The rehearsal room was a small one with the dimensions and look of a kindergarten class. A long coat closet covered by an accordion-fold wooden sliding door. There were old speakers and amplifiers and beer crates and shoes and wigs and men's clothing and a bed. Several foot-tall risers stacked in the middle of the room made us look like a primary school choir. Benji handed me an electric guitar and sat down on an arm chair. He didn't bother to invite me to sit, so I found a stool and perched myself on it. Mo had followed us and he, too looked for something to sit on.

'I have never used an electric guitar' I said, hoping I wasn't butting in. Benji ignored me. I was young and eager. He was mature and experienced. He took things slow, he had probably seen a lot. This was going to be fun; a wonderful school for now.

Mo opened his mouth to say something but Benji's stony look floored him. We saw he had picked a bass guitar and was strumming.

'That's a bass guitar,' Benji said to him. To me he said. 'I want you to sit upright and relax. Like this.' He demonstrated. 'Hold your guitar like this.'

'Uh, sure,' I said. He was telling me things I already knew. The only person he was teaching was Mo. What did he think of me, a novice to guitar? I said, 'Let's hear it for Mo.'

I began to play the intro. I was amazed at how soft and easy electric guitar was. The strings were lighter, and easier to press down. It was sweet—a few simple chords underneath a charming little melody, very sweet. I did a pretty good job, but something didn't sound quite right. Before I finished the few chords, I noticed Benji had set a piece of paper on his knee and leaned forward to peer at the guitar. 'Let me hear it again,' he said. 'This is an electric guitar, why do you pick the strings like it's an acoustic? Just be gentle. Just glide and feel the sound. Glide and don't muzzle the strings.'

I played the short piece again. This time he watched my hands, my wrists, my thumb, my shoulders. When I finished the second time, he looked up at me.

'You don't have to try too hard,' he said. Both he and Mo laughed a little, and Mo let out a good-natured growl. 'What?' I asked, confused.

Benji beamed, 'You're a natural.'

'I've been telling him that exact same thing for almost an hour,' Mo lied. 'It's me you need to teach.'

'Okay,' Benji said, 'let me show you something.' He pulled another guitar from behind some cartons and played a simple Zaïrean rumba pattern. I gestured that I wanted to sit next to him, and Mo stood to let me. Once I was settled in, I started playing what I'd just heard Benji play.

'*Omera*,' Benji almost shouted, 'you're already playing it better than I do.'

I smiled at him. 'I bought myself an acoustic guitar in 1975. All I have done ever since is play, play, play. Now I need to learn songs.'

'So, what are you doing that I'm not doing?' he asked.

'Teach me,' I said and turned to look at him.

He said, 'You're playing the notes just fine, but not the music.' I shook my head slightly: I had heard this before. He looked for another way to explain it. 'Think of it like dancing. Open your heart and feel it. You don't just stand this way...'—he raised his arms stiffly and froze, then moved them a couple of times, freezing in each position— 'and then this way and then this. Dancing is about the way you move from one position to another.'

I began playing the piece again, this time playing soulfully, like I'd heard Benji do. He stopped me. 'Music is the same way. You have to get the right notes, but the music is also in how you get from note to note, how you move through the phrase.' He

112

switched his playing to be more fluid, more melodic. Then he stopped and stood up. 'Now, play it again. But this time don't play C-F-G-B-C. Play the phrase.'

I started playing again. It was a little more melodic but still kind of stiff. 'Relax, Abonyo. Don't worry so much about individual notes, you've got those down. Now relax and play the phrases.'

I did seem to relax a bit. At least his playing improved my style a little: it became more like music. 'See,' Benji said, 'it's better already. A couple more times and you'll have this down and right.'

That made me glad, so I pinned. I sweated.

When I finished, he looked at me. This time he was smiling. 'Thanks, Abonyo. That's much better.'

'No problem, Benji,' I smiled back. 'I'm just learning to stay relaxed and be musical.'

Opija popped into the room and asked if everything was okay. He watched me play too. As I played I heard someone singing along. It was Opija. He was caught up in it, so was I. He was glad, so was I.

After a while Opija told me to stop. He marveled at how condescending he thought I sounded. I brushed it off thinking I probably sounded the same way sometimes, or better. I looked up and saw Mo's piercing eyes staring at me. I smiled at him and he reciprocated. Something about him and everything that had just happened made me want to smile.

'*Mambo yote,*' Opija said. He was applauding me.

'*Mambo bado,*' I told him.

9.

So after an hour and a half of playing, we called it a day. Opija said he wanted to see me in performance that evening. Then he walked out the door.

Mo later directed me out of the bar into the sun. I followed him to a tea and *mandazi* café. We sat in the corner. A young girl came up and took our order. We sat there and conversed as we waited for our tea.

After the tea arrived, Mo proceeded to tell me about his life. As he was talking, I sat there and sipped my tea and munched my *mandazi* watching him tell the story of his childhood and life as a goat herder in the Kano plains. I caught myself suddenly feeling some compassion for him. I realized, as he talked away, that we were similar in a lot of ways. We were both hunters, we were both aggressive. A while ago, he had walked with me from the hot sun into Olindas Bar and I was as hopeless as an empty bag. Now I had a job, my talent had won it all for me. What about him? He had stood by me, he was still standing by me. His story was grim and moving. He had escaped poverty, he had a useless father. Now he had to be his own man and take care of his family; he had a wife and a son. He was training as a carpenter but he wanted to be better than that.

The hard times had taken its toll on our country. We were experiencing great hard times in the country with the *goro goro* hunger spell and the yellow maize donations.

He kept saying, 'I was going to tell you about my childhood. Interesting enough, our story sounds the same. I was raised in the floods of Kano. I grew up eating *mawele* because my mother couldn't afford rice.' He told me how poverty got him to where he was today. How hard his mother had to work, doing *otong'o* labour on the rice farms to feed him and his four brothers and two sisters. Throughout the entire time, I listened attentively and interjected some questions here and there. He was a really good guy. When he finally finished his story, it was clear he was pleading with me not to abandon him, to take him with me. I asked him about his level of education and he looked away.

I stood and paid for our teas and *mandazis*. He tried to remove money from his pocket but I beat him to it and paid. I said, 'It's the least I can do for monopolizing your time and making you tell me your boring life story. Look, Mo, I am no better than you. I have many brothers and one sister. I want you to learn to play that bass. Either that or learn to sing. That's the only way to get out of poverty, the way I see it.'

He nodded at me. At that moment I knew how bossy I was. I knew I was a leader of men. I knew men would listen to me. I knew that I was talented and it depended on how well I used that talent. I was learning fast: people with talent were respected because they were above ordinary mortals. My father had told me to use it to make money, become rich and famous. He was right, I could see. Money was the only thing standing between me and power. I could see it now that an opening had been made for me.

We returned to the bar. So while we were waiting for the other bandsmen, I started strumming some standards and Opija sang them, and he was a really good singer! I was pumped. Then the drummer and bassist arrived. Drummer was a tall and cool looking guy called Odongo but Opija introduced him as KSK. Whatever that meant. The bass player was a stout man-boy who introduced himself as Onyango Otoyo. Spark, added Opija. Opija really delighted in giving out nicknames. I wondered aloud what his nickname was. Dr. Nico Pedhos, he said. 'And these are not nicknames,' he explained. 'These are stage names. Music is supposed to be beautiful and musicians need to have sweet sounding names.' Pedhos, he was. He continued to be the same cool laid back guy and I had begun to like, the one who had offered me a job and changed my life. Soon Benz Benji Obat the solo player joined us followed by another guy who looked youngish, dressy, wide-eyed and deadpan.

The dressy kid introduced himself as Kasule Opete. Para Para, Opija completed for him. 'Rhythm guitar,' he said boastfully. 'I play the fine style... Lokassa ya Mbongo's 'dry' strumming.' He went on to explain that the style inspired the African All-Stars' huge and popular breakdowns. Opija said the kid was a Ugandan who recently fled the country following the bloody ouster of Amin.

The other musicians soon bundled in. I quickly summed up the band. Opija, though a tenor singer, shared lead singer position a soft-voiced handsome guy blessed with boyish looks and a swanky stage swagger. He went by the name of 'Mawazo Ya Pesa,' although his real name was Mark Pascal Omondi. His dark-rimmed spectacles and his strong jawline and bony cheeks on a long face made him look like Malcolm X. He was a gentle suburban-bred youth who had all the pass keys to the polite society. He was smooth and elegant, but masculine unlike the other eunuchs in this band. The backing singer was a sickly-looking and frighteningly thin youth dressed up in *omboto* clothing that smelled funny. He was called Paul Harrington McDonald Onyata 'Pong Bando.'

The band was complete. Opija then suggested we all sit down at the table and he introduced me. It was then that I witnessed one of the most extreme Jekyll and Hyde moments I've ever seen.

It didn't take too long for me to figure out that this whole experience was going to be pretty ridiculous. Opija sat down, and his demeanor changed immediately, as if he was suddenly a pastor running a baptismal class. He proceeded to pull out a handwritten paper that had all the 'rules' we would be following.

Leaning forward to address me, he said, 'OK, here's the deal, Abonyo,' and he proceeded to read every rule in its entirety...each one started with 'Every member shall....' and there were things on there from 'arrive fifteen minutes early to every rehearsal and gig' to 'know the set list by heart' to 'wear the agreed upon clothing' to 'contribute to band funding needs as they arise' to 'constantly maintaining professionalism and excellence in all we do' and things like that. The rest of us started to look at each other coolly, drummer KSK Odongo was even smiling. But me... I was like 'Is this guy serious?' Of course these rules were being read *to me*. I was the newcomer and this was my welcome party to Kisumu Delta Force.

As if that by itself wasn't bad enough, once he was done

reading 'the rules', he said 'OK, item two: set list. These are the songs we will be playing' and proceeded to pass out a handwritten set list to the drummer to read it aloud. It was a set list of 20+ songs for me to learn. I didn't know whether it was an appropriate set list for a gigging cover band like this one. It had songs from just about every different genre: rumba, benga, soukous, Tanzanian pop, Kenyan Swahili pop, and some were totally obscure songs by little known artists. Most of the music was standard fare, Zaïrean sets, standards, hits of the times and past.

At this point Mo and I just kind of looked at each other again, realizing what was happening, and Mo appeared as if he was getting ready to bounce.

I sat there boxed, speechless, and frozen to my seat. The drummer then gave me the song list. I was told that the other members already knew all these songs and that they all had played them before, so I just assumed that I would basically be subbing.

10.

I then started woodshedding to learn all the songs, though I already knew many of them from my father's collection. I ditched my social life and there wasn't time for home life. Sleep was the thing when I got home.

Within a few weeks I had mastered most of them.

Finally I was up on stage pounding my heart out under all the stage lights. I was forced to take my shirt off after the second song because I looked like I had just come out of a pool and my extra baggy sweat-soaked jeans were not making the show go any easier. Fortunately the rumba solo leads were not so intense, I found a way to play. In rumba music, the lead singer and rhythm guitarist took the brunt of the abuse. The solo guitarist only served to fill in parts and later play the long sweet dance riffs, the *sebene*. Whether it was rain or sweat, electric guitar solo lead

117

completed the circuit for a well-grounded rumba.

I quickly settled in this band and adapted its atmosphere and conditions. KDF were not too shabby either, moving from beep-beep experimentalists to fully fledged urban African band within a couple of years, complete with fractured egos and the traditional musical differences along the way.

The official history of the band had Nicholas Opija forming the band in Kondele in 1978 together with Orwa Jasolo and then discovering the drummer KSK Odongo and a couple of guitarists in Osiepe nightclub, recruiting singers and soaring to fame and fortune in 1979 after being mistaken for Ramogi's band due to Orwa's participation. As a consequence, to seal their deal, Jasolo, who was a veteran musician, refused to have Nicholas as his boss.

Well, here we were. Nicholas now had the band to himself and he could run it the way he liked. For starters KDF did not have their own material; it was not a band of salty, seasoned pros. So as a young wide-eyed teenage boy who was mastering solo guitar, this was my place. These guys knew more about gigging that I knew. The strength of the band was in the vocal section, particularly the main singer Mawazo Ya Pesa. He had a high tenor voice, warm but with an urgent quaver, that could slide up to a womanly falsetto. His voice scaled the highest notes I never imagined possible or real. He could sing with a relaxed flowing delivery which was admirable. He was twenty-four, although he looked about eighteen, and had solid church lineage with both parents staunch Adventists. Perhaps more than anyone (except the boss Opija himself), fans absolutely adored Mawazo. And, they had good reason. He played an essential role in so many of Delta Force's biggest songs. Bless his high voice, he was charismatic enough to make cadavers dance at the nearby Russia mortuary. His voice blended well that of boss Opija. Opija was called Dr. Nico Pedhos because his voice set the pace for Mawazo's. The singing style was he would sing a line in a straight confident alto and then Mawazo would repeat that verse with a piercing soprano. But Opija, being the owner and leader of the band, had the command of everything. His singing made some cry and some laugh, some jealous and some simply sit up and take notice. He had played music professionally in Norway. I learned many things about this ugly guy. He was an accountant. He was the school chorus director, the church musician, the band leader, the husband, the lover of women. He was always whispering words of wisdom in my ears. Boy, but that breath. Even when he spoke while you stood next to him or while you looked the other way, you couldn't avoid it ... *for sure*! When I say I was in hell, I was in hell. I *had* to communicate with him. Break? no break... continuous music the whole evening... the whole time, no breaks.

I quickly developed a semi-personal bond with Mawazo.

The sickly youth called Onyata 'Pong Bando' who dressed up in horrendous-smelling *omboto* clothing had a funny style. When singing, he would always have a guitar strapped on. It was part of his stage persona given that he was a failed guitarist. This guy though weak-looking and very thin, was super talented too. He was the big voice of the band. He had a strong baritone, deep and rumbling like thunder, but sweet, with tearing emotion. He loved to wear untucked long sleeve button down shirts as these were long enough to cover his waist and butt. In between songs, he liked to talk to the audience a lot.

The instrumentalists had passion and played with a measure of perfection. Benji played solo guitar with a sort of desperation and easy fluidity that challenged and unmasked my underlying lack of solid technical foundry. I always wanted to play like him. He always seemed haughty. Of course it was not a secret that I was poised to replace him. I knew Opija liked my youthful passion, eagerness and enthusiasm, good looks notwithstanding. Benji worked as a music teacher at a secondary school. He always talked negative of Opija. He was leaving the band. He was always distracted and broke too many strings while playing *sebenes*. I think the reason Opija hired me was because he didn't feel too secure with Benji.

Drummer KSK Odongo had an interesting nickname:

Gentlemen's Gentleman. He got that nickname due to the fact that he loved to address people as gentlemen, yet he was the gentleman himself. He seemed really cool and alert and smart. He never wore cleaned-up *omboto* like all of us, he bought his outfit from Sir Henry's next to Ann & Agnes in town. He walked with a comb and a shoe brush in his pocket. He was a gentleman. He had perfect Colgate-white teeth and he spoke in English only. It became evident that as a drummer, he always had the best seat in the place, able to observe everything from awkward encounters, to crazy dancing, and best of all, the dynamics of men and women behaving badly on the dance floor! As a drummer, he held everything together. He was always the backbone of the band and he was a true gentleman.

Mo Thwaka hang around with the band doing a little bit here, a little bit there like sometimes manning the entrance, carrying beer crates, clobbering disorderly drunks and bad guys, running errands like being sent to call women, buy cigarettes and Big G. He was a tough man with enormous energy and a dynamic drive that left you standing. He was always at it, going hard at it. He raved hard around the band like a train and I could trust him with anything. He had loyalty too. He virtually lived at Olindas and had lots of time to practice the bass guitar. And; surprisingly, his tunes were making sense.

Mo's wife, Akumu, used to come to Olindas every so often and soon got herself employed as a waitress. She was big and gruff and swarthy like Mo. Like her husband, she was loud, thick-headed and arrogant with a lot of village in her. She was the kind of woman who beat men and she used to boast she didn't need Mo to protect her. Once when she came to serve at our table and leaned over, her armpit came within inches of my face and I nearly fainted.

KDF

IN

KONDELE

T had been six months now. It was late in the night. The weather was warm. Kisumu was roaring and breathing around me. I pushed my hands deep into the pockets of my corduroy trousers and tramped on the sidewalk of Jomo Kenyatta Highway somewhere past Lake Primary School headed towards Kisumu Girls, towards Bus Stand. From there I will get to Kisumu Boys then cross past Aga Khan and General and the park and find my way on Achieng Oneko Road. Heading home.

It was past midnight according to my new Oris. *Mambo yote.* Dear God, it was late. It was a Friday and we'd played an extended gig. Performance was awesome good! Clever arrangements, lots of interaction with the crowd... the guys were off the hook! Everything had been fine save for Mo Thwaka's poor performance. He'd been practicing and today was his debut performance. The song was Wanyik's 'Sina Makosa.' Man, it was horrible. Poor Mo. I doubt if he was going to make it ...he'd been trying so hard yet he had no talent. Hm. Luckily Spark Onyango was on stand-by and covered quickly. Nobody noticed.

Kisumu was silent, it slept. I checked my surrounding. A few stray cats. Some mad or homeless people are burning what smelled like tyre. Up in the sky it was clear; full moon and no stars visible. Reminded me of Dorry... she loved the moon.

A car cruised past towards the bus stand, slowed down at the Caltex Petrol Station, its yellow and red rear lights blinking out the darkness and the dimness. It's indicator winked as it turned into the petrol station, quiet and alone. It was a red Ford Cortina.

123

I was thinking that soon I will be able to afford one like that. Or even a Datsun 160J, Joginder Singh's machine. Ha, maybe the powerful new Peugeot 504. Yea. Hm, Mercedes Benz, why not? *Obengo!*

I felt glad in my heart about many things. Kisumu was so cool at night. I felt so safe now with Idi Amin vanquished in Uganda recently. My feet were crunching on stones and kicking at tins and dirt.

It was Friday... no. No, it was past midnight. It was Saturday morning; Sabbath. Filled me with guilt. I had promised Mama that I'd go to church *for her.* It had been a while. Now I needed to do it *for me.* I owed it to God for this opening. I planned to go see the pastor, at least to have a talk. I needed to make it to become rich and famous. This was the beginning of my journey into music, it scared me still. In the six months I had been with Kisumu Delta Force, I'd become wiser and worldlier. Here I was on the first lap and growing up and casting away all the innocence and inhibitions and trying to understand the kind of man I was. Still didn't know who I was, I was still afraid of life. I saw myself in many memorable moments as an unaccomplished musician. Just a budding guitarist.

That future was now, and those long term goals were becoming short. I wanted the countless hours of work I did on music to be self—sustaining and as this was my only job, I didn't want it to be poorly paying. I wanted some success with tastes of this life, I wanted it to be rewarding.

I didn't even know the kind of music I want to make. I was primarily a rumba-and-any-African-music kind of guy. But I wanted to concentrate on the classic benga which my father was pushing me to play. Not Collela's benga, no. I had my own ideas. I wanted some-thing urban. As Benji, our solo guitarist, was now taken up by his music teaching job and played less gigs, I had become the main solo player. Heck, Opija was not interested in recording...that thing was just not in his head. I suggested to him that I had some songs I wanted to record and it was like talking to a stone. Honestly, I didn't think I wanted to be in this band playing bubblegum cover songs of great musicians. Where was I going with this?

With Benz Benji gone, nobody cared if I played anything right, nobody complained. I was still a crappy guitarist, I knew. I could not play scales right, and I hardly ever sat down to practice. I still had trouble with F-chord. And I had awful right-hand technique... my tempo had been known to swing from too fast to too slow without ever hitting 'just right'. To Opija, it was continuous music. To me it was inhaling horrible raunchy breath for hours... playing in a bar and doing nothing about recording some songs. The crowd loved the band, they danced away and we had a nice time. The job ended at 11pm each night, and I could hardly wait until it was over. I mean, I was counting the minutes... at 5 minutes until 11pm, Olindas came up and whispered something to KSK the bandleader... and I was glad it was over for the day. Time to go get some sleep after a hard night's work.

Each Friday Opija shouted: 'Overtime! *Mambo yote!* The band loved it because they were paid handsomely for an hour of overtime... like 50 shillings or more. I was like, 'God! One more hour! My fingers are burning...!' Yes it was that bad.

I'll never forget that night I finally confronted boss Opija and said, 'Sir, don't you think we need to record? Yeah, record an album and go on tour like a real band?'

'*Real band?!*' he had demanded, 'Look here kid, you are nothing but a novice. A greenhorn. A trainee guitarist. We are training you *and paying you instead of you paying us!* So at least be grateful. Don't tell me how to run my band!'

Was this guy serious? He was worse than Idi Amin and his soldiers who had been roasted by machine gun fire out of Uganda.

Imagine the amount of bad breath I inhaled in that brief moment of fury. Just imagine. I had belly aches for two days... but, I didn't complain (that was *really* hard for me to do), or act unprofessional. I continued playing gigs like a damn fool. But I was no fool. Yeah. I was no fool.

I was patient. Riana... my Riana had said that to me. 'Just be patient and learn everything.'

'And then? What am I going to do?'

She said, 'You aren't even twenty, Otis. You have a whole life ahead of you. Be patient.' She was the only person who called me Otis. To others I was Otii. To my family I was Owiro. In primary I had been Owish or Owinye. In secondary I was O'Waya or O'Wired or O'Weird. In music now I was Otis Dundos.

Hey! Thanks. But you, Nico Pedhos, my boss, good regular dental care goes along way, my friend. Taking a breath near you is the most horrific experience I've ever encountered. Stuck in muck!

Still patient I was. I tramped past Kisumu Boys, past Aga Khan Hospital, crossed the roundabout and moved on past Old Nyanza General Hospital towards Mayfair. On Achieng Oneko Road. Towards Kenyatta Sports Ground. Towards Milimani. Towards home.

Of course I was patient. As patient as a vulture.

2.

A lot had been happening. In Nairobi, Issa Juma, that dynamic, raspy-voiced vocalist quit Les Wanyika and formed his Super Wanyika group this year. Bwammy wa Lumona had left Mangelepa and decamped to the newly-formed Viva Makale. To prove that they could still carry the riot without their captain, Mangelepa had released two fine new hits, *Amua* and *Dracula*. Massive, they were. Maindusa Moustang had moved to the frontline as solo guitarist and Mayombo Ambassadeur had taken over the rhythm guitar. And Lovy Mokolo Longomba, the sweet voiced singer had left Super Mazembe to join Shika Shika then formed his Super Lovy. Samba Mapangala had eventually ditched Les Kinoirs and formed a new group, Virunga. He did so sensationally with a hit single entitled 'Virunga' on ASL label.

Moreno Batamba had laid claim to the song 'Pili Mswahili.' Through a press interview, he sought to set the record straight and put to question Baba Gaston's claims of ownership of the song. He wanted Gaston's name taken off the record. Meanwhile he had a new hit 'Dunia Ni Duara' with his favourite back-up singer, Coco Zigo Mike.

Things were happening in the music scene, musicians were busy men. In Kinshasa, Franco and TP OK Jazz had just released the sweet and bruising 'Liyanzi Ekoti Ngai Na Motema,' simply known as 'Munsi.' It was a fantastic song of this year. We were rehearsing all the songs on the album. They were like nothing I had ever heard... majestic. Pure gold. As we were rehearsing, Mawazo Ya Pesa promised to give a spirited interpretation of 'Mbawu,' the song composer Simaro Massiya fondly called 'Decision Echange Maloba.' The challenging part was the lack of horns in Delta Force, so I normally had to play the sax parts with guitar. It was a nerve wracking act of improvisation. But I did it out of love for OK Jazz. I was reading the album sleeves and seeing photos of men like Ntesa Dalienst, Simaro Lutumba, Djo Mpoyi, Gerry Dialungana, Lukoki Diatho and Papa Noel. Kasule Para Para knew so much about these men. He told us wonderful stories of these great men and the Kinshasa music scene. To men, names like Franco, Tabu Ley, and Verkys were so big... so large. So legendary. I sat down with Kasule many times to hear stories of these men and how they created such solid and mature music. I was mesmerized. I kept it in my heart that one day when I got rich and famous, I was going to go to Zaïre to meet these fellows.

We were rehearsing 'Munsi' and I thought the sound quality was horrible. We normally practiced in Olindas dressing room. Spark was drunk, so nodded at Mo. They traded places. Spark staggered out of the room. Mo took Spark's guitar. Benji was playing mi-solo and Para Para was tuning his instrument. He was good on rhythm guitar as a disciple of Lokassa but I wanted him to tune into the dumpy style of Gégé Mangaya. We both agreed with 'Mwalimu' Benji that it was essential for Para Para to use the

6ths and the 10th.

'Work a lot with 10ths,' Benji said. He demonstrated. 'Like this.' And he played ran smoothly through a patter. 'See.' He kept paying. 'This is good for Franco... for OK Jazz. See? I'm *in* the key of G still.' He stopped and looked up. 'Okay? The 10ths work best. For 'Munsi' you need a polyrhythm.'

'What's a polyrhythm?' I felt compelled to ask..

Benji scratched his beard. 'What I mean by polyrhythm is that when you listen to a typical OK Jazz style... and can pick each part whether it is a guitar line or a sung line...each part is a distinct rhythm that is layered on another. For 'Munsi', just use three sets of chord shapes. Very simple.'

'Thank you, sir,'

For about ten minutes, Benji and Para Para went through it soulfully with Benji pointing out little flaws here and there.

'I love the way you are feeling it yourself too,' I said.

Benji gave me a stony look. 'You have to love it to make it, Abonyo. Most of our African styles are either in minor or major scales. Let's see the lick in relation to bass and drums. Mo.'

Mo shifted uncomfortably in front of his amp. We ran through the set and we all had our attention on the bass. From where I sat, it boomed. At that moment Opija entered wielding another new OK Jazz album which he said he had just bought at Victoria Music Store. We couldn't wait to listen to it and the song 'Bina Na Ngai Na Respect' ruffled our feathers.

'Bina Na Ngai Na Respect' had me up all night slapping myself senseless around my room and bouncing off the walls. It was going to be the best thing for a long *long* time.

All in all, I was *really* glad I was doing this and this was a good start. This band held together (like a newly married couple) and we were doing fine. We now had 30+ songs (some I really liked, some I was not too crazy about). I had been scrambling to learn/find my style in/get some planned solo ideas in.

If I had had the foresight to do this from the start I could have really progressed a *lot* faster. *Mambo bado.*

3.

'Bina Na Ngai Na Respect.' This lovely rumba composition came with interesting gossip. It was really a functional song. Hm. Made Dalienst the most talked-about singer. Respect for married women, as a virtue, inspired the song. Franco was confronted by a nasty situation in 1980 when married women used to throng his shows at the OK Jazz Une Deux Trois Club in Kinshasa and husbands used to complain. Franco argued that married women just loved the music of OK Jazz. But Ntesa Dalienst observed that married women needed to be treated with respect inside the club. Thus he composed this song which was now the finest dance rhumba that (I believed) was going to scale OK jazz career for the next decade: 'Bina Na Ngai Na Respect' (Dance With Me With Respect) was packaged in the *Le Quart de Siècle de Franco de Mi Amor et le T.P. O.K. Jazz* series on the new Edipop label, marked as Volume 1. Meaning we were going to see more of this solid and mature rumba sound!

In this song, a married woman says: *'I just love the music of OK Jazz, so when you see me rolling my buttocks here in this dance floor, dance with me with respect because I am a married woman.'*

I loved Dalienst as did everybody else. He was the new star of OK Jazz now, alongside Djo Mpoy, Kiambukuta, Ndombe and Wuta May. With 'Munsi – (Liyanzi Ekoti Ngai Na Motema)' and Papa Noel's 'Mobali Malamu' it was going to be remembered for a long time that the early part of '81 was very much Dalienst's. More *Le Quart de Siècle* albums rolled out and we sapped them up. By the time Franco ended the *Le Quart de Siècle* series towards the end of the year, there were four new OK Jazz albums in the market, all of them containing hits such as 'Sandoka', 'Bimansha', 'Mandola', 'Tailleur', 'Fabrice' and 'Coupe de Monde.'

In these frightful days that OK Jazz ruled rumba, I loved music. I loved Zaïrean music. People could see my star was rising and KDF, here in Kondele, was starting to draw good crowds because of my magical playing. Magical? Yeah. You heard me. I was magical, no joke. I was not the fresh-faced kid who used to twist and screw his face trying riffs he wasn't capable of two years ago. Too much practice and I'd surely come of age. Really come a long way. I now embellished fire when I played the extended climax dance scores, the *sebenes*. When I say 'embellish' I mean I made my guitar wail and scream in the style of my idols like Bavon Marie Marie, Michelino and Manuaku. These three were the guitarists I adored. I wanted to play like them. I made my guitar scream in exquisite embrace. I played hard, syncopated *sebenes*. All over Kisumu, people talked of that terrific kid who played lead guitar like a Zaïrean at Olindas Bar in Kondele.

People came to Olindas to see me play. I was the sensation.

Mo Thwaka had also improved tremendously. You know, I don't believe what many instrumentalists say about bass as an easier instrument to just jump right into and play (rather boringly) than a solo lead guitar. I had profound respect for instruments and found it essential to make myself think along guitar melodies all the time, both rhythm and solo than to play 'traditional bass' supported by rhythm along with the drums. What makes bass easier, perhaps, is the fact that the basic bass has four strings instead of six and many bass lines are very basic.

What makes bass 'inferior' is what guitarists themselves say. Most bass players have tried unsuccessfully to master solo or rhythm techniques before setting on bass. That's why rumba bass players are commonly known as or thought of as 'failed solo guitarists'. Most of us African guitarists try to self-teach ourselves guitar and fail (as it's very difficult to avoid bad techniques of self-teaching) and move onto another instrument. Bass just happens to be considered by myth to be a 4-stringed guitar with the same roles and functions as a guitar but easier.

I tried my hand on bass too, after discovering that I was also good on rhythm guitar and soon learned how easy it was. I later learned that bass players, usually, are some of the best rhythm guitarists ever. Bopol Mansiamina from Mode Success was a great rhythm guitarist apparently but he was also a bass player.

I was thinking of asking Opija to replace Spark with Mo.

Apparently he had the same thought. The whole band knew that Spark was egotistical, inconsistent and unreliable. He was an electrician (that's how he got the nickname Spark, anyway) and liked to say that he was earning more fixing electricity.

'I want him to go?' Opija confided in KSK once.

'How will that happen?' asked the drummer.

Yeah. How was this going to happen? Search me.

'May the best man win,' replied Opija.

So I told Mo that it was necessary for him to fight his own fight. Mo smiled. It was a warm sweet smile. It looked to me like he was happy to have an ally. What I didn't know was that for a long time Mo had decided that the bass player position was his. He practiced hard until he was able to play, then he decided to take over Spark's place. And don't you think Spark was a soft lad. The guy was hot like charcoal. And tough. He was an electrician, a man you didn't want to mess with.

I was convinced Mo arranged the 'accidents' which frustrated Spark away. Imagine an evening of work and we are setting up, and Spark discovers his guitar is locked in the rehearsal room and no one knows where the keys are. Oops. Then another time Spark is attacked by thugs on his way from Obunga where he lived and got his hand badly smashed. Double oops. I mean if they were true thugs, why couldn't they smash anywhere else... balls, legs, ribs, face etc. Why only the hands. The fingers.

Well, Sparks went to hospital for two months and Mo was the new bass player. He earned the nickname 'Commando' from Opija.

Then one evening after two months, Spark shows up. He's drunk. We can hardly contain the guy, and he's yelling about the band plotting to kill him so Mo can take his place.

He starts bitching real bad and he's dangerous.

Senji... swaini... tumbafu!'

He reminds Mo that he is an illiterate nincompoop who cannot even write his name. We tell him his job is still there and he is sick and need to recover first. He seems okay with that that for a quarter of a second. Then he rises again, he keeps on grumbling. His hands are still bandaged, so at least we are certain he won't try anything stupid like starting a fight (he would be a danger to himself).

About two weeks later, Spark's recovered enough to play. By now Opija appears to have decided on Mo because, to him, Mo has the right image for a bass guitar player: he is tall, huge, dark skinned and manly. So Spark is encouraged to take up second rhythm guitar or mi-solo (which he can play very well too). Spark grudgingly accepts his new position and the band backs him up. But he still has his eyes on the bass.

What happens next is we witness Mo and Spark display an open fight during a gig. With guitars. I was having too much fun but slowly they began to stop running songs together and seemed indecisive about which song was next. No time for voting, one of them would just start playing one of his tunes, expecting us to jump in. Worked okay briefly but it was obvious there was a competition afoot. I thought it was part of their shtick. Soon I wasn't getting any cues, they were sabotaging each other with bad notes, volume increases, and tempo changes.

Luckily it was break time before it was noticeable. The two headed outside and by the time we got there, it was a full on fist fight! Both guys were six foot plus and around 100 plus kgs. They managed to bloody their clothes and injure their hands, but it wasn't till they had to play again that I realized they had injured their hands pretty bad. They couldn't play guitars. There were too many bum notes and Spark broke three strings. Too many times we were out of sync. I spent the rest of the night, nearly in tears from laughing at every bad note struck! It wouldn't have been quite so funny if these idiots had realized how ridiculous they sounded! The crowed didn't seem to mind though, and stamped and bumped and swayed and clapped and whistled as noisily as always.

Then Mo 'accidentally' knocked over Spark's beer that was sitting on top of a nearby speaker, and it poured *into* his amp.

The guitarist immediately righted the spilled beer bottle, but the damage was done. He twisted knobs and pushed buttons, but the amp was dead. We suggested running through the PA, as the mains were behind us. Nothing. Spark was enraged. He packed up his stuff, loudly cursing at band and patrons alike, yelling he'd never been so insulted or treated badly as he stomped out. As a result of which somebody was going to die.

We were absolutely speechless.

We were looking at our bass guitarist, asking him, 'Now look what you just did.' Mo was equally bewildered. I had never seen this side of him before. Of course Spark was back the next evening. He remained glum and silent but we sensed something was terribly wrong.

The band was pumped up. New line up was; thus, Opija (lead singer), Mawazo (singer), Onyata (singer), me (soloist), Benji (mi-solo), Spark (bass), Mo (bass), KSK (Drummer), Para Para (rhythm guitar). Opija appeared to be very happy with this new lineup. He appointed KSK as the bandleader and gave me a brand new Gibson with a set of picks. I knew it was a bribe. I was capable of being the bandleader, the band could've voted for me. The Gibson, though, became my most beloved possession. He wanted Mo to take a junior position, maybe learn to play percussion—the tumba drums.

Peace prevailed. Warm nice feelings all round.

One evening I found Mo sitting all alone in the dressing room tuning his guitar.

'How are you holding out, brother?' I asked. 'Aren't you supposed to be perfecting your tumba skills?'

He looked at me with blood-red eyes and wiped his brow. 'Don't worry, Abonyo,' he said. 'I'm the bass player of KDF. Watch me.'

Whatever he meant by that came to pass.

Towards the end of the year, Sam Olindas threw the band a party to celebrate his birthday. Beer was sold at half price, so it was a free-for-all jamboree and all geeks and nerds of Kondele turned up. The place was overcrowded and spilled over. People were drinking on the road outside. Suddenly trouble hit us close and square. A fight broke out between a couple of *odiangabus*. Number one *odiangabu* threw a full Tusker bottle at number two, who ducked, and the bottle and its contents made a direct hit to the bridge of my Les Paul. Since all the inputs were on that part, the offending beverage quickly achieved entry.

The Gibson become instantly tipsy, playing all sorts of noises it had been unable to previously produce, without any direction from myself. My bandmates tell me, although I don't remember this part, that I then flew off the stage to take *odiangabu* number one in a throat grip and announced his imminent departure from the planet. Now, I'm not really a fighter, but I think I saw a bad scene about to unfold if I retreated... including damage to my most beloved instrument. So, I slunked back and the *odiangabu* pushed me and raised a beer bottle to hit me. Spark reacted. He jumped off the stage and cold-cocked him as hard as he could... band still playing. The *odiangabu* went down like a ton of bricks, and Spark helped me climb back on stage just in time to unleash another irresistible benga *sebene*. Next thing two guys were carrying the *odiangabu* off the dance floor and we never saw him again (albeit alive).

Well, folks; you see? The Kisumuans in that room loved it.

They took him to Russia. Come next evening the *odiangabu* was dead.

You know what happens after this? Police. You know what they say this is? Murder (only I knew it wasn't). I won the war of words with the cops and they said they believed me and I could see it in their eyes that they believe me. But then, the guy was dead. Complicated things for Spark and me. Didn't matter whether it was an accident or not. Didn't matter whether I was right or wrong. All that was up to the judge. And, man, it appeared everything was against Spark. More than a hundred people saw him hit the *odiangabu*.

Long story short, Spark went to Kodiaga to serve four years

for manslaughter and Mo became KDF's regular bass player.

Soon the band was faced with another problem. We had no electrician to do the wiring. Spark Onyango used to do the wiring and all the connections. The big sound of Delta Force was the result of his skills.

Weeks later, Mo came over to Pandpieri to help me construct a small store for Mama's miller.

'Did you do it?' I asked him as we sorted out pieces of timber and *mabati* looking for what we could use.

'What?' he asked. 'Spark?'

'Yeah.'

Mo was cool and calmly told me, 'I know I can trust you to tell you the truth. I set it up. Sorry that guy died.' He paused and nodded. 'I wish there was another way. That was the only way.' He paused again for a long time and was in deep thought. Then he looked at me. 'What would you have done if you were me?'

I said nothing. I knew we were both survivors and Kisumu had limited opportunities. He did what he had to do.

Mo was speaking. 'It wasn't my idea though.'

I stared at him. 'Who's was it?'

He smiled. 'Guess.'

'I can't guess.'

'Well, I'll tell you one day when you buy me a beer.'

4.

Year two with Kisumu Delta Force, we had a party at home. My older bro Odingo had completed his undergraduate at University of Nairobi and was proceeding to South Africa for his postgraduate on a grant scholarship program. Ouru, had done 'O' Level the previous year and had not performed very well. He wanted to go to the army. Agwenge was in form 1, Tom was in class five, sister Akong'o was in class four, brother Timbe was in class two and sister Obera was in class one. Sister Akinyi was soon joining nursery and little brother Hawi was turning one. He was named Hawi ... rightly so. He nearly killed Mama during birth. After the party at home, the rest of the year seemed uneventful. As a matter of fact, everything else seemed uneventful.

One evening Riana came to Olindas Bar. Remember Riana?

Now, don't you forget that she never really approved of me as a musician. She never liked what mattered most to me: music. She saw musicians as either dangerous and unpredictable shrapnels or dregs of society and didn't even appreciate it when I played the guitar. I tried going to their house in Milimani to play guitar and sing a song by her window as all hopeless romantics do and guess what I got: her uncle yells at me to shut up or he will call the police. Second time I try it again. It's a Sunday morning and her folks must be in church. Here I am singing my heart out when I hear something like a growl. My eyes pop open. It's a dog! In seconds I am running down the street with dogs in hot pursuit.

Love, stupid.

Riana, who never came out to my gigs (better for both of us) was in this year twenty, like me. We'd been friends for more than two years now. For some reason (boredom, curiosity—who knows?), she decided to come to Kondele that night. On this one particular Sunday there was a bit of a bad vibe in the pub; the atmosphere was very heavy. We were just rattling through our set. I was warming up on some scales while Mo and the guys were getting their things set up when I felt a sharp jab in my back.

I looked up. It was Para Para. 'Hey, your girl's out there in trouble.'

Mo and I dashed out and found Riana fighting and kicking some lad. I knew the lad, he had been a decent local physical fitness instructor at one time before a nut in his brain went loose with excessive bhang smoking. He normally volunteered to station himself at the door of Olindas as 'bouncer.' Mo grabbed the back of the lad's shirt with his thick hand, flung him so he went sliding across the muddy road face down, and kept on rolling in the mud and into the puddle of dirty water on the other side of the road. People who were walking about the streets turned to look vaguely and went about their businesses. The unfortunate lad got up, ran away like a thief.

I turned around to find Riana. She was nearly mortified.

Needless to say the poor thing was ruffled pretty bad. She always argued with me that music was a dangerous business. Now, how could I still convince her it was not. She looked at me with the saddest look I had ever seen on her face as she backed away from the door of the bar, and said, 'I'll see you in church on Sato. Take care.'

Now what.

Now WHAT.

NOW WHAT!

In the days that followed I tried fruitlessly to realign myself with Riana. Tried to make her understand I was profoundly sorry. But, as with all things of this nature, there were invisible lines drawn, unspoken but understood limits that we could never cross. Or, actually, that I could never cross. You see, it was somehow OK for her to call me and tell me about her latest boyfriend and how he treated her like a queen. But it was not OK for me to talk about the women in my life (what few there were...) because that hurt her feelings. I know, this sounds incredibly masochistic, but those were the rules, and I stood by them and tried to quell the little flutter in my heart and the twisting knot of agonizing pain in my gut I felt every time Riana started dating someone new. That's not even mentioning the times I'd met her to sings songs for her.

Yeah, I know. Love's a bitch. So here I was, laying my soul for the most important woman in my life, and there were still rules I had to follow. Nothing too personal. Nothing even vaguely sexual. Safe things, like poems and books and nice talks. Possibly a hug.

But nothing personal, private... nothing that she could cherish and treasure for the rest of her life as having come from my hands and heart.

5.

Opija decided to rename the band Nico Opija and Delta Force. He feared I was slowly taking over the band. People had told me to take over the band. I was made to believe I was the best asset in the band. Because of me, the band was youthful and played with a mature solid confidence. There was good competition and everyone in the band was suddenly trying to be the best. The band had a way of kicking off every gig with a funky number called 'You Can Do It,' originally done by Slim Ali. Opija liked to open with it because he found it impossible to sit still through my infectious groove and funky guitar riffs (which seemed to have that same effect on audiences where we played). This song also had limited lead guitar parts and allowed room for Opija to exercise his alto voice prowess. We dragged out this addictive groove for as long as ten minutes sometimes, just to capture the audience and keep them entranced. Then we encored into our usual numbers.

This afternoon, out in the open air, the Slim Ali song seeped out from the stage like blue smoke and enveloped nearly everyone who was going by like sirens at Lake Victoria. When we finished the first song, we played the evergreen 'Bina Na Ngai Na Respect'. We had a large crowd pushing toward the stage, trying to dance and get closer at the same time to watch us.

We were in Kibuye market, playing in the open. We were promoting New Blue Omo, courtesy of East African Industries. The whole thing had been organized by Mrs. Odera (or Mama Iva), the regional sales representative with EAI. She was one of those disturbingly stunning elderly women who unnerved you with their presence. She had come to the Olindas once to promote Omo and loved us. And... pssst... she was secretly hitting on me. It had started with the awful teasing that had me wondering what the hell was going on. We never spoke more than four phrases to each other before that evening. She smiled at me in greeting. Pretty elderly women jazzed me. So much symmetry in a single creation. Such viewing pleasure. They were like an oddity that I couldn't solve. She invited me to join her for a drink since I looked rather low. I thought, why not? Even her name was pretty. Mama Iva. Sounded like a nice, sweet person right? She knew (I knew too,) that I was interested in her, and she was trying to encourage me without tipping her schmaltziness off. She had a basically happy marriage, as far as the straight emotional aspects of the relationship went. It was just that the sexual side had all but died. This is something I didn't know existed in marriages and she educated me about it. I normally thought that marriages were bedlams of hot sex every night. I mean I didn't see how such a voluptuous woman could miss sex. If she were mine I reckoned I would make love to her at every given opportunity. She laughed long and hard at my logic and reckoned that I was totally inexperienced due to my young age. Couples got bored of each other, she said. Sex even disappeared, she made me learn. Still I didn't see how. I think it was my reasoning that fired up her interest. I was young, virile and eager with enough energy and would be fun.

Kibuye market had grown from its humble beginnings and had now turned into one of the biggest open air markets here in Kisumu. I had earlier heard Mama Iva saying that Kibuye now served the whole of Nyanza, Western Province and the Rift Valley. That it had grown into a hub of economic activities never witnessed in any part of the province especially on Sundays. As a kid just barely seven years ago, I remember accompanying my grandmother who used to sell tobacco leaves at the small market. Also at the market were Nubian women selling lime juice, *mahamuris*, pancakes and samosas. Now I could see other merchandise like *omboto* (second hand clothes) had appeared. People from Maragoli and Kisii and Nandi regions had started bringing farm produce and this begun the unstoppable growth of Kibuye even with the persistent effort by the municipal council to stamp it out.

Mama Iva had insisted on the band having this concert here today, on Sunday, hoping to boost Omo sales.

We were wearing New Blue Omo T-Shirts and New Blue Omo caps and there was a large New Blue Omo banner as backdrop on the huge raised wooden stage we were performing on.

The MC was a high-spirited eloquent fellow who spoke the most brilliant and the funniest Kiswahili I ever heard. He implored and pleaded with people to make New Blue Omo their Number One detergent. And man, that guy could talk. He jabbered non-stop and yodeled and danced and said all the good things I ever
heard about New Blue Omo.

Fortunately he gave us a chance to play. Next we played 'Munsi' and it was mesmerizing hear Mawazo and Onyata sing:

Munsi ee, nakolinga yo te mama
Oh Munsi eeh ee maamaa...

On the third song, while I was dancing through a rhythm guitar interlude, I spotted something on the periphery of the crowd. A face. *My father.* I looked again to see if it was really him. He was standing behind the gaggle of dancers, gazing up at me, smirking, bobbing a little on his right foot, his arms folded across his chest. My father. He looked like he was studying me. I caught his eye from the stage and he gave me a smile. One of his friends was bobbing manically beside him, waving their hands, bumping up against all the other dancers, bumping shoulders with my father to try to get him to dance too. My father kept his eyes on me and looked stony and seemingly not quite ready to believe he was seeing me playing rumba, even though he had discovered at least one way or another that I was actively involved in rumba and not benga as he had earlier advised.

The condition under which my father had shut down my mother and gave me a nod and a wink to be a musician was that I play benga music. He was even ready to connect me with the likes of Owino Ja Shirati, Collela Mazee and Ochieng Nelly... the heavyweights of benga music. POK producer Oluoch Kanindo was also his good friend.

Even the hardest, coldest man can't resist a benga musician. Make no mistakes, benga music is an aphrodisiac in and of itself. Nyanza had a ripe market for benga music. Plus, like my father argued, it was our music. Well, he was right. What he did not know was it usually did not work just to tell someone that you're a benga musician, but once they saw you in action, saw you performing with the band and saw the audience surrendering to the groove and pushing to get closer to you, they were hooked. It was like shooting fish in a barrel.

What my father didn't see, of course, was that I had started my journey with this band whose performances were in a bar where we had limited audience. I played to the dictates of my boss and I got very little real action. If we could have played Nyanza province circuit as a benga band, I would have been in hog heaven. I would have maybe really made my debut as a benga guitarist. But now here I was, out for general public consumption, and I was being pleasantly consumed by the likes of Nicholas Opija. There were hundreds of men and women here who loved rumba, dancing to the music and watching. Their adulation wasn't lost on me, but I seemed to only have eyes for my father, standing there with his arms across his chest, a trilby hat cocked backwards on his head.

We only performed five songs and were called back to the stage for one encore. Afterwards, the band broke down our gear and distributed free Omo and other giveaways to the audience as Mama Iva gave charming marketing speeches and flashy girls dipped a dirty shirt into bleached water in a trough and made the foolish audience believe it was detergent. The women in the crowd loved this part. For me it was all theater. Mawazo jumped down off the stage to find girls, most of who were too young, who laughed at all his jokes. He flirted and acted like he enjoyed their advances and eyeballed some of the young girls who couldn't hide their attractions. If I was particularly feeling lost, it wasn't for my father. I might've availed myself to one of them, but I took my mind off it and packed my guitar.

My father stood at a distance for a while with his friends, watching me schmooze and shake hands. Then, after a while, when I looked over toward him, he was gone. I heard Mawazo inviting a bunch of girls out for drinks, his arm slung over their shoulder as they pulled him away.

6.

It was my first time at Sunset. I had dinner with ... you guess who. After dinner, Mawazo and I sat on the back porch nursing drinks and reflecting on the mystery of old rich women and young musicians. We were laughing that we were caught up in this and he reckoned it was a cool way to make some dough on the side. Then Mama Iva strolled over. Barefoot, she was clad in cut-off denim shorts with beige cotton and polyester silk-screened t-shirt with the slogan *I Shot JR*. She could've done better with a simple updo straightened and hot-combed hair pulled back into a single pony tail than the long beaded braids she had.

She bent over us and said, in her best sales-woman impression: 'Let's see, which one of you is Dundos?' Pointing at my buddy, she added, 'Are *you* Otis Dundos?'

Taking about as much as he could stand, Mawazo curtly excused himself and went away inside the hotel as if to go for a drink. But we knew where he was headed. Mama Iva had some friend in the hotel and she had asked me to bring along my mate to serve one of them. Mama Iva, never missing a beat, shook my hand and calmly said, 'So, you must be Dundos. Hello. Remember me? Mama Iva? You know, the female sales rep from EAI?'

She must be kidding me. Was she drunk? Was she merely putting on a show? My smile faded as my stomach shrunk into an icy little knot. Despite the heat and humidity, I felt a cold wave of fear slide up my back, making the hair on the nape of my neck stand up. Mama Iva tightened her grip on my hand and pulled me up to my feet. 'We're going for a walk,' she whispered into my ear. 'Just try and be nice to an old lady, understand?'

As we strode past the opened screen door, with Mama Iva's hands tightly gripping my shoulders, I could hear someone say, 'Oh God! She's grabbing him *right now!*'

They were Donna and Alice, both friends of Mama Iva.

This was followed by a harsh 'Shh!'—then I saw Donna press her face up against the insect screen. 'Mama Iva,' she said with a giggle, 'you are really sick...'

'Have fun too, dear,' Mama Iva cheerfully replied, as she escorted me to her room, which was just a few doors away. I soon realized that abducting me now wasn't such a crazy idea, since Riana had broken up with me recently.

'Why do we continue doing this?' I asked, without any preamble.

I knew she would pretend she didn't know what I was talking about instantly, and I didn't want to preface it, give her time to build defenses.

There was the slightest of pauses, and then, 'I don't know. All I know is I don't want to stop.'

We sat in comfortable silence for a few moments. And then she asked, 'Can you be discreet?'

'For the danger I'm getting myself into, for the obvious danger I want to be more than discreet. My career is very young.'

She chuckled at my exaggeration. 'I have as much to lose here as you do, perhaps more,' she said pointedly. 'I have a husband and kids. A family. My job with EAI. Reputation. My husband. I love him.'

'I know you do. But, apparently, you're not as married as he thinks you are.'

There was a long pause. 'I suppose you're right,' she conceded. 'But I do not want to divorce my husband, Dundos boy. I'm not

143

in love with you.'

'Neither am I. I have Riana.'

'I know about her, you told me,' she said.

Another long pause.

'You must behave well in public, don't show any hints, okay?' she said.

'I'm not stupid. Maybe young but not stupid.'

'What about your band mate?'

'Mawazo doesn't have a big mouth, he can be trusted. It's you to sew up your two friends.'

Mama Iva sat up, slapping at a mosquito on her neck. 'Don't mind those two. So how are we going to do this?' she asked.

'I don't know. I'm waiting for suggestions.'

'It's not like I've never done this before!' she snapped.

'Madam, I wasn't saying you hadn't. It's just that... well, you and I have both obviously been thinking about this for a long time. Do you have any ideas?'

When she answered, her voice was so soft and distant, I wondered if she was speaking to me...or something that was not quite there, not quite real. 'When I think of you...of us...all I see is you and I together in glorious physical harmony.' She fell silent. 'I suppose that sounds corny. Can I tell you something?'

'Yes?' My own voice had dropped a few decibels.

'I knew the instant I laid eyes on you that... we would be wonderful together. In bed. Last time you made me reach there.'

I didn't believe what I heard. 'Did you... did you really?'

'I did, honey. You made me...no one has ever. You're e tiger.'

I didn't what what to make of this. 'You mean you never...?'

'Yes.' she fairly cried. 'Let's do it again.'

Although she was old, Mama Iva had fine sexy moves. I liked the look in her eyes now. She was a dame who had class, came from the old school. She could drink and curse with the best of them and still could outclass anyone in the social uppity world including royalty!

Kisumu stop, I want to alight.

7.

One night at Olindas, as we were winding up, a girl wandered in. No one paid much attention as Opija casually joined her and they sat in one of the booths. Ten minutes later, Opija bade us farewell for the night and took the girl with him and they disappeared in the dark night of Kondele.

Freaked? Hm. To us this had now become normal. This was Opija. Nicholas Opija was a well-known womanizer with shameless audacity. He delighted in boasting about his conquests. You probably know many men like him here in Kisumu. This guy was a chick 'magnet', Damn! He wasn't particularly good looking, remember. You are probably holding your breath thinking about his bad breath and saying *yak* imagining him kissing some soft lips somewhere. I don't know how he did it, but he had a chain of women. Someone said he had a very outgoing type A personality. Maybe. Another someone said he had a charm, that he carried *ther nyang* in his wallet.

His conquests were frequent (several times a week) and as diverse as night and day. From the Plain Jane to the most unusual exotic and sophisticated Atienos and Nafulas and Mrs. So-and-sos. He became kind of a 'hero' in a strange way for me. Don't get me wrong, I always had girlfriends (and an occasional Mama Iva) but I just didn't have that magic, charisma, (mojo?) or whatever it was he possessed (did I mention access to large quantities of controlled substances like Mo?) But he really didn't need any substances because I saw him first-hand in action numerous times at parties and gigs. Women would approach him, start conversing. They would have some laughs and the next thing you know he and the next conquest were gone. It was freaking uncanny.

You want to sympathize with his wife. I'll think twice if I were you. He was married to this hefty, hot-headed Norwegian woman. It was said this woman was the source of his wealth. Legend had it he had gone to Norway as a student and took up music. Then they started a band, this band.

Lotta, she was called. She was as smart as all the white

women I had known. She probably knew of her husband's womanizing and decided not to do anything about it. Not with the four kids he had given her and the beautiful home he had built for her in the Nandi Hills with a breathtaking view of Kisumu town and Lake Victoria and the distant Nyabondo Plateau. She was content with life here in this beautiful African town and with her work as a high school English teacher. And she loved Opija. She came to the bar occasionally to sit and get drunk as she watched us perform. I looked out for these moments as the bar got more crowded while we played, and at that moment they would be in the midst of a standing ovation. They would be kissing and caressing. The band would be in shock.

Lotta would often get drunk and sometimes act un-lady-like. She would want to dance with other men! One night she wanted to dance with me and Opija wouldn't have it.

Lotta intervened and said: 'Turn the f...ing sound down!'

I looked at her in amazement. The band brought the volume down 50%. The wife walked up, and stood at the front of the stage screaming at me! Said this was her band playing here and she could dance with whomever she desired and right now she desired to dance with me! The audience realized what was happening, and started booing her and chanting '*Mzungu malaya.*' Over and over! Opija got freaky scared and went to hide in an inner room. Sam Olindas was wide-eyed, and stood there looking tense, his large eyes rolling in terror.

I did dance with Lotta. People cheered and whistled. She held me so tight and ground her body on me. I saw stars. Red, green and yellow ones.

Later KSK and Mo escorted her out of the bar to her car and I apologised profusely to my boss!

Anyways, one night we had a big Christmas gig at Nyanza Exclusive Club, which was attended by Indians, VIPs, politicians and some Kisumu big shots. We had been hired to play from 9:00 pm to 1:00 am by the private club president. The beer was already flowing and the stereo blasting when we got there to set-up. A few of the private club guys were beyond inebriated and acting like a bunch of drunken idiots which was par for the course if you ever played any private clubs. Well, there were lots of good-looking young women who appeared to be dates or wives of the club members throwing the soiree. One hot woman (wearing distinct cyan outfit, long and fitting) caught my attention since she had walked by us several times checking things out as we unloaded and began the set-up. I asked about her and was told (with a lot of sshhhs) that she was the wife of the club owner and this was her party.

About thirty minutes into the set-up I noticed Opija's red coat slung over a speaker and he was nowhere to be seen. Since he was the MC, the party couldn't get started. So KSK and I got Benji to sit in my place and had the band play some instrumental sets while I moved around trying to find our boss. Not long after, out of nowhere, Opija came rustling in with a boyish grin but he looked as flustered as a rooster. His afro was ruffled and he was trying to pad it back in place. He proceeded with a very quick sound check. Then KSK handed him the mike and I hastily helped him put on his coat and he got the party started. We played about ten songs, mostly OK Jazz rumba and the VIPs danced. During a brief interlude, I found my boss outside smoking a cigarette, I had noticed all along that his fly was open and now I told him about it. You can imagine his shock and embarrassment.

During the second half, the woman in blue (with her husband right behind her holding on to her hand) made her way through the drunken dancers right up to the front of the stage and she started eyeing and grinning at you-know-who. This grin was different though, not a flirtatious type, but a more intimate look. I blew it off since Opija's reputation was now unbecoming. But to hit on such a glamorous woman in such a place. And the way her high society husband was so enamored with her! The poor man had no clue what was going on. I surmised that Opija would get her number and link up with her on a rainy day. After

147

the set, I jokingly mentioned to Opija that he had an admirer and he said yeah. Said they had already 'met' just after we had arrived. Evidently they had 'met' earlier when the rest of the band were too busy to notice the encounter. How fast?

He explained that she pulled off the whole thing. He was fixing his bow tie and then saw the lady in blue motioning to him to come over to this secluded corner where she was standing by herself. They talked briefly and then she grabbed him by the hand and took him to the restroom. There it happened...he serviced her with a quickie. Banged her against the wall while she clung on him. She then gave him her private line number and said she had to get back to her husband because if she didn't he would come looking for her. Then it was clear to me. It happened the time we were looking for him. It explained the boyish crap-eating grin and his ruffled afro and his open super fly. I thought to myself: this man was beyond redemption. After he had finished his short graphic explanation of his latest sexual conquest, I didn't know whether to laugh or cry or throw up! After all, it was no big surprise to me, opportunity (once again) presented itself and Opija acted upon it.

During the third set, Opija opened the first song and sang a lovely ballad straight at the lady in blue. She stood so close, taken by it. Swept by it. We were transfixed as Opija sang his heart out, brought out a rare vocal distinction, hit the highest notes I never knew he could do. It was a plain bass and drums rumba number and the words came out. Came out and charmed the woman to the bone.

Mawazo and Onyata sang the next song. We talked a little more and then split up to have some food before the final set. I went out to get a much-needed beer. As I walked towards the keg, feeling a little high-flown and wondering if he even knew her name, that little voice of reason inside my head said, 'That lucky lady charmer with a foul breath... someday he will get caught.'

Opija joined me, a beer in hand. He was in a happy mood. So I took advantage. 'Watch it, she's going to be coming back at you, boss,' I said. 'You shagged her well with that song.'

He smiled, 'You certainly have my attention.'

'How's she?'

He shrugged. 'Not so good. Average.'

'Married women are becoming too bold. What happened to virtues, sensibility and marriage vows? I keep wondering.'

He lit a cigarette, took a deep puff. 'Women are made for men, Abonyo. To keep men young and focused.'

'Really? I didn't know. Women destroy men.'

'Hardly. Maybe fools.'

'My father used to say this: when you eat too much fish without being careful one day a bone will get stuck in your throat.'

He glared at me. 'Why are you telling me all this, Abonyo?'

'Because you are my boss and I begin to think you take your life as a joke.'

'Because of women? I'm an artist, you know. It's natural.'

'Yeah, I know. But that's somebody's wife.'

'Do you know how many married women Franco has slept with? Do you know what killed Bavon Marie Marie?'

"What?'

'Woman. Her name is Lucy. She was Bavon's girl. But Franco was sleeping with her?'

I glared at him.

'Eh?' he beamed. 'Do you know the real story behind 'Bina Na Ngai Na Respect?'

'No,' I told him.

'When you look at me what do you see?'

I laughed and shifted in my feet.

'You see nothing. I have no feeling for anyone except me what benefits me. But you, you're a real artist. You care too much. Feel too much. Why do you care too much? Nobody cares about you.'

We jawed about it for a while then went back into the hall.

8.

The days of a thief are numbered, so they say. You know that popular thing they say about a thief and his forty days. Truly those the gods choose to destroy they first make mad. Opija had been having an affair with more married women. I knew at least four. Mama Iva had been furious, he had tried to seduce her. One night we were blowing the roof off Olindas Bar, when Mo nudged me in the middle of a song and gave me the universal 'check that out over there' look.

There was *the* woman on the dance floor, not at all unattractive, dancing by herself in a slowly widening hole in the crowd.

'Can you imagine Opija has stooped so low?' asked Mo.

'You mean he's sleeping with that thing?' asked Mawazo.

At first, I thought, 'Okay, what's the big deal?' but as I watched, the deal became apparent. She was perhaps the worst dancer that had ever lived. I mean, we'd all seen people who couldn't really dance, but this was something special. Limbs just sort of flailing away at completely random intervals. She seemed completely on the verge of falling over at every given moment, but her eyes were clear and she was enjoying herself and didn't really seem drunk.

During the break after the song, Mo and I laughed and said, 'Well, she's having fun... so there you go.' Opija came for the second half and took over.

As the night progressed, as Opija sang, she was out there for almost every single song just sort of thrashing away in her own little circle with other dancers just trying to stay out of the range of her wildly flailing limbs. Of course the whole band had been entertained by her for some time, and we'd all been laughing amongst ourselves all night.

At the end of maybe the third set, I and the rest of the band were a little slow getting off stage. Opija excused himself saying he was going to see Sam Olindas in his office, and went into one of the inner room. I watched and after ten minutes, saw the woman get up too and follow him. I kept myself busy changing my guitar string which had broken. Mo had disappeared off somewhere. KSK was changing batteries in one of his pedals, and Para Para was tuning his guitar. I think KSK was adjusting his control console for our rumba galore show, which he loved very much. As I was settling myself to tune my guitar, I noticed what appeared to be the woman (who'd been dancing weirdly before) staggering towards my side of the stage. She looked highly intoxicated.

I pretended to be involved in guitar fixing and waved her over to Para Para who was on my left. I glanced over to see him glaring back at me with the look of death. The woman stumbled her way over to him, knocking over the mic stand in the process. She walked in front of the drums, behind me, as KSK was setting up to the drummer's mic.

I continued to concentrate on tuning the Les Paul. Then I heard a curious splashing sound behind me. I turned to look and my hair stood on end: the woman was throwing up on the drummer's floor toms, crash, and ride cymbals. KSK, having pretty much set himself up in a corner, was trying to get away over his hi-hat. He kind of succeeded. He knocked over the hi-hat and a little crash cymbal, with the crash cymbal almost hitting Para Para.

The drunk woman was 'rescued' by a bar maid and a bouncer and was being escorted out of the stage. She was frothing in the mouth and murmuring. The bar maid, laughing so hard she could barely speak straight, got some rags and went to clean up the drums while KSK (madder than a rained-on-rooster) went to the changing room to clean himself up.

I saw the bouncer struggling with the woman. He called for help. Then I saw it: she had suddenly become heavy. A bomb of panic exploded.

At that very moment, Opija, appeared into the bar in his underwear staggering real bad. He had such a Devil-awful look on his face. 'I'm dying,' he managed to say, 'I've been poisoned. She...

she has poisoned me.' He was pointing a shaking finger at the woman who was now lying on the floor twitching and convulsing. Then he too started frothing in the mouth. He sank down to the floor in slow motion. We stood there speechless with our mouths open for five seconds as we watched our Nicholas Opija jerking with his eyes all white.

I jumped onto the stage and dashed to where Opija lay. Murmurs and movements of confusion started and wailing soon commenced. Everyone shouted, made suggestions and swarmed around us. They clenched, fretted and watched as Para Para helped me lift Opija.

Sam Olindas bounded into the room and instantly summed up the situation. 'My car,' he shouted, 'Bring them to my car.' He fought his massive weight to the entrance. People were crowding into the bar. We gathered them up, battled our way through the throng and managed to stuff them into Olindas' 504.

The medics at Russia worked like ordinary civil servants who had seen many men and women die. To them this was just another one. I am sure I am right to blame them. I am sure they let Opija die slowly. We stood there watching as they asked us details of names and such while they should have been saving his life. Opija was still breathing silently, his heart beating weakly. A man in white long coat who would be a clinical officer rudely asked us what happened. We said it was poisoning. He asked us how we knew it was poisoning. We told them to do anything to save his life and they told us to let them do their work and asked us to leave the room.

So we stood outside waiting. Waiting for our Opija to die. Sam Olindas was weeping. It wasn't the first time I had seen a grown up cry. First time was 1969 when I watched Chief Ogwang cane my father... witnessed the draconian experience of seeing my father wailing like a woman.

Half an hour later and the man in white came out with that stony look that confirms the worst. He asked about next of kin.

We were looking at him with fear and expectation. The he

pronounced the word of doom.

'He is dead. The woman too. They are dead. Is he her husband?'

This in itself was like a death sentence. I didn't know how to handle this. I felt the world plop down around me. I had hoped that somehow he would pull through. Well, folks, this was my third or fourth encounter with death. Not a good feeling, especially if the dead man is your boss. It terrified and confused me on some level; filled me with a deep sense of loss and made me vulnerable. Death had always been a mysterious thing for me. An ugly monster that cut lives suddenly without warning. Even if it's a guy you hate, you will love them and feel sorrow for them when they are dead. Did you know it was very difficult watching Sam Olindas weeping like a child without my eyes leaking? I had to stop a few times for the words to console him, to stop him blubbering. It made death even more terrifying to me. Has anyone else dealt with death without being terribly upset or am I weird? I mean, why was I feeling so terrible about the death of the man I hated for taking his whole life as a joke? A man who messed up families by sleeping with married women? A man who couldn't allow me to exercise my artistic freedom in his band. Why was I feeling so bad... why was I crying? Death, as ugly as it is, has an uncanny way of uniting even the darndest of enemies. I wondered from the reactions of Sam Olindas to that of the nurses and medical workers who had little difficulty at dealing with a death. It all baffled me... everything was strange and I felt emptiness.

Nicholas Okoth Opija. 1948 – 1982

Husband, accountant, bandleader, singer, businessman. Survived by: first wife Gaudencia Akoth Opija and two daughters and two sons; second wife Lotta Fajnova Opija and four daughters.

And mother, father, eight brothers, four sisters, cousins, uncles... where does this end?

RIP Dr. Nico Pedhos. *Ondiek Marach!*

153

9.

The band went into mourning. Two weeks later, we buried him at his home in Suna Migori. The eulogy of the greatest man was read, tears were shed. The neat camphor coffin was lowered into fresh earth.

Questions were asked, cops came to Olindas Bar. We recorded statements, arrests were made. But one big question remained unanswered: Who did it? The husband of his dead lover? Possible. His wife? Unlikely. Other business enemies? Who and why.

The husband of the dead women was convicted and sent to serve at Kodiaga on death row. Then people forgot.

Two weeks after we buried our lovable Opija, his ghost came to haunt us. We relaxing at Olindas one Sunday mid-morning playing draughts and drinking and smoking cigarettes when we heard a commotion. To look up I saw a fat policeman sweating and running. There was tension in the air and I wondered what was wrong.

An old barber who ran a *kinyozi* next to Olindas bar asked, 'You haven't heard? It's been on the radio. Police are told to be civilians. The country has been taken over by the army.'

We ran into the *kinyozi* and heard the announcement again and again and again. *'Polisi wawe kama raia.'* It was the voice of Leonard Mambo Mbotella. And he was vocalizing the dark rumblings of what was really a coup, and scared us to death. Immediately Sam Olindas closed the bar and we ran to our respective homes.

Kenya was on the edge. Suddenly.

There followed hours of heightened fear and tension. There was one grim reality in my mind: that Kenya had gone to the dogs. We all saw what the military rule had done to Uganda and I didn't want it. Well, every business shut and people retreated to their homes and waited expecting the worst. In Pandpieri, people stood in small groups swapping rumours. It was like everything had stopped: music had stopped on the radio. Fear suddenly yanked in. A Ugandan living nearby was terror-stricken. He had escaped the horrors of war in Uganda and was just beginning to settle here. And here it was again. Her fear terrified the whole of Pandpieri. Mama prayed ceaselessly. Our father, on the other hand, was trying to contact relatives in Uganda. He was looking for a boat to take his family away.

Then news leaked in: the coup leader was a Luo. My father changed his mind about taking us to Uganda. He shaved his beard and went to celebrate with his friends in Nyalenda.

In hours to follow, Kenya appeared to have hit a dead end. We had fear of basic services stopping, fear of food supplies diminishing, and fear of our entire economy going haywire. We had real fear. Fear of the army coming to Kisumu to shoot us. Malicious rumours were continuously fed into our own bloodstream; the scariest being the thought the Ugandans and Tanzanians were using the opportunity to attack us.

Fear reigned supreme. The reality of Kenya being ruled by military regimes was unfolding. Riana came to our house and we weighed our options; our options were horrible, and our hopes were collapsing at a crucial moment. And in that dark moment, Riana hugged me and told me she loved me.

After ridiculously long hours with hopes destroyed and complete exhaustion setting in, one of radio's loudest and most poisonous voices suddenly cut in the still air telling us to thank God. Things were okay.

Then we heard Moi's voice on the radio.

Riana screamed with delight. The coup had been quashed. On the radio, they called it an attempt that had been quickly suppressed by loyalist forces led by the Army and GSU. The Luo guy who led the coup and his allies fled to Tanzania. His name was Ochuka and the newspapers said he was a psycho! Many people in Kisumu casually wondered how many 'other' Luo boys went down with him in that unfortunate sump. My father returned home looking glum.

Fear turned to chaos swiftly. For three days we lived through its grip and rode the climax of the chaos like a horrible recording before we returned to our normal lives. People asked questions. Many questions. Many loud-mouthed liars in Kisumu had so many answers to give why the Kenya Airforce to planned this coup, said they were expecting it. They did do this to punish Moi to neglecting the Luo nation. I, on the other hand loved this active president of ours who went around preaching about soil erosion, who was planting trees and building gabions all over the country. What motivated this plot against him? The newspapers then reported that the rebels did not even succeeded in assassinating several leading officials and in occupying the government center of Nairobi, they failed to assassinate the President or secure control of State House. Their supporters in the Army made attempts to capitalize on their actions, but divisions within the military, combined with civilian anger at the coup, they were unable to achieve a change of government. Facing overwhelming opposition as the Army moved against them, the rebels surrendered in barely twelve hours.

But my father had many reasons for hating Moi. Hadn't he sacked Oginga from Cotton Lint? Hadn't he detained journalists and lecturers for printing and circulating *Pambana*? Hadn't he denied Oginga the registration of Radet? Wasn't he marginalizing the Luo? How many Luo ministers were there in the Cabinet anyway?

You know, my father could talk so long and so bad about Moi till cows came home. That Moi's government was restored; that (*really?*) Moi went back to work? To rule again. And Oginga's fortunes were in simmers?

And... yes, he shared many peoples' regret that the coup failed.

In Nairobi, the aftermath was bloody marred by burning and shooting and looting and arrests of KAF rebels and University students and looters. Looting went on for days. Soldiers brutally cracked down KAF rebels in Nairobi. Most of the arrests happened during that early period of maximum confusion and fear. In the total confusion and disorder of that week, many innocent people were shot on the streets of Nairobi.

Soon Nairobi returned to normal. But the people's confidence in the government was poisoned by the violent rage and blood of August 1.

We soon returned to work at Olindas. Nobody in the band seemed to be in the mood to play. The bar was always almost empty. Sam Olindas asked me to step in as 'acting bandleader' for some time while he pursued a new contractual agreement with Lotta (Opija's widow). I was, of course, excited about this offer. This was the opportunity I was waiting for to turn this group into a professional orchestra. Little did I know KSK, who was the actual bandleader, was a black mamba. Him with his smooth talks. He had always appeared mature and independent minded. He turned out to be a snake with his own twisted schemes. He managed to convince Lotta that the 'new people' in the band' were here to take the band from her. New people in the band were, of course, Mo Thwaka and I. Next thing I knew, Lotta called us to a meeting at her house and guess who were also in the meeting: Benz Benji Obat. It sunk on me, even as I pleaded, that I no longer had a job. They were willing to let me stay on one condition: Mo had to leave. They gave me time to think about it and dismissed me. Of course I couldn't perform in the band without Mo who was always my protector. Without him, I would be a lone ranger in the band and I would be pushed around and driven to mere fingers on guitars strings. I rounded up Mo and we weighed our options.

Long story short, I quit my buddies to step up a notch.

10.

So, anyway, feeling like a miserable, self-damning loser, I spent the second week of August wrapped up in myself. Art in me commanded me to seek solitude. Even if I wanted some loving, it was beyond reach. Riana was spending time with her new boyfriend, Mark.

Anyway, I was sitting on the shores of Lake Victoria at Hippo Point attacking the little options I had in my head when something inside me snapped. It snapped like a true inspiration. I remembered it, Mama Iva was in town. I wasn't going to be sorry for my feelings anymore. I was going to give my life a new facelift. I had an idea. I went to a lingerie shop at Alpha Plaza. I spoke to a salesclerk and explained what I was looking for. Something classy and sexy at the same time, something beautiful and precious and wonderful, just like the way I imagined. Something that will provoke the strongest emotions in a woman of taste and class.

The salesclerk smiled at me and asked about size. I had all that information in my head. Size D or something. I gave her a description.

She beamed at me. 'That's a super *big* mama,' she whispered.

In a short while, she found what I wanted. She brought it out for me to see and I nodded. She wrapped it in front of me. It was a lacy bra, emerald green with black lace trimming. I'd seen it on a mannequin, and knew immediately how Mama Iva's massive tits would look in it. A little part of me was sad that I'd never get to see her in it. A couple of weeks ago I was planning to get her a present along those lines, and she somehow found out about it and was kidding me on the phone.

But this time it was different. I wasn't doing this for fun, it was a means to an end. I asked the sales clerk for a small card, like the one you send with flowers. I thought for a moment, and then remembered a little ditty from Shakespeare I had read in Mr. Patterson's old books in our house:

> 'To me, fair friend, you never can be old
> For as you were when first your eye I eyed,
> Such seems your beauty still.'

158

I wrote it on the card and taped it to the outside of the box. I planned to drop it off at her hotel that night or the next night. In the afternoon Mo Thwaka came around to Pandpieri and we had to go and help my father with off-loading some crates at Ogongo, and that turned into a four hour marathon.

Next day I was sitting in the sun day dreaming when my sister Akong'o told me Riana wanted to see me. They had been together an hour ago and she sent Akong'o with a message that I go see her as soon as I could, she was alone.

I took my bike and rode over. She was alone in the sitting room.

'What's the matter, honey?'

'That bastard Mark! I broke up with him today!' She started crying, long wracking sobs that tugged at my heart. I went to her, sat on the couch, and gathered her shaking form into my arms, doing my wonderful best friend routine.

She felt wonderful in my arms, like she belonged there. I was just over six feet, and Riana stood five-nine. Five-eleven in heels, so when we danced on those rare occasions, her head fitted wonderfully on my shoulder. I chased those thoughts out of my head as I stroked her back.

'What happened?' I asked softly.

'Otis, Mark is cheating on me with my best friend...' she started, and I knew this was going to suck big time. Riana continued, 'Mark... wants...' She sighed, looking around, searching for the words, searching for a way to tell me what I already knew.

'Mark wants to make love to you.' I said it, and Riana's head snapped around.

'He *told* you?'

'Of course not.' I laughed.

'Then how did you know?'

'Because Mark and I are both men. And I know how men think.'

'Oh.' Her voice was quiet. I knew that Riana was a virgin.

159

'We broke up, Otis. Broke up for good.' She dissolved into another round of crying, and I let her get it out of her system. We had this routine down in the past. Riana would cry, I would hold her, I would tell her what a bastard her guy was and that he didn't know what he was giving up (and thus saying without saying that I knew what he was giving up and I was ready, anytime, to take up the slack... but that was part of the dynamics of the relationship).

If that wasn't a conversational, emotional and every other kind of optional land mine, I didn't know what was. She asked me for help. Could I help her dump him? I stalled for time, thoughtfully stroking the sprouting beard on my chin.

'Is this what you really want?' I finally managed to ask, falling back on that old therapist's trick of answering a question with a question.

'Well, I do love him...' As she trailed off thinking about *that* particular topic, I felt my guts knot up in agony. 'But,' she continued, 'I'm not sure I'm ready for this.'

'Did you tell him you want a break up?'

Riana was silent for a long moment, and then she slowly nodded. 'Yeah. He told me to give him another chance if I really love him...' She smiled ruefully, knowing that I understood the position she was in.

'So what's the point. He'll never change.'

'We broke up, Otis,' she said softly. 'I mean it.'

Finally, all cried out, she asked, 'Otis, what are your plans tonight?'

'I don't have any,' I said.

'Oh, good. I'd hate to be alone.' It sort of annoyed me that she automatically assumed that I'd spend the night with her, but there wasn't much I could do about it now. At the back of my mind was my date with Mama Iva. I knew Mama Iva was getting impatient waiting for me at Kisumu Hotel.

Well, Riana made tea. We drank, ate biscuits, talked, told silly jokes and laughed (just like in my fantasy). We sat down to

160

watch *An Officer and a Gentleman* on VOK TV. She loved that 'filim', and as usual, was in tears by the end. I must admit, I was also a little damp around the edges, and she knew it. I didn't care if she did or not.

We sat in silence, with her head on my chest as the credits rolled, and then the screen went to commercial.

'Otis, why can't I meet someone kind and sweet and warm and funny and sensitive?' she asked. I'd heard this perhaps a hundred times before, and each time I had kept silent. My arm was around her shoulder, and my hand reflexively closed, gripping her tightly, so great was my sudden anger.

Keeping my voice even so as not to let on, I finally said what I'd been waiting to say for as long as I can remember. 'Yeah, it must be pretty tough to find someone like that. I mean, someone so funny that you can just order them to come to you whenever you're sad and they'll cheer you up. Someone so warm that whenever something happens to you, either good or bad, the first thing you want to do is call him and share it with him. It's so hard to find someone sensitive, someone who cries with you at the end of *An Officer and a Gentleman*. Someone so sweet that they write you poems for your birthday.'

I had done all of those things, and I knew she knew it. Sarcastically, I added, 'Yeah... must be real tough finding someone like that.'

Riana molded her body against mine. I could feel the dual pressure of her bodacious breasts against my chest. She levered my neck, bringing my face to hers, closer... closer.

And then we kissed. Really kissed, for the first time. Her lips were soft and hot and slightly moist, just as I'd always imagined them. It was a soft, friendly kiss at first, scared and slightly tentative. As the passion grew to overtake us, the pressure increased in little leaps and bounds until we were kissing hungrily, trying to consume each other through our mouths. My arms went around her, crushing her body against mine. Years of accumulated passion and denial welled out of my body, transmitted to hers through the kiss. She could feel my need, my hunger for her, for every soft, sweet, tender inch of her, and she responded, grasping my shoulders with her hands, pulling me hard.

Looking at me deep in the eyes, Riana said something that made me warm inside. 'Some day when I decide on this and when everything is right, you will be the first. It doesn't matter if we'll still be friends or if you'll be married but I will give it to you. Just know that.'

Good point. The entirety of our physical contact over the past four years had been two wonderful hugs, some slow dancing at a mutual friend's wedding, several kisses on cheeks. Here and now, this kiss marked a turning point and it confused me.

It was over in an instant, but it was an instant that would be burning into my mind forever.

I saw Mama Iva at Kisumu Hotel that night. She wanted to know my whereabouts of the afternoon and I told her I had to see Riana. She didn't say a word. I dropped my hand from her shoulder and reached for a beer. I was disgusted with myself for feeling nothing for this wonderful woman after kissing Riana this evening.

I told her I had a present for her. She looked up at me. Suddenly, I was scared. She was going to freak. I knew it.

I handed her the box and watched as she opened it, ready with an excuse or an explanations, expecting her to go ballistic as soon as she saw it.

Amazingly enough, that didn't happen. She read the card and smiled at me. Then she folded back the tissue paper and saw what it was. Squealing, she lifted it by the straps and held it in front of her.

'It's sexy,' she breathed. 'And my favorite color!' She looked at me, held her head to one side and asked, 'Dinos, do you know I'm a married woman?'

I shrugged.

She suddenly leaned over and kissed me straight on the lips.

Then she turned went into the bedroom, slamming the door behind her. I knew that she was trying it on, and I wondered if she remembered what I'd said about giving her sexy gifts. I turned my attention to the TV and tried hard not to imagine. Not imagine that it was Riana (and not Mama Iva) stripping her clothes off to try this new bra on. I flipped around and found some choir singing 'Joy To The World' on TV and watched the sopranos reaching for those high notes. My mind began to drift and fantasize, and in my dream I imagined me and Riana married, watching our children opening presents and giggling. I saw myself standing behind Riana, my arms around her waist, both of us in comfortable, fuzzy bathrobes as we watched our kids open their gifts. I got lost in that comfortable fantasy, turning it over and over, looking at it from different angles, the way a film director might, looking for the best shot.

And then, as always, that sad little tug at my heart as the fantasy machine ran out of steam and told me that it would never be, that I was chasing rainbows again, that I should be happy with things the way they stood, and that I should find someone to love, someone that would love me as much as I loved Riana.

I heard the door open behind me, and I looked at my watch. It was 12:30am. Mama Iva had been in her bedroom for thirty minutes.

Then I detected that she was standing in the doorway to her bedroom. Curious, I looked over my shoulder and felt my heart seize and the breath lock in my chest.

Mama Iva was standing in the doorway, leaning against one arm held above her head, all her weight on one leg, the other bent slightly and held forward of the other... a model's pose. And she was modeling my lingerie. It was the only stitch she had on her voluptuous body.

'Like it?' she said. Her voice was a husky, deep-throated whisper.

I was speechless. I nodded softly. 'I remembered what you said a few days ago... about me being so poor I can't afford to buy you a gift.

She fed me with a warm smile. 'And then I remembered what you said to me on the phone this afternoon about surprising me. And you mended fences with me and then I finally listened to what you had to say. Baby boy, you really *did it* this time. No man has ever bought me a bra before. Panties, yes. But never a bra. And like many men admit, my big tits are my best sexual arsenal.'

Still speechless, all I did was blink and drool.

She held her arms. 'Come here, baby boy' she said, softer still. I stared at her, my mouth dropping open. Surely, she couldn't mean.... could she? My question and prayers were both answered when she crooked her finger at me. 'Right now I feel so confused and so in love I can do anything you ask me.'

'Anything?' I asked.

She nodded. 'Kiss or suffer or... whatever,' she said.

That was more poignant. I gave her my best goofy expression, a roll/shrug of the shoulder.

She nodded, her eager eyes searching mine. 'Anything.'

On shaking legs I stood and walked to her. She dropped the arm that had been on the jump and let it fall on my shoulder. She curled her fingers, and she was suddenly scratching the back of my neck lazily, as one might scratch a cat behind the ears. Believe me, if I could have, I would have purred. Her touch on my skin, this electrical, sexual touch sent bolts of passion shooting through my body. I wanted so desperately to feel and smell and taste every inch of her that I shook with desire.

'I want you to make love to me, Dinos boy. Tonight. Just once. Maybe twice. Depends. But make it good, okay.'

Considering my options, I thought that if this was going to happen yet again, then discretion was the better part of valor. A voice in me said, 'Allow this most perfect night of love, for this magical married woman, end as it has already begun, with a single soul-burning kiss that will branded be into her memory and she will love you forever. She will change your life for the better.

She's game for you, Otis.'

Even if I never touched Riana again, I knew my remembrance of making love to this wonderful married woman in her hotel room bed this night would be replayed in my mind again and again.

And suddenly, it was clear. As clear as Lake Victoria on an April morning. My, Oh my! I was getting addicted to committing sin of fornication by sleeping with this married woman again and again. Still kissing her, I took her hand and led her into the bedroom. The only light on was the bedside table lamp, and it had a red handkerchief draped over it, giving the room and eerie, ethereal glow. Struggling hard not to drop her, like she was made of porcelain, I laid her on the bed and stood above her, admiring.

Her devotion to me was immeasurable. When the storm was over, we lay poleaxed, stupefied, mesmerized and half comatose.

11.

A few weeks later, Mama Iva packed me in her car. She took me to see a queer called Fortune Man. I asked question and she hushed me, said she knew what she was doing. I remained tense as she drove to remote parts of Kisumu rural to commune with a man who will give me 'fortune' two months or so before she could take me to Nairobi. This trip kicked narly senses in, alerting me to another poignant episode in my spirituality. Mama had recently found me to be 'spiritually bankrupt.' We were on a spiritual quest; Mama Iva wanted a 'Man of God' to 'pray' for me. The woods surrounding the Fortune Man home were deep and creepy, a few creeks ran amok, the recent rainstorms had inundated the area with wetness, now making everything still very crisp and clean—and muddy.

We eventually reached the place. The compound was fenced with *ojuok* hedge. Mama Iva faced me and took a deep breath. 'This is something you have to do. If you don't you won't succeed as a musician,' she said.

'Nothing wrong with prayers,' I said.

Mama Iva didn't reply but only prompted me to follow her.

She sighed. She appeared tense herself. 'You can tell me whether to go ahead with this or you can back out now. It's upto you. I'm doing this for you. Come.'

We entered the compound. It was a place not from this world. It had a mud-walled house that was literally falling away. A little earth tremor and it would crash and powder away like a puff of dust. A frail looking man sat under a *dwele* tree. He didn't even pay us any attention. A sick looking dog regarded us nonchalantly with bloodshot eyes.

'We have come to see you,' Mama Iva said to the man. He sat with a near empty mind. The he looked up and got on his feet. He led the way into the dreadful house. After some ritual of lighting candles and pausing up and down chanting strange words and singing, he sat down and spoke. Said I needed peace, tranquility. Said I needed another life in another world.

I wondered what he meant. I had always prided myself with the thought that I was fairly well grounded to the Earth and that there was only *one* Earth. I didn't believe in claptrap; psychic abilities, ghosts, phantoms, generalized goofy shit unexplained magic.

The strange man said I was yet to know.

A tingling came to the back of my neck and crept into my psyche. Ghosts, phantoms, people claiming to have psychic abilities had never moved me. But this strange man spooked me. He wrinkled his nose and narrowed his eyes. Suddenly, something new to his 'ability' came. Like peering through a cardboard paper roll, with the 'scenery' around mixing colours and melting into cone shape. Very casually, he gave me some bizarre facts about my life. Three times I was meant to die. The first time? When my father taught me to swim. Did I know I was to die that night? Secondly, Magak's death was meant to be mine. And third: Oliver died in my place! My soul was protected for my future destiny. And with that, I could suddenly see across the lake and into the semi dense brush and bushes in Pandpieri country beyond and beyond that! At the end of the 'cone' the vision was a little blurry. I developed a sudden unwanted headache and the experience dissolved.

How did he know these incidences that had happened so many years ago? I had told no one. I had even forgotten them.

I sat still for a long time; the tingling to the nape of my neck still remained, but now in the context of rendering me ill, like being flush with a fever or lake sickness.

It passed within a few minutes.

I had a question for this strange man. 'What do you do?'

He cleared his throat. 'I commune with nature. I fix destinies of men. I remove ill luck and bad omens from their paths. I restore luck and good fortune stolen from humans by other human forces.'

Mama Iva was mystified by way things were developing.

At first there was a bit of dizziness to contend with, then I saw the strange man, in an odd sort of way. It was like looking through a cone, my peripheral vision was a mixture of mixed colors all running into one another. I could zoom forward, side to side, and even backwards.

Turning to Mama Iva, I said, 'What then?'

The strange man spoke. 'I need a soul. In your family. Name anyone. It must be done within two full moons.'

So this is what it comes to. Everything now fell into place. Zaireans called it *ndoki*. You nominated a soul within your family in exchange for fame. Franco had sacrificed his brother Bavon Marie Marie. As if reading my thoughts, the strange man began a long tale about the musicians and politicians who had visited him to buy fortunes. And some of the names shook me down to the ground.

I stalled. Mama Iva prodded me. Then she leaned close. 'Nominate that useless drunkard brother of yours.' she whispered harshly. 'I don't have much time to do this.'

I fumbled for words. 'Keya,' came out the words. Just came out.

'That will be fine. Your brother, right?'

I nodded.

There was a long moment of eerie silence. Then Fortune Man spoke, 'You realize once a name is mentioned and the sacrifice is made, you cannot undo it. So I want you to be absolutely sure.'

My mind was blank, my heart was almost tearing my chest. I felt Mama Iva shuffling beside me. 'This is what you need,' she whispered.

'Yes,'

After that things happened as if in a dream. A one hundred shilling note was pressed into my hands and instructions given.

'Give it the soul you choose to sacrifice. This will give you ten years of fame. Then you get twenty years of darkness and it's all over.'

Together with that he gave me a shiny pebble. 'Take this and keep it in your wallet. You will control every situation for the next ten years.'

That's how the spooky episode unfolded. The development of 'special powers' in whatever capacity were left to develop on their own. The powers will come into effect as soon as the item of sacrifice (the one hundred shilling note) was used by the sacrificial human. I felt that I hated this and that whatever was happening to me shouldn't happen.

Fortune Man sat back to explain his powers and his methods. He used the waves of the lake, the breezes in the air that swooned in the boughs of the trees surrounding his small hovel. These lake breezes had spirits in them, bad and good. The squeak/groan of the windmill, the croaking of the froggies at the pond, the trickle of water in the stream, the crickets, and the breezes wafting the millet and maize field.

I found it incredibly strange the way he had recalled my childhood tragedies. Weird to fathom from the get go. A sickness welled up in the pit of my stomach—the same sickness I got when out on fishing boats at the lake.

Later that night I couldn't sleep. There were measures to deal with such happenings. Bile formed in my throat and something warm trickled down my temples. The calmness I sought was being a little elusive; my vision was blurred as was my memory. When sleep finally came, I dreamt of Fortune Man.

A few days later, Keya came into our bedroom while I was asleep. In my dreams, I heard him moving around. Then I woke and he slipped out of the room. After he'd left, I realized he had stolen my money. Taken all the money in my wallet *including the Fortune Man's note.* I hurriedly went after him in an attempt to retrieve Fortune Man's note, found him in a *chang'aa* den in Nyalenda and he had drunk all the money and had not a cent.

I knew then that I had sacrificed him.

I called Mama Iva. Her reaction skewed me. 'If his death makes you richer, what does it matter? What use was his life to him anyway? He's better and more useful dead than alive. It's called sacrifice. You will make a lot of money, use it to take care of his family.'

I knew it, she was about to tell me I was not the first musician to sacrifice his brother's soul. She started giving me the names and I asked her to spare me the yarn.

When Riana called me a few weeks later, I told her I was going to Nairobi. 'Nairobi? With this coup? Are you crazy? What about me? Are you leaving me?'

BUT
THIS
IS NAIROBI

I had always been a dreamer and what got me to Nairobi was a dream, literally. To chase the Kenyan dream, every Kenyan must be in Nairobi.

Mostly I wanted, in Nairobi, to become a more evolved artist. Nairobi was the perfect, moist setting to give succor to a young, romantic heart. I had abandoned the non-industrial Kisumu town of my childhoods: our sunny lakeside town, which had raised me into a man and given me much to see and experience, but nothing to hope for and to live for. Kisumu with its sleeping Lake Victoria had nothing more to give me. A town that moved too slowly and sometimes didn't move at all. A town that my expectations had quickly outgrown. But many folk liked the small town appeal, except of course, the school going youth. As kids neared teenage the lameness of a 'small town' became all too apparent and they yearned for the nearby towns and cities.

I was too antsy to stay here now. A dwindling sense of self-confidence in my creative work at the loss of my hope to lead Kisumu Delta Force made me re-think my future and look at what opportunities Kisumu had left for me. Honestly, I couldn't see any and my options were racing towards zero. The one conviction over the last few weeks was the nagging feeling that I needed to make a huge change in my life and get the hell out of this town. You know, really, the truth is that Kisumu normally has little to offer us after high school. That's why many of us headed for Nairobi. Many left Kisumu pretty young because they thought that there was another way to live, outside the parameters of an organised homely society in which we had been brought up. I, too, was embracing every young person's big city dream of Nairobi with its opportunities, many cars and its streets teeming with masses of people who moved too fast with a purpose, going somewhere. A city with high-rise buildings that had elevators in them and the spectacular landmarks I had only seen on calendars like Kenyatta International Conference Centre and Hilton Hotel. Not forgetting the lovely Uhuru Park, traffic lights on roads, funky cafés, and the time to partake in such havens. Fulfilling the dream to me was to come here and start on my journey as a guitarist.

2.

Sitting in the waiting room of the offices of Akamba Bus, I felt very much like the newcomer I was, with my dusty safari bag, my chewed-up tweed guitar case and my corduroy trousers, and obviously displaced look. In the bag were my clothes, underwear, vinyl (singles and LPs), a few books and dreams. That was all I had. There were not many people in the waiting room, it was five o'clock, and I had to wait an hour before Mama Iva would come to pick me up. I'd taken a, whatever, six-year old *Drum* magazine they had there on the table and read that rather than just looking into space and feeling uncomfortable. I pretended to read the magazine, looked at my hands, stared at posters of Sportsman cigarettes and Raymond blankets on the wall.

There was a young couple right across from me just chatting and giggling. They looked like well-up Nairobi kids. The guy had oily Ray Parker curly kit hair and wore the latest Azzaro shirt and Zico jeans and stiletto shoes. The girl had parachute pants and jelly bracelets, and very big teased Afro hair. I couldn't stuff my face in a magazine, not because I was distracted by them: I was looking at them and feeling rotten. I was in my early twenties and they couldn't be much younger than me yet they looked too good. It was tough though because even if I pretended to do something, I was still worrying that the young couple could see my anxiety and they could think I was a weird, grumpy Kisumu man. And from the way the guy was staring at me, I could act stupid out of nervousness, smile or laugh a little and then I could feel like an idiot from Kisumu who'd just come to Nairobi for the first time. I was going to lose my goddamned mind with all these funny looks shot at me. Heck, I was having enough mental conversations within the fray that was Nairobi!

By the time Mama Iva showed up I was freaked right down and out. It was some minutes past six. She wore a floral chiffon dress with a ruffled bodice like something a lactating Sunday school teacher might wear. She took me on a drive to heaven with wide roads and dazzling city night lights eventually turning up in a nice estate called Nairobi West. Ha, welcome to suburbia. Beautiful place. Clean. We went upstairs into a furnished bedsitter. She explained that she owned this building and I could use the bedsitter for as long as I wanted. She was going to pay for my meals and other needs. What? I was like, what?

'This is Nairobi,' she explained, giving me a seductive wink. 'The caretaker must never find out. He could tell my husband. Not that I care. This is my flat. Well, it's good to exercise respect... if he comes around just tell him you are a tenant and that I brought you here, Okay Dundos boy?'

I faced her and nodded. Then I asked about work.

She looked to me, she tried hard to keep her smile down. 'Don't worry about that. I know why I brought you here. I will find something, I will connect you with a band soon, suitable one. For now *kaa square*. Just relax here...the city is not safe with this coup which has just happened, so it will take a while for things to get back to normal. We can't even go out to a dance, you know.'

She pushed me and I plopped on the bed and thought about Riana and Kisumu behind me. I felt her weight on top of me and I went flush, my mind whirred and I could scarcely breathe. 'You okay?' she whispered. I just shrugged and made a "I dunno" face. Familiar lustful feelings invaded us, she worked my trousers down.

3.

I came to Nairobi at the time of austerity and fear. I found a Nairobi that was knotted in fear following the coup attempt; smarting with its aftermath.

A shrouded metropolis, this was Nairobi.

But to me, the overwhelming newness of City experience was at once scary, exciting, overwhelming, and exhilarating all rolled into one big unknown bundle. The old Kisumu was falling away into memory like a another day, perhaps rapidly, perhaps slowly, and life took on a new complexion in Nairobi. Maybe, it was just my expectations. I realized that my high expectations had moved me forward from who I was toward who I was going to be. '*Kaa square,*' I was constantly told. 'This is Nairobi.' Means stay cool or sit tight. Not that the person I had been was bad, or that the person I was going to be was some great attainment. It was simply the ebb and flow of life. A new 'normal' had prevailed. New rules, new routines, new experiences, new dreams, new perspectives, new expectations. If the old was a less-than-desirable circumstance, the new seemed shiny and promising. For one, I had to smoothen my rusty Kiswahili in order to communicate. I wasn't going to be using my DhoLuo very much.

Three days and I had gotten the hang of it. I had gotten into an odd-yellow-painted Kenya Bus that attracted scowls of disapproval from the other drivers in Fords or Datsuns or Peugeots lining up at an Esso petrol stations (the coup had brought fuel shortage). And can you imagine the fare had shot up? Fifty cents! I had only five shillings in my pocket, now I had fifty cents less. I went to town, to Cameo and paid two shillings to watch *The French Connection* and heard whispers and rumours of so-and-so who had just been picked up by Special Branch. Later that night I appeared to have gotten into trouble with Mama Iva; she wanted me to keep off the city center and stay indoors for a while. I was not to leave the room and venture into town for a few weeks. Day four; she brought into the bedsitter this black and white Sanyo TV. Being tired of being told to *kaa square,* I spent days and nights glued to it, watching Kiswahili dramas and the like. I watched some nice flicks and dramas: *Dallas, ABC Moonlighting, Different Strokes, Good Times, Fist of Fury, Six Million Dollar Man and Bionic Woman, Incredible Hulk, Saber Riders* were amongst my favourites.

And I got a big load of info about the coup, news on trials of the Airforce rebels, all of it. They were still bagging the rebels and the bandits and the looters, and a fat *mzungu* called Patrick Shaw was a busy man. I heard the mere mention of his name made a bandit shit or pee in his pants.

You know what he did, he shot them. Man, he was famous for shooting down bandits and bank robbers... let me just say bad guys. Patrick Shaw was licensed to kill; he did not negotiate with you, he gunned you down even when you were kneeling and begging for mercy. Then he waddled away leaving the spoils to the undertaker.

On the Sanyo telly, I was used to seeing the footage of the man who would be president, my brother Brigadier Ochuka and I thought he certainly didn't look the part. Not with that beard, not with that cocky look. I didn't think he was an intelligent man. Look what shit he had brought our beautiful country, what a shame. I mean, why get drunk on the day you are going to be president? You don't put the cart before the horse... you don't start celebrating and get drunk before you get power, you get power first. I thought Mobutu, Bokassa, Gadhafi, Idi Amin and Doe were a lot smarter here. I mean Amin didn't get drunk till he had real power in his hands. Anyway, I continued watching: more rebels and University students who were sympathetic to the coup were still being picked up. Cops were in business being jittery for nothing and extorting bribes. They had a good reason to brand you a rebel, a KAF sympathizer or a looter if you didn't co-operate.

Weeks later, the city was safe again. I was free from the *kaa square* routine now, I thought. I filled my evenings going to the city center and joined other immigrants catching our first sights of Kenyatta International Conference Centre. I did a lot of walking. Given the profoundly walking culture of Kisumu, I was an anomaly as I walked everywhere and glimpsed at apartments I would never live in, restaurants I wanted to eat at but never got around to, and bars where I wanted to drink at with friends I didn't have yet. Nairobi was my compromise, one of many in a lifetime. I was trying to connect with this new culture and I was just hanging there. Nairobi urban speech patterns and street styles lent themselves to snappy call response mutual name calling, bragging and storytelling in Sheng. I knew I shouldn't complain but I was going through the wringer. I buggered it on the culture shock front. Bud Spencer and Terence Hill comic action at Cameo could have provided an escape. Upstairs in Mad House was the last place I wanted to be on some overly cold Saturday afternoon for 'boogies', if it wasn't for the superb line up of funk which I hated. I carried my acoustic guitar with me all over Nairobi for many days, carting it in its heavy reinforced case from city center to Nairobi West on Kenya Buses, dragging it through the streets of the city. And I'm glad I did. Not just because playing on park benches at Uhuru Park helped me make friends, but because it helped the policemen (who were hunting KAF rebels) less suspicious. Once a roomful of thespians at Kenya National Theatre sung 'Harambee Harambee Tuimbe Pamoja' at the top of their lungs together (badly), and I followed with acoustic guitar. The ice was pretty much broken. People started interacting with me, it made glad. Glad because nothing could make them feel any more self-conscious.

Nairobi provided a warming newness. For the first time I was using tissue paper instead of newspaper. I was eating meat a lot and I liked that. In the mornings I showered with warm water.

I would tune in to VOK General Service, which rotated bands every week on their *Salaams* programs...from Issa Juma to DDC Milimani Park to Vijana Jazz to Moreno Batamba. The songs which were thumping on VOK's National Service this year were Nyboma's 'Double Double', Mangwana's 'Maria Tebbo,' Franco's 'Odongo (Co-operation),' Tabu Ley's 'Maze' and Super Mazembe's 'Salima.' Les Wanyika and Super Wanyika too were prominent on the radio.

So popular was 'Maze' that it brought a new vocabulary among the youth who took to calling their pals *mazee*. I found out from a Zaïrean friend that *Maze* in Zaïre is a woman's name. But many Kenyans who loved this rumba-soukous song and now called their buddies *mazee* couldn't get a word. I loved how Pascal-Emmanuel Sinamoyi Tabu aka Tabu Ley Rochereau made his own line shine—*I love you, baby touch me* sounded so magical. I loved that line. It was a sexy line and I liked it and I sang it many times. One Saturday in November I read in *The Standard* that André 'Damoiseau' Kambite, the man who played solo guitar in *Maze* and *Kele ByBy* was dead. Oops!

On my lucky evenings they played my favourite old OK Jazz and I wallowed in the full spectrum of majestic rumba. I soon became restless, I was a clueless young man and I was too restless. I loathed what was on the radio. The local music scene wasn't really what excited me, and I listened to LP's of bands from Zaïre, South Africa, and many more from African countries. At Garden Square, I could sit by one of my idols: Mangelepa, Virunga, Viva Makale, and learn new guitar techniques from men like Siama. This was really a time to be inspired. I couldn't find work, I knew a guitarist could be immune and invisible here, I knew. Like any artist, he could be a nobody, I knew. On the flipside, he could rise above the clouds and be a rainbow in the sky. He could be misled by the immense strength of his stardom and its shadowy motor, but that was far as it went in his head. In this city, nobody cared if I was a guitarist, I soon learned.

Of course I kept tabs with home. Younger brother Agwenge was in form three, so I wrote letters to my parents, back home to see if the little money I had sent had been received and if everything was copacetic with my family. Ouru had completed his 'O' Level in '80 and was not eager to continue further with books. He was more active in sports and spent time playing rugby with Indian kids. Tom was in class seven and was sitting his CPE that year, so I sent him a card. Sister Akong'o will be a candidate too, next year. Others: Timbe, Achieng Obera and Akinyi were all in primary, Akinyi had joined class one this year. Yes, I was settling down. Yes, Nairobi was safer. No, I hadn't gotten a job. No, I wouldn't be coming back in a while. Yes, I received an occasional aerogramme from bro Odingo in South Africa.

4.

Soon I was hustling, toiling away at uncool *kibarua* jobs at Industrial Area to live for the next day and earn the requisite weekly shillings to supplement Mama Iva's love-payouts. She told me to tune in on National Service and listen to *Yours For the Asking, Sundowner* and *Midday Melodies*. She was soon connecting me with a 'progressive' band which *did not* need my benga solo guitar.

The 'progressive' band was called African Heritage. Yeah, you know them. African Heritage. She took me to meet this heavily built guy in navy crew-neck sweater, and asked him to take me in as a guitarist. Me and this guy, we recognized each other as kindred spirits from South Nyanza and by the end of the day he had hired me to work part-time as guitarist. Later I learned that the reason he hired me so fast was they (the band) owed Mama Iva some sort of favour. Man, these guys were 'heavy'. They looked even cuter than they sounded. Heavily built men...muscular. Clad in expensive African wax print designer clothes, these guys were famous for their high-fashion wardrobes. I sat in with them during rehearsal, I attended their shows. It was a privilege for a guy like me to sit with these glamour guys. It was more than a dream-come-true; it was transformation. Literally. One time I was playing with a third rate cover band in Kondele, Kisumu, the next I am here in Nairobi playing with this swanky pro band. I mean these guys were international.

We performed in places like Hilton, InterContinetal, Six Eighty... how did I come into this? Because of woman. I had thoughts going on inside my head: how was it easy for Mama Iva to shove me into this band? Very soon I knew why. She was having an ... er...um... you-know-what with one of them, that was why I was introduced to the leader as 'my nephew.'

Later I confronted her about it and she gave me a piece of advice. 'You better not let him know about us. I am merely helping you here, you asked me to get you to come to Nairobi and I did. Now, as a musician, use this opportunity to build your career. There are so many bands here in Nairobi you can work with. Besides these guys don't really like your style. I'd use this as a springboard, if I were you.'

Yeah? Right. I swallowed that. Of course I wasn't sore, why should I? I was grateful.

African Heritage had been formed by Alan Donovan, a *mzungu* who knew how to make money on African art. This *mzungu* had his own ideas about what African music should be when he plucked Job Seda from Black Savage to form the group. African Heritage, really was his business empire and did shows of various African wear and artifacts. They didn't like my style. They tried to teach me 'African music.' What about their style? Well, they called it African funk and said it was hardcore, a sound which fused African rhythms with rock and soul, and they sounded more like Osibisa. Honestly I didn't like their style one bit. Kit drums, bass, percussion, saxophone... hardly any guitar. It was not popular even. On the other hand, I had no choice. Mama Iva had put me up with them. I had nowhere to go since she was paying my rent.

So I did what I had to do. I was getting my act together, man. So we practiced the songs from their albums—which I was heartily sick of. Pretty soon I found myself performing every Saturday afternoon at the African Heritage café on Kenyatta Avenue. We played some gigs in Carnivore; my first on stage since leaving Kisumu. To my severe and enchanted astonishment, I enjoyed it. I kept in the background and played shakers, toms and congas, but mostly, acoustic guitar riffs. I soon picked up many of their other tunes. I dressed in their colourful African garbs, I stood there primitively sober and extravagantly cute in their extravagant costumes and I smiled a lot the way I was wanted to. I grew a beard and increased weight. I was one of them. We played night clubs and VIP shows and fashions shows and cultural events. We were always on the move, always on the road. I learned to play their kind of bass and did bass solos during some of their performances. Then I came to the startling realization that African Heritage clearly had an inclination to Western music (something that irked me). We were supposed to be an enigma of Africa, weren't we? Why were we trying to create rock with Afro infections? Why did our sets include songs with gentle, two-chord *bossa nova* guitar behind intricately meaningless vocals? There were rumba songs, alright, but they tilted toward salsa, zouk and several desultory South African ballads and some Soweto jitterbugs. The only pure African thing there was the drumming, but even that was not Kenyan.

I played along, tumbled along and I didn't know where this was taking me even as Nairobi's indecorous nightlife had swallowed me.

I met other Nairobi musicians and had to act the part of a fine lead guitarist. Then there were the standard props and rules: to be a musician here in Nairobi, I had to act in a certain way, dress differently... it was weird. I took long, hard looks at the lifestyle. I tried to protest but was reminded over and over again that this was Nairobi. It was like rubbing salt in a wound. Deep down I always knew I was a good guy. This new life taught me many bad things. I met so many well-known musicians whom I had respected, names I had read in *Nation* pop scene and in magazines like *Viva* and *Drum*. I met them in the flesh here in Nairobi. And got sucked up in their private lives and was shocked. These guys were filthy and nasty and I wondered how in God's name they were still alive. Many were hooked on women, bhang, *miraa* and drink. Many didn't have their own homes and lived with friends. I met some elderly musicians who had deserted their families. One had incurable syphilis, several were on treatment for STDs. It was a constant source of frustration and anger with many artists I met. I chose to look at it a bit differently. I took my chances and picked my life as carefully as a clown picks his hat.

These rogue men of music were forcing me into all the bad behavior of musicians: women and drugs. I didn't like smoking herb, it didn't do anything for me. When I first tested with drugs, I had to stop. I had to stop because the whole mood had just dropped, the bottom had dropped out, and I remember thinking then it was time to stop it. Coke and maybe some grass to balance it out. I was never completely crazy with drugs. I'd been introduced to it and at first it seemed OK, like anything that's new and stimulating. When you start working your way through it, you start thinking: 'Mmm, this is not so cool an idea,' especially when you start getting those terrible comedowns. A singer I met for the first time, called Russi, who was a local compère, brought me down to The Cavern on Tom Mboya Street, and that was when I had cocaine for the first. I told Russi about my sinuses, and he said, 'This'll clear it.' Rambo, another well-known guitarist gave me a smile of approval, I tried it... and nearly hit the roof. I closed my eyes. I had never tripped so hard in my life. I made a silent vow to curb my intake. There was laughter galore, and I rushed out into Tom Mboya Street, trying to breathe the effects out. I remember a small time journalist who knew me saying, 'What's wrong, Dinos?' and I said, 'Nothing, I'm just a bit giddy.'

Many musicians I met later were so chummy, so I'm it went without saying that the drug-taking didn't start or stop with me. The plain and simple fact was drug-taking was fashionable and cool, and most of these Nairobi musicians wanted to be a part of it. My no was a firm NO. No drugs. But women; here I must confess I had no escape. Chances of bedding young sophisticated liberated working class women in Nairobi was always in the offing. When you played with the African Heritage, they kept coming.

Yeah, the opportunity with these attractive middle class women was abundant. Being one of the Heritage's gave me class. Status. We had our own troupe of girls who stuck around us like bodyguards. Many of these were the models who used to work for the African Heritage Fashion House. But we often got around them to the sex-starved crazy women who waited to waylay us backstage or in hotel lobbies. I did countless one-night stands. I thought I was choosy but I got my types. The one girl I imagined I fell in love with was Angelou Adoyo, a half-caste woman who was about my age.

Her mother was Luo and her father was born of British stork in Nairobi.

When I first saw Angelou I was playing congas during a show at Six Eighty. And time stopped. Literally. She was dancing so close and she was so enchanting with a really great body. Soft supple skin. A perfectly shape, soft eyes, soft complexion, adorable. She wore stripped semi-designer jeans with a frilly lacey powder blue top with jillions of blue daisy-like flowers all over it. The 'point five' girl appeared to be tomboyish, her hair pulled to a single long pony. She was pretty, not outstanding or astounding or drop-dead, just a pretty-faced half caste girl but not overly so. But the body, oh, my. Good thing with Nairobi was the girls were so beautiful and so willing. No sweat. it was a pure delight. Pure.

I danced with her, had to. She wasn't a good dancer, she was stiff, well poised and stared straight ahead as I held her. Nervously I licked my lips and brushed a finger against her face. She wasn't startled and continued to give no reaction whatsoever. We hugged and swayed and slowly—very slowly, she eased my hands down to the small of her back. I found this inappropriate—but oh well.

More hugging and swaying.

Slowly, though, I *did* begin some 'exploration.'

Angelou *did* , too.

Soon and very soon we got together, romped about and I nailed her that very night. It was fantastic! It was no brainer, she was game for it. We boffed and shared my bed. She was a very strange girl. Very. To be so cute and so classy and waste that beauty on musicians like us who were bums? I didn't get it. I found her odd. Weird. A bubbly personality, perky, over friendly, giddy, and the whole works. She spoke fine Nairobi English and was a professional. She was a graphic designer working with an advertising agency known and Ebb & Flo. And I discovered, to my chagrin, that she lived in her rented apartment in Adams Arcade and had her own car, an old

Mercedes pimped with stereo, pumped speakers and spicy music. She used to describe me as being so handsome and so young with a baby face and wanted me to write a song for her.

Over time she invited me to her parents place. It was nice, very nice 2-storey misplaced Colonial home in Kileleshwa, complete with statuary, hedges, front yard pond, trees, Roman style pillars. A backyard pool was included. Large family room, separate dining room, large kitchen, air conditioned.

Such things and more that made her special to me.

I tried to win her and have her for me only. I tried and tried and tried. But actually failed to fully comprehend why oh why I was drawn to this carefree girl. The reasoning behind my desire was to have a relationship with her; hers was to have fun.

At least once a week I took her out and we spent the night either at my place or at hers.

Meanwhile...

I couldn't let Mama Iva find out about her. Mama Iva who was a trusted lecherous perv, had me on a leash. Mama Iva was a selfish, demanding and controlling bitch. She had no desire to leave her husband or end her marriage, so she was just enjoying life romping around with young boys in torrid illicit affairs. Frankly, all Mama Iva demanded of me was the once-a-week loving that blew the living daylights out of her. I was content to play that part, I was young and virile. I remembered the callous way she'd treated me, the easy ways she found to crush my spirit and trample my feelings. The mean manner in which she fought off women around me. Mama Iva had a cruel streak in her, something she didn't hesitate to use when she wanted to get her kicks. She sometimes delighted in seeing me bend to her will, seeing me flush with anger or embarrassment when her venomous tongue hit the mark. She was a bitch through and through, and I'd fallen into the ultimate vanity, thinking I could get out easily. You bet I was always thinking of a way out.

Having Angelou now opened my eyes to my need for

freedom. I needed a young girl I really fancied for love and I needed her. I knew she was the woman I wanted to be with. Full of life and happiness and joy and wonder, she gave off her beauty in waves. Watching her walk across a room was a treat in and of itself. Like I said, for me, it had been instant.

Sad thing is for her... well, it hadn't been. The stark, naked truth of the matter was that Angelou was only attracted to me as a musician. To me it was conquest, to her it was adventure. I was handsome, sexy, masculine...but above all, a guitarist. Whatever it is that attracts women to musicians, I just don't know. We had become wonderfully close friends, and I fell quietly, desperately in love with her. Maybe not so quietly, though. When it became apparent to Angelou what my feelings for her were, she told me as gently but as firmly as possible that she just didn't... couldn't...feel the same way about me. She took the emotional responsibility off her shoulders and thrust it squarely onto mine. It became obvious that I was once again in *not* control of my life, that Angelou wanted nothing to do with me in... that way.

I tried to break away and be strong. As a man, I had to be on top of my emotions. So to get back at Angelou I soon found someone. Joy, she was called. She possessed all kinds of sunshiny persona. Medium sized breasts, big cantaloupes. Bubbly personality and attitude. She was a model, a teen model and she was working for African Heritage Fashion House and many local magazines such as *Viva, Drum* and *True Love*. She had two commercial to her credit advertising Ambi perfume and Susana Pomade. I lusted after Joy with the lust only the truly infatuated and completely unsatisfied can. She was smallish and had a wonderfully warm smile, and dark, intelligent eyes that drew me in like a buglight. If I were to open my personal mental dictionary and look up the word 'perfection', Joy's smiling face would be staring right back at me. And, if you listened to her personal definition of 'perfect man,' I fitted the bill completely... except for one crucial detail.

She wanted someone 'funny, warm, sensitive, caring, not afraid to show his emotions...' And then, always, she would add, to my chagrin, '...oh, and sexually attractive.'

Angelou soon learned about Joy. Did she even care? A small, very private smile tugged at the corners of her mouth. She smacked her lips, grinned and slyly eyed me. Quietly, almost too quiet to hear,. she said, 'I think if I were you as a young musician I wouldn't get into a serious relationship with a girl. You are not even twenty five, man. You and I can have fun without commitment and enjoy life. This is 1982, we have just survived the coup and, thank God, we are alive. It's December, man. Enjoy life.' I said nothing. You know, she was probably right.

You gather now that I was a romantic at heart. But it was hopeless, wasn't it? I think I just needed to surround myself with a woman who really loved me. I thought things were going on smoothly and I loved Nairobi and all the good things I was getting.

The band was gearing for a new album and everybody was encouraged to bring in their compositions. I had written my first song and shared it with the band. It was a silly thing called 'Kisumu Girl' and it was about lovers in Kisumu. It was inspired by a silly rhyme we used to sing in primary school. I wrote down the lyrics on a piece of paper and worked out the chords. It went like this:

> When you know
> When you know (amigo)
> When you know what to do...
>
> As I am a Kisumu girl,
> I will marry a Kisumu boy
> But a Kisumu boy is far away
> I will look for another one
>
> CHORUS:

You will be the witness for my dear
You will be the witness for my love

The band listened to it and thought it was funny. The lyrics were nothing, the trick lay in the guitar hooks. But surprisingly, the producer liked it. They wanted a chorus sing-along song that even children could identify with. Something like Osibisa's 'Happy Little Children.' We included it in the album. You can guess how happy that made me. When they went to studio to record, I accompanied them playing guitar and *kayamba* shakers.

We were in it for a better part of that month and at the end of January 1983 we had laid all the tracks and produced the master. We took a break and went to a party. Most of the band, the media, showbiz personalities and the entire African Heritage fraternity was going to meet at Papasha De Luxe and have an old fashioned party with some bands joining the African Heritage on stage. The party was great, lively. At one point, one of the female executives of Ebb & Flo asked me if I would rumba with her, so I looked at Angelou and she gave me the go-ahead nod. We took to the floor, with graceful glides and sweeps of grandeur. She was good to hold and floated around the dance floor. On our third chorus of 'Let Me Love You' I accidentally bumped into the indomitable Mama Iva. She shoed my dancer off and took over. After the song ended, she went off somewhere to get drinks. I felt someone tap me on the shoulder. I turned: Joy. I apologized and Joy looked me in the eyes and ran out of the room, as if Cinderella had just heard the first chime of midnight.

Thinking I might have hurt her, I ran after her and she had exited to the outside balcony, overlooking the busy Nairobi night.

I approached her and said, 'I'm sorry...I hope I didn't hurt you.'

She burst into tears. 'Dino,' she blurted, 'I got a job this afternoon, I've got an eighteen month contract with BAT to do a commercial for Embassy cigarette but I can't take it.'

'Why?'

'Otis, I'm pregnant.'

'Shit, sorry to hear that. When does the commercial start?'

'Rehearsals start in March. I'll be in my fourth month.'

'Does the father know?'

'Not yet, but I'm about to tell him... Dino, you're the father?'

'What? Oh, no... no way. How can you be sure?'

'You're the only guy I had sex with for three months.'

I felt a sudden urge to jump off the balcony and land in the middle of the street.

And like a despicable rat, I exclaimed, 'Oh no, you're not blaming this on me.'

In an automatic response she turned and slapped me hard across the cheek. 'You bastard...you goddamned, bastard.'

She ran down the stairs and into the street of Nairobi nights, waved at a Kenya Bus, got in and went off.

5.

To shorten the chain of events, I called her on Monday and she agreed to meet me to discuss the matter. She was for abortion (albeit illegal). I still had enough Adventist upbringing to offer to suffer for doing the sinful thing: I wouldn't marry her, but I'll support her through the pregnancy term, give the baby a name, and then we could put it up for adoption. I had already thought hard about that.

Without my knowledge, Joy had gone ahead and signed with the Embassy cigarette commercial. I didn't have any idea as to what she was thinking. Two days later, I called her through the ad agency and she told me she was starting rehearsals and shootings in parts of Nairobi and Rift valley.

'What about the baby?'

'Don't worry Otis, I know how to take care of that problem,' she said, trying to reassure me.

Two months passed. I called the ad agency several times and was told they were in the 'field.' Then they were back in Nairobi to shoot the final part of the commercial. She still wouldn't take my calls, so I decided to leave her to it. The anger was going to wear off and she was going to come back. Then on the following Friday night, someone knocked on my door. It was a handsome guy, in his thirties. I opened the door and he asked, 'Are you Otis Dundos?'

I nodded.

'My name is Muaka. I think you have a friend named Joy. May I come in?'

'Sure, yes. I've tried to call her all week and got no answer. Is she alright?'

'No, I'm afraid Joy is dead.'

My heart stopped. The world stopped. Everything stood still. My muscles forgot their use. Some very cold electricity wracked through my skin. I sank to the couch... and the guy reached out to me. I hung in the limbo... heard no sound. Then just as fast, the universe flooded back into my ears and to my senses with an almost deafening crescendo.

Faintly I caught the words. 'It was an accident... the police ruled out suicide, but it looks like she did it accidentally, on purpose. She was rehearsing and told one of the other models she was going to fall down a flight of stairs in an effort to abort her baby. You knew she was pregnant?'

Again, I nodded.

'She must have tried too hard...when she fell, she broke her neck. The baby was still-born. It was a boy.'

I began to cry, whimpering, at first, but then I lost control and went to pieces. Muaka came over and tried to embrace me, to give me the 'support' he thought I needed. I brushed him. He stood there awkwardly as I wept. Not sobbed, wept. Blared

it up like a four year old. That was where this story started...
and that was where this story ended. That I didn't love this
girl? I couldn't have been more wrong.

But...

The kid? My kid... my boy! Oh, no. I cried hard and
angrily.

I went to City Mortuary to find out for myself. Muaka
volunteered to take me, but I told him not to bother. I
preferred to handle this matter on my own. The pathologist's
pm report confirmed it: she, indeed, was three months'
pregnant. Tired and guilty, I bribed the attendant into letting
me see the body. He took me into the stinking house of the
dead lined with rubber coated cold rooms. He yanked open a
door and a gush of chocking formalin smell hit me in the face
and pained in my ears. I followed him into the room. He
pulled open a drawer and made to go but I pulled him back
and made him stay with me. I looked into Joy's face. She had
turned so black that she looked like something molded out of
clay. Her face looked small and pinched and her eyes were
swollen. I reached out a shaking hand and touched her cold
forehead and her hair. In my mind was a picture of her round,
soft face. I saw her shy, hideous smile, the smile that had
appeared on numerous covers of *Drum*, *Viva* and *True Love*
magazines. I heard myself whisper, 'I love you, Joy. Be in peace.
I'm sorry, forgive me, joy.' I heard something like her voice
whispering in my ear and I smiled at the little puffy clay—face
that had once been Joy. I gently closed the drawer and stood
back.

I followed the attendant out of the death house into the
sunshine outside. There was a feeling of death all over me and
something about Joy filled me with dread and left a sour taste
in my mouth. I thought how lonely death is. They say death is
the only connection between us and God. Is it why death
leaves so much emptiness and loneliness? I mean when a
person dies and leave us, why is there so much loneliness? Joy,

crammed and frozen inside made death so ugly made death look so upsetting.

I felt ill. A burning sensation seethed in my stomach. I was sweating and feeling terribly hung up.

I stood there in the sun looking lost and out of place. The attendant approached me and offered me a cigarette. I did not smoke much, but I accepted it. I needed it. He asked if this was my first *real* experience with death and I nodded.

6.

The following days I carried my cloud of loss to work, to the beats of African Heritage. I was not myself, kept hitting bum notes. People saw it. I stayed inside my room for one week, ate nothing, said nothing, drunk only water. I didn't let anybody know that I was mourning, just said I was sick. Mama Iva, in particular, was so concerned. She thought I was in one of my artistic mood swings and kept off.

On the second week I went into rehearsal with the African Heritage. But when they went to perform at Hilton, I went to Nairobi Cinema with Angelou. To say the least, the very least, she was the one I told the truth.

There was a long pause, Angelou seemed to be in a trance, her eyes were closed—opening only when she heard movement. She was angry. 'I told you not to fall in love, she admonished. 'Look at the emotional burden you've brought on yourself. Now, I'm your friend, so am I supposed to carry this burden too?'

For a time she had tried penetrating the mysterious confounding boundary wall. She asked me questions, consoled me, and told me everything will be alright. To no avail. I was in another world, in deep mourning. There were dozens and dozens of "universes" beyond, all selectable and plausible. She was an artist and she saw through me, she assumed strongly that at least one of the many worlds I was traipsing through was the land of the dead. But its exact placement was a little vague, how far away would that put me from Joy and my son?

She had to bring me back.

Some nights I told her to drive to some lonely spot in Adams Arcade and we just stayed silent in the car. She really tried to mend my broken heart, that half-caste woman. Even though she was an alcoholic and smoked weed, she had a heart of gold. She was a good person, a person I could trust and confide in.

For two months that followed, I was falling apart. It was almost as if I was underwater... as if everything around me was floating far from me. As if even the very air was afraid to fill my gasping lungs lest it got tainted by my disorientation. My life was at crossroads: one part of me was dying and a new part was coming alive. While this was happening, there were lots of things banging inside my head. I was in a state of floating contemplation that could be anything from a few hours with a bottle of whiskey that I couldn't really afford to weeks of soulful, shuddering, silent blankness. For a long time I waded in this silence with the knowledge that something sinister was afoot. It just floated there whispering on the brink of subconscious thoughts, never allowing me enough entry to be prepared.

I floundered about aimlessly seeking my way. Was this then a possible chance at redemption?

Well, if so, I'd blown it...

I may have been trying to escape the reality of the situation but Joy haunted me into the deep private chambers of my heart. To begin with, the artist in me demanded a transformation. I was quitting African Heritage. I never mentioned it to anyone but I was quitting. I stole out like a thief, moved out of Mama Iva's bedsitter in Nairobi West with my guitar and my clothes and moved into an apartment in Mathare North. I spent most of my days going to MacMillan

Library to read. Read books on philosophy. I was on a quest for self-discovery. Angelou came to this odd part of the city, to Mathare North to visit me in the flat. First time she puked; she admonished me, said I didn't belong here in this slum. You guess she was probably right. You walked into this room and saw this was beyond roach cube. The sink in the shared bathroom was held up by bricks and a sisal ropes. The kitchen corner looked like someone blew soot up the wall using firewood. Angelou said the room smelled like turpentine. The place was *haunted!* She and I heard distant screams from within the room in the midnight hour and in the morning we all shared the fact that we had the strangest dreams. The whole experience with cheap housing was the weirdest any of us had ever had, and being experienced by a guy and a lady who had never lived in slums.

Then her visits were frequent. We smoked weed, rolled all over the bed and on the floor groaning and grinding and panting. And she didn't stop till she'd drained me out. Only then she left me empty and hollow. And I slept, slept long till the hunger in my belly bit. I didn't know which day it was, which month it was. I had no radio, I didn't read newspapers, nothing. The army might have taken over the country and I wouldn't have known until I saw people running about screaming and heard gunfire.

My mind was not properly made. First were the superstitions tied to my quitting: Joy. I needed to be as far away from her as possible. African Heritage was one of the things tied to her. Mama Iva too. I didn't want her to baby me for long. I was at war with myself over survival versus conscience: did I really want to quit the African Heritage? What then? Where would I go from here? I was still a nobody in the Nairobi music scene. Nobody. I was yet to make myself. If I quit now, what else. On the other hand, how was playing with African Heritage helping develop my own skills as a guitar player when guitar was not their most prominent instrument? Being with African Heritage, I had gained some clout and respect for being a part of something really cool and organised. But who what was I? A solo guitarist! Promoting them was not giving me perspective in terms of personal style. I undoubtedly had to find means to better promote myself.

News filtered in: African Heritage had a one month contract to back the Zaïrean singer, Nguashi N'Timbo. I was not to play in that contract and I figured that I was going to take a one-month leave while they backed the soft spoken N'Timbo who was in Nairobi this year promoting his song 'Shauri Yako' done in Kiswahili with Orchestre Festival du Zaïre. What I didn't know was that Ntimbo had been in East Africa for most of last year (1982). The newspapers reported that he did many singles which became part of recordings that he licensed to Melodica.

At the end of that month I would know whether I was quitting or staying. Weeks dragged, the month passed. No events. By the end of it, I was pretty distraught. I did not want to be in the band, it wasn't really what I wanted. Mama Iva found me and tried to reason things out. Here I was with this fantastic opportunity; I was in one of the most envious of all positions one could ever be in. To be an up'n'coming star, a darling of the women and an idol of the youth. I was honoured to be one amongst the members of a band of this ranking... I was a Heritage. It mightn't have been what I was ultimately looking for. But with African Heritage, I had a chance to propel myself to the uncharted waters, didn't I.

She talked to me.

Angelou talked to me. People talked to me.

The few friends I had made wanted me to stay in African Heritage. But at this point, my conviction was absolute. Conscience won over survival. I had to come of age and had to be myself. I focused more on how I could be a better person to those around me—or even to those I didn't really love—but I stopped short of admitting exactly how much a temporary state of affairs could fracture my relationship with myself. I wanted, more than anything, to be a man. A good man. A man people responded positively to. I was getting concerned about how my attitude, talks and behavior affected other people around me. It occurred to me that my childhood hadn't prepared me for the many challenges I was facing now. My father hadn't prepared me enough to be a man.

I had to be a man. Thus another journey began, a new journey.

After a month of depressing weariness, my life was hardly falling into place. But suffice to say that in my life's highs and lows, the past few years had been parked firmly in the struggle to succeed as a guitarist. To be painfully honest, the past few years had been difficult for me.

In fact, the last time I'd remembered feeling like I was on one of life's distinct highs was early 1980 when I was active in church before I started venturing into full time music, particularly the months I was actively playing for Gloryland and trying to please Riana. I felt like I was in this philosophical playground of self-discovery; my thinking was clear, my senses were heightened, my awareness was keen. Look where I was now. How better to wriggle my way out of this dark space than to mimic where I was when I wasn't feeling on top of the world? Surely going cold-turkey from one existence in lakeside Kisumu would bring the same rewards this time, right?

Let me see...

The past few weeks had driven home a point. I made friends with many young Luos in Mathare North and saw that living in this slum with their families was no mean task. Life could be very difficult for many of these Luos living in urban decay. The fight to get out of situations like this could be full of disappointment and setbacks, I saw. I had always considered myself not a slum person since I came from a humble rural home but seeing my fellow Luos fighting poverty in this slum made me see it was not their choice. I used to talk with them in DhoLuo and observed that many of them here were genuinely honest and hardworking people who just couldn't go back home because either they had no homes to return to or things were worse at home. They needed a little friendliness and encouragement since this was the *only* life they had.

I smoked weed and danced around many flat many times but could never get to the heart of facing the reality of starting over. That I had to be a man and succeed was a foregone conclusion. Now I needed Nairobi to inspire me. Real men worked and achieved, didn't they? I didn't know about other guitarists, but; for me, guitar playing was a kind of meditation. Suddenly I was mindful. This mindfulness meant I was to stop dreaming and start living entirely in the present, even if just for a few moments—a skill that most of us artistes, with our crazy lives and hectic schedules, had a hard time cultivating.

Two months and a half into the new year, things started to lift. The timing coincided (actually, it was hardly a coincidence) with a conscious effort to work (really work) hard, to put away the idle dreaming-and-staying-up-late-watching-weekend-movies-and-procrastiting-whilst-eating-bread-and-milk-and-feeling-sorry-for-myself *shenzi* mode of 'living today for the next day' that I'd slumped into as of late. I cut my sleeping hours to eight. I bought rumba vinyls and practiced to perfect the rumba and soukous finger picking techniques. I took myself to Garden Square to watch Zaïrean bands rehearsing instead of people-watching at Uhuru Park. I researched every Zaïrean-related music out there and spent an absurd amount of money getting the ones that actually seemed very close to what I wanted to hear, and every day I learned a new technique and improved my style. And every day I was reminded that it was one small thing I was doing to be better.

It suddenly dawned on me that every minute counted, and I didn't want to spend them sitting in this dreary room in this dreary semi-slum thinking of the best way to get inspired waiting for something to strike me. I had to go for it. I will say, at this point, that I took a cue from Retro Rumba du Zaïre Band—who went a whole month without a solo guitarist and approached me through mutual acquaintances—and learned that somehow my reputation as a guitarist wasn't bad after all, which made me feel what somebody feels when you get to the shore after escaping drowning in high water. It jazzed me terribly when I learnt that the moan whose shoes I was stepping into was a giant known as Mose Se Fan Fan. In that year, Mose Se, a celebrity Zaïrean star of rank, was up about Nairobi. He had been a solo guitarist and ex-OK jazz. Fan Fan's outing here with Retro Rumba du Zaïre Band now disturbed and upset me. I hate to see stars falling down and Mose Se had been an International star. Anyone who had played with OK Jazz was, without any doubt, an International star. More to it, Mose Se had been a big name in OK Jazz. You know he really made that hit *Djemalasi*. What was he doing in Nairobi walking on foot and doing lowly recordings in River Road? And guess some of the people he was working with? Moreno, Pele Ondindia, Kasalo Kyanga and Coco Zigo. Related: the Retro Rumba gesture was a God-send (at least, I hoped it was) after Mose Se ditched them and moved to Tanzania.

Somebody had once told me to keep off Zaïrean bands. He was probably right. Zaïrean bands were too soppy and often more commercial than artistic. Zaïrean artistes thought they were the best and their bands always had no openings for Kenyan artistes. And if, as a Kenyan you managed to get into one of them, the first thing you had to do was learn Lingala. They assimilated you. You didn't have a chance to grow as an individual Kenyan talent.

Sad thing, Zaïrean bands were the rulers of the game. I had to learn. I considered myself a troubadour still. I was a guitarist who wanted to play the hard benga solo (which was similar to Zaïrean rumba or *soukous* solos). This was me, it was my natural style. It was what I loved playing and it was what I played naturally and enjoyed. There's not much more to say. The point is I wasn't here in Nairobi to party and have a good time, but rather to get experience and connect with the serene part of myself that flourished three years during my first go-round with Kisumu Delta Force. That part of me was there, it turned out it never left. It was just that like anything vital, it needed nourishment. It required me to do exactly what I was doing now; to get the best I could from Nairobi City then go back and start a musical enterprise in Kisumu. For Kisumu, dear ladies and gentlemen, I was a homeboy and was forever going to remain a homeboy. Like every hearty Kisumuan, my allegiance remained.

7.

I was ready to let the transcendence begin. I was attempting to kick the smuck to retool my life. Because I spent many months brooding in Mathare North, the unfortunate effect of not starting to play again was to cause things to grind to a total, screeching halt. Broke and without meaningful work of *any* kind, I was taking every gig, no matter how little it paid, no matter how dire the prospects. In this year, Nairobi was awash with many expatriate Zaïrean bands. What I loved about the Zaïreans was their unquestionable commitment to performing the music they loved. I spent months listening to many Zaïrean bands, going to see as many performances as possible. There were plenty others complete with magical stage acts and spiky guitars, following bright-eyed in the wake of a trail blazed fierce new competitors, most notably Samba Mapangala and Virunga.

The most dynamic Zaïrean and most committed, Samba was always inviting along random people he wanted to use in his band. Okello Jose had done a long stint in his band during the glorious Le Kinoirs days. Besides his manager, Tabu Osusa and his drummer, Onyango Shaban, he wanted another Luo artiste to have a Kenyan face in his band. I was never sure if he was trying to suck me up or what. If he 'drugged' his musicians along, though, I was instantly sure to dislike him. But, folks, Samba was big this year. It's doesn't matter whether; listening to the music of Virunga was like being forced to eat Dunga *dek* as a kid; the more it was forced, the more unpleasant your mind made it taste. What I'm trying to say is Virunga didn't even have the best solo guitar player, so I wondered what made them tick. Until I watched them perform at Garden Square.

The week I made contact with Retro Rumba, rumours swirled in that Moreno had just joined Virunga and they were touring the country promoting the single 'Mabiala'. To me this looked like a wrong move since Moreno was already a star who had managed to create his significant cranky bad guy image with semblance of fame taken from his eponymous hit 'Pili Mswahili,' wisely sung in Kiswahili. His other credit-crunch busting compositions were 'Dunia Ni Duara,' and 'Urembo Si Hoja'. As a matter of fact, Moreno was a definite grower. Initially, you could have struggled to see past his baritone, which had all the garbled messiness of hardcore, whilst falling just short on the aggression and rebellion that usually characterised his chosen Kiswahili genre. His lovable 'Urembo Si Hoja' had featured one woman I adored: Nana Akumu.

The name Akumu, you guess, created the magic-held affinity of the Luos in Nairobi to Nana. Akumu is a rare and beautiful Luo name, so that made her our sister. Akumu's husband, Tabu Nkotela Kiombwe and I were good pals for a time and I used to have some hearty moments with him educating my young mind on the art of creating good music. His outfit was Orch. Pepe Lepe which wasn't a known band. But he was a cool sober-minded guy. Nana, on the other hand, was an artistic recluse who was difficult to ignore and hard to control. With her indie outfit called Bana Ekanga, she had recorded for herself the super groovy 'Haraka Haina Baraka' on Editions Shika Shika label (absolutely amazing). I had seen her live shows a couple of times I could see her free spirit and why she couldn't get along with her husband. Nana could get down and raunchy. That woman was dynamite. She took a different direction. 'Haraka Haina Baraka' sprung out of the old and new friendships she had made here in Nairobi. She was satisfied that she ended up a solo artist. Major bands were all politics, she believed. She didn't want to end up losing her soul to the devil along the way. Reflecting on her circuitous path, Moreno believed she did the right thing by sticking her guts out and going it alone.

Around the same time it appeared Lovy Mokolo Longomba had done his time with Shika Shika and Orchestre Lovy and was back in Super Mazembe. Back to where he had begun. He was regularly recording with Mazembe as Bana Likasi and touring with them and challenging Madjo Maduley on lead vocals.

I never really cared much for Lovy's early solo career—people said he was hasty. Others said he was full of hot air after the spotlight Mazembe gave him. I always loved Lovy. I remembered his performance of the single 'Nanga' on Sanyo Top of the Pops, with that strange climbing-frame-mic-stand. But Lovy in the new nefarious Nairobi scene was like nothing else I could admire. With Lovy, I had instantly become a Mazembe fan, and I'd pretty much stuck with him through the short and often sweet years that made the early '80s. But he Lovy I was seeing now was a family man with problems. That was why he was so restless.

Shika Shika, which Lovy regularly 'prostituted' with, was being led by Jimmy Moni Mambo and had Frantal Tabu on guitar. Wow! What can I say about this band? They were brilliant, they had come on so much since the last time I saw them early in 1981when they toured Kisumu. Things got loud whenever Moni Mambo took to the stage on many occasions at Jeans Bar in Nairobi West and Hallians. With their abrasive, cartoonish vocals and shock-tactic lyrics, Shika Shika wanted to be everyone's taste. In a market that was becoming increasingly saturated with second-rate soukous and Baba Gaston offspring, it was refreshing to hear a troupe of young musicians making original, cutting-edge soukous music for *vijana*.

Zack Shivachi, a friendly River Road session rhythm guitarist (who hated Zaïreans like I did) had introduced me to his friend, the omnipresent rhythm guitarist Siama. We used to call him Mwalimu because of he loved schooling us. He was always showing you some hook on the guitar. The guy was here and there and everywhere. And if you didn't have Siama in your recording, you had no recording. It appeared like Siama alone could drive a rhythm Nairobi loved to sway to. He created strong, substantive songs driven by his memorable rhythm guitar chops, mirroring a depth of experience portrayed with integrity.

In this confusion, some chirpy cockney new guy had written a popular single which went like 'Wangare Twende Dance Na Lemba Lemba'. The song had a classic clash soukous feel and while it wasn't a serious number (to me), it still had a feel of comedy that the mainstream Nairobi music scene was used to be getting from Shika Shika and Viva Makale. The new guy who sang this one called himself 'Sauti Ya Simba'. His name was Lessa Lassan, he had played with Dr. Nico and African Fiesta and indeed his style was poignantly Fiesta. He had also come around from Zaïre and decided to make Nairobi his home too. He was mostly recording with members of Shika Shika like Frantal on an out-fit called Popolipo and had hits like 'Owiti' and 'Tobias Oduori.' I spent months trying to meet him. Well, I finally found him in Cantina Club after waiting for an hour and a half. It was already starting to get sweaty with the amount of people in the bar, and I was tired of the hardships of being a broke guitar student who couldn't afford a soda at a bar where nothing (and I mean nothing) came cheap. Lessa Lassan and I had a heart to heart. The guy was a charming talker. A warm-hearted big man with a funny voice. I loved him. I picked up some new experience from our encounter and moved on to find the next Zaïrean band.

Shivachi again introduced me to Ilunga Mabuluki, the leader of Black Devils. In the Devils' fraternity I met many hard working men of music, very serious. One of them was Botango Bedjil Mofranck, popularly known as BB. I used to accompany BB to Ainsworth Club to see Sammy Kasule in concert. Sammy had just released a sizzler known as 'Here To Play Music'. He used to refer to himself as The Grunts and Guitar Man owing to his ability to sing and play bass guitar at the same time. He had an outfit called Radi. I really respected this guy for his seriousness and his forthrightness. He took his music seriously and I could see he was destined for bigger things. We sat down and he warmly recounted his moments in Taso Stephanou's Makonde and about Orchestra Somajeko International and his lovable song 'Maria Wandaka.'

The urban scandals of bands provided an interesting kaleidoscope in the Nairobi scene. Urban? Yes, but more than that. Even though the scandalous trio of Viva Makale, Shika Shika and Moja One had been around for the best part of two years, it was only last year that they'd really made an impact on the music scene. Viva Makale, an outfit fronted by the tenor sax player George Kalombo Mwanza and featuring Coco Zigo and Bwammy, had recorded the whimsical and eclectic 'Akamba,' a song that took the style of 'driving a double.' Meaning to the locals it was a praise of some kind for the Kamba tribe or something just Kamba since you heard hoots such as 'Masaku, Kitui, Kangundo' in it. But at a private level, the song was sung in Lingala and it was dealing with domestic woes of a couple. It worked in a funky, retro-soukous vocal and Bwammy put a bombastic spin on solo guitar with Siama stringing the memorable rhythm guitar chops. Coco Zigo's cheerfully mongrel animations made it orotund. He was one of the best dancers I had ever watched, splendid. The end-product, with great jeer, flourished a plenty. Kalombo managed put together another sizzler called 'Bibi Mudogo.' Then the party for Viva Makale appeared to have ended there and Bwammy went back to Mangelepa, briefly taking Coco Zigo with him to star in the hit 'Lisapo.'

But scandalous thing is Viva Makale, Shika Shika and Moja One were indie bands with no fixed musicians or instruments. With the exception of the singers Lovy Longomba and Dago Mayombe and the bassist Nsillu Wa Ba Nsillu 'Manitcho', the three bands used to share the following musicians: Chery Matumona (solo guitar), Bibi Ley (guitar), Tabu Frantal (guitar), Siama Matuzungidi (rhythm guitar), Thomy Kabea Lomboto (bass guitar), Coco Zigo (vocal), Moreno Batamba (vocal), Jimmy Monimambo (vocal), Fataki Lokassa (vocal), Tambwe Mandola (vocal), Lawi Somana (sax), Kalombo (sax), Tshamusoke (trumpet), Lava Machine(drums), Onyango Shaban (drums).

Talk of scandal. It didn't matter whether you were Moja One or Shika Shika or Viva Makale or Super Lovy... if you wanted rhythm it was Siama. If you wanted solo guitar, it was Frantal. If you wanted bass, it was Nsillu or Thomy Lomboto. If you wanted good vocals, you had Coco Zigo, Fataki Lokassa and Dago Mayombe.

And, you know, I almost forgot the honey-voiced Fataki Lokassa 'Masumbuko Ya Dunia' who greatly inspired my move into music in 1975. His indie band was Bana Ngenge Popote. He was an exciting showman whose voice was heard in Super Mazembe's epic 'Annivasaire Dixieme' album. Other times he played with Moja One where he teamed with Coco Zigo, guitarist Siama and drummer Lava Machine. But most of the time he was a regular member of Virunga. Bana Ngenge was just an idle side show.

Ochieng' Kabaselleh alias Kallé, alias Mbuta Kidi, alias Obwogo Kwach wuod Ogolla, alias Mbuta Masanga was a big name up here in Nairobi too. His real name was Hadjoullas Nyapanji Ochieng Ogolla and he was a big boisterous man. But he was a fine composer. Regularly he was associated with Lunna Kidi Masanga, his indie band. He was always very adept at walking the fine line between two dramatically different musical styles be it benga or rumba-soukous, liberal and conservative. He was extremely adroit at working through the muck and using different musicians to come up with good music. Although he liked to work with Zaïrean artists and a host of River Road session musicians like Owacha Willy, Oswaga Ley, Willy Mazeras and Onyango Shaban, his main solo guitarist was Anzino Osundwa of Mazadijo.

Now the giants...

Mangelepa, Les Wanyika, Maroon Commandos and Super Mazembe represented the amalgamation of four musical giants whose careers created a wealth of experience spanning a decade and producing a bedlam of good experience and an impressive repertoire.

Mangelepa was a seven-piece orchestra whose horn-enhanced take on African jazz was straight from the lo-fi, speaker-shuddering rulebook of Orchestre Bella Bella in the '70s. Mangelepa was awfully creative and frighteningly energetic and sometimes took matters to extremes. These men had everything you could possibly want in a band: a very well-polished horn section, a mean looking drummer, hyper-singers (including an all singing all dancing sensation) walking bass and funky guitars. In Mangelepa style, things were bent and twisted... guitars and sax notes were bent and twisted. Mazembe, on the other hand, could bring a smile to everyone's faces and a leak in their pants. The things that struck me were the amazing fluidity of singers Longwa and Katele's syrupy voices and the virtuoso guitarist Bookerlose's energy. Added to Atia-Jo, the bass player with a hell of a long winding name:

Mwanza wa Mwanza Mulunguluke what-else-*yawa*, Rapok Kayembe (rhythm guitar), Kassongo Songoley (rhythm guitar) and Dodo Doris (drums), the band was a relatively new dinosaur pile-up. The lesser known luminaries in the band were the likes of Revo, Nene, Rondo Kandolo, Charles Atei, Lobe Mapako Roddy, Loboko 'Pasi' Bua Mangala, Kitenge Ngoi Wa Kitombole and Musa Olokwiso. I loved the Mazembe of Katele Alley/Longwa era. I didn't really fancy the Super Mazembe of the Lovy Longomba and Kassongo Wa Kanema era. The output was too monotonous and superficial.

Guitarist Bibi Ley Kaba Kaba was tumbling along with what was left of Les Kinoirs after heavy weights like Samba, Okello, Madjo Maduley and Pele Ondindia left. Okello and Madjo Maduley joined Super Mazembe while Pele Ondidia turned up in Samba's newly formed Virunga.

Mention the name Samba Mapangala and you had one of the most successful and respected of the recent tidal wave of unashamed singer-songwriters to have broken the mainstream and broken Baba Gaston's lineup. Virunga immediately conjured up notions of heart-felt and beautifully crafted songs in people's minds—and, of course, their plaintive, expressive voices which gave Samba's work that extra edge on his striking debut.

Seeing Samba and Virunga on show was an experience. I went to Starlight after an interesting wait at Kencom bus stop (involving a chance meeting with a young lady who knew me and who would later attempt to *katia* me). I finally took her along with me, we boarded a bus, which the conductor said would be heading up Valley Road. Arriving at about 7pm, there was already a lengthy queue outside the venue. I held the girl's hand and battled my way through the scrum of fancy dressy students and fans that seemed to be permanently hanging about near the door of the club, skipped past the street drinkers getting out of the cold, and headed upstairs. We got into arguments with bouncers over the 'Over 18's' rule.

The girl was apparently under 18. At about 7:30, as everyone else was running down to the front, we decided to join them all. Taking the enthusiasm and energy of rumba-soukous as their starting point, Virunga then packed in the shunting riffs, twitching vocals and bass-heavy grooves, to create something that was more innovative and individual than the usual disco-punk fair.

I had read somewhere that Starlight Club owner and legendary club impresario Robbie William Fisher Armstrong had been putting bands here regularly since the 1960s, and the pub had built a bit of a reputation with gigs from OS Africa Band and a myriad of latter day funky soukous bands going down a storm. When Samba and Virunga burst into the scene last year, he turned the Starlight into the hottest live music nightspot in town. Through his Virunga machine, he rotated men. Talented men. Some of the faces I used to see were of Coco Zigo Mike, Fataki Lokassa 'Masumbuko Ya Dunia', Jean Claude Mulamba, Dago Mayombe and (occasionally) Moreno along with Ottis on vocals. Coco Zigo was a great vocalist and also a very disruptive force on stage. On guitar were men such as Nsilu wa Ba Nsillu Manitcho, Sammy Mansita Nzola, Django Nkulu Mwilambwe, Bejos, Siama Matuzungidi and Beya Mikobi Dibuba. And many others who came on brief *nzong nzing* flings. Their line-up was completed with funky drums from Onyango Shaban and Willy. Lava Machine soon replaced Willy on drums and the trumpeter Kodila was soon a regular feature. By then 'Solo Sax' Lawi Somana had left to join Tabu Ley. A real mixed bag here; the Virunga era fused with funky disco, threw in some hard Franco and Tabu Ley rumba harmonies and sprinkled on some heavy Zaïko riffage. Now coming towards a conclusion for this year, Virunga had been a useful platform for a number of Nairobi bands wishing to showcase their music to the city, whatever their genre.

8.

The band Retro Rumba Du Zaïre had come to Nairobi last year. There had been a story about them in *Nation*. They came as the backing band for solo guitarist Mose Se who now them. So they had an opening that I could fill.

I met   band's leader shortly. Dodoly was his name. I wanted to get close to him. To observe how Zaïreans ran their bands and what made them tick. We met not even knowing what each other looked like up until the meeting. We sat at a café in Accra Road and had tea with *mandazis*. As we ate, he filled in the story of his group in broken Kiswahili and where he couldn't find a word he used Lingala and repeated in French. His words had too much Bantu prefix *ba*. To mean *wandugu*, he said *ba-ndugu*. To mean *waitaimba*, he said *batayimba*. To mean *wamekuja*, he said *bamekuya*. My knowledge of Lingala was kindergarten, so we struggled through it and found that we could at least communicate with me constantly saying, 'Can you say that again, more slowly.' He asked me if I played music, to which I responded, yes. Guitar? He asked. Yes, I said. *'Muzuri, eh?'* he asked. I nodded and smiled. He asked me if I wanted to come to the club they were playing in at Ngara and jam. He expected me to play like Manuaku, he said. Who's Manuaku? I asked. Manuaku was the guitarist of Zaïko Langa Langa. He also wanted me to play like Matima. Their style was called soukous. I had heard about it: In the 70s, when I was growing up, this hot, guitar-based sound called soukous—itself an evolution of Zaïrean rumba— sprang out of Zaïre. Soukous was fast-growing. This band Retro-Rumba was actually one of the many Zaïrean bands importing it here. In Zaïre soukous was associated with bands such as Zaïko Langa Langa, Isifi and Viva La Musica. I used to hear of a singer called Evoloko and I asked Dodoly about him. He had recently formed a new group called Langa Langa Stars, Dodoly told me. He asked me if I would be comfortable playing soukous and he gave me some cassettes to go listen to.

I was very reluctant and refused on multiple occasions. After more personal consultation, I said that I would in fact come to his house to play guitar. I wanted him to see me as a novice.

Don't ask me why.

Okay, let me tell you why: I wanted an experience with a Zaïrean band. Plain and simple. Within weeks, I had rehearsed enough with them to play their gigs.

The club was called Tete La Dhahabu in Ngara. This particular venue was an alley-night-club-restaurant, very low-key. The sort of place a plate of meat was charged higher than a prostitute. In fact I talked to the bandleader that day to complain about how depressing this place looked and about *my* security! He gaped at me, meaning he didn't know what I meant. I said to myself I wouldn't be playing with them for more than six months. I would pick up the experience I needed and move on. While we were setting up and discussing the set lists, I saw immediately that they had good players but no vocals! Too late now, time to go, bar was packed! I was expecting some serious grief from the bar owner and promoter, instead he wanted us to be the house band. I met him when he tripped, sat down with a beer watching us set up. He was a rather portly and elderly Kikuyu fellow who knew very little about music. His name? Kamau, he told me. 'Just play,' he said. Are you kidding me? 'What about the lead singer?' I asked. 'There's a good man,' he said.

That good man turned out to be... oh, what a man! Big, swarthy, unkempt with staring eyes. He was wearing red polyester stretch pants and a black polo neck sweater. His name? Biggy Tembo. His real name? I asked? Yes, from Tanzania. Why, his accent screams Tanzanian? He played in Dar with Bima Lee. Oh yeah? Well, his Tanzanian accent and slightly gooney name of Biggy Tembo put me at ease.

Luckily, this big guy Tembo had been doing this a while and could speak Lingala! Unfortunately, he only knew the words to a nursery school vocabulary. So we watched him struggle. At first, he made up words, or worse, just babbled. Later in the evening, after a little 'lubrication' he got brave and started spewing fairly suggestive lyrics that brought the band to near convulsive laughter.

Somehow, we got through it. Weeks followed and we played every evening at Tete and had the best time for the next four months. Lots of solos, and most surprisingly, no one, not even Kamau the club owner noticed that the band was not in sync. Me? I was at home playing in this band. This was my Uni, man. I was learning... learning, picking skills. We played lilting, rippling, soukous dance groove that seemed to smile from every register, with melody and rhythm inseparable. I felt better and less guilty. For once I was playing *real* African music. Doesn't matter whether it was Zaïrean. Certainly it was much better than the Western noise African Heritage put me through. I was not frightened, I loved Zaïrean and my style flourished. They started calling me *Cherahani* due to my fast finger picking style.

The music was joyous. Biggy sang melodies that coursed through the patterns like vines on a trellis.

I discovered the Zaïreans well-kept secret: stamina and love for music. They truly (I mean truly) enjoyed their music. To them music was everything. They played it with passion. Passion akin to making love to a woman you truly love. I wanted to be part of this. The Zaïrean touch came through in gleaming, circular guitar lines that went skipping through arpeggios or lilting through scales. The songs we played had one or many of those lines, catchy and infinitely repeatable. I shared my notes with the rhythm guitar player's and our lines criss-crossed with three-part vocal harmonies, which in turn (in many cases) split for call-and-response singing. Most songs started with the slow melodious rumba patterns before bursting into soukous where I played fast dance notes.

Because I was always listening to music with an ear towards learning how to play it, I had become adept at working out how the different pieces fitted together, and what made each of them work, apart and together.

In months that followed, I tried to hang out with Biggy and found him strange. He was always chewing *miraa* and he loved the company of Ngara prostitutes and wimps. I knew he was a heavy bhang smoker and various other pills, but there was a notorious one called Revolver because it was such a big trip. Zaïrean musicians were all taking these pills to keep themselves awake, to work these incredible hours in this all-night place. And so the prostitutes and waiters, when they'd see the musicians falling over with tiredness or with drink, they'd give you the pill. You'd take the pill, you'd be talking, you'd sober up, you could work almost endlessly—until the pill wore off, then you'd have to have another. Biggy had gone beyond comprehension. He was smoking marijuana for breakfast. Nobody could communicate with him because he was just glazed eyes all the time.

I refused to touch hard drugs. No, dread, no. Biggy, Dodoly, the prostitutes...all offered. But no. Marijuana... weed, yes I smoked. *Miraa*... yes I chewed. Prostitutes I picked occasionally, especially when Angelou and I were on bad terms or when my taste buds craved for new and different women.

Aside from the increased formal appreciation of music, I had also become much more appreciative of the work that a musician had to do to make a song work. Songs I might have (heck) totally dismissed at one point I listened to quite seriously today because I knew how difficult it was to make even a bad song sound good.

We worked hard to improve our style. We incorporated an eclectic range of influences. The combined effect felt something like a distillation of sunshine. Bandleader Dodoly seemed grateful to have two East Africans in the band, so he couldn't be accused of being totally Zairean. The band was East African, he said to the press. They called me *likembe ya Retro*. He never once complained when I was late for gigs because those days I was so broke I used to walk on foot from Mathare North where I lived. Perhaps if he had been a boss and not a buddy, he could have taken my advice and made me the bandleader as a strategic move to confuse the officials who were harassing him all the time in the wake of the Government's crackdown on foreign musicians. He wouldn't take my advice to make me a front, he trusted Kamau more and they kept bribing the officials.

In August, Kamau was arrested for habouring illegal aliens in his club and soon after Baba Gaston came for Retro Rumba Du Zaïre. He was taking them to Tanzania. That left me, the soloist who played liked a sewing machine, with the responsibility of finding a new band to perform at Tete La Dhahabu, with the caveat that my life depended on it, and that I'd have to really go out of my way to do this or form a new band because, well, I had to have a job.

Biggy and I sat together and weighed our options. He, in particular, couldn't gamble. He wanted something long-term. He was nearly thirty years old and he would have gone back to Dar if he could. He couldn't. His wife was Kenyan and he had two kids. The only means of feeding his family was his voice. Luck soon came his way. Issa Juma needed a singer, so off he went to join Super Wanyika.

9.

Personally I didn't feel I had a lighter baggage. I had the burden of focusing on the next chapter of my dreams. I could confidently say that I had accomplished my dream of playing with a Zaïrean band and it had put my perspective in place. African Heritage had put in me a sense of big band discipline and class. Retro Rumba? Well, it opened my eyes to the real raunchy world of music. I saw the cold, and nefarious heart of Nairobi's music business and it made me know the kind of guitarist I was going to be.

Life hadn't improved much; I was still walking on foot from Mathare North to the city center to get 'lifts' from Zaïrean bands at Garden Square. I soon became a guitar harlot and participated in the *nzong nzing* flings with Zaïrean bands. I became so fluent in Lingala I could tear a Zaïrean to pieces in bitter verbal exchange. I lived on the edge and lived for the next day, smoked weed, womanized and worked with River Road session musicians. I usually languished around with these guys around some well-known or dingy little-known recording studios on River Road waiting for clients to hire us for a recording. The man who schooled me most was Zack Shivachi. Zack played rhythm well and had been at it since the '70s, playing guitar on tracks for DK, Kamaru, Kakai Kilonzo and many others. The Kikuyu artists got the attention, but it was Zack and the other studio pros that were crucial in crafting the sound for their hit songs. At the time, they were usually unaccredited, paid a scale wage for their sessions. The best of the bunch that got plenty of work included Osumbax Rateng, Owacha Willy, Okech Ombasa, Berry Guya, Vinny 'Redman', Ondiek Nzoi, Steven Sakwa, Peter Owino Rachar, bassist Swalleh Yussuf, solo guitarists Anzino Osundwa, Roland Isese, drummer Juma Othech and Odongo 'Manila' Guya, and for them the pay was excellent. Redman was the busiest of the bunch. Anzino was the finest. For guys with the chops to make a living in music, it was a great alternative to going on the road or trying to make it with a band.

From the River Road sessions, I learned that studio work required very creative and versatile musicians, and if you were late, you'd better have a good excuse (like Redman's salt'n'pepper stories about lacking bus fare). Since their work was anonymous by design, you didn't read much about the life of these studio pros. But Peter Owino Rachar, who looked at me as his kid brother, was kind enough to share his story, explaining what it was like playing for the Kikuyus and making them rich. He told me how he helped turn DK's '*I Love You*' into a hit, and what happened during a typical session. These River Road guys could have made the finest band since it was a group of made up of a few drummers, singers and guitarists that were on first call for Top 10 records. Few like Anzino and Osumba built a reputation in the business as individual musicians—not as part of a group. Anzino led his Mazadijo while Osumba led his Sega Sega. Anzino was also the key soloist for Ochieng Kabaselleh who (apart from having his own Lunna Kidi Masanga band) had recently recorded a few singles with Mazadijo including 'Wuora Ogolla Adoyo,' 'Princes Lako,' and 'Kasuku.' The reputation of these River Road musicians was built primarily on their expertise and their association with the many hit records. Sometimes it seemed as though we were part of the same few bands because when recording an album you might find a drummer from this group and the next day it was the same drummer wearing the same clothes. For example, much of Kamaru's records were made in a studio band comprised of musicians from this group. The Kilimambogo band of Kakai, Kabaselleh's Lunna Kidi and most spinoff Kamba and Kikuyu albums were made by players from this group too.

The River Road tempo sucked me in and the only thing I still kept of my old life was Angelou. We used to meet and I used to tell her my problems and she used to listen. She knew I was stuck and she used to support me with money. She eventually convinced me to swallow my pride and look for Mama Iva.

I couldn't do that.

So instead, she contacted Mama Iva and asked her to contact me. Can you imagine? Well, Mama Iva did find me. And began about rearranging me, I expected it. For starters, we would begin from where we left: move back into her generous bosom and into her abode. I moved from Mathare North back to Nairobi West. We spent a whole day in bed and talked. She soon learned about my musical journey since December 1982 and where I was headed. She saw I was stuck.

Slim Ali, she said.

I knew Slim Ali. Everybody knew Slim Ali. I knew Hodi Boys. Everybody knew Hodi Boys. It wasn't what I wanted at this point. Did I have a choice? She asked. This was the best she could do for me. She stressed to me she was a lover of Kenya music and would always support Kenyan bands since they supported her New Blue Omo campaigns.

I reluctantly accepted her offer, though my mind was open.

10.

Rehearsal, breakthrough. 'Let me have some coffee and then I'll listen,' said a groggy voice like that of a mother to a child who rises early and eager on a Sunday morning. It was September '83, and the voice was that of Slim Ali, who was speaking from his bedroom to me and his band mates who were outside the door. And thank you Mama Iva. May God bless you for saving me once again. I thank you fair lady for making this connection. I didn't know much about him, but we had come to his house. We had walked through the driveway and into the detached garage in the back. We had walked in settled in the jamming space which was small: a horde. It was then, as Mama Iva and I stood waiting, that I discovered this guy Slim Ali was a speed user, which made the funky bass on his soul music even quicker.

I reflected: Nairobi had now swallowed many of these Mombasa-born artistes. I was always a great admirer of Kelly Brown's outlandish styles. As a kid awakening to music in Kisumu, I used to wonder if that huge afro he adorned was real. And what of that tight fitting trouser? I used to admire him a lot. He used to look like one of the Jackson Fives. He used to sing with the Beavers at Rocka Bye in Mombasa before coming here. Cally the Bushman, he was called then. And he was realistic like me. You don't count in music or anything unless you were in Nairobi. Unlike Saidi Travolta Mohamed, he didn't shylock his soul. He rebaptised as Kelly brown and skirted above men like Ali de Rocky, Ishmael Jingo and Feisal Brown to join the Sharks in Nairobi's Club Bonanga. The popular crooner Ali de Rocky followed; he made a name here too. These men of music all came here from Mombasa, escaped. Just like me. Mombasa, through its alienation of 'outside' music was eager to build a sound of its own. Nothing affected its slumberous peace. Not even the benga and rumba from upcountry. And the ways of the WaSwahili were forever magical. They had come up with *chakacha*, a spectacular wedding musical fanfare laced with the tantalizing effects of *taarab*. This was where even the most conservatives of VIPs and MPs began to dance and sigh and hobnob with ordinary folk. Mombasa, really, had produced musicians of soul. Deejay Abdul Haq used to argue that the heart of Mombasa's appeal was centered on its ability to give birth to its product instead of annexing it like Nairobi. He was probably right. If he was, why (then) did all these glamorous sons of Mombasa who wrote so beautiful songs for her (like the Harrisons and their Mushrooms) leave the city for Nairobi?

Mr. Ali's voice rattled me out of my reverie. 'Welcome to the Hodi Boys empire, kid.' he told me. He drawled in Kiswahili rich in the cadences of Abdalla Mwasimba. 'You have a song, *mwanangu?*'

I nodded.

The song was 'Kiswahili.'

Let me sing it:

> *Kiswahili....*
> *Mi' nasema....*

'That's it.'

'That's it?'

I nodded.

'And you think it's something for Hodi Boys?'

Again I nodded.

'Eh? And what do you want to call it?

'Kiswahili.'

Mr. Ali knotted his brows, gave me and Hodi Boys a listen and agreed to sign the song to his record label that day. It had been a long dark road to getting there, but Mr. Dino Otieno Owiro alias Otis Dundos had a deal. And thank you Mama Iva. May God bless you abundantly.

I was overwhelmed and somehow learned to play their style right there and right then. We were going to jam and we were going to record 'Kiswahili' live in their style.

I rehearsed with the Hodi Boys. We released the song as a single on a 45. It was well received. It was a hard groovy dance number. And it served the purpose I wanted: it made my name in the musical circles. It had my name on it. Yes, Dino Otis Dundos. And it was pristine. People heard it on the radio. My father heard in Kisumu and called. Wanted to know why I was doing this. This wasn't benga? I found some words to say to him. That I was a man on a vertical learning curve. I had had to start somewhere. To make a name first. Still he didn't understand. It didn't bother me one bit, though. I had so many things on my mind.

For the next two months, I teamed with Slim Ali and Hodi Boys at JKIA. Those two months schooled me. For once, I was in an open arena. I met many musicians. You see, the African Heritage was a closed society; you had to play by their rules. Retro Rumba was plain club rumba and soukous Zaïrean style that allowed me to fully engage my lead guitar prowess. But the Hodi Boys were different. Or was it their style? And look, here I had my first single, a 45.

One evening during a gig at JKIA, Mama Iva came in accompanied by a well-dressed gentleman. He asked if we could play 'Kisumu Girl'. The band looked at me, so I apologized and told him that we didn't know that song. He told me that there was a Shs. 200 tip for us if we played it. Well, the band didn't know it, so I played the main riff, which I quickly taught to the rest of the band and we played that for about five minutes, after which he handed me what I thought were two Shs. 100 bills, but they were actually eight bills: Shs. 800.

That man had been, to me (until that moment), just a name. A big name. The name you only read in the newspaper and heard on radio and saw on TV. Ochieng Kamau, the man in charge of marketing at the record company, Attamaxx KRC! Can you even imagine this? The man behind the name! Ochieng Kamau himself.

Pretty soon they wanted me to do an album. The producer Justin Bomboko himself called me to a meeting at their offices in Hurligham. Mama Iva again had made the right connection. She accompanied me to this meeting.

I experienced happiness, total happiness.

I felt it searing my heart. I remembered Kisumu and all the people who were going to listen to it: Riana, Mama, my brothers and sisters, the members of Kisumu Delta Force: Mo Thwaka, Mawazo Ya Pesa, KSK Odongo... all of them.

I said, yes, I would. And Mama Iva pouted.

I closed myself up and worked. Worked through the many songs I had written in exercise books. Just words of lyrics. I had chord progressions and melodies in my head. I played one or two for Attamaxx guys once and they told me to continue writing more. I wanted to challenge myself. I wanted to make something that was as much a representation of my personal, creative self as possible. So, I started with what was in my head and nothing else knowing that by the end of the month I would need to present six or seven complete songs. I just took it step-by-step and day by day. I had a Sanyo tape recorder, so I would hum tunes going da-da-da-da... and tili-lililii and record it on tape. Song one, I wrote. Song two, I wrote. Song three, I wrote. Song four, I wrote. Song five, I wrote. Song six, I wrote. And more. Wacky rhythms, neat leads, florid saxos, throbbing bass, extended *sebenes*, all tucked away in my elephant's memory.

The album was to be called what? There were many suggestions. And the makeshift band? Well, I had two problems. One, what to call the band. I had names like:

> Lake Victoria Squad
> Victorians
> Gulf Band
> Lake
> Victoria
> Kisumu
> Victoria Boys
> The Victorians
> Victoria ODW

VICTORIA
FOR
VICTORY

NOW I was happy. Things were working. No longer was I the new guy in town. Kisumu was tucked away like an odd blackboard jungle. There were days I missed home, but it was a no-go for now. I wasn't going to Kisumu anytime soon. Nairobi was home now, much as I felt closed off. I felt far less open to meeting new people, making new friends and actively working with professional musicians. After a year of meeting new people and going out all the time, I was sweetly and fatigued. Adjusting to big changes and challenges in my personal life surely fatigued me.

Suddenly I had a reason to live and I was flung into the thinking roller-coaster... thinking and putting things in focus for this new album. I detested distraction. Some common but ugly demons of competition, jealousy, and entitlement had started to rear their heads. Men and women who had supported me here in Nairobi suddenly wanted a parcel of my cake. And what is worse, they were demanding for it. When I got here in Nairobi, I entered the new community as an eager novice with a commitment to ideals of community and a more holistic way of participating in the music rat race. I was prepared for this. In my heart I believed that music, as an art, was not a zero sum game. With talent, patience, persistence, and diligence, opportunities always came and the success or merits of any other bands were irrelevant. Nevertheless, everyone airing their their own opinion, bickering, talking shit and publicly critiquing each did not really help anybody. It isolated and divided us. It soured us. It was poison. I'm saying this because I had made a few friends who I really valued. Yeah, men and women had greatly helped me along the way and I was ever grateful. It was much easier to keep those ideals close back then. I wasn't emotionally investing in anyone or any projects yet. I was just talented and ambitious, and I was being driven by people who valued my talent, but I knew the long term goals were pretty far away and I was achieving my short term goals and enjoying the process. I was inspired by what was happening around me (the great music being made and the rapid visibility of the Nairobi scene) and excited about becoming a part of it. In the future.

We went into rehearsals, stripped the songs down to six. I had collected some good musicians including a keyboard player from African Heritage, Loh Zom from Makali Vibrations and (guess who?) Owacha Willy, Redman, Wally Amalemba and Swalleh. Yeah, the best of River Road too.

I had written some perfect Kiswahili poetry for a song called 'Talaka.' I sang the lyrics out and I knew the person whose voice would bring a boisterous interpretation to this song: Biggy Tembo. We invited him, asked him to sit in with the band on a few tunes. 'Talaka' came roaring out of the speakers. He sang the opening line:

'Sijui mimi nitaanzia wapi... !'

We knew things were going to get weird(er) at that point. In the middle of 'Talaka' (where Biggy rambles on in a scat style) he brought a rare distinction that scared me. He sung the words like they were written for him:

Nani anaweza kufanya nicheke mpaka dunia igeuke?
Nani anaweza kucjua siku akaifanya iwe mwaka?

224

Nani anaweza vunja milima ya ndoa yaa—ngu?

It was amazing how well the 'Talaka' theme worked with Biggy's relaxed baritone.

Besides the new material, we had a high-tech remake of 'Kisumu Girl,' and another fine jazzy material of an expatriate South African composer, saxophonist and arranger, Eddy Blacky Mphalele. It took us more than two months to record and I swear it nearly killed me. The stress of it. Honestly I was never prepared for this, never knew producing album took this amount of energy. We were recording in Attamaxx KRC Studio in Hurligham and for those two months we saw nothing of Hurligham except when we went for some walks in the evenings. The record company men were very strict on us. Producer Justin Bomboko (well, I'll just call him JB as he liked to be called), had a lot of pressure from the head of marketing, Ochieng Kamau, to ensure that he got the best from us and packaged a selling album. JB brought along the production engineer, a peculiar perfectionist with a wry sense of humour called Jimmy Makossa. JB was a great talker, an enthusiastic party-goer and a back-slapping practical joker who often laced our beers with vodka, guffawing when they caught on. But JB was more than a spoofer. He was a taskmaster and a skull duggerer. He said he thought he was going to be a poet or novelist. He wanted to be a respectable pan Africanist, wear Nigerian *agbada* or Zaïrean *abacost*. Only one problem: music hit him in midriff. He rode us hard through the musical scale with a keen ear for flaws.

We'd start at seven in the morning and go right through to the small wee hours. It was a tedious process: JB the taskmaster'd fry your nerves. Jimmy Makossa was sensitive to the type of music that would fill the market demand he had envisaged. He had a good ear for sound and he knew what would sell and what wouldn't. Many lyrics had to be rewritten. Many songs were dropped and 'Kiswahili' was picked to fill space. He made the technicians and engineers work in shifts to accomplish targets and deadlines. And when we complained that he had made us work on one track for almost a week, he told us that some bands spent four months on a single track. Eddy, on the other hand, was a professional with enough experience and he had an ear for good music. His wide knowledge of instruments also helped a great deal. He was a master at balancing everything in the studio: strings, horns, drums, congas, vocals, rhythm. He, too, didn't leave the studio until morning, having delivered a wonderful sweet, tender, sincere performance.

Going through this, I learned that there more to producing a song than just mere words about a guy expressing his desire for a girl. People wanted music they could identify with. I really didn't think much of it at first, though, certainly not in the sense of: 'Really, all this great effort to make my name!' Then I realized why I was to be made a star: it wasn't just for the fact that I could write songs, I had the look and pull of a star.

I also marveled at the power good instrumentation could bring to a song. The original version of 'Kiswahili' had been plain and racy with overlapping rhythm guitar and packed drumming. It was fast with abrupt gear changes. But when we rerecorded it, and Eddy added the volume and the jazzy effects and horn arrangements, it was richer, denser slower and sweeter. It even had a soft Jazzy flavor to it. After that, I thought: 'This is spectacular.' The new version of 'Kisumu Girl' was given the same treatment. To thank Eddy, I put his composition 'African Sunset' number two on side B of the album. The first song "Kwa Nini?' discussed things girls shouldn't do and it was very important to me. At a very personal level, that is. Another song 'Tusonge Mbele' discussed the need for courage to move on from one moment of disappointment or failure. Many of the themes I dealt with were based on my personal experience. 'Adoyo Nyar Kano' was a special dedication to Angelou.

At the end of it, JB gave a nod. 'This is going to be a hit,' he told me and winked. 'You are the right image we want too. What do you want to call the album?'

226

'Kaa Square,' I said.

And *Kaa Square* it became. Following this was a much needed break. There was going to be remixing, the pressing at Polygram and sleeve design.

I went away.

From the proceeds of my debut *Kaa Square* album and a loan from Mama Iva, I did what every musician does: bought my first set of instruments. This was more of a long term plan. I knew I would have a band soon. For a while I was comfortable.

I did some radical changes in my personal life like moving to a bigger house in Donholm Estate, changing my wardrobe, cultivating an identity through my dress code. I didn't mind creating an artistic appearance (no suits required!) but yeah, with this new found fame that had brought tons of friends and fans, I was a role model, wasn't I? I didn't want to be portrayed by the media as a sloppy celebrity. JB explained to me that (really) I was in this uncertain career that involved the hurly-burly of late nights in bars with prostitutes and shady characters, thugs and broke, fake social climbers, alcoholics or just mean-gutted whores. Maybe the press perceived some musicians this way because Nairobi was teeming with all the not-so-successful musicians who tried to 'make it' but ended up failing to make anything like 'a living'.

In Nairobi I had seen enough musicians who were 'professional' and loved their jobs; then there were musicians who were bums and gave us musicians a bad name as undependable dregs of society. We were associated with drugs, womanizing, alcohol abuse, and we were irresponsible and unreliable cons. Yeah, musicians were notorious for making young nubile school girls pregnant and dumping them. They slept with married women and broke homes and got away with it. Yet they had no homes themselves. Me? I had dignity, man. No coincidence that now I also had an identity as a guitarist. I had gotten far with my guitar, life was now intense.

Life was moving fast. I had a brain. I had a name to protect.

I had to have an image, not just a dress code and a hairstyle but a personality. I had seen fine examples of brilliant musicians like Baba Gaston, Owino Misiani, Samba, Longwa Didos, Sammy Kasule and Slim Ali who were successful artists, businessmen and family men.

Income came in from Attamaxx KRC. JB visited me every now and then to see my next plans. I had more songs but we couldn't record them as Victoria ODW, not just yet.

The Hodi Boys single 'Kiswahili' and the album 'Kaa Square' were still very much in the market and selling well.

I had a lot on my plate, music-wise.

2.

My beginnings as a solo guitarist and songwriter had been flagged off. I now developed a unique way of writing news songs. My thoughts were the seeds of creation. I picked up a guitar, fingered a chord, and strummed, and music came out. What could be more rewarding? I played, music happened. Instantly. And if I tried something tricky, I could hear on the spot whether it worked or not. If I was trying to figure out a song, I'd try all manner of different things, until suddenly I hit the strings a few times and the song I was trying to learn started coming out. I sold my material to most of the recording bands but saved most of my finest to Black Devils Makali, a really inspiring new teenage band.

After a close liaison with Frank Ilunga Mabuluki, the leader of Devils, I wrote songs of deep and blunt agony, culled from the threshold of my existence and experience. The multi-layered soukous, Jazz and reggae sound the Devils featured inspired me to create my own style which was plain and confined as a confessional. It was a style I loved. A style not fast but loose-edged, not grinding but throbbing steadily. I had dreams popularizing it and making it a Kenyan sound.

I had swell moments around town with Black Devils' men. 'Grunts & guitars' man Sammy Kasule now sang sexed up Afro-funk for the modern age. I always remembered him fondly during the time he used to be backed by Radi and Somajeko. It appeared Sammy had come of age and by this time he was teaming up with Black Devils, BB Mofranck, Frantal Tabu, Zembi Okeno, Siama, Onyango Shaban and others. To me he was always a kind of serious Afro-funk guy. I have no doubt Sammy was one of Nairobi's most talented, and rather unfortunately, overlooked stars. *Kasule*, his new solo LP, should have gone a long way to help give the man the attention he deserved. In the Black Devils' fraternity I soon made good friends with 'Goldfinger' Tégé Zoba, the all-round rhythm guitarist who was to become my very close friend. Tégé Zoba wasn't the best-looking guy, or the most charming. He loved to wear wax print or tie'n'dye shirts with large abstract repeats on them and they were hated by everyone. The designs were so outrageously unique I could have sworn he used to make them himself. What he did possess was persistence. 'Don't worry guys, everything's fine!' was his catch phrase. Whenever things were going wrong, he never lost his nerve, he stayed optimistic and persistently worked at it. If he had to go to every good-looking girl in the bar, he would probably leave with one, including, once, the winner of the Miss Ugliest Girl In Nairobi contest. He was an all-rounder here in Nairobi. He knew which band was doing what and playing where. He knew all the clubs. He knew the inside story of nearly all musicians. If there was anybody who could write a book on the inside story of Nairobi's pop scene in the '80s, it was Tégé.

In November when the Black Devils were invited to Uganda for a series of charity concerts, Tégé remained and moved on to play for a while with Ali Magobeni in City Blues. I had a little Afro song I had written one lunch hour at a café in Donholm as I waited for Angelou. It was called 'Hapana.' Yeah. Just that. It was to be a hit and it was to be a signature tune and it was to be overplayed on radio and in disco halls and it would refuse to go away from peoples lips. It would depress me because each time my name would be mentioned, that song would come to mind. It would depress me because I was not an Afro artiste. Okay, this is how it went: when I showed Tégé the words on the piece of paper and lipped out the chords and strummed my guitar, he immediately wanted to rehearse it. So we went my apartment. My apartment was a studio. In my living room was a complete band gear with the drum set in the middle. Guitars, mics and all. What I lacked were speakers and amps. We rehearsed the song the whole day. Tégé provided the drifting wafts of a lone electric guitar on a Casio keyboard and I ushered the jerky twangs of acoustic guitar. We sang through the thing soulfully like nerds whose lives depended on music.

One afternoon we invited Ali Magobeni and Mama Iva for a hearing. We were having drinks with Tégé and Angelou on the porch when the two men arrived. I invited them in and asked Tégé to play the song for them as I was discussing some money issues with Angelou. Her mother had recently lost her job at the bank and was depending on her, so she needed a loan. The two gentlemen were inside for about thirty minutes and when they came out they all wore grins. The grin on Magobeni's face was even broader. We got busy the following week. Initially I wanted to do a single and the single came out. Went on air and became an instant hit, went on to top the charts. People pushed me, so I took courage, called Attamaxx and suggested an album on the strength of the single.

'You have some songs to fill the dish?' JB asked. 'You know Attamaxx is a house of pros. We don't believe in recording on a whim, you know. We control our stuff. Send me the cassette and let's see. Then don't call me, I'll call you.' And hung up on me.

Before sending umpteen unopened packages to be followed with umpteen-times-ten futile phone calls, it made sense to talk to some Nairobi-based working musicians. I might gain a little insight, or better, a friendly break. Most of the musicians I talked to recorded with Attamaxx so it was easy enough to pester them out of their phone numbers, with which to pester them some more.

I applied this strategy to the best of my inchoate abilities and struck gold in the dirt with the entry of the gregarious Baba Gaston. A talented musician-writer, Gaston was long on experience, his band creating and employing some of Nairobi's best musicians. He had been told about me and he quickly encouraged me to use the new album to launch my own band. That was natural for him to say: he was a bandmaker.

I was specific about the life of the album; what suggestions was he offering regarding promoting it in the competitive market?

On the phone, Gaston was gracious, explaining in animated detail what club owners would expect from an album by a brand new band and how to leverage that first no-paying off-night gig into a second no-paying off-night gig at a different place.

'It's easy-after the first one,' he said, ' you call the second one and tell them you played the first one and it was boffo and you keep bugging them and sooner or later you're in the second one. Just don't expect a lot of money until you can fill the place.'

I pressed Gaston as to what might be a good a successful first 'real' album. He kept on pushing for the band and I kept talking about the album. We were not getting anywhere. I could practically hear him thinking: 'Let's see, Garden Square is crummy enough to take in a new band at the moment, Starlight is not too crummy but putting a band next to Samba is real peril, and like meddling with a bomb. So if they bomb you, it won't besmirch my good name... Hmm, let's see...'

He paused and recommended that I consider bringing in some big names in the mix. 'Consider going back to Kisumu and grab that space. You can play some spiced-up benga and create a name for it. But Nairobi... ah ah.'

I scheduled lyric writing sessions with others and we sat and wrote lyrics together while listening to demos. At first I had a session in my apartment with Magobeni, Tégé and BB to come up with guitar parts to the songs (a few of the 'sounds' we recorded that day actually made it into one of the final tracks). In a few days, we recorded vocal tracks in Melodica and sent the sessions to JB in Attamaxx to mix them. But Attamaxx wouldn't put their money on the thing, so I went to Andrew Crawford where I started out recording all 6 songs in a 4-hour session in December with a makeshift band that brought in the likes of BB, Ayub, Zembi, Onyango Shaban and some well-known session musicians. Shivachi on rhythm, Sammy on bass, Anzino on mi-solo, Lobe on tenor sax. In a month, we were in studio for nerve-wracking rehearsals. It was hectic. Many musicians didn't turn up; many didn't trust me and demanded that I pay them upfront. I made many last minute replacement calls. We had a bedlam of talent and experience and proceeded to develop those recordings as much as possible by mixing them and Sammy recording overdubs. Eddy Blacky was still in town, so I had additional sessions with him to come up with keyboard parts for all the songs.

My only composition was the cover song 'Hapana.' The other songs were by different people and were credited to them. Throughout this entire process, my fellow bandmates and producer for the final production constantly gave me feedback and helped to shape the songs. It was a blast. My team of experts played the final mixes in the studio, made a few adjustments after-wards, and then it was done. The album was pressed in Polygram Studios in Industrial Area and released on Polyder label. Zembi brought in a family friend to create the artwork.

When the album got into the market, Chege Wa Gachamba gave me a great write-up. He posed a question.

Question: 'Are you now a reggae/Afro artiste?'

The answer: 'No.'

3.

Things were looking good. I had money in the bank and in my wallet, dreams in my head and my whole life in front of me. Then a disaster struck. Disaster that, once again, changed the entire course of my life. I had a violent quarrel with Angelou. She had been my number one for many months and we had some joint investments. I had even suggested marriage and she was game for the idea. She had softened up as she grew older and had matured in many ways. First she stopped smoking, reduced her drinking and started behaving like a wife around me.

Then we quarreled. The cause of the quarrel: woman. I had been secretly dating an irresistibly charming girl called Achieng. Now, just in case you didn't know, Achiengs are dangerous women. It was just sex, but Angelou found us in bed one afternoon and hell broke loose. We yelled at each other and she called me all sorts of names—and, boy, she knew them. Then she did the unthinkable, she locked the door from outside, locked me and Achieng inside and went to the petrol station. In the meantime I did the wise thing that probably saved my life: I dialed 999. Angelou returned and doused the house and set it on fire. We were rescued with minor burns but the entire house was burnt to cinders. All my materials possessions, all my dreams... everything turned to ashes.

I did not sulk for long.

I took a leaf from Issa Juma's new record that said 'Matatizo Nimeyazoea.' I simply said, 'Haizuru, that's life.' Angelou was saved trying to torch herself, she suffered minor burns too.

I had more shocks: Angelou was pregnant. I met her mother for the first time. She came to see me, to talk to me. Introduced herself as Sabina Akoth Smith from Kano Kobura. I wondered briefly after Smith; her British husband had divorced her. She clarified that, said it was only a separation and she liked the name because she still loved her husband. She and I had similar socio-cultural backgrounds. She had grown up in Kisumu too, spoke my kind of DhoLuo. We connected very well, she was really warm and charming and we discussed her daughter's conduct. She tried to convince me about my love for her daughter. 'I know you love Adoyo,' she kept saying. 'I have talked to her and she is willing to change if you will forgive her and take her back.' She loved the song I had composed and recorded for her daughter, 'Adoyo Nyar Kano. 'The words said:

> Kano ma Kobura
> Adoyo unyuolo nyar berna
> Adoyo ma aluongo mana ni Angelou
> Rapudo ber ka min mare
> Lando omako chunya

In the months that followed after new year, music grew and progressed. Competition became fierce. Musicians worked too hard, were overworked. Studios were busy, VOK National Service was changing bands every day. The African Heritage was now firmly in the hands of Job Seda who had now changed his name to Ayub Ogada. Nairobi was now a city of new music. The likes of The Mighty Cavaliers, Ishmael Jingo, Hodi Boys, Kelly Brown, Steele Beauttah, De Rocky, Magobeni, Saidi Travolta and Fadhili were less heard of. Many had either flown abroad, were in semi-retirement or just not active.

Sammy Kasule and B.B. Mo-Franck had teamed up and joined Frantal Tabu's new super group called Vundumuna. 'Ildephonse Supersax' Tabu Ngongo been invited, thus weakening Mangelepa who relied on Ngongo's super solo sax. We all knew that with the massive talent of the instrumentalist Mo-Franck (a musical schoolmate of Ray Lema), Vundumuna was set to be the ultimate crossover band Nairobi had ever known. Already in this age of Breakdance, they were grabbing the attention of the young elite. I used to go to Carnivore for their Wednesday and Saturday night gigs and the place was jammed beyond capacity. You couldn't get a place to stand, leave alone dance. Apart from the institutional status at the Carnivore, they were also recording a lot and Ochieng Kabaselleh had recorded a fine single with them called 'Milicento.'

The power of Orchestra Vundumuna suddenly caused

Virunga to crackle. Samba was having difficulties paying his musicians, the newspapers wrote. The band was bloated with too many stars. We watched helplessly as Virunga fragmented then exploded and a new band called Ibeba System was formed out of the crumbs. And it was led by (guess who?) Virunga's solo guitarist Sammy Mansita Nzola. The likes of Kasongo Wa Kanema, Siama, Coco Zigo, Pele Ondindia and Onyango Shaban were the first to jump into the newly created Ibeba group while 'Manytcho' Nsilu Wa Ba Nsilu made the significant move to Vundumuna. Fataki Lokassa tumbled along with Samba together with Virunga's manager Tabu Osusa.

The combined force of Vundumuna and Ibeba soon smoked Virunga into near obscurity. Ibeba took over from Virunga at Starlight and they were now the hottest soukous band in town. So hot were Ibeba with a neat mix of their own *soukous* and covers that even Moreno and Lovy Longomba were moonlighting with them. Sammy Kasule, on the other hand, was a busy man. He had gone to England and recorded his version of 'Shauri Yako' which was groovy and quite awakening with nice drum arrangement and a remarkable lead guitar. While it did not beat the original Ntimbo version, one felt it was a great effort at creating a crossover hit. I used to play Sammy's version and I felt it religiously well ploughed. He now mainly worked with Vundumuna, and as part of another group, Africa Jambo Jambo. There were rumours that he wanted to leave Africa because he felt his music was more appreciated in Europe.

Moreno had remained with Moja One but was more often heard performing with Sheila Tett and Margaret Safari in Kenya Blue Stars. Tsk! Tsk! Tsk! Coco Zigo had converted to Islam and changed his last name to Hussein. Samba had done the same and added Omar to his name. There were a great many new groups with amazing talents and stamina, the most prominent ones being Earthquake, Star 7, Gravity, Makali Vibrations, Makonde, Mandingo, Lunna Kiddi, Maroon Commandos and many others that featured Kenya's ideal sound: benga. From Mombasa were the Roots, Them Mushrooms and Safari Sound. In western Kenya were Shirati Jazz, Victoria Kings A, Victoria Kings B and Victoria Kings C, and Jolly Boys.

One day I was sitting at a café somewhere in Tom Mboya Street having some idle tete'-a-tete' with Tégé Zoba. He was wearing one of his usual crazy wax print shirts, this one had large abstracts repeats of an irate man chasing a fat woman. He had two Scotch and waters... I had two Cokes with a twist. He had eaten Indian food earlier and had a faint odour of garlic on his breath. The combination of garlic and Scotch aromas, had always repulsed me. So I looked away and guess who I saw: Biggy Tembo. Then I remembered I had called him to this meeting.

This was in the early months of '84. My brother Ouru had recently joined the '82 Airforce and was at Eastleigh Airbase. It was moments like this when you stopped and thought long and hard about the direction your musical career was taking and I had many things to be happy for. Things were working good. One, Angelou and I had gotten back together. The other, I was finally putting together a band. My Urban Benga band.

Biggy Tembo came, sat down and ordered food. He was part of this: he was one of the few good men I had in my circles. Being older, more experienced, and more talented than we were, I needed him. Remember he was a large man, 6ft 4in about 130 kgs, and abrasive as a *matatu* tout. He was the epitome of a rumba singer: he loved to take matters in his own hands! With that baritone. We had picked him up a few months after he quit Super Wanyika and was hanging around with the River Road music harlots lending his voice in good-for-nothing recordings for cheap money. You know them, don't you? Redman, Osumbax, Anzino, Shivachi and the whole gang the length of River Road.

Fast forward about a month, and we had a band in place. I had used all my saving to purchase guitars, drum set and speakers. Mama Iva helped me acquire the rest of the equipment on condition that I will pay her back as soon as we made our first album. Meaning she had a stake in the band. That was okay by me for all the good reasons. Pendo, a fat woman with a voice of gold was our regular singer. Tégé Zoba who now liked to be called 'Goldfinger' played rhythm guitar. Swalleh was picking up on bass. I played solo guitar.

So we were set. We still didn't have a drummer. I wanted KSK Odongo. I also wanted Mo on bass. I traveled to Kisumu and arrived at Olindas Bar in Kondele where I found Delta Force performing with pathetic instruments. 'Gentlemen's Gentleman' KSK Odongo appeared to be the only sober man in the group. Even the silver-voiced boy Mawazo was half drunk and emaciated, and was wearing jeans with bags on its knees for non-stop wear and zero wash. Sam Olindas immediately took me to one side: he knew I had come to pick the best men from Delta Force and he accused me of wanting to wreck the band.

In answer, I quoted Kiambukuta's famous statement: *'Mutu na mutu na ndenge na ye. (Everyone for himself)'*

I rounded up KSK and put in my bargain. 'Look. Gentlemen's Gentleman, I know you have ambitions and you have eyes. But look, the days of KDF are over. I have always known you wanted to push Spark from the leadership seat and do things your way. That's why you set him up and got him locked up at Kodiaga. I wanted to do that too in '82.

See, you don't have the means to do that as long as Spark is alive. So in the meantime as you weigh your options in life, you can come and play for me in my new band. Just for a while.'

In less than a week, 'Gentlemen's Gentleman' KSK Odongo turned up in Nairobi and brought with him Mawazo Ya Pesa and Mo Thwaka. The three Kisumuans were visiting Nairobi for the first time. I appointed KSK to be our bandleader and vice president of the orchestra. I made some hard convincing to Tégé Zoba and Biggy Tembo and reasoned that I only wanted KSK to be the visual leader of the group, due to his cool appearance and his talent as a good speaker with his brilliant command of the English language and his classy manners. KSK was a man with personality, characterized by extravagant and fine clothing.

The band was called Victoria ODW. We went into rehearsals and mastered many popular covers.

Mama Iva stepped in to make use of her position as Friend of the Orchestra and after two weeks, she suggested we needed to replace Pendo, our female singer, (unfortunately one of our band mates created the cardinal sin of bands and started sleeping with her), so we sent word around for a new girl. The first girl that showed up sang a few songs and we told her we would let her know after we heard the tape recording later. Well, Mo Thwaka had to walk her out as we were behind locked fences so when she left KSK Odongo was behind the drums and happened to say, 'man did you hear that? She was so flat; I can sing those songs better than her!' We did not hire her, so Pendo continued to sing for us. But after a while her bedside manners disgusted me. She was a really cheap flirt with hot pants. Her grisly manner was a yellow caution light to everyone she met. I had to cut her off my team. I contacted Zembi and she brought in a young lady we both knew well, a lady with more virtues. She was a painter called Ayo Achieng Massikkinni. She was outstanding in every way; voice, attitude, looks—and she really knew how to hold a room. I had known her for a few months when she participated in my last recording as a backing vocalist. After that I met her once or twice and found out she was a true artist. In fact, she was a melodic force of nature whose pleasingly quirky persona was so persuasive that she actually made you want to stick more with her. Her fashion sense was admirable: shoulder pads and leotards that made her look hot. Her classic Banyala beauty made her the girl you could take home to your parents. But her wild streak made her the perfect companion for a night on Club Boomerang. She joined us and became the seventh member of the new band. A little sophisticated, I only worried about how she would entertain the rowdy Kisumu suburban crowd.

On her insistence, I had gone to her place to see her paintings. Ayo was very bright, very fleshy, had a nice body. When she spoke and was excited (which was often) she babbled in multiple languages all at the same time in the same sentence. Soon enough we were becoming best mates. And we looked into each other's eyes, we dissolved into each other. But that's what we did, round about that time, that's what we did a lot. And it was amazing. You're looking into each other's eyes and you would want to look away, but you wouldn't, and you could see yourself in the other person. It was a very freaky experience and I was totally blown away.

Another time at her place and I caught the strong scent of marijuana wafting along the air, she smiled. I wasn't a toker myself but knew what the implications of those who did—er, that it usually meant musicians smoking the hemp were usually zoinked out of their minds and thusly were easy to mess with.

Happy Smoke, she called it.

There was something disturbing about it. I asked her, 'How do you come back from it? How do you then lead a normal life after that?' And the answer was, 'You don't.' After that I'd got to get trepanned or I'd try to pry her out from inside my skull. I had to make a decision which way this stupid thing with feeling was going to go.

Suffice it to say from then on Ayo became a part of my shenanigans. Her marijuana smoking made my hair whirl at first. She was a heavy smoker and couldn't do anything without it... singing, making love, being in the mood. Name it.

Mama Iva didn't like Ayo.

She didn't scare her though; she only made her know she was aware. She didn't regarded Ayo as an invasion or a pest, and she didn't cause trouble, she smiled to hugged Ayo for helping her.

4.

In naming my band Victoria ODW, I was being different. I didn't like the way Africans named their bands orchestra such-and-such or put the word Jazz band at the end of their bands names. I admired the way Western groups were. Boney M, Kool and the Gang, the Beatles etc.

My first responsibility was to find work for the band. But I was facing dead ends. I wanted to get a good nightclub contract for my inexperienced band. The clubs I had my eyes on were Hallians, Equator, Arcadia on Koinange Street, Pasha Club on Kimathi Street and Club Camey. They were all taken. I had some ideas for records but the big recording labels CBS, Polgram and AIT were battling to stay afloat. JB said, 'Wait, I'll contact you.' I soon hooked up with a 'bookie' who was going to help us get gigs. He worked as radio announcer with VOK National Service and had the loudest mouth in the Nairobi music scene. He took us in and gave us all the free publicity we needed on the radio. He connected us with a bar in Langata. He informed Mama Iva, who told me, 'it's a small bar.' I met him a couple of times and he said, 'Just bring a small drum kit, practice amps only and your guitars.' We packed up and got ready.

Arriving at the venue, we found that there had been no advance publicity of our appearance. The only thing we had seen was a small sign at the entrance which said 'Kenyan Youth Band in the lounge at 7:00 PM'.

When we started our first number, it was for the bartender; there were no customers. After a short conference, we figured we had better do a warm-up first, to try and draw in an audience. We really didn't have a warm-up routine to fall back on, but we didn't want to start our choreographed performance without an audience.

Ayo took the bull by the horns and started a high tempo Tanzanian pop number. I think it was Black Warriors' 'Nawashukuru Wazai Wangu.' As she got further into the number, Mo Thwaka added the bass. Then KSKS rolled the drums and soon I was chording along. Other musician dropped in. Mawazo accompanied on the shakers and Tégé came in right at the last as Swalleh cracked a double rim shot on his big floor toms. The intro to our first number had been revised, improvised and distorted out of recognition. It was all a suitable fanfare for the entry of the star, Ayo, in an outfit that looked sprayed on.

An audience began to drift in, a middle aged man and his girl. By the end of the second Tanzanian pop number, we had the house quarter way full. Another two songs and it was bursting on the seams. The set was almost one hour long, and we pumped the audience and got them on their feet in a genuine roar of excitement; not in approval of our work, but as part of it. They asked us to play either 'Maze' or 'Odongo.'

We played in this bar for a month then, following my plan, I decided it was time to go to Kisumu. This was something I had up my sleeve: I was going to make Kisumu the base for the band. I had discussed this with Tégé and he had given the idea a nod.

5.

This had been an incredible journey. I could now say I'd gone a notch higher as a solo guitarist; I was now better equipped at making music. I had gained more experience working with musicians, vocalists, engineers, and mixers to collectively move towards a similar goal. This year 1984 was important for many reasons. It was the year I became the most street smart (or perhaps the least stoned)

I had grown up, and cast away innocence. Still I didn't know who I was, I was still afraid of life. The combination of mindfulness and almost willful mediocrity made me ease up on myself and just be for a little while, clearing my head and soothing the tensions that built up over the course of my two-year sojourn here in Nairobi. Yeah, I was trying to be a man. An accomplished man.

The accolades and press exposure I got were not enough, I still saw myself in many memorable moments as a budding musician. I only knew I was a good guitarist. I'd met many crappy guitarists over the course of my life in Nairobi, and a few great ones. I counted myself lucky. Being a guitarist myself created a connection between us, given us something to talk about. Guitarists were always giving each other little gifts—showing each other how to play a tricky part of a song, teaching each other new chords or new ways to make old chords, sharing licks and riffs with each other.

And I knew there was a good reason for my existence: I puddled along under vast breeding and strictures and consciousness enough to squash a giant into a thimble, but every once in a while I got to feeling stifled and claustrophobic. We musicians always make the world a better place. My gift, in that note, to you is to make you happy, thus showing you that you can do to be happy. We create perfect harmony in melody because we say true things. We make people smile and dance. We provoke, entertain and teach. That's why we get famous. Just listening to music is often enough to help ease the stress of our day-to-day lives; making music is a thousand times more effective.

As 'schooling' months in Nairobi came to an end, it was more than appropriate that I made a final piece of investment that encompassed the last four years of my life. Now I was not only a solo-lead player, but a songwriter and a band owner.

And somewhere along there, the intense vulnerability of how I looked without knowing exactly how I wanted to look caused my thinking to stop. There was no moment of clarity, no wash of sage wisdom. Instead, there was space. Space created by my own conscious efforts; space carved out by what I was not doing this month... this year. It was only when I realized I'd stopped feeling desperate for December 31st 1984 to arrive—the last day of my days in Nairobi—that I saw I'd let go of the anxiety that wanted to plague me the first week of my return to Kisumu.

Folks, don't be fooled by the romantic '80s Nairobi pop nostalgia. For two years I was in the thick of it. I saw most of it, lived through it, and made up a fantastic amount on my own. Let me tell you, there was nothing romantic; much of the time it was awful. Nairobi pop music had the coldest, coldest heart. Most musicians in general were overrated sellouts and untalented posers. Producers like JB were thieves and leeches... clever pirates. Why do you think he jumped to producing my music in audio cassettes (which were easy to reproduce) instead of vinyl which I preferred?

But I kept fond memories of playing with great bands like African Heritage, Hodi Boys and Black Devils Makali. Lots of psychedelic experiences with glamorous women and hard drinking rascals were sideshows in this music school. All in a good cause, of course.

LAKE
VICTORIA
BREEZE

THE bar was packed to capacity and the crowd was chanting 'Vic—Toria! Vic—Toria! Vic—Toria!' That only meant one thing: I was needed up on stage. We were *finally* in Kisumu and it was about time! A succession of large shows had honed the band's act to near perfection. I'd figured out what delighted the crowds and blatantly played to the lowest common denominator.

From the underground fringe of the music scene, Victoria had crashed the mainstream with a vengeance. For the crowds that turned out for the Kisumu concerts weren't just the trendies and students, but the office workers, the students and the elite— the people KSK had always insisted we needed to reach. We were at our regular venue, Kisumu Shore Resort club on the shores of Lake Victoria where we normally merged with the club's resident band, KS Jazz, to create big band sound with saxophones and trumpets and congas and traditional cow skin drums. Saturday nights, our shows at KS Resort were resounding and riotous, climaxing in a crescendo that left the entire clubhouse drained of energy. Our shows normally went until almost midnight. Mostly on weekends when played to a packed house, the bar did a phenomenal business, so we made one person glad: Uncle Ratego Kwer.

See, Kisumu Shore Resort was on the grounds of his vast lakeside residential home, covering over twenty acres. Uncle owned every stone, every tree, every spoon including all the sand on beach. One was pleasantly surprised by the size of the place. It used to be Kisumu Vacation Ranch before Uncle bought it from the previous Indian owners some years back. My uncle's dream was to create the ultimate relaxation paradise in form of hotel, lodging resort club of the future. In this fantastic setting on these shores, just on the outskirts of Kisumu town, he had built a relaxing holiday resort for the family, for tourists and for fun lovers.

Uncle always said it was a great gamble, I didn't think so. Lake Victoria; our beautiful, old, lake community resource could turn any investment into a profitable venture. When we were young Uncle used to be a senior officer in General Idi Amin's army in Uganda. A brigadier. He used to visit us in Pandpieri and he enjoyed going to Dunga's Lake Victoria the best of all. I think he had it in his head that he will make enough money and invest in a lakefront resort for his retirement. When Amin was defeated, Uncle crossed into Kenya and bought the property. Then he went underground for some numbing years. He later resurfaced and built this resort. And it became a haven for all types of water-related fun, canoeing, swimming, speed boat skiing or taking in evenings of sunsets.

On a closer look, the KS Resort was archaic in look and feel. Some people found it to be rather dark and costly. Others found it enchanting and dreamlike with its 1950s colonial-style architecture. The scenery and grounds were impeccable with long winding roads and beautifully maintained landscaping. The clubhouse where we performed was located on a much larger property just down the hill from the lodge. It was separated from the main lodge house by about 200 metres so that the guests will not be disturbed by the live band noise. Negatively/daunting to fathom, our fans had to drive or walk to get to the club and it was an inconvenient walk. The clubhouse offered spacious dining and dancing areas as well as a casual dining terrace overlooking what might have been mistaken for a golf course. The dancing floor space was extended onto the soft green grass and right onto the vast sandy shores of Lake Victoria. This view was breathtaking, especially during sunset. Quaint liquor bars and drinking tables were set up around the dancing grounds. The club grounds were amazing; during our shows, we had seen some couples necking on the plush grass grounds.

My uncle wanted the best in live entertainment for the club. As soon as the sound of Victoria ODW appeared to mature up, before I finished defining the style I called Urban Benga, he snapped us up like a lizard. We supplied benga and rumba varieties to please all kinds of music lovers. Weekends here were filled with concerts, parties, weddings, couplings and meetings.

I knew the reason Uncle had invited me to play at his club was a means to fulfill part of his unfulfilled dreams. You see, Uncle had been a musician too, himself. A musician of sorts, he was better known as an artist and music was just one of his outlets. Only he never fulfilled his dream because he had a family. But like all jacks of all trades, he was never perfect. He never excelled in any field. And he was never famous. He had played saxophone with groups such as Black Devils in Uganda and that was about what it was in terms of his experience. He was well aware, of course, of the significance of music. According to him, none of us would pretend to understand it, much less attempt to perform it as it should be performed—as he said he performed it, years ago. Of course Uncle knew that no one else in Kisumu had ever been able to give the music its proper range of expression and feeling, so infinitely complex and at the same time so hauntingly simple and melodic like I was trying to do, not even his incompetent five-piece band, KS Jazz, which he was trying to turn into a jazz quartet without much success.

For two months this had been our base.

Two months ago on a bright sunny morning when I landed with my band from Nairobi, my uncle personally came to receive us at the Railway Station. His '70s fashion sense really was timeless. Even with his big bushy beard, Uncle still looked like the same awkward and highly not unlike Isaac Hayes or some other chap from the James Brown era. Years and ageing had added bulk to his physique and he looked tough and sporting a canvas khaki hunting hat, large Yves Chantal shades, sideburns, moustaches and goatee beard. He looked more like the Godfather. The only thing that he had discarded was his bushy afro. He had driven me to the clubhouse to have a look around. It had seemed a large modest club for me and his wife and Tabitha looked enthusiastically on as I complained about the sign out front. I saw Victoria ODW's name was only just a little smaller than Kisumu Resort Clubhouse.

'Hmm,' Uncle Ratego thought, scratching his jaw, 'what do you think?'

I had shrugged, thinking of the many opportunities I had left in Nairobi. As if reading my mind, Uncle spoke. 'You don't want to play that game, Owiro Odundo, *okewa*' he said as he exposed a gleaming row of dental camouflage. 'Remember, you're practically unknown so you need to establish your own territory. Here in Kisumu.'

He was right. My band needed to play and gain more experience and playing at KS Resort was made a world of difference.

So it had been two busy months.

2.

This evening was another much-awaited Friday Night show. It was about time but it did not make a lot of sense waiting while the audience filed in. Victoria ODW dressed and made up backstage then went through the pre-gig huddle. Ayo had a personal hug and kiss for each one of the band and urged them to 'just have some fun'. Then KSK and Mo Thwaka appeared onstage and started to plug up, while the youthful and agile KS percussionist, Kayembe Flavien, was whistling aloud and working at the control the sound board—a massive Selecon set up Uncle had recently imported—and lighting was taken care of by the club's regular crew. The KS Jazz saxophonist Tom-Tom and trumpetist Kasule Mopero, elderly and ceremonious old men smoked and looked nonchalant while Tégé Zoba and Mawazo Ya Pesa drank sodas and chit-chatted with some girls.

The club's crew was friendly and co-operative and Mo Thwaka had few problems working with them. If there was any tension between the bands it evidently didn't come from the club boys or KS Jazz band. We had no stage manager now but KSK knew how to set up after his years of experience with Kisumu Delta Force and Mo was always hanging around him picking up skills.

We had only twenty minutes for a sound check, but, as the opening act, Biggy Tembo had to accept such shenanigans. He understood the politics and came prepared. He had all the levels set in double quick time—the advantage of being ingenious.

Five minutes to go. I slipped into the dressing room at the back. The only people I ever allowed here were KSK and Ayo. Others like Mawazo, Mo and Mary-Goretti just made a habit of bursting in. It was small, clean, spaciously arranged and brightly lit, and as dressing rooms go, it wasn't bad. I read books here, picked my nose and practiced on my guitar.

' What are you playing tonight, Didi?' Mary-Goretti asked

I grimaced tiredly. '*Muziki*, Mary-Go.'

'*Wewe.*'

'*Nini?*' I observed with humour; '*En ang'o?*' I laughed.

I doused my hi-tope fade hair with gel and picked up a comb. Mary-Goretti came to stand beside me. I didn't have to introduce her, you could tell it from the way she was behaving around me. That told it all, yeah? I was her dream and I hated it. We both faced the mirror. She eyed me as I carefully ran the comb through my hair. I watched her too. She was my heart's prize. She was kind, funny, brilliant, beautiful, and as intensely in love with me. She was also a gorgeous, tall (really tall) woman with a perfect body (to my eyes) and a model's face, and about seven years my junior. The one month we had been dating was the happiest of my life. She stood now in a tight blue tee that said 'Sweetest Girl

In 1985' in pink sparkling letters, and a pair of white shorts that ended somewhere above mid-thigh. Light amounts of make-up perfectly accented her tan, magazine-cover face.

I said, 'Get me my shirt.' She fetched my frilled navy blue shirt. She continued to watch me as I dressed.

'What are you singing *for me* tonight, honey?'

'Uh, something good, baby.'

'Start with 'Dada We!''

'Get me my mocs.'

She obeyed, fetched my shoes. I sat down to put on shoes. 'Didi, start with 'Dada We!'

'Mary-Go, tonight is Biggy Tembo's show.'

'What kind of a man are you, Didi?'

'Several kinds.'

'Didi, you're the band leader.'

'No, I'm not. KSK is. Look, Mary-Go, I'll sing something romantic for you, okay? I promise.'

There was a tap on the door and in bounced Mawazo Ya Pesa in his velvet trimmed drape jacket and white silk pants.

'It's hot in here,' he said in his trade mark soft voice. So soft you continually begged his pardon. He noticed Mary-Goretti and comic-bowed, his blow-waved curlyk hair rolling down. Then he extended her a delicate hand, bent his knees and waist, 'So-so-sor-ry Miss Afrika,' he cooed. His grin disappeared for one dead moment. It returned, valiant and toothy above his plump velvet bow-tie. We all laughed, Mawazo the loudest. He cut his laughter short.

'Otis boss,' he said innocently, his eyes honest. 'The gig.'

'I know,' I said and handed him the program.

'Can we kick it? *Wachwade?*'

'Hold a bit. I'm looking for my belt. Seen my belt, honey?'

Tégé Zoba walked in through the door. He had the usual hangover look. 'Otis Dundos!'

'What, Goldfinger?' I turned to Mary-Goretti. 'Get me some cologne.' She handed me a tall perfume canister. I moved over to the mirrored wall and sprayed it over my hair.

Tégé coughed. 'Uncle is coming up. He is not a happy old man.'

'Then you better get the hell out of here. Get me some cigarettes, honey.'

Tégé looked smug. He turned to Mawazo, 'Let's go.' They ran out of the room. Mary-Goretti handed me a pack of Embassy. I lit one and regarded my image in the mirror as I smoked. Drums sticks hit three times followed with a drum/cymbal barrage and then the whole band came in and hit a break. A blast of jazzy instrumental guitar and sax music slowly came and created the initial pre-show warm-up routine.

I turned to Mary-Goretti. 'Time to go, Mary-Go.'

She came, held my arm and we made our way out of the room. The salon of the KS Resort Clubhouse was designed in confusedly nautical style with lots of seating and dancing spaces. The entire length of the wall was a mural depicting the culture of the Luo people. On a tiny central space several people stood to watch Victoria ODW prepare. Elderly men and women were seated on the tables nursing drinks. Most people on the dancing floor near the band were youth, many of them the drongos and dumbass kids who adored me. Girls looked dressy in multi-coloured outfits, chewing gum and snickering with joy. Young guys were draped in baggy trousers, T-shirts, windbreakers, mocs, bow-ties and coats with sleeves folded or pulled up.

I loved the way the dancing floor space was extended onto soft green grass and right onto the vast sandy shores of Lake Victoria. I loved this view of the lake, especially during sunset like now. The lake sparkled and the colours danced upon it.

Mary-Goretti followed me along the short corridor. A few friends and fans called, '*Koro* Otiii! I nodded, smiled and waved. We reached the stage and I gave Mary-Goretti a smack on the cheek and jumped upstage. My appearance caused a sensation and more people pressed to the stage front, a tumultuous cheer suddenly ensuring. The applause was polite and restrained.

The instrumental session went on with the Magical Duo Kasule Mopero and Tom-Tom facing each other, conducting a sax and trumpet conversation. Biggy Tembo was smoking a joint instead of conducting the orchestra. Flavien handed me my guitar and I gave a nod to Biggy Tembo.

'Dada We!' I told him. He conducted the instrumental intro to a halt. While he charmed the crowd his unfunny greetings into the mic, Mawazo appeared from the back and took the mic at the extreme left. I looked around. Mo Thwaka and Tégé Zoba were strapping their guitars across their chests. Behind sat 'Gentlemen's Gentleman' KSK forever unchanged, as always looking sleek and dapper, and wearing a toothy gentleman's smile. Flavien ducked in behind his kit of two hefty Congas tumba drums and three thin talking drums. Good billing was deservedly given to him when set his drums into what he called African talking.

Like a soft explosion, KSK did his multiple hits on the snare drums, repeated with a double on the tenor drums and did a smash on the cymbals. He hit a break then did a gentle cascading roll. We all joined in the medley of a well-rehearsed rumba-soukous with Swahili *ngoma*. Ayo took the mic. The tone of voice of *Dada We!* was inexpressibly up-lifting; quite an overbearingly memorable dance-to-me tune with such affecting words too (if you could listen), produced a very joyous effect. It created a mood, an emotion, a response. When the chorus line came everyone joined in with us. It went up a long melodic tempo and the sax players replied to each line of chorus with my guitar filling the small empty parts. Then came the humour part where Biggy Tembo carried on a conversation with Ayo. All instruments simmered down.

Then it hit a stop.

And you thought it ended there.

Then the snare drums struck a double or a triple and the instruments picked up. Then the *ngoma* climax reached and instruments dropped one by one and eventually the bass and drums remained. The closely packed up *ngoma* picked pace with incredible speed, power, and fluidity. The drums literally called for hard dance. We now achieved a maddening pop from the crowd; the *ngoma* had everyone shaking with us, chanting and clapping, some laughing; and, this... this.... was just really good pieces of music. The girls (well, the women) were energetically twisting and rolling their hips. The *Chakacha* ingredient assumed that everyone (particularity every woman) should sing as much as dance. What the young nubile girls did with that sexy hip-rolling known as *kibwebwe* was suggestive but legal, so it seemed. It was a compulsive Swahili practice to express oneself best with body language (spontaneity notwithstanding), resulting largely from a culture of a merry people. A number of white people on the dance floor were enjoying it and trying to follow the gyrations of the women and girls, not being able to comprehend and partake in yet another triumphantly private Swahili music.

> *Na utarudi......rudi na utapenda!*
> *Zako hasira furaha waacha wapi*
> *Ndugu...(Weeh!)...Dada...(Weeh!).... toto.....(Weeeh!)*
> *Cheza ngoma.*

All hip-rollers gained eminence, singularly so immensely. Dance scaled the heights. Biggy Tembo raised his arms to say, *'Kata sasa!'* His voice so rending, but its resonance quickly worked out of an impression in mind. The silence he demanded we offered, we got intimate and low-key almost in a style of syncopated slowdown. Flavien was nearly tearing his Conga *tumba* drums with KSK Odongo drumming it along with greater relaxation, speed and power. Tom-Tom underscored this performance with a constantly fretting sax. Now Tom-Tom dropped his sax and it was like a wet blanket was lifted off. The *ngoma* and the drumming was more distinct and the mood too.

My eyes caught Mary-Goretti , she was all smiles, dancing very close to the stage. With her was Sheri, Mawazo's girl. They shouted something but I couldn't hear a thing in the blare. So I just nodded and waved. The *ngoma* session went on for about ten minutes then KSK hit the snares and did a triple on the cymbals. I and the other instrumentalists joined, first to come being Mo's with a rolling bass. Then Tégé keyed in rhythm guitar taking us up a soukous tempo. The sax-answered-vocals completed the score, bringing the song to an end.

Next on the menu was my old song 'Kwa Nini?' The dance version only needed solo-lead, rhythm guitar, bass, drums and sax. The rest of the band cleared off the stage. The last to go was Mawazo Ya Pesa who joined Sheri and disappeared with her towards the lakeshore. The crowd formed a rowdy bar just near the stage and Mary-Goretti was there sitting directly before me. I smiled at her and she smiled back, her eyes eager.

'Look,' I told Mo, 'just play the groove.'

'Okay.'

'When it drives let it drive.'

'Okay.'

I turned to Tégé and patted him on the shoulder. 'Stay on the 6th.'

'I know.'

'Right.' I turned to KSK. 'Ready?'

'Ready.'

'Okay... two, three, four...'

We hit softly into it. The guitar I was playing was a Gibson which made my name in Nairobi last year. My finger style arrangements had a restless, passionate intensity born of a restless soul that I was. Each time I played this song, I wanted to make the craftsmanship and expression just phenomenal. I wanted to make this song amazing, I wanted the guitar solo to sound more beautiful. I wanted the pain and hurt from the guitar's ripple effect to be mind- blowing. As we played the extended lead guitar intro, the band's eyes were hard on me. Nothing should go wrong, they knew how I felt about this song. The drums were restrained and the instrumentation was subtle. I first played long notes and then rhythm guitar picked up cue on a lingering tempo, slowly rising like a moaning voice then the bass joined a sweet interruption. Now we continued to rise, a multiple of quivers and ripples and ripples higher and higher, registering different variations. Then the drums rolled and struck and the instrumental was bubbling, slow-building and heart-rendering. Highly aroused by the delicate magical balance, Biggy Tembo vocalised right into the instrumental mix with his most fervent syrupy baritone. He drew the words from the large larynx in his large chest as he went down on his knees. He cried with my song, I cried too. His voice kept rising, and so did the quivering notes of my guitar. He sang an emotionally-packed line and I saw the chords in his neck sticking out. I heard the gasp and I plucked a master note repeatedly and the drums hit a snare and the cymbals crashed and KSK did another triple on the snare and managed a master rebound as we kept building it up. Biggy's voice, tender yet strained, cried to the world with prolonged pangs of anguish and of meticulous phrasing of diction. As always, we improvised and played a *sebene* for dance enthusiasts in the crowd. On and on, we achieved the fiery, spontaneous feel that owed as much to my meld as a fine soloist's grasp of syncopated soukous rhythms and sophisticated harmonies with Mo and Tégé's ability to juggle rhythm, bass, chords, and drive melody.

'Kwa nini?' the song that helped make my name in Nairobi had grown into a timeless testimony that lasted six minutes and thirty-five seconds. Each time I brought the song to an end, it revealed an unguarded side to me. I shed light tears. My Guitar offered a dynamic, shifting kaleidoscope of nylon-string colours that showcased my vulnerable artistic qualities, while, at the same time, demonstrating my formidable chops.

Then we launched into OK Jazz's 'Talaka', a song I enjoy playing as a guitarist because it was less challenging and had some nice rumba breaks. Halfway through the song, a friendly, chemically enhanced Uncle Ratego decided to join on stage. He was always down for having fun, so Biggy Tembo let him sing

257

backups with him. Into the charged *sebene* guitar solo we went, which was fun but a little intense and which I had spent some shed time on, and my rig suddenly went completely fast. I couldn't rant and rave enough to express my enjoyment each song we played.

Biggy Tembo resumed the lead vocal on the next song. We quickly coordinated and swung straight into 'Usilie,' a grinding and percolating rumba. Mawazo Ya Pesa emerged from the crowd and jumped upstage. He took his position next to Ayo. 'Kisumu Girl' followed, again sung by Mawazo. Ayo, looking smoking hot in a sparkly one-shouldered red dress, next sang 'Masumbuko Ya Dunia.' Complex syncopated rhythms, intricate counterpoints, and cascading arpeggiated runs graced the wonderfully crafted composition called 'Masumbuko.'

Then Biggy Tembo and Ayo's did a lovely duet on Afrisa's 'Loyenge.' Towards the end of it, I beckoned Benz Benji Obat and handed him my guitar. I joined Mary-Goretti. 'How do you like our show, baby?'

'*Wa—andafuuul*,' she shouted with her crispy Luo accent to be heard above the blare. 'Didi, you cry when you play.'

'Emotion.' I smiled and held her hands. 'It's hot here, let's go out. We fought our way through while my fans patted me, thumped me, touched my shirt and called my name. We got to the shore stood on the sand. The cold wind from the lake cooled me, soothed me.

Mary-Goretti said. 'Let's dance.'

'I'm tired.'

'Oh, I'll get drinks then.'

'Hurry, baby.'

'Hug me first, Didi. Hey!'

I took up into her eyes. 'You're cute!' I held her and kissed her.

'Okay, let me go, take this.' I took her small pouch and idly watched her disappear into the crowd. I shrugged, closed my eyes and thought about my music. Every night my music with Victoria

ODW appeared to get better and better. It was amazing to listen to our performance and imagine that all that was crafted so perfectly with little or no help from a recording studio. I was so talented, it sometimes amazed me. People loved me. It was impulse. I'd come a long way now in the showbiz to know that that every entertainment wasn't necessarily the same. A song could not be played the same and the audience always responded differently. I loved applause. In the applause was love. The noise that particularly accompanied my music was something I greatly valued. It made me feel loved and appreciated. It also gave me some power: when I wanted people to listen they listened. I got my fans to receive my message through what I sang to them. When my fans cheered me it was embrace. When they yelled it was an encouragement.

Mary-Goretti came back with the drinks.

3.

My inspiration hit the metronome motorlode one evening when Biggy Tembo and I went to Victoria Music Store. I was told about the latest: 'Candidat Na Biso Mobutu.' Delivered by the Grand Master Luambo Makiadi Franco and the OK Jazz machine. I thought I had heard the best when I heard 'Chacun Pour Soi' and 'Mamou.' But this! I said, 'He can do this... he *can* do this!' Yeah, it challenged me. Even last year at Action Centre in Kondele, hearing the techno 'Lisanga Ya Banganga' and 'Omona Wapi' go from rage to thunder against the Omega One disco's speakers in a set of pure rumba wonder was a reminder of the Zaïreans' terrifying prowess of creativity. I wanted to spend most of my days in a studio creating music.

This inspiration stayed with me throughout the next four weeks of intense rehearsals at KS Resort basement. I knew how this album was going to be made. Biggy Tembo was going to sing all the six songs. I wrote the songs with his voice in mind. This was going to be Victoria's first album and we were all looking forward to it. Composing the songs for the new album was a less strenuous. I had no real worries about anything; I knew I wanted to write some music that was out of the ordinary, but really, I felt unease from the get go. Quite characteristic of me, I shut myself in my no-man's land of creative fantasy. And I had Lake Victoria, so I could get all the tranquil moments. I had an exercise book, a pencil and my acoustic guitar, the one I bought with scrap metal money from Ojal in 1975. In the evenings I went to some remote parts of the shore that had rocks jutting out of the water. Upon the rocks, I sat

and hummed, wrote down words, verses, poetry.

I hummed and tunes came. I wrote the words for 'Mother's Rules.'

> While I was on my way to Pandpieri
> I met a young woman
> I asked her to marry me
> She told me: 'Let's live together!'
> I went back home
> In order to ask my mother
> My mother gave me permission to marry
> *(Stanza repeated)*
>
> But my son, said my mother, I give you three rules
> The first one: never love a woman for her beauty
> The second one: her face shouldn't be too attractive!
> The third one: mind the one who talks in her sleep!
> The fourth one: let her cook first and let me taste the food!
> The fifth one: keep awa from the one called *odhi-oduogo!*
> Mother's rules ... Listen son, listen!
>
> *(Instrumental Interlude)*
>
> But my son, said my mother, I give you three rules
> The first one: never love a woman for her beauty
> The second one: her face shouldn't be too attractive!

The third one: mind the one who talks in her sleep!
The fourth one: let her cook first and let me taste the food!
The fifth one: keep awa from the one called *odhi-oduogo!*
Mother's rules ... Listen son, listen!

I had some serious ideas to work instruments into the heavy material that was growing in my mind. And it got to a point where that spontaneous feeling that can produce wonders was almost lost. I sat down with the band one evening and explained my ideas.

They looked around and smiled at each other... they were looking at our songwriting situation. I could see they didn't believe we could pull this off on our own without the help of Nairobi's seasoned session musicians or experienced studio hands. The passion kind of dwindled, so this was really depressing. I knew I just had to find a way to that kind of passion and let it be alive longer.

I had a plan. I was going to get the band to rehearse the songs and then play them live for our fans for some time.

Another thing I planned on doing, once we had rehearsed the current ten songs and record them 'live' on tape 'as is' (the good, bad, and ugly), I was going to get the band to play them out regularly and then we were going to select from our 'live recording' the ones that were good and refined.

After a while, I was going to try recording the sets again 'as is' and see if we had evolved, devolved, or gotten stagnant.

We went through with it like that for two months. Then we had six songs to perfect. We ploughed through with more ideas in order to 'stuff the hollow men'. I was very keen to let the guys more into the songs beforehand so they could work with their parts more and well, be part of the creative process. We rehearsed, rehearsed for almost three weeks. The stuff improved and sounded fresh, new. We were treading new territories. During rehearsals it was growing together nicely. We finally recorded the demos on tape. We finished all the songs but one before we entered the studio!

I had to go Nairobi next. I walked into Attamaxx's new studio offices. I walked in and JB was reading *Men Only* magazine while talking on the phone. 'I'll have to call you back,' he said into the other end of the receiver as soon as he saw me. He hung the phone up, put the magazine down and pushed off some papers from his desk. 'Not a very smart thing, what you did,' he said to me. 'Going to Kisumu and leaving all the money here.' I rolled my eyes. They had heard nothing about me for close to a year since 'Hapana.'

'I am here to negotiate,' I said, sitting down. 'I want to do another album.'

'I am not letting you go Otieno Owiro Dundos. If I did could you imagine the controversy? I can see the headlines now. 'Boy star migrates to Kisumu leaving all the money," he said. I rolled my eyes again.

'Fine then, as long as you don't ask me to sign any contract. I have six songs; I'll go into the recording studio as Orchestra Victoria ODW, put down my bits and be done with it. One album... one album,' I said.

'I want to propose something big. I have changed a lot of rules since you left. I want to propose a way to take care of your career for the next five, six, seven years. A contract is for...' He ruffled through papers. 'Ah,' he said smiling devilishly. 'Five albums, thirty tours, twenty-two singles, all with promotion of course, and the clincher...' He said smiling. 'This must take no longer than 6 years. Do you want me to calculate what you will make?'

'No,' I said. I had expected this, had been prepared for it. I had been told about this, had been warned.

JB gasped.

'Two hundred thousand a year and we take care of everything including distribution.'

Uncle had prepared me well for this. Uncle was my guy: he

had a mix of darkness in his soul that resonated for a kid who came of age into the pre-Independence poverty and tyranny of our neo-Colonial capitalist rulers. He understood the politics that made some people rich and some poor forever. JB would try and get me into the epic snare-roll built in a contract like this and bleed me for six years—his circa KShs. 200,000 a year sounded so much like Idi Amin's bombs. It was almost comical. Make me an offer like this as young and clueless as I was, and then tie me down. Question: just where did he get all these ideas from? That's what I got for expecting Attamaxx to do everything to me and make my name. They were in control over artists, clever bastards. What if things didn't turn out well? What if my records didn't sell? Weren't we now in the age of discos and DJs than live music entertainment? Omega One and Funkatec in Kisumu were taking away all the youthful fans already. So much of it that I was already thinking of a way to blend my live music with disco. In Kisumu there were disco jokers (DJs) who were already bragging they could keep two turntables going in a mix that was 'tight as *pier jamach*' (in a heavy DhoLuo accent, the hardest phrase I'd ever had to transcribe). But that didn't even matter for now: my problem now was to create music that would be played in discos!

JB was saying something. 'This is the best deal ever, Dinos. Don't let things get into your head, you're still a nobody. I made you.

'And now you're breaking me.'

'Fine. I will give you time to think about this. How about we do the album you have then?'

I got up and left. Left that office.

Left Nairobi.

The answer lay with Uncle in Kisumu.

4.

In downtown Kisumu town was the 4-track recording studio

called Shashi/ Hindochar which had been established in 1971 as a way to fill a need for a live-sounding tracking room.

At the time the two-room facility, housed in a nondescript building near Patel and Mithun Mansion, was a small studio; tiny, smoke-filled setup and in such cramped quarters there just wasn't enough space to set everyone up at the same time and still maintain some separation. The building itself was large and awesome with high cathedral-like ceilings and plenty of empty ground around it built in the 1920s as a Hindu Temple. In the 1960s it was used by Yasha Yogi as his Kisumu center for Transcendental Meditation. Soon after that, it was converted into a recording studio. It was one of the first 4-track studios in Kisumu. Although there had been major renovations since then, it was still the same state-of-the-art recording studio that Kisumuan orchestras recorded in 40+ years ago. According to local lore, the building was haunted by the ghost of a guitarist who committed suicide there. The ghost supposedly roamed the hallways at night, drinking leftover booze. Hm.

Uncle purchased it this year and named it Lakeshore Studios. I went there to inspect it and was shocked at what I saw: the console was mushy, the recording rooms and mics mediocre. The studio reeked of cigarette smoke (among other substances). Shards of 2-inch tape hung from the ceiling and clients were always locked out of the studio for weeks—sometimes months at a time waiting for their pre-production tapes. They were told to come back after two weeks while their tracks, overdubs, mixes and masters were rushed to Nairobi's commercial studios. The basement had years of crap. As most basements (or attics) do. Old furniture, portable pools, canoes, tables, toilets, and generalized crap crammed the place. It wasn't cramped but it was dark. Far in the back, though, there was a ceiling light fixture. With a new bulb there was light! The basement was a little musty, but dry. Air was provided by a basement window.

My recommendation: keep the existing clients, sack all the workers, refurbish the place and employ professionals. This was how Engineer John Onditi, who previously engineered at Tahamaki Sound Recorders in Nairobi in 1978, became the studio manager/ chief engineer. He was a revered professional; he was the only one who could operate all the equipment. He had a good ear for final product and would record and dub over and over until it was right. He immediately suggested change of recording equipment and Uncle imported a multitrack analogue tape and other state-of-the-art equipment such as the Trident A Range console and Fender guitars, bringing the studio into the professional recording end of the market. The place was upgraded to three rooms— A, B and C— and they were still pretty dead-sounding. So a major renovation was done which resulted in a very large modern studio, high and rectangular. The control room was up some stairs at one end, with the desk to the left of a window that looked down on the main room. For the backing tracks, the bands were going to play in there as a live unit, with the drums in the center of the back wall, bass to the left, solo-lead and rhythm guitars to the right and the keyboards immediately in front, under the window. The walls were covered and padded with heavy baffles, high ceilings were created. The works.

Producer/engineer Jeff Omolo, also a session guitarist who had performed and recorded with several Nyanza benga bands since the 1970s was brought back from an early retirement. He had vast experience with how music was recorded and mixed and he knew how to create an ambiance that was atypical of many benga bands. He possessed sharp knowledge of how sound was enamored with reverbs and delays—anything to make them sound clean and up-tempo.

I spent time in the studios during the renovation seeing installation of vintage preamps and other gear that played a role in great-sounding records. I helped with the wiring the musical instruments, set up heavy analog tape machines, black boxes etc.

Opening the doors on the studios space with the Trident A Range console, Engineer Onditi told me that Lakeshore Studios was going to become known as one of Western Kenya's premier tracking rooms, hosting sessions for Victoria ODW and other bands.

Recording good music, I now learned, was more collaborative. People needed each other to do sessions. Everybody involved was required to know what pieces of gear, mics and audio formats they were going to record and mix down to.

This was very important to me as Victoria ODW were virtually going to be living in Lakeshore Studios. At night, while the watchmen will be chasing stray cats and sitting gloomy-faced in the cold, while street children were sleeping, the thieves hustling and prostitutes roaming the streets outside this nondescript building near Patel and Mithun Mansion, Onditi and his team were going to be working to produce and engineer several albums for me.

My next mission was how to convince Uncle to make me a partner in this studio.

Tégé Zoba asked, what next? There were critical questions: did the personnel at Lakeshore have experience and expertise with record production? Yes. What about record marketing? Distribution and promotion? What we were going into was akin to self-production which was easier said than done, he told me. There was also the issue of the label. In today's industry, the way he saw it, you either were on your own, or you were signed to a label. I agreed. An artist should look to get signed once they'd taken their own career as far as they could. If, at that point, you were not satisfied with your reach and/or income, you'd try to find a label... but only then! Doing so before taking it to that ceiling, in his opinion, was a cop out. It was giving up in a way because the tools were out there and if you could use them correctly, you could earn an income from your music, keeping 100% of the profits. If you were on a label, you could see 0% of profits if you were not a hit (obviously, if this was the result of the deal I had recently signed with Lakeshore after ditching Attamaxx, Victoria ODW would probably get a nice check upfront, but after that, we were not going to see a cent).

I began to see things. Solution? I asked him? Take the risk, make nice records (nice meant good sound) have our own label but subcontract marketing and distribution of finished product to Attamaxx. I frowned at that.

5.

The 2-month gestation period behind our *Lake Victoria Breeze* album and its evergreen hit single 'Anyango Nyar Nam' saw Lakeshore studio perfectionism and improvisations taken to extremes. And despite the success, the experience helped to convince engineers John Onditi and Jeff Omolo that there had to be another way to make records!

Making it had been teeth grinding, you know. We didn't actually know what the budget was, Uncle (the producer) just told me 'Right, you've got three weeks to do it,' and without the pressure of having to do a certain style of record, we just did what felt right with the time given. Having already routined and rehearsed hard for weeks and weeks, we played the six songs live. The band would just run through a number in the studio and then dive straight in while Uncle and the engineers looked at us from across the studio. Still, although the original plan was to lay down all the backing tracks before recording overdubs, this wasn't strictly adhered to: once a backing track was deemed satisfactory, there was a tendency to take it a little further and do some overdubs. Then we listened to the replay of the recorded sound.

My guitar parts were very easy since I had most of them worked out and the overdubs were simple—they were double—tracks, guitars with more effects or embellishments here and there. However, there were very few over-overdubs. They were mainly just single overdubs, and there was very, very little comping on that album. In terms of the vocals, I had the best team. We'd do just one track and if it wasn't right we'd redo it, and if it still wasn't right we'd maybe drop in one or two bits, but generally there was very little comping. We didn't really have the time. The musicians were in form and we recorded most songs in one or two takes. Ayo's silk-smooth vocals, like audible chocolate, and Biggy Tembos' baritone were surprisingly a perfect match. This was Biggy's second time in a record studio and he seemed resigned to give his best. His voice was as deep and rich as ever, and the lack of fast soukous drumming and loud guitars allowed him to forgo the over-singing trap he sometimes fell into. Tracks like 'Sigalagala' and 'Nimezoea Tabu' were beautiful, sunny tracks that soared with joy. Mawazo Ya Pesa, too, managed to strip down his sound without falling into the trap that many artists found themselves in, that of stripping too much away and becoming boring. His cutting, literate lyrics also kept the listener from becoming complacent; melancholy and bitter. As we worked through it. I sometimes had a sinking feeling the album sounded like it was written post breakup and pre-recovery. There were enough bits of sonic imagination to keep the listener awake and admiring Mawazo's fierce delivery. Then engineer Jeff realized we needed an echo chamber for the song 'Kit Maro Otama' which was Ayo's hip swiveling new style rumba. There was none and in the end we improvised. The improvisation saw Ayo singing her heart out inside a toilet bowl! Something we were to talk about for days to come.

By now I thought I knew the tricks of recording good music. I had just a few of my own thoughts and experiences regarding practice/rehearsal and recording band practices. Often in Nairobi, it was common to hear someone saying 'it pays to really rehearse well and to record several sessions' and I agreed and now with my debut recording in my band, I was just trying to emphasize that it *really* was essential to do three or four takes of a single song and then later make a choice. In Nairobi studios, things were done rather hurriedly. You *thought* you had a good song but how well-tuned was your band? The advantage was that over there you dealt with well-selected seasoned pros who knew a good sound so we often recorded one take and took the master to Polygram. I always felt I wasn't exercising my artistic freedom, rather I was spoon-fed. But here now I was in charge. We recorded many versions of the first three songs played the tapes three nights a week. Of course I knew how they sounded but I could almost guarantee my fans were going be surprised if the records came out the way I wanted.

Well, we worked through it and I thought it the sound quality would be horrible. We practiced in the basement, cinderblock walls...there was so much reflection of bass and nodes that once, when I complained Mo's bass was *way* too mushy sounding and loud, we traded places... I went and stood right in front of his amp, he stood where I usually did. We both agreed, in front of his amp it was quiet, where I stood it boomed.

We spent weeks and recorded one of our sets. Got it home and jolly... it wasn't all that bad. We played the tape with the pan a little and I was amazed. We recorded the whole month (cutting out jabber in between songs, and false starts) over and over again. I could finally hear what the audience would have heard. I had experienced that in Nairobi when it seemed like you were in a jam, ideas came flowing, cool stuff, finding new riffs, mind working overtime, ears working overtime... and then you heard it back and said to the rhythm guitarist 'that's horrible, I thought we could minimize the variations, it should sound like it's Kenyan! Meanwhile, the band members had already started falling asleep.

On a song like 'Gor Mahia Pek Pile', I had to play a damp solo and thought 'ouch... I *blew* that' and the engineer said, 'damn, that wasn't what I thought it would sound like'. Here the stripped-down guitar sound, scattershot percussion and frantic vocals brought to mind the sound of Choc Stars, a contemporary aggregation.

Afterwards when it seemed like it was over, I gave the musicians a week off and had to work at the songs when listening back to not repeat the 'ouch' thought process. Many times I needed to hear it with fresh ears and I thought 'ooohh... that was kind of a nice little riff there... and it builds up pretty nicely.'

Finally it was over. Finally I could call a few people to criticize the recording. Finally I understood why that solo I did and thought blew chunks on 'Gor Mahia Pek Pile' was so well received and people came up and said 'that was *great!*' Or why the solo I was so proud of, the one I thought was 'perfect' was shrugged at. When I asked Tégé and the others what they thought of that song, I got a guarded 'yeah... that one.. it was okay, it was good.'

The recording of album was my most intimate and low-key yet. There were no bum tunes to be found. I called in Super Mazembe's drummer Dodo Doris to play snare drums. Victoria Kings B senior member and bassist Odongo Agwata came in to play on the three classic benga tracks, but mostly the album had the make and the feel of Victoria ODW. I brought Odongo in because I wanted the best benga bass and I knew he could give me that, plus we had the bass hooked up to an Ampeg SVT. My guitar went through a Roland JC120, close-miked with a Shure SM57, same for Goldfinger Tégé Zoba's guitar. We were using Fenders, so we got the superior sound on the guitars. Banking on this as the musical palette through which the unknown band from Kisumu was going to make its entry into the overcrowded pool, we carried innovations with the sure prospect to make this record succeed in a way that most similar over-produced albums failed to do. On the song 'Anyango Nyar Nam' I wanted something purely artistic like what Simaro recently achieved with 'Faute Ya Commercante.' I had acoustic guitars, restrained bass drums, hi-hat packed snare drums and subtle brass section on this one. And this record was unique in many ways: everybody was eager to be the best. Tégé Zoba's had an opportunity to play long gentle rhythm scores: the strings on 'Safari Ya Mbali,' the rippling guitars of 'Anyango Nyar Nam,' the gauzy pedal steel of 'Hera Mar Mbese,' the sweet call-and-response background vocals and *dodo* beat of 'Kisumo Ka.'

The album made for good listening for everyone else. As it

happened, Uncle was very, very excited. This was the first project for the studio since he bought it and refurbished it. We said we wanted to do it on our own and he pretty much left us to it. Uncle didn't need to be reminded that he was growing old gracefully, he was dancing in the studio, doing some amazing foot works. He even sang backing vocals in 'Kisumo Ka.' The 70s may have been the golden age for creative output, and some of the guys who were there may have ended up making some of the best records of their lives. But we were here to prove that 80s was not over yet and we were getting in the middle of it with even better records.

One other thing to consider was the cover design. A paste-up artist from Nyanza Printers did what I thought was good enough. The credits were as follows:

> Biggy 'Mukubwa' Tembo— lead vocals
> Omondi Pascal aka Mawazo ya Pesa— vocals
> Ayo 'Super Girl' Achieng Massikkinni — vocals
> Dinos Otis Dundos — solo guitar
> Benz Benji Obat — first rhythm guitar
> Tégé Zoba 'Goldifinger' — second rhythm guitar
> 'Commando' Mo Thwaka — bass guitar
> Odongo Agwata — bass guitar
> 'Gentlemens Gentleman' KSK Odongo — drums
> Dodo Doris – snare drums
> Recorded and mastered at Lakeshore Studios Ltd, Kisumu.
> A Phonogram production in collaboration with JoJo
> Productions. Manufactured by Polygram Records.
> Marketing and distribution by Attamaxx Records.

Listening to it, I felt the benga-tinged instrumentation defined a new kind of benga music for the next generation. We took a three week break. In my mind I wanted to be back in the studio in December for our second album.

6.

Angelou called me from Nairobi during the last week we were in studio. She normally called me at KS Resort using her office phone. She had been trying to reach me and was given the studio's new number.

'Hello.'

Her call skewed me. I had a queasy feeling even as I put aside my stresses with the record and tried to play Mr. Jollyman. Tried to find words to cheer her up. I told her we were in studio finishing a great album. Then it occurred to me that she was not speaking. So I stopped and heard her soft breathing.

'Adoyo?'

'Dinos.'

Her voice was still (undeniably) intoxicating. Rich and thick and guttural, a deception in itself. Soft, low... a mellifluous rumble of synonyms. I could see her face, I could see the dark bewitching eyes. I could see her thick lips slightly parted and enchanting down to a painting.

And I knew it even before she spoke it. 'Dino, I am glad things are working well for you down there in Kisumu but I need a name for your son.'

Dramatic pause for me to grunt and for her to take a deep breath and draw a soft sigh over the wire. My adrenalin rose and I felt heat in my face. I felt maddening thumping in my ribcage. Honestly I didn't know what to say. I floundered for a word. Stalled. Stared blankly. I couldn't say it surprised me much, I had been expecting it. We had kept in touch and it was a difficult pregnancy for *me* as it was for her. She was sickly and nauseated for most of the term. I soaked in it to my bones. She called me every other day to call me names and I swallowed in all the bad words and all the names she hurtled at me. And the way she ranted like a mad women it sounded like she would die the next day. I came to the point that lingering restless grief usually drove one to. That point where you can only feel redemption by knowing that another can hurt just like you do. I came to a point where I committed a crime against morality. I wanted the child to be born so I would free myself. For sure she was now my ex; the imperfect wife. Lousy cook. I wanted to love her and we went through a lot during my Nairobi years, was still hurt by her. She gave sex that felt like a thousand bees were buzzing hot sweet honey on my body while delightful fingers massaged me and seductive lips poured kisses and thrilling words. I mean that woman could banshee scream and proclaim things in Luo during orgasm. I missed that.

So? Now...

She was the mother of my son. Hm, that softened me. The thought that somehow now we were tied for life.

So I cracked a bit: 'So then?'

Now the baby was born and she sounded like she had returned to her old jovial self. Ebb & Flo gave her six months maternity leave, she told me. She was calm. Her voice was softer than usual. She sighed long and tiredly. Then asked, 'What name do you want me to give him?' She asked that question from the side like a faded afterthought.

She told me that she didn't expect much from me. She had become a different woman. Meaning? Her life was now her baby, who she was going to bring him up as a single mother. That softened something in me instantly. When I tried to put in a routine argument about my rights as a dad, she dismissed me as a dreamer. Said that she couldn't trust me to be a father; I was too young and yet to grow up. I was an artist and; for that matter, very turbulent. She knew what she was doing and I should count myself lucky. Did you hear that? I tried to ignore that 'talk-down' tone, tried not to feel like she was trying to prove a point to me. Tried to imagine that the reason she already knew the future she was going to give my son was she thought I was an undeserving bastard who had made her pregnant by accident. See, she still maintained it in her head that I was not good enough for her, her voice said it all. She didn't seem to care that I was sensitive... about being left out of my son's life. All she needed, she added, was financial support. But if I couldn't do that, it was OK, she'll manage.

Our conversation seemed scripted... strained. The only thing that boiled my blood was that this enchanting half-caste woman had made me a father at the age of twenty-three.

'He has your eyes, Dino. And your Indian nose. I will call him Dinos Otieno Owiro Junior.'

7.

Days later, I wafted between shame and guilt and more guilt to the verge of resentment towards bits and pieces of my past. I found it harder and harder to tell anybody about my son in Nairobi, but realized I had to find a friend and a relative to confide in. I picked on Uncle and KSK but it became difficult for me to express myself to them. I didn't want any lectures on parental responsibility. In my mind I was faced with gory reality as an absentee father who sat back and watched an undeniably innocent young woman get dragged down into the long road of single motherhood. And I was doing nothing about it.

I ended up confiding in Ayo. Thankfully Ayo did crack a moment of grief out of me. I visited her one morning at her single room in Ondiek Estate. I found her dreary-eyed battling a hangover, smoking and wearing a short flowered dress and playing loud music.

Apart from singing, Ayo made a living as a painter and, like her Nairobi rooms, this room was always full of oil paintings, an easel, drawings, boards, books on the floor, an acoustic guitar, empty beer bottles and many odd objects Ayo picked on the way along her artistic journey. After her supremely effusive hugs and suggestive touches and fondling she went straight for my emotional jugular. But first she announced that she was having her exhibition soon, she had thirty pieces of oil on canvas that were going to be framed.

I could have sworn my nostrils got a whiff of Happy Smoke.

Ayo was a rambunctious girl, a city girl, a street wise girl. Coming from a broken family and with her mom working long hours for the Nairobi City Council, Ayo was on her own from a very early age. Growing up in Dandora, she got away with a lot of stuff but ventured into those dark areas mostly out of curiosity. Smoking pot was one, heisting beer from the local neighborhood liquor stores was another. The 'heisting' went from lifting small bottles of Vodka to stuffing audio cassettes down her pants at Ebrahims.

Often times she got away with it.

Not always.

'So, tell me, Indian boy. I hear your Nairobi woman gave birth.' There was no way she could have known already unless, of course, Angelou herself told her. So I made her listen to me; she listened to me. I sat down next to her and told her. Then she laughed. Laughed long and hard. Coughed so hard in the stitches I thought she was going to break her tiny frame. She knew Angelou very well from our Nairobi marathons. She asked questions (a lot of them), and laughed frequently even though I had said nothing funny. I couldn't know if she was being friendly, or if this was her way of making me feel like a human wreck sitting here next to her on her blue Vono bed.

Like most singers, Ayo possessed a hard, coarse, cracking voice that thudded inside your skull. One that hit you square in the face and made your ears ring. And she spoke so rapidly you almost didn't hear what she said. It was quite a huge contrast from the syrupy soft voice she sang with. Now she admonished me in that voice that stung my eardrums with a pneumatic drill and demanded of me to make a point of going to Nairobi soon to see my son. I felt slightly flustered; my jaw dropped. I don't really know how to phrase this but... she was right. She had a son too, she revealed to me. Six years old and living with her parents in Kakamega.

I wanted to ask her about it. Then I opened my mouth to ask

her about it. But Ayo flipped the story over the way you stop music on a record player and turn over a 45 before the music has reached climax. I had an automatic giggle for her unbelievably funny jokes. This Luhya woman was a talker. She was all talk and never gave you a chance to talk. She said something, even asked something and before you responded she had found an answer for you and said it. She didn't really care what you said, she dominated a conversation. She was a wild woman who drank like a man, could holler like a village idiot, could laugh till her eyes streamed with tears, yet cry at the same time. I mean really weep with laughter. She was practical about private things like her sexuality. No pun, her vibes scared me. Yet I trusted her and was very open with her.

We talked, laughed and puffed Happy Smoke.

Fascinating.

We exhausted all jokes and laughed our heads to exhaustion. She sat up, picked the acoustic guitar. She had a song she wanted me to include in our next album, she was going to sing it. I sat up quickly. She stroked the acoustic lightly, speculatively; my heart glowed.

'*Nataka Baba*, it's the name of this one,' she rapped, smiling. She touched and strummed the strings again, and the music rose and died, lost notes without a tune. And she brushed the light strings and the very air shimmered and changed color. With a deep in-draw of breath, she began to sing.

> *Uliacha mama, na ukaniibia*
> *mapendo yoo—ote ya baba,*
> *Ulituacha ukasema utarudi...*
> *Sina namna, sina chochote*

The first lyrics ran, sung low and sweet in Ayo's mellow far-off fog voice. The rest of the song—I clutched at it, heard each word and tried to remember, but lost them all. They brushed me, touched me, then melted away, back into the fog, here and gone

276

again so swift that I could not remember quite what they had been. With the lyrics, the music; wistful and melancholy and full of secrets, pulled at me, crying, whispering promises of a thousand tales untold. All around the air was full of color.

Words, music, light; Ayo put them all together and wove it for her vision and fertile imagination.

She hit the end and for a moment I forgot where I was. I clapped clumsily and she went on with another round of whooping laughter. As we smoked weed, she looked at me with moist sultry eyes. She fed me with a quirky smile—one of the traits I liked about her beauty, and said these words to me: 'You know, Dundos, weed makes me ache. Now I ache.' I knew what Ayo wanted. It always happened after we smoked weed. Her warm eyes told me. Ayo had been my secret lover from our Nairobi days. And it was getting serious: she wanted happiness. She wanted a relationship now and I had to sort it out. I was OK with a secret affair. And what was happiness to her more than the sex which she craved for like a lioness on a kill?

'Close the door and make this woman happy,' she whispered, pulling off her flowered dress. It was the only stitch on her body.

8.

The album *Lake Victoria Breeze* was out in the shops and on radio. I felt the butterflies of nervousness evolve. It was an oddly sweet feeling you get that finally your life was getting into proper perspective. After years of struggle to succeed, I was fighting the reality that I may finally succeed and cross one big hurdle in my path to finally becoming an accomplished musician.

My very inward parts felt magnified as I visited locations within Pandpieri that reminded me of happy and sad occasions. The oppressive yolk of unrelenting struggle in my formative years became a reminder as I watched the transformations in different locations in these mid years of the 1980s. I suddenly begun to see things. When taking Mary-Goretti to see an Indian movie, it occurred to me that we still had only two old film theaters since the '60s. Nothing much had changed since the '60s and the Colonial times. Many individuals and family members I observed put my wheels to whirling. Kisumu was a typical Africana, small town, close knit families, good clean folk who were God-fearing and were sheltered from the perils of crime, not like Nairobi. I was also overwhelmed with the joyous memories of walking downtown with my mother as we shopped in various stores. That joy I felt, exceeded any previous sadness. I was glad to have grown into a man without having to leave Kisumu like most young people had done. I was coming of age in my home in this docile sunny town. I had my family and friends around me. And I had a chance to help my parents educate my younger brothers and sisters.

My child hood home held so many strong emotions inside. I will always come back to Kisumu weary and worn out after years of travel. And on the day I will lay to rest, my remains will be buried in this land.

I became an uncle at age twenty-three when my elder bro Keya had recently turned up from Mombasa and married a beautiful Luhya woman called Rose. This year the woman, *nyamalo* as we called her, had given him a baby boy. I guess to be a twenty-three year old grandfather is something what happened when you were number three of eleven children. More nieces and nephews were going to be born.

I distinctly recalled conversations with my sisters Akong'o, Obera and Akinyi where we wondered what sort of adults our brothers would turn out to be as we became men. Odingo had just completed his Masters degree in the South African university where he was lecturing. We had spoken on phone recently and he confirmed that he had received my album, I had mailed it. He was happy that my career was taking off, that my name was soon going to be known. We were all happy things were working well for him as they were working for me. My father continued to maintain his job as a tow truck driver and fishnet artisan; Keya went to work at the service station where Ouru recently worked out of. Ouru was very much in the army and active in the forces' rugby team. Agwenge was still mysterious; he was seventeen and had done his 'O'Level last year and didn't get enough points to go 'A' Level. We wanted him to repeat but Uncle thought he should join the armed forces or the police. He took on sidelined private teaching; told me he wanted to be like me, he wanted to sing. Mama said, 'Don't start misleading your brother into that life.' My father said, 'Take care of your brother.' Tom was fifteen and in form two while Akong'o was thirteen and in form one. Bro Timbe was ten and in class five. Sis Obera was eight and in class three while our youngest sis, Akinyi was aged seven and in class two. Our last born Hawi was in nursery.

Now that's my family.

We were not alone.

It wasn't just us, nor ants or cockroaches or mice.

It was relatives!

There were my cousins and uncles and aunts staying with us in Fort Jesus. Almost half of my cousins were teenagers or older. They had been living at Fort Jesus for some time, but their future seemed cloudy and they did not know where they were all actually headed. Many of them were employed at KS Resort. I think two or three joined the University, some migrated to Nairobi. But the relatives as a whole had to put on the persona of a family in need. We were a blended family, a combination of families living together with hopes for tomorrow.

One of my nieces in particular was a very gifted fine artist. Aluoch was her name. During my visit to Fort Jesus in Pandpieri, I found her and we spent time chatting about creative endeavors and we actually hoped to share some collaborative projects in the near future. She was picking up skills in graphic design for print and I thought I could engage her to design my album sleeves.

We spent some time shooting photos together and later she came to KS Resort and took photos of the band during

279

performance. Mama was still tight-lipped over my music career. Occasionally I went to Pandpieri to help my sister Akinyi with her homework and observed that half of the kitchen garden at the back of the house was overgrown with weed and needed to be cleared, and maybe Mama could start a poultry, but she said no, that wasn't even possible, in a voice that seemed to want to ask me whether I was certain I was really convinced that I wanted to spend the rest of my life playing guitar in a band full of sinners and actually calling music for drunks in a bar my career.

I attempted to switch to another topic but she asked me what I hated most; asked me to build my own *simba*. Odingo had built his before he went to South Africa and I was the next in line and Ouru may want to come home too and become a man too and he will need to build his *simba*. Not after I and built mine; of course. So. Maybe I didn't want to be found to be in the way, did I?

I knew what was coming next: when was I lastly in church? When did I last participate in the Holy Communion? I would sit there brittle with guilt and anger. I had observed my father playing mum to Mama's harsh and direct offensives and I knew it paid. Mama was always on my case, she was always on *our* case. Mama was a correctional facility; she ruled our home with an iron fist. She never spared you.

I always believed it was Mama who held our family together with prayer. Each night Mama prayed for each one of us (eleven of us plus our father). The thing I found my family cherished most (especially Mama and younger siblings) our love for Jesus Christ. Sabbath keeping was paramount. This made our family close and in constant desire to bond together. When Odingo went to South Africa, Mama had my father install a telephone in the house so she could talk with him. During my last year in Nairobi, she called me regularly. I was truly thankful in my heart for our need to bond together as family even if there was no love in it because we satisfied huge amounts of physical needs. Our reunions were vital and they helped us maintain unity. I knew that as a third born in a family of eleven, I was required to uphold some responsibility for the family unit. I had a role to play as a senior member, I had many younger siblings to take care of.

Mama said that since my elder bro Keya, who recently returned, was an alcoholic and not very sober in the head, greater responsibility was left to our father, Odingo and me. Odingo was far away in South Africa and my father was fast ageing. That left greater responsibility on me.

9.

Weeks turned into months. *Lake Victoria Breeze* was a makeweight album and the sales were steady, thanks to Attamaxx who did a good job with marketing and distribution. The song that was constantly played on the radio, in bars and in discos was 'Anyango Nyar Nam.' I got calls from as far as Abidjan. I transformed the band and Uncle became our manager. I now only had the artistic burden in my hands. All the other aspects of running the band, paying salaries, arranging shows, coordinating business with Attamaxx were in the hands of Uncle. We were in studio again for another album. Around the time that the *Golden Horizon* sessions began toward the end of '85, bassist Mo Thwaka left to join Kisumu Delta Force and was replaced by Odongo Agwata, while second rhythm guitar player Onyango Odol was added to a line-up that also included Kayembe Flavien and saxophonist Tom-Tom and trumpetist Kasule Mopero, fleshing out Victoria's sound and enabling it to be more experimental and downright up-tempo. This, after all, was what band manager Uncle Ratego Kwer was after: creating a consistently dark and evocative mood by way of sparse musical arrangements and plaintive vocals buried deep within the reverb-laden mix. My musicians got wacky as the confidence of experience turned the men into professionals. With the money that came, my musicians picked bad habits.

Did I say Mo Thwaka left? He didn't leave, I sacked him. He had become stone alcoholic. I mean this guy would do a shot of whiskey and follow it with Vodka. After doing the shot he would pour some of the beer into the shot glass to get any sediment left from the shot. One evening we had played a couple of sets, I saw him making his rounds. He must have had at least ten shots of whatever while on our 25 minute break. We were getting ready to start our last set and I saw our bassist staggering back to the stage with one eye shut. He stumbled onto the stage and put his bass on. We were opening the set with the remake of Simaro's 'Faute Ya Commercante.' Man, that song required serious sober bass. So he was standing on stage blowing like a flag in the wind. He plucked one note of the song then started to fall backwards hitting the wall in the back of the stage. He crashed and just slid down the wall and lay on the floor with his bass in his hand. One of our sound crew picked him up and laid him down on one of KSK's drum cases on wheels and wheeled him into the band room. Flavien jumped in quickly and picked the bass guitar. We finished the set with poor bass. We later took Mo to Russia and left him there. He got out the next day and where do you think the first place he went to? His local *chang'aa* den in Kaloleni. He got arrested and I refused to get him out. His wife Akumu came to me talking tough and threatening me, so I was compelled to get him out of jail. But he never was to play with the band. Instead I hired Jalupo, the KS Jazz bassist.

Then I went to Nairobi for crucial business matters.

Thanks to budgetary constraints, the entire *Golden Horizon* album took a total of six weeks to record and mix, which, although about 40 per cent shorter than the time accorded the preceding Victoria albums, still spoke volumes for the ingenuity, craft and rapid-fire innovation of the musicians and technicians. It sounded brilliant. Again Biggy Tembo's voice dominated it. Biggy Tembo even earned a nickname from fellow band members; they called him The Voice of the Orchestra. I traveled with the master to Nairobi for pressing at Attamaxx.

282

In my absence, Mo Thwaka returned to the band and took his place. Uncle let him back after he swore he would control his alcohol consumption. Ayo was in Nairobi exhibiting her abstracts at Gallery Watatu, so we took longer in Nairobi. Plus, you guess, I was spending some time with Angelou, babysitting my eight-month son, watching him pulling at things and stuffing them in his mouth. And as I watched him, as I watched his innocence, my life changed forever because I suddenly made some powerful decisions that led to my transformation. I decided I would do everything to make sure he got a bright future. I made the decision that he would have opportunities that I never had as a child and as a teenager. I decided I would never waste my time again.

Whenever I told Ayo I was going to see Angelou and my kid, her reaction mildly surprised me. She gave me a hard look and gave me a flicker of a nod. I thought I saw a sneer on her face. Ayo was getting all possessive around me and she was pushing Mary-Goretti away. And I was not comfortable with what I was beginning to feel for her. How could I (for the life of me) be falling for this eroded bitch? She was six years older than me for crying out loud!

Soon she was done with her art exhibition and we returned to Kisumu. Back to our world. Back to my problems. One evening I returned to my house in Milimani and found Mo Thwaka and his wife Akumu sitting side by side in my living room being served tea by my little sister Obera. Mo was looking cleaned up; he was clean shaven and had a haircut. He was wearing a suit with red tie. Akumu, wearing a *kitenge* with a massive headscarf, greeted me and went straight into the matter. She had been told that I had sacked Mo and she wanted to know why. How could she help? She said she knew the problem was with Mo: his drinking and womanizing. Mo sat the whole time saying nothing and looking at the carpet while Akumu did all the yapping. Akumu admonished him like a child. I had a long talk with Mo and made him know that the only reason I was ever going to spare his ass was due to our time together playing with Delta Force in Kondele. I may have had a soft spot for him because he was the one who helped push my career when I met him in Kondele in 1980. But the band was an institution and rules were rules. No band member (me included) was going to go renegade and get away with it. And he was not special. I made it clear to him that he was still suspended and would not be performing with the band for a while. He will hang with the band and still get his salary, but I was not allowing him to participate in gigs till his conduct improved. And not only that, all his salary will now be paid to his wife and he will only get gig allowances, per diems and part of the currency notes thrown at us by fans during performances. I expected Mo to protest that; he didn't. Right there and then I knew how much he feared his wife.

One afternoon we were at one of our usual haunts, a little bar on the bank of River Nyando in Ahero. This place was an old 30-by-50 makeshift bar with an extension built up on stilts (yes really) because it was literally on the river bank and you never knew when Nyando broke its banks. We always had a fun crowd there, and I always liked to take my younger brother Agwenge along. He liked to sing a couple of Tabu Ley tunes. He had some talent and since he was so hell-bent on becoming a singer, Ayo encouraged me to train him so he will not end up playing with inferior benga bands in Kisumu and burn himself out.

This particular night was Agwenge's eighteenth birthday, and he was partying especially hard. Mo Thwaka was drinking with a grizzled old *mzee*, most of the night. This guy was probably in his sixties, short stocky, big white beard, white side burns and gray hair dotted with white. Under other circumstances he could have been mistaken for a radical politician in Jaramogi Oginga Odinga's newly formed Radet movement... except for the grimy jeans, beat up leather jacket, and beer belly. Anyway, Mo and this guy were getting along famously, drinking, dancing, and chasing girls, generally having a great time. About the middle of the night, I noticed it looked like they were having a war of words at the bar, and a couple minutes later, Mo knocked the old guy off his bar stool, jumped on him, and proceeded to beat the living sh#@%!t out of him. It took about four other large men to pull Mo off, and get the old guy outside to safety. A while later, when we were taking a break, I approached Mo and asked him what had happened. He said, 'Oh that's just my father, don't mind him.'

Long story short: Mo's father, Mzee Frank turned out to be a fantastic singer and joined Victoria. He was blessed with a voice for singing Luo traditional songs; a *dengo* voice.

10.

Golden Horizon and came out in September and was well received. Through the remainder of that year till 1986, the album was not only pervasive but quite inescapable. Two songs were real hits, the most loved being 'Jessica' was KSK's tale of an unfaithful wife who has run away with another man. The song, sung by Biggy Tembo, is a cockhold husband's lamentations. It was a huge national hit. You could hear it in buses, bars, shops, friends' houses in Kisumu, Nakuru, Kakamega, Eldoret, Nairobi and Mombasa. It was No. 1 on radio, and VOK's Elizabeth Obege made it her favourite. But it was a sad song. The initial sounds of strings and the solo guitar notes all warned the listeners to get out their hankies.

I got a call from Mama Iva one Friday morning informing me that she had a promotion that Saturday at Kakamega, a large outdoor event. Being dependent on playing music for a major portion of my income, Uncle's first question was: what does it pay? The answer: nothing, but we'd get the band's name on the radio, there would be a big crowd and it would be great publicity for the band. Besides I owed her. I reluctantly agreed to do the gig.

When I met the band the next day to load up, I noticed they were packing many more speaker cabinets than we normally used. We just had the usual 100 watt 6 channel powered board that we used for small gigs, no extra power amps. I tried to explain that adding stacks of speakers to a 100 watt head would not give us a *big* sound, but my advice fell on deaf ears.

We were packed and headed for the promotion with truckloads of unnecessary speakers and Uncle's 'welding' generator (there was no power in the field where we were playing, so a generator was required). Our first tour was moved around in a couple of vans, with everyone finding places on top of the amps and speakers. When we arrived at the venue, I was informed that we would be running a snake, so that the generator could run sound out front, on the 6 channel 'vocals only' P.A. with giant stacks of speakers! We fired up the generator, plugged our gear in, and blew every single fuse in every piece of equipment on stage! It turned out the 'welding' generator was set to generate DC, as opposed to the AC current that our equipment required.

We replaced all the fuses in the nick of time and finally began
playing. Unfortunately, the snake we were using had no return cable to send a signal back to the monitors, so the singer had daisy-chained several short guitar cables back from the board to the monitors alongside the snake. Halfway through the first song someone tripped over the makeshift monitor cable system, killing the monitors! This happened about half a dozen times before someone finally found some duct tape and taped the cords together.

The applause was polite and restrained. An announcer welcomed us as, 'Coming all the way from Kisumu.' Mawazo Ya Pesa launched straight in, not leaving the audience time to form any opinions about the band

We did the 'overture' straight out of the Zaïrean band videos we had recently watched—a cut from Evoloko Joker's 'Eliyo.' KSK treated it as a warm up, lustily thrashing around the kit with tons of cymbal crashes. Biggy Tembo then set up a simple 4 beat for our first number, 'Kisumu Girl.' He invited Ayo on the mic.

Ayo's entry onstage was spectacular and I could feel the

audience buzzing. Above the droning, distorted guitar she strode to the front and belted out the opening verse. Immediately, she eyeballed some young guy in the front row and frightened the shit out of him. In no time at all, the crowd warmed.

'Anyango Nyar Nam' was followed by four breakneck numbers from the new *Golden Horizon* album played as rapidly as Biggy Tembo could manage. We were blitzing the audience with our no-holds-barred fury as we rattled through number after number. It was almost with relief that Mawazo ya Pesa did the little intro part for 'Unanichoma Ndani Ya Roho' as he wasn't sure how long he could sustain the pace.

When the promotion ended I breathed a sigh of relief. This horrible gig was finally over! It was just at that time that I heard an overdressed Mama Iva announce (previously unknown to me) that the band would be back tomorrow, same time, same place.

Back in the hotel and I had the most unexpected visitor: Riana! She was working in Kakamega, at the post office and heard I was in town. Over the years, we had kept in touch via telephone, telegrams and some letters. The last I heard of her was two years ago, she had broken with her boyfriend and was a broken woman. I had sent her two aerogrammes which she didn't reply, so I forgot about her, but I guess she always was in my subconscious because you cannot imagine my joy when I saw her after so long. She came to the hotel! And, for her sake, was reacting to me exactly how I had thought she would. When she saw me, she ran up and threw her arms around me in a warm greeting, oblivious of people in my room, including Ayo and Mary-Goretti. Her innocent brown eyes looked up at me from behind long, nice braids as she listened eagerly to my (rather boring) story of how I had missed her over the years and it was amazing how beautiful and grown-up she looked. Chubby and mature, a biggish woman with great hips in a maxi skirt. Her beauty was on display, probably for my sake more than anything. She wanted to give me every chance to admire her, be proud and have a good look.

She touched my face and tugged at my nose. 'Otis! Look at

you, boy. How handsome you look with your Indian nose. I can see you have become a real musician, eh?'

As I said, her devotion to me was immeasurable. She still had her wicked sense of humor, though, which I suspected was behind the performance I was now watching.

'Let me tell you, though,' Tégé was grinning, 'I saw this big woman jumping and dancing hard and screaming and I swear she would have jumped on me in a heartbeat. I could tell it!'

My jaw begged permission to go slack with shock. I denied it, but was surely tempted. Tégé had always been coarse, but he hadn't known Riana ten minutes yet and he was saying these things?

Mary-Goretti made an exaggerated pouty face and looked up at me. 'Didi, I hope you told her you were saving yourself for me?' I quietly sighed in relief that she was not choosing to take Riana too seriously.

Tégé laughed. 'I tell you what; since you have all these fine women around you: Mary-Goretti, Ayo etc, etc. Why don't I get lucky with this fleshy new one, huh?'

Furious, I opened my mouth to shout this vulgar idiot out of my room. The idea alone was offensive enough, but to say such a thing to a woman you've just met? Your boss' girl? My arms tightened and released an involuntary reaction I got when I was pissed.

Ayo got up, picked up her jacket and walked out of the room furious. Before I had a chance to say a word, however, the situation defused. Mary-Goretti laughed. 'Oh, that's so sweet of you, Larry! I hope she was a good girl for such a nice man. Yesterday. You can have she, go ahead?'

'Hey people,' said Riana, 'stop being stupid, Otieno is just an old friend. We come from way back. 1980.'

'Nobody takes my jokes too seriously,' Tégé said with such certainty that I almost thought he was serious. Riana nodded her approval, before turning to me and rolling her eyes. I stifled a smile. Mary-Goretti on the other hand gave me a look that said she was only indulging this charming newcomer for my sake. I silently told her I loved her.

'See,' Riana said cheerfully, 'he was never my guy. He's yours.'

'He-ey guys,' Tégé said, 'I've been so entranced in the heat of the moment that I haven't hardly noticed our guest has luggage.'

We all looked and saw Riana did have a light suitcase.

Riana spoke directly to me. 'Why don't you show me where to put my suitcase Otis? Then I can buy you a soda and we can catch up a little bit. The hotel is full, I can't get a room and I must be in Mumias before eleven in the morning?'

I groaned inwardly. I ignored Mary-Goretti's confused look, but I knew I'd have to explain it to her later.

11.

Our band played extended the New Blue Omo promo shows to Bungoma and Mumias and we indulged heavily in the libations. After the shows we packed up and went to the hotel to crash. The next morning I went to the van and trailer to find that we had been robbed! The thief had apparently opened the trailer. Both of my basses were gone (one of them was a KShs. 12,000, hand-made imported American bass) the keyboard rack, the cymbals and kick drum were all gone too.

That day we filed a police report and visited every bar, electronic shops music stores in the area to make them aware of the crime in case the thief turned up to sell them the stuff. We finally had to move on and go to the next town to play another show. The phone rang about an hour before the gig. We got our gear. On the phone was the police o.c.p.d. And they pieced the night together for us. *The trailer had not been locked!* When we hit the highway with the trailer doors flung open, some gear just fell out. Someone was nice enough to grab what they found and turned it into the police. The other half of the gear ended up back at the venue. The next day we spent about seven hours retrieving our gear.

On our trip back to Kisumu, I could afford a smile. Seeing Riana had made this trip worthwhile.

LIVE

RECORDINGS

OF

EURO AFRICAN TOUR

WE were in the studio for a great part of early '86 recording and the first album of that year was *Wend Osote* featuring Ayo on vocals. She brought heart and profundity to the album. Amazingly, Ayo's seductive mix of romantic ballads and smart sexy glamour with tongue-in-cheek lyrics still seemed to possess the much needed hit potential to make the album storm the airwaves. A savage indictment of the band's 80s era was in the making from our seat in Kisumu. Deep down I knew I was creating music that was going to be remembered for years to come. This year Ayo had replaced Biggy Tembo as the lead voice of the band and this was her second album.

From horror to hilarity, I saw it all!

The band members lived fast, loose and hard, and had a following that was, to be kind, a bit rowdy. We had built a cult following that went beyond the Luo nation, beyond the boundaries of Kenya and East Africa. Our music was alive in people's lips, in bars and in discos. Our songs were analysed in newspapers and discussed on radio. As fame stole me over, there was never a shortage of argumentative characters in the band that were ready to challenge my leadership and stand up to me with uniquely craptastic noise. When I suspended Mo Thwaka for drinking and being disorderly, he threatened (so Nilotic style with his spot-on boozy rasp) to get a witchdoctor from Nyahera to kill me. He railed at me. Said I was a bad man, that I was controlled by an impulse that made me delight in wickedness. Bad man?

Maybe I was. But Mo Thwaka was a socially challenged trash of a man who was basking and making coffins in Kondele when I had picked him out of the dirt and cleaned him up six years ago. What did gratitude mean to him and his wife? To me he was an immensely hot-aired social climber; a drinking drifter who claimed to have helped me get a grip in music. A fly I knew how to swat. I told him to go rumba with his mother. I told him to show me that he could even write his name.

When I edged Biggy Tembo out of the position of lead vocalist and replaced him with Ayo for artistic reasons (I wanted variety and transition), he called me an idiot. I thought he was going cracked on drugs and he was tripping and I didn't know what to do with him. When KSK demanded more money than I thought he was entitled to and I said no, he called me a hyena. He cursed and swore like a market madman and decided the grass was definitely greener somewhere else right at that moment. I found him to be a hopelessly immature and narcissistic musician who was always dreaming of re-establishing Delta Force. I knew that he and the two other men who felt they made me into what I had become thought they were entitled to the band's fortunes and were therefore better treated as untouchables. People told me to fire them; to me this would be like junking the Mercedes just because it had a broken spring.

At least Biggy had some sense: that competing in Victoria ODW was a zero sum game. He quickly captured perfectly the desperate and belittling status of vocalist and looked for every opportunity to pitch his ideas to the president of the orchestra (that's me) and earn a living singing lead parts during live performances and doing backing vocals during our recordings. The man eventually accepted his position and took in the reality that he would never be a vocalist in frontline again.

Uncle said I had a twisted mind and a mean streak which worried him. He told me these men were wrecking the band and Ayo said I should crack the whip and sack them. Uncle wondered why I had chosen to buy myself a car yet I had money problems with everyone. I knew I was difficult to confront, yes, but some of my actions warranted some explanation. For example, I edged Biggy out because he started getting this dreadful melancholy and I was not comfortable with a drug addict in my band. Uncle once told me with love and brutal honesty that he understood that my impoverished childhood, awkward adolescence, and horrifying early adult years were responsible for my selfish motivations. But my meanness was something that he couldn't fathom. He said this because by now, my cut in all recordings and shows was sixty percent; the rest forty was shared by the band. And that was the bone of contention. People argued with me about this all the time. I knew I left a wake of misery and heartbreak in the band as I was eaten up by the inspiration/compulsion/drive/ ambition to be a better musician. But, wasn't I entitled to the fruits of my hard work? I literally lived in the studio. I was always preoccupied; even when walking I was always singing things inside my head.

So much for hard work.

I felt I was entitled all the material things I had acquired and all the standard props that came with the grandeur of fame: fine wine, expensive watches, nice shoes, leather jackets, a well-furnished house, nice food, perfumes and a car. I had a Volvo and was thinking of getting a Merc. Yet the senior members of the band (in particular Goldfinger, KSK, Mo and Biggy) wanted to bring me in guilty. When I bought the Merc, somebody slashed the tyre and made and an ugly scratch on the paintwork. I moved into a rented house in lower Milimani and barred the band from coming to my house for fear they would slash my leather sofas with razors, drink my whiskey and steal my cassettes, my albums and my novels. Mawazo ya Pesa had popped in one afternoon and went on to tell the others about what a mighty telly I had and about my KShs. 10,000 Kenwood music system.

Life's little surprises and showbiz politics weren't helping the band in creative transition all the time. With a dangerous swagger and infuriating charm, I took matters into my own hands. I knew what was good for the band; I worked too hard to maintain a balance in recording and performance. I knew the musicians I could count on and I knew the snakes in my band. Personally, I knew I was as complicated and nuanced as some of my songs, at times eerily serene with moments of overwhelming madness. I called this hard work. Work? An act of cerebral stewing. Or I was a man confronted by the difficulties of too much artistic freedom. Every musician has been there: when life seems to be wildly spinning away from you, the only thing you can control is your music. I thus asked the question, what happens when you lose control of the music too? No, I didn't want that to happen to me. I didn't want to be distracted. I worked pretty hard and did everything on my terms. I had always known it: I was a leader of men. My hard work was a natural extension of my uncompromising vision to find total freedom. I didn't want my art to fail me; I wanted to be as rich and as famous as Franco. I was not going to spend time developing individuals in my band; I was going to develop the band. I was going to open doors for musicians to walk in and out whenever they felt like. Brutal in my emotional inquisition, I had subjected my musicians to a ruthless scrutiny in search of perfection in compositions.

Uncle told me to tone down my dirty words from soap-and-water mouth that I was beginning to sound like Idi Amin.

2.

In early 1987, I ventured into business and opened a club on top of Mama's Rusinga Island General Store. I called it Koch Koch and it became a popular meeting place for the band. A pudgy old man manned it. We called him Ong'any though that wasn't his real. The club had a large open area for dancing and such, crystal ball, a mega stereo booth on a stage and a jillion tables scattered out in a large "U" shape. I had my own private office here. It had an excellent view of Lake Victoria and it was large enough to sit ten people, so I used to hold meetings in it. I sat here with the band many times for meeting and parties. I wrote most of the songs here.

Pretty soon I had enough songs and we were in studio again to record *Tiacha!*, an album that was the complete incarnation of my dreams and aspirations and was made of loosely connected guitar sequences. *Tiacha!* was written for the common man. It featured Mawazo ya Pesa and my brother Agwenge on lead vocals and had Mzee Frank as one of the backing vocalists. It had long complicated abstract guitars arrangements and gear changes and was considered hardly danceable. All the lead guitar parts were played interchangeably by me and Bookerlose from Super Mazembe. Yes, I wanted racy soukous guitars and Bookerlose was the man with the hardest hand. I respected people with talent, remember. Bookerlose had a fast sliding style which was his own; his hooks dashed with the amazing fluidity of Manuaku and his gear changes frighteningly spontaneous like Beniko. Some songs were utterly self-indulgent with a real slant toward art-house soukous in the style of Langa Langa Stars. I yelled a lot in the studio but in the end we were pulling it through. The album was skipping along with a rueful comic sensibility.

Phone rings at 3pm on Sunday morning when I'm in the studio hunched over the console with engineers Onditi and Jeff doing overdubs on 'Kik Iyanya.' I grudgingly take off my headphones and click my tongue at the rude interruption.

A deep, gravelly voice asks, 'Can you be on stage, set up ready to play by 9:30? Tomorrow? Someone's coming from Nairobi to see you.'

I paused just enough for him to introduce himself, which made try ne politely ask, 'Where do you want to take us, sir?'

To which he says sounding distant, 'I want to see what you guys can play for me so that I can bring you across here for a month during summer.'

Did you hear that? Summer! That could only mean one thing. 'Where are you calling from, sir?'

'London, *sir*. I am the owner of African Dawn. I promote

African pop. We want some benga here in summer, do you think you can come?'

Now... picture this scene. Just picture it. If you were me, what would you do? Or say? This guy was a legend, I recognized that voice from URTNA. Miruka Obange. I couldn't contain my excitement! London? A month!

This was going to be EPIC.

You bet I gave the proposal a quick wink and nod.

Fast forward to meeting his agent at KS Resort. The agent turned out to be sniffy Nairobian who was very well versed in African music. After exchanging pleasantries, he introduced himself as Kabs Kababana. He gave me an expensive full colour business card with African Dawn logo and his name on it, plus his contacts. I sat him down with drinks and jumped on stage. After quickly assigning harmony parts, and subtle clues I would get from whomever wasn't playing to the tune, we hit it off. Quick sound check brought the crowd forward and we were soon into the full-bore of rumba and Urban Benga. First song, our masterpiece 'Anyango Nyar Nam.' I could see the shock in the Nairobian's face. He said we were awesome! He liked the band's clever arrangements, lots of interaction with the crowd. 'You guys are off the hook!' he said. Next songs, he was shaking his legs like an apeshit drunk.

Next day he was fresh and we sat together with Uncle and Mama Iva drawing the plans for the European Tour. We will be touring Europe in two months for a series of shows. He needed the names of the musicians for Miruka Obange (in London) to make out the visas.

I was started taking the London tour seriously and started preparing for it.

Practice! Practice Practice!

We were in the middle of it when problems started. Problems with KSK Odongo. His twin brother Opiyo was dead and he literally fell apart. Soon after burying his brother, he was swimming in debt and was on the verge of returning to his hometown to work in his father's sugarcane farm. He asked me for a loan, which I gave him. He asked for another loan, which I gave him. Then came the shocker: he quit. Later I heard he was struggling to re-establish Delta Force and had used the loan I had given him to buy new instruments. The rumour was confirmed when he turned up with members of Delta Force at Lakeside Studio to record a single. I swung into action and stifled the production of the single and seized the new musical instruments. He had a choice and a motivation. The choice: play for me or face his decline. The motivation: pay me my money back and save his ass. He soon returned to Victoria and walked into his position of vice president of the orchestra. But he was a troubled man and he sunk into a downward spiral of jealousy and insanity.

One night, four weeks into our European Tour, we were playing at KS Resort and I noticed a little guy sitting at the bar watching me play. This was during the first set, so I didn't give it a second thought as I was used to admirers standing close watching me play. The next set he was leaning against the wall across the dance floor from the stage, but directly in front of me. He just stood against the wall for the entire set staring at me. He smoked his cigarette, drank his beer, but other than that, no movement.

About halfway through that set, between songs, the little guy started walking toward me. What's all this now? What's this guy upto? Did I bone his wife or what? I'm thinking; whatever it is...here it comes! I was playing a Les Paul Custom at the time, so at least I had a nice hefty piece of wood to defend myself with.

He gets halfway across the dance floor, stops and smiles at me. After regaining my composure, I smiled back and pull down my feathers. We're getting ready to play again after a break and the little guy comes up to us and asks if he can sit it on a song. He didn't seem drunk, so I asked him what he wanted to play. In answer, he went to the drum kit, took the sticks from KSK, and pushed him out of the seat. He started playing and it was an awesome vintage vibe. He hit the drums right, he was tuned super tight, and did an amazing combination of a left-side snare and cymbals. And as he bashed the cymbals away, his foot maintained a steady pattern on the bass drum. He produced a palette of sounds and textures and allowed for plenty of contrast from cymbal to cymbal. Overall, he produced the huge sound and energy of a soukous band! He possessed styles that I didn't know existed. I asked him his name.

'Pajos. Pajos Mwana N'Dilli,' he said with a lilting Zaïrean accent. I thought I didn't hear him right. I don't know if we physically hit a break with our instruments all at once, but it appeared the band suddenly reacted tumultuously. I didn't believe this guy. Zaïrean and Tanzanian musicians lied a lot. Everyone said they were someone and played with this guy or that band and he said he was Orchestre Siza Kosa's famed drummer, Pajos? So I had to go figure this out. None of us believed him. Well, we knew the all-time favourite Siza Kosa song 'Angelina' and we started the song and he played it just like the record. A lot of drummers can play it just like the record, so we still have our doubts.

Pajos then got up and said, *'Nazokende kolala. Nalembi na ngai. Nalali pardo lobi.'* He went away among the crowd.

After the night was over, I found Uncle and told him about the mysterious drummer who claimed he played with Orchestre Siza Kosa. Uncle said he could prove whether the guy was a phony or not: he had some old Siza Kosa videos he had bought in Kinshasa. We went to his office and turned the video on and he played a Siza Kosa video. It was the 'Didi Ekosila Te' video and sure enough, there was the little guy with the harsh Zaïrean accent on the drum kit, in the video!

That's how Pajos Mwana N'Djilli became the new drummer and put my problems with 'Gentlemen's Gentleman' KSK to rest. Later on I learned that the whole thing had been set up by Mama Iva who had been unhappy with the rogue conduct of KSK. She had picked Pajos in Nairobi, brought him to Kisumu and coached him on what to do. KSK soon slunk away to join Delta Force.

3.

I was on the phone with Miruka in London and Kabs in Nairobi. The European Tour itinerary was taking shape. They wanted a 3-week tour of Europe, meaning not just UK but Germany and Netherlands.

'Europe? I asked.

'Yes,' Kabs said. 'European Tour.'

I smiled.

He explained that the continent's high population density meant less travel time between gigs (read: money spent), and most countries had a large appetite for music (read: money made), and many genres did well (read: audience). I had given him the names of ten people; Mama Iva and Uncle wouldn't be in this trip (thank God). Kabs came to Kisumu again to stew things and prop us up. We needed to polish our dances, he noted.

I put Ayo in charge of the whole thing and quickly two choreographers were found: a guy and a lady. The guy we got was pretty overqualified but open to doing it for the fun of it, and the lady was a real classroom choreographer/lead dancer who was young lady and quite full of herself. She had no understanding of our music and would make ridiculous musical requests, and made life generally miserable for the singers Mawazo, Biggy, Ayo, Agwenge and Mzee Frank. It was evident that she was an amateur, as she had little to no formal dance training and disappointingly little natural ability. But the training was rigorous and focused on the songs we would play during the tour. We all got a bunch of satisfaction out of this exchange, which took place immediately after another of Ayo's inane musical directions.

Ayo: Have you ever even worked with dancers before?

choreographer/lead dancer: Sure I have.

Ayo: (incredulously): Oh really? Where?

Choreographer/lead dancer (nonchalant): French Cultural Centre, Nairobi.

Ayo: I was there and don't remember seeing you.

Choreographer/lead dancer: (silence)

She learned the lesson that we all took to heart as working musicians—be humble, because you never know who you're talking to. Later on Ayo brought in six professional dancers: three girls and three boys. They were put on a vigorous training and performed live with us as their and mastered our music and polished our skills.

Around this time, Franco and TP OK Jazz tour came to Kisumu and we were hastily requested to curtain raise the event at Moi Stadium. It was a wonderful opportunity to meet the man, the grandmaster in flesh and we got soaked in the thick of it. Franco and the mighty orchestra were late with two hours and we played their songs throughout that time. When the band arrived amid chaos, Franco himself hugged me and I shook hands with men like Madilu, Simaro, Josky. They started and got into it but it seemed like the crowd couldn't get enough. Then there was a sound like thunder and we all saw the walls of Moi Stadium falling down like a piece of mattress and a huge crowd streamed in. We saw it; saw fans literally pushing and bringing down the walls of the stadium upon hearing Franco plucking his guitar while they were still outside while the police ran for their lives. Very soon, someone decided to switch off the electricity and all of a sudden the booming guitars and electric drums went dead. Most musicians would have thrown up their hands and waited for power to be restored before continuing, not Franco. He encouraged his vocalists to keep on singing and what sweet voices they had. Very soon power was restored again and Luambo could play till the end.

At the end of it I felt I was chummy with this great man Franco. While he autographed my copy of 'Mario,' I asked him the source of his magical talent and success.

'Ndoki,' he said with a big smile.

I nodded with curiosity. 'Ya solo nandimi.' Meaning I agreed.

I recalled my meeting with Fortune Man.

The next day when Franco and OK Jazz left Kisumu amid chaos, we had not been paid. I left Uncle to grapple with the greedy promoters and it took weeks before I saw the cheque and when I saw it, the amount shocked me.

I cast my sight on the European Tour. Things were taking shape. The original contract with the African Dawn called for our appearance for three weeks. If we increased business they would keep us longer. They were negotiating to have us perform in the Philip Morris, Heineken, and Camel Jazz Festivals. They sought my opinion about it. We agreed. Uncle and the band were ecstatic. It was then that I had an inspiration. I had in mind to record an album or two in UK and make use of their sophisticated studio equipment.

I called Uncle; we were all in agreement with only one minor problem of having the tour extended. Uncle kind of laughed, said he was happy that things were going so well. Said that he had already talked to Kabs asked for more money and African Dawn had agreed to pay in case the tour went beyond three weeks.

That afternoon, the band was sitting at our usual table in the coffee bar of KS Resort. I explained the extended tour. That we probably would be on the road for at least one month. The boys looked rather forlorn as they realized that we were going to leave within a couple of days.

Then KSK returned.

He told me he wanted to re-occupy his position of vice-president and help me make my dreams come true. I had some words to say to him. 'You know, KSK, I respect you but your prostitution is not good for your career. You know you don't have the means to re-establish Delta Force. You cannot record at Lakeshore as long as I am alive. But you can work for me. You and I come from a long way. Remember the days we used to eat half bread with water in Kondele? You know me? I am eager to cut off small bands posing competition for me here in Kisumu. You can come and work for me or you can leave town.'

KSK looked glum, he nodded.

The next night we were told that the VOK General Service was going to do an interview with Uncle and me through its weekly *Wajue Wanamuziki* radio program. The interview was to be part of a promotional feature highlighting and promoting our tour of Europe.

The interview went well and on Saturday, it was in Daily Nation's *Pop Scene.*

4.

In July, the first European headline tour had started. It was the first time I had been outside the borders of Kenya, it was the first time we had flown in a plane. The KLM plane touched down at Frankfurt Airport at about 7am. We were really excited to land in the fourth country in Europe and the first foreign country we were visiting. There was the hustle and confusion of disembarking into a new land, into a new environment. The day was dreary and raining in Frankfurt, Germany. The immigration was surprised, asked what kind of group this was. The band was 18-piece with six dancers, singers Mawazo, Ayo, Biggy, and Mzee Frank; guitarists Tégé Zoba, Mo Thwaka, Kayembe Flavien; drummers KSK and Pajos, and saxophonists Tom-Tom and trumpetist Kasule Mopero. The climate was quite pleasant hovering about 10 to 18 degrees Celsius. Outside the airport, Miruka Obange was waiting to receive us as well as preparing us for an unforgettable travel experience. He was a 6-foot-tall man who wore his hair in dreadlocks and turned heads whenever he entered a room. We reached Frankfurt Hauptbahnof (where he said his ex-wife lived) in about 20 minutes. After breakfast and a few hours of random conversations, we headed out to do local walk-about around downtown Frankfurt. This being the first foreign city I visited, I loved it. It was clean and gloomy with rain occasionally washing it over and over even in summer. I was able to appreciate more than a few things in the city, the best part being the architecture. All roadside restaurants were small and sold turkey and were overcrowded by neat old men reading huge newspapers and smoking pipes. Biggy quickly discovered that drugs and European women were within easy reach. Tégé found some cool Dutch wax print shirts, and whilst we were walking around, there was a lady with a microphone and a camera man in the street, asking people to say things in German and English that was written on a board, and filming them. Well Mo suckered right into that one, while the rest of us gave it a quick swerve.

We had an early morning the following day, as we had reservations made on the train to Amsterdam. It was about 550 kms from Frankfurt and the train covered the distance in about 4 hours. The Europeans in the trains had never seen so many thuggish-looking black people and somehow race came into the picture and into conversations. Ignore them, Miruka told us in Kiswahili. He explained that the train could hit a top speed of about 300kmph more than a few times and it was quite a comfortable ride with the first class tickets he had booked for us. We reached Amsterdam at around noon. After a delayed visit to the Tourist Information Centre (with a long line of freaking tourists!), we quickly put down a high-level agenda for the day.

I found Amsterdam to be dirtier than I imagined after seeing Frankfurt. It could have been a lot neater. I, for sure, did not expect people to pee on the roads like they did in Nairobi. As much as the city was clumsy, it still had an inexplicable charm to it. Blame it on the unstoppable tourists or the undying activities happening in the city or perhaps the numerous canals that acted as veins to the city. Miruka warned us about racism. Said this city, like all European cities (except London) could be very scary for black people. He said there was a fifty-fifty chance something really bad could happen to you because of your skin colour.

So we stuck together and started off visiting some customary nice sites, buildings, museums, which (in my opinion) were so-so. In the afternoon our destination was Uttrecht, a city in Holland near Amsterdam, was where we were going to be accommodated for the first seven days of the tour. After almost 2 hours, we reached there by night. Miruka's sponsor and partner for the

Amsterdam tour, Mr. Claudius took over. He was a publicist and musicologist who ran a recording studio, Altstadt, and brought foreign bands to Holland during summer. He took us to Altstadt, his home studio. It was nice and spacious with all facilities and accommodated eighteen men and women comfortably. Before having dinner we sat in a large rehearsal room and Mr. Claudius explained to us that he didn't expect a dismal performance like the one he got from the South African band he brought in last year. He had listened to some of our albums but he had to see us in action. He explained he wanted us to perform in Holland, Belgium, Germany, Spain and Ireland. He was taking this summer show seriously and he had printed T-shirts, caps and posters. He wanted us to keep the shows typically African. Thus we set up did a mock performance.

Next day he took us to the local radio known as Hot Spot FM and we did extended interviews on the program *Werk* and had our music played. Ayo appeared sick, was vomiting and had a fever. So I sat with her in Mr. Cladius's car while Miruka's car followed, then the mini bus carrying the rest of the band. There was one place where hookers did their business in boats anchored in a canal. Even on this Sunday morning, there were some for the business. My men made their picks and flirted and laughed. Then we went to a picturesque castle on a beautiful canal side. Later on, we went to see the real landmarks of Holland. Wind mills. I was excited to see two big and beautiful wind mills near a canal. Unfortunately it was not working. Ayo took lots of photos.

Our extensive tour begun at the Paradiso Venue. There had been no advance publicity of our appearance. The only thing we had seen was a small sign at the entrance which said 'African Folk Music from Kenya in the lounge at 7:00 PM.'

We had a very eclectic repertoire and I was surprised at the large number of Africans in attendance. Lots of Kenyans in attendance were excited and spoke to us in Kiswahili. I explained to the band that I wanted us to put an experience through one of the most exciting and energetic acts ever seen in this city. We first warmed the crowds with everything from gospel numbers to some American soul and jazz and African traditional music. World music had now become a marketable commodity, so coming from Africa made us part of it. Someone requested 'some Paul Simon' and even though we were playing rumba standards we wanted to oblige them. Yes, we did play some numbers from Paul Simon's *Graceland*. Ayo and Biggy gave an exuberant interpretation of 'Under African Skies.' I had personally never played any Simon's tunes, but his music wasn't exactly technically demanding on the lead and bass. So I went along with it. We made it through what I thought was a pretty decent renditions of 'Diamonds on The Soles of Their Shoes,' and 'You Can Call Me Al,' and Mawazo sang pretty well. Simon's songs were pretty relaxed and laid-back, definitely not what you would call lively. At the end of the first set, a middle-aged woman (who evidently was not the requester) came up and said, with what seemed like genuine exasperation and no humor, 'Play something *faster*, guys! We're not dead yet! Play us some reggae.' It was as though she was offended that we were trying to bore her to sleep with slow music. One of us could have said 'Excuse me, Madame, but that we are not a reggae band,' but I think we were all basically too stunned to speak.

During the second part of our show, we launched straight into rumba, benga and soukous and it appeared we made a connection with the crowd.

At the beginning of the night it was obvious the crowd had been drinking quite a bit. After about 3 or 4 songs, they moseyed up to me (while we are playing) and tried to dance like our dancers. We launched into set 6 and after 2 songs we had the place hopping. Almost everyone was on the floor dancing. We kept up the momentum and moved from one up-tempo dance favorite to another, and Mr. Cladius drunkenly leaned on my guitar and said, 'Play a slow song next.' Ok, so we played a slow song: 'Anyango Nyar Nam,' and towards the end of that song he told me, 'you have to play slow songs for the rest of the night.'

He was asking for almost two full sets of ballads... I had the answer. Most of Ayo's songs from our recent *Wend Osote* album were slow songs laced with rumba elements.

Ayo's performance stole the night at Paradiso Venue...to taste her voice and realize she truly had that intangible quality that wrapped around the audience and enveloped them into her world. Her songs evoked thought and a kind of painful bliss that made even the most apprehensive listener of girl-guitar-acoustica stand and take notice. Was it Urban Benga? What was it? Was it rumba? No one even knew. If you saw Ayo live it was even harder to define as she really beat you to her own rhythm, literally. She stopped, gazed out into the distance as if accessing some cosmic information, and then continued on her melodic stream. Watching her was like viewing someone through their bedroom window when they were uninhibited, open, and honest.

We had the dance floor packed during the fast songs, and about three quarters packed for the slow songs. Later on that night, Miruka told me that he was dancing with a different woman each song and doing his best to grope, and that was easier to do when the song was slow. We played other more ballads, and then something mid tempo—the dance floor was packed again. Mr. Claudius came right up to me and said, 'That's too fast, play slow songs.' I said that I would see what we could do, but we didn't know enough ballads to play a set and a half worth.

We took a break and Ayo excused herself, said she was not feeling well. So we played the next few sets without her. At the end of it, I went to Ayo's room and found her on the floor of the toilet retching and coughing throwing up. I said it was the weather and dismissed it as such.

She shook her head. 'I'm pregnant, Dinos,' she said.

5.

From Paradiso Venue, we moved to The Concertgebouw and Odeon Theatre in Amsterdam. We later played for 100,000 people in open-air music festivals throughout the city. We played a really popular upscale dance numbers for the remaining three nights of our Amsterdam date. Word had spread around the city about this majestic and energetic folk group from Africa and our shows were jammed every night and the owners got a lot of business.

Crazy things happened. On a number of occasions a girl would come in and flash their new boob job to the band. But our last night was extra special. Two ladies came in and one proceeded to put on quite a show, one displaying her new tattoos to us and she even flashed her 'other goods' to the crowd. But it was the other girl that really got my attention. As the leader and solo guitarist, I was upfront leading the band through a number, when she came up on stage, faced me (her back to the crowd), and lifts her skirt to reveal her pantyless crotch. Yeah, there were witches all over the world, not only Africa. Just imagine. She started riding my leg! Ayo stepped up and pried her off my leg. We all saw her naked crotch before Ayo pushed her away into the crowd. We didn't miss a beat but the band (and me) was just awestruck.

My experience with the real Amsterdam became a wide-eyed wonder of the year. The band had managed to connect spectacularly with the Dutch fans and it was Ayo that they were screaming loudest for. It was from this leg of the tour that a further the first live album appeared. The album titled *Victoria ODW – Live in Amsterdam* came out on the small Dutch label, Marlestone and was recorded at the Altstadt.

The tour continued to UK. The prestigious Royal Albert Hall in Kensington was the first stop. The evening started very late, in part because the promoters were clearly waiting for the hall to fill with fans. By the time the show begun, well after midnight, a nice sized crowd had formed and we had about 30,000 London fans. The show collided with the annual two-night African music festival. London was a beehive of activity and, like Amsterdam, it frightened me. For once it was hotter than our Kisumu and dirtier than I had imagined. The city was *en fete* with the rough and tumble of football terrace hooliganism, which was also flowing on to the streets during summer.

We met in the lounge immediately after dropping our bags in our rooms, Miruka handed us over to the local promoter and his staff who were super helpful. So over and above, it was a fabulous evening. Our tour manager here was an intelligent-looking impeccably dressed middle-aged English woman who introduced herself as Pam and made sure we were comfortable. She was rather tall being just over three inches taller than me, trim, proper, and a little strict. She sat us down on the longue and explained the dos-and-don'ts. Then she was charming enough to crack the champagne. There was the usual sound check and dinner routine, and it was nice to see that Royal Albert Hall had a good size stage. The dance hall was awesome and, unlike Amsterdam, things looked professional here and the instruments were superb. It was like somebody thought we were a big band like Franco and OK Jazz. Once we had finished sound checking, we were driven back to the hotel where we found Miruka waiting for us with some Dutch journalists. We were conducted through some interviews and KSK filled in many questions.

When asked to define our music, the obvious answer I gave was benga; I didn't say we were developing it.

Many questions pissed me off, like 'Why is your music so Zaïrean sounding?'

I normally expected this annoying question and I normally had a short answer, rehearsed like a nursery school rhyme. 'Zaïrean music and benga both use the guitar as the driving force. We derived our music from the eight-string *nyatiti* while they derived theirs from the *likembe*. That is the reason for the similarity, mainly. We have developed our music over the years by borrowing styles and techniques from them and they too have borrowed from us. They have our bass while we have their melody in the solo guitar and rhythm guitar style. In benga instruments follow singers while in Zaïrean style, singers follow

310

instruments. There are similarities and there are differences. Benga and rumba are two styles but we are all Africans and we live in the same environment and share similar circumstances. That we sound alike cannot be a misnomer because we draw our inspirations from the same environment. We encounter the same problems and we sing about the same things mostly.'

Then we were rushed off to lunch. We hit the stage at six. Pajos was trying to get a balance on the drum seat for best performance; it was important that he be seen while not beating the rest of us into submission. Instrumentalists Tégé and Flavien adjusted their strings against my middle C. By the time we had adjusted everything, we barely had time to catch a breath before starting our session. The singers and the dancers bounded in from the rows of dressing booths.

We were made to understand this venue had been made famous when Franco and OK Jazz performed here two years ago. Many African students throughout Britain had bought tickets and were arriving here in coaches and by trains for this Sunday show. After a short conference, we figured we had better do a warm-up first, to try and draw in an audience. We really didn't have a warm-up routine to fall back on, but we didn't want to start our choreographed performance without a good audience.

His usual print shirts riddled with abstracts of falling elephants, Tégé Zoba, introduced the band. The elephant repeats on his shirt were like red pins and a deluge of Katarikawe's dreams. Even before his words sank in, Pajos struck the drums with a sound like exploding bombs and went off into packed ethnic percussion. We started off with the high tempo 'Earthy Sounds of Africa,' a traditional drum-sax-and-flute-driven eclectic dance musical where our dancers were eager to stage live ensemble variations. The costumes varied from sublime to outrageous, constantly resurrecting vintage styles yet still showing fashion for a modern expression. Soon I was chording along and we played low-keyed primal rhythms, fused with the earthy, drum-driven tones of Africa while our dancers did energetic dances. KSK had tambourines and Biggy and Mzee Frank had shakers, giving this number a real tingling *ojawa* sound. We created a high energy, sensual yet elegant atmosphere and we soon inspired, uplifted and connected every audience to themselves and to us.

The place was warm and noisy and filling up. By the end of the second dance musical, it was spilling over. The dancers had seduced the audience into immediate connection with the performance, stimulating all the senses of African magic as it pulled the Londoners from the mundane world into one of exalted reverie and passion.

We were ready start our show now, the traditional dance was designed to bring the audience to the same level as they were now. But first we let the saxophonists Tom-Tom and Mopero get a bit of the spotlight during the musical by playing out some jazzy charades. Then with a raised hand, I signaled the start of our show and the band did a breakneck segue into a spirited number featuring throbbing bass and leaping guitars. All the four guitars came alive in action: me, Flavien Tégé and Mo. On this number, Mawazo ya Pesa made use of his vocal prowess, ably assisted by Ayo.

The orchestration was in full gear with a fast-tempoed, biting benga. 'Hera Mar Mbese,' merged into 'Anyango Nyar Nam'. Other songs followed in sequence. It was a very skillfully created piece of material. It was also a piece of material that we loved to do. The rhythm held the thing together, softly, masterfully. My solo was fast and screaming, while faintly in the background, the bass could be heard played with a bow. Occasionally the bright tinkle of a triangle sparkled against the almost velvety sounds. Tégé had, with great finesse, woven the melody, then the tempo of 'Anyango Nyar Nam' so that the piece transformed into the mournful strains of 'Lek' to the joyful, excitement of 'Kit Maro Otama.'

The piece was almost fifteen minutes long, ending with Tégé jumping up and down as his finger hit every string on the guitar, with Pajos Mwana N'Dilli ricocheting from one percussion surface to another. Mo was plucking and pounding his bass with solid energy. My body melded into my guitar as my entire being literally rocked with vitality. We could feel the intensive power being projected from the audience as we all became a single vibrating, then resonant entity.

The show was a good one, though we had a few technical problems as Pajo's bottom snare drum skin broke, and later he had a bit of a monitor problem mid set, but these were soon overcome with a bit of banter to the audience, and it was a good show. It was a very enthusiastic audience, and we noticed on this tour that a lot of young people were in the audience which was great.

The last note had been played. I looked over at Ayo. She momentarily caught my gaze and flashed me a grin. Her plaited hair had been flying all over the place and beaded locks clung to her face. Her skin glowed with perspiration.

She stepped forward for the last chorus line and Mawazo put an arm over her shoulder. 'Nataka Baba,' she announced, before resuming singing. The message was quickly relayed among the instrumentalists and Pajos pounded us into the fast Kiswahili number. 'Nataka Baba' is a song Ayo loved because she had written it for me. Hearing her throat shredding vocal work, I couldn't imagine she was soon to be mother to my child. It was normally long, wordy and expressive but during live shows, we normally reduced the lyrics to a few verses of the chorus before guitars took over on long dance scores.

At the onset of *sebene*, Ayo moved to the front and dazzled the house, enthralled the crowd with wild sexy gyrations of her hips. The hall lit up with a rowdy exaltation of a strip club seduction. She began with a relaxed provocative brew of elaborate sinuous routines, sensually throwing her arms and legs in alternating sequences to the beat. The beat piked up and she was rotating her waist all the way down and up. The crowd loved this and the roar was deafening. When the snares did a quick hit and she twitched, when the cymbals smashed and she jerked, when the drums rolled she dropped on her buttocks. Hard, so hard she could have broken a bone. Her movements of hard tit juggling and wild hip gyrations were all framed within the tight kaleidoscopic structure of an African ritual dance. We all saw beautiful, bawdy energy that had never existed before in her. She was hard and hot in it for a good fifteen minutes. The amalgamation of energy, technique and culture created a groundbreaking style of dance primal, visceral, sexy, yet also triumphantly African. She appeared to be in a trance, I thought I saw her slip and stutter and was going for a pretty bad fall but Mawazo leaped in and caught her. She could have had a bad fall and got a bad twist on her leg but it was covered as part of a crazy dance routine. Mawazo stooped a little and picked her up, held her close. I was standing close and the fretboard of my Les Paul jutted out in front. Ayo half turned and brushed her body against me, my arm twined around her neck and her lips brushed my ears. Faintly I caught the words. 'I could've hurt our baby.' None in the band would have any idea that she ever said those words to me above the blare. Now I believed her.

Audiences love drama and cabarets of this kind. The audience was on its feet in a veritable roar of excitement; not in approval of our work, but as part of it. We were drained. I looked at Tégé, his shirt was soaked. Pajos was dripping. Ayo was all smiles.

The night was madness, madness. Madness. Four hours of Victoria was never enough. Tour manager Pam and Miruka were all smiles. She said we take a break. The gig was working, I could see. I only wondered what the British press was going to write. Victoria had seized their audience right in front of their noses and I doubted the journalists would be too happy about it. I was told the last concert in this venue by a Swedish rock band was a flop. And here we were, an unknown band of African savages lighting up this place with our frighteningly private music and lyrics they couldn't understand.

314

Twenty minutes later, however, the audience was still baying for an encore and African Dawn weren't going to go into that. Not that Miruka cared a feather—this was simply the business and everyone took their chances and gave it their best shot. Eventually, after 40 minutes, African Dawn personnel had to go on and try to swing the audience back. Miruka listened for a while from the wings and thought the crowd was a lot eager for more. He had no doubt they were going to hear more. Royal Albert Hall crew was a little less cooperative. Their management asked the band to shorten their set—already, the politics was starting to undercut them. Pam insisted they had a contract and they'll play right up to the last minute. Any beef about their set and she'll have African Dawn's lawyers crawling all over them. But African Dawn had to eat crow and accept that the venue management were bound by London City Council license and was going to blow them off the stage for night anyway.

The applause rolled behind us as we made our way offstage. Normally, there'd be a twenty minute interval before the headline for no greater purpose than to allow the crowd to forget about the last act. We took this time to sign autographs and have pictures taken with the hall crew, plus exchange pleasantries and contacts with our curtain raiser, a local 5-piece rock band called Razors who incidentally did a fine set for a young bunch of lads. We willed around pouring with sweat signing more autographs and shaking hands with African students and talking to Kenyans in Kiswahili. Ayo was absolutely ecstatic and hugged and kissed everyone. Then it was quickly off into the van and back to the hotel. Time to change and wind down before the usual review.

Back at the hotel we were met by a few fans wanting autographs and a guitar signed, so we did this. Then some members of the band, Mo and Co., hit the bar in celebratory mode, and others went to their rooms. Pam gave me a number and I made a call to a doctor to see Ayo because of her knee, but it was late in the night, and he would only be able to see her in the morning. I took Ayo to her room. The hotel had some pain killers, ointment and bandage. So I put her in the tub for a hot bath, put the ointment and bandage on, gave her a couple of pain killers, and tucked her in bed.

I rejoined Pam in the lobby.

'Great show, Mr. Otis Dundos,' she said as I sat.

I nodded and shrugged.

'You came out locked and loaded.'

I shrugged again.

'Mr. Otis, I didn't know you could do that African finger picking style for all those long hours. How are you going to get through the tour playing that fast? You mind your hands, pal, and don't tear up your fingers.'

I held up my fingers at her. 'I am a seasoned player.'

'Not ready for the Hammersmith frame yet?' she asked.

'Sounds fine,' I said, grinning. Hammersmith Palais de Danse was our next venue here in London.

We sat talking. In a quasi manner she couldn't understood musicians' motivations: there *was* an unseen force putting them all into doing the narly things they wouldn't normally do. She was quite well-spoken with fine English manners and she told me about London and the English. I had always loved English history and she was delighted to know that. She was surprised that I was only twenty-five and had my career roaring. To which I asked her age: thirty-four. I looked away so I wouldn't scare her if my eyes clouded. Wait, why would I care if she saw my eyes cloud in front of her? Her age should never concern me. Why was I becoming shy or self-conscious? It suddenly occurred to me that what I was feeling was what I normally felt when in the presence of Riana. Honestly it was hard to explain what thirty minutes out of the life of someone like Pam meant. She was born in Rochdale, Greater Manchester. She told me that she spent several years working as a jobbing model and it was not until 1978, when she was 24 that a New York agent signed her up and she decided to go fully into modeling. She worked in the US and did journalism and public relations. She returned to UK with her husband ,in

1983 and worked as a freelance journalist for a while until her daughter was born. Then she developed interest in music and joined African Dawn as tours publicity manager.

It was amazing to see how energetic she was, the personal edge to everything she said was what inspired me as an artist. She asked me to tell her about myself and Africa. I told I knew very little about Africa and was just getting to know Kenya. I told her about my music, my family, my surroundings in Kisumu, my life, my dreams, my fumblings, my... my celebration of life, freedom, and fulfillment. All that. Me. I felt her emotions, sensations. Immediately she knew how to connect with me. She offered me an opportunity to gloat/share/ wonder with her. She looked up at me and I was startled by her eyes, they were bright blue. We carried an honest, funny, and sassy conversation about ourselves, England, Kenya and music till about one in the morning.

In those hours she stripped down to her most primitive level, you'd think we'd become wonderfully clear, instinctive, perfectly functioning animals. Suddenly I became utterly polite, listened. I was just a wide-eyed African boy who had worked so hard at playing guitar and running my band ruthlessly and recording prolifically till I found myself here in London. I hadn't gotten much out of high school. I still had a long way to go and talking with intelligent people increased my thirst for knowledge and exposure.

Presently she yawned and said, 'I have to leave you now.'

'Thanks,' I said, 'I need plenty of rest.'

'The young African body not as frisky as it was?' she chuckled. Then she pulled a fast one. 'Tell me, I notice things. Your female colleague... what's her name?'

'Ayo.' I sat up.

'How does she put up with an artist like you? I never would.'

'We get along.' I offered a meager smile.

'You do?' she asked, then, sensing she was sending me an odd question of some sort, she gulped and pursed her lips.

'She's really reliable,' I replied. 'Very reliable!' I added, pointedly. 'She's an artist too.'

'Reliable artist? Good grief! Otis, dear, trust me you don't need an artist for a lover. As an artist you need too much love than a fellow artist can give. Artists are selfish beings.' She got to her feet. 'Make sure you limber up the stairs and do press-ups for your wrists and fingers.'

'I will, Ma'am.'

'Ma'am?' She frowned, eyes narrowed, for a moment, then she shrugged, turning to me and grinning. 'I just can't get used to it. Just call me Pam for now, huh?'

'Sure, uhm, Pam.'

'See you for breakfast, what, about ten, eleven?'

'Sure. Thanks.'

She put her hands on my shoulders and kissed my cheek; she was almost my height in her heels.

I made phone call to Angelou to talk to my son, Junior. I also called my parents and talked with Mama and my father.

Victoria ODW weren't exactly the talk of the town the next morning, but it was clear, the buzz had started. *The Guardian* wanted to do a story and sent a reporter around. TV24 wanted a 10-minute video of the gig and an interview with Ayo. Sales of our albums were steadily growing and it was expected to chart within the next day or so.

I knocked on Ayo's door to take her down for breakfast, and she had a slight limp, said her leg was feeling a little better after a good rest. The doctor came in to examine her early in the morning and said that she may need an operation. They put her knee in a soft cast for 4 days and she was able to walk okay, and stand up on stage, so she was going to make it through the tour fine.

I picked up the new OK Jazz album, *Special 30 Ans par le Poète Simaro et le Grand Maître Franco,* from the hotel's music store and had been playing it all morning. On the cover I loved the picture of Grand Master Luambo Makiadi Franco sitting looking jovial, well-fed and smiling together with his vice president, Le Poète Lutumba Simaro. Now what wouldn't I give to be in that chair!

The album presented rumba odemba at its finest. The sound was grand, big and exquisitely sweet. Excellent guitars and barrage of all talents existing in OK Jazz: the horns, guitars, drums, vocals. In guitar I could hear Gerry Dialungana's hard-finger signature tune, Simaro's trademark captivating rhythm and Dizzy's tingling mi-solo licks. And I also picked out Mantuika and 'Nono' Nedule Papa Noel. On the vocals I easily picked out Madillu, Malage de Lugendo, Kiesse, Pépé Ndombe Opetum, Lokombe, Djo Mpoyi and Kikame. I was not sure whether it was Decca or Makabi on bass, but I definitely picked out Makabi's style on 'Testament Ya Bowule,' while 'Tala Merci Ba Pesaka Na Mbua' and 'Vaccination Ya Ba Soucis' definitely had Decca. My favourite was 'Aminata Na Zangi Visa' which brought the best (perhaps) in Lokombe's fresh, high-spirited vocal score and had the rare participation of Djo Mpoyi.

The album was a bedlam of exquisite rumba variety and orchestral discipline in the grand big band style. OK Jazz had managed to give us another masterpiece that was heavy on emotion with very neat classic arrangements. Franco's participation in this one was zero, so his attention-grabbing photo on the sleeve was just for laughs. Probably just the big name. I knew the whole project was composed, arranged and directed by Simaro. His touch and sound just shone through on every song beautifully. It will be played many a time in my room for sure on this tour.

6.

Hammersmith Palais. We got ready and headed to this place. And, like Royal Albert, found it mobbed. Mobbed that we really had to manoeuvre ourselves to get on and off the stage with security in yellow jackets onstage providing barricades. I looked at the mass of people who were here to see us and felt butterflies in my stomach. Must have been more than two thousand! Hammersmith was to pose a chemical romance for the band. It was spectacularly diva-esque: it was like all half naked young English women were there. I heard whistles and close by were two young girls waving and smiling. I would have just blown it off, but one of the chicks caught my attention. She was wearing these tight jeans that could have passed for being painted on. And a halter top that had this metal ring that went around her neck holding the top up. After a smoky start with the traditional dance musical, I went over, followed by Flavien. We talked for a bit; gave off a few laughs, a few smiles, and they wanted to know our names. After the introductions, we got back on stage as the traditional dance ended and we got the second set going.

The band crashed in, and the pastel pinks and blues of the starry stage backdrop turned a stark black and white. Biggy Tembo sauntered in, sporting a trilby, scarf, wax print shirt and corduroy trousers: a bit Jazz Age. We were doing hard rumba number real cool and vintage style with Biggy pouring out his heart over the speakers. The familiar hit 'Ja Nyadhi' boasted warm horns, and and explored the slightly controversial age-old narrative (well, revolutionary to men) that African women would commandeer a man with frustrations till he pursues pleasure in another woman. It was steady, groovy and grinding with steady up-tempo beat and everyone was dancing real cool. The two girls were dancing too close and getting real naughty. Wasn't long before the Tégé and drummer KSK were watching too.

We got the second set done and Mawazo Ya Pesa with his blazer and tie entered flanked by Biggy Tembo. They entered walking slowly with Ayo in their midst. The hall lit up. Ayo, apparently, was the one people want to see. Too bad she had a bad leg and she had a laminate. And so she wasn't quite going to nail the neurosis or eccentricity the crowd might have been after. Hammersmith wasn't going to see much action from her. The action man, instead, was Mawazo. Tonight's set was going to

draw from his bulging kitbag of hits. We launched into the new
song 'Ukipanda Bei Uta Shuka Bei!' in which he executed a nifty
little dance routine with the rotund male backing singers Biggy
and Mzee Frank. When Mawazo hit high notes, his voice had the
power to bring the hairs on your arms to attention. I gave the
somewhat excessive guitar solos. One by one the crowd twigged.
It was a chemical romance! Cue delirium. People went absolutely
apeshit. Only different from before. As we launched into our
mopus operandi 'Kisumu Girl', faces beamed and when the parts of
'Kisumu Girl' were replaced by 'London Girl' joy and excitement
flooded the place. Then came the flirty 'Maria,' and Bado
Nakupenda', whose new head-banging direction prompted a little
segue into Wanyika's 'Sina Makosa' as a coda.

What really clinched Mawazo's star status wasn't all this,
though. Wasn't his baby-oil smeared chest. It was excellent that
he had great abs, and he certainly had the right to wear his shiny
jackets wide open: it was the way he moved. Mawazo could walk
eight or ten kilometers on stage during a single four-hour show.
Even when he was standing still, he was dancing, measuring every
twitch, shrugging and dirty-laughing, moving in exquisite
staccato. Not everyone who mithered into the microphone of
Victoria ODW should have been expected to impress with the
vigour of a Mawazo.

We had assessed the mood and realized that what worked
here were songs with twilight ambience. New songs came thick
and fast; 'Le Le Le!' (a bruising power ballad), 'African Woman'
and the disturbingly saccharine 'Syphilis Cure' ('I'm still soggy
from No Cure,' crooned Mawazo). Then the room twigged en
masse to the faintly sinister 'Guok Motho (Dead Dog).' Slim Ali's
'You Can Do It' was well received; Mawazo gave it a sunny-day
one-dimension-ality.

Next Biggy Tembo roamed the stage like Serengeti's angriest
rhino, doing elephant dances, adjusting the band's amplifiers. He
broke his microphone and got a new one by dismantling a piece
of the drum kit.

'That was amazing,' chirped Pam at the end of four groggy hours. 'They're going to be the biggest band in the world,' someone remarked. Disturbingly Miruka was nowhere to be seen. Palais promotions and events coordinator spoke to the jeering crowd. 'Come October, there'll be no stopping the march of The Black Parade. We will invite this sensational band from Africa here again. Victoria ODW!'

My ears were ringing. As the band mooched offstage, a punk in a cream suit struggled onstage and grabbed the microphone to make a speech on behalf of the Palais's loyal supporters: 'Get out here and play us some music!' Pam nodded at Palais officials who in turn nodded at me. Victoria ODW returned for an encore, but seemingly inspired by the invasion, the stage was now swarming with yellow jackets. KSK would not tolerate it. 'Is this a security area or a stage,' he barked, sarcastically. To the band, he shouted, 'Let's get out of here.' And he walked offstage. 'Nigger,' someone shouted in the crowd. I panicked. Some fans were spouting awful racist nonsense. Television cameras caught that. I looked around and saw Pam with her mouth hanging. You got that wrong, KSK. This wasn't a security area.

To me, our show at Hammersmith was very successful artistically. We offered vintage rumba, we galvanised it into the premier sex-charged African savage energy like what we did at Royal Albert yesterday. Here in the Palais we seemed to have our version unsexed, preserved in aspic, served with *pili pili*.

I was glad, I was glad, I was glad.

Laugh, laugh, laugh.

With a flourish.

Next? Dublin, Ireland. We arrived at the hotel just in time for breakfast, so that was great. Our hotel was the Westbury, tucked back behind Grafton Street. Everyone piled off the bus, and there was an amazing array of bus heads at the breakfast tables, myself included, but this did not faze the staffs, who were most helpful in cooking us fresh eggs etc. After that it was time to wonder around the city, find a girl to seduce, get drunk, get a bit of extra shuteye. We walked around Dublin; we were just roaming around the streets. Tégé went looking for his lethal shirts. Biggy probably was looking for drugs and prostitutes. I couldn't find a mango or a banana. So I sat with Ayo at a roadside restaurant eating Irish stew, bacon and cabbage.

Pam found me and handed me a photocopy of the newspaper ad that she had prepared for the Dublin concert. I wanted to be in a quiet room with a woman, to make consummation. But I had to go into the city to find a music shop to get some guitar spare parts. The volume pot on my number one guitar needed changing, and also I wanted to pick up a few other things that we needed to keep the show running smoothly. Ayo's leg was feeling a little better, so we went out for a walk around the shops. Well a hobble or limp around the shops more like it. Still it was good her knee was feeling good enough to do this. As the hotel was literally in the middle of the shopping centre, we went in search of baby's clothing for her unborn child.

Five minutes down the road and bingo we had them. Whilst out, KSK came looking for me with a message from Pam, saying the original plans had changed and the goalposts moved. We had to go down earlier than planned. So it was back to the hotel for a quick shower, down to the gig, and stay down, as it was 20km away. At the sound check a big cheer went up, as Miruka had flown over from London with my new Carparelli guitar, much needed guitar picks, a fresh stock of merchandising with items that were running low, and some tye'n'dye stage shirts for the band and myself that we had ordered from a company in Scotland.

The venue was The Baggot Inn and we were on stage at 8pm. We went for the sound check and stayed around just case. The sound check went well; it was a huge hanger of a hall, so the sound was probably going to be bouncing around off the walls and we would need some people in to soak it up with dance. There was support act, and luckily we did not have to worry, as there were enough people there to soak up the sound, and it was a most enjoyable concert. The band wasted no time in creating havoc with harmony rhythms, screaming solos, polyrythmic mi-solos, and manic take on vocals and dances with as much a build into the primal fury of rumba, benga and soukous. Focused and relentless throughout, every song barely seemed to register a couple minutes before ceasing and eclipsing into another. Infectious and groovy throughout, the crowd steadily grew across the course of the set, partly because of pure sweetness of African melody, partly due to what was to come. The band was all in good form, and there were lots of smiles around the stage, which was always good; and to be honest, it was infectious; as we saw the audience react with us. After the show it wasn't long before we went back to the hotel for quick shut-eye as we had a 7.30am wake up with an 8.30am leave.

We stayed in Dublin for an extra day. KSK and I had a session at Dublin's Windmill Lane Studios getting our concert tapes in order, making use of the equipment and the engineers. Finally we had a master tape that I called *Dublin Show*.

In the afternoon, Pam took me into the city to see the zoo, Book of Kells, Temple Bar, St. Stephen's Green and Grafton Street. There were lots of nooks and crannies and Dublin depressed me to the bone. Probably I was just homesick. Pam hated the place too, hated the Irish.

We spent the evening at a Travelodge drowning warm Irish lager and she was gazing longingly at me over her glass. I didn't need to put any effort into seducing her; there was tension, a fire. I told her about Ayo and she said she didn't care. I sensed a frustrated libido, I tried not to sympathize. I smiled at her; it was difficult, though, to read this English woman's face, she generally beheld a rather stoic face. But there were flashes in her eyes and a quivering on the corners of her lips. She was game for it. We finally got drunk kissing and over-the-clothes fumbling. When we kissed, it was a kiss to write home about. Neither of us cared about the foul Irish lager breath, or the prying eyes of white people in that bar. We just felt each other through our lips and experienced it. She reluctantly pulled away from my lips, got up and persuaded the man at the front desk to let us have a room for an hour for four pounds. Instead of feeling like I had satisfied some need to make love to a white woman, I felt a bit empty and seedy.

7.

Given exhaustion that reached a near bursting point, I have to admit the idea of three marathon weeks of Victoria ODW music wasn't exactly enticing and perhaps much to the chagrin of some members of the band: this tour was wearing and tearing us.

I felt it possible that cutting loose and skipping out altogether and going back home (also admittedly, I discovered I was not a long distance runner and was yet to learn the art of keeping alive being on the road for many weeks) was what my body and mind needed.

Miruka would have none of it, 'You have to cover it!' he roared, refusing to let me skip out so we hunkered down to Belfast, steeled our resolve, and were as prepared as we could be.

When the band took the stage, I let Flavien play solo guitar while I let loose in a room-crushing 'Demented Aggression' with Pam in some mature lovemaking. Flavien carried the solo guitar part very well and covered me good. For someone unversed in the ways of Victoria, the transition from newer and slower 'serious' songs to older, frantic, and seemingly 'campy' songs was a fascinating one to behold. Across the fifteen-song set list; however, most of it sort of bled together at times, regardless of era, the hilarious banter that introduced 'Pili Pili' and 'Kisumu Girl' being standouts, along with encore staples 'Nashikitika' and 'Ruka Ukuta.' Though largely inaudible in the din of the venue, the bass playing of Mo was particular feast for the gig, though long documented, it was nonetheless fantastic.

Meeting the members of Vijana Jazz from Tanzania provided an escape. We got real chummy and sat sipping pints in a Belfast hotel bar. We got so tipsy and so noisy the gaping Irish might have thought—if they could see our faces and make nothing of our Kiswahili—we were just African musicians, abroad for work, catching up over a beer; chatting about going home, about the families, wives, partners and problems they had left behind, about the future.

Vijana Jazz was in great shape and I was happy to be in the fraternity. Singer and bandleader Hemedi Chiriku Maneti, with a solid *pamba moto hawamu ya pili* tag to him, (one that was occasionally clad-fitting for the band's malleable music) was livelier than I had ever known. That his band wasn't drawing many crowds didn't prevent him from unfurling some adventurous vocal takes, as heard on my favourite track 'Mundinde,' where he benefits greatly from back-up gang vocals of Saidi Khamisi, Gotagota, Fredy Benjamin, and spurts of melodic guitars of Shaaban Wanted and CID Shakashia including bassist Baker Semhando. Vijana Jazz (like Juwata Jazz, Bima Le, Dar International and DDC Milimani Park) functioned largely in their own sphere of rich poetic Swahili pop with strong Tanzanian recipe. Maneti had somehow crossed the ever-difficult divide between power Swahili pop and majestic rumba and had incorporated horns whose personnel, Trumpetists Mnyupe and Mawazo Hunja, and saxophonists Kimeza and Rashidi Pembe were in the tour too. Drummer Abou Semhando added progressive percussive power that completed the circle for the band. The one guy who missed this overseas outing was 'Commando' Hamza Kalala, the dynamic solo guitarist who had recently left Vijana Jazz to form his Bantu Group band. MDJ Eddie Fondo had featured him recently in his weekly program *Wajue Wanamuziki* when Vijana Jazz came to Nairobi for a series of shows promoting their latest single, 'Mama Wa Kambo.' It was revealed this was Kalala's last recording with the group.

During our last night in Belfast, Victoria ODW was staying the night and I had a room in an annex at the back of the rambling property. Ayo retired around three. The place was quiet as everyone, except Flavien and the two old men Tom-Tom and Kasule Mopero, disappeared with Irish women. Throughout the tour I had known I was hoarding a notorious bunch of men who loved flirting white women, getting good kisses, and a dramatic drunken connection, followed by a swift exit. And with the 10 gigs we'd played, the boys had the opportunity to connect with many attractive women. Flavien said it was as simple as clicking your fingers and summoning some amorous fan to your backstage tiger-printed love dungeon. I couldn't possibly enjoy myself wondering if these women who starved for sex from my men had my band's songs mentally sound tracking our foreplay. I knew, with the notoriety of virile he-goats like Mo Thwaka, a year from today a lot of European women were going to be nursing brown curly-haired babies.

I was dozing too, mainly from the effect of Irish Heinken. I'd tried reading Yeats for a while but my eyes lost their focus. After the excitement of the gig it was difficult to calm down. In years gone past he would've smoked a joint but I'd got out of the habit. So I found my way to my room. I woke suddenly to the door inching open. I looked at the clock and found it was 4am. That time was beyond unsocial. I didn't realize such an hour existed unless I was still partying. My stomach was a bit churny too; too much Heinken and lemonades probably, and the punch at the party was evil. The window was open and I could hear the sound of the wind in the branches. It will be dawn soon. I heard my front door open and close, then a few seconds later the door to my room opened. My heart beat hard. A dark figure knelt at my bedside and I could smell perfume.

I heard a woman's voice. 'Dundos?'

'Ah?'

'It's Pam. Can't sleep, I...'

She shucked her jeans, removed her shoes and jeans and sweater and tossed them on the floor. She stood very poised and calmly in pale pink 'thong' undies. Then she was inside the sheet with the agility of a cat. And she smelled clean and wondrous.

'She won't be coming in, I hope?' She was referring to Ayo. I had made it clear to her I didn't want Ayo to know about this, she could cause an ungodly upset and that would be bad for the tour.

'Don't worry about her; she is recovering from her injured leg and...what about your husband?'

'Don't ask about him,' Pam said, coldly. 'We haven't lived together for over a year.'

'Eh? You never said!'

'Why should I? He keeps shop out there in Anaheim while I pay all the bills. He screws his young starlets and leaves me the h—hhell alone. A perfect marriage!'

I kissed her and she pressed her body against mine, her arms going around me, pulling me tightly against her. Despite her raging emotions her passion surprised and even scared me a little.

Her hand slid to my buttocks and inside my shorts to grip a glute. 'I don't give a damn how well I convince you, Dundos. I'm actually relieved I don't have to go through the pretense. Like all old men, he needs the young things around to prove he's not getting old.'

She paused and sniffed, 'If you need to know, I've always wanted to settle down in a good, committed relationship with... Oh, God, spare me, Dundos? What am I saying? You'll take whatever's going and live it up because you can. You play because you love the attention, just like the rest. You've got good genes and a rare natural talent. Women flock to you and why shouldn't you enjoy yourself? Hell, if I was in your position I wouldn't hesitate to get as much action as I could manage.'

Her arms around me were out of this world, her breath gently panting in my right ear, closer to Mars than Earth. They say you cannot hear a scream in outer space, possibly because you can't think at all. I held her soft body in my arms and wondered how easy it had been for me to make love to this well-learned socialite white woman. How fast it had been. She was refined, articulate, strong, persuasive, argumentative, beautiful and she'd become my dearest, dearest friend. But after sleeping with her, I knew she was a melodramatic, romantic, and insecure thirty-four-year old. I soon found it impossible to relax in her presence, a feeling I began to resent having in 'the workplace' and behind Ayo's back. Pam was hypnotized by me, and felt weak as she watched me flex my guitar arm every moment I played harder riffs. She got a giddy feeling of excitement when I touched her. Two seconds we'd be talking and two seconds later we'd be grappling in an embrace. It happened so quickly we each took each other by surprise. I remembered turning and smiling into her face and little else following that. I figured we tripped a few memories and just ran with the script. I remembered her doing things no woman had done to me, taking me in her mouth and straddling my face so I could return the favour. I remembered Pam rising above me as she impaled herself and sank back with a sigh. Most of all, I remembered tossing her on her back as if she was a bag of spuds. She was smiling with surprise and anticipation and I held off till she begged me to not to do it so hard.

She was soft and supple and engaged me with enthusiasm. Her long nails dug into my butts and she heaved off the bed at me, amid growls and gasps. She was mindless of the noise and I couldn't have cared less. I thought to myself what if the band wasn't sleeping and, what if I thought the band would be listening in but were in fact listening, it was a fleeting thought. What if it was an open secret?

'Oh Dundos!' she howled with lust towards the climax. 'Uh, Dundos!'

I still cannot understand what draws beautiful high society women (career, class and all) into the arms and beds of musicians like us who are jerks most of the time. It happened a lot in Kenya, now Europe was even worse. Here it was madness. I am a guy with standards as a leader of men in a band, and often it kept me from getting laid, and then I usually got frustrated. It was very much my problem; I wouldn't want to blame anyone else for it. I didn't think Pam was trying to duck her responsibility for her issues, either. If I read her right, she just wanted some loving company and maybe some thoughtful discussion about the tension that cropped up between career, dignity, and libido. It was wicked hard to be firing on all three of those cylinders at once. For all the haters out there, why is that such a boring topic? It interested the hell out of me. Sometimes things aren't just meant to be. Getting some action on a whirlwind tour seemed like one of those things. Not every situation in life is conducive to getting laid. In fact, you can be unlucky and go through life in environments that aren't really helpful to finding someone. The universe works against you sometimes.

Besides, long ago before I succumbed to Ayo's seductions, I used to feel like such a creeper if I tried to hit on (and possible have sex with) a girl in the band. And it doesn't reflect on the individual women either—Ayo was probably a cool person and we could talk and have a great conversation, and I obviously admired her musical talents, but it was a line I shouldn't have crossed. You know what they say: God did not create a perfect being.

In UK now, here in Belfast, my musicians were making goddamned fools of themselves. I was witnessing flirts getting into flings and into awkward relationships. We were in London getting ready waiting for African Dawn to finish drawing up the last leg of the tour to Copenhagen and Helsinki. During the first set, some woman clad in a business skirt suit had come up from the pool area and sat behind us on some benches next to our drummer KSK. The lady was full-figured and very well-endowed by the hand of our Maker, if you know what I mean. Loisa, she was called. It appeared that this woman had her mind set on KSK since she was eyeing him like a cat ready to pounce on an unsuspecting mouse. Anyway, KSK had a full complement of drums including the double bass kicks, and a high drum throne with a quart bottle of beer between his legs. We finished the set and after mingling I noticed that Loisa was about 3 sheets to the wind and KSK was close behind at about 2.5.

We began the second set and about half way through this

rather long improvisational section of an unrecorded song we were perfecting for my Kondele buddy Mo as his first composition and I realized that there are no drum beats, nothing at all. We turned around and saw what appeared to be KSK who had fallen over backwards onto the floor still on his drum stool, the beer between his legs, and his back on top of Loisa who was showing all her well-endowed self to the shocked host, hostess and guests in the dance hall. Drums and cymbals with stands were laid out all over and there was beer flowing out of the bottle onto KSK, Loisa and the carpet. Pajos and I went to his aid, helped clean up the mess, had a good laugh, and Pajos took over the drums, finished the gig.

Later we found out from KSK that during that song, Loisa couldn't wait any longer and made her move on him. She apparently came from behind and placed a breast on each of his shoulders and started shaking and shimmying. Of course KSK freaked, lost his balance and fell over backwards screaming as he fell right on top of Loisa. This display of buffoonery and pandemonium was later deemed by me 'Accident Ya Belfast' in a song.

KSK did later link up with Loisa (for good or bad).

Throughout the night I would play my guitar solos and either walked up to the edge of the stage and perch on a monitor or walk around the stage and interact with the other band members.

And I heard mind boggling stories.

Flavien slept with this really cute shy law student once. Afterward she told him she'd just lost her virginity to him. Mawazo had death threats hung on him from two English women and got so scared he couldn't go out on his own.

On a side note, Pam told me there were a lot of Caribbean bands from decades ago that had been detained in the UK to do shows/record because of all the illegitimate kids they created (see: alimony, support etc....) it was the funniest thing cracking on these guys who thought they had the world by the balls back then but now these (idiots) had a half a dozen women draining them dry on a monetary level—priceless! As a musician I am *so* glad I avoided that whole baby mama drama by selecting Pam who was sober, mature and knew what she wanted.

8.

I had a message in Pam's answering machine, message from sis Akong'o asking me to call home urgently. I made the call and Mama answered the phone and there was a nervous tremor in her tone which alarmed me.

'*Keya Nyasaye oomo.*'

My big bro Keya was dead. What? Suicide. How?

In my mind something stirred. I felt at odds with it, but it was familiar. It had been done. I heard a high pitched whine that settled to a low drone, there was a haze that filled my eyes, and then cleared. I smelled the smoldering bushfire, something gnarly wafted along on the listlessly woodsy air; something dead lingered there, too.

I felt the cold air whispers of Fortune Man.

Whatever it was seemed to have passed. I thought for a moment I was catching something. I didn't know, not for sure. I was stunned. Once again I would be haunted by circumstances.

Fortune Man. It had come to pass. Ten years of fame and fortune. Then what? Twenty years of darkness.

Weird prophecy.

I tried to focus. Mama had found his body in our banana garden. I kept screaming over and over again, 'No, no no, not Keya! Anyone but Keya!' It was surreal. I was stunned. I had forgotten my vow to support him build his *simba* this year and *go dala* (establish his own home) next year. I would be haunted by circumstances. It was not his fault that he had been born the weakest person in the family; he was born that way with his many faults.

He was thirty years. It was ruled as a suicide, but those of us that knew him believed that it wasn't intentional. My brother Ouru thought he was frustrated by his wife's infidelity. He took his own life to get away from his pain, but he never would have wanted to escape life like that. He'd never wanted to hurt people like this. He was a tired man. Mama was always harsh on him; my brothers always blamed him for letting the family down as an elder brother. Nobody wanted anything to do with him. He was a liability to us, a useless man who could not even take good care of his own family. He had not built his own *simba* and traditionally he had locked us up since we could never come out of our father's homestead until he got out first. If you had put this coincidence in a movie script or book plot, no one would believe it... but here it was... truth... not fiction.

His son Petro Okoth Okomo had been born with cerebral palsy.

Reason for this? His mother Nyamalo, used to drink heavily when carrying him.

Pam was with me and she cried with me.

We exited in total solemnity, each going their own way. As I walked east toward Fifth Avenue, I could hear the tolling of St. Patty's Cathedral's bell. It was drawing me near. When I reached, a handful of Irish, those that couldn't get inside the church, were on their knees in the street and on the sidewalks, praying, crossing themselves, saying rosaries. The sight of this sent chills through my body.

My last moment with my brother.

He had come to my house to get the money I had promised him. I couldn't give him the money because previously when I gave him, he disappeared for two weeks drinking. Another time he used his wife Nyamalo to get money from me, still with the pretext of using it to build his *simba* and they used the money to finance their *chang'aa* business. I guess you probably have a similar brother or relative in your family, the kind of person you don't know what to do with.

I told him to keep himself busy watching TV, gave him the remote control, and headed to the shower. After a long, cold, shower, I came out and he was sitting there watching TV. I dressed up, went out to buy milk and bread, came back and he was still glued to the telly. I sat down on the sofa with him and saw he was watching *Vioja Mahakamani*. This disturbed me a bit; it wasn't like him at all. The last time I left him alone he stole my electric iron. Another time he stole my nice clothes and shoes which he sold.

'Oh, you like *Vioja Mahakamani.*'

He grabbed the remote and sat back down, looking at me with a confused look on his face. I said 'Sorry,' took the remote, and switched off the telly. I could see his reflection in the window next to the telly. He was kind of smirking. Then he saw me looking at him so he refocused his attention to the telly and I heard him give a quiet little sigh.

'*Thu, aol yawa,*' I faintly heard the words. Problem was, I could give him money and that evening he would be drunk and messy and yelling at Mama, threatening her. And I would be blamed for giving him money.

I found a tape, fed it into the VCR and we watched a movie. Later I made tea and we drank together in silence. I watched him drink three cups and gobble down margarine-sandwiched bread like a man who had not eaten for days.

Now Keya was dead. It felt me with terror than guilt. If only I had been a little patient with him. If only I had a little less harder to understand him, to help him instead of judging him and being harsh to him like the rest of us. After all, he was my elder brother. He was like my father. I got in touch with my brother Odingo in South Africa. He, too, couldn't make it for the burial. I sent money to my father, enough to cover the funeral expenses.

THE
GREAT
DEFECTION

THE album titled *Victoria ODW – Live In Amsterdam* came out on the small Dutch label, Marlestone, and was recorded at the Altstadt. We had only four days to do live recordings on the radio show *Werk* on the album. On the second day, recording begun at Altstadt Studios in Uttrecht under direction of producer Mr. Claudius. The English producer for our UK shows, Matt Lange of Stegno Africa passed all rights and tasks to Mr. Claudius on this LP because he was exhausted after producing *African Victoria Conquers England* and *Victoria Live in Hammersmith Palais*. Lange proved incompatible with the band's style and our collaboration had ended, with eight backing tracks scrapped. By African Dawn's suggestion, Stegno Africa replaced him with a Mr. Nigel Whitleman, who had engineered some African albums.

So we returned to London with the master tape for Lange to reproduce at Stegno Africa and market in UK on behalf of African Dawn and Altstadt, and to meet Nigel. On eve of our scheduled meeting, just outside Sheffield, Nigel had a nasty accident in his car and nearly died. So we never recorded an album in London. Before we left Europe, Altstadt and Stegno Africa re-issued the complete tour show on LP and video reverting to the original order of songs and adding a further five songs not issued on the original LP under the new titles of *Live In Amsterdam 1987* and *Live In London 1987*. The albums were released in Europe and the U.S.A. on the Stegno Africa and Marlestone labels.

Miruka pulled me to one side and said, 'I can see your music has become international, why don't you use your name? Because I can see this band is a vehicle for you.' In Europe I had learned what I had known all along. That as a musician you had to record and record and record.

With the good-selling albums and total record sales exceeding 3 million, it seemed safe to say 'mission accomplished.' African Dawn suggested a farewell party.

Party?

The party was a private affair. It had the usual post-concert characters. Pam was in high spirits welcoming guests and laughing a lot. Miruka drunkenly wandered around and trying to talk to me about next summer. There were hot young things in short skirts, casually-dressed journalists, etc. But there were also some people that stood out a bit; their clothes were nicer, more businesslike, less street casual. There was a woman journalist who didn't appear as if the music scene was her usual beat, and there was a guy with a radio crew who, from listening to him, did pop culture in general, not just music and bands.

Pam was in high heels. Heels; she preferred flatties and only wore high heels once or twice when I insisted because they brought her ass up to the right level when I took her from behind. As she brushed her lips across my cheek I smelled her perfume: Cinnabar; my favourite. I exchanged pleasantries thinking, So much for taking the afternoon off.

Pam had gotten me a suit and tie and I had gotten a haircut. We all got into our best. With guests giving bewildered looks at Tégé's goatwhore shirt (hey, he had to change into something less infuriating after leaving the venue) we exchanged anecdotes, ate, drank and journeyed off into the waiting night, fully slaughtered and still listening to music from our latest LPs pumping softly out of the speakers.

The voice on the speakers was Ayo's, breaking out of the thicket of dense instrument on a 'Nataka Baba,' and it was unlikely we could ever go back. Flutter was in my stomach. It was just a small flutter; Ayo had disappeared as soon as she saw me enter the room and I got myself a drink and moved to the back, situating myself in a perfect watching spot. Forty minutes later, people were drunk and mindless. I saw Ayo and Mawazo. I was watching, well— the room at large, but, of course, focusing on Ayo.

She was trying to talk to Mawazo. He was talking to the woman journalist, and then he gracefully handed her off to KSK. A white guy from a radio company came up, whispered in her ear, and then she was chatting amicably with the radio personality.

Ayo was charming with distant smile. She was perfectly balanced with a thoughtful pause, a smooth answer that seemed to please her interviewer. The man's professionally pitched voice was lost in the din as he asked a question. I couldn't hear Ayo's answer, but she looked amused, saying something that had Mr. Radio laughing.

I was doing my damndest to stop gnawing at my current bone of choice when Mawazo once again inserted himself in the picture and into my consciousness, and started his game of upping-the biggest-prick stakes. He timed it perfectly and as soon as the radio guy moved off with his crew, he; almost cat-like, zoomed through the crowd and was right next to Ayo. At that moment Ayo had started to look around, and I was hoping that what she was looking for was me. I never did get to find out, however, due to the interloper.

My plastic drink cup crinkled in my hand, and I forced myself to unclench. I turned my body away a bit and backed up even closer to the dark wall and tried to make it so I was social-balling with the small, animated group of guests who were mingling freely with the band. Any other time they would have been fantastic and engrossing makers of music enjoying themselves, with their palatable excitement to have had performed all these summer shows and got to be part of this farewell gathering.

But it was an illusion, needless to say. I was staring at the woman I had made love to that very afternoon, the woman who was carrying my child, and the suggestive conversation she was having with a rumoured other... lover? Sex buddy? Whatever. It was obvious.

Mawazo's face was impossible to read, especially since he kept Turning away from my line of site. But he looked turned on, I could tell that much. He wasn't dripping or drooling; at least he didn't seem to be. But I knew Ayo and what her words could do to a man.

This wasn't good. I should have looked away, I knew that. Especially when Mawazo put his hand on Ayo's waist and she shrieked with laughter.

Was that wicked grin and glance out of the corner of his eye from the man for me? I wouldn't be surprised. I hunched back even further, but still watching, still torturing myself.

Something was working out: as I had noticed, Mawazo liked Ayo a lot, and from what I could see, things hadn't just started today. Ayo was an entity close enough to himself to distract him.

She said something in his ear and he screeched with laughter. His mouth moved as he chewed his gum; since he was a none-smoker, he always had a piece of gum in there, chewing along. It wasn't quite as visually cool as smoking, I thought, as it made him seem a bit like a snarky teenager.

I made the mistake of moving back and a young girl got in my way and started a loud conversation. My eyes drifted across the room again, and Mawazo's attention snapped on me.

Ayo, too, noticed me then, looked straight at me.

I sighed. Mawazo's eyes were fixed on me. He made to go but she held him. She took a deep breath, her nostrils flared. Her eyes never left me.

At this point just before I interrupted her private party, she must have slipped in some completely ridiculous joke to keep Mawazo, her scintillating conversation partner, engaged. She looked unconvinced, but did continue with her spiel. And it was indeed a spiel; I had to wonder if this was going to wind up with him getting laid, or getting a pitch to join up in her love for art or Happy Smoke. Usually this wouldn't matter, as it could be a challenge.

Tonight it did.

I had been off his game lately with women, that was for sure.

And it was really pissing me off. Ayo was fading from my view, I could tell. And I wasn't completely positive she actually *cared* that she was.

It all whittled to sex, didn't it? Effing S.E.X. Somehow, Mo had always warned me that Mawazo and Ayo would sleep together. In his mind, he'd simply been waiting for the right moment. I'd known Ayo was a front, a beard, from the beginning; the singer was (maybe) only slightly sexually attracted to me. It amused me that Ayo was so concerned about her own image that she felt it was necessary to get coital with me and even conceive her second child, but as the term 'girlfriend' came into perspective, her own personal priorities reigned over the goatshit crazy noise machine she called a Victoria ODW. It became a fun fiction for her for the convenience of bringing her art to reality and achieving her own fame.

Ayo had issues, personal and otherwise. She had had an unhappy childhood satisfied only by personal gratification. She had lived way, way—way out from any other girl (or boy for that matter) so making friends hadn't been easy. Her suffering and fending for herself from an early age induced in her an uncanny appetite for art.

She was curious.

Though demure the young teen was very naughty; she maintained the innocence regardless of her naughtiness. Her demure charisma was astounding to her young lovers in Dandora where they lived. Such a sweet girl, very caring for her young sisters, buddy—buddy with her ghetto pals, and 'demon in the sack!' She liked sex; she liked 'presenting' herself while she was paid by whoever.

Her life took the route of degrading debauchery.

341

The sensation(s) were wondrous and had to be repeated.

She always thought she would be caught; she sort of feared it but then welcomed it, too. She didn't know why. She just thought she would be caught by her parents.

So she had potential, besides. She was an artist; she had ideas and loved taking charge of life. Getting into trouble to get give good pieces of herself to earn money to keep her going was an easy indulgence—so she found boys to fill that void. So Mawazo wasn't just sleeping with her, her was fulfilling an uncanny void at the center of her soul. I'd figured that out instantly. We had been having sweet sex, even this afternoon. So then my mind had moved forward: why was she dashing her libido on me? That was what I didn't understand for the longest time. She was an independent woman when we'd first met; she had been a lot more flirtatious. It wasn't the flirtation of someone asexual—it was the flirtation of a nymph with a maniac need to be consumed.

2.

Hours later Pam and I were having goodbye romp. It was getting really intense with Ayo's husky yet tender voice wafting from the music system on the hit 'Yawa Tera Uru Mos,' controlling the charged sexual atmosphere in the room. We were practically yelling and moaning at the same time. When we were quiet for one second, we heard the floor creak. I got up to peak through the door that combines the two bedrooms and there was Ayo, sitting on the bed next to us.

Ayo's eyes were wide. And I was wound up like a coiled spring.

My eyes adjusted to the dim light and found she was dressed in a black nightie—the lacey top revealing a great deal of her ample cleavage.

'You are really doing this? With *her?*' Her voice scraped my nerves like fingernails on a blackboard. '*Part of you lives in me...*'

The words hit Pam hard, like being punched in the stomach. Her lip quivered as the tears formed.

Then Ayo's hand collided hard with my cheek, leaving a mark. I wanted to tell her something like it was just sex but the words didn't come out, Ayo walked away from the room too quickly. She couldn't let us see her cry.

Pam put her arm around me and we both grinned at each other, sniggering. We shared a Marlboro and fell asleep. Late into the night the music from the party had died down. Further down the hall a woman was moaning. I opened my eyes and listened carefully for a while. The moaning sounded familiar.

'I hope I don't sound like that,' Pam whispered.

'Shit, I hope they finish soon,' I chuckled, 'or we're not going to get any sleep.'

'Must be Mo and some Irish bitch,' Pam told me.

'I guess!' I said, before settling back down. I listened carefully until the noises died down. I was hearing Ayo's voice and I was cool.

'That sounds like an African woman.'

'It's Ayo,' I said.

Pam cleared her head and faced me.

'Why is she doing this?'

'To get back at me.'

'Is it a member of the band?'

I shook my head. I couldn't tell her it was Mawazo. 'It's some white guy. A fan. Irish.'

'I, I have a confession,' she said. Her voice sounded soft and lacking in confidence. I hadn't heard that tone in her before.

'She never really got over you, y'know? She's in love with you. Like I am.' I heard something in her voice that struck a chord deep inside me. *Like I am.* Those three simple sentences were said with a level of conviction and passion, and even a hint of frustration I had never heard in a woman's voice before.

'Pam, we had a scene. We agreed to break it up as soon as we return to Kenya. I only care for her because she is such a sensational singer and she is carrying my baby!'

Next morning we unbuckled, packed up and got out of the rooms, got ready and to unwind before the flight home. I found Ayo's room empty, door open. There, too, was the heavy stench of marijuana smoke lingering lifelessly in the room despite the heavy presence of incense. I had gone there to give her calcium tablets which I found among my things.

I went back and got into the shower. Pam mooched around the room naked talking on the phone. An hour later, Ayo came. She was 'high' smoking a joint. A crooked smile played across her full, crimson lips. She raised her dark eyes up to find Pam standing naked before me. The world froze; it took Pam a good five minutes to cover herself. Each and every tick of the second hand caused Ayo some sort of pain; sharp at first, like a fresh paper cut, then it deadened to the slow lull that occurs beneath a bruise.

'I only came here to tell you that I want a break from you as soon as we get back home. As soon as you pay me all my dues. Then I will do a solo album with the band and retire from this business. But I want you to know that as bad as you are, Otis, part of you lives in me. Our bond is deeper than the child I'm carrying.'

She walked quickly away from the room, leaving her voice ringing in my mind. Those words instantly became a permanent part of unwanted memories, playing on a loop inside of me. I could still feel the iciness of her fingertips... and the bonded of a shared love of art and music.

What about Mawazo? But that flirtation, and a bit more here and there, was all he'd ever gotten. Not love, nothing to worry about since he had been a pawn in our duel. He'd discovered the joy of screwing the lead female singer of the band first time we hit Europe, so it'd come to no surprise to him when he'd overheard people talking about him. State his position and clear his name? He couldn't, Ayo was smart enough, too smart.

So why use Mawazo to hurt my guts?

344

I didn't know. All I was willing to admit to myself was that my relationship with Ayo had gotten to me, and, annoyingly, now Mawazo was getting to me, too.

3.

Africa, East Africa, Kenya.

We got back home on a sweaty Friday. In Europe I was mobbed by fans, in Nairobi at the airport I was mobbed by the press, with camera clicking like tiny grenades. In a classic coming-full-circle, I had entered the public consciousness. The feeling I got as we stood there waving and smiling sheepishly at screaming fans was like getting the last gasps of air squeezed out of me by a lion. In the live setting, my high-profile performances in Europe left the riffs and heaviness rumble through my body. Now as I bathed in the glorious aftermath, getting warming showers of accolades here in Nairobi, I felt like I'd been through a vigorous workout without having moved a muscle.

We found Kenya waiting for us. I understood the meaning of the phrase *It's Good to be Home*. One of the people waiting for me was Angelou and my son Junior. The happiest man and woman were probably Uncle and Mama Iva. Uncle was clad in an XXL *Live In Amsterdam* T-shirt I had sent him. On steroids and culled from a riff from a recent bout of diabetes, he appeared a bit weak. But still as band manager, he wanted to cherish his own illusions of money over our tour. Oh, big time. Uncle threw a great party, but what happened at that party? Liquor, ladies and all kinds of things.

Media coverage continued for weeks after (recorded) we were back after twelve unforgettable concerts across Europe. Reason for the success? We played for audiences that appreciated us and took us seriously for the first time. So, I think, playing in Europe and being treated to a certain musical and artistic respect was eye-opening and really encouraging to the band. It made us realize that what we were doing was substantial, was artistic, and was respectable rather than just this pop commodity that we always felt like in Kenya, because of the way audience received us and the way the press and the organisers conducted us and promoted our music. That success in Europe told us that our music was more than just African stuff.

The journalist interviewing us at VOK General Service blinked. Ayo put in another point: 'We guys of Victoria had an amazing moment on the tour when we were out for a walk in Ireland and came across a group of Irish people trying to do *Roteke* dance steps in a park. That made us feel; really famous.' Mawazo showed him some nice pictures of Hamburg. The newest photos he wanted reprinted in Daily Nation *Pop Scene*.

KSK said, 'I'm the vice president of Victoria. Have a look at the press quotes from the tour.'

And there were some things to come: in the moment we were cutting the tour video and Attamaxx was going to announce its launch at a concert in Nairobi later that month.

In another interview with the press they wanted details of the hilarious times in London. There had been reports of KSK threatening to beat a fan who called him a nigger. We laughed at that. How many people genuinely liked our music? I showed them the over-fifty guest books and photos of autographs we made. I explained: 'As you can also see in the guest book, the organizers of the tour, African Dawn, let us know: read here, here.' It read: 'You were the stars of this year's summer festival. Your energy, talent and music made this a real highlight.'

Ayo chuckled. She asked the journalist, 'Why are you not thanking us? Say thanks, say it, come on.'

'Thanks,' said the journalist.

Ayo laughed. 'For us *wana* Victoria, it was great being part of such an excellent London African music festival especially being presented right before many world famous and adorable musicians. We hope to be able to show a video of our tour soon.'

'I hear you have plans to leave Victoria soon,' the journalist asked Ayo. 'To go solo?'

For a second Ayo looked coy or coquettish. Then laughter tore out of her lungs. She made hard laughing rounds among the band members present in the interview room. Eventually she played her stitches down and said incredulously 'Where did you get that silly rumour from? I am the princess of Victoria. Can't you see? Victoria pulled off the London tour because of me. Didn't you see my picture in *The Guardian*. I am the star of Victoria. I can't leave? I am the power girl among these brash Victorian men, how can I leave? I am enjoying my seat here as Princess of the Orchestra.'

'Our princess.'

Tégé added, 'Ayo is part and parcel of Victoria.'

And Flavien said, 'Ayo is with us for life. Omnipresent.'

'Like M'Bilia Bel in Afrisa,' Pajos remarked.

Then Ayo said, 'The day I die, Victoria will sing songs at my funeral.'

4.

To upscale more publicity, Uncle drafted a letter, purportedly written by me, which was published in Daily Nation *Letters to the Editor* column. In that piece, I gave thanks to all the organisers, technicians, promoters, supporters and fans & especially to African Dawn, Stegno Africa and Mr. Claudius in Holland. Many European artists did our concert and tour posters and spiced up our publicity with clever graphics. A very big *Thank You* went to our Kenyan (read Kisumu) fans who received us like celebrities.

From now on, anything I did, the press took a note. One newspaper stated that I had created my legacy in three years. I think that was insane. My legacy was yet to come. This was only the beginning. A month later two very special guests were present for a special live show at KS Resort. This was Matt Lange of Stegno Africa and Miruka of African Dawn who had come to present each member of the band with a car. Stegno Africa had printed thousands of T-shirts and caps which were sold as our merchandise. Each member of the group became a star in his own right.

Towards the end of the year, the tour albums were still selling well, and the band was in a hiatus. Attamaxx sold records and videos under license from Altstadt and Stegno labels. In commercial terms, Attamaxx was not making much money from distribution of Marlestone and Stegno labels and Attamaxx had to fight Altstadt and Stegno Africa to get the labels to license it to manufacture and release the albums under its label. I was in the picture and was quite happy with the work the European labels were doing. Thanks to their broad marketing networks, our records were available in all the major cities of the world. *African Victoria Conquers England* and *Victoria Live in Hammersmith Palais* went gold out of the box and had since been certified for sales of two million copies. I knew there were often many implications regarding the contracts; however, which resulted in bands like ours making less.

So while Attamaxx was fighting with Stegno Africa over control of production and marketing rights, my brain was stewing. I learned one thing: that we musicians are well-oiled money making machines for record companies. That was it. Why would a Whiteman who had never set foot on an African soil get on a plane to land in Nairobi and travel five grueling hours on rough Kenyan highways that ruts and rises like a roiling sea (rough because I had traveled on smooth European motorways) to a dusty, sleepy town called Kisumu to spend fortune and present fourteen salon cars to a pack of black African nerds if it's not to make money?

How much did we make? Apparently not that much. Taxes took a sizeable chunk of the lot. In Britain they had a greedy tax system called value added tax which all musicians dreaded. Then we had to pay for promotions, nobody will come to the concert if nobody knows it is on. We had to pay for tour personnel like roadies, people to do all the lighting, sound technicians, stage set up and a whole gamut more. Often in London we had to have opening acts that had to be paid. Then we had travel expenses, accommodation for everybody working on the tour, all the flights and food as well, and on top of that, we had to pay for the venues.

I shared my bitterness with Tégé and we knew that unless we had our own studios and pressing plants and labels like Franco, we would forever have no control over our hard earned money. Even if we concentrated only touring and concerts, we were only making most money for promoters. I mean sure there were overheads but if you played to 20,000 people and charged KShs.40 per ticket, you made a cool KShs. 800,000 per show. Add to merchandise sales at the gig and you could be looking at around KShs.1 million per show, play 30 shows in a year and we would have made KShs.30 million from tours alone, obviously after paying the overhead costs, this will be reduced. Now I could understand why many musicians I knew had refused to record and were concentrating on tours and night club engagements.

5.

The band was in hiatus for most of 1988. One fine morning in April, Ayo gave birth to a bouncing baby boy. The birth of my son united us and humbled Ayo in a very profound way, made her connect with my family. I saw a side of her I had never seen before: a pleasant Maragoli mother. It moved me and pained my heart knowing well my son was never going to have a perfect family.

Mama suggested the name Okello after her uncle who was a musician. Holding him in her arms, Mama declared said, 'Your tiny breaths declare God's greatness. Your high pitched cries shout loud His sovereignty. Your precious frame pronounces the vast creativity of our God.' To me Mama said, 'Congratulations, Owiro my son! You have given me my fourth grandson. We have been so blessed, and stretched and on our knees before God daily. I want you to be involved in the life of this child!'

She passed the crying kid back to me. As I held him for the first time, I looked over every square inch of his body. I loved him at first sight. He had my eyes and nose. I thought about my first born son, Junior, now three years and living with her mother Angelou in Nairobi. I had recently visited them to celebrate his third birthday. I had bought Angelou a four bedroom bungalow in Woodley and settled them. Angelou's mother had moved into the bungalow with them to babysit Junior.

I would now put more effort building my band. No more procrastination, I was now a father of two boys. I would work more than one hundred hours a week. I also decided to set long-term goals for my life. I was twenty-six, so I was no longer young.

As the year neared its end, our fortunes had waxed and waned. Mo Thwaka and his father Mzee Frank had already sold their cars and Mo Thwaka's wife, Akumu, had been around to complain to me, to ask for money. Mo demand for another car.

KSK needed to finish his five bedroom house and wanted money. Mawazo Ya Pesa, Ayo, Pajos, Flavien... all of them, they had squandered their money fast enough and wanted more money. Forget all the excuses, forget Mzee Frank's scraggly beard and his lie of being robbed by thugs in Kaloleni; the real problem with these men and woman always boiled down to greed and petty jealousy. I had paid them in lumpsum all they were entitled as far as the tour was concerned; our lawyers had opened accounts for the likes of Flavien, Pajos, Mo Thwaka and Mzee Frank. I had bought them furniture and opened a hair salon business for Mo Thwaka's wife in lieu of royalties.

What's next, hair-pulling and time-outs?

And more demands and ultimatums! But mainly because courting comparisons to *me* was always lame, no exceptions. Did they even know the burden, the strain, the stress of keeping a band afloat. Everything, right down to broken guitar strings, was on my tab. I stayed awake at night thinking while they romped many drunken delights inside the thighs of harlots.

They knew the band's account was still flush with money from the European labels and more money was still streaming in from royalties. We had made enough to keep us living for years. But I wanted the men to get back to work.

So I had to cut short the recovery brake and get the band ready to start off again with more concerts and hopefully a new album soon! That meant a lot of work but we were looking forward to that.

A day after I paid massive advances to my musicians, I was so mad I decided to go hide in Kakamega for a while and see Riana. I called her. She was delighted that I could still remember her, famous as I was. There was deep eagerness in her voice when we spoke on the phone.

'Come Otis,' she said. 'It will be a great honour to spend Christmas with a famous man.'

Famous man, indeed.

Fame, fame, fatal fame/It can play hideous tricks on the brain.

Fame is, I think, just a disgusting by-product of what we artists do. Sure, there are some perks. But who wants to get hounded every waking moment? Who wants to get into the rut of reckless competition and one-upping? I think with our impoverished African living, being famous is more important than being content with life, because money can get you what you need to get yanked out of the vicious circle, pull you from the bottom of the food chain and make you be content. You can buy a big house and even build a bigger house for your mother. Your mother can stop walking to the market. You can even hire servants to take care of her. Along with being famous comes money and *money makes the world go round*. Literally. It's being content with your life. To be content is to have everything you value in life. Some people do not value fame and fortune and money. Then what's more important? When I was a little boy growing up in sun-drenched Pandpieri, like most young boys, I would pretend to be a rich pop icon, with flashy sun-glares and a smashing smile, waving at make-believe crowds and twanging at an imaginary guitar. I had dreams to be famous.

But, alas! Here it was... or it seemed to be. Fame to me, really, was something that I had factorized and toiled to achieve. But, once beyond, it was no more what I really wanted! So. It is essential to be content with yourself and comprehend... Or it just won't pay off. Okay, you are right I had worked hard day and night to get famous, so I could as well live with it and play to its rules.

Which were?

One: smile endlessly

Two: Dress well and watch your step and say all good things and smile because press cameras are watching.

Three: smile endlessly.

Four: Be ready to dish out money.

The hard part was the attention. I couldn't even pick my nose. I couldn't go down to Lwang'ni hotel like a normal Kisumuan for fresh *ngégé* without causing a scene with people in awe of me. When I ate, they watched. I couldn't even reach to the part of tilapia I loved most: the head. I wanted to crack the massive skull, break open the engine, get to the brain and suck sweetness from the eyes like any Luo. But I was who I was now. I couldn't.

The hard part was every day you have to be in a good mood, because that was what people expect. People laugh at even your stale jokes. You say things, anything and people will laugh. People found everything I said funny. One time I was told that Odago, my former classmate in Primary, was dead. I spoke words that signified the simple age-old condolence and said, 'RIP Odd-hag-goo.' People hooped with laughter. Another time I sent Mzee Frank to call for me a woman I wanted and he was too slow and the woman went without my emissary getting to her. Mzee Frank returned looking a bit flustered without the woman and I called him an idiot. Do you know the hangers-on around me (including Mzee Frank himself) laughed at that.

I soon learned to get good at it. I hated all the people who flocked around ready to spoon me, ready to feed me, even ready to brush my teeth for me and clean my shoes. I couldn't hide in a kiosk and eat *mbuta* and save some money like a normal Luo in Kisumu. Suddenly I was expected to eat at Sunset and I was losing money. And when I went to Sunset to eat, I had my usual pack of hangers-on and they too feasted. They were Uncle, Mzee Frank, my brother Agwenge and a hoard of free loaders who offered free body-guard services. I tell you it was a real drag sometimes. I couldn't sit down in a bar on a hot Kisumu afternoon for a cold beer and nurse my own thoughts and compose a song. When I was quiet for a moment wearing a stony face trying to think, someone would ask, 'What's the matter *jatelo?*'

In this life I had two new lessons: one; money doesn't equate to happiness in our consumer capitalist culture. James Brown was right: money doesn't change you one bit, you are always the same person inside. Your ego is telling you that you would be happy with money and it probably would be fun for a while but eventually you'd feel even emptier than before. Two, the vultures and mongrels waiting to scavenge after your money are human beings, and there are plenty of them. They come in all shapes and sizes with all manner of proposals and schemes. They can die in your place for you.

But honestly. Honestly, why didn't I enjoy all the attention? Honestly, in the beginning, it was really tough. Coming from Pandpieri, I was just a dreamy kid who had a dream, which was to go to become rich, have a career and to be able to support my family. To have a dream like that and, you know, you're not ready. Like everything else God gives us, fame comes with a great responsibility tag. With vermin and bugs and leeches attached.

I took a few days off and went to be with Riana. Christmas was around the corner. I drove my brand new Mercedes 200E all the way alone. There was deep longing in her eyes when she received me in Kakamega. She took me to her house where she allowed me to hug her and kiss her.

Hours later she had cooked a delicious meal and we had eaten. She had gone to do the dishes and we carried on an engaging conversation as she finished tiding her kitchen. She sat across from me at the kitchen table eyeing me, almost reading my thoughts. At first she was not at ease at my presence and regarded me with mixed feelings. It was clear in my eyes that my desire to have her to myself increased beyond imagination. She looked yummy and voluptuous.

Something was going to happen.

She played dumb. 'What?'

I reminded her of the promise she made to me in 1982!

She blushed, grinned. 'It's not like I've forgotten,' she said.

'Oh well... you meant it.'

She looked at me with longing. Mulling my words over for a moment she suddenly understand and broke out into a wide beaming smile. She reared her head back. 'Otis, you know that was seven years ago, *bwana*. I was young and emotionally wounded. Remember. You made me happy.' The ulterior motive, of course, was to get her into a romantic mood. Of course, there were the typical complications with that...

'So, you want to back off?'

'No.'

So we moved to her bedroom where I helped her change her bed sheets. And she kept saying she was not ready. She found things to keep herself busy... brushing her teeth, loosening her braids, the like. Busting a virgin is every man's delight—she was confused or even nervous. Afraid even. Not hysterical, though. Where she was and/or how she had gotten to where she was to agree to this she didn't know—but it was terrifying.

She continued to look at me with longing She knew instinctively that she was going to give herself to me today after all these years. She faced me and told me something that uplifted me. 'Otis, It's not just about the promise I made to you in 1980, I need you. It may not be love, it may be physical. You know me, how difficult and stuck up I can be. Like a woman, I need a man. A man I can trust. I'm twenty-six years old.'

'You trust me?' I asked.

She nodded. 'Can you imagine I do. Despite the things you do to women, I know you. I know you're a good guy who can be trusted. I knew you when you were a nobody and couldn't afford to have a girlfriend. You loved me and waited. I pushed you away and even though you knew my boyfriends, you were patient. You understood me more than anyone.'

She had been the most kind to me during my tumultuous days of post-high school. She had been friendly, very friendly, charming, but had never dated me. She was flighty although flirty. But she was strict and kept her set of rules. I had desired her then and I greatly respected her.

'I'm not a good guy anymore.'

'I don't care. Come.'

So I took a bold step. I took her in my arms and kissed her. Then I moved back to an arm's length—just so enough so that she could feast her eyes on my bulge. Her eyes *did* rest on the bulge, I made no bones about it and took her hand put it on the bulge. I waited for her reaction and saw guarded fear in her eyes. She was staring at it hungrily.

On trembling legs she stood, leaning against the bed for support. Then she dropped down and plopped on the bed. Taking a deep breath, she pulled herself together and sat on the edge.

'I want you, Riana.'

'I know, Otis. Please take me slow.'

There was no sentiment from her, though. There was a look of confusion. Panic was still a part of her, too. Then a shade of disgust and 'how dare you' and mixed emotions flooded her until she was embarrassed and contemptuous.

'My name is Otis Dundos,' I told her.

'So you think being famous makes you get anything you want?'

I laughed. 'I'm still the same person.'

She blushed, couldn't answer but only stare at me in mild disbelief. Then, 'Otis, you know I've never done this?'

I had my turn to smile. She reminded me she also knew that I had a bad reputation with women. She knew about Mama Iva, Angelou and Mary-Goretti.

Very timidly I took a step forward, coming a few inches closer to the still sitting stunned woman. She locked her eyes onto my bulge.

'Don't be afraid.'

'Okay.'

'You will like it.' And I made the bold move, took it out.

Riana put her hand to her mouth.

'You see how stupid I am?'

'It's okay. I'm proud of you for waiting so long.'

Riana closed her eyes. 'Oh, Otis,' she said aloud. Her mouth fell open, 'Oh Dinos!' she moaned. Her confusion seemed to mount. She knew that there was no escape... she was going to give herself to me. *Finally* it was going to happen. Again, how she had come to be in such a predicament she didn't know. After pulling herself together somehow, she concluded her fate was sealed. She raised herself up and got onto her feet.

Compliance!

No sniveling, no crying, no bickering, not even an 'ahmmm', just firm twenty-six year old fingers pushing down hip-hugging jeans to reveal thunderous thighs.

'W—what else should I do?'

I was taken aback by that question. I knew that it meant something, led up to something more. With her mind running in search of a thought to grasp, Riana knew that we knew nothing more mattered than what was to happen. But still...

Totally naked, she moved to stand before me. She was breathing hard and so was I. 'Darling, I'm not like you. I have no experience, so you have to teach me.'

I took a turn at blushing, smiling, nodding my head. 'Relax.'

She bowed her head, her long straight braids covering the

356

side of her face and her continuing blushing. In minutes dramatically nature took over. There was some raunchous groping, kissing, suckling, and romping/rolling on the bed and the floor. Afterwards there were questions that she wanted to ask me. Things we wanted to talk about. Like why we had not used protection in this frighteningly dangerous age of killer HIV/AIDS. But they were regarded as way too intrusive and/or just too embarrassing to ask.

I stayed with her for two weeks. Till new year. We spent the entire days and nights eating, talking, loving, smooching, groping and coupling until we were drained. Her stamina perplexed me.

6.

Mary-Goretti and I had grown apart. We were together on this day, a Sunday. We were up at our old haunt, in the rumbling Colonial-era bungalow constructed in my ten acre property near Kong'er in Nandi Escarpment. It was a rustic bungalow nestled into a hillside and I called it DreamScape. I had bought this property with my first royalty check in November of 1985. The five bedroom house was handmade from the natural resources in the area. It had been built in the 1950s and had a strong farm appeal. It was quaint. It was picturesque. The area was not too desolate, chocked with jutting boulders and small trickling springs, patches of sparse grass and wildflowers. The bungalow surroundings were clustered by a couple of small outbuildings, a large woodpile, a barn, a cow pen, a fish pond, a well and a large garden in full ripeness ready for plucking. It was a complete and perfect farm picture. I had cows, goats, dogs and chickens and they enhanced the feel of being in the country and country life.

The sun was not too hot for the day, there was a cooling breeze. We'd eaten lunch, and I had fed the dogs. We were just cuddling—nothing more. I wanted to talk before anything happened, because I didn't know how she was going to react to what I had to say.

I said it. 'I don't know how much longer I can deal with this.'

'The separations, you mean. The coming and going,' she replied, understanding completely.

'Right.'

'I'll admit it, Otieno, I've thought the same thing.' That was strange, she never called me by my name, it had always been Didi.

Something had happened between her and my younger bro. First of all, I found out that Agwenge had taken her out on their first date the night after I came back from Kakamega. Second of all, Agwenge finally dumped his girlfriend Auma. As the big brother, I confronted Agwenge and he denied dating Mary-Goretti. As for Auma, he said (he thought) he'd stayed with her for so long purely out of inertia, but he finally got sick of her. And Ayo overheard him telling me.

I gave it to Mary-Goretti. 'Look. I think the only reason for us to put ourselves through all of that is if we were almost sure we had a future. And I don't know if we do anymore. First of all, I am too young to even think about that. And, second of all, my trip to Europe brought home a few truths. I think we want different things out of life. You want marriage and I cannot give it to you.'

It was unusual for me to talk to Mary-Goretti like this. She wasn't strong-willed, wasn't smart and; certainly, she wasn't the type of person who would sit well with platitudes. And couldn't die to keep me. She was not that type of girl, no she had no grasp.

She looked at me, startled, then sighed. 'You've been killing yourself for months to bring this up.'

I sat up. 'What?'

'Now you're a millionaire, Didi' she said with a little grin. 'So, you want to buy me out and dump me and get someone of your class, huh... like Riana?'

'I'm not seeing anyone, Mary-Go. My art is compelling me to float free for a while.'

'Okay,' she said, throwing me a soft look of despair.

I hesitated, 'You can find another guy. Provided it's not my brother. I don't want to judge you as a slut who sleeps with brothers.'

She gave me a long stare. 'You know my weaknesses. I'm not a fighter. You know how soft I am. But I don't want to be taken advantage of.'

'I know you're not made like that.'

She took a breath and then looked up at me with a little come-hither grin. 'There's no way I can let you go, Didi. You are in my heart. Mark my words. We will always be together.'

'We agreed,' I said with a laugh, and reached for her. Slowly she began to undress. Her emotional outbursts were nipped and nullified, but she still trembled and shook as she peeled off her clothing.

Later on I rounded Agwenge up. He felt compelled to give me an apology: he captivated me through a series of subtle shimmers and soft confessions on why he did it. To me he was still a foolish little brother, always dimwitted. And he'd waited the few months, and waited some more, and the little foolish bro actually had the temerity to be rather charming and apologetic. He was so sincere it was painful, he had morality issues with me for sleeping with Mary-Goretti that I had to fight not to sympathize with him. Also, whatever it was that he and Mary-Goretti were doing together, it was making him mature, more confident. Mary-Goretti was paying more and more attention to him, and he didn't feel it was his own fault.

What really made it hard for me to hate Mary-Goretti was fairly simple: my brother was innocent. Mary-Goretti did what she did because of my growing circle of women. She told me she was still in love with me. The way she looked at me, the way she always drew me. The way she looked as if she'd get down on her knees and beg me to take her back. It was impossible to ignore, and it caused rage.

I couldn't think of the last time a woman had looked at me like that. Not that it mattered, of course, and it wasn't like she hung around me long enough for her to get that sickeningly close to me.

I couldn't hate my brother. He didn't know the situation, the politics... he didn't even know Mary-Goretti was playing with him to get at me. But it all seemed unfair, somehow. He didn't want to think further into why, but several aspects of the situation pissed him off. This made him want to do something about it. What that was, he wasn't sure yet. He was a young adult experiencing love and sexuality of a woman for the first time.

Ayo's entry to his debacle was unwarranted: Mary-Goretti was uptight about Ayo, and it was for all the wrong reasons. After watching them closely, I had the distinct impression Mary-Goretti didn't understand what was going on in the head of her own love toy. Ha. Not a clue. She was blatantly ignoring her own emotions. She was insensitive to Agwenge's unfolding love as she popped a new piece of chewing gum, not even noticing when Agwenge called her sweetheart and stalked her around Kisumu. No matter how cool my brother was, no matter how dimwitted he was in other ways, he was his own man and his understanding of his own weakness was pathetic compared to Mary-Goretti's sure sense of her needs and wants.

Agwenge was yet to grow up and fully understand women. He didn't understand how Mary-Goretti could find it convenient to forgive me (for cheating on her) and still slip into my bed any time she felt like. Ayo told me to get Mary-Goretti to love him back. For the love of a brother.

7.

We experienced transitions at the beginning of the New Year. We were rehearsing for our new album. But it was not coming very well due to mounting tension in the band. We were still in one piece; there was the solid core of nine of us who'd known each other for a while—me, Tégé, KSK, Ayo, Mo, Mawazo, Mzee

Frank, Pajos and Biggy. Pajos not as long as us other six, but since he'd been with us for almost a year, he was now part of the band. I considered Tégé and Ayo two of my closest friends and I knew they were aware of their positions. We had differences and Ayo and KSK had expressed that they wanted to go on their own ways.

My eyes were open—the band dynamics were different now, it was clear. But I knew how to play this scene. I'd played in three bands Delta Force and African Heritage in the first life; and, later in life, in adult age, in Retro Rumba Du Zaïre and nothing major— but enough to know myself: I was a pain in the ass. As a normal African fellow, I think I was good to get along with. But as 'fellow band mate' I could drive you right into the wall.

The 'problem' was my ear for perfection. I had the physical attributes to be a great instrumentalist. I knew my music and I could hear all the parts in my head. And if someone else in the band screwed up, I was the first person to hear it. I could hear a bum note almost before you played it. If the player was not dead-on, I would hear it and I would bug you to death about it.

To pull this album through, I decided to play things down, bend my rules and exercise some artistic freedom. I was trying to be good and I promised myself I wouldn't be so much of a martinet this time round. Not with the dissenting elements in the band. I became harder on myself than I was on anyone else, sleeping less and accommodating the band at my home and throwing parties every weekend, though I'll admit they did notice that I was playing a front.

However, while polishing a song, Mo stood up to me about the way the bass should go. I wanted a walking bass; he was insisting on a running bass. It quickly became apparent that I wasn't going to have a way on this one. Mo was as quick with his ear as I was. And he was even harder on himself than I was. He had also become very hard to confront lately. I was mad; I didn't want to be challenged.

As an added bonus, I could play bass, and not too badly

either. I decided to either drive Mo absolutely crazy or relieve him.

I was coolly advised that I had to make myself gentler by necessity, because of Mo. I quickly glommed onto his working methods—the first couple of run-throughs of an unfamiliar song, he played like shit. After a couple of trips through it, he was perfect. He had to work his way into it. Ayo and I, because of our good ears, wanted to play it perfectly from the get-go. Mo didn't care about that, he got to that point. As soon as we all got used to that, we were fine.

I wanted to have Biggy Tembo as lead vocalist on this number because our Urban Benga had slowed down. But his drug use was upsetting and he was getting sloppy and unreal. The European Tour had exposed him to harder drugs than he'd been into and so his songs were taking on more references to getting high. Until that point we had made rather mild, oblique references to *njaga*. We were disappointed that he was getting into hard drugs because we didn't really know how we could help him. We just hoped it wouldn't go too far. In actual fact, he did end up clean but this was the period when he was on it and had a steady supply. But soon he ran out of the drugs he had smuggled from Europe and went apart. It was a tough period for Biggy, but often that adversity and craziness can lead to good art, as I think it did in this case. I hated that, and I hated the fact that the hard stuff he had picked up in Europe was pulling him away from his work. Within weeks of our tour in Europe, Biggy was taking drugs daily and I became more and more worried. I couldn't reach him when he was tripping, but when the effects wore off he would be normal until he took it again.

Biggy's wife complained *to me* about her husband's drug use. When Biggy was tripping she felt as if she was living with a stranger. He would be distant, so spaced-out that he couldn't talk coherently. He then destroyed his ego and didn't believe he could do anything.

I stopped taking weed. I mean I just couldn't stand it. I had dropped it for I don't know how long. Then I started taking it when I started dating Ayo. It made our sex stormy. We were going through a whole game that everybody went through. And I destroyed myself. I was slowly putting myself together after our European Tour, bit by bit, over a six-month period.

I had firmly made Ayo to stop, she was breastfeeding, but I guess she had gone too far into it and withdrawal was taking its toll on her nerves. Sometimes, it just came; and with a vengeance. She hated me, she would scream. There was one day that Ayo, in between songs and just started crying.

Attamaxx supplied us with a new singer to stand in Ayo's place for a while when it would be necessary for her to babysit. Belinda Auma Aseela was quiet and sweet, and very good-natured. I loved her smile; it was the prettiest thing I'd ever seen. I got the impression that because of her shyness, she was a bit of an outsider. Ayo and I talked about this once, and she saw the same things I did—that Aseela was learning to get a bit out of her shell and being part of the band. At first she was really so-so shy girl, not overly outgoing, mostly reserved. She was most comfortable in long flowing dresses. A tall woman with soft complexion, she was very pleasing for the eyes to behold. Like Ayo, her idol was M'Bilia Bel. She wanted to sing like Abeti or M'Pongo Love. She adored Tina Turner and Diana Ross. But she was; really, a fine singer... very sweet rich voice, heavier than Ayo's and huskier. A nice steadying influence. Maybe sexier... maybe. She was multi-talented. She could play good score on electric guitar (and occasionally accompanied the band in mi-solo) or the acoustic guitar. She could even play the keyboard, and chipped in on the vocal harmonies, so she did more than add flavour to Ayo's songs. Heck, she was a good dancer too.

Her life was heavily shaped—and ultimately transformed—by music. As a high school student, she was a triple XXL M'Pongo Love fan, but it was Yvonne Chaka Chaka's South African soul that changed her life and inspired her to express herself. She set up her transition from heavy-busted and shy girl into a confrontational chick very honestly and courageously.

And her journey? She had worked with Earthquake band in Nairobi, played some cool shows. Earthquake was sleepless, thrilling and dangerous. And then it was over. Because of that, she quickly started to loosen up. Gradually she became a mother and matured up.

It was rather amazing to watch her blossom. She turned out to be sassy and smart. We noticed she quickly starting throwing little looks across her over at Biggy Tembo! I was uncomfortable with this. My flings with Ayo had engendered 'indiscipline' in Victoria. The whispering and rumours about their 'friendship' soon affected me. She seemed defensive, with a bit of a chip on her shoulder, waiting for someone to make a comment. Nobody did. The rest of the band just treated her like a new band member—which was what she wanted.

I asked her if she wanted a solo or two on the new album and she reacted with complete horror! Evidently, that scared the hell out of her—but she pitched right in on the harmonies. But she didn't want to be benga's second female singer. You see, since Kenyan benga music was a male-dominated field, I was one of the first to break that mould with the addition of female vocalist when Ayo filled her position in a more permanent basis in 1984.

Another singer had joined us. Sam Ouma 'Ojua Kali Man' was; well, a little different. He wasn't what he seemed at first glance. He was fairly thin and not very tall. His afro was styled in the lines of his idol, Djo Mpoyi, and he tended to walk around singing Djo's songs, chains hanging off his jeans... that sort of thing. He looked like; well, we called them Kisumu hippies. You know the type, you see them in Kisumu all the time squinting at the hot sun and saying they are from Milimani when in real fact some of them are from Nyalenda and Pandpieri. You might have called them greasers or something like that. But he wasn't. He was a very nice guy... very nice and very serious. He just liked to project the image of a burnout. Not that he never lit up a cigarette, never drank a beer. And he was up-to-the-task. He had that screechy, crying voice, a voice with tears in it. Hearing him sing 'Mandola' would make you think Djo Mpoy himself was in the room

His appointment was by design: to replace Mawazo, just like Aseela had been hired to mark track Ayo.

As much as the two new singers added energy in the band, cracks started to appear. Competition was stiff and everyone was fighting to win my favour. I thought this was healthy, but I sniffed trouble. Something deadly; more deadly than all the interpersonal stuff, was steaming beneath the carpet. Problem was most band members didn't know what was going on. Aseela just stumbled on it by accident and rushed over to inform me. It was a Sunday, after another fine productive rehearsal, Aseela came looking found me at Tégé's house. He lived right across the street from the East View Hotel.

I wanted Tégé to recommend a bassist who could replace Mo. Tégé stared at me. 'Mo?'

'Yes. Mo Thwaka!'

Just then Aseela burst in breathing heavily and sweat streaking from her face. 'I think you need to know that KSK is planning to ditch us and reform Delta Force.'

Then she gave us the details: Mawazo, Mo and Biggy were in it. I wish I had had a camera to take a picture of the look on Tégé's face. He was flabbergasted—and shocked right into his eyeballs.

Aseela said, 'I think the new singer Sam Ouma is in the class of Mawazo, so we have a perfect replacement.' She was trying to sound nonchalant—and failing completely. Oh, make no mistake about it; Aseela knew exactly what she was doing. It was just one of the reasons she was one of my favourite people. I had asked her to spy and report everything to me.

I got up. 'See,' I said to Tégé. 'We need a bassist.'

'I have a bass player in mind,' Aseela said.

'Bring him on,' I said.

I got home, my phone started ringing. It was Agwenge asking if I thought he should ask Mary-Goretti out.

'Only if you have an ounce of brains,' I shouted at him. 'This time I will crack the whip on you. You know the rules of the band.'

Then Ayo called and said she wanted to see me. I reminded her that she her child was almost one year old. Then, later, Aseela called, telling me what a great time she had shopping with Ayo, buying clothes for the baby.

I saw Aseela in a way that I had never seen her. She could take charge of things. Oh, she knew how to survive—she knew what an outcast I'd been in Nairobi till I formed Victoria. What I couldn't tell her is that I'd lived a life where it went a lot longer than that. That disbelieving gratitude at a gesture of loyalty from Aseela surprised me sweetly. Well, I completely understood that. She was proving herself loyal and pertinent. And when Ayo's time came, when she will be gushing and gnashing with labour pains, I wouldn't get a raging case of the warm-and-fuzzies. I knew Aseela would be there to make sure everything went well.

Later on Tégé called to say he thought he had a bassist in mind who could match Mo's image and style. Salaries were due, so I had time to deal with my rogue musicians. I had at least a month to sort things out. What Aseela and Tégé didn't know was the invisible hand behind KSK's moves. I knew many ways to play this game. One was to acquire a studio.

My decision to pull Victoria from KS Resort had irked Uncle. We were only of use to him while we played in the club and recorded in his studio. Overall, live, of course, was where Victoria really shone. The band had always made its bones on stage but come '88, following the success of the European Tour, we were going to stop club performance as we hit the road and we had already engaged many promoters. OK Jazz, Afrisa and Zaïko were certainly big influences on us musically and just seeing how they could still go out and play for the masses after all these years was really inspiring.

I had gone to Uncle's office and requested him to get a new band to replace Victoria at KS Resort.

I made my point. 'Let's be honest, Uncle, we didn't shine out the way we did to come back here to play clubs. No progressive band that has graced international limelight ever comes back to play clubs for the rest of their career. If they do, they don't know their value. I want to play arenas. I want to play stadiums. I want Victoria to be constantly on the road.'

Uncle looked levelly at me without blinking. Then he said, 'I think the European Tour really got in your head. You forget you are an African in the African soil. OK Jazz and Afrisa play large concerts in Europe and USA and still come back to play clubs and bars in Kinshasa.' He paused for one dreary spell. Then, 'Don't count on me as the manager of your band. I have resigned. I have already reported you to your mother, you stupid boy.'

I lay in a stupor. Then I began to chuckle.

Bloodlines, oh bloodlines. Problem with relatives is they saw you as something they owned. He still didn't get it. We had gained international exposure, Victoria slammed out such a heavy and massive sound that really belonged in sports arenas and stadiums instead of small clubs. I never was going to perform at clubs like KS Resort again. After two years of playing mostly cheap or free shows through tinny PAs at every underground dive in the country, I could get taken for granted like the way the local musicians were taken for granted by the hipster glitterati. I had a fan base I had created that I now had to develop. But Uncle's nephew-boy-meets-the-godfather-Uncle style made plenty of nonsense to non-ironic heshers, unrepentant classic rockers, disaffected stoners and un-schooled Kisumu mob. I was not part of this. They say life gives you opportunities to exploit and manipulate. Europe had given me the exposure I needed and I was going to capitalize on it to move up to the next level.

A month later, on a wet February evening, Riana called me. She was in Kisumu, could we meet? Yeah, why not.

'Koch Koch,' she suggested. 'In an hour.'

'Okay,' I said and she hung up.

I didn't know why but I had butterflies in my stomach, I felt nervous and at odds about something was amiss. Something gnawed at me and I didn't know what—or what to do about it— if anything.

When the rain at last let up (some) I eased out of my car and walked briskly in the rain and paused just under the canopy of a supermarket. I still had that uneasy feeling and I didn't like it. I. At length I made my way along following the signs towards downtown Oginga Odinga Street. In minutes, I got to Koch Koch and went into my large office to remove my jacket then returned to the club area where the main shindig would take place. I was early; the place was not crowded yet. Soft music filled the place. Off to one side in a corner was a small open bar. Ong'any waved at me, all smiles.

Then—

'Hi!' spoke up a voice from behind me. Gave me a sudden jab-flinch. I nearly came out of my shirt. I turned and there she was all smiles, blazing eyes of fire, too much perfume. I searched my mind while focusing in on the image next to me. Riana was looking blazing, cute bimbo. She had gained more weight.She was way too chipper, and looked *nothing* like she sounded on the phone. I relaxed. I held her, took her in my arms, as massive as she was. As I made to kiss her, she brought her mouth to my ears. 'Otis, I'm pregnant.'

8.

We were knee deep in the rehearsals. Suddenly Uncle walked in with two middle aged fellas. They looked nice fella in good clothes. But Uncle seemed to be "up to something." This was not good. He appeared to be apprehensive, shifty, and sneaky. Then told us to stop and move our things the hell out of *his* studio. The two nice fellas started breaking things up. The band was shocked, Aseela stared at him, and she was getting pissed. I was amused. Pure jealousy. And to think he was my mother's younger brother. He loved money like a prostitute, he had realized he couldn't control me and was turning to Delta Force. But if he was a real businessman (instead of the corrupt greedy opportunist he was) he could have let me continue using the studio. After all I was paying and I was a prolific recorder. I knew the problem: I had cut him out of royalties and his role as Victoria's manager was purely administrative.

I had an option. I called Attamaxx. They were enthusiastic and I was gearing myself to transfer the un-finished recording to their Nairobi studios when I got a call from a Mr. Kiguta from a company called TopAfric Promotions in Rwanda. We were to tour Burundi. We were to participate in an up-coming show in March which was a two days away. While we were preparing for this, the same Mr. Kiguta wanted us to tour Zambia in August. Things started unfolding and Mr. Kiguta came to Kisumu to have me sign the contracts. Our Burundi tour had sold out; we were moving our March date to Bujumbura for two weeks.

The show of support for this tour was absolutely overwhelming and I wanted to be sure that we could play for as many as possible within our tight schedule. All tickets purchased for the Bujumbura date were being honored at the various venues, and a limited amount of additional tickets were to be sold by vendors at the same venues. The TopAfric Promotions' two weeks' Bujumbura tour couldn't have come at the right time. It provided me with a much needed escape from the volatility of Kisumu rebellions. I would be away to focus and put things in perspective. I knew what would happen in my absence, I knew KSK and Kisumu Delta Force would occupy KS resort.

I had to have Mawazo, Biggy and Mo on this tour since they were the core band. For now I was feeling the heat; I was getting burnt down by their indifference and incorporation. I very well knew somebody was working to sabotage me; and as a result, I wanted to buck against that. It was like a straitjacket. Because these guys were members of the band they knew all the songs. I had to run my music through them, and if they purposed not to play to their best or not play at all, I was toast. They were not bound by any contract to Victoria. After a while, I just felt I wanted to scream, and hand them the sack. They could fix me if they wanted to and a lot of money was at stake: tickets had been bought and I had been paid up front. They could play some really obscure, weird, obtuse game to sink me and; of course, no one would hold them accountable. Taking a hiatus was my reaction against the war inside my head. I had to free myself out of that straitjacket. Weeks passed and I had to get creative and focused for Bujumbura. The fear of getting into a room with traitors and snakes in my band and making music flop was real and terrifying.

I needed a backup plan real quick. Tégé had suggestions which I bought: we would be in Bujumbura two weeks before the concert and find a local band we could use to back us up incase Mawazo, Biggy and Mo turned frigid. I went up to Akumu's salon in Wananchi and paid her Mo's salary for that month. I needed her to talk to Mo, to tell him not to misbehave during the tour. She stuffed the notes in her massive breasts (without even counting) and told me not to worry.

Long story short, KSK's plans stalled. Mawazo, Biggy and Mo did come with the band to Burundi. The promoters required us to come with our musical instruments. The sound system included mics, cables, amplifiers, speakers, anti-feedback devices, and our master control board. Special lighting had been added. All this equipment was newly acquired during our European tour, and was my most treasured material possession. The promoters agreed to cover shipping costs. It all had to be transported with us on road trucks. I tasked Tégé, Agwenge, and one engineer to ensure the equipment was all in and packed well. That meant that one of them had to take charge of the loading to make certain the truckers took good care of our equipment. Nothing was to go ahead of us.

Upon arriving in Bujumbura we found it was an election year and the country was in a campaign mood. So we tried to blend in by being Kenyans and cool and indifferent in the volatile atmosphere. We were to perform in support of one presidential candidate. We pulled up and met our new 'tour buddies' for the next ten shows: Empire Bakuba. Some good pals rolled through: Dilu Dilumona, Papy Tex, Emoro, Pepe Kallé, Doris Ebuya, Kinanga 737, Bileku Djuona Mumbafu and a pile of other old timers of that band. We had a great time and as soon as the last note of the Bakuba set was played it was time to get down to business. Our bassist, Mo, mysteriously disappeared in a puff of 'smoke' so Tégé and I two-stepped our lards down to the venue to get the party started right—and we needed a bassist! Good for us, Aseela could step in and play bass.

The first show was over few in a few hours and it was real fun... great stadium crowd and rowdy people in charged campaign fever! I think this was the first time Empire Bakuba played here too despite being French. The bill featured many other smaller Burundian bands as well and, man, I saw a bedlam of talent. Hidden gold. The first band of some idiot kids playing American imitations jumped about the stage like monkeys with their street punk just to warm up the crowd... doing breakdance or robot or rapping or reggae or whatever noise it was. Our turn came and we played a shorter set due to too many bands... that sucked! Empire Bakuba was up next and they were fantastic on stage with Pepe Kallé roaming like an elephant and Emoro the pygmy doing breakneck acrobatics. They made me feel like 10 years ago: singing those old soukous romantic songs and making me feel good and having our own Biggy Tembo as guest vocal on 'Bitoto' was good too!

My brother Agwenge got mad that I wasn't letting him get a bit of the limelight which he thought he was entitled. Bloodlines, oh here we go again. Twenty minutes before we got onstage, I got a call from my father in Kisumu demanding to know why I was frustrating my little brother's talent yet I should be his keeper. The tone of his voice let me miffed me. My family had been peeved when Agwenge didn't accompany me to Europe. I felt conflicted. Should I fix my family problems right before we hit the stage to deliver a powerful set or should I risk *both* my brother *and* father stewing for another forty-five minutes. I decided since I was already in the process of being cut out of my family over my brother, I might as well put my work first and sort my brother later. From that moment on, I assigned Aseela with the duty of grooming my brother, to sharpen his vocal skills. My brother was a squeaky singer, no great voice. He couldn't hit high notes, he was a tenor and the band had very few songs that could match his voice.

We played a really fun set and Empire Bakuba was great. I've never seen so many Bantus dancing to a band in my life. I went outside to 'make things right' with my brother. He accepted my apology which calmed my conscience somewhat.

After two days in Bujumbura we made our way down to Rumonge on the shores of Lake Tanganyika. We took time to this small port because the roads were freaky muddy after a crazy rainy the night before. What a beautiful location lost in between the mountains. There was a good atmosphere and everybody was trying to relax a little before the show and the only way to do that was to go dipping in Lake Tanganyika. We dove in and tossed in the cold water. After that we headed to the show and the turnout was better than expected.

The show was great and the crowd was awesome. We had some percussion problems onstage which Pajos and I ignored through the first half of the set. Mid-way through I sensed something was wrong because Tégé started doing his patented 'don't-worry-guys-everything's-fine routine.'

Mawazo's unsure laugh between songs steamed burned my anxiety. It progressively got worse and worse until I turned around and noticed that Pajos had suddenly shape-shifted into a chimpanzee and was playing standing up. Frightened of becoming a confusing rumbabilly act, we suggested maybe skipping our last song but Tégé was up for the challenge! We began our last song. One verse and it was over and before we said 'Merci beacoup!' Pajos was already outside round back throwing his arms in frustrations with his drums, looking for a carpenter. All in all, it was a great show with a totally cool ending that was unpredictable. Those were the best kind, anyway.

We got into other towns with our promoters and tour personnel and the politicians and played shows at stadiums and in makeshift stages in marketplaces to drum up support for the presidential candidate. It was not a very exciting tour but we were being paid, so we just went on with it and enjoyed the tide. They treated us to some nice food and we were surprised they had *ugali* here!

Then we had a free-time-hit on the last town! By that I mean we split up. Mo and Biggy drank themselves C-minuses, Aseela went to practice her clarinet skills in a hotel room occupied by a male member of Empire Bakuba, Mawazo, Mo and my brother Agwenge went looking for girls at an impromptu party in the hills outside our hotel in the company of some members of Bakuba, and Tégé went shopping for his lethal print shirts. I remained drinking beer and writing songs. I danced to 'King Sa' by the Afrisa and was joined by some senior members of Bakuba; we got hiccups and we all caught up with old jokes and I sharpened my Lingala.

I got time to call Ayo; she was tired and complained too much.

I also called Angelou and she was delighted. During breakfast next morning, men and women of Empire Bakuba and Victoria could hardly lift their heads and were half asleep. We were about three hours late for our next gig! Pajos put 'Kisumu Girl' on volume 1,000 and everyone woke up cursing and before we knew, it was time to hit the road and we were three hours late to play our powerfully moving live set in other provincial towns of Burundi. Some old Tanzanian buddies showed up which amped us up to the tits. Guess who they were? Juwata Jazz on tour.

All in all, it was a tight and aggressive tour.

We blasted through our sets for rigorous hours. We had a great show even though our turnout definitely affected the campaign rallies by opposition parties, but we made the most of it.

9.

After two weeks of it, we were pumped. We were packing our equipment, doing last minute bar visits in Bujumbura and bidding farewell, as well as toying with the idea of extending our tour of this beautiful tiny country. A promoter wanted to take us across the border to Zaïre. Though I initially wanted to boogey into Lubumbashi then sashay up north to Goma, plans changed. The band would not do any of this... we were tired and wanted to go home. So we swapped out vans from the rental company and hit the road for the border. We were driving along the lake towards the border. We checked the weather systems and no freak storms were scheduled immediately in front of us so we felt mildly *sawa sawa* about the drive.

Lake Tanganyika was angry that day! The magnificent lake was around us, ahead of us and in the sky! Evening was coming on strong, there was no traffic on the interstate highway and there were still storms about but none were close. About three hours outside Bujumbura we noticed some pretty heavy lightning and thunder up ahead, but no rain. From seemingly out of nowhere hail starting pouring down. We pulled over, and within seconds of the first hail stone hitting, we started getting whupped up by massive hailstones the size of soft balls (the sport kind)! Our windshield started cracking and then majorly got taken out by the stones. It was terrifying and so strange! Some quick and straight up miraculous manoeuvring led us through a ditch, over the highway and into a metal covered carport of a private residence.

Everyone got nasty bangs. Aseela, sitting next to me, screamed and screamed and screamed. My head hurt. Really badly. My tongue felt swollen. Opening my eyes only created a new myriad of discomfort and distortions.

'Holy shit!' somebody murmured.

'My head!'

'Is everyone okay?'

Band members were struggling to get out of the van. Some were laughing.

'Don't be so sure,' Aseela replied dryly. I tried sitting up, that was a bad idea. Very bad. My neck, arms, stomach, every 'fiber of his being' ached or was on fire. 'Shit!'

'Just take it easy, I'm here.'

'Where the hell is here?'

I could barely focus in on Aseela, it was her voice but her 'form' was distorted. It looked like I was the one who got the worst banging. The others were all good. The driver helped me out, spread me on the grass. Aseela came to kneel beside me in the rain while others ran off to get shelter. It would be a while longer before I came to my senses.

A little while later, I was fine. Aseela helped me to my feet.

'Is everyone alright?' I asked.

She didn't speak but gave him the One-Finger-Reply.

The hail and lightning storm surrounding us continued for another hour or so. In that time we noticed our back window had been completely blown out (didn't exist) and I became concerned that gear had flown out. When the storm calmed down we inspected our stuff and (smile) it was all there. Luckily the trucks carrying our equipment had gone ahead of us, ahead of the storm. We covered our stuff with Pajos's drum rug and drove with our hazards on into Rwanda with a brutally smashed windshield. We crossed into Kigali and pulled into a rest stop area. A few of the band members (Mo & Co.) filtered out into the bleak of the night, heading for the restrooms, snack bar, and the pure darkness beyond the rest stop area lights (for a leg stretch and frolic.) We checked into a hotel around 12:30am, glass shards and all. The clerk came out and saw our totaled van and took pity on us. We were assigned into different rooms. Armed with Vodka, lemonade, Coke and ice, I got the band into the hotel's bar to celebrate our health, safety and not dying, and we kicked back and breathed sighs of relief. Biggy Tembo smoked up his joint then casually strolled to the restrooms.

Our promoter linked up with us the next day in Kigali. We played two packed shows... last shows of this great tour! We got to the place early and we found out it was an open air fest and the worst is that it was raining bad. I could not even breathe because my ribs ached bad due to pressure exerted by the guitar. Even when it was time for Victoria to end up the show, things continued to go over and over the wildly! Perhaps it was due to the fact that we were playing for Francophone audiences, but this was one of the liveliest shows I'd ever seen in my life and definitely the best time of my life. There was time for hooking the beautiful Rwandan women, time for some pictures and getting drunk before spending the night at the hotel. The party was almost over and nobody wanted it to stop. We were packing up and Biggy got sick and had to be hospitalized for two days... malaria. So we took advantage and continued our romp. Rwandan women made Biggy, Mawazo and Mo forget the rest of their shitty rebellions!

My Rwandan woman... her name? Marie-Jeanne. Was the most beautiful thing I had ever conquered. Time for some drinks and making love after the show could have killed me. They say you can never die because of sex, they are wrong. It was killing Mo. Hahahaa. I couldn't get enough and neither could the band. In situations like this, the best you could do is to be brutal and call for a stop. I went knocking on hotel doors.

Before the night trip to Uganda... see you later in Kigali!

We left for our long drive home even if we were getting used to it! Our journey to Uganda began in the van with some easy morning listening to the respectable quality hot soukous of Choc Stars and Grand Zaïko Wawa and two hours later degenerated into all of us aggressively and emotionally singing along with Madilu and Franco in 'Mamou.' Everyone was super amped to be going back home to Kenya, and I was pretty stoked about going to Attamaxx to get new engagements and work out some deals on how to package, market and distribute our Rwanda and Burundi shows. Shed a tear, pour out some deep and personal grief.

I slept and had a dream that Riana and Angelou were sisters. My mind was flood with a mix-mash of memories—past-present-and otherwise. My was slightly confused, trying to hold on to whatever new reality he was in. Reality? What a concept! I felt awful. Resting wherever I was best. I drifted off to sleep, awakening now and then with bouts of hysteria! Nothing made sense, oh how my head hurt. My stomach was in knots, it felt as though seething throughout my innards was one of those fuses from the cartoons.

In spite of the hard raining we got to Kampala pretty early and at the lunch time we went to shop. Finally we were back in Kisumu. I went home to Fort Jesus in Pandpieri to relax and unwind.

10.

'Gentlemen's Gentlemen' KSK Odongo, the vice president of the orchestra, eventually pulled the carpet under my feet. He quit, taking with him Mo, Biggy, Mawazo and Flavien. What made me sore was that he had the audacity to call the press and, flanked by Uncle, made imprudent statements that 'the whole band' had 'decamped' from Victoria *and went back to* Kisumu Delta Force because I was mean, tight-fisted, brutal and hard to get along with. That I was not allowing anyone to exercise artistic freedom. He even hinted that Ayo was also soon ditching Victoria.

My mind was in a blur, whirring, spinning out of control. Too many questions with no answers.

This was not good; no, not good at all.

Truth was the soft-spoken KSK was a cat who was trying to fool people. He had always been a fascinating combination of conflicting characters. Always hid under the cloak'n'dagger façade of the perfect gentlemen with perfect Colgate-white teeth, with a smile to kill. To me he was often presenting as the classic cut-and-run renegade yet remaining a solid, reliable craftsman. Yet he was walking away almost as soon as the band became an established and cherished Urban Benga sensation here in Kisumu. Such devilish impulses were a bit puzzling, but KSK now appeared to have pulled it off. I was so angry I could've bashed a head. I sat down and wondered after the motivations and implications of his decision. For one thing I knew his source of his instigation was *my own* source of instigation three years earlier: Uncle Owiny Ratego Kwer and his money.

I was not amused. This was ugly.

'This is really getting annoying,' remarked Aseela.

I had no comment, he just clamped my mouth. I wanted to write a rejoinder to the press but Tégé and Ayo advised me not to. It was better for him thinking he had won. Time was going to judge him in the artistic battle.

The moral of the KSK story: it was hard for Urban Benga not to be dicey if musicians were dicey, or even not willing to be slightly loyal and committed. What sense was there in creating a story about beautiful music born from a scrap of paper fished from the trash? And that's the story of Kisumu Delta Force so far. A story of restlessness and vendetta. Taking away men like Biggy Tembo, Mo Thwaka was quite a relief, though. My only disappointment was losing the valuable talent of Mawazo Ya Pesa, a man who had the power to enthral crowds and sang like passion struck him. And Uncle? A man who was in his retirement after stealing millions of Ugandans' shilling and was better off building a church for his own redemption. And... hey! Wasn't he better off posting random flyers inviting people to the launch of his memoirs? If his life was anything worth writing about. And will they (KDF) meet his expectations. Then there were the internal problems existing in KDF: will Spark Onyango agree to play second fiddle to KSK? And hey, hey, hey... I soon learned that Benz Benji Obat was back in the group in solo guitar!

They had planned their exit well; they released 'Kisumu Animal Dance.' It had some good songs and they received good press coverage and good airplay (Uncle's money was working) but to me it was less a nursery school album than a product from heavyweights like Mawazo, Mo, Biggy and KSK. It sounded wild, monotonous and unhealthy with confusing arrangements. The voices and drumming were excellent. The guitars? Ah-ah. Definitely lacked my touch, they only pulled it off due to the professionalism of Lakeshore's engineers. (Animal Dance? What kind of animal exactly? Definitely mangy dogs.) And Biggy Tembo's new singing with an XXL throaty growl—making him sound like a mating bull dog or lion—was repulsive to people like us who knew his old smooth drug-free baritone. As for Mo, he was an idiot who didn't even know how to write his name.

I was not grumbling while they were celebrating Delta Force's birthday that night, I was watching things. With Benz Benji Obat injecting some good old *Sulwe*-era slobber into his Gibson power chords and intricately unraveling *ywora nena* solos, I could sense (sadly) that something was clearly not in sync. Wrong move Uncle. Mo, Mawazo, Biggy and Flavien could get by just on their deftly rendered covers, but they were dependent pawns. I knew the weakness in Delta Force from the beginning: no could not write strikingly intense originals, given the glaring example of the demented chaos of tunes in their good songs like 'Dr. John Obare' and 'Nyar Mara' which still sounded like flat-out-oldies despite the engineers explosive attempts to create up-tempo sounds. Technology hardly ever makes good music, art does.

Well, a good slice of Victoria's fans predictably fell for KSK's dodge and ditched us overnight in preference to a new sensation— that was simply the business. I would figure out how to deal with this and it would only be a matter of time. There was little time to breathe let alone struggle to think up a plan.

11.

The music press always adored Victoria. Many journalists were my personal friends. How I survived the dissertations soon became a matter of debate in the press and on radio. I received phone calls asking how I was going to replace Mawazo. When one journalist asserted that Delta Force was an extension of Victoria, I called the newspaper house and stated that our stream of Urban Benga and that of Delta was akin to comparing a VW Beetle and a Mercedes Benz.

One female journalist had especially loved 'Gentlemen's Gentleman' KSK and she wondered how I was going to survive without my vice president. Most fans missed Ayo. Despite the organic, evolutionary process of her music, and the sincere way in which its form and content collided to create her own shifting Urban Benga style of, press were often desperate to stick the dub step label to Ayo as performer. In a way, it was this keenness to relate the 32-year-old woman to what was perceived to be 'of the moment' that made much press about her music irrelevant to what she actually did as an artist. Yet another expressed confidence that I was going to weather the storm. My energetic style of playing made the guitar powerful. My literate and beguiling lyrics—a startlingly fresh take on Urban Benga's classic themes—added layers of mystery and humour to Victoria's evocative and energized guitar work, and cast me as Urban Benga's most original and unlikely front man. For a jaded pop press the mix was irresistible.

A week after Delta Force released their debut album, I was falling apart. I was getting increasingly agitated, which was causing my artistic output to take on a definite dark and wild streak. God heard my silent prayers from Heaven. He answered them.

One afternoon in May, Aseela and I were in Victoria Music Store; we were conducting a small investigating on a piracy racket. The music store owner had found some bootleg copies of our albums in his stock and alerted me. A young policeman had been come with us. As we were working through it, the policeman showed me a hand-written piece of paper. It was headed 'There's No Mathematics in Love' and it had words of verse that read like this:

You call me a slut; anyways it's a casual insult
You can call me a slut because you can't have me
You can't have me because I made my rules
You call me a malaya; Yet, don't you know:
One plus one is two; And one times one is one
Count the times we have shared and the value of that time
Calculate the value of the loving I have given you, *wewe bwana*
And you say I don't take your money because my love is free
What kind of a girl do you think I am?
You cannot turn me on and off like a switch
I am a woman and I can have the same loving as you

You call me a slut; anyways it's a casual insult
I want to be lonely in love than alive with you and dead.
Drop your attitude that I'm supposed to be a virgin, are you?
Men made me be the woman I am, don't worry
If a woman wears a sexy dress men call her a slut and a *malaya*.
Men say she's dirty and evil, yet sometimes it's just a bikini
It's as if women having sex is soo wrong,
while men doing it isn't.
I am a woman and I can have the same loving as you

If you're ready to love, don't calculate.
If you're ready to love, (I say) don't calculate.
You're ready to lose so you can win my love, *oh oh bwana wee. x3*
I give my heart to you. (Eh-eh) x3

If you're serious show me;
don't talk while I need you to sweep me off my feet
Don't look sad and admit you're broke, *bwana.*

381

I am a beautiful mature Luo woman with dignity here in
Kisumu
Words in the mouth of men lost their meaning centuries ago
We women know better now;
A man still has to be a man to love like a man
Then I will leave John and George and give all the love to you

Don't calculate the losses Mama yo yo yo x3
Do you know why?
There's no mathematics in love.
Don't calculate petrol in my car and food in a restaurant
And money for making my hair and polishing my nails
Don't calculate what you give me to give my mother
I repeat don't calculate what you give me to give my mother

Don't calculate fine wine from Germany
and nice *kitenge* from Bruxelles
And expensive perfume from Paris...
Don't calculate and bargain
about the cows and cash you gave for my bride price
And don't calculate the money you give me
for my brother's school fees
Don't calculate my sister's college money
Because she's your sister-in-law oh—oh—oh!
She's your sister-in-law eh—eh—eh! x3

There is no algebra in money for food.
And multiplication and subtraction in house rent and petrol
There's no equation in money for clothes and perfume and wine
And no hard algebra in making me adorable for your love
For all your Kisumu friends to see...
Yawa what a beautiful woman you have here in Kisumu.

There's no mathematics in love. (Heh!) x3

382

This composition made me a bit twitchy. Handed the piece of paper to Aseela and turned to the policeman, 'You can sing?'

He nodded.

'Sing it,' I said.

He sang out the words and his voice amazed me. It was deep and gravelly with a range of multiple octaves. It was scratchy with a soulful sandpaper rasp to it and it had a deep spiritual quality.

My hands must have been shaking as I looked from the policeman to the piece of paper in my hands. Oddly, hearing him sing didn't measure with the unusual rush of burst of adrenalin in my blood. The words of poetry; the lyrics mellowed me out on that score. Still, I was thinking that this song was too wordy. Very much unlike our style of short lyrics and much instrumentation.

Aseela appeared to have wandered off into thought.

'What's your name?' I asked.

'Opiyo.'

'Opiyo?'

The policeman nodded. 'Willy Wilberforce Opiyo.'

I asked him what inspired him to write this song. He mulled, thought, hummed, and seemed to be talking to himself. Explained he was NOT a mathematically significant genius. We talked and he explained that women and their love for money always fascinated him.

'So is this from personal exp—'

He cut me short. 'Imagination,' he said.

Aseela grabbed my arm, and gave me a sharp smile. She said. 'This is poetry, let's record it!'

We went into rehearsals over the next two months. Willy Wilberforce Opiyo, who had quickly earned the nickname 'The Poet' accompanied us. He wrote all the songs, we selected twelve and recorded two versions of the album at AIT, under supervision of Felix Jakomo: one was a slow ballad that featured Willy as the lead singer backed by the heaven-made trio Aseela, Agwenge and

Mzee Frank, and another was hard and driving, and featured Sammy Ouma 'Ojua Kali Man' and another new singer known as Oroko Afelo who had joined us, coming from Ochieng Kabasele's Lunna Kiddi. His husky tenor was blessed with a distinctively taught, tremulous vibrato, and a throaty chuckle that was going to pepper our later work. I rebaptised him as Roki Fela. Felix chose the second version and pressed the vinyl at Polygram. When the album came out, 'The Poet' Opiyo Willy quit his job and joined Victoria.

Towards the end of the years I was in Nairobi, accompanied by Tégé and Aseela, to oversee the production. Our trip to Nairobi coincided with the first installation of Makombora Music Series, organized by Attamaxx. JB had been pretty mad with me for ditching him and choosing to work with Felix and AIT on my *greatest* album. We had been invited and I took the opportunity to introduce our forthcoming album. I paid a journalist to do an epic article about 'There's No Mathematics In Love' as a one-of-a-kind album. Then there was a short interview with me incisively centered on Kisumu music scene and my band. In the interview I gave insights on the forthcoming album.

In between things, I took time to work out a good marketing strategy. In a brief tryst with JB and Ochieng Kamau, things were sorted and a deal was worked out with Attamaxx to market and distribute the new album. Our primary market in Nyanza, it was noted, was now being shared with KDF. I had to do things smartly. JB reckoned Victoria had a solid fan base that ought to provide us with a living regardless, but we shouldn't expect to be making the sort of money we were growing used to. Now was the time to consolidate and diversify. We had to break into new markets with the new album. I made calls to Pam and distribution deals were discussed with African Dawn. Strategies were drawn. To begin with, we needed a captivating sleeve design.

Felix of AIT hired at least five different graphic designers. We reviewed at least one hundred concepts. And each of them needed other options, just in case everything disintegrated.

One night as I slept, it came to my mind like a dream that Angelou was Nairobi's best graphic designer.

I spoke to her the next morning and explained to her my reason for calling her. Yes, she was aware of my frustrations with jacket design proposals for my album, Attamaxx had approached her already. And it made no sense for her to seriously consider helping me out. Frankly, she could see the need for a captivating design as far as the market was concerned, with a lot of bands doing the same thing. She only wondered why I really thought she should help me.

I told her I knew her talents and I trusted she would give me the design I needed and she thanked me for my faith in her. Then she also asked me how I was getting along with my women and moved the conversation into risky territory. Right there and then I knew that if there was going to be any deal at all with Angelou I needed to be honest. She liked truth and honesty. I explained about my competition with KDF and about losing half of my musicians and why I needed this album to make a good point. She was quiet, but, surprisingly understanding.

'I want everyone coming to Makombora to see this album,' I told her.

'Is Ayo coming?' she asked.

'Yes.'

'Ah,' she chuckled, 'to keep an eye on you?'

'Yes and no. Ayo wants to quit the band...'

'And Aseela wants to take her place and keep you in her bed?'

'No.'

'Whereas you, on the other hand, fancied a little skinny dipping with your ex?'

'I beg your pardon?'

'Me.'

'Something like that. I cannot resist you.'

'I'm not fighting over you, Dino. You keep your Victorian women, it'll make things easier.'

'But...'

'But nothing, Dino. I'm actually relaxed about this. Maybe I'm finally getting over you, huh? I figure there are lots of spunky toyboys around, so...'

'Hey?'

'Hey, what, Dino? When you slept with those women, were you thinking of me?'

'Actually, I was, Adoyo, I...'

'Damn, Dino, and here's me thinking you were finally becoming open and honest. Obviously, you've still a long way to go.'

'I was...'

Switching to DhoLuo, she rapped, 'See you next year when your son goes to class one, Baba Junior, bye.'

I threw the phone across the room and went to sulk in the toilet. Perfect. Great. Retrieving the phone again, I called Felix on his direct line and asked him to get me get the top level advertising agencies in Nairobi.

'What about your designer woman?' he wanted to know.

I shrugged. 'Don't ask.'

12.

'There's No Mathematics In Love' was going to hit big. Despite the album's expected success, I toned down my vibes. During an interview, I was hard-pressed to comment on a damning statement made by KSK. He had called me a manipulative pop opportunist. I backed away from that bold attack and wondered why the press was helping my enemies viciously attack with outspoken reviews yet I was Urban Benga's reining hero.

I didn't want to sound as the most articulate, contrary, and witty pop star able to subject himself to the strange ritual of the interview process. I knew Journalists could count on me to give good story, with each new interview eliciting bucket loads of outrageously memorable quotes on a number of distinctly rumba and Urban Benga subjects. But I was not interested in attacking anyone. I didn't want to start engaging with KSK, it would make him popular. I walked my path and asked to judged by the next album, not rhetoric.

Through the press, I stated that the beautiful ones were not yet born; the good days of Victoria were yet to come. I knew what I wanted for Victoria, I stated. And I knew where I was going. Of course, I knew how to use the press to help me advance business. Television appearances and music press interviews were always the main avenues of promotion for Victoria releases.

Pam gave birth to a baby boy in mid-May. She called me. She had picked an African name for her son: Daudi. She recently sent me a photo with her sweet smile. I thought I was a lucky guy: three kids in one year. In the picture, Pam was wearing stripes, *de rigueur* and looked a bit like a Dutch woman.

THERE'S
NO
MATHEMATICS
IN LOVE

WHEN you have a good song, the world is yours. The new album *There's No Mathematics In Love* brought a gush of freshness. It was superb... it was one tidy package of good songs. Besides its *auteur composituer*, 'The Poet' Opiyo Willy, it featured two the new sensational newcomers: Oroko Afelo aka Roki Fela and Sam Ojua Kali Man. Of course I'll swank about them. They were smart, extremely talented, devoted. And good looking. But wait till I tell you about their voices. 'There's No Mathematics In Love' was a hefty and super long song playing a full 10 minutes and 56 seconds. This song simply came out and touched the nerve of the moment and said what many people were thinking.

There was some significance to this. A mathematical significance. Yeah, a whiff of money, if you what I'm saying.

Critics and fans alike were in thrall. On radio it was another one of those endless requests on daily, sometimes hourly, basis. Wow, this particular song 'There's No Mathematics In Love' was popular with girls. Male DJs often played it in hopes that they'd get lots of calls from the female listening audience. 'Mr Right' DJ Eddie Fondo loved it... featured it heavily on his *Chaguo Lako* program. One can only imagine what horrors the KBC management visited upon 'Mr Rrrrright' for this extraordinary break in playlist protocol. The same song two or three times in row? On a whim? In fact by this time, the Victorian presence in the music press was impossible to ignore, I daresay. It was stunning and daunting too. We hadn't done anything different from what we'd done all along — play music. I think the fact tha tthe songs concerned us all played a role. The emphasis now was on 'forward,' because the Victoria's best days and worst days were behind us—particularly when we were without our one consistent spark of youthful energy, Mawazo Ya Pesa. I was starting over and I had many things in my head. I now wanted to concentrate on recording LPs than going on tour. I wanted to define the ideal sound for the band, create a new identity.

'There's No Mathematic In Love' was a little bit in the soukous vein with extended *sebenes* (a platter that can best be described as 'soukous benga' with guitar solos and animations that wormed their way into our sound subtly but oh-so-effectively). You could hear the rhythm guitar throughout the song playing counter lines. This was East African guitar influence. Many people agreed that the solo lead and rhythm guitar combination was smart. The album boasted a more refined direct sound full of powerful songs, beautiful melodies, catchy riffs and sophisticated arrangements. I felt it was too up-tempo.... not anywhere near the standards I wanted to set. It lacked the depth I imagined I could create. Yes, it was a brand new beginning for the newcomers in the band. But... artistically, it was zero. I felt we were a bit inconsistent. I remember taking my time in the studio a bit getting to *the core of things* and throwing it in for the first time, not being particularly excited about what I figured would be a modestly good progressive power release amongst a tide of new titles.

How wrong was I? Where to begin... hey presto! Like a rabbit out of the hat, people gobbled it up.

So in the end I was glad. Really... really during the past quarter of the new year, I had every reason to be glad. The band had stabilized with exceptional new talent! Our music reveled in a rich conglomeration of fine tones, capable vocal work, strong riffing and electronic effects, all topped off with just enough virtuosic flair to snap your neck to now and again. With the fresh new talent brought in by the younger new musicians, we moved into a new phase and everything suddenly changed. Victoria was lethal. With the addition of Roki Fela and Sam Ojua Kali Man to Victoria, the band had now dropped some of its slicker Kisumu Urban Benga sound and had embraced a more soulful rumba Zaïrean style that included scorching raunchier and far more exciting *sebenes*. Still we were moving, trying to find something not just Zaïrean but *African*. Stylized storytelling in vocals, intense live performances... all the new energy and innovation made devoted wilder fan base. And that's how 'There's No Mathematic In Love' listened—carrying itself straight through to the end. I must at this point call out vocalist Roki Fela for absolutely stellar vocals. This energetic singer sounded like the love child of modern Moreno Batamba.

The Poet' Opiyo Willy's other interesting composition 'Wasichana Wacha Tabia Mbaya', started as a slow rumba duet featuring Ojua Kali Man's smooth liquid soprano and Aseela's love of melismatic, pop-worthy, and yet commanding tenor vocals. Then halfway down, it built into a call-and-response affair with hard questions asked and no answers given. Then it burst into a *soukous* score with riveting *sebene*.

Yes, Victoria had more power and more variety in the vocal section than we needed. Sam Ojua Kali Man was set to be another dynamic singer and showman after Mawazo. He brought exciting innovation: he introduced the new dance style *Sammyyyyiii Business*. When he yelled 'Sammyyyiii,' the backing singers answered 'Business.' Mzee Frank sang backing vocals throughout and his voice had a sweet, shadowy quality that insinuated its way deep into the inner heart of a lyric, displaying a singular kicked-back, smoldering soul passion that enabled him to navigate, quite credibly, thank you, as both a boss roots radical and a lively Luo benga chanter. But Roki Fela was the one who truly stood out. He was emotional, straining his voice to its limits so that his entire body seemed to vibrate while he sang. His vocal style and his outstanding talent as charismatic stage rover and showman were well caught here in 'There's No Mathematic In Love.' He got a new nickname: 'Ndugu Ya Kasuku.' He was the big parrot who's colorful; free flights of evocative, beyond-scat vocal lines gave the band such a distinctive new sound. He also boasted a signature sound all his own, particularly noticeable when he snarled out his sharper-edged lines. Despite everything else going on around him—the guitar and the remarkably tight and synchronous rhythm work—he was really a show-stopper.

So. Here we were. 'There's No Mathematics In Love.'

Accolades came and the song stayed at the top of Polygrams Top Ten list for a good part of the year. We played some amazing shows and had the best time talking about the record and hearing stories from devoted fans; the people that had been with us ever since our KS Resort days. It was indeed a privilege to have their support, dear old Kisumuans. And thanks for inspiring us. Afterwards the song was nominated The Best Song of the Year.

Suffice it to say I was witnessing 'newness' in the band; one that appeared to upset the ceremonious dark old hands and voices. Ayo was, indeed, starting to show the strain with increasingly wild mood swings and bouts of bad temper. She could be haughty and arrogant one minute then the life of the party the next. Eventually she dramatically gave her seat to Aseela, stormed off into semi-retirement in Nairobi. She had an offer of a solo exhibition at the opening of a new gallery that had induced her to spend so much time in her house putting oil on canvas over the next long months. As I well knew, it was an offer few painters would be able to resist. The remaining old guard, Tégé Zoba, appeared to be losing his grip. He got sick. He was quitting the band for personal and artistic reasons. Well, I soon heard it said he was on his way to rejoin Black Devils. He wasn't able to play again. Sorry Tégé, we almost got famous. Soon after we tore up the whole lakeside town with our tunes and became the leading band here in Kisumu *minus our Tégé.*

Right, let's air this out right away: he had wanted me to appoint him to be the vice president of the orchestra. But he had his own hang-ups. He was nearly thirty-five years old and his son was twelve and he needed to be re-united with his family and be near his son in Nairobi. Come to think of it: I never knew he had a wife all these years... that guy was a first class womanizer who lived for the next day. Did age just catch up with him? I couldn't tell. Victoria's heartfelt, disarming, exhilarating and totally unexpected queer rumbastic Urban Benga could exist without ruffling feathers on an old musician with a penchant for reggae music. Smart musicians evolve or die—the audience is irrelevant, or should be. Tégé Zoba didn't evolve with us, he went a different direction. Maybe his reason for quitting could be justified... I also heard (not from him) that he wanted to reconcile his new-found Rastafarian beliefs with the Taitta culture of his people. He had been skeptical of the band's eclectic musical fusion and left to follow his dream, to play reggae. By the time the first half of the year ended, he was playing with Black Devils Makali in Nairobi. So I needed a rhythmist. I brought in Benz to fill in for a while but I needed a rhythmist.

2.

During a visit to Nairobi, I saw a community of rural-looking blind Kamba beggars playing music at a street corner. Wailing out Christian songs and rattling their crude instruments, they called themselves Street Corner Evangelists but to me, they were just rowdy bunch of awful singing, feet stamping and hands clapping beggars hitting tins cans, beating cow skin drums and rattling pebble-filled tin can shakers to attract coins.

The small troupe consisted of three drummers, one guitarist and four women singers. It was their guitarist who caught my eye. Blind and ragged and dirty, he played lead electric guitar perfectly. The guitar was a tattered Japanese model. They had managed to connect it to speakers via a small amp and powered it using car battery. The sound was perfect. I was so caught up I gave them lots of money and made friends with them.

I kept coming to that street corner every day. I had read the literature of blind musicians; the artists who derived their power from the darkness and deeper concentration. I wanted to see the power of this blind musician after reading tales of men like Steve Kekana, Blind Boy Fuller, Blind Blake, Blind Lemon Jafferson and Stevie Wonder. I began to talk to him and found him to be warm and cordial. I got his name: Roga Roga. I learned that he was born blind as a result of a family curse. All his siblings were blind. He was rough and direct with an honesty that lacked sentimentality. Although he was not educated, his artistry as a folk guitarist lay in the honesty and integrity of his self-expression. Beyond being a guitar player, he was a pained believer in Jesus seeking Salvation. But since he was not an educated or thinking Christian, his life was ruled by superstition.

Days later, I took him to Attamaxx studios and gave him the 'real' instrument. We watched him play. I watched him play holding his notes and releasing the melody. He had that quality of coming up to the note and never quite hitting it. That was a very inexact technique, but it gave you the quarter-tones and all of the strange nuances. Blind Roga Roga had great dexterity and fabulous syncopation; he could keep his thumb going real strong. He had the best left-hand vibrato – the absolute best. Very light touch, real light, and really fast. But that vibrato, I think you can only do it by wiggling your notes just right.

To my ears, it sounded as if.... how did Blind Roga Roga achieve his distinctive guitar sound? Sheer instinct, someone told me. I got it: instinct.

I played to him all the songs in our *There's No Mathematics In Love* album and he quickly learned them—*all of them!* He had great dexterity because he could play all of our sparking melody lines. He had fabulous syncopation; he could keep his thumb going really strong. He was so good—I mean, he was just so *good*!

Convincing him to join my band was no brainer. To him it was dream-come-true. The blind Kamba beggars he played with soon got another blind guitarist, so it wasn't much of a loss to them either. They were more than happy to have one of their own get a 'real job.'

And I hired the bassist, G-Chord Ajuma Ouma who had previously played with Mandingo, and was willing to change his style to suit ours. It had been a tough choice to make bringing in musicians who did not match our style, but I was willing to take the gamble for two reasons.

One, I was tired of working with home boys.

Two, I wanted to change the style of Victoria to techno and Afro, and needed more experienced hands.

3.

I sat on the balcony of Koch Koch, a western tuxedo, new boots, fancy gold watch, manicure, trim the whole nine yards. Koch Koch was now more than bar for the band to stop in for a quick drink. Now it was our headquarters. The news of the town was still hot with the still unexplained decision of Uncle to terminate our contract with Lakeside Studios and we had lost the law suit he had filed last year. Now I was required to pay him close to one and a half million shillings. I was drinking and feeling like a man with great stress and deep fear. I had no happiness and did not want to be happy. I was a man on brink of disaster and death.

I was waiting for our new manager 'His Excellency Ambassador' Okoth Ochot to take me to KBC studios to record an interview with Omuga Kabisai. I wanted to set some records straight to our fans. Not that I cared much, Okoth Ochot had suggested that I needed to focus and the one thing I didn't want to lose were my fans. He was a publicity professional; an in-demand-on-the-fashion-art-celebrity- sort of fellow. He had replaced Uncle as our new manager. His plans for 1988 included rehearsing for our new album while picking up the occasional gig within a 200 mile radius. After shambling around Kisumu for some time and spending more than we were making, I tried to sit with my musician and work on some ideas. I was putting more emphasis on vocals and harmony other than melody, and I was focusing on music with social messages. In total I had five singers all singing together in my new choral intensive style.

The law suit by Uncle had depressed me for many months. Today there had been a ruling and it went to his favour leaving me relieved minus one and half a million shillings. Not that losing the money worried me: I didn't have much to worry about money. Massive revenue came from the sales of our European Tour records and our other new albums including *There's No Mathematics In Love*. All members of Victoria who had participated in the tour and the recordings were receiving their monthly payments in lieu of royalties. But losing that lawsuit left me a mentally and spiritually exhausted, a wandering shadow of the man I once was. It meant now we were to permanently vacate Lakeshore Studios. I was however glad I had officially cut links with Uncle and now firmly in control of the band after the departure of the old guards. I could sit down to make use of artistic freedom. *But I needed that studio.*

We would now be running our meeting and rehearsals at Koch Koch. I had recently converted the backrooms of the bar as Victoria's rehearsal studio and meeting point.

After a session with Omuga Kabisai, I parted ways with my manager and headed for Koch Koch to brood and sulk and plan my next move. I found Aseela on balcony with her guitar scribbling things on the back of an envelope.

'Hey, what's here?' I asked.

She looked at me. 'I'm writing a song. Buy me a beer.'

'Can I see?'

'Why not?' She handed me the envelope. Scribbled in pencil were nice words of Kiswahili poetry. She titled it 'Roho Inakufa'.

'Good girl,' I congratulated her.

'So tell me the bad news. So we've officially lost Lakeshore.'

I nodded. 'We've lost the studio.'

Aseela heaved a heavy sigh. 'What are your plans? Are we

going to make this place our base?'

I nodded. 'This place has been our base for almost a year now.'

We spent the rest of the evening drinking and chatting and loosening up. In the night, we were joined by 'The Poet' Opiyo Willy who had come to 'polish' the song Aseela was writing.

It was times like these that I tried to draw on my 'other life'. Life that pissed me off. Pissed me off more than the woman I had recently slept with who slapped me with thunderous *nyach* (gonorrhea). Adhiambo, she was called. She was a soft hustler who hang around musicians with an attitude I reckoned irrational. The fact that most men of music were drawn to her like fruit flies to a rotten orange confounded me. And she reminded me of Mary-Goretti.

Talking of which... Mary-Goretti had recently come to DreamScape 'to visit'.

She had put on a lot of weight since becoming Agwenge's wife. She was going to be a big woman, I could see.

I knew, deep down, that anything I had with Mary-Goretti was a bonus. I knew—and it proved to me, every time she called, which was often—that we had forged a friendship that was utterly unshakable, despite the fact that she was romantically involved with my kid brother. I also knew that the friendship was based on the perverted part: sex. The sex, I didn't want, she forced. And I knew I wanted her to be happy. She wasn't. I could hear it in her voice. Saw it in her eyes.

'You just came to visit, huh? What about your husband?'

She gave a dramatic shudder and dabbed at smudged mascara. 'Please? P—please? Didi?' She reached across, grasped my hand and sniffled disgustingly.

I pulled roughly away. I had begun to dislike Mary-Goretti and now all I could see was how ugly and loathsome she looked. Sly, flirtatious eyes, too much make-up, cheap weave, pushy tits, calculated little-girl charm and gushing, counterfeit innocence. I also saw a grasping gold digger.

Mary-Goretti had never been open about our fling, refusing to discuss it. I split with her as soon as she announced her marriage to my brother. In fact, we had only seen each other two or three times this year since Agwenge took over her life but in her thick head she always thought she belonged to me. She still sneaked into my house and left her bras and panties in my drawer. She still left her cheap earrings on my bedside table and her chemises and blouses in my wardrobe.

When I asked why she was being so generous with her adultery, she'd smiled wickedly and pulled me into the bedroom. Age-old Adamic weakness of man towards woman and rusty personal principles rather than compassion induced me to have sex with her.

But I was still sulky, just a little bit. It compelled me to think of the two women I felt I truly respected: Mama Iva and Riana. I respected them because they respected themselves.

So, in an attempt to shrug off the sulkiness, I put aside any kind of thoughts of love and romance...and, arrgghh damn, sex... and concentrated on what I had. A home in the hills, some land. Money. Freedom. Some property here in Kisumu. And the band. And what did I miss most? Ayo immediately came to my mind. With Ayo gone, I needed—well, not a shoulder to cry on, because I was handling it well. I needed a sympathetic ear. Mama Iva was the best listener out of all my female friends with the possible exception of Riana—and Riana was nowhere to be found. She had disappeared to Kakamega to literally to figuratively exorcise her personal demons, regrettably including the ghost of her lover.

Towards the end of July of the year, the band took a six month break. His Excellency Ambassador Okoth Ochot went to Nairobi to work out some deals with Attamaxx. He had some ideas and I gave him a chance. The break was not meant to be, due in part to eminent burn-out due to exhaustion, extensive over-performing, over-partying, in-fighting, and disagreements with Attamaxx, another law suit by Uncle, and a notable incident of Mzee Frank getting himself banned from the Sunset Hotel for stealing ashtrays.

So I got in touch with His Excellency Ambassador Okoth Ochot and informed him I was coming to Nairobi. Then I called Mama Iva. She wanted to know how I was coping after losing so much money to my uncle. I said I was fine with it. And, on one level, I was. On another level? I was sulky.

'Be my guest,' she said. 'Come to Nairobi, Indian boy. Come to your love nest, make an old woman happy.'

Nairobi, I went.

Mama Iva was happy. Nairobi soaked me in the wonders of mature love. Consummation was as wild and as frightening as I expected. As always I experienced true passion, a combination of brutality and perpetually unsatisfied desire. She made me share her wildest debauchery with reckless abandon.

Then we shared a pillow and talked. She couldn't understand why Uncle wouldn't throw us out of Lakeside, she said she thought I knew I will need to set up my own studio. But in the meantime, Victoria necessarily had to continue recording at Attamaxx in Nairobi. Secondly Attamaxx and Polygram had talked of presenting us with a gold disc for 'There's No Mathematics In Love.'

Next day I called JB and asked to discuss gold disc deal with Attamaxx. He asked me to meet him at Attamaxx's newly refurbished club in Hurligham, called The Place. He wanted me to see *the place*, his brainchild.

I did meet JB at his club. Beside a few regular customers, the place was nearly empty. We made our way to the back of the bar where we sat down in a booth, well hidden from most of the people in the bar. Even though I enjoyed and appreciated my fan base, this was one of those times I preferred not to be bothered for autographs or pictures. JB overlooked the bar. He was right: this was *The Place*. There were many ornaments and decorations referring to the bar's urban Nairobi theme but they were obviously put together so the whole thing wouldn't seem overdone or ridiculous. There were some familiar benga tunes coming out of the speakers, adding to the relaxed and toned down atmosphere of the bar.

I said, 'You know, if it wasn't for you bringing me here I would have probably never found this place, and even if, by coincidence I would have walked down this street I still wouldn't have noticed it.'

'That's the whole point.' JB explained, 'We could have gone to Hallians or Garden Square or something like that but believe me, when you live in Nairobi you're happy there are places not overrun by Lingala music. Only people familiar with this city will know of this place since it's new. It probably won't be that crowded either... so let's go in. It's freezing out here.'

With that said we entered the bar. JB was right. He ordered two Pilsners. 'You can drink whatever beer you want, as long as it's a Pilsner.' JB ruled. 'I'm not paying for it, they are promoting it here. We have crates and crates of the lot.'

'Good then, I should relax my tired bones.' I said.

'What?' JB asked a bit confused.

'Wasn't that Kalenga Nzaazi's line in 'Ni Mimi Tu?' I asked.

'Yeah it was,' JB answered, 'but I will stick to my promotional gimmicks. Free beer is unheard of in this country and it's not my idea of building clientele here. Maybe you should write a song about this, invent and patent a Pilsner-phrase!'

We both laughed at that.

'You know I could come to this bar just for the cool atmosphere here to compose new music.' I said. I felt the conversation was drying out a bit and talking music, I knew, was always one of the best ways to revive a conversation. I was right again.

'Oh, sure,' JB agreed. 'So you have another album that could topple 'There's No Mathematics In Love'?' he asked.

'I have all sorts of music bubbling up here.' I tapped my forehead. 'So have you been listening to me lately?' I asked.

'I've been listening to a lot of the stuff you recorded at

Lakeshore... the likes contained in *Lake Victoria Breeze* album like 'Anyango Nyar Nam' actually,' JB answered. 'Apparently my bet is Ayo was the best of your lot, so I've been listening to her quite a bit lately. And I suggest this: do an album with her again.'

'Without Mawazo?'

'With Sam Ojua Kali Man. Ayo's one of people's favourites.' JB said. I wondered whether that was a good idea. As a producer, JB always knew what would sell. But I knew he wanted to recreate our old sound which still sold well. I knew he was even capable of getting Mawazo Ya Pesa to sing with Ayo. He knew the singer had a big following but he was completely insecure. 'She's a class act all the way,' he continued.

We drank in silence for a few moments. Then JB spoke. 'There was this one song I thought was awesome,' he said, 'I can't remember the name but I went something like...'

Suddenly softly he began singing the song:

> I would dial the number
> just to listen to your breath.
> And I would stand inside my hell
> and hold the hand of death.

That was 'Mary Magdalene' also known as ' Adundo Nyar Jo Nam' from Ayo's *Wend Osote* album of '86.

'Come out of your thoughts,' I spoke 'I love that song too. It's one of my favourites.' I was amazed how good JB's singing sounded. Even though he was getting tipsy, it still sounded amazing. I knew JB was a great actor but I never thought the guy could sing as well.

'Or how about her latest tune.' JB continued. 'I love this song 'Ayibu' from your *Live In Amsterdam* album.'

Suddenly and without warning he sang as loud as he could:

> *Ooh inauma nikifikiriiiiiaaahhaahh...*
> *Waniuwa uwa na tena inuma uma*

Waniuwa uwa na tena inauma uma

He even imitated the guitar-chords from the song. The entire bar looked at us for a few seconds, but it didn't make JB stop because everybody was laughing at his sudden performance.

'I think they heard you at Mombasa Island!' I laughed.

'Let's discuss your gold disc then,' he said. His terms were very simple: he wanted ten percent of all sales. Yeah, your guess is as good as mine: bribe.

I told him I needed to sleep over this and he told me to take my time.

4.

I found His Excellency Ambassador Okoth Ochot near Hilton. He was excited and pleased with himself. He had a job for the band. The wind seemed like it could cut through anything with its freezing breath. Nonetheless the streets of the city were busy, crowded and alive. From time to time we passed a street-hawker selling pirated copies of my songs. There were people standing in long queues waiting for their buses. The atmosphere of the evening rush-hour was quite a picture onto itself. Nothing much was said during the walk to Six Eighty Hotel except that he wanted me to meet someone.

Turned out he was an elderly man who was gnawing on a sandwich and reeking of bad body odor. Joseph was his name. He was a consultant working in the health sector and he was organizing an AIDS awareness campaign and wanted Victoria to go over across and do a series of concerts in Uganda.

I was not game for this idea. I pushed along for the sake of Mr. Manager was enthusiastic about it. For starters, Joseph the Ugandan appeared to be putting a show, said this was the first time he experienced the real Nairobi. He found the statue of Mzee Jomo Kenyatta at the KICC mesmerizing. Many times when he visited Nairobi, his experience was limited to his hotel-room and Nairobi Cinema. He had immediately fallen in love with the beauty and the character of this vibrant city, so he inhaled its atmosphere as if it were some reviving drug.

From time to time he would ask His Excellency about the things he saw on those streets. Whether it was regular tourist-information or more specific details about the way people were acting, His Excellency was happy to give all the explanation he could give. He too loved this city and he was happy Joseph could appreciate it too. It was funny to see how this seemingly pointless conversation began to break down some of the walls between us.

Suddenly Joseph said to me: 'How much do you charge for doing an AIDS concert with us?'

I had an answer ready in mind. 'Fifty thousand per day,' I told him.

We were standing in the Six Eighty's bar drinking on his account. From the outside, Kenyatta Avenue looked very inviting. The decorations on the bar immediately gave away the traditional Kenyan look and feel. Joseph was amazed by the somber mood of this seemingly very entertaining bar.

I was still gauging him. Something about him wasn't right. He never maintained a direct eye contact. And I doubted if he was indeed a businessman: he had no value for time.

Then Joseph sat down and opened his briefcase. He quickly took us through the details of the project. He wanted twenty days in Uganda. The client was Uganda National AIDS Control Council and I would meet them in Uganda.

AIDS always scared me. In Kisumu it was spreading like wild fire in these frightening months late 80s. In 1985 my father had summoned his entire family members and informed us of a new sexually transmitted disease called AIDS. The shocking thing was that this disease, like the dreaded *chira*, had no cure. What startled and scared me most was the stigma that came with this disease. When it killed you nobody was allowed to touch your contaminated body, you were wrapped up in a black polythene bag and quickly buried in the presence of health workers and the police. I was witnessing such scary incidents of people succumbing to AIDS especially in Kisumu. Over the last few years there had been an exodus of ladies from Uganda who, because of instability in their country, crossed into our country looking for jobs in large numbers. Most of them were employed as housemaids and barmaids. Already at this time the effects of AIDS were much known in Uganda than in Kenya. The ladies, some of whom may had already contracted the disease, still looked normal and very attractive to the young men around the lake who were highly impressed by the humbleness and etiquette displayed by the foreign beauties. Young men started marrying them and taking them to their rural areas. Their numbers increased in bars and prostitution became lucrative and widespread. Acquiring sex became a zero-sum game. Men were sharing women not knowing the consequences. Life was good and money was in people's pockets because of the uncorrupted economy. Beer flowed. Men wined dined danced and wenched in the mushrooming bars and clubs around town. With cheap sex and plenty of money, who cared about Government posters and billboards reading AIDS KILLS, HELP CRUSH AIDS along the roads.

'Hey... are you in the mood to go with it!' Joseph startled me out of my reverie.

We talked a bit more, set the time and the place where we would meet each other tomorrow and then we said goodbyes. We watched as Joseph walked back the elevators, to his hotel room.

Before entering the elevator Joseph raised his arm as a final goodbye.

His Excellency Ambassador Okoth Ochot and I then parted when I had to go see Mama Iva. She and I walked through the cold streets of the city hand in hand going nowhere, saying not a word. We were not in the mood for anything. We eventually took a taxi back to Nairobi West. Though it was freezing, there was an entirely different coldness plaguing me. I couldn't say it was a bad evening and Joseph appeared a fantastic guy and fifty thousand a day for twenty days was good money, given they were taking care of all expenses. But with that came the realization that all I could want in this life was to make more money. It was the first time I was getting into a deal like this using music to teach people about the dangers of AIDS. My mood started to shift as I became more and more saddened over the fact that my chances of making the world a better place were little to none. AIDS was a monster that wouldn't be easy to tame. But I would give it a try.

Within a few minutes, we were at Mama Iva's private apartment, I immediately went to her stereo. Pulled an album out of its case and, at a low volume, let the song play. I softly sang along as I danced. Mama Iva stared at me silently then went to the fridge for a drink. No word was spoken between us.

The lyrics of the song filled the room:

> I would dial the number
> just to listen to your breath.
> And I would stand inside my hell
> and hold the hand of death.

When the song ended and Mama Iva's glass was empty, I went to bed. Sad about my life but happy with the idea I would spend some days playing music with positive messages gave me some hope.

5.

Orchestra Victoria arrived in Kampala four nights later in style. The band has no history with Ugandan audiences, and when we appeared in that small city, we found our shows had been advertised. There were posters all over, much of it were messages on HIV/AIDS awareness. You have to understand, we were a simple band. We thought we sucked and we tried really hard to make good records and we practiced. We didn't feel like the biggest; certainly not the best band in Africa, there was the legendary Franco and OK Jazz. We just felt like the same eight dorks that were touring in a van in Western Kenya four years ago, that hadn't changed even after we got lucky and went on tour to Europe.

But Kisumu and Kampala were not very far apart, we were famous here as much. Our records were played here and we were imitated. The Mugogo Stadium was a perfect venue for Ugandans to see this legendary band in a very intimate setting. The venue had a very great and relaxing feel, making each show there a special event. And the new Victoria only elevated that feel to another level. All the vocalists had great stage presence and the amazing front woman was 'Queen of Sheba' Aseela. The Ugandan fans were shouting for Mawazo and Ayo. But the band playing live with new experienced musicians was sure a good sign of transition. We played a short, but solid set. In fact as were warming up while (Joseph and his team gave their vibes on the dangers of HIV/AIDS and distributed T-shirts and condoms to screaming fans) I told Roki Fela and Sam Ojua Kali Man that it was time to test our capability as a reformed band. We had not rehearsed for this concert, many musicians had been called back from holidays. Nevertheless, our set was solid, and the band was in great shape and we played our parts flawlessly. Because of the short nature of our set, Victoria concentrated on our most known songs, and gave the fans the maximum value out of our performance. You could clearly see that all the band members were enjoying themselves on stage and had a great time.

Joseph's itinerary indicated that we would be touring Uganda for the next seven days.

The audience went totally crazy at our gigs and lived through every moment with the band. It miffed me that Ugandan fans had incredible amount of energy. This was an educational tour, so we limited our sets and moderated the performances like it was modern psychosis. Through subtle improvisations, we managed to raise awareness on HIV/AIDS and to endear ourselves to people who were looking for something beyond a good time.

We were psyched and got inspired to play more of this tour in terms of sending messages. Not having a functional AIDS song in our repertoire was not a problem because we improvised and composed on there and then on the stage. Then it was the last of hopefully a bunch of shows around the Mt. Elgon area as well as the band traveling to the northwest through Gulu. His Excellency Ambassador Okoth Ochot and I accompanied Joseph to Kampala to their offices then we went to the bank to have him transfer our money into Victoria's account. He did the transfer and showed me the documents. He gave me a copy of the transfer slip. Then we parted when His Excellency Ambassador Okoth Ochot and I boarded a midday bus to Gulu to join the band and Joseph took a flight to Nairobi.

We wrapped up the tour, played three shows for the Northern Uganda communities. We had to be escorted by soldiers with machine guns throughout in compliance with the Ugandan government's security alert about this region being the most dangerous in the country. But playing jammed shows and getting mobbed by eager crowds, it didn't look like there was any danger. What these northerners needed was a good time, downright dance. There were frequent announcements of guerrilla activities in that region. We returned to Kampala in readiness for the trip home. I went to the bank. No money had been sighted.

No money had been transferred!

Love it, hate it, cry about it, even go stark raving mad: a glorious mess. Plain and simple. We had been conned. Joseph could not be traced. The bank knew nothing of the transfer, they asked me for a copy of the transfer slip Joseph had given me and I couldn't find it.

This was Africa, the place where smart birds would take your money and spend it on crap and line their wallets while you sweated. You want to know why we're in such an economic mess?

It's because of those smart birds like Joseph taking risks with other people's money, but we'll not blame it on these schlumps because it's easier and people can relate better to the idea of irresponsible politicians and government officials getting wealthy through corruption while we watch. Some poor fellow just decides to go to parliament and he fools people during campaigns and makes promises and gets elected. And then suddenly he's a millionaire. So when we see this, we're motivated. As soon as an opportunity comes, we jump at it. Ours is not a society of hard working men and women, it's a society of greedy grabbers and it's been so since Independence.

Can I borrow one thousand dollars now? To take my band back to Kenya? The journalists at the press conference said nothing.

6.

Joseph ran off to USA, we soon knew. His Excellency Ambassador Okoth Ochot was trying to track him down through his contacts. I soon put it behind my mind as a bad dream and turned up in Nairobi with the tapes to produce the new album *Victoria Live In Uganda.*

Recording in Nairobi had by now endeared us to new sounds. At Attamaxx, I met BB Mofranck. He was in Nairobi on a short visit from Japan. With him was the saxophonist Tabu Ngongo. We sat down in Attamaxx waiting room and swapped yarns about music.

'Put some wind in your music,' the soft spoken Tabu said.

'Beg your pardon?'

'Saxophone.'

I understood. Tabu's other name was 'Ildephonse Supersax'

And B.B. Mo-Franck had heaps of advice on what made his Vundumuna succeed as an Afro pop act. 'Change your style,' he said. 'Try and be African. Sing in English. Don't use Luo words.

Match the success of 'There's No Mathematics In Love.' Don't go back into benga even if your version is urban... that is for Kisumu which you are not. You have demonstrated that you are bigger.'

I pondered that. Nairobi was giving me all sorts of wacky ideas. The other day Mama Iva suggested that I do a song for Kanu. For Moi. Singing praise songs for politicians and well-off business people was not my cup of tea. I loathed the idea. Now I came to terms with the contemplation to go into a new area: functional music.

I asked Tabu Ngongo if he had any good saxophonist in mind. He snorted rudely. Then he turned to B.B. Mo-Franck and there was a brief interlude while they jabbered away in Lingala and French.

Two hours later, an elderly man with a saxophone case joined us in Attamaxx waiting room. From the respectful way Tabu and BB greeted him, he must have been a man with some weight. His name, I was told, was Vicky Bashakado. The two Zaïreans told him I was in need of a saxophonist. He sighed and rolled his shoulders and put his beady eyes on me. Then, very methodically, he opened his sax case.

His sax had not been played for over five years, he said. Then he lifted his instrument and held it up, his eyes lit up with a warm admiration. Once the mouthpiece touched his lips, his entire body relaxed and he closed his eyes. He blew lightly and a sharp, lonely sound hung in the air. He blew into the mouthpiece again, harder this time and sustained the note, clear and achingly sweet. His long, dexterous fingers lovingly manipulated the keys as he continued to expel air into the mouthpiece. Light and sound permeated every cell of his body and spilled over into the room. He was transported to another universe.

Over the next few days I hung out with this old man and made a connection. He seemed smaller, almost frail compared to his dominating stage presence. He stood a bit less than six feet tall. He was fit, trim, and solidly built, and his moustache was still quite dark. But his beard and the hair on his head had gone

411

mostly white, and when he walked he moved gingerly, perhaps the lingering effect of some prostate trouble a while back.

Long story short, Vicky agreed to work for me in my band.

7.

The week was full of events. I ran into Ayo. I ran into her at Attamaxx where I took the tapes for the production of the *Victoria Live In Uganda* album and she was in the middle of recording her first solo album.

I walked in on her in the studio right in the middle of a session. She was recording with Attamaxx's studio band. She had been in Kisumu a few times last month to get help with her lyrics and had consulted 'The Poet' Opiyo Willy a lot. She was seated in a booth in the recording area behind the corrugated metal screens in the 30 x 25 x 18-foot live area recording her parts while the band played live in the studio. She had huge headphones and she was singing, curling and pursing and flipping her lips behind a large mic. Everyone in the studio was looking intently at her.

Standing behind a corrugated screen at the back of the control room was Attamaxx studio's *de facto* chief engineer, Meja Okilo. He saw me and beckoned hastily as he went up the stairs into the control room. I crossed over, went up the stairs. The control room was long and thin, with a large window to the right of the console overlooking the main recording area, which was about one storey high and had a few screens suspended from the ceiling to break things up. It was quite a good-sized room, with one end slightly under the control room, and it was live but not too live. I perched myself on a stool and looked around. The control room was complemented by a 36-channel Harrison Series 24 console, Urei 813B main monitors and a 24-track Studer A820 recorder running Ampex tape at 30ips.

Looking through the window into the live room, I caught Ayo's eyes. She looked at me and looked at me hard as sang through her part neatly without missing a lyric. I saw that most of the studio musicians hadn't changed. Lee Kinyua's drums were located in the far-left corner of the live area, next to Radiglo on bass, while Cliff Oswaga and Joan Magero—one of only two women vocalists, along with Ayo— faced them, so that their guitar mics were pointing away from the screened-off kit to minimize leakage. In terms of the co-production roles, Eddy Blacky Mphalele largely directed operations, saying 'Let's do this next,' or 'Let's try that,' while also overlapping with Jimmy Makossa when deciding what sounded good, where a song should be heading and how to best achieve this.

I watched the mother of my son sing and my cup boiled over. She looked more attractive—her eyes registering every line of the lyric. My heart was screaming with excitement. Ayo was always a confident vocalist; she was also quite picky about pitching, so sometimes she could be more sensitive than other people. That was why her tracks normally had to be re-recorded last after everything has been put on tape. She normally insisted on this. She thought her pitching was a weakness, although I didn't consider it to be much of a problem.

During the break, Ayo and I found something to sit on in the tape machine deck at the back of the control room. We hugged and kissed and held each other. She had a sensible choice of short dress showing those one litre Coca Cola bottle *madiaba* legs of hers. She had on a white tee with a green open shirt over it, and accessorized by a silver necklace with an elephant on it I'd seen her wear several times. It was all tight, so it wasn't exactly slob-like by nature. She looked actually quite good when you could see the legs. I just wished she would sort the hair. Surely she could find a colour of weave that complimented her dark complexion. She was lovely, nonetheless. A hair colour change wouldn't make all the difference!

We sat down to drink sodas. I asked about the recording and she said it was quite a tough discipline being forced to record everything on 23 tracks while allowing for the time code. We chit-chatted mindlessly for about five minutes before Meja Okilo came up the stairs from the studio to remind Ayo that she had two minutes left.

Ayo finished her soda. 'Dino.' Her hand reached out and grabbed my shoulder before I could whirl and turn, and held it tight. Startled, I turned to look at her. Her nostrils dilated, she nodded rapidly. 'You look fine.'

Then she smiled, sharp and yet discomfortingly friendly, and used her other hand to take my chin and tap me on the cheekbone with a long finger. 'More than fine, really. Handsome.' Her thoughtful tone of voice was almost as if she was talking to herself.

I was still not sure if it was because of the unexpected touch of her hand, or the random intimacy between two people who'd had an awkward relationship and had a baby together and fell apart and weren't completely sure whether a thing still existed. She made me uncomfortable. All I was aware of at the moment was a searing realization that this woman wanted me. Badly, intimately... *sexually*. And right behind that, was a sly devil's question of how (exactly) Ayo would make that clear.

I stepped back, getting myself out of reach of both her touch and that really dangerous thought. I could feel my cheeks burn, and my voice was full of false cheer.

'Lt's talk later. Sometime. Get back to work.' I winced.

She held her gaze. 'Stay with me, Otis. Stay here for a little while. Please.' I was not sure whether I heard those words. With a wink, she ran down the stairs and strode back to her recording booth. I sat there for a moment pondering her words.

8.

Ayo dominated my living daylights for the next two weeks. She drew me into the world of her sultry delights in Nairobi's underworld in Eastlands. She made me 'form' her a band and appeared poised to dominate a man's world. I recruited men and hastily put a band in place in less than a week. Most of the men were burnt-out Nairobi session musicians and Attamaxx readily supplied the instruments.

For two weeks, I acted the solo guitar player in this band along with a drummer, my new sax player Vicky, a bass player, and two female vocalists. We also had a guy who played keyboards and harmonica. Ayo was the so-called leader and 'manager' of the band.

For some days we played a few gigs together. They were rough and I felt the band was going nowhere. Ayo thought she could get them to do a live performance at Eastland's Benga Marathon that had a regularly scheduled live show featuring local bands in Eastlands. There was also the added bonus of obtaining a broadcast quality video that she could use for promo purposes. It would also give this woman an opportunity to really showcase her 'talent' as a bandleader. Therefore, I decided to support her.

I convinced Ochieng Kamau and JB to give them a hearing. The venue was Attamaxx's The Place club. When she arrived along with the bass player (who was boinking her at the time), it was obvious that she was half drunk. They emerged from a hired *matatu* with drinks in hand. What? Boozing up while driving to the gig. Swell. They unloaded and set up their gear just in time for the start of the show. I joined them on stage and took one of the cheap guitars they had, quickly tuned it. Things went south immediately. She missed her cue to come in on her lead vocals during the first song and gave me the stink-eye as if I was the one to blame. She was singing flat on every song. Even worse, her bass player boyfriend, whose instrument was out of tune, was stepping on everyone's vocals, my guitar solos and even her pathetic attempts at playing keyboard which generally consisted of just hammering the same chord couplet over and over and over.

In between sets, the 'host' of the program was interviewing her. She had a look on her face that was a cross between a drowning-man-look and a scowl. Her answers were terse and dismissive and showed contempt for the small audience as well as her fellow band members.

I saw JB grab a microphone. I heard him announce my name over the P.A. and he motioned for me to approach the stage. When I got there, he had a simple statement.

'Give me something to puke in.' To which I responded by placing a trash container in front of him.

After vomiting profusely into the can, he walked off the stage and into the men's room, all the while cursing and muttering things.

I followed him into the men's room and found him pissing. 'What is the meaning of this?' he asked as he was pissing furiously. 'What game are you playing at?'

I fumbled for words.

'Is this thing meant to embarrass me, eh?' he asked as he shook his thing. 'Me? I have a reputation to keep. For Attamaxx and for our respected customers.' He stuffed his thing in his jeans and faced me. 'Tell me why?' he almost wailed.

I shrugged. 'Trust me I don't know the meaning of this. Ayo is an accomplished artiste. A fine and disciplined girl, you know that.'

JB glared at me, his face set, his nostrils twitching. Then he spoke. 'I'm cutting her off *my* studio as soon as that damned album is finished. Do you have a problem? No, you don't.'

'Please...'

'I'm pissed off!' he yelled. He zipped up his pants and walked out of the toilet.

During the second set, JB and the officials of Attamaxx all got up and left. We were playing a blues song in G, while she was pathetically playing a harmonica in a completely different key, with obviously embarrassing results along with the out-of-tune sax honking away. Mercifully, the show was over after a few more songs.

Later that evening in my presence, she was ranting and raving to her boyfriend and the drummer about how they blew the show and a litany of other complaints and that she was bragging about 'firing' them from the band after they were done with playing two upcoming booked gigs. The drummer tipped off the other band members as to her intentions. I saw where this was going. I wanted to take that pressure away from her. I consider how embarrassing this thing was and how badly it was damaging our reputations, mine, especially.

Next day I called a meeting and dissolved the band.

When she got to know about it, Ayo was up in arms against me. 'You are evil,' she yelled at me, 'Your walk is evil, your talks are evil, your head is full of evil thoughts. It doesn't matter to you that I'm the mother of your child! BUT I HATE YOOOOUUUU!"

I agreed with her. My mother had once said, 'In future you will be a bad man, a very bad man.'

'I'm evil but I'm protecting you from self-destruction. You are trying to destroy me, you put up that show to damage my image in front of Attamaxx and my fans.'

'YOU ARE EVVIILLLL!' she yelled. She picked an ashtray and hurled it at me. She didn't mean it to scare me; she meant it to break my skull. I saw it coming for my skull, I ducked. It whizzed by very close and made its way through the curtain, through the window glass into the street outside.

Then she came tearing at me with her claws. I held her, and escaped with an ugly scratch on my temple. I held her and her teeth landed on my arm. She sank her teeth into my flesh and I beat her real bad. Thumped her soundly on her back and on her cheeks. She broke down, started crying. Still I held her. As she cried, she told me I was evil. I had used her to build my career. I made her pregnant and dumped her. I didn't care for the pains she was going through as a single mother. Did I pause for one moment to think she too, was an artist and an independent spirit. I was running away from my responsibilities, was not concerned about parenting. What about her? She had always given that yarn before about me putting my artistic independence above everybody around me. Pam's name often worsened the wound in the middle of her chest. Both inside and out, she was a wreck. Over and over again, she told herself she hated Pam, it was worse. That was the trouble: as much as she wanted to hate me for ultimately leaving her broken, it was impossible for her to say it.

It took finally the wound on her leg to finally snap Ayo out of her tantrums. She had gotten fallen while running in the rain in the precincts of Dandora on her own. She had slipped downhill in the black cotton soil mud, crashing her leg on a boulder.

Later Ayo had calmed down, 'Sorry, sweetie. I didn't mean...'

More whimpering.

There was an anxiety in her voice that virtually drove me out of my senses and put me on an emotional roller coaster whereupon I wondered why it took her so long to pour her grief this way, even plot to destroy me. I normally thought that she was unlike other women, that she was an independent-minded artist.

'Take me back Otis,' she whispered. 'Take me back if you can.'

I nodded. She reached up and took my big, warm hands into her tiny, cold ones. She snuggled down against me on the sofa. We seemed to meld together perfectly; a match made in heaven... though that may have been a bit of a stretch. For whatever reason, though, I was almost sure that she needed to warm her nest and be her man, it was not love. The new version of her, sardonic and hopeless, *wanted* me. The old version of her stopped trying to resurface and let the dark monster take over. Part of her enjoyed it, and another part felt lost, like it didn't belong.

In the days that followed, I found myself spending days and nights in Ayo's house in Dandora. I held my two year old son, Okello. I watched him find his way around the tiny flat pulling at things. Late in the night after he'd slept, his mother and I nestled on the couch and watched bootleg videos of *Emanuelle,* the ones Ayo had smuggled out of Europe. I made Ayo confront her demons. We found a name for her album. I wanted a title that reflected her general state of body and mind. *Dawn of a New Era*, I suggested. I wasn't sure if Ayo was being serious or on a wind up mission, but I suggested a name that symbolized a new beginning.

The record hit the shops in August of 1989.

I played the album, listened. All the songs were derived from personal experiences. I clearly saw Ayo understood the promiscuous hard drinking and violent life she sang about because she lived it. She could deliver her songs with such emotion. She knew firsthand about struggle for love and heartbreak. She didn't attack men, she blamed women for letting men run them over and dump them and hurt them again and again. We took time to critique the album and found some flaws in some songs. She explained to me her songwriting technique. Like most good singers, she always had a sense as to whether or not she could improve on a vocal, but always tried to avoid doing too many takes. When she was working on her songs, she liked to try different options. All in all *Dawn of a New Era* was a quality, hooky album that succeeded in meshing two things that many artists had difficulty in properly combining: pop-influenced female vocals (which could be dull or flat sounding in many African bands) and genuinely interesting progressive rumba. It also had a couple of extremely good bass riffs (particularly prominent and badass in the haunting 'Siku Nitakufa') that I really loved. In the first part of the song, I played the fills after every vocal line, and then in the second part, the reeds played the fills during the choruses and the copper during my solos. The lyrics gave listeners personal glimpses into life lived on an emotional roller coaster: the 'voyage' at the heart of the record was a misguided love affair. Her lamentable choices, sung with heart-torn regrets and played with ragged glory by the experienced hands of Attamaxx studio band, went down as easy as red hot knife inside Blue Band margarine. After a few years full time musical career with Victoria, and a few months of nothing at all, it seemed like the time was right and hey presto! A fantastic new album *Dawn of a New Era* was born. Ah, you bet new record deals were set up for Ayo by Attamaxx.

For all this, it didn't succeed in truly pushing the envelope to 'phenomenal', as many compositions lacked a certain climactic resolution that I sought. In addition, I felt that the males supporting vocals were a bit rough, and there was little to write home about lyrically. The style was an improvement from Victoria, however, and an indication that Ayo, as a musical graduate of Victoria, was well capable of excelling in the course that she'd chosen for herself.

In my heart of hearts, was a sucker for Ayo's alt-urban Kenyan sound and this 1989 release was up to her usual high standards. She was articulate, strong, persuasive, argumentative, and beautiful—and she was my dearest, dearest friend. I took a moment to look at the photo on the cover of the album. It was beautiful; an ageless, blue-tinged androgynous Ayo giving something off-camera: the 100-metre stare. I especially liked it because it captured her at a peculiar, transitional moment in her career.

When I returned to Kisumu, the elderly saxophonist, Vicky came with me. He quickly settled in the band and even got a new name: Mifupa Ya Zamani.

9.

I returned to Kisumu to be confronted with some family problems: my sister Akong'o was dating 'The Poet' Opiyo Willy Wilberforce, the composer, the singer, the former policeman. How this happened no one could tell. Except I blamed myself for it more than Mama blamed me.

Akong'o had completed her KCPE at Lwak Girls with a C+ and I wanted to sponsor her to do nursing. She was staying with me. The musicians often came to my place and even my sister, a good convent girl, fell under the spell of Willy, the singer with a sweet tongue who had all the philosophical things to say about women and love. Unknown to me, she often visited him at his place. Things came to a head when (while I was away in Nairobi) she refused to go back to my house and it seemed as though their affair would become a topic. But Roki Fela, who was the acting deputy bandleader and who was trying to connect Akong'o with a Busia-based businessman named Ruganda, told Willy to pack his bag; he was being fired from the band for misconduct.

Then Willy did the unthinkable, he celebrated Akong'o in song. Roki Fela too (not much of a composer) wrote a song for Ruganda who loved Akong'o too and when the two song-subjects met they hit it off. This caused real problems for Roki because the Ugandan would buy drinks for the whole band during concerts and in the name the young woman Roki sang about. It dawned on Roki he had lost the battle, so he contacted me. Willy, too, realized the danger of elevating his girlfriend Akong'o to celebrity with an unrecorded composition: she could be snatched away by the rich man. So Willy went to my father to declare his interest in marrying Akong'o.

As soon as I landed in Kisumu, it was Willy who came complaining to me. I called my sister and she told me she had made up her mind to get married to Willy. While my father appeared not to have a problem with the idea, Mama was flatly against it. The Ugandan businessman came around and he, too, declared his interest in marrying Akong'o. He left my father with a lot of money and bottles of whiskey and wine.

Willy then took advantage of my father's support and married my sister.

My family responded with muted acquiescence to the news. Neither parent questioned Akong'o's decision, or asked if she was aware of the difficulties ahead. There was no pre-nuptial passing on of parental advice or enthusiastic discussion of any wedding or marriage arrangements. All the usual elements of an engagement were absent. I was a bit puzzled: mine was the kind of family that did not ignore the elephant in the room. With no one admitting to a problem, it was impossible to address it. An invisible gulf lay between Akong'o and her husband, no doubt filled with the questions they couldn't bring themselves to ask. My siblings also kept their distance; once married it was as though Akong'o ceased to exist.

Suffice to say the whole drama miffed me. The philosophically-minded Willy actually had the temerity to seduce and win the heart of my sister and convince her to marry him! Akong'o of all people! She could never date musicians... swore never to date one. I believed her when she normally said she will take her time in life, study and become a nurse and then get married to a doctor. I believed her. I couldn't believe that the man who actually broke her vow and literally swept her off her feet was a singer of lower ranking in Victoria.

I gave them one of my houses in Okore Estate to live in. I visited them there one evening to find out how they were coping, hoping to wipe cobwebs out of my sister's eyes and get her out of the damned marriage. Akong'o never expected me. As I closed the door behind me with a shaking hand, I saw her fighting her instinct to run through it. Much as none of my family had visited her, it appeared she was intent to work on her marriage.

I asked Akong'o if she was really married to this man and she nodded. 'I love Willy.'

I sat with Willy, my brother-in-law relaxing and talking. We shared some of his moments with Victoria. Then he fished out his classic *There's No Mathematics In Love* album and put the needle on his other composition 'Mwanamke Si Gari.' We laughed over the lyrics:

> A woman is not like vehicle
> Try owning one
> A vehicle breaks down and stalls but
> a woman breaks down and bolts.
> Try owning one

Can women who are addicted to alcohol
be in a steady and faithful relationship?
Ooohhh? Mama! Ooohhh? Mama!

Any woman however simple you think
she is a complex machine.
Try owning one

I had hardly ever paid much attention to this particular song maybe because it was overshadowed by Willy's other compositions including the masterpiece 'There's No Mathematics In Love'. I had listened to all the songs in the albums hundreds of times, but today as I sat with my brother-in-law, all of a sudden the words had new meaning to me. I wasn't ever going to listen to this song the same again. He was such a creative composer; his songs had form and structure. They were not instant hits, they were hidden gold. They were songs that were going to be listened to for many years to come. Actually Willy was always philosophical said true things about human relationships. He touched the hearts of many women, many of whom expressed great admiration for his compositions. Women loved to listen to these songs in which pangs of yearning and denial were typically unmistakable. That was why we called him 'The Poet'. His songs could make women cry. His other song 'Wasichana Wacha Tabia Mbaya' was already our lovable hard-hitting anthemic song in disco and on radio, and was soon to be a classic.

On a lighter note, I asked Willy how he did it. How he, a singer and an artist of low ranking, convinced my sister, an upright, principled, strict SDA Sabbath keeper, hard-to-impress, no-nonsense and focused kind of person.

'Poetry,' he said.

Poetry, indeed.

Akong'o, on the other hand, wanted to know when I was going to marry. My family wanted me to marry. It had come to a point when my father summoned me twice to discuss it. My mother had, on many occasions, gotten a girl for me. She was concerned because my younger brother Ouru had recently brought a girl home to her; a girl he intended to marry. Now my younger sister was married too. Yeah, the pressure was immense. Personally I detested this pressure. I was busy. Plus my life was fine, so I reckoned. I no longer wanted to see Mama because of this unnecessary pressure.

On my way from my sister's place, I stopped by a *kinyozi* at Kibuye Shopping Centre. It was a decent place for a haircut, and I liked the one male stylist. He was good, and quick, and did a decent job. He was busy when I walked in, so I thumbed through the stack of hair styling magazines on the coffee table.

'What a sorry place for a superstar?' a deep manly voice said to my right.

Mo Thwaka!

'Yes, sure it is, Mo,' I replied, taking in the well-built former Victoria's bass player, his face recently nicely furred up with a new beard. About a month's worth of stubble, which was turning into a nice black beard, high up on his cheeks, and already nice and thick across his strong jaw, and around his thick lips.

It was one of those rare breaks in the dry September; he must have spotted my pick-up in the parking. This rugged looking young lion told me he was on his way to the gym. He had also taken advantage of the few hours of the hot and dry weather to wear a tight sleeveless T-shirt and a pair of cutoffs. When he bent his arm to pick up a magazine, his bicep flexed nicely and the rough outline of a fat nipple pushed against his shirt. Unlike me, he was doing his best to maintain of his youth and despite his heavy drinking, he was in god shape.

We jawed for a bit, talking about music, our European tour and the weather. He had a big smile and we seemed to be hitting it off quite well. He started telling me about Delta Force and KSK's management problems, and I was wondering where this was leading to when my barber came to my rescue and told me he was ready for me. I quickly excused myself.

'I'll see you around. I'll send my wife for my royalty cheque next week.' he said.

I nodded, and went off for my haircut. My barber made quick work on the wild bush of hair on my head. He shampooed it, conditioned it, used Pressol to liven it, then he fluffed it and gave it shape. He trimmed up my beard nicely, and we had our usual discussion about his chick and his *mitumba* business. As I went back to the counter to pay up, Mo Thwaka was there, settling up with his stylist. I decided to roll the dice.

'Still here?' I asked.

'Yeah, I decided I needed a haircut too. I'm going to the audition tonight for Benga Chamber; I've run out of work.'

Orchestra Benga Chamber was a new band in Kisumu.

'You are out of work?' I asked simply. I was in no mood to get into Delta Force gossip with him; I knew where to get the information on my rival band if I wanted to.

'Well, haven't you heard Delta Force is *kaput*, since Spark Onyango hanged himself last week and killed not only himself but our Mombasa tour.'

That item on Onyango's death had jarred me a bit. I doubted if it was suicide. But why was the party ending so soon in Delta Force? When they first appeared, they were so dreary, so mechanical, and now soon out of print.

I found myself asking Mo why he was quitting.

'Well regrouping that band after Spark will take some time and when it does, I doubt if they will emerge stronger than one would expect. There are two groups within the orchestra.'

Two groups within the orchestra simply meant weak leadership. I thought primarily they wanted to sell some records and make some dough instead of fighting. Couldn't blame them. I liked competition and I felt the cold slap of reality when I learned it could cause problems. Mo Thwaka was feeble-minded still that was why he failed to see that Spark Onyango's death wasn't suicide; it was elimination. I only wondered which faction Mo belonged. You know, Delta Force never ceased to amuse me.

It appeared like their Urban Benga act consisted of revolving bouts of whining, slacking, scrimping, bitching and tantrums, with a little soukous and body putty thrown in for good measure.

When Nicholas Opija, er, RIP Dr. Nico Pedhos, formed this 'group,' he was in danger of becoming a can-we-really-make-it cover band. But luckily most people had never heard of a Luo band playing such rumbastic Kisumu town Urban Benga, so the fans never noticed that the band had no material of its own. By the time I arrived on the scene, Delta Force was already battling their inability to procure a mainstream audience. Then the 'group' began to splinter shortly after I joined and the formidable Spark Onyango left and Opija failed to hire pros and the 'group' got noticeably worse because the two prominent members who left (Benz Benji Obat and Spark Onyango) never really quit. Until Opija died and there was nothing left. The 'first faction' got back and the 'second faction' that included KSK and Co. left *en masse* to join me in Victoria. When KSK and Co. moved back to take over Delta Force after tasting professionalism in Victoria, he attempted to introduce new changes. And the 'first faction' grew tired of his ranting. But for a short few months, it was as if he was going to change the band as we knew it. Didn't happen. Or did it? I saw them in action on two separate occasions and you could sense they weren't going to unite and connect with their fans. Nothing was going to change the band, not even Uncle's money. The real owners of Delta Force were the 'first faction' which had the support of Opija's widow, Lotta. They were a cult band whether they played Urban Benga, rumba, or whatever... that was the way it was. It was a hard thing to accept. At least I knew, judging from all the loving gossip I was getting from men like Mo, *I was going places.*

Before I knew it, Mo Thwaka was a regular guest at our shows. Not long afterwards, Mawazo Ya Pesa left KDF and approached Mama Iva to ask if I could have him back in Victoria. He was nursing a broken ankle. But if you were under the impression that the hardest-working vocalist in the game would use the injury (which happened after he hopped offstage at a Kilio Cha Kengele concert to greet his fans) as an excuse to relax in Victoria, forget it.

Mama Iva, like me, had a soft spot for Mawazo on account of his talent. She brought him around to my house one weekend.

'You sure you want to ditch KSK?' I asked.

'KSK is no boss,' Mawazo said softly, very softly. 'You're the boss.'

'Boss, indeed,' I wondered aloud.

Yes, but I was trying to make him understood limitations. He read my eyes, and pulled himself up. Reading his red eyes, magic without the glasses, I had pity on him.

I offered him beer and relaxed happily at the sensational singer's lapse into bawdy vernacular and felt very comfortable listening to him making so much heart-felt confessions.

'I hope you know the politics of music here in Kisumu,' I said.

He knew what I was talking about. The invisible hand of Uncle was upsetting things and messing careers of young musicians.

'Your uncle does not know that the real cause of problems in KDF is Lotta. Now Spark is dead and Benz, you, is weak. So Lotta is facing problems. She owes your uncle so much money. Your uncle is pressuring her to sell the orchestra to him. It's blackmail and it's a zero-sum game. But me, I'm getting married and I need job.'

I knew that entire story. 'You took the words right out of my mouth,' I said. 'What will happen to KSK's line-up?'

Mawazo laughed. 'KSK thinks he can get musicians. He does not know he needs money to run a band and this is Kisumu.'

Mama Iva's eyes bugged slightly in surprise. She said, 'I was just going to tell you that you have a fairy godmother, Mawazo Ya Pesa. Right now I'm your god-send.' She turned to me and said, 'I want to see Mawazo in Victoria.'

I was listening. And I was thinking. Having Mawazo alongside Ojua Kali Man and Roki Fela was a great idea. For such a stoner, Mawazo was an incredible showman. And he could be just in time to walk our incredibly prolific path this year. Surely his talents could result in another new record, and next year I could have him with us on tour to have him sing his songs which the fans loved. Yeah? Yeah. And if anything about Mawazo's return was anything to go by, nonchalant vibes about Victoria's dreams-come-true and a never-ending supply of sticky old guards coming home to roost made for great music all over again. And to me, we weren't breaking any bands; we were dipping into our own pot.

Then Biggy Tembo. He, too, stumbled back into the warm bosom of Victoria. Like a dreadful virus bursting out of remission, this long-overdue return from KDF's garage scums guaranteed better growth for Victoria to induce chills, fever and mass hysteria in the band. I knew what to do: split the band into two. I wasn't going to be confused with inferior, funny-named units out of Kisumu, this gaggle of malefactors crawled *back* into my band and distinguished themselves as some of the most outrageously delinquent musicians this side of the Sahara. These men were really weird weirdos (who else would tame a hop-head like Biggy Tembo?)

And Gentlemen's Gentleman—now transformed into Mr. Right—deftly failed to exploit bedlam of talent. In the end as we watched KDF fall apart, he degenerated into a filthy, screamy nerd. Eventually Uncle's visionary cultural wherewithal lost ground. He, too, put the kibosh in. He dumped KDF and, faced with dim options, he sent Tom-Tom, Kasule Mopero and Flavien back to KS Jazz. When KSK eventually turned to me for help, it was the best thing he could've done. In my mind, he ably represented the most glorious lows to which Urban Benga could withstand. I counted his gains and losses and found out he exemplified such grimy circumstances by some classics contained in two epochal albums.

KSK, as always, wanted to be the vice president of Victoria. Even his mutual grin had a reluctant quality as if to say words to the effect that he almost regretted things would get warm so quickly between us. Our journey together over the last few years was such a passionate one; I always forgave him and took him back when he turned up hungry and dirty. Like characters in a well-wrought drama, our dance would linger over days, weeks, and seasons with requisite steps and missteps, possible brief changes of partners, and time to sit out a number or two. Then his infidelity would rise again.

Not anymore. For him the door was shut. It was *pata*, hasp, bolt and lock. Rivet, nail and screw. All of everything; something like finally locking out a dog turned mongrel. Victoria was too good for him. Bigger than life, grander than reality, beyond imagination, and a dump.

Wordlessly KSK returned KDF.

10.

Then the worst thing that could ever happen happened. Africa's king of rumba, the Grand Master L'Okanga L'Ndju Luambo Makiadi, otherwise known as Franco died. The deep-seated Kenyan blustering part-riot, which always gobbled Franco's influential rumba odemba in OK Jazz was now dissolved in a tremor of remorse as Africa and, indeed, the whole world mourned Franco. An outward searching that alighted on the music scene saw Baba Gaston, sponsored by Sterns, travel to Kisumu to request us to back him up on an album commemorating Franco. My former rhythmist, Tégé Zoba, called me from Mombasa and pleaded with me to agree to Baba Gaston's proposal. My band had been praised for playing benga without any Congolese influence, and I always detested rumba and was reluctant to agree. But my father had always advised me not to resist any opportunity to try venturing into new styles. 'Don't be one thing only,' he told me. 'Try many styles and explore. Develop your style only after you have explored thoroughly. You are still young and many years ahead of you to find your own path.'

So I, together with my eleven musicians, accompanied Baba Gaston to Nairobi where we were given residence and rehearsing facility in a run-down apartment in Racecourse. We slept on bunkers like solders, we rehearsed in the small room sitting on beds and on speakers. We ate bread and milk and chips. We rehearsed and rehearsed hard for two months. Baba Gaston conducted us through the whole orchestral score. The whole thing was captivating and so magical. Rumba music was so dynamic and so spellbinding that for some time, we toyed around with the idea of transforming Victoria into a 'full-service' rumba band. We had the opportunity to interact with many Nairobi-based Congolese session men and women, and they taught my young musicians some very bad habits. There was never a shortage of women, and grass was never in short supply.

Baba Gaston used to be against all the bad habits musicians were exposed to. But he was level-headed. 'You have to be very strong to survive in this business,' he told me once. 'As a band leader, you are the leader of thieves, lazy-bones, drunks and harlots in your band. You can't make money at this crazy racket if you're honest or just a good boy. If you have discipline and self-control, you are safe. But if, like me, you have a front, you're making money—or expect to.'

We worked on his material, writing songs, strumming guitars and playing tapes for two months then joined up with some of the finest and most professional session men I had seen yet at AIT studios to bring out an almost therapeutic relief with the frighteningly expensive *Africa Toleli Luambo Makiadi* album.

This album was about recreating a hero out of a dead legend. OK Jazz were not merely masters of the classic rumba sound, they embodied the best qualities of the rumba ethos: unerring positivity, hope and—in the old fashioned sense of the word—the fantastic.

Franco was one of my earliest musical heroes. His orchestra's heavily cultivated image of innovation and affluence was at first a response to the economic and social depression of 1960s Kinshasa, but this didn't muddy the luminous wonder of Franco's songwriting and guitar playing prowess, musicianship and production, which went on to enhance—in some cases rescue— the careers of Vicky Longomba, Essous, Edo Nganga, Brazzos, Mujos, Musekiwa, Kwamy, Simaro, Youlou, Bavon Marie-Marie, Boyibanda, Verkys, Checain Lola, Mangwana, Michelino, Kiambukuta, Papa Noel, Mosese Fan-Fan, Ndombe, Dalienst, Dialungana, Malekani, Dizzy, Mpoyi, Madilu, Malage, Carlito, Nana and Baniel (not to mention his huge influence on pop music of Africa).

We performed in many Nairobi venues with Baba Gaston on the strength of that album. Trading on high rumba octane, getting ourselves together as a rumba outfit, we were selling our ease for unease. Unknown to me, there was mutiny in my band. My musicians was afraid that we were transforming into a rumba outfit, while we were forgetting our base in Kisumu as well as the very important allegiance to our faithful lakeside Urban Benga fans. I was, therefore, forced to cut short and go back home.

But, wait a minute: *what a machine Franco was!* He performed, toured, flirted, danced and recorded up until his stroke two months ago on October 12th.

But 1989 was not a good year. I also lost my friend, guitarist Bookerlose to AIDS.

11.

We had ushered in another new year with no ceremony. In 1990 *There's No Mathematics In Love* was now three years old. We were needed to have a new album. A man known in some hefty circles as Chris Tetemeko was very close to me. He inspired me into African praise singing. Tetemeko was a wealthy politician and a friend of Felix Jakomo of AIT who bought me a house in Nairobi in order for me to record a song about him. I pocketed eight hundred thousand shillings and told him we had a deal. I was listening to a lot of old Mangelepa and I wanted to make an Afro-rock record that was really upbeat and hard-hitting.

For just three and a half months, Victoria had gone dandy with the release of 'Chris Tetemeko (La Ardhi)' which heralded a return to the Victoria's old-school sound. It was an album with ten highly worked-over songs that were identifiably Victorian. My counterpoint guitar riffs, together with Mawazo and Biggy's dyspeptic vocals, created a distinction. It was laced with early '80s late-night energy and lyrical self-doubt, a few synths and downbeats for modern measure.

It turned out to be a gleaming showcase for Mawazo's powerful, emotionally resonant voice and knack for relentless melodic hooks and big, anthemic choruses. The album enabled the band to evolve musically while aiming to satisfy its many long-time fans. Going in to the writing sessions, Aseela, who was directing the project, said, 'Let's not try to sound like anything. Let's just jam, and see what happens.' Aseela was big in this one, really. She co-wrote every song with either one of the band-mates or talented collaborators as Mawazo ya Pesa, and Biggy Tembo. She arranged the album and you could tell it by her love of dense instrumentation. I let her get away with it for the sake of experiment. When recording the album, I used six guitars, conga drums, wind instruments, a rich brass section and (for the first time in our recording history) a keyboard. We came up with some pretty interesting tunes that sounded nothing like anything we'd done before. Even though some of them didn't make it into the album, the process stretched us and took us to new places.

It was the first time I said, 'It doesn't sound like us, but I can see us doing that.'

'The Poet' Willy wrote the flagship track 'Chris Tetemeko'. It was to turn out to be another of Opiyo Willy's most critical and most successful piece of poetry. It was one of those songs that jumped out at you the first time you heard it because you liked the music but didn't pay attention to the lyrics. It was one of those songs that gave you a quick word of advice before it ended. It took us three days to nail the song, with two dozen takes and three final cuts from which to make a selection. The producer put on strings for one of the cuts over Opiyo Willy's objections. A rush was sent off to Attamaxx post haste and the word came back they were satisfied. The band could now relax and get on with the real work.

You could hear our risk-taking on such primal, slithering rockers as hard-driving first single 'Rafiki Yangu,' which *Daily Nation* pop column praised for its 'wind-in-your-eyes hook and leather-glove-to-the-sky chorus' calling it 'the ideal soundtrack for hitting the road.' The songs reflected the confident swagger of some of Victoria's favorite hands. Credits on the back of the sleeve read as follows:

> *Vocals*: Omondi Pascal aka Mawazo ya Pesa, Roki Fela 'Ndugu Ya Kasuku, Sam 'Business' Ojua Kali Man, Biggy 'Mukubwa' Tembo, Queen Belinda Aseela, Mzee Frank, 'The Poet' Opiyo Willy
> *Lead Guitar:* Dino Otis Dundos
> *Solo Guitar:* Frantal Tabu
> *Benga Solo Guitar:* Collela Mazee
> *First Rhythm Guitar:* Roga Roga
> *Second Rhythm Guitar:* Siama and Onyango Odol
> *Bass:* Nsillu Wa Ba Nasillu 'Manytcho' and Sammy Kasule
> *Keyboard:* Belinda Aseela & BB MoFranck
> *Drums:* Onyango Shaban and Pajos
> *Tenor sax:* Lobe Mapako Roddy
> *Trumpets:* Kush Malombe and Shal Tumba
> *Congas:* Jerry Spatacus
> *Arranged by:* Belinda Aseela

As you can see, this was a weighty album made up mainly of Nairobian pros. It was very much a Nairobi affair with a tight grip on Urban Benga.

BROTHERLY
LOVE

I N early 1990 we were on safari to Mombasa where we were lined up for a series of shows organized by our manager His Excellency Ambassador Okoth Ochot and sponsored by Attamaxx to promote our ant's pants *Chris Tetemeko La Ardhi* album. Mombasa was always a magical place. Besides eating *mnazi*, we hoped to buy more Le Seigneur Tabu Ley Rochereau-esque silver & turquoise flares for our cool stage look, and hopefully rub elbs with Them Mushrooms.

My brother Agwenge did not come with us, he was partly sick and partly upset with me. He had not fitted well in Victoria's musical rhythms and drumbeats lately. He appeared to be losing his grip and his diminishing weight and energy were subjects of scornful rumours. At first I thought he was depressed by the whining of his wife. Then he appeared angry and agitated and easily irritable.

Then he wanted his own album. That annoyed me.

What did he know about making music? Did he even know how tread the line between melodic Urban Benga and pop-infused heavy rumba. He was an airy-fairy who couldn't stand without me, so his seat in my orchestra was a warm extension of brotherly love. Here's the bone of contention: he had composed a highly melodic Kiswahili number titled 'Ndegele', which we included in the *Chris Tetemeko La Ardhi* album.

The song rode the success of the album. And suddenly Agwenge was full of hot air. Now he wanted to be the star feature of *his own* album. What he should've known before getting carried away was that I was still struggling to stay on the grip of things. It didn't come easy. I failed to convince him. I failed to make him understand that 'Ndegele', rode *only* on the technicality of my guitar work and Aseela's arrangement placed decidedly within the realm of heavy rumba.

Well, Agwenge wanted a solo album. He came around to my apartment one evening and showed me his songs. They were well stringed poetic words of love written with horrible handwriting on the pages of a ruled exercise book. He even had a title in mind: *You Came Too Soon.* I tried to reason with him: he was the first salaried member of the band to request to go solo. I tried to explain to him the dangers of going solo. He will no longer receive monthly salary and he will eat from his sweat. Moreover he was setting a bad precedent. He was my brother, he was family. If I allowed him to go solo, all the other singers who knew they were better than him will rise up too.

Then I lost my cool. 'Listen, *omera*, you can flush your frapping tantrums and airs but you are in no position to do a solo album. To do that will sign your musical obituary.'

'Meaning?'

'Victoria has its rules, *omera*. We have harmony. I emphasize not only musical harmony, but group harmony.'

'Meaning?'

'No.'

'No?'

'Yes! No.'

'Fine.' He walked away.

The irony here was that Agwenge, my second younger brother whom I adored and who was raised number five out of eleven in Pandpieri, in all likelihood segregated his environmentally cranked oddballs from any future you'd wish on a family member. He was every inch the band member from hell precisely as he was the kid brother from hell. In fact, my father's advice was almost bad enough to serve as reliable guidance. 'Just help your brother.' That was it. Short of getting childish about it, our father's advice simply did the opposite.

Next thing, Mary-Goretti called me. She was pregnant Agwenge was faced with the prospect of becoming a father. It definitely sparked something in him, Mary Goretti told me, and led to the burning drive to record *You Came Too Soon*.

'The songs are about realizing that today could have been the day that someone would be blowing out the candles,' Mary-Goretti said. Then she told me something that jarred me: she had lost her first child. It just hit me pretty hard. I remember visiting my brother in his house and he was bawling. I didn't realize that my brother's wife had suffered a miscarriage a year before. It was a pretty emotional moment.

Mary-Goretti said, 'Do it, Didi. For the love of a brother.'

Agwenge soon stopped playing with the band and told people that I was jealous of his talents.

When we came back from Mombasa, he had left an extra space. He quickly teamed up with 'The Poet' Opiyo Willy (who was now his bro-in-law too and) who had the effect of allowing the words to shine more brightly. I sought him out and he told me something about himself that jarred me. Something that made me change my mind.

We rehearsed and recorded *You Came Too Soon* at Attamaxx in two months. I put this album under Victoria's repertoire. On the cover the title read: *Otis Dundos Presents Agwenge Lwanda with Orchestra Victoria ODW.* Aseela and 'The Poet' Opiyo Willy sawed off and sand-papered the zig-zaggy ideas that Agwenge picked up from his journey here in Kisumu; the life that had slipped into really nice pop across the board. And no one could have done it any better than the last-ditch ex-Delta Force heavyweight he chose to include. I'm talking about Mawazo Ya Pesa. He and Mawazo had paired up and connected. They dressed hip too: skinny ties, curls, bright collarless shirts. On this album's cover, the two pencil-mustached singers could almost pass for New Kids On The Block, if not for Agwenge's smoking jacket (nothing underneath, natch) that looked almost the same as the one El DeBarge wore on the cover of Rhythm Of The Night in 1985. The album revealed my brother's most intense moment, but it was not a brooding affair, nor was it preoccupied with people going their separate ways—further evidence that my brother had ventured out of his comfort zone. During one of his moments of fame, Agwenge explained to pop journalists how he did it.

'My ship has sailed,' he said. 'I want to do something that is a little more charming in the lyrical take, so I started reflecting on when I met my wife as opposed to dwelling on the hard times. This is for my wife.'

My brother-in-law Opiyo Willy sneaked in another poetically rich number called 'Finally' which we worked hardest on with the result that it was the most artistically successful. It was a slow rumba ballad whose lyrics were rapidly sung. The lyrics (in English)were quite thought-provoking. This was the number that became the tour de force for the album. The lyric had blown everyone away and the tune had a haunting beauty. It was slow, rolling to a faintly rumbastic style, with a scorching solo from my Fender in the bridge. The sound was sparse and reminded everyone of the hopelessness of life.

But Agwenge was sick and visibly sickening bad. When the album went into the market, he went to hospital. In December of that year, I was in Nairobi again. His Excellency Ambassador Okoth Ochot had connected me with a promoter who had taken advantage of renewed outburst in the wake of *You Came Too Soon* and *Chris Tetemeko La Ardhi* albums. He wanted to take Victoria across to Dar es Salaam.

I politely declined. The band took a needed break.

2.

I was relaxing at DreamScape enjoying cool breeze from the

formidable plateau. Warm sunshine filtered through the thick heavy tree tops gently kissed my brow; the day was bliss, kind of boring, but bliss just the same. I had been reading a book, wiling away the hours listening to music. I playing the latest OK Jazz release I fished out of Victoria Music Store recently, an excellent number called 'Tonton Zala Sérieux' by Nono Nedule 'Papa Noël'.

Like any impatient artist, I was day-dreaming and trying to put some order into my mind. It felt like I had come of age and was now used to putting time and energy and blood and sweat and soul into something. It seemed so often to lead to wanting the power to define that thing for other people, and that got inside me and festered there. We are artists are taught to be individualistic and closed-off to the world, and it takes hard work not to be.

Aseela had recently added some revolution into our performances. We had borrowed dances and animations from Zaïreans and she put together a dancing troupe which included up to six female dancers lead by herself. Our acts were backed by a burlesque revue and had a traditional drummer's routine. Since the dance routines changed monthly and were heavily choreographed, Aseela researched a lot. She got together with the dancers and the traditional drummers for weekly rehearsals that ran our shows. Our new dance style included *Moko Mach, Sammyyyy Business* and *Viatu Namba Ngapi*. Also we had some comic acts. For instance when doing *Sammyyyy Business*, Ojua Kali man would brandish a briefcase. The fans loved that. I thought we were done with eccentricity when we lost Tégé's crazy shirts. Well, Mawazo came up with something to make you jeer and whoop with laughter: long shoes. Mawazo had developed the new dance style *Viatu Namba Ngapi* in which you moved your body hard without shifting your feet. The paraphernalia that accompanied this show were long coats and clownish long shoes, so long he couldn't walk in them. They were at least number thirty... as long as an arm. Then there was Vicky's military gear:

440

the trombone.

G-Chord's fat bass-plucking, string-surging sleekness was a testament to how much experience had changed our music. Yeah, like any seasoned artist, I struggled with the question of identity and artistic freedom. Identity is a vital thing in popular African music. What you sound like is never as important as how the audience relate to your personality. Identity is something constantly at the forefront of my mind. It riled me how journalists always tore into my music and dug up Zaïrean influences in it. My idols, fans... they didn't have a problem with that. It was music. People's suggestions on music, my kind of music, made me rethink my style. I was trying to come up with something new all the time. I was perfecting my Urban Benga.

Yeah, Victoria was struggling with identity, I noticed it when a freelance journalist watched our show in Dar es Salaam and asked why I came up with the name Victoria. I do not think we had any identity. I had taken the name Victoria because we wanted to be an urban band, and provide an alternative to benga. This is what I always said to the journalist. It is not true, I had better names. The truth is this: the finest benga artiste in business, Dr. Collela Mazee, was using the name Victoria. He was a friend of Uncle and he occasionally came to KS Resort before our European tour. Dr. Collela had a personal desire to extend use of the name Victoria Kings and he implored upon me to respect Ochieng Nelly, the pioneer of pop benga. Ochieng Nelly's band was the first in line of the Victoria Kings benga bands, and was rightly called Victoria Kings A. Dr. Collela stated that he followed Ochieng Nelly in importance and thus relegated his own band to second position; thus his band was Victoria Kings B. Awino Lawi was another unique and very creative Benga artiste who had played with Collela, his band was Victoria Kings C. We did not have any problem with being the last in line, we had surprises, and our benga was different. It was Urban Benga.

Ideas for songs came to me as soon as I had confronted my ghosts: I needed to talk with my father to get ideas of my songs. I needed my songs to have positive meaning. I needed to talk to people whose opinions I highly respected. My pastor, Riana, Mama.

Themes for my songs?

Well, let's see? Religion, political affiliation, youth, love, and unemployment, guilt and fear, ambition, uncomfortable situations, or stereotype... I wanted to create music extremely fresh, contemporary, and full of rhythm, melody, energy, and passion. For love songs, I dug into my own experiences and the experiences of the people I knew. I asked fundamental questions: what exactly is it that men and women looked for in each other? We saw how people got married and met their exes and still wanted to get along with them 'for old times' sake' and women still flirted with their former boyfriends (married or not)... what did men look for in women that made them decide 'this is the one' ....and what did women look for in men? And if you chose 'wrong' partner, were you supposed to spend the rest of your living with a 'mistake?'

At a deeper level I wanted my music to communicate poignant messages about humankind and its beauty, hope and social evolution. In my next album I was going to hinge my songs on themes close to my heart. Songs that were going to spell my true identity. This was the '90s and the music scene was getting overcrowded. There was mediocrity and there was pure gold too. And Loketo was showing us that you could not expect a growing mass of fans to shun a rarified, occasionally difficult, protracted dance floor experience. People no longer wanted to ride the rumba-lit ride, hear some words of poetry in a song to sing to their girlfriends and go home. People were in soukous train and wanted hard dance. You had to take part and play the thing down to the ground. I wanted to create this kind of distinction. The music that I had made so far had an emotional connection which triggered moments from my youth and new post-youth experiences. But now I wanted to do the whole relationship thing with the crowd that I watched Loketo do in videos. Once I established that connection, I would be eating out of my hand. For now? A little affection on stage was a good tool to use. If I could pull it off and it looked genuine, sure, why not?'

Achieving identity was about establishing who I was to my audience. The dynamics within the band were important. Half the battle was to show the audience how much I cared about them and about how each member of my band enjoyed keeping our act together. A lot of bands I had seen in Nairobi just walked through the moves and you knew they were only there because they'd been paid. The intimacy within Victoria ODW was going to be built now. I didn't want to be afraid to show my affection to the audience: they were going to feed us the energy I created once I had them on my side. The fans, the enthusiasts in disco halls, the sober dads in record shops, the *jua kali* worker in Kondele and Manyata, the fisherman in Dunga, the market seller in *Chiro Mbero*, everyone who listened to our music and bought it... they were not at all fickled emotional freaks—they were smart.

But first things first: make a change. Get a new identity. I arrived at a simple decision. All I was going to write about were going to be based on aspects of life in Kisumu.

It wasn't that long ago that I realized I have been pushing people away and, for the life of me, I couldn't figure out why. I sat here today and wondered, 'What makes me push the people that care about me so far away?' I realized that it was my insecurities, my fears, my sense of self that had been driving the people I loved the most out of my life. Losing the best musicians was no coincidence. I had spent most of my life breaking rules, shouldn't I stop now? And as my maturity peaked, some things became clearer. Some say the best things in life happen when you least expect them. This was certainly the case for me. Here I was twenty-eight year old musician, a little intimidating artist. I had no one to blame but myself for this situation. Sure I had an inadequate child hood and poor people skills. But don't get me wrong. I was not a total loser; I had fought my way around this world until I was a leader of men, a businessman and the owner of an enterprise.

Victoria, my enterprise; I had employed men and women—picked talented losers from the roadside, cleaned them up and gave them a life and a future; I had created some good songs people loved and identified with. I had contributed in making the world a better place. Songs were like children. Sometimes you were closer to one than the other. But there wasn't a song that felt better than any of the others. But if something did not work, I didn't release it.

3.

I was inspired to do another album; an album that was going to show my coming of age and confidence. I was anxious to explore a softer side: I wanted to do an instrumentally rich album. We were known for hard-hitting anthemic Urban Benga. But with Aseela's influence and inspired with the success of *Chris Tetemeko La Ardhi* which she arranged, I now wanted to take my feet off the accelerator pedal a little bit, allow the guitar tones to come out a little more, play things down and still be heavy. As usual I took ideas from our reservoir of unrecorded songs. We always had ideas floating around; we always had new songs and new ideas.

I picked the best musicians in Victoria; we sat in a circle and we started brainstorming. We started out by playing more canned pieces where someone would bring in a song then it turned into a whole new project. The meanderings of the songs were determined by the performance and everyone contributed ideas. Since we were not constrained for time and we were not working with a deadline, we went through it leisurely. We were doing the rehearsals at DreamScape in warm weather and in a lot of ways it was really enjoyable to not have any constraints. Literally we would have somebody start playing an idea and the band would find a tonal center and people would start coming up with ideas and start riffing off. It was really about listening; there was a kind of participatory dance going on between all the players when we could hear each other at our best.

The task of figuring out the pieces for the album fell in the laps of Roki Fela and Aseela, and they sifted through hours of material to find what sounded right. Aseela ploughed through the muddle. The first gem we picked for polishing was a neat song called 'Luopean,' composed by Ojua Kali Man.

The project got a boost as more experienced hands came on board. Word had gone round that we were making the Album of Albums. The structured machine of Victoria with parts and measures pivoted naturally when Ayo Achieng Massikkinni arrived from Nairobi and came on board with her whole arsenal of ideas. We tore through the rehearsal creating music, and our method also let us honestly evaluate how good the songs, players, arrangements were and we identified 'blind spot' problems with songs. Aseela wanted the environment and personal experiences to influences us where we took things. Writing songs, she stressed, was a personal journey. She wanted the band to match the vibes of our surroundings in a way because we were making it up as we went, as well as trying to get influence from each other. She picked a mic and sang; words poured out:

> You used to sleep on reed mat
> *Mama yo!*
> Your sister bought a mattress,
> you said you want blanket
> *Mama yo!*
> You said you needed a blanket,
> now you want a bed
> *Mama yo!*
> A man's life is never over
> *Mama yo!*
> Luck shows up unannounced it's never too late
> *Mama yo!*
> I know we will succeed someday my child!
> *Ee Mama ee!*

'What is that called?' I asked

'Call it whatever you want,' she said. 'Often the material determines when it's done. The music has its own natural flows and breaks. The music grows and determines its own path.'

She had a point. We African musicians cannot read music. In recording African music, we can pick up and chord and sing upto a point where a new movement begun or the definitive end. We build it together and we innovate as we go. We don't music, we just work through it and panel-beat it into shape.

We rehearsed for three months and in June the plate was full. I knew what I wanted to call this album: *Luopean.* JB agreed to produce it and signed it to Attamaxx record label. He picked Jimmy Makossa to engineer Eddy who had recently engineered *Chris Tetemeko La Ardhi,* but was in Zimbabwe.

The music was being created on the fly with no performance being entirely the same. While recording at Attamaxx, we would go into the session with the idea of creating on the spot and the tape was rolling. The engineers were like, 'Oh, the tape is rolling? Let's just start playing.' And things sort of evolved where somebody might introduce some sort of musical idea or texture. A lot of times it was really about the bed texture and people started playing with that and then the songs developed a short evolutionary life as we were playing. A few pieces like, 'Attitude' and 'Onja Intro,' were actually warm-up pieces leading up to more structured pieces while recording. *Luopean* had our version of Ngaushi N'Timbo's classic 'Shauri Yako' – we did it as soulfully as Starzo Ya Estha and Festival du Zaïre did it in the original recording with finely blended vocals of Sam Ojua Kali Man, Aseela and Mzee Frank. Of course, like most people, I hated the grumpy rip-it-up Mazembe version and the flat and monotonous Afrisa version. We also had 'Mado,' Celi Bitchou's tale of an unfaithful woman: our version was so modern and polished as to dazzle. In it, 'Mifupa Ya Zamani' Vicky had room to demonstrate his saxophone prowess.

The rest was original material.

I explained to Jimmy that I wanted to get a more unusual sound than that on the previous albums, something different to the standard recording. As an engineer, he was very, very keen to experiment, and JB encouraged me to do this, so as co-producer, he was in charge of the musical direction while I took care of the sonic direction. Jimmy got a better guitar amp and supplied better guitars. He changed me to a Fender Jazzmaster—and he also had the Gibson that I'd used on my first *Kaa Square* album seven years ago. You didn't want to lean on that thing too heavily.

To achieve the correct African groove effect, I worked with the engineers on the drums. It really was the drum sound that largely defined the album's sonic direction. Meja Okilo the co-engineer had just arrived on the scene at that time, and he gave us a little education on how the Zaïreans did it. He had worked with Zaïko Langa Langa Nkolo Mboka and he told us how to mic the entire drum kit with C-ducers. I had initially tested the mic on other instruments, not drums, but when I briefly tested it on drums, I thought, 'Man, it sounds fantastic like that.' There was absolutely no spill between the different drums when you used a C-ducer. Each drum was completely separate. Every part of the kit was therefore miked with C-ducers—kick, snare, hi-hat, three or four Rototoms and two crash cymbals—and this gave us a very, very contained drum sound with no space at all. Everything was right up close, there was no ambiance whatsoever, and we then used reverbs and delays to give up the shapes and the sizes. The fact that the drums had such little ambiance and were so sterile and cold really set up the mood we loved.

So basically, Pajos had to record his drums alone, or, in the best case scenario, with G-Chord accompanying via headphones. Having recorded the cymbals this way, we also did cymbal overdubs because we wanted a very, very heavily compressed sound that totally sustained. You could hear that on a couple of songs, including 'Shauri Yako' —when the cymbals crashed there was a click followed by a long, long sustaining cymbal. It hissed for about 20 seconds.

For the first time, in the studio, Ayo dueted with Aseela on the chorus. They sang together, side by side, sharing one mic in the vocal booth with their arms around each other. It was all too much for Ayo and I took her out and down to the pub after the session.

I would later add my many guitar parts (as was the new fashion) on top of the recorded rhythm section. In guitar I showed off my impeccable double-pronged attack. We were prepared. Prepared because the dominant value in popular music now was perfection. Perfection of each individual part trumped the quality of the overall interaction of the band. And perfection could only be achieved via perfect separation of the components of the mix, so that every error could be fixed, and every nuance massaged for maximum technical correctness.

Luopean achieved what I wanted. With it, we had come into the homestretch with heart-wrenching Urban Benga ballads. It was an exhilarating, pivotal album from a band bred to exceed. It was one of those things where people were going to get it or not. We didn't spend a lot of time worrying about 'What's the PR for this particular thing going to be?' In a lot of ways that was liberating because it put a lot in the lap of the listener. It felt like something very new sounding... for lack of a better word, experimental. People were going to gravitate towards that kind of thing; and that was just fine with me.

4.

Attamaxx threw a thanksgiving party at The Place, Nairobi to celebrate the success of *Luopean* recording. It was a Friday and about ten bands were playing and it was jolly rowdy. The bands were awesome and slick and cool too. There was definitely a bongo player in one of the bands band. And there were some primitive upcountry benga squads too. There was a bedlam of new talent being showcased by some new bands Attamaxx had recently signed up. So we dedicated our shortened set to allow many of the new bands which, definitely Attamaxx, wanted to be present. We got two hours at 12:00am and took the stage. And celebrate we did, with stretched out and ramped up performances of material taken almost entirely from the *Luopean* album, featuring jaw-dropping virtuosity from Victoria's four ferociously gifted male vocalists.

At 1:35am, I handed my guitar to the new guitarist, Ominde Nyang', and went to the gents to smoke a joint. Things had loosened up and a drunken Mama Iva insisted on critiquing our show! G-Chord was told to play bass like a man, which considering his gender, seemed pretty reasonable! Victoria had about ten minutes left before another took the stage and Mama Iva went on ranting saying it was Girl Time. Aseela walked into the stage and grabbed Mawazo's mic. The band started playing her songs. Minutes later Ayo walked in and stopped the band; she requested for one of her songs. Aseela said no... absolutely no! 'This is my time, wait for yours, lady!' It was an assured night of pop mess glory. The two ladies, Ayo and Aseela, had some sort of problem between them. At the start things were cool and they did a marvelous duet on 'Wasichana Wacha Tabia Mbaya'. After that things turned sour and we saw there was a problem. They would flip each other off during performance; mutter insults at each other between songs... that sort of thing. It started early in the first set and got worse.

There was an attack then a sabotage then confusion descended.

The first choruses faded into groovy finger-snaps and some sort of backwards-tracked harp samples. The vocals were playful rather than portentous; deeply un-performance-like. People stopped dancing. Now came the riff, and oh what a riff. Four distorted power chords instantly unrecognizable.

Drummer, Pajos, got enraged and fumed. He stopped playing and you know what happens when drum and bass goes silent in the middle of a song. So everything stopped and I stormed back in and got the gig restarted.

Ayo composed herself with massive effort and sang a nice ballad, and hit the high A in chest voice. Roki Fela (who was backing her up on vocal) whispered to me that he felt like a peacock and I told him to hold it out a little longer. Aseela's voice cracked hideously just as the sound guy hit the delay hold button. It sounded like a rooster getting killed with a pen knife and fighting for its life. Utterly humiliating. Even my industrial strength aqua net hair spray couldn't hold my head high after that.

About halfway through the second set Ayo flipped one bird too many and Aseela lost it. She yelled 'What are you doing, stupid slut!' and took off her (*reeaally* nice expensive looking) shoes, slammed it into Roki Fela's back so hard the burly singer staggered out of her way. Aseela stormed across the stage toward the Ayo wielding her shoe. She pushed Mzee Frank out of her way like tissue paper and charged at Ayo. Ayo saw her coming and stepped out from behind a guitar rack looking for something to defend herself with. They started ducking it out, on stage, in the middle of a song!

Fortunately neither of them knew how to fight and they were basically flailing at each other like a couple of primary school girls. There was little chance of serious physical damage; only panting like hens and pulling at each other's clothes and tearing off each other's braids and leaving ugly scratch marks on each other's faces.

The band instead of stopping the song and dealing with their feuding band mates, opted to keep playing. The song, of course, just fell apart. Phrasing and meter died a horrible death! After about eight or ten measures of this, the drummer and guitar players finally stopped playing, stepped away from their instruments and separated their fighting band mates. G-Chord charged out of the stage cursing loudly, Ojua Kali Man got hold of Roga Roga and moved him to a dark corner to pout.

Try to picture in your mind, a seven piece band, half of which is engaged in little girl fisticuffs, the other half soldiering forward because 'the show must go on'. It was like a scene that got edited out of a really bad movie. The saddest crash and burn of a live performance I'd ever seen!

By the time they were pulled apart with blood pouring out of their noses, the only stitches they had on were their undies, and Ayo, gasping, panting and rising like mercury in a high school lab thermometer, was in the process of ripping Aseela's off. As they were pulled apart, she yanked it off. Vicky tried to drown off the noise and jeer from the audience by raucous sax noise as Aseela went down with her legs splayed. I moved in then, ripped off my coat and dashed into the stage to wrap it round Aseela. Ayo flung herself in between us and either pushed the naked woman or punched me, I don't know. Aseela did a serious skid-and- roll on her buttocks while I staggered, spun in mid-air before finding myself breaking hard into a guitar with strings ringing and stinging and breaking. Aseela rose groggily on all fours, and as I reached out a hand to her, I was vaguely conscious of Mawazo and a younger bouncer at my flanks, steadying me as well as staring down between her legs. The crowd of dancers stood somewhat flummoxed, bewildered, bemused, and miffed hard.

5.

The rest of the year seemed uneventful... as a matter of fact, everything else seemed uneventful. Victoria went into hiatus in July. The band started to become very fatigued and very tired. I felt now that we needed to take a break and an opportunity to recharge our batteries as we barely had any time of. So I was persuaded to finally take a break! The band and I took a well-earned rest after a whirlwind nine years. I was ready to make this long break last: something like seven months to one year. We weren't a talentless band that needed to keep polluting the airwaves, or else people would quickly forget about us. As much as I was the sort of artist who would put out a large number of records, I didn't think we needed another album rolling out this year or next.

Sounds a bit nebulous.

I was fired up for the future of Victoria as we got into the '90s and *Luopean* already told people we were still hit makers. The future was certain in terms of the band's label situation, as we completed our contract with longtime label Attamaxx. I was keen on these aspects and about my personal aspirations.

I was alone and sadness sucked at life as I packed my guitar. I lay low and kept out of sight and did some things. I was overseeing the construction of some of my houses in Wigot, Kisumu. I avoided the public, avoided Gor Mahia matches. I got tons of letters and postcards from fans which I trashed without reading. I turned down numerous tour proposals and new record deals. I kept the phone off the hook. Instead I sought audience of my workers, the construction workers at my building sites, my newspaper vendor, my house cleaner and my cook. I had the windows of my car tinted and gave my driver holiday.

I took to compulsive reading. Read newspapers, magazines and novels. The days consisted of veg'ing on the couch watching TV, zzzing, snoring, eating, farting, reading, dreaming, nightmaring, worrying, talking to myself. I went to home Pandpieri only when I knew Mama was at work at Rusinga Island General Store because I didn't want her to remind that I was nearly thirty years old with no wife.

I looked Riana up. She had broken up with her boyfriend. We got together and she told me my daughter was nearly two and living with her mother in Kakamega. She had lost her job at the post office and was broke. She wanted to borrow me money. She had plans; wanted to go to Britain. She was careful now and took morning-after pills each time we mated. We went for a nice jaunt with my family's two dogs through my father's neighborhood of Pandpieri, got good fish and gabbed up a storm. There were multiple trips to the Sunset Hotel, and the overeating continued, as was my new-found occupation: drinking. Ten kilos heavier, I was quickly told that I needed to get away and be fit, so Riana and I got into my station wagon some days and shampooed it over to South Nyanza.

I wanted to be in the islands... in water places.

Mfang'ano Island provided a perfect escape.

My fans and buddies Okech Simba and Okeyo and their wives put us up and took us out for a nice dinner, and then we headed for some sights in the hills. We were greeted by suspicious-looking islanders who took great care of us. They gave us a site at the foot of one of the hills with a creek nearby where we fixed our tent. The air was sticky, muggy, and downright unpleasant. It was hard to breath but Riana pushed me and we climbed up the rusty rocky hill (which was all of about a hundred feet or so). At the top we surveyed the area around; it was quite a sight to see and much more to behold.

We got down and found some cool wetland and tried to catch fish. Trees dotted the landscape. When there was a chanced breeze, the air was overly scented with the scent of pine. Fragrant wildflowers and wild weed-mint and catnip, also were present. Riana noted how the breeze, wafting through the pines and other deciduous trees, was not unlike the sounds of the lake.

She was mostly speechless, not about the surroundings or the newness. Something was bugging her, had been bugging her ever since we landed on this island. She had many questions—most of which I already explored trying to convince her we couldn't be an item. We were in love, granted. And that was about the closest we were going to be anything item. My bringing her home to this island had changed her perspective. She reckoned with herself I brought her to the island to welcome her into my home.

'I don't think we're meant to be an item, though,' I commented as we soaked our tootsies in the nearby creek.

'What do you mean?'

'It's complicated.'

'It's not, Otis. This is us. You and me. We can make it work.'

'This is different than the first love; I loved you for real in 1980; whatever this is, it's different now.'

'And I love you now. For real.'

'We're different people now.'

'No, we're not. We're mature and we know what we want.'

'No, we're mature and know that what we had in 1980 was innocence.'

She was in deep thought. 'It's funny, you know. You loved me so-so much and I couldn't reciprocate; couldn't feel a thing for you except sympathy for a dear friendship. Which was great. You waited and it was good. But now, I really feel for you... feel it so deep and tremble and get wet just looking at you; yet you can't feel a thing for me. Just can't, see? Yet, like 1980, we're together.'

'Riana, we will always be together. Whenever we will be apart we will always miss each other. Yet we will always find each other and get together and find love. But what will we do with it? We're together now, Riana. Let's fish,' I said.

I was teaching her how to catch fish and she was not concentrating. 'I will always love you, Otis. My vows shall remain unbroken, unlike you.'

Upon seeing a rather large albino perch in the deep (and wide) creek, I drove in with cloths on and easily caught it. We pried off its scales, cut it up and we sought out some sustenance.

Which was not hard to do; nearby there were equally large fruits and veggies. 'We are *really* someplace else!' I commented.

Riana sighed. 'I like this place. It's so cut-off. Let's and spend a week.'

'Do you have enough...'

'I don't care, I could get pregnant again and I don't care.'

'Riana stop.'

'Otis, dear, I'm a different woman. I hate to pin you down over anything but facts are facts. And fact is this: we are tied together for life more than before and the reality is...'

'Riana, I provide support for my daughter.'

'Yes, you do but...'

'We have sex anytime you call me.'

'Do you think that's all? What I want... dear God. I am a woman. And what I want is more than what you give. What I want is you.'

'Riana, let me tell you that of all people, I respect you. And you know that. You're beautiful, you're smart and you're self-respecting. But now you're beginning to nag and you sound like a tart.'

She sighed. 'I want a perfect marriage, Otis. That's all. Your daughter is growing and she will soon need a father.'

Riana still tried to finger out how if this was merely a dream of some sort—how the hell could there be such realism? Pain, joy, anguish, peace. Physical and mental satisfaction; good sex. How could two people bond so well and refuse to be an item? She didn't understand it, but I did. And I didn't try, not that I didn't care. I had at the beginning, but it gave me a migraine and I quit and just "went with it." Some things are not meant to be, no matter how good or convenient and suitable they seem. It was a law of life and Riana either couldn't fathom it or didn't want to accept it.

There was a sun, not as bright or as warm as the one we were used to in Kisumu. After noshing we curled up with one another and fell to a blissful sleep. I watched the moons fade and nighttime take over the new landscape. I heard various birds and other "wildlife", there was some sound far off that annoyed me, but I was too tired to pay it much attention—besides, it was far off always anyways.

It was dark. Damn dark. In the sky above—which was equally dark, there were (at least) a few jillion stars. No constellations were discernible, but there were stars just the same. Riana had awoken firstly, the need to pee awakening her. The air was brisk and a might chilly, the fire had died down and there was a sort of curious "funk" in the air.

It wasn't me. I snored peacefully on. Riana crept just a few feet away and did her business. Her peeing clamped shut when there was heard a voracious sound. It was from some animal—some *big* animal and he (it) was damn close. Too close.

She screamed. 'Otis!'

I was awake. 'What the fuck was that!?' I yelled--like Riana knew.

'I don't know *what* it is, I just want to know *where* it is!'

Although that didn't really seem to matter as the Voracious Loud Mouth seemed to be way too close, somewhere in our immediate vicinity.

Then it stopped and I felt more than saw it float away into the darkness. Riana clung to me hard. It took seconds before I knew what *it* was. And I broke into an exhausted laughter.

'What is it, honey?' Riana asked.

'It's nothing, there's no danger, let's go back to sleep.'

'But what is it? Tell me please.'

'This is Mfang'ano Island; the safest place on earth.'

She seemed delirious, but still.

I couldn't tell her it was *just* a night runner. That would scare her more.

The next morning we broke our camp up and headed for the shopping centre. We found a nice bar in a cool show place by the lake. Okech Simba's buddies and some Subas came along and we enjoyed some hearty moments chatting and eating and drinking! We ended up back at Okech's bar around 2:30am and tarried till the next day. After that we hit the sack, tipsy. I dreamt I was married to Riana and that my life was mellow! Then we awoke next morning to the worst disaster of our safari so far... we couldn't find Riana's bag and the thing she valued most in there was her Franol tablets sac! Suddenly a scare of her getting an asthma attack became real. Okech Simba took us over to his neighbourhood village for a bit of post-holiday ragery! We hired an *andururu* speedboat and cut through the water for Mbita. Then we got in the wagon and headed back to Kisumu.

Next I went to Nairobi, to Ayo. No trip to Nairobi was ever complete without spending at least one night with Ayo. As you can see, her Racecourse house had become somewhat of a shrine to me, with floor to ceiling graffiti. Every time Ayo painted, she messed up her walls with oil paint. The landlord put a fresh coat of paint over it all—and the cycle begun again. It wasn't long before the walls were filled again with colours as rich as the imagination in her soul. Poetry, messages to me, and song summed her life.

We'd been kissing, touching, laughing, tussling. I had been drunk. I'd been physically turned on—and mentally very turned on—but it was in a strange, non-aggressive way, brewing underneath the booze and the churning emotions and staring at her in awe. I was a bumbling idiot. I was fairly certain that I spoke in one word answers only when spoken to and laughed at everything she said, even if it wasn't that funny. It had been fun, and at the time, when, breathless, we'd broken apart. But by the end of the month, we were making love less and less. We were quarreling more and more. We were making goggle eyes at each other with my son while I was strumming my guitar and when she left I scribbled entries in my journal and played with my son. He had just learned to call me daddy. His eyes got big and he pulled at my beard, played with my big arms and jumped up and down on my hairy chest. Other times I was asleep on the coach while Ayo would be cooking lunch, and his tiny hands on my beard startled me and I hollered at him and his laughter made me smile.

6.

August ended and September started, and life continued pretty much as it had before, with exceptions. What was really worrying me was my past relationships. I had dated several women, ruined so many chances. It was normal if you were a musician. They kept coming. I was a decent guy, great guitarist, emotionally stable. But I think my indecisiveness on settling down showed through and I couldn't seem to fully connect. That I ruined some fine young women literally worried the crap out of me. I honestly felt, if I changed completely like I was trying to do, I certainly could make at least one woman happy. Riana, to begin with, was a nice person. With her it was not just the female thing, it was love and companionship. Angelou recently told me I was getting old. (Haha, Angelou thought I was actually like the biggest kid alive).

Ayo was a problem. But Ayo was now just a constant, low-level pissy pest that was forever in my nerves. Since she was now downright malicious, there was nothing else for it. She got to me at some level, of course, but I'd never, ever show it after the first time she needled me about Angelou.

The scribbling, sneezing, farthings, daydreaming, all stopped when Angelou sent me a nicely phrased hand-written letter which was delivered at the offices of Attamaxx where I was doing some part-time work as music arranger. The letter was brief and to the point: she wanted to see me. About what? You guess it right: our son. I always said that it could wait provided the kid wasn't sick, and I could always push aside her demands. Gave her a good reason to call me irresponsible. I wasn't really irresponsible, the boy was still young and I was looking for some good money which I will give her soon. I was busy working... look, the band wasn't even bringing in much to the extent that I now had to take a part-time job.

And before I could blink on it, she got me. I found Angelou waiting for me at the reception. She looked me over with very tired eyes and a cocked eyebrow, her hair untidily pulled back into a ponytail and a scuzzy black hoody on.

'Adoyo *ber*,' I said in greetings.

'*Ber ahinya, Baba Junior.*' She squinted at me. 'So there are times you come in on cue.'

I winced, nodded. 'You wanted to see me?'

'That's not the shirt you were wearing last week,' she said in DhoLuo.

'No.'

458

'Wasn't that the shirt you said Ayo bought you for Christmas?'

I nodded, shrugged.

'Ah.' She got onto her feet with straight ahead eyes and pursed lips and I was surprised at how much weight she had put. She looked good and yummy. She still dressed like a designer and she had on black jeans but her thighs were thunderous in them. 'Dinos, the mother of your son needs breakfast.'

So we ended up in a scuzzy diner called Tobina with tasty food and an entertaining mix of blurry-eyed patrons. It was all yellow walls, green whicker seats and the trendy at-your-table ordering, and it was oddly comforting.

Angelou was quiet for a good two, three minutes after we ordered cocoa or tea, French fries, meat pies and sausages, and it wasn't until she had her hands wrapped around a cup of hot cocoa or tea that she spoke. I had mentally zombified, suspecting I was about to have a conversation I'd never had before with a woman, and a cold sense of dread had been building since I decided to meet her after she had been trying to see me for over a week.

'So.' Angelou peered at me over the rim of her cocoa cup. 'Are you still sleeping with her?'

I smiled at her. The cocoa was waking me up, but I still didn't know what to do but dance around a bit. 'Do you mind?'

Unfortunately, she seemed to actually take my bad joke seriously, and blinked at me. 'Oh! So, you'll tell me what you have with her is what you have with me, correct?' She smiled. 'Just sex with the mothers of your boys!'

I found it easy to lie, I know I could have, but at that moment I realized I was cornered and the manner in which women normally dug into my inner guilt with truth angered me. What I really wanted was an ear for all the things I couldn't tell anyone. Including the ridiculous joy I got in sleeping with different women who knew each other. It came to me now how selfish I was, how I was exploiting my fame and money and financial security. Her palpable relief that there might be another explanation was not heartening, but I soldiered on. 'Well, actually I... we really broke up.' I didn't want to meet her eyes s her facial expression changed again. 'Then she called me and said....'

'Said you come to Nairobi to spend holiday with your son. Does that also mean...' She paused. 'Sleep with her?'

'Yeeesss. Yeah, it does.'

Angelou's face was a study.

And she stared at me, so intently I thought she was going to burn holes through my face, and it hit me this was probably a very, very bad idea. She'd always struck me as open minded, independent-minded, but, obviously, this wasn't the case. It was bad. 'The Poet' Opiyo Willy was right: once you sleep with a woman you're hooked. But once you have a child with her, you're at her beck and call and you're toast. There's no such thing as parting ways here in Africa, never.

'Well, I hate you,' she exploded. 'I *knew* it. God, I'm *so* stupid to have hoped otherwise! Stupid, stupid, stupid!'

'Sorry.' I said timidly.

'Oh, God, no.' She waved her hand at me dismissively. 'Don't be sorry. Really, I was starting to wonder, I really was.' She let her face fall onto her palm, and looked at me wistfully from her sideways eyes. 'It's just not *fair*, you know?'

'Did you really care?' I asked, curious and a bit horrified.

'You can't just hurt people, it's not right. You can't just run from your responsibilities and say you do what you do because you are an artist. We are human beings, Dino. You can't just mess our lives like this.' She said the last almost accusingly, and I winced again. 'We are not bimbos to date for five seconds and then you just float away leaving us holding the baby. It makes no sense to me, because you never seemed actually *involved*, you know? Even, like, in a lust sense. And then I started to think that it's about time you settled down with me and brought up Junior instead of running around sleeping with women who wants you because of your money. Did you ever think you're not growing any younger? You just... well, like, *like* to make women have a crush on you. No love, just desire... desire. These women will kill you, *nakwambia.*'

I was speechless, and relieved, because she obviously wasn't disgusted. But I was still shocked because, obviously, I wasn't floating through my world unnoticed.

'You look surprised.' She said, and she smiled adorably, reaching out to touch my hand. 'Is it because I'm not telling you the nice lies you're used to hearing, or is it because I had you figured out?'

'I...' I thought about it, and, instinctively, put my fingers on top of hers, staring at our two hands. 'I guess, I guess you're probably right.'

'Ooooh, I of course I'm right, Dinos.' She gave my hand a warm squeeze. 'I might still sleep with you, you know, so you don't break any other hearts more than you've broken mine. It's called love, buddy. Remember the times.'

I laughed. 'I'm *so* good at heartbreaking? Is that what you're saying here? Oh God, I don't believe this.'

She patted my hand then withdrew her own. 'Now that we're talking, I want to get to that eventually. That fucking drives me nuts.'

The grumpy 50-year-old waitress dropped more sausages on the table from roughly five feet before shuffling away, and Angelou picked one. She resumed her batter.

'So. You hooked up with Ayo because you are insecure? I was wondering what will make you have babies and run away. So: Spill.' She gobbled her sausage and munched into her French fries, and poked what was left of it in my general direction for emphasis. 'Go on.'

'You want to know?'

'If you have trouble saying it, *please* feel free to draw it. Actually, can I request it?'

She lifted her eyebrows at me, and I laughed.

'God, Angelou, it was surreal. 'You have to understand. I'm an artist.'

461

'Wait, what was that?' She stopped me and probed at a comment that was meant as a throwaway. While Angelou might have been flakey, she wasn't at all stupid.

I decided to make the point. 'I said I think it's my artistic drive. I'm so mad at myself, because I'm totally out of control. I fear.' I said, giving up on stabbing at my uneaten meat pie. 'What am I doing is probably what artists have done for centuries, hooking up with you women for comfort?'

Angelou gazed at me, her eyes written with disbelief.

I continued. 'I'm a musician, you never stop being a musician, and it's just like how artists never stop painting. Poets never stop writing poetry. I'm a musician, I'm an artist, Music is my passion, it's my therapy, it's my first love and I feel like... yeah, it took a lifetime for me to fully discover and control it.'

'Please, spare me.'

Angelou laughed, laughed long. 'This is ridiculous. You are messing women's lives to sort your artistic ego, is that it? Is this legal? Let me remind you: who isn't the artist here, huh? Me? Ayo?'

I said nothing.

'It makes *no* sense!' She said, breaking out of intent listening mode for the first time in ten minutes. 'Listen to yourself, Dino, Oh my God. So you're saying—and have been saying the whole time—that you're both ashamed you screwed around with us, and what a whore *we* are for giving you comfort, but let me tell you this, *mazee*: you're the whore and you will be punished.'

'Uh.' I was jolted, and also trying to ignore the fact that the fresh-faced kiddish couple a couple of tables down from us had stopped their kiddish chattering to listen to our conversation. Angelou, in all her infinite personality, was pretty loud.

'Yap.'

'Well...,' I flailed, because to me, emotionally, this logic made so much sense. Until I said it to someone else. A reason not to tell anyone, really. 'Just... what do I have for my pride in this life other than what I have in my hands?'

'It's not your band, brother. It's the three boys God has given you with three different women. Stop.' She reminded me helpfully.

I rubbed my eyes. 'Okay. What sort of a man am I? I feel like I've taken advantage of everybody around me. I have nothing to feel I gained, or gave. Basically, I feel guilty and I fear.'

'Dino, sweetie, stop that. So you're really sorry, yes?'

I nodded. I blinked. 'You're not the person I knew. You're... different.' I said quietly, feeling suddenly emotionally lost. 'You're wonderful... you're... you're...'

'Tough?' she supplied.

'Tough.' I shrugged awkwardly, and looked up to look in her eyes. 'And there was a time I was actually going to marry you. I didn't want to lose you. I didn't want to feel that way, the way I feel now—as if the clock was always ticking. That I was instantly hooked on my music which took away my love,' Angelou had that gleam in her eye as if she was going to yell at me and I shook my head, 'I loved you.'

'You did?' She was aghast.

'Not in a mature way,' I corrected hastily, 'Not like now, I guess. It seemed like it was a love for teens. The kind of love we musicians write songs about. I guess that kind of love doesn't exist.'

Her bulbous nostrils flared. 'Baba Junior.'

'You don't believe me?'

'No.' She said quietly, almost sadly. 'Do you still...?'

I shrugged. 'I'm not sure, Adoyo. I'm so rotten now. I've done some pretty rum things I'm not sure I could love a woman like you.'

If I wasn't looking keenly at her beautiful face, I could have sworn I saw a ripple of disappointment. She quickly blinked as if fighting back tears, and looked away.

'You're human, that's why you have sex in the first place. You have feelings and you can love. You just want to shut doors of your heart. I have a problem with your weakness, Dino. You are unable to conquer your fears. So sad to think Mom thinks so highly of you.'

I winced. I had met her mom several times, and like many people, found her charming and caustically entertaining.

We glared at each other. The waiter cleared our plates, and she put her head on her arms on the table, looking thoughtful, I did the same, and we stared at each other bemusedly over our arms.

I felt so much better talking to her, like maybe I wasn't such a loser getting attached to a beautiful ghost as I had convinced myself I was. She had always been a rare person I was completely comfortable around, and suddenly I felt relaxed. She'd hit a nerve, though, that I needed clarified.

'How's Junior?' I asked.

She let her head drop completely and was now looking at me out of the corner of her eyes, suddenly melancholy. 'He's fine, Dino. I don't ever want him to be as selfish and as mean-gutted as you. I can put up with you since we're joined for life. I can handle you, he can't.'

I thought about that, and was confused. 'How do you know me so well?'

'Because... I'm a real artist, just like you. You're you, and I'm me. We both want power. But you're an artist who has managed to build power. People *want* to attach themselves to you. People like me who have nothing.'

Angelou's whole body language changed as she straightened up from the table, the air seemed to change with her, and suddenly she looked downright angry. Reflectively I also pulled back. 'And that, *that's* like really annoying, Dino, you have no idea.'

And the comfort was gone. I tensed. Suddenly I was desperate and angry myself.

She just made an annoyed sound, clicked her tongue against the roof of her mouth. 'Oh, *shenzi*, I'm going to cry, let's go.'

She stood up and rushed out of the restaurant. I dropped money on the table and stumbled after her. One of the waiters gave me a sympathetic smile.

She was leaning against my car, looking at the cloudy morning sky over the nearby Treasury Building with a lost look on her face.

'Adoyo....'

'Dinos.' She was suddenly hugging me to the point where I didn't have any breath. 'I like you so, so, so much and it's not fair that you can't like me but it's even worse because you just don't *get* it that we are joined for life. You don't get it at all.'

'Adoyo...' I said helplessly. 'You have no idea how much I wish I could like you like that too. I hate that I somehow hurt you. You're beautiful, and wonderful, and I wouldn't deserve you, and... I regret losing you.'

'*Ever* losing me. Can't believe that but Thanks.'

'Welcome.'

Silence.

Then she sighed. 'Oh, Dino,' She looked at me in a way that made me feel like the lowest level of scum for unloading my ridiculous problems on her, and then kissed me lightly on the lips. 'You're an idiot, and I'm really not in a position right now to try to correct that. And I'm angry because it's almost insulting that you don't get it, and it's stupid of me to think so.'

I was at a loss for words because there was none that could, er, help, but she didn't really want any.

'Let me go home.' Was all she said in a way less of unhappiness but of crashing comprehension, and she sat in my car for a good thirty seconds looking stunned 'Let me go home, I'm not working.'

I thought she was on leave. Hopefully that would get her mind off of me and to where it should actually be with her son.

'Dino,' she began, 'Don't worry about school or tuition, we've taken care of that... but I have a bit of bad news and you're not going to believe it. I lost my job at Ebb & Flo.'

7.

I returned to Kisumu. Mama called me. I understood the apparent weariness in her voice as much as I understood the sick feeling in my stomach. She had just been told about it. I learned of it a week ago. May Goretti had visited me in the night. She confirmed the rumour that Agwenge was HIV positive.

Yeah, it was now well known: my brother Agwenge was HIV positive. It only confirmed my worst fears. I had noticed my brother's deteriorating health for many months. When I found the ratty apartment he and Mary-Goretti lived in and knocked on the door, there was no answer. I heard what sounded like crying inside, so I just went in. I didn't know what to expect, but I was ready for sadness and anything that will make me puke. Lamplight and sobs spilled into the passageway. Perhaps she really was upset? Unsure whether I was offering a shoulder to cry on or looking for one, I tiptoed to the open doorway and choked on well-intentioned words of comfort. Agwenge was sprawled on his back over the king-sized bed, cursing softly while Mary-Goretti struggled to make him eat rice. The heartfelt sobs were those of a woman mightily frustrated—her own grief and burden alarmingly on view as she bent to her toil of the till-death-do-us-part vow..

Agwenge looked up, stretched out a hand and yelled, 'Get this stupid prostitute off me. She gave me AIDS!'

The room seemed to shrink and I felt huge and ungainly, uncomfortable in the spotlight of attention. Mary-Goretti stood up whispered pathetically, '*Shemeji*, your brother is really sick.'

'Is it AIDS?' I asked. She nodded, lowered her gaze and sniffed. 'He thinks it's me who gave it to him.'

I glared at her and shook my head. I walked over to the bedside and tugged at my brother, '*Omera*, how are you feeling?'

Agwenge sat up. 'I'm sick, *omera*. I'm not well, *omera*. I have AIDS. I don't want to leave Mary a widow and reliant on you. I don't want to leave my son.'

They say AIDS in the family is a curse.

466

I struggled for words. I normally had no words to say in such situations. He didn't seem to be in pain, he didn't seem to be suffering. He was wholly conscious and in command of his wits, and able to speak clearly. I thought what my brother lacked was courage. He was in denial. By this I don't mean the lack of fear which some people with AIDS have, which enables them to do very dangerous or frightening things because they have no idea what it is to be afraid. I mean a courage which overcomes real fear, while actually experiencing it. He was admitting he had AIDS and fighting its consequences, albeit badly.

I didn't have much of this myself, so I recognized it (and envied it) in others. I had a memory which I could place precisely in time (maybe 1977 in Pandpieri), of the two of us scrambling on our rooftop, the sort of crazy escapade that boys of our generation still went on, where we should not have been. A moment came when, unable to climb back over the steep slates, the only way down was to jump over a high gap on to a narrow ledge. I couldn't do it. Agwenge, young as he was, used his own courage (the real thing can always communicate itself to others) to show me, and persuade me, that I could.

I had spent most of the day so far responding, with regrettable brevity, to the many kind and thoughtful expressions of sympathy that I had received, some from complete strangers.

AIDS scared me to death. So, odd as it would be if this were a wholly private matter, I thought it would be strange if I did not shed a tear, partly to thank my brother for his brevity and partly to express my sympathy for my closest living relative, someone who, in many ways, I had known better than all my siblings due to our work as musicians. And someone whose woman I had shared.

I had to get on well with him now, better than in the past few months, better than the coming death and eulogy and blankness after he will be gone. So we pretended nothing was really wrong and we relaxed and swapped stories about music, about songs and about our colleagues in Victoria.

Time passed, dusk approached. Agwenge had taken Piriton and conked off.

I got on my feet.

Mary-Goretti was feeding the baby. She said, 'You can't leave me alone in this house with *him*. Stay the night.'

I wanted to go home, not spend the night under the same roof as the woman I despised. Perhaps that was evil, but necessary. She was so beaten down that she didn't even care that I saw her crying, or saw the way she was living. She had no pride left.

So I decided to stay a while and talk. At that moment, we heard voices and members of my family entered the small sitting room. They were my father, Mama, my sisters... entire family.

8.

I got Agwenge admitted at Lake Nursing Home and I hired a private doctor to attend to him. Sighing, trying not to moan, quite disgusted with my own stupidity, I hurt all over. Yeah, guilt ate me. I agonized over it and lost sleeps for many nights. My brother's AIDS became an issue and scared the living shit out of me. I got thoroughly shit-faced and hung over for two days.

I had to confront myself and go for a test.

I visited Agwenge in hospital and watched him trying to move his right arm and saw he couldn't. It shocked me how fast he had deteriorated. I felt sick, too, in body and mind. I watched Agwenge cranking one eye open cautiously, then the other. He looked about his surroundings, determined my location, and finally settled his gaze on me and on Mary-Goretti and on Mama and on dear family and co-conspirators in his debacle.

'Well, *omera*,' mused Agwenge rising against the wall, 'I had a dream. A dream about a tour. We were in Bujumbura again. It was so beautiful.'

Mary-Goretti and I both laughed, evidently pleased at his condition and his secure detention in the hospital bed, rather than in anticipation of his speedy recovery, which I doubted would happen immediately, especially if I had to go back to school to learn to understand all the 'complications' his doctor talked about. To my best knowledge, AIDS represented such horrible and terrifying things as crabs, syphilis, gonorrhea, genital warts. AIDS was a disease of shame. I was hearing words like 'unsafe sex' or 'unprotected sex' and I was getting some ideas for a new functional song.

Agwenge sat up saying seriously, 'The doctors say I will be fine next week to be discharged.'

He was staring at me through narrowed eyes now, and I faltered and loosened my grip. Mary-Goretti trailed her fingers down his body, nails brushing his skin as if they were someone else's, and I watched them, fascinated. My mind went in one direction in the brief span of silence, down the road of boozy self-flagellation: idiot, idiot, idiot! Would this be the last encounter? Could such a deeply held and long-lived secret, so much dirty laundry, so many skeletons in various closets, be sustained? Should it be?

Two days ago I had asked his doctor what he thought my brother's probable life expectancy was at that point, given the medical treatments available. I learned that Agwenge's prognoses was very poor. It was likely that he would continue in relatively good health for a few months to a year and would appear to be healthy during that period. As his immune system was increasingly weakened, he would become more and more vulnerable to opportunistic infections. It was likely that the first such infection would strike Agwenge quite hard. Because of the especially virulent nature of Agwenge's infection, it seemed likely that the first, or almost certainly the second opportunistic infection would overwhelm his body and either result in death or a period of severe illness leading to death. This was evidenced by the extremely sudden drop in Agwenge's T-cell count and the rapid rise in his viral load. The doc said Agwenge's prognoses was not good and whatever that meant? I had asked him for an accurate opinion he could form based on his test results and the information available to the medical community now.

'Pray,' was what he said in reply.

'Are you kidding me, doc.'

'He nodded.' You know I'm not a miracle maker. Jesus is.'

Go to hell, I said in my raging thoughts.

The days dragged by as I watched my brother deteriorate. His fingernails were bitten while he was tense and angrily abrupt with his wife. In an unsuccessful attempt to clear my mind of thoughts of untimely death, I wandered down to Dunga to the beach and jogged up and down the narrow strip of sand. It didn't help, so I went to DreamScape, strummed my guitar, hung out with my father, and went on a physical fitness binge.

Many times I went looking for Riana at the single room she was sharing with her friend in Milimani. Many times I didn't find her. Either she was busy or she was avoiding me. Could I get away with simply yelling 'goodnight', or should I break into the house? Not wanting to bother her neighbors, I spent my days at Koch Koch. Often I was joined by Mo Thwaka, who had recently become a close buddy again.

I quit smoking and curtailed my drinking (boilermakers anyway), and embarked on a self-designed fitness program that included jogging and pull-ups out on a gym near Robert Ouko.

9.

Luopean was set to become the greatest accomplishment of my life. Hadn't it been heavily pirated. It was. Barely three months after I returned to Kisumu, JB called me with bad news: they had busted a River Road racket in Nairobi and tons and tons of bootleg copies of *Luopean* were among the lot found. They were pirating *Luopean* the way they had pirated my other albums and there was nothing I could do about it. My sources had told me that there were more cassette versions of the album than the LPs.

Meaning pirates were making more money than me. Every song is such a long, painful labour, more painful than pregnancy and childbirth—you can imagine how terrible it feels to see that work being taken by strangers, duplicated in Nairobi's River Road and distributed for little money and buyers made to believe it is coming from me. I spent months rehearsing and producing a song—so the pirating of my work felt like a brutal kick in the gut. I worked hard and loved getting paid for the work I did. I'm pretty sure the rest of you love getting paid for your work too. And it seemed to me like I was targeted for clean rip-off from the beginning.

As early as 1986 as soon as we released *Lake Victoria Breeze*, the issue of piracy had confronted us when I discovered bootleg copies of the album in a Nairobi music store. I asked Attamaxx how feasible it was that the thieves were so smart to copy my songs and still sell it in the same market. How was that possible? The answer was simple: the thieves were selling the bootleg copies cheap since they had incurred no production overheads. Then I saw cassette versions of my albums in the market and it riled me because my music had never been issued on cassettes. I hated cassettes because they killed the quality of good stereo. I was an audiophile, so I really cared about bitrate or codec quality. Nothing was ever going to replace vinyl. There was this short-sighted, really silly phrase reading: 'Home Taping Is Killing Music – And It's Illegal' that was printed on the back of LP covers to discourage people from buying pirated music on quality grounds. At one point it used to make me feel good that someone was warning pirates to stay away from our work. Only now, seeing the scratchy, dusty, strangely otherworldly and awful-sounding bootleg copies of my music on cassette did I know how schizophrenic this sweet-and-sour phrase was. Suddenly I hated to see it in the back of my LPs... what purpose was it serving there except to remind me that someone was ripping me off anyway whether I liked it or not. No way was anyone going to fight home-taping. Piracy, that frightening beast, was ripping our lives away from under our feet. There was a well-known genial, verbose, sneering-voiced River Road bootlegger known as Macharia who had duplicating machines and was so impossibly prolific and daring. He was large, brash and intoxicating. I wanted to nail him real bad. He was the one responsible for thousands of bootleg copies of our music in Uganda, Malawi, West Africa. That he wasn't the kingpin in this racket, I didn't know. But I knew he was the man responsible for my poor harvest of records for many years. There were even whispers that he was working in cohorts with the producing houses such as Attamaxx with a particular brand of off-kilter strangeness that'd, quite strangely, eventually made the production and distribution companies stay in business by offering poor quality low-budget back-door cassettes.

Someone whispered to me that this was something I couldn't deal with because it was bordering on political corruption. Question I asked: did they know rampant piracy in Kenya was hampering the music industry's growth? Answer: who cared about music and musicians. Were there even copyright laws in place? First we had Zaïreans competing us out unfairly and second we had thieving pirates operating in broad daylight.

But even if Macharia the bootlegger were wealthy and had political connections, that didn't give him a right to rip us off. I was so mad I wanted to go to these countries where our music was being sold. I was told Nigeria was a good market for bootleg copies of our music.

But again was the irony of technology. Young people loved my music but couldn't really afford the shelf prices, so they taped my songs straight off the airwaves onto cassettes. People recorded out LPs onto cassettes and swapped these cassettes with friends. By now, sales of cassettes even surpassed the sales of vinyl. Home taping was widespread and nobody was guilty of fleecing a musician of his hard-earned money. Music piracy was legalized. The cassette was the standard format for tape recording and thus the standard for music piracy. All our hits had been massively pirated in Nairobi and my figures told me that a good number of those who had our cassettes hadn't acquired genuine copies from the shops. A good example was the anthemic 'There's No Mathematics In Love' which was overplayed and massively pirated within three months of the album's release. Attamaxx investigations revealed that over 1 million bootleg copies were sold in USA and Europe.

Reasons piracy cases were rising and continuing to down press us was overpricing of genuine copies due to high production costs at the Polygram pressing plant where Attamaxx and all the others took their master tapes. The big record labels such as POK of Oluoch Kanindo, Polydor, ASL, CBS, Polygram and EMI were struggling to maintain their grips and balances. A decline in music sales due to home copying had indeed resulted in less revenue for the music industry, negatively influencing the investments in new music and thereby ruining the future of the industry. EMI had (in a few years back) folded up and sold out to AIT.

The cassette had challenged the disc as the most popular format and the number of LPs sold gradually declined while sales of cassettes increased rapidly. Now you could walk by a market stall that had your bootleg recordings on sale and it was business as usual.

I would say music piracy is irony, lack of respect, blatant theft and hypocrisy. Wrapped into one little perfect bundle. Wow. That's a very one-sided, short-sighted response, and certainly not the greatest solution for those who create works from their own labour and creativity—authors, song writers, musicians, composers, painters, journalists, film makers etc. Think of the industries this crime affects. Why should someone be able to get for free what was created by someone else? I can't walk into a supermarket and just walk out with packet of milk because it's just a copy. Does it make sense? What exactly is the difference? The difference is that if you walk out with a packet of milk it's not there anymore, but if you copy a song the original is still there. Surprised you needed to ask really.

Someone asked how much, just how much of that $222,000 that African Dawn collected from our 1987 European Tour actually came to us. Not even twenty percent. And come to think of it; musicians are paid a pittance in royalties from airplay on radio and from performances. Their greatest opportunity to earn an income from their craft is by live performances *and* cassette sales.

I swore never to record again, only an occasional live show. I wasn't going to spend my sleepless nights creating music for the sharks and the hyenas to steal and get richer than me.

8TH
ANNIVERSARY

T seemed like I had been playing for so long. By 1991, it was kind of the last ditch—either this was happening or it wasn't. What threw us far out of sync was our five-record contract with Attamaxx which was eating us alive. *Luopean* was our fourth under that deal. In the six months since the album was massively pirated, both the music business and the dominant aesthetics shifted. The band members wouldn't go anywhere near my studio garage in DreamScape—where we'd had dingy rehearsal spaces for three years—to rehearse. But soon enough Attamaxx wanted us back on tour to promote *Luopean*. And just as they wanted us to begin recording. But out of sight, we didn't rehearse as much as we didn't party. Our manager His Excellency Ambassador Okoth Ochot had eventually found a smart lawyer who charged me KShs. 200,000 to smash the Attamaxx contract and set us free.

I knew a way another out. I called Pam. I asked her to come to Kenya.

And that's how 1991 marked the start of things. I wasn't feeling so good... I was wary like a South Nyanzan. I had become reclusive and a little paranoid. After close to a year in the wilderness, there were even rumours that I had died. I was twitching. But why? Nine years from the time it all begun, Victoria had been preserved in vinyl, lionized in print and immortalized on countless magazine covers. In an age filled with endless re-unions and many chartbusters, Victoria was now part of the Urban Benga pantheon. So why was I wary? What's more, it was turning into a feeling of dread. I was twenty-nine, you know...way too old and wise to handle any situation. That made me a better band leader. I think when I formed Victoria, we were trying hard to make it seem like it came naturally. And I think now we embraced the fact that it was hard work

But in 1991, in the months-long interim, I was seriously out of step with my music and fashion. Those who didn't believe my death rumours lamented that I had gone from incendiary star to middle-aged burn-out. That I had fallen because I had not released any good music since *Luopean*.

There was trepidation that we would have been gone from people's hearts and minds somewhat, and that we would have to, kind of, start over again at a lower level. Many close to me pushed me to regroup the band and record or do a press interview. Things were really happening, though. I was on the cusp of a belated career revival with Victoria. People didn't know that piracy had forced me to stop and rethink things. People didn't know I wanted to be in charge of my own production and distribution. That I wanted to keep a close watch on how my music was moving. I was looking forward to Pam coming to Kenya in June for purely business reasons: she was coming to help me market my music in Europe. She was coming to have me sign the deal with African Dawn.

Then something happened which peeved my pet into action.

At the beginning the year, Kisumu Delta Force suffered another significant rebellion when one of its less talented guitarist, Ominde Nyang', organised a new group that eventually decimated KSK's lineup. The new group was known as Victoria Academy and guess who were the first jump aboard: Mawazo Ya Pesa, Biggy Tembo and Mo Thwaka.

And guess who was behind it: Uncle.

Victoria Academy? I asked.

'Yeah,' I was told. 'We are the children of Victoria,' Ominde told me. He was not meaning the lake; he meant they were a legal offshoot from my Victoria! Like they were the training school of Victoria, and proudly so. Of course it was all guff made by Uncle to get back at me for ditching him. What a daft quack. Couldn't they use a little imagination? I was soon faced with another big problem: Academy became the most gloriously dangerous of Kisumu groups and for a while they overshadowed Victoria. It was baffling... I had never taken Ominde Nyang' seriously even when he took over from Benz Benji Obat. I had only seen him as an affable hard-drinking rascal musician with a stupid sense of humor, a long handlebar moustache and a little adequate gift for the guitar.

My main singer Sam Ojua Kali Man (who had always surprised me with his erratic progress as a solo voyager) was flirting with them and had been featured in their debut single, 'Ka Maili (Emi'gwonyo)'. Aseela, too, was whoring with this new group. Her association with them was somewhat justifiable: she had to be near Biggy. It was no longer a secret that she was having a troublesome sexual relationship with the hop-head baritone who had a big influence over her and at least I knew he had stringed her up in drugs too. In the early days they could often be seen marauding together downtown. They lived in each other's pockets for several years straight and shared beds whenever we toured. I won't get into it, but they had been uncomfortably close. She confessed to it to me that it was just sex and she was smart enough. Thinking about the relationship, consummate concubine is what came to my mind and I sympathized with Aseela. Biggy was still legally married.

I knew I would lose Ojua Kali Man to Victoria Academy. But Aseela I had to retain.

Now you see the root of my wariness, don't you? There were no words in my head, no songs in my thoughts. Only a vision of the cows I would bring to DreamScape, my plateau home and sun on golden grass. I was deeply embarrassed. How do you respond to two singers you love leaving you when you've slaved to keep them for nearly four years? Aren't singers such ungrateful whores? Why? Instrumentalists were okay, it's singers who were giving me the most headaches. My singers had always been transitional.

From Biggy Tembo to Mawazo to Ayo and now I was losing Ojua Kali Man and Aseela.

Academy managed to attract the kind of fans that were too snobby to go see Mawazo, Biggy and Ojua Kali Man, but behave just the same, if not worse than Victoria's fan base. The fans during the pre-Academy era used to be cool, reserved, primarily intelligent human beings who enjoyed a good time, a few beers, maybe one or two underhand dance floor caresses and a raucous encore, but listened. But the entry of Academy caused problems. They preached dance and hard noisy *kwassa kwassa* and *madiaba* dance in the soukous vein. Jokes aside, Academy, *really*, was a trimmed down Victoria but with more power and imagination. While my Victoria was the sober and homely TP Ok Jazz and Afrisa, they were the Zaïkos and Kiams and Trio Madjesis and Wenges. While we were the established conservatives with a respectful mature sound, they were the careless youthful rebels with nothing to lose.

I had to find an antivirus.

His Excellency Ambassador Okoth Ochot's intel provided a reprieve. His idea was: *create a solid vocal squad and power it with hard dance.* We agreed we couldn't take competition with men like Mawazo, Ojua Kali Man and Biggy Tembo lightly. So I reorganized Victoria, gave power to the vocal section. To replace Ojua Kali Man, I didn't miss a beat and hired a new singer called Paulo Opapo aka Poli Poposso from Sulwe Boys Band, who had a dynamic soprano voice, sweet, liquid and musical, sometimes shrilly but always almost syrupy in its quality. He could reach an exalted level with charming in-draws of breath, flowing easily from the pits of emotion to the high ranges of desire and pain. He didn't possess the stamina of Ojua Kali Man and Roki Fela, but he had something special: he was a romantic crooner who gave 'The Poet' Opiyo Willy's songs new meaning.

Things really couldn't have been better. And then they got really shitty. One day, a guy by the name of Okach showed up with a ton of muscle and a standoffish attitude. This guy apparently had his fifteen minutes of fame riding the coattails of Biggy Tembo with his particularly generic baritone. But now, it was clear that he was just a washed up, bitter asshole by the time he had made his way to our little musical oasis. He operated a shop on the side and the only thing that made sense was the very similarity of his voice to Biggy Tembo's. He performed Biggy Tembo's old hit with such amazing accuracy fans soon started calling him Okach Biggy. He had come from a struggling band known as Heka Heka, a Kisii band based in Manyata Gonda.

Victoria's vocal force was created and 'The Poet' Opiyo Willy had a name: 'The Five Bosses.' The idea was to have my five singers singing together and The Five Bosses represented a powerful vocal unit. Their vocal definition: Roki Fela—taught, tremulous vibrato; Poli Poposo—piercing and dangerous soprano; Aseela—controlled, emotional, rich, husky, sexy; Mzee Frank—fragile, and Willy—frantic and breathy. They made a loaded vocal power house. Given that in the new arrangement, they all sang together, their voices challenged the instrumentalists. Our musical arrangements chopped rhythms together in disordered formations that had never been tried before in Victoria, really created new impressions. Given that the five vocalists attacked the same verses together, their voices created heart-jeering ripples, sometimes flew in all directions. With fans cheering and raising the usual ruckus and as smoke and lights filled the air, I smelt power. Victoria now didn't play the cool Urban Benga, it was hard benga! It was because of all the tonal colors caused by the abrupt key modulations in the break juxtaposed to the funky rumbastic *sebenes*. The *sebene* rhythm beat played in this period was called 'Wayoro Ayora' as you could hear Roki shout in some points. It went like this:

> 'Ayora, eh eh eh, ayora.
> Ayora, eh eh eh, ayora.
> Wayoro ayora.
> (Yawa) Wayoro ayora.

Ayora, eh eh eh, ayora.
Ayora, eh eh eh, ayora.

The power of 'The Five Bosses' was first tested at Attamaxx's 1991 Makombora Music Series in Nairobi's Nyayo Stadium. And it didn't take long for the scrum outside to get ugly. Having tickets, which went on sale that day and sold out instantly, didn't guarantee entry. The line stretched around the corner, and for most people, that was as far as they got. Even those who made it inside had to endure an hours-long wait. The sheer magic of 'The Five Bosses' held the fans in awe. The singing was powerful as each singer sought to sing at their best. The new kid Poposso with his high soprano ringing big in the mix beat Roki Fela and Aseela to it... he stole the show. It was a great gamble, it was awesome. Makombora was the ideal wrestling ground. Victoria floored all the bands including the Zaïreans and took the prize.

2.

Winning this year's coveted Makombora Music Series' Band of the Year award put us on a higher scale. We were witnessing our 8th anniversary as a recharged band and the sense of being the top band of that moment engulfed me with feeling of goodness and achievement. So many troublesome years had passed. And over these years, as age, fame, addiction and creative foment interceded, my vision striated. A lot had happened. I had achieved success and fulfillment. Since *Lake Victoria Breeze* our first album eight years ago, Victoria ODW was embracing a new equilibrium, one that weighed each member's voice more equally. Or something like that. Now I was standing at the shore looking at a beautiful horizon.

Fulfillment?

Big ticket concerts and hordes of clawing fans aren't enough awful things that can be said about fulfillment. Well, after eight years I still felt I was still beginning. I still wanted to create a dependable band. After eight years, I was considering adding some tech-focused resolutions to my New Year's to-do list for the band: improve the sound, yeah.

Kodachrome-sharp snapshots: tension, sickness and death, new marriages, suicides, extreme highs and heart-breaking lows, fallouts, chock-full of amazing performances, new record pirates, awful album sales, bank loans, Pam pushing me to sign the Afrikan Dawn contract, ghosts and more ghosts.

Real life, mercifully, was far richer than songs on vinyl records. I'd had my head split and my heart ruined on the day it became apparent that my brother Agwenge had AIDS. Mary-Goretti, she cursed her luck with girlish modesty, but almost immediately brightened. It amazed me how quickly she accepted the hand of fate in her family matters. To me that was sublime. She had accepted the reality and could now deal with the problem. And who's to say the sun shone less brightly? Agwenge, on the other hand, was clinging to denial with his claws when everybody could see he was sicker than a dog. He was planning to make a song about himself, which, I worried, might somehow tip the already precarious balance of our family life.

From the sublime to the ridiculous, the old saying went; but there was nothing ridiculous even about the long story of Uncle taking for his third wife a school girl. And now this; now the very embodiment of shame; myth came cropping right here in our lakeside town. It was numbing, mind-bending, and top secret marriage. No one got wind of it till much later. Mama was kept in the dark. Life went on and for every iota of lost excitement there was precisely the same enhancement of dignity.

That's how it was in Kisumu town, Western Kenya, April, 1991. It was official: Uncle had a new wife this year. His third. Maria, she was called. So young, a school girl. The poor girl was hardly seventeen when Uncle plucked her from form three. Call it whatever... statutory rape. Who among men could confront Uncle about it when her own father accepted it. Besides Uncle had an effective magic wand: his wallet.

But while we were trying to come to terms with Uncle's new marriage, a major tragedy hit our family close and square: Ogongo where our father worked went belly-up.

That meant my father was without a job.

Many Kisumuans know about Ogongo in Dunga. By all means this was the largest fish cannery in the Western region. Built in the '60s on the tip of the Kavirondo Gulf as an Indian company, it later became a parastatal when the government intervened to rescue it from imminent collapse in 1982 then renamed it Ogongo Fisheries (1983) Ltd. It had a workforce of two thousand by the time my father was promoted as head of mechanized trawling in March 1982 at a salary of less than Sh.1,500 when most employees were earning Sh. 800 per month. Every 15th of the month one would witness a large number of people outside the gate. Most of them had come after their debtors and relatives. The advance money for the workers was only Sh.200 while officers, as the management staff were referred to, got a percentage according to their grade. My father used to take home Sh. 800 as his *libandhi* (advance).

Ogongo, as I have said, was an Indian company and all the heads of the departments were Indians who could hardly speak English, leave alone Kiswahili. With three working shifts, Ogongo was a very vibrant company until the first African managers took over and brought it down with corruption, nepotisn, favouritism and outright theft. Stories went round of how one African manager would just go to accounts department and take large sums of money to go to his home without accounting for it. At the time of its collapse, Ogongo was employing more than two-thirds of its workforce from one location. It was said the managers used to go to the village where they were given a few heads of cattle as inducement for employing their kin. A fishnet repairer was employed as deputy chief engineer. People with no education were placed to head sections. Only people from the same clans as the managers were promoted on the merit system. Just before the closure of Ogongo, a manager and a senior government officer carted away all the fishing nets and other valuable gear to unknown place. Now Ogongo was no more and thousands including my father became jobless.

I called my bro Odingo and we resolved to give him a loan to start a trawling business.

This was his dream.

3.

Yes, all this and more was happening in this year. While our town was pregnant with expectation due to Oginga's new political energy, another monster was consuming us down here in Kisumu: AIDS. One of my unrecorded songs was a scathing attack on careless Kisumu women who were spreading this epidemic. When one of my verses said *wet with blood between the legs*, people were shocked. I was concerning AIDs and my careless sisters. The upsetting black dots on Agwenge's skin, culminating in his violent outbursts aimed at Mary-Goretti as missiles, tripped my jumpy-jumpy rookie scribble brain to compose a real AIDS song for Kisumu. It was ironic, because the main secret to being an artist is to be ruthlessly methodical. Planning the work and working the plan. Well, this AIDS song, like all the rest, followed my usual pattern of songwriting. I sat the band in a half-circle and we rehearsed together, filling the gaps as we went along. I had one clear message: there is no cure for AIDS. We were better off without it because it was a killer! We performed the song during an AIDS awareness seminar at the Kisumu Social Hall. This was appropriate because the show dovetailed almost perfectly Agwenge's decision of becoming the first infected Luo to go public. He got out of his death bed and was driven to *Sosial* in his Datsun. Watching him make his way across the stage, supported by his wife and Ayo, to the mic stand, we were all afraid he had decided to die on stage. The song was Ayo's 'Siku Nitakufa' from the marvelous '89 *Dawn of A New Era* album. He roared through the opening number, earning shouts of encouragement from his friends, fans and several top-flight Kisumu hooligans scattered in the crowd.

> The Day I die, how's it going to be?
> How is it going to feel like to die.
> Fleeing away from this life to another life?
> Where will I go? How will it feel like dying?
> Am I just going to walk away from my body

And that's as far as he went. Barely through the opening lyrics, he couldn't go on and faltered out even as the beat continued going steadily. We saw him falling and rushed to him. He was walked out of stage in one of the most touching and upsetting moments of my life and driven back to his hospital bed.

And now there were things I hated most: one, the untouchable man in Moi's government who had murdered our Robert Ouko, two, the men who mismanaged and brought down Ogongo, three, AIDS which was killing my brother and, four, Aseela's relationship with Biggy Tembo.

AIDs and life sickened me. I wanted a change, something artsy to inspire me. I was going to spend the middle of the year writing Victoria some good one-offs, because these seemed to be Attamaxx's specialty. The hiatus following our heavily pirated *Luopean* album gave me the opportunity to compose some more songs. The lyrics I came up with were inspired by the emotional upheavals I'd undergone following my family's winds of bad fate and the political waves sweeping across Kenya. When we were innocent kids growing up in Pandpieri, we knew nothing about Kenya's ruling political class contributing nothing to develop the kerosene-lamp-lit, poverty-ridden, anesthetizing, under-developed Kisumu town due to complex personal issues between two old men who had played their parts in riding our country of the Colonialists; one who had created a power (which Moi had inherited) and seemed like the most productive and another who was a bitter rebel. But subversive politics of Jaramogi Oginga Odinga were his own folly. Why did he support Kenyatta to presidency when he could have fought his own battle and win like a man. After all, the British loved him and hated Kenyatta who was 'a leader to darkness and death'. Remember Oginga brought the Russians who build our hospital and some people, instead of helping, came down to the hospital to shoot us and kill us.

Instead of fretting, I was writing, and it felt good to create. I was told to tee off on His Excellency Ambassador Okoth Ochot. Personally, in my bad heart, I was getting fed up with him. He hadn't gotten us a gig in over five months. Time and time again he stumbled on about how everything was speculative and tentative yet it was clear he had no plan. He kept coming with stories and excuses and I was going to fire him for sure.

I think he sensed it. And in his vast epic of recent and current plans, one special serpent's tooth surfaced: the guy could really work under pressure. He came up with the Zambian tour. That surprised me, I must admit.

I gave him the chance to try for a little grit in the aftertaste of our 8th year in show business as a band, but he was so over-the-top enroute to another of his many dream stations or just panting to please me to be excused whether everyone in the band lived happily ever after or ended up starving and roasting in Kisumu hellfire of a sun. His Excellency Ambassador Okoth Ochot was, after all, a Kisumuan. If I didn't know my fellow Kisumuans, if I didn't know life then I didn't know him. And if I didn't know about my fellow Luos, then no-one did. See, I relied on Kisumu to build my wealth, and that made my Kisumu fans part of an immense family. You can see why. I always felt that the reason Nairobi produced the majority of great musicians was not because it took immense dedication, skill, practice, talent and luck to make the place sound habitable in the first place. Kisumu offered me that and more: we loved music and we could do a hard dance. The Zaïreans knew this. What Nairobi offered was hard money and classy clubs, nothing more. But Kisumu... *yawa* wait until I tell you. We love music. That's all. But we lack power. Money is power.

His Excellency Ambassador Okoth Ochot's best-laid plans of mice and men were things I just had to hope on, you know, to warm him up for what was to come, like a singer preparing for a rowdy matinee audience. Not the proverbial grinding crash of sensational fiction, but closer akin to the satisfying crunch one gets when he or she slaps a mosquito on the cheek.

While His Excellency Ambassador Okoth Ochot was putting final screws on the Zambian tour, I was lobbying for a gold disc. *Luopean* had sold close to one million copies in East and central Africa, and was selling in Europe as well. I was on the phone a lot demanding from Attamaxx why on earth it wasn't happening. I had recently passed the book onto my lawyers even.

It was an unpleasant *upumbavu* and intellectual arrogance on their part as producers to wait till our lawyers put pressure on them to agree to present us with the gold disc that we rightly deserved. Really, what did Attamaxx think of our image and reputation? To a musician whose legacy included the founding innovator of the entire benga movement, and a host of other essential luminaries, I felt if I didn't have the horsepower to show the world my numerous gold discs, I simply didn't stand a chance of keeping up with the pressure. It's hard enough to acquire a status, but it's harder enough to keep it. In music you need to sell records and the only indicator of winning sales is a gold disc, which is a symbol of achievement. If you think I'm wrong, ask Kisumuans. Which band recorded as prolifically as we did? Worked as hard? Toured as much in only eight years? Traveled and performed abroad as well?

That challenge might be the biggest mountain range out there to cross. Usually the 'overnight successes' you read about Victoria on *Daily Nation, Drum, True Love* or *The Standard* was a fallacy because we had been working hard at it for years. People who didn't live in Kisumu only found out about us when the newspapers wrote one good article for a change. People were overwhelmed by Kisumu every day and moved back to Nairobi or other towns that were easier for them to navigate. Bands that got attention in Nairobi got it because reviewers lived in Nairobi and kept an eye out for new things. It was unfair to judge people for being ambitious and wanting to better their chances of being seen. And how did Kisumu happen? It didn't. It evolved. A long time ago people just don't know.

I went to that Nairobi, went up to *Nation* and made my demands.

Suddenly it happened. Suddenly Attamaxx yielded. Suddenly we got the gold disc for *Luopean*.

Aseela broke the news. 'Hey,' she exclaimed enthusiastically, 'We got it!'

Aseela was enthused, too, and the rest of the band too. It had to happen, I knew. The acceptance ceremony was brought to Sunset Hotel, Kisumu.

I gave an compelling speech; a stoic face, facing the audience, denouncing Attamaxx as a ruse of the local music, giving the press falsities in the generosities to come. Kisumuans almost cried with joy as they watched me receiving the gold disc on TV.

Attamaxx's JB got all choked up. So did Ochieng Kamau, and other Attamaxx officials. JB kept, remembering how last October he brought in the first tapes of our album and how I made a forecast with him that not only would the album win a gold disc, but within a year we'd be making another great album.

The event was a shmoozefest and the industry's equivalent of the trading floor at a merchant bank swamped Kisumu Sunset Hotel. People came from all over. All the heavy weights of African music were there. Sterns, Mazadis, Polygram, AIT, Studio Veve were all represented. Here was where deals were negotiated, artists courted and signed and honchos sussed out their rival's marketing strategy. Just how much intel was gathered at these events was anyone's guess, but there were gatherings everywhere, anytime, in the week leading up to the big night.

All in all, for me it was just another day at the studio. The gold disc and the success of *Luopean* had done a lot of good. Miruka of Afrikan Dawn called me from London and told me that Pam will be coming to Nairobi to pave way for his company's business negotiations with us. He was not happy with our contract with Attamaxx and the fact that we were still using their label.

Somehow this got to the press.

Question people asked: would it be feasible to cut links with Attamaxx?

Quite a relief. Good riddance, even.

4.

I found momentum swinging our way early in the year. The gold disc added new spark to our hitherto dying fire. Victoria felt good together. Without question we could reform and knock over the crowds again. Kisumu was the home of the second act and embraced stars that came back from the dead.

But at what cost, I wondered?

Could I and His Excellency Ambassador Okoth Ochot survive a revival? The Ambassador, who eschewed the 'celebrity bullshit' but still ran the gamut of show business to earn a living at the same time, seemed to be enjoying the reflected attention of being Victoria's ambassador. Perhaps show business had stalked up to him from behind and seduced him with its glamour and falsehood? Here, at the gold disc award ceremony, everything seemed possible.

Kisumu, thank you. For support.

People; nonetheless, were beginning to understand. No longer was the question, 'Where do we go from here,' knocking ceaselessly in my head. The band suddenly had new energy: the sound was mature. Living and surviving in Kisumu as a band was no longer a very hard thing to do. Victoria was a mixing ground of temper-tantrum queens, older companioned couples, lithe twinks bucking for a bang, muscled men who changed their afros to curlykits weekly. An interesting group of people in a comfortable open-air space, hey, it was the boiler-hot Kisumu, and what do you expect?

Anyways, that was what the promotional literature on His Excellency Ambassador Okoth Ochot's Zambia tour said—who am I, aside from a smartass, to question it?

Now, in terms of sound maturity; our new combative style of the Five Bosses vocal attack had been concerning me lately. While it successfully made us blow out Ominde Nyang's Victoria Academy, it had its challenges. It couldn't work with our older songs which people loved so much. And I'm sure Kisumuans saw it—it was a problem. It was the old-stuff-to-new-stuff phenomena, to which a remarkable number of people seemed not to adhere to. Most of our fans were as old as we were and preferred our older songs. My old singers who had since decamped from my group were very well in the mix.

Thing is, if a band changes their sound, it's okay to fans as long as the new sound appeals to the fans. When fans complained of overdose of one style called Urban Benga, we listened. I had always made sure the band maintained a unity of purpose: cosmopolitan Kisumuans were dedicated to throwback guitar-driven Urban Benga and the downtown or even village lifestyle that went with it. But now weren't we beginning to sound like a stripped down Langa Langa Stars, or a cross between that Zaïrean band and Virunga. Roki Fela didn't like too much layering of the instruments, particularly guitar, preferring a less engineered sound. I agreed with him inwardly. He figured folks could better imagine the stripped down sound, as many kids liked to dream of being with the band. I agreed again. The new vocal innovation had driven up our beat.

The Five Bosses were always hit verses at the same time.

Their sound was easier to understand and reproduce live. The key to their hitherto success, however, was clearly the showcasing of combined vocals on record and their image on stage as a live act. To lose this image would render the band to just another hack outfit and condemn them to playing in pubs the rest of their career. Although the music had changed, I guess it was the entertainment on stage that counted, and we still had one. I think it was one of the many hallmarks that made a great band; a band that was always looking to take their music further and experiment, go into unchartered waters. Look at some of the greatest bands of all time: Franco's TPOK Jazz, Tabu Ley's Afrisa, Zaïko, Kiam etc and you will see how different the first albums were from the last ones. It was a completely different sound, but the same band. But I mostly agreed. A lot of bands went in a different direction, this was nothing new or life-changing. For better, for worse, for mediocre. Growth was productive and healthy. What people needed to start doing was listening to an album as an individual piece of work, instead of making the band itself one big musical blob of work.

This year was the golden age of the band. Victoria air guitar'd her drum stick, and tapped her foot the whole way through. Melody became completely oblivious. Sweetest thing you ever felt. I had imagination of it happening like that. We were still adored for one thing: love songs. Folks love love songs, and ours was now enriched not by the sax of Vicky—the old pro who mimicked his every move on stage and who would make sax fill in empty spaces between verses—but by the five powerful voices combined. We didn't miss a beat! You were sucked into the beat of hard hitting drums, steady shakers, steady tumbas, captivating rhythms, criss-crossing double solo guitars, thudding and grumbling bass, the heart-rending vocals... it was magic as always.

What about the softer side of Victoria group? The softer side was the world of men like Vicky Mifupa Ya Zamani, Pajos, Mzee Frank, Roga Roga and of the cordiality of associations between the band members and the unity it brought. Mzee Frank in his trademark white linen shirt and black pants was hatless for a change and his friendship with Super Mazembe's Katele was no more about *chang'aa* hunting in White House, Ondiek Estate than it was now about comparing notes in voice education. Roga Roga appeared to have discovered more freedom and was constantly in frantic communication in sign language with Vicky: the only man who had patience. People called him a 'beloved queer' but I used to talk to him in sign language and knew he was no queer. He was a nice guy, very serious.

But then man who becoming destitute was Vicky Mifupa ya Zamani. Vicky rarely found his own performances and record dates satisfying, no matter how much they pleased his audiences. He developed his own honking, gut-bucket style of sax playing which characterised some of the most exciting music of the 1960s and 1970s. Being really a rumba saxophone master, he always preferred the solitude of the backyards and the trees. You might have thought it strange that Vicky, at age 63, would want to spend a minimum of five hours each afternoon playing his horn in his backyard in Migosi. Five hours' practice was a very full day for most musicians between gigs but *Mzee* Vicky had the training and discipline of a professional. Somehow his reputation as quirky and unapproachable loner was more than an image he had cultivated, it was who he really was. A man who respected his age and his work, the Bible-quoting *mzee* didn't chit-chat on a conventional level. He was very thoughtful, very intelligent and didn't hide his feelings. He spoke his mind and this had nothing to do with age, I knew many slovenly and unprincipled liars like Mzee Frank.

Like most of my instrumentalists, Vicky came to my band to not only to fulfill his own dream but to lend a hand, share and build and create new experience. We called him The Teacher. Over the years we had many lengthy discussions about recording techniques and musical aesthetics. I can say with absolutely no reservations that we achieved the best recorded sound of my career in these last two years with Vicky's clever suggestions. The dazzlingly quick improvisational brilliance added his own quirky cerebralism and humor He could make his sax-talk, sometimes we carried on rigorous sax guitar conversations.

5.

And eventually Afrikan Dawn wrote a letter to me signed by Pam promising to finance a double album. The first album of the year with the full participation of The Five Bosses was going to be made. Since *Luopean* had been massively pirated, I didn't want to record again but His Excellency Ambassador Okoth Ochot had other ideas. 'Do it like Franco,' he insisted. 'Keep one step of the bootleggers by continually releasing new titles.'

He was right. *In 1983 alone Franco and TP OK Jazz recorded eleven albums, and all were hits!*

The artistic direction and the arrangement for this record following the band's vocal section reorganization was problematic. In the past the band had had at least four periods of vocal distinctions: the Biggy Tembo era, the Ayo era, the Mawazo/ Agwenge era, the Aseela/Roki Fela/Ojua Kali Man era and now The Five Bosses. While each period had produced significant improvement to the band and re-engineered the sound, the creation of the new sound posed problems. The new sound had to be better to be accepted. And you can imagine how singers always dominated the band. Replacing Biggy Tembo (who was vocally strong) with Ayo especially proved problematic. And don't forget Ayo is a woman!

Now.

An album with all The Five Bosses on each song was proving to be a serious challenge. Should the band stick to the same formula that worked in the past or change tack? A more sophisticated sound, perhaps, now we could chisel a good working budget? Or maybe we should stick to what we knew and take a gamble with the fact that the public wouldn't tire of the same old shit? Logic suggested if the public liked our previous records why wouldn't they want the latest one from Victoria? Loyalty works, yeah?

Getting the songs to fit with the vocal scale was the next technical hurdle. Remember we were competing Victoria Academy which had the dynamic trio of Biggy Tembo, Mawazo Ya Pesa and Sam Ojua Kali Man. When it seemed like I was getting tired of this again, His Excellency Ambassador Okoth Ochot stepped in with words of wisdom. 'Allow the band a free hand in this one,' he said. 'This is the style Verkys used to manage Langa Langa Stars.' He was right. My Five Bosses were designed to sound like Langa Langa Stars.

But where were these wonderful songs going to come from? I called a meeting and asked each member of the band to compose a song or two. But of course the privilege fell in favour of the five vocalists only. And you guess they were more than happy. They'd had little time for composition and had been flat out working. An album could be fleshed out with outtakes from previous sessions, sure, but they needed a good 5 or 6 new numbers to build around.

'The Poet' Opiyo Willy was now appointed a key arranger and was for more acoustic work. His composition was taken from one of his unrecorded songs. He liked simple arrangements of well-crafted songs and wanted a sound like what Franco and Tabu Ley achieved with the '83 'Hommage A Kabaselle'. He opined that many a weak song could be disguised by over-engineering, vocal prowess of The Five Bosses and lavish layering. A corny lyric could be drowned out or rendered unimportant by the use of standard vocal hooks and fine guitar works.

Aseela took charge of things. The new kid, Poposo, who was a romantic crooner with a penchant for heartfelt ballads, had a song he wanted to sing, but it wasn't original. It was by an old benga singer and it was called 'Abondo'. Abondo is the name of a hardy cactus tree that grows in many parts of rural Nyanza. It was a folkore song of desire, of loss and of mourning. The song was both pretty and soulful, but Aseela didn't like it on principle.

She hit back with a beautifully choral song called 'Ayom Yom Kom Iwe Ne Ng'a' and she determined to sing the lead with the rest of the singers replying to her lead parts in a call-and-response fashion. It didn't take a great leap of the imagination who the *ayom yom* was and Sam Ojua Kali Man was going to be riled.

For the new Victoria sound, the lyrics were primary. The melody was to come after 'The Poet' Opiyo Willy wrote first and foremost, after he had scrawled lines in an exercise book. Willy had an ear for good sound and preferred loaded slant rhymes for the Five Bosses. There was a reworking of his song 'Naomba Utulivu'. This song was a spin-off of the same one we recorded in our 1990 *Chris Tetemeko* album. However, the lyrics were quite different. This song was about our push for reckless greed. We tend to push people out of our way to advance ourselves. We knock people over to climb the ladder to power and positions and this only leaves us without friends once we reach those high towers. We are wrapped up in our own worlds and care less for others. We hurt people without caring, even our loved ones. We find it easy to hurt others and offer no apology. The song asked:

> How do you deal with the relationships
> In your life? Are you knocking people around
> physically, emotionally; With your words or in some
> other way; While you achieve your own ends?
> *Jirekebishe.*

Roki Fela argued a lot with Aseela who appeared to be having an upper hand in this recording. Aseela had more than six compositions she was convinced were hits. Hits, she argued, were sometimes constructed from even less and Super Wanyika, in particular, had the reputation of coming up with songs within five minutes of recording. She saw little reason why Victoria couldn't come up with stuff in the studio, now they had the luxury of a bit of time. Needless to say she meant, without referring to relief from not having heavyweights like Ayo and Ojua Kali Man, that she now had artistic freedom. Well, I was seeing many of her hitherto-hidden talents. One was leadership over men, another was a domineering character.

A good album was clearly going to impact on any future negotiations and His Excellency Ambassador Okoth Ochot insisted we put as much effort into it as possible. By the state of Kenya's industry, two years at the top was reckoned to be the life expectancy of a band. I wanted to break that expectation and push Victoria's career out another two years. But much depended on how well the band worked together and whether internal tensions would boil over.

Attamaxx had made enough out of the band over the last eight years to give us the artistic freedom we, as seasoned pros, could make good use of. There was no need for them making things difficult for Victoria over the innovative shift in vocal section when they were working with the rival Victoria Academy who we were competing. So if they thought they were sweetly being good to us and at the same time working with our rivals and calling it business, it was time to unpack. I put a call to Pam who put a call to Polygram and AIT. I later learned how Pam put the weights on His Excellency Ambassador Okoth Ochot to severe the links 'permanently' with Attamaxx and she asked him to make use of his friendship with his friend Felix Jakomo. The Ambassador lamented that Attamaxx either had no faith in Victoria or were getting back at us for arm-twisting them to present us with gold disc. In any case, believing, perhaps, that the band had little more to give after *Luopean*. He and I now had to deal with AIT's honchos at their production meetings. I wanted a fuller, more refined sound with higher production values. AIT wanted at least two hits from the album—appropriate for mainstream rumba and benga radio formats. Like it or not, we were confronted with a new industry now, and its demand for profit.

We recorded *8th Anniversary* at AIT on our new Victoria label. I left most of the arranging to band members, with the exception of my own composition, and most of the arrangements you heard in most of our Attamaxx recordings were not my own either but Attamaxx's studio arrangers. Attamxx knew their market and presented their productions in absolute terms, I could say. Perhaps people never understood how good I was when I wanted the record to sound artistic. When recording *Luopean*, I stood my ground and had most of the arranging done by me and my bandmates. I wanted to replicate the success of that great album in this new recording. So I was glad I was working with AIT on this one. Roga Roga and I doubled on lead and rhythm guitars with Benz laying down the melody on second rhythm while Aseela devised a descant. To this Roga Roga added some fingerpicking acoustic guitar and me, later, some work with the brushes. Mifupa Ya Zamani and Lobe Mapako put a resounding blow on the horns but in the end we settled for Mifupa's single-note tenor sax while Mzee Frank blew a tin whistle but none of Victoria was competent on this difficult instrument more than I was comfortable with Aseela's keyboard. In some songs, the keyboard had to be discarded in favour of flutes and shakers. I used the tremolo, frequency, depth, and reverb and the absolute mind boggling fingerpicking that fingers could play. The scratchy guitar sound had to stay, the band insisted. Like the effect Issa Juma achieved with 'Anifa.' I felt it was too experimental, so could we confine it to only one or two songs? I meant it for any of Willy's artistic compositions. For the rest of the songs? Simple was better, insisted Aseela. She talked long and hard with AIT to come up with an agreement. The producer, Felix, was under as much pressure to produce a saleable product, both because of AIT reputation and his percentage of the gross.

The recording session was relaxed with the engineers at AIT happy to allow Victoria to work around our commitments. The Five Bosses sang their hearts out with all the passion. Aseela's voice shone and glitzed richly rang throughout, in lead and backing roles. And I was seeing new energy in this woman. This was her album to direct and arrange, it gave her an opportunity to show her vocal prowess. She was at her best. To reach the highest notes, she always sang with her eyes closed pressing her fingers against her temple.

Felix would sit in with us during the initial sessions and I hoped I'd be able to please him enough to get rid of him as soon as possible. He had been a dominating presence throughout the sessions to make sure it was so AIT had all the latest gadgetry to play with.

The invited artists included Frantal Tabu, Lobe Mapako Rodi, Atia-Jo, Onyango Odol and Dr. Collela Mazee. A trickle of visitors came and went as we worked, including Angelou. I grabbed Ayo for some cameo backing vocals and she went away chuffed with herself. It'd been a good while since anyone had asked her to sing.

Finally it was done and it had been a grueling three months and it was no big ceremony even. Aseela's smile, as she wiped sweat off her forehead with tissue, told it all: it had been hard work sweetly. But her brilliant smile suggested happiness.

The cover was done by AIT's graphic designer. I wanted a group photo of the band on the cover and shots were taken. There was nothing fancy about the shot, no make-up or clever studio poses. I selected one in which the musicians all looked like middle-aged African dads and moms. On the back of the sleeve, only guitarist G-Chord lacked facial hair, and tenor sax Vicky Mifupa Ya Zamani was, of course, wearing his ubiquitous 'godfather' hat. The music? Up-tempo, Utopian, rich and dense instrumentation, a non-stop relaxed groove secure in its manliness, embracing 'Family' and 'Happiness' (two song titles), assuring a mature audience that could survive these 'changing Times,' of the early '90s.

The personnel line-up of *8th Anniversary* included:

Vocals: Roki Fela 'Ndugu Ya Kasuku', Queen Belinda Aseela, Mzee Frank, 'Power Voice' Poli Poposso, 'The Poet' Opiyo Willy, Okach Biggy

Guest vocalist: Ayo
Lead Guitar: Dino Otis Dundos
Solo Guitar: Frantal Tabu
First Rhythm Guitar: Roga Roga
Second Rhythm Guitar: Benz Benji Obat
Bass: Ajuma Ouma G-Chord & Atia Jo
Keyboard: Belinda Aseela
Drums: Pajos Mwana N'djilli
Alto sax: Vicky Mifupa Ya Zamani
Tenor sax: Lobe Mapako Roddy
Congas: Kaput Ja Manyata

This superb double-vinyl album put our discography at fourteen albums and pegged Victoria as pioneers of both 'quiet storm' and 'retronuevo' Urban Benga and rumba, reaffirming the band's 'top band' position in our lakeside town and Western Kenya. But newspaper reviews took matters too far. Look at what a journalist said: 'The band sounds like a dedicated husband still madly in love with his wife after all these eight years.' In other words: *as reliable as his band.*

Victoria Academy, are you listening?

As this album was on our label and we had a new producer, I had freedom to design the marketing and distribution. I got in touch with Pam in UK and she advised me on what to do to hit the bootleggers below the belt. Her plan was simple: *release the cassettes first and let the hyenas grab them then release the expensive LPs later.* So I first signed the release of the album on seal-wrapped pre-recorded cassettes to be retailed at the same price as that of the inferior pirate copies and then distribution team delivered them to the African markets and people grabbed them. Two months later I signed the release of the disc with an expensive-looking cover and all the lyrics printed on paper and inserted in the jacket for fans to master the words of the songs. Pam's idea worked! Many of the fans who had bought the cassettes preferred their music on vinyl than on cassettes. During our time with Attamaxx, they controlled my music and all the production and only sold the end-product. I believe it was their monopoly and their unfair control that denied us good access to overseas market. With AIT and now on our own label, I was dealing with licensees and other would-be second party producers.

6.

The new era with Roki Fela, Aseela, 'The Poete' Opiyo Willy, Mzee Frank, Poposso and Okach Biggy became one of the highpoints of Victoria's career. I wanted to see my group achieving another international recognition, particularly with the first visit of a Kenyan group to southern Africa. Primarily we were headlining this tour in Zambia to showcase The Five Bosses and promote *8th Anniversary*. His Excellency Ambassador Okoth Ochot was a busy man. Dates were being finalized. Mr. Kiguta of TopAfric Promotions had been in touch with me. Our records were selling well in that country, so the expectations were pretty high.

Victoria assembled and began rehearsing for the tour. In between things, Mr. Kiguta came down to Kisumu to meet me and I signed a 10-day contract. Watching the ink of my signature dry on the paper, I smiled. We were going to earn three times what we made out of the Burundi Tour. In just ten days! Mr. Kiguta beamed and said to me one of the nicest words I've ever heard from a promoter: 'I still love Victoria on record but they've never gotten good money out of me for a live show since the Burundi Tour.' This show was to be bigger, with more equipment and, perhaps, more at stake. A stadium concert was planned for Lusaka. Apart from Victoria's original crew, TopAfric Promotions, acquired a full-time lighting team, sound assistants, five stage hands for moving the gear, and a minder—a six foot ex-gang member. Victoria had never played outdoors for so many years since the Kampala debacle so it was very much a step into the unknown. All the songs in the new album were to be showcased, of course, plus *Luopean*—revamped and rearranged.

Aseela took personal charge of things as tour manager and was already busy selecting the band's wardrobe for the tour. Of late she had been bitchy, moody, and difficult to judge her mood. A week before the tour, she was hospitalized with complications of abortion. Maybe if I'd known what I could do about her drug-related problems—the migraines, the addiction to painkillers, the depressive illnesses—I'd have been more understanding. But I found her honesty amazing. Something made me want to treat this like it was just a minor social gaff. Perhaps you'd call this a confession: Aseela was a woman who aroused my interest. It had been a given admission that she was beautiful and innocent and successful. I could see that when I hired her. Since then, though, I had noticed her buoyant capacity to be bossy, even though her routine demeanor was feminine, mature and respectable.

Biggy Tembo introduced her to drugs and it irked me. She wasn't afraid to confess to me her love for Biggy and couldn't help it despite the damage the relationship was doing to her health and her career. She would marry him if he proposed. I believed her; I could see it in her eyes. Why was she aborting his child then?

Her eyes bore into me... eyes red with fire.

'Never mind the question,' I said.

'He forced me to do it,' she said and her eyes clouded with tears. 'His wife forced him.'

She was determined to go on that tour and the band certainly couldn't do without her but she was in a terrible shape. Runny-nosed and dreary-eyed, she was clearly losing a grip on herself even if she didn't want to admit it. She was visibly sick.

One of our dancing girls volunteered to care for Aseela during the tour; she insisted on someone she could trust and her sister, Akoth, was put on the payroll. The host could just squeeze comfortably into the tour bus—a 48-seat Scania with a massive wheels. Somewhere behind, the gear was being transported by a rented semi, towed by an Isuzu-powered loader. After a week's winding up, we hit the road for the first of massive concerts in the major population centres. Bookings had been heavy, with a likely turn out of around 120,000 for our first Lusaka gig at the Independence Stadium. It was faintly reminiscent of Bujumbura, but this country had a far larger population and the band was near overwhelmed by the response. It was horrendous, from start to finish. The start was awful because we got the wrong gate, then we got on the stage, perspiring, having held up an entire plane of journalists. And the gig was terrible. Opening for us were bands like Harari, Zam Zam, Earthworks, Deadly Black Savages (what kind of a name was this, anyway?). It was a phenomenal lineup, and we were the headliners. But it was a fantastic opportunity. We couldn't go on stage because Mr. Kiguta, was fiercely negotiating matters with sniffy businessmen or politicians—who, I suppose, had their hearts in the wrong place—who were trying to promote the policies of Frederick Chiluba, but it was the wrong place and the wrong time. Supporters of Kaunda were booing and throwing things at them, and that was unpleasant enough. Anyway, we finally got on stage and we were five songs into the show when Mr. Kiguta ran the businessmen off and refused to have them back on despite the fact that it appeared they had paid him handsomely to gain some publicity for Chiluba.

Mr. Kiguta said: 'I'm not going to let a bunch of confused politicians ruin this show for the people who deserve it. We are here to dance, so let's dance.'

Mr. Kiguta had a lot of temper tantrums. I could see he had a lot of weight here in Zambia in matters business and politics. And he was just as corrupt as any normal businessman you met in Kenya. He couldn't stop it; fame and the whole fine promoter thing was just a side-show for him. The reason he had us here was to build support for new MMD party administration and it was my good guess President Chiluba must have paid him well.

Aseela had not shaken off her morbid sentimentality,

something somehow life-affirming, but ultimately tragic about her struggle to escape her fate. She was still walking up her path to full recovery but had not kicked large daily puffs of marijuana. After the debut concert gig, however, she was in good spirits. But something was missing. We didn't see her assured stage performance, powerful vocals, well-crafted stage movements and promising animations... the only thing that we saw was she was *very* disappointing. She was lackluster and her voice was never the greatest at the best of times.

Two days later she appeared to have gotten a good grip on herself and had amazing new stamina. She was back to her bossy self and took charge of things. And we went out there and played our hearts out. The names the fans were screaming for were Mawazo, Biggy and Ayo. Sometimes even the first note of the evening would be wrong, and we'd all get off on the wrong foot. At the end of the gig our crew backed our rental truck into the marquee and every penny we made was grabbed by Mr. Kiguta who had loads of things to complain about. He quarreled us like school children and I hated him outright. Maybe I hated him because his greed reminded me of my own greed. He had paid us well upfront and he appeared hell-bent to recoup massively. And I knew there and then that this swarthy lunatic was going to go to any length to milk us, even make us do more shows than we agreed on the contract.

He took me to one side and said, 'I'll pay you extra to do extra shows at the Caltex Lounge.'

The Caltex Lounge was a functions center not far from the Kaunda Hall where we had performed two shows. There Mr. Kiguta had laid on a buffet and drinks for the band and crew. Security barred the entrances and the invited were ushered in through a back exit. Even the promoter couldn't slip out unnoticed. Fans were still outside and liable to pounce on anyone leaving.

Victoria t-shirts were in abundance and anyone who had any role to play acquired themselves one. A local entrepreneur had been contracted by Mr. Kiguta to run them off to his own design, blatantly ripping off the band's name. His Excellency Ambassador Okoth Ochot realized he had to seal up the merchandising deals or more of this was liable to happen. A lucrative revenue stream for the band was going into the pockets of people who had no connection with Victoria.

We carried the routine of playing large open air venues during the day and the Caltex Lounge as the evening encores for six consecutive days. Things almost fell apart on the seventh day of our tour, in the outskirts of Lusaka. We had played a good set to a practically empty room that was part of a club filled with pasty juiced-up bigots. After watching a few fights break out and nearly getting into a few ourselves, we decided to head back to the home of some 'Party' friends of Mr. Kiguta who had offered to put us up for the night. On the way back to the car, I thought we were safely into small-talk, largely about what Kenyans do that Zambians don't when the bottom of the entire situation fell out: all I remember is Aseela screaming at one of the Zambians for boasting about a football match their national football team, Chipolopolo FC, lost to Harambee Stars, and the Zambian guy apologizing profusely—in a horrible English accent. It was that simple. People were still a bit old-fashioned that way up here. Still a bit old-fashioned about a lot of things, I could see. It was hilarious, really, but we couldn't see that because we had just had it with each other. It was like arguing with your girlfriend about nothing because you can't figure out what's actually bothering you, except in this case your girlfriend keeps affecting an offensive accent and is yelling at herself about it while all you want to do is just shut her up you could think.

On the eighth day, after loading in our equipment for a show at a modest club known as Lusa Small, we got chummy with the soloist of a band from South Africa named Deadly Black Savages (or something equally lugubrious). Although his band was slated to open, his bandmates were nowhere to be found. We comforted him, tried to convince Lusa Small's sound guy to have their set delayed and even helped find a parking spot for their van when the rest of the band finally showed up. In exchange, Deadly Black Savages (or whatever) insisted on playing second in our slot. They parked their asses at the bar upstairs and simply refused to go on. Eventually, we were forced by the sound guy to go on first, before most of our fans had even arrived.

Deadly Black Savages continued drinking upstairs through our entire set while their soloist joined us on stage. His name was Steve and he picked his guitar lightly, augmenting it occasionally with casually flashy tricks. He seemed as surprised and delighted by what he was doing as the audience was impressed with his showman appeal and kept going seemingly showing off. He was a fine player and embellished some good riffs for two songs.

Then the performance really hit and Roki Fela 'Ndugu Ya Kasuku' sang an extended version of 'There's No Mathematics In Love'. His distinctive bark and quivering vibrato, coupled with his lovable chuckle carried the song. The crowd loved this song which somebody had pirated here and so huge was its popularity people even sang along the vocal parts. Roki Fela performed it with great love, ease, control and enthusiasm. Holding out the mic at the audience, he made them respond to his calls. When he sang one verse, the audience answered the next verse.

> Don't calculate petrol and food in a restaurant
> And money for making my hair and polishing my nails
> Don't calculate what you give me to give my mother
> Don't calculate fine wine from
> Germany and nice kitenge from Bruxelles
> And expensive perfume from Paris...
> Don't calculate and bargain
> about the cows and cash you gave for my bride price
> And don't calculate the
> money you give me for my brother's school fees
> Don't calculate my sister's college money
> Because she's your sister oh—oh!

Roki stole the show at Lusa Small. He sweated pints and pints through it and was showered with money. Women screamed, some tore off their blouses and flashed bare breasts.

At the end of it as we were winding up, Mr. Kiguta asked the crowd to make a date with the band for the mega show at Lusaka Stadium tomorrow.

But Lusaka Stadium gig turned out to be the worst that I've ever played. I felt really (bloody awfully) sick. It was flu and bad fever. But to be fair, the sizable, if a little subdued, crowd on hand at Lusa Small on our ninth night came to Lusaka Stadium to hear Roki Fela spin yarns and crack gags, they came to hear that voice. Roki was trashed, stumbling around the stage, mumbling into the mic before he finally gave up and crashed down on the drum riser while the rest of the band played around him.

I found out later that by that point in the tour, Victoria were so sick of being heckled by the Lusaka crowds that they had simply stopped trying. But it pissed me off because I was there hoping to do a killer show. I wanted to maintain Roki's standard.

Hours at Lusaka Stadium were grueling; things were taking a frightening nose-dive. I saw that tour as; well and yeah, Victoria was indeed god-awful. Roki Fela could barely squeak out a sound. He handed 'The Poet' Opiyo Willy his mic and staggered backstage in one of the most upsetting moments in the history of Victoria. Our Poet took charge and delivered the remainder of the song. I sometimes found Opiyo Willy's voice nasal and irritating as hell on record, but live, it took on a whole new dimension of torture. The sucky part was due to the fact that there were more girls in the audience and 'There's No Mathematics In Love' was always a lady' choices. They thought we were amazing, not to have stopped in the middle of the song, but kept everything going, completing the song undaunted.

Poposso came on cue and we played a few songs from the *8th Anniversary* album which had little effect because they were unknown. Then we played a Franco song. When we finished that song Mr. Kiguta asked the crowd what they wanted to hear. A few of were yelling out Paul Simon songs, others wanted more Victoria, but a bunch of middle-aged guys in the front row kept screaming for more Franco. I looked at them and said, 'I guess it's another Franco song'. I was up front and off to the side of the stage and saw Mr. Kiguta turn his back to us and say sarcastically to the band 'Franco, yeh!' And we did. It really sucked. But all the screaming Zambians up front sure were happy.

Benz who was accompanying us on rhythm guitar was in an even worse mood than the rest. After about 45 minutes-and halfway through a song he smashed his guitar and walked off. Unbelievably, we got a standing ovation out of it, as the crowd seemed to think that what happened was part of the show, but it really wasn't. Just a freak thing that happened that really became the bad stroke of our show that night.

Hell broke loose, expectedly.

That was it. Riots and police tear gas threatened to stop the show. And basically something hit me—a stone hurled by an angry fan—during our last song. I have no idea what happened next. I came to and woke up before I hit the floor, but not before hitting my head on the microphone. I looked around me and I was seeing everything in weird multiple dimensions, and the band seemed to be playing a completely different song to me. Everyone looked at me in horror, including the audience, and I strummed along for the rest of the song, hoping no one would notice. I could barely move on stage. I might as well have been dead. But you can't really go out there and explain to the audience that you're sick, so they probably just thought I was a boring and horrible musician. That was embarrassing. I didn't throw up on stage, but I almost did. I had to keep turning round, and I probably looked really green. It was awful, I tell you.

I guess I spent a long time there bamboozled. Then I sunk under because by the time I woke up I found the promoter had locked us in a room screaming and demanding his money.

'You fucking hypocrite,' he screamed. 'You think this is

Nairobi!?'

Hyena, vulture, shameless thief, hypocrite, carnivore were among the words he called me. I nearly slugged him.

'Shameless thief,' he shouted, 'tis is not Nairobi. You will pay!'

He seized our equipment and threatened me with legal action.

A short while later, his men bundled in Aseela, Roki Fela, G-Chord and Poposso into the room and I saw them sick and shivering, with some of them vomiting.

Mr Kiguta came to a rude realization that things were really out of ordinary. He put his head back, his expression cold. His voice was a grinding monotone. 'Is this poisoning? Call a doctor, take them to hospital.'

We were diagnosed with malaria. Only Mzee Frank and Willy escaped it. Roki Fela suffered real bad and was even hospitalized for two days. It puzzled me a bit at first because I was from a malaria prone area of Western Kenya and had never had malaria since my early childhood. The doctor told me it was a different strain.

We got some shoddy reviews on radio, saying the vocals sounded weak, but no one mentioned that I was sick. It was really depressing. Not that I believe in giving excuses. What seemed to be a total embarrassment became a much talked about event that day. A few days later, I and the band were winding up the tour. We played the last venue of the tour then security saw us out the back exit into waiting cabs and back to Mr. Kiguta's office. He chopped off a sizeable chunk of our allowances then handed us over to his transport manager and went off for his other business. He was so pissed off he had no nice words of (even) goodbye.

We were not leaving till the next morning. So His Excellency Ambassador Okoth Ochot booked got us a paying gig at Lusa Small.

7.

We got back to Kisumu and into a load of grief. 'Gentlemens' Gentleman' KSK Odongo was dead...and *shit!* Rumours were flying all over Kisumu and people called it suicide.

He was found sitting on his drum stool behind his new electric drum set (recently bought using Uncle's money) in the Olindas rehearsal room. He had been fooling around with electric connect-ions and electrocuted himself when he wanted to connect wires and bit off at live wire with his teeth. I wanted to believe it was an accident. KSK wasn't that courageous or careless... the guy loved himself. I mean KSK wasn't the kind of artist who would mess his own life. The guy walked with a mirror, comb and shoe brush in his pockets. The guy showered twice a day and complained a lot about Kisumu heat. The guy hated to sweat, detested the smell of sweat and kept away from the hot sun as much as he could. The guy always wore well pressed shirts and when sitting on a chair, he would remove his hanky and dust the seat first. When he ate fish, he never ate the head. He only wore jeans and T-shirt on weekends and his jeans were not like Mo's which never saw water: they were always washed. When the blue started fading, he gave them away. You should've seen his bed room. You should've seen the bed he slept in, he slept like a king. No I didn't believe KSK was capable of messing himself by taking away the life he loved so. I wasn't particularly sorry for him since committing suicide means taking one's own life. And that is doing something stupid. The Sunday keepers say your soul goes straight to hell and you have no chance of redemption. And death scares me... suicide scares me more.

So you can imagine how pissed off I was to learn that he had left a note for me to educate his son. I didn't even know he had a son... so conservative he was I didn't even know his woman. I only knew he dated several high class working women, the refined liberated women of Kisumu. It didn't jar me, it only angered me. When a close friend-turned-foe suddenly dies, how does it affect you? What are you supposed to do. I think my twenty-nine year old mind couldn't really wonder about KSK's last thoughts as his soul rushed out of his body. I'd seen a few deaths... Oliver, Magak, Nicholas Opija, my bro Keya, Spark Onyango and I don't think these deaths affected me that much. I think the way you respond to a guy's death has to do with how they treated you during their lives. When a guy went through his life like he was of no use to society and he was better dead and no one will miss him, you feel nothing for him when he finally dies. I think so far I hadn't lost someone really dear to me, someone I really 'lost.'

Then the rude realization that we were still family musically hit me. My life played a brief vista of our times together and I couldn't really appreciate that 'Gentlemen's Gentleman' KSK Odongo was the same drummer who was my deputy for four years. I could only see him as the dim-witted traitor who was always walking out on me to recreate Delta Force. Reason for suicide? No one knew but many attributed it to the failure of Delta Force especially after Ominde Nyang' organized the rebellion that resulted in the birth of Victoria Academy. But was this enough reason for the guy to kill himself? I didn't think so. I know people kill themselves for all sorts of funny reasons. During my high school in Kisumu Day, a classmate killed himself for being jilted by a girl. But in KSK's case, there had to be another reason. But this wasn't any business of mine; I had other things in my head.

I didn't go to the Russia mortuary; no way was I going to go. Eyes were on me, but I didn't bother myself. No, dread, no, I wasn't going into that mortuary. Never wanted to see the body. I was asked about his last wishes... about his boy and I said I said I was going to think about it. But deep inside I was angered. Why me? What about his brothers and sisters? His parents...relatives. Maybe he had died penniless but whose fault was that? I gave him all the opportunities. He gave me hell, eventually stabbed me in the back and nearly destroyed my band. What about the cars I gave him which he crashed? What about the way he attacked me in song calling me fake millionaire? No, I didn't think I would do anything about those last wishes. And I wasn't going to consult anybody because I knew they will try to reason with me to educate the boy. He couldn't be really penniless, what about his royalties? What about his rental houses? This was another scheme to rip me off.

No way. Sorry KSK.

Instead I suggested a fundraising.

I booked *Sosial* for the celebration of KSK's life and fundraising for burial expenses. It shocked me the number of people who turned up. Uncle too attended with his hot school-girl wife, Maria. At one end, a stage had been set up and a roster of bands and musicians had been organised to entertain the mourners. A brief appearance of the still-living still-willing members of KSK's faction of Kisumu Delta Force was to be followed by a cameo from Victoria Academy. I had refused to put Victoria on the program, so Victoria didn't participate.

Tears and sadness lasted till nightfall, then the event took the shape of a free dance and the place was rocking and cops on beat had been in to wonder if this was a dance party or what kind of a funeral service this was with high volume and dancing people. The place was jumping and pumping and Ayo sparkled as she shared the stage with Mawazo. Academy could only play our records since they had no material of their own, so it was like old times, I thought, and what a shame someone like KSK who was so much loved had to die.

When Academy launched on 'Anyango Nyar Nam' I could take it no more. Someone handed me a guitar and I strapped it on and got on stage. But I couldn't play right. At the end of the song, Mo took issues with me about it. 'What's up, *bwana*? You're playing off key,' he grumbled.

I shrugged and snorted harshly. 'That last *sebene* part on 'Anyango' is open string, I dampen the strings with my hand, then strum over the pickup. I don't have my plectrum?'

'Your hands soft, *jatelo*?'

'I haven't played seriously in weeks.'

'It showed!'

'*Wacha*. Knock it off, you Kondele man.'

Next was 'The Poet' Opiyo Willy's all-time Kisumu anthem 'Wasichana Wacha Tabia Mbaya', off the *There's No Mathematics In Love* album. I was back on stage in a flash and we started the warming benga-rumba groove. In the original recording this song was a duet featuring Agwenge's smooth controlled off-colour soprano and Aseela's love of melismatic, pop-worthy, and yet commanding tenor. But in this performance Agwenge's part was played by Ayo. 'The Poet' Opiyo Willy's songs were normally very wordy and the crowd loved the true things 'The Poet' loved to tell. Indeed during Opiyo Willy's era, our music had slowed down and the singers had room to talk... to say things. To provoke people and make people laugh at themselves. Listening in to the vocal bantering between Aseela and Ayo was to watch a duel. The two women actually quarreled each other through the song, each one trying to out-do the other much to the delight of the fans.

'They'll be fighting in a minute,' Roki Fela warned, whispered to me.

'*Hapana*,' I whispered back. 'Ayo's having fun, it's Aseela who's taking things too seriously. Look at her face. But I love these women. They go back a long way.'

Then a long way down, we built it into a call-and-response affair with hard questions asked and no answers given. Then it burst into a *soukous* score with riveting *sebene*.

There was a brief interlude and we were all nursing drinks and talking in the cool air outside. I took a much needed breather, downed a soda and walked about greeting people. Ayo was drunk and getting sad. 'Seems everyone thinks the world of him,' she said and she sighed. 'Women especially.' She was talking about KSK. My eyes scanned the crowd and I took in a number of smartly-dressed important-looking women.

'Which one?' I asked.

'There,' Ayo pointed. I saw a nice looking woman with a well-rounded face, sobbing piteously and being comforted by two other women. She was a looker even in such grief. She was biggish and well-dressed. She was important-looking; could have been woman of force and strength like my Mama Iva.

'Who's she?'

Ayo shrugged. 'All I know is that she is a bank manager.'

'Wow. She looks older than him.'

'Obviously. There are others. I doubt if we will carry this funeral through without women tearing their clothes.'

'Nonsense. He didn't marry any of them. Does he have other kids?'

'Possible. The one who bore his son with was here. I can't see her now.'

Biggy Tembo joined us then, just arriving. After shaking hands with me like Moi greeting Babangida, he asked, 'Where's KSK?'

'You mean the body? Russia,' he was told.

'Why not Lake Nursing? With my pal Agwenge, huh?' he asked, reached for the Guinness Aseela held out for him. Lake Nursing Home was the hospital where my brother Awenge was admitted with kidney complications.

'Ai yawa!' Aseela patted Biggy Tembo on the shoulder. 'Achieng Ayo knows this big man better than anyone. You could've gotten married to him. Long before I joined Victoria.'

Ayo was on her. 'Ask yourself why you're perfect for Biggy? Hm. Married man!'

'Give me the short version?' Aseela replied. 'I don't *really* love him.' She kissed Biggy Tembo openly on the lips and laughed delightedly.

'You don't love him?' Mawazo Ya Pesa put in. 'I think you do. One big happy family. I could write a song about this. For *Wana Academy*.'

'Why the love?' asked Ojua Kali Man.

'Sababu gani? Kwani hauoni, maze?,' replied Aseela. 'For one, we're not attached. He's married, that means I have my freedom. Two, I don't really love him, not in the emotional sense...we get along fine. Hey! Don't forget I'm artist.'

'Three?' asked Okach Biggy.

'Ah, three?' Aseela sighed. 'Three? I couldn't ever marry him but I could have a baby with him in a heartbeat.'

'Yeah, but keep love out, it complicates things.'

'Says who?'

"Says the Love Doctor. The Poet Opiyo Willy.'

Everybody laughed.

'Huh? How so?' Ayo asked. 'You don't want the bastard to cheat on you?'

Aseela nodded. 'I want to establish control. Freedom.'

That made me remember Aseela's recent abortion. 'I think you love him, don't deny it,' I said.

Aseela protested. She let out a long sigh, came close to me and whispered in my ear, 'Are you thinking about the abortion? It seemed a natural thing to do at the time.'

It amused me. She was sweet on him--mostly out of desperation.

And we carried on poking at each other and laughing and having fun like secondary school students. Mawazo then announced he had recently given out an engagement ring to his sweetheart.

Ayo beamed, faked out a genuine concern. 'Amazing. Hey, did you do it the traditional way? Luo chicks like it traditional. Y'know, on bended knees?'

'Ah?,' Mawazo grinned, 'No.'

'No?' 'The Poet' Opiyo Willy spoke for the first time. 'Oh, no, no. No. I don't get it. Oh, Ayo, that's a good one. I'll have to remember that on my next song. *On bended knees*. Well, we are musicians, aren't we? We sing about love and manners and tell men how to treat women like ladies and we show women how to love men. Right? Right?'

'Right,' somebody yessed him.

'But... really we can't be the perfect people we want the people to be. We are slobs for most of the time. Haha!'

515

'I know,' said Mawazo. *'Poleni basi.'*

I turned then to look at Mawazo. I had noticed how bad he looked some days ago when I met him at Lakeshore Studios. Today he still looked no better; he had lost almost half his weight, his laughs ended up in tearing coughs.

I took him to one side and demanded to know from him what was wrong... why was he in such bad shape and he told me he was recently diagnosed with TB and typhoid. He had quit smoking. As we talked, a young woman approached us and Mawazo introduced her to me as Judy, his fiancée. The young woman looked at me with wonder and said she was a great fan of mine. She looked cheerful and innocent. She told me she was a nurse and I only hoped she was now going to take good care of Mawazo. I only hoped whatever was eating him alive was not what I thought it was.

We chit-chatted, avoiding the newsworthy topics, for almost an hour. Ayo sashayed around serving drinks. Aseela was most amused, so carefree and chipper. The two went on yapping, mostly Aseela doing all the yapping, yapping enough for the two of them.

After filling his noggin with beer that only sought to give him migraines, Biggy Tembo announced he was not feeling well. He was leaving. Aseela put her arm around his neck and the two of them disappeared in the dark of the night.

Academy performed again and I joined them accompanying them in guitar. Then other bands played and the night wore itself out. Late in the midnight hour as we got drunk and gossiped, I learned from Mo that KSK was HIV positive. *Arum tidi* the bird of death was perching: more deaths were knocking.

The funeral service was held in the old Catholic church near Kibuye—only the second time, Mawazo said, that he'd set foot in a church. There were more people outside than in the sanctuary and the pews were almost empty. I accompanied the immediate family and a few friends to KSK's home village of Sega Ugambe in Ugenya where they held a private ceremony before the cheap cypress coffin was lowered into the earth.

And that was how 'Gentlemen's Gentleman' KSK Odongo completed his thirty-three year old journey.

8.

Pam was finally coming. She had been trying to get me for the past two weeks I was embroiled in KSK's funeral. She was coming in less than a week, her telegram said. And she wanted me to meet her at JKIA, Nairobi.

She was coming with my son.

You guess I couldn't hide my excitement. My passion for that articulate English woman had endured these three years and now, it seemed we'd finally put it to bed and moved ahead with it. Thinking about her, I normally felt a strange kind of disappointment and sense of loss. I often read her long letters in fine handwriting and wondered if we ever would have made the distance together—whether it remained a 'might have been'—or would the distrust still come between us? Her, on the other hand, couldn't. On numerous occasions she expressed confidence that we will meet and share the passion but not live together. Our love, she reckoned, was built on a dream. I recalled how I felt her emotions and sensations the first time we spoke. Immediately she knew how to connect with me the night of our highly successful premier show at Royal Albert Hall in Kensington, London in the summer of '87. And then there was the memory of her kisses, long and controlled yet insistent, irresistible and orgasmic.

When she emerged from the International Arrivals at JKIA, my still-alcohol-addled brain reflected joy and happiness through a paradoxical kaleidoscope of sensation and disconnect. My forehead made a light thud against the window of my soul as I closed my eyes and attempted to will the last of my drunkenness away. Trailing her was a brown boy with bushy afro. When Pam saw me and pointed, the boy ran to me and I ran to him and scooped him up and tossed him in the midair drawing shrieks of laughter from him attracting the attention of the entire lounge.

Pam was a beauty to behold.

Watching her move towards me, it struck me that she was seven years older than me. But it didn't matter; the longing and the eagerness in those deep blue eyes drank me up. Her age never really worried me. She was a woman who affected me at a deeper level. Even now after these years, I found myself becoming shy or self-conscious in her presence. I still felt about her what I normally felt when in the presence of Riana. I didn't want to hug her; I wanted to break the wall of mounting pressure. So, with my heart beating, still holding my son, I held her arm and walked her to where my car was parked.

In the car, she wondered why I couldn't even kiss her. I couldn't admit my sudden shyness as I held my third son. His tiny fingers gently brushed my shoulder, grasped my back and I held him tight to me. Then I pried his hands off and scrutinized his face. I was looking at a finer version of myself. It amazed me that me my boys always looked too handsome... Junior, Okello and now this tiny one called Daudi.

I thought of Junior and Okello, and more about Okello I felt sad and happy. His dashing smile, his puppy-like affection and soft sloppy touches. His unmistakable sweetness and affection was similar to Daudi's who, despite barely knowing me, was touching my face and bawling when taken away from me.

The next day we were in Kisumu relaxing and catching up in DreamScape. Pam fell head over heels in love with the place. She loved the house and the eucalyptus and the surrounding plateau. We had reached the place by night and she remained outside as I took the bags in. She remained outside admiring the place. When I rejoined her, she was leaning on the car; her back pressed against the door, and looked at my ghostly reflection, warm tones superimposed over the cool blues of the Kisumu night. Glimmering in the distance was Lake Victoria, appearing as if it was the edge of the world.

Jowi, one of my dogs jumped up and began barking, growling, and doing what dogs do when confronted with an adversary. Jowi was, however, smart enough to know not to mess his owner's guests and settled for barking.

'This place is beautiful, Dino,' she whispered.

'It's ten acres of property,' I told her. 'I want to make some money and turn it into a ranch. A real ranch for my retirement.'

'Yes,' she said simply. 'That's just great. It's so cool and fresh up in this place.'

'Every white person falls in love with Africa at first sight. Come on let's go inside.'

And as she admired my lonely home, I couldn't hide my fascination with her... could hardly believe this magnificent English woman was in love with me.

Then she leaned upwards to give me a kiss. It was short and reassuring. It made my spines tingle with promise. And it made the entire world seem peaceful, even if just for a few moments. After two hours of reminiscence, four glasses of wine and a pleasurable browse through photo albums, I held her hand and took her to my bedroom.

Sex happened and she was as insatiable as I remembered.

Hours later I was holding her, not saying a word. She looked too beautiful if it were not for the fact that she was crying and telling me about her divorce and the stigma of having a black child in a racist country. The fact that she was half-naked could have distracted me into drooling sexual feelings again. I couldn't dare; Daudi was in my lap.

Days later, I gathered courage and took her to meet my family and Mama liked her. Pam connected so wonderfully with the family, and was on joking terms with my brothers and sisters. Then I left Daudi with my sisters and we went back to DreamScape for more passion and intimacy. As we made love, I searched her face, but her look of honest pleasure was unambiguous. Her reaction was equally generous and she was as noisy and as insatiable as I remembered.

After the bliss faded, we could think straight and talk. She was interested in my plans for the band and was thrilled that my vision was to be continued, at least for a time. I shared her excitement about a proposal Miruka had made. He was interested in having us do another extended tour of Europe again and he wanted the entire band. We laughed at memories of our '87 tour, of the arguments and disagreements that had to be sorted before any decision could be taken about a concert, and marveled at how excellently the tour had turned out. People were still talking about it.

Then she switched on to a sad story.

'It broke my heart to have to do what I did. I think I got pregnant deliberately, y'know? Perhaps I thought I might hold on a little longer? Oh, God, I feel so foolish.'

'Why?'

'Because it's not right. It's actually what Millie Jackson sang about. I'm still in love with you but *loving you is wrong*. I thought I'd forget, but, I couldn't. I just had to see you. And now you're back in my life and it's just the same—just the same old feelings driving me crazy.'

'I couldn't forget you too, Pam...'

'Don't tell me that!' she snapped. 'My heart jumps right out of my chest when you say that. You hardly ever replied to my letters and whenever we spoke on the phone it was like I was forcing you. You were always in a hurry to go. All you care about is your band... your music. Nothing else.'

Here goes, the same tongue-lashing. And I thought this one was different. She was a well-spoken, socialite English woman with fine English manners. How did she get so fast into the quarreling gear like all my women? Maybe Angelou was right that the fault was with me. All these women treated me the same... like I was the villain or the devil incarnate. Riana, Angelou, Ayo, Mary-Goretti and now Pam. All of them.

'Actually,' I replied, 'I think I'm treating you well.'

'For now,' she commented. 'Because I'm here. Because I'm

here to help you market your music in Europe, yes. That's why I'm thinking of never leaving you, never getting you out of my sight.'

I heaved a heavy sigh and said, 'I'm sorry about your divorce, Pam.'

She nodded and turned to face the left side of the double bed. Then she said, 'I tried to make things up with my husband and he was ready to forgive me. But I couldn't. I had Daudi and... and...'

'He was black,' I finished for her.

Pam turned and nodded. 'It couldn't work, *thanks* to you. Now it's even more complicated.'

I glared at her. She looked straight into my eyes for one chilling moment. When she spoke, it was a whisper so fragile like falling leaves. 'Why do I love you like this, Dino? Why did I sacrifice my life? And when I see you, it's so... so silly.' She smiled. 'No promises? No commitment? What's this you put in me, huh? Can you please tell me?'

'Whatever you say,'

She looked at me. I smiled back. I returned the look calmly for as long as I could.

'Whatever I say?' she acknowledged, before squeezing in next to me. I draped my arm over her shoulders and she rested her head against me. The awful realization of what I'd refused to accept for four years slowly flooded my heart, drowning me in sadness. I had never stopped loving Pam. That was why I had stuck myself out the back of beyond. That was why I spent my days alone and miserable.

She was speaking so soft it was like she was speaking in my heart. 'My whole life was is so hopelessly screwed. I was on anti-depressants. I was sick.'

There was a slight lingering worry about her sadness that told me how lonely she was. I tightened my arms around her. I mulled, considered then shrugged. Clouds of pity gathered around my eyes.

'I had to come to you.'

I bit the bullet on that one. Good enough. I smiled.

She leaned forward and turned her head to look into my eyes. 'I want you to be a good daddy to Daudi. I want him to grow up thinking the world of you and I don't want him knowing what a whore you are. I want the best for him and I don't want him growing up in a racist country. I see the way your family loves him and he feels love for the first time in his life.'

All in the Family. I was obliging, very. My smile turned to a notion...'Did the divorce affect your daughter terribly?'

'I can't tell. She took it gratefully, and she told me to move on with my life. She lives with her daddy. You should ask about me now... my life and my future is Daudi,' she concluded. 'Will you help me raise him, Dino?'

Sadness, a thousand times worse because it was of my own making, engulfed my being and I dropped my head onto my arms and howled.

'Yes I will Pam.' I answered seriously.

'Really? You are so unpredictable.'

Maybe yes, maybe no. And we slept.

The next morning was light, clear, warm and breathless. A hint of mimosa on the air, rising mists turning hills into receding cut-outs, a callistemon splashing its scarlet among the green. Goats bleating in the grevilleas, and little herds boys shouting in unison. The Kisumu man-made world of noise, heat, concrete and stress didn't exist in these hills. It was a day in which nothing bad could happen.

The weather was too perfect to spoil. The program was simple: rehearsal. I had called the band to my home. A numbing depression dragged at my heart as I nailed up the garage-turned-studio door with spare timber and locked the cottage—a useless precaution considering every garage window was broken. After calling in to say good morning to Pam, I went outside to get some sunlight and read the newspaper and ended up in the garage tuning my guitar.

Pam came looking for me, asked me to help her prepare breakfast. Like all my women, she had the depressing habit of trying to possess me. We made and took breakfast. Then the band members arrived one by one and we got down to work. We were rehearsing as usual and she kept interrupting us, wanting to talk.

The conversation hadn't been much. I'd shuffled my feet, she'd asked me again what I thought of her settling permanently here in Kenya while looking at me intently. She could find something to do here. She could try her modeling career in Nairobi, combine it with her journalism. She could use her savings to start a public relations agency. How did she manage to make me feel so much like I was under a microscope? After I'd haltingly told her it was unthinkable raising the boy in Kenya and that I wanted them in England where they belonged, there'd been an uncomfortable pause.

'I'm not turning you away.' I said suddenly, looking at her, desperately hoping she believed me. 'I just want my son to be brought up in England. There's too much suffering here. You won't even fit in.'

'Is it about your other woman Ayo?' Pam wasn't smiling, and I couldn't tell if this was a joke or not. Especially not from behind a shimmering wall of whiskey hangover.

'Ah.'

'Owiro! *Omera* get back here we finish this thing, *bwana.*' someone yelled. A band member, with clear exasperation in his voice.

'*Yaye!*' I looked over my shoulder, sighed, and looked back, where Roki Fela was staring blankly at me with blazing eyes. He stopped, looked at the ground, and appeared to make a decision before turning back to me. 'If you have.... time, you can come here so that we continue with rehearsals. You are holding us back, *bwana.*'

I wrinkled my brow. 'Where's Benz?' Benz Benji Obat had joined recently again after KSK's death. Victoria and Academy had each gotten a good share of Delta Force's musicians.

He gave me a wry look and his half-smile. 'Benz can't play what you want and you know it.' My mind stuttered, halted, and I probably winced.

I looked at Pam. 'You better go back to work,' she suggested, 'I'll need someone to take me to Pandpieri to get Daudi.'

'Call me sister Akong'o'

I got back to the rehearsal and asked for my guitar which I tuned absent-mindedly thinking about my problems. How long was Pam planning on staying here caught up in her love for me when her real mission was to bag my band for Afrikan Dawn? There was no way she could ever resign from Afrikan Dawn and her story about resigning was crap. She had managed to tear us away from Attamaxx and AIT.

To where?

Then it occurred to me that African Dawn was keen to take over record marketing and distribution in East Africa and cut Sterns out of this region. That was why I had been persuaded to start my own label.

'Aaaah—aah....eeh.' Poposso's singing shattered my reverie and I became alert, although it was such a subtle shift I couldn't have said his facial expression actually changed in a way that I could tell outside my gut.

'Okay,' I said. 'Stop. Let's start. Sing that again!"

The singer stopped and everyone looked at me. The band laughed at me. I was visibly lost. It rankled me. But no, I thought, I wasn't ready for this, I wanted some clarity. Pam had brought confusion, not inspiration. And I wanted to make sure the business was right. Right now, it did take a minute, but everything was so great. I was inspired again, I was excited, it felt like I was a new artist. It just felt right, right now.

Slowly we worked on a chord progression, we built a beat. The instrumentalists worked slowly and created a plane that the singers, The Five Bosses, wallowed in.

Later in the afternoon, Pam had left me alone to work and went with Akong'o to Pandpieri. We rehearsed till six then called it a day. The musicians hoped on my pick up and I drove to Kondele where I normally dropped them to find means to their respective homes. After dropping them, I had at least an hour to kill before I would drive to Pandpieri to pick up Pam and Daudi.

The 4-wheel pick-up's high fuel consumption no longer buoyed me. I couldn't face a lonely evening, so I drove aimlessly, ending up outside the Aseela's at Arina. She had asked me to go to her place if I could. She had skipped the rehearsals and only called me in the evening; said she needed company, friendly company. I, on the other hand, didn't need Pam's smug certainties.

Aseela opened the door cautiously; then threw it wide in welcome. She was wearing a blue dress that showed her great figure. Her sweet smile appeared to ask, 'Hey you came after all?' I explained that life was dull and so much music business didn't fill the hole in my heart; neither did the fatty takeaway she normally brought me for lunch. Aseela had just turned nasty when Pam came and I didn't know why.

'You skipped the rehearsals today. Again.'

She ignored the question. 'Give me a break, *bwana,*' she said. 'A drink will do. I'll buy, come on. Let me get my jacket.'

So we found ourselves at Koch Koch and ordered lager. As we drank, I glanced across and caught her staring tight-lipped at me. She couldn't fool me, I knew she had a burning issue. It made a bit more sense. I waited until lager had loosened her then asked if everything was okay.

With a faraway look in her eyes, Aseela appeared to deliberate on where to begin. She begun slowly and, with an emotion-filled voice, told me about everything. About why Biggy Tembo was avoiding her all these weeks. About all the things that he put her through then he left her. And about her feelings for the burly singer who had messed her life. And why she now wanted to kill herself. I didn't move the whole time as she talked.

'Kill yourself? Why?'

'I don't know Dino. I've loved him for so long that I'm not sure of myself anymore. I want to be with him and all, but I want to think about this to see if this is what I really want. I want peace... to rest.'

I frowned slightly but immediately lit up. 'I don't get it. Biggy loves you too, I think. He *could* leave his wife for you.'

She called a waiter and ordered another whiskey. Now she had that look of hers that made me uncomfortable: looking stern and unapproachable. Aseela's alcohol abuse was something that often riled me. When she begun, she wouldn't stop till she probably hit a black out. As a person, she was ardent and energetic. It was even fair to say that she was a young woman of few words at first. When I hired her in 1988, the only thing that drew my attention to the then 22-year-old singer was the fact she was soft-spoken and full of respect. She uttered not a word until after her second song and thereafter limited herself to the most perfunctory of yesses and thank-yous.

Now she was grown, mature, spoilt and crudely bashed. But she still wasn't really a talkative person. So for her to be talking this much, she must have been really upset.

But in a blink she would take to the sky like an eagle when irked. Like the way she became irate when a journalist wrote shit about the affable ending of one of her songs in our *8th Anniversary* album.

Her drink came and she drank quickly. She smiled sadly. 'I want to tell you a sad story, Dino. Don't pity me. It's about ending my relationship with Biggy and my life. You've always respected me, thank you. I know you probably think rotten of me but I agree Biggy has been my greatest weakness. How it started? He made the move one night here at Koch Koch when we were both apeshit drunk and slobbered me with wet kisses.'

She had been unaccountably unhappy when she woke up to find herself cuddled up against him the next morning. That her hand had been lying lightly on his manhood had just been the frosting on the cake. They both stayed close to each other until Biggy started to drift her off into the most contented sleep in his drug life. He introduced her to marijuana and she accepted because it made their love making more pleasurable. She found, too, that this took a lot of emotional stress off her mind. Then he took her deeper into more harder drugs and before she knew it, she was using syringes. Then one time he took her to a club in Nairobi and asked her to have sex with his friend. She walked out, but he followed her and slapped her. Told her if she couldn't do it, he was leaving her. She loved him and couldn't afford to lose him. Weighing the pros and cons, she decided that she was undecided by the whole thing. She still needed time to think. Too many thoughts began to converge in her mind so Biggy started to sing, something he always knew would calm her down. She eventually yielded and he dragged her into his sordid life of perverted sex. She changed lovers frequently.

'Now he has AIDS and he is blaming me for it. I'm so bashed, Dino. There's no way I can continue living this life.'

AIDS? I wasn't surprised.

'Have you tested?'

She shook her head. She continued to hold my hand and gaze at me with such compassion that the lies that bind could no longer be sustained. 'I'm sorry, Dino. I'm not a careless lady. But Biggy hated condoms. His friends too... oh Good grief. I want to die. I know you now you think so low and rotten of me but I did what I did for love. I wanted to please Biggy and now I'm not sure if it has cost me my life. Hey, don't look at me like that, I never said I'm anybody's angel. I know you want me to be a nice girl and you've told me time and time again, but sorry I can't be. I'm spoiled deep down in my heart and I don't give a damn that I'm a bad girl. *Telo Owadgi* Odingo, don't you know that I'm an artiste and I'm just as messed up you are. We are all messed up. We carry the burden of entertaining and educating people to make the world a better place. We can't be good people; we're artistes. As for Biggy, I love him and if loving him is wrong, I don't want to do right. Heck, I don't care that I am his mistress... what a shame. I don't care. I love him and I could die for him. I'll die but it's okay. I'm an *artist*.'

I looked up sharply. 'You can't live your life and die for someone, Auma. Your life is yours, not Biggy's. You can't live your life for him. It simply isn't right being a priority in someone's life when to him you're only an option. Life is given to us by God. It doesn't belong to us. We can either accept it as a precious gift, enjoying it as much as possible, or squander it on greed, lust and trivial disputes. To look for meaning and purpose in nature is a form of insanity to which I am glad I have never succumbed. But don't worry too much, you've told me your story. You had to tell someone like me to get it off your chest. You're still our queen in the band. Do me a favour, go test yourself and let me know the results.'

The rest of the evening was not like old times. Aseela looked sad, sobbed and sobbed and sobbed as she drank. Blew her nose and sobbed silently. Then she smiled. Wiping her tears, her voice husky, she said she was happy. Her burden had been lifted, guilt was gone, and we relaxed in our friendship.

She had more surprises as we were getting ready to leave. Taking a deep breath, closing her eyes and sniveling, she took my hand. 'There's something else....' She sniffed.

I smiled at her and nodded. Waited.

With another strange far-away look on her face, she spoke. 'I... I'm pregnant again.'

The words of the troubled woman barely entered my tortured ears; my mind virtually caught a fire as I reeled withering on my drunken state. My mind cleared instantly. My mouth hung open. 'Again?'

She nodded.

'Biggy again?'

Again she nodded.

I hated Biggy now. There he was, having (supposedly) cleaned up his act after the drug-fueled craziness of the Nairobi years. But his elevated position as singer of good ranking in Victoria from '85 till '88 should have sobered him instead of taking him off on the crazy journey he was still languishing on, still way off in the future. After all wasn't he the oldest musician in the Victoria family and didn't he have the most serious family? A wife who adored him and three boys to raise? Look what he done to Aseela. He had now dragged a young woman into a life of sordidness and taken away her self-worth, the mindless perv.

'Auma, I told you...'

'Dundos, I know. I know what you told me... heck, Abonyo *telo owadgi* Odingo you did nothing but tell me... I know you love me and I thank you. I know you told me time and time again all these years to break away from Biggy... I know. People have told me, everybody is against it. My mother is not talking to me because of it. Frankly, I don't know what he did to me. I know shit happens but why can't I open my eyes and see. I mean, I'm in this with my eyes and ears wide open and I know the whole thing is fucked up. People say he bewitched me. I know he consults witchdoctors. I can't break away and he has taken away my decency. I... I want to die. I have become something beyond the scope of decency.'

'Knock it off, Auma, stop rumbling and feeling sorry for yourself. You made your bed, you lie on it. I want Biggy to bear responsibility now. Enough is enough.'

'I don't want to tell him he's the father; he wouldn't let me keep it.'

'Good gracious, how could you? How could you be so.... so...'

'Careless,' she supplied.

'Yes. Careless!'

'It happened. It happens. I'm a woman.'

'So how are you going to deal with it?;

She snuggled closer, looking at me intently in the eyes, her eyes strangely intense and radiant. 'What if we say it's yours, huh?'

I gulped and shook my head No, 'What? Seriously? No. hell NO.'

'I need your help. Biggy respects you... even fears you. We could create a story that you and I are... you know... And he'll be okay with it since you're our big boss and I'm a beautiful woman, the Queen of Victoria. As long as it's you, Dinos, he'll be okay. And that's the only way I'll save this baby's life.'

I shook my head. No. 'No, Auma. I'm afraid that's not going to happen. I'll give you a choice, sweetie,'

She nodded eagerly, looking at me intensely, giving me *that look*. 'I don't think you're ready for motherhood now.'

She heaved a heavy sigh, gulped down her drink. 'Okay? Why not? I'm a woman like any.'

'You're a beautiful woman.'

'I know. Men tell me. I'm a broken woman now.'

I rolled my eyes, paused. 'There's the *other* thing you can do other than leave with guilt,' I said.

She leaned forward with an 'uh, like what?' look on her face.

I leaned closer to her ear and made a sound like a flushing toilet.

Aseela made a face. She furled her lips, shook her head '*Chieth*,' she hissed, 'nice haul. Look *telo Owadgi* Odingo, if you're thinking abortion, forget it. I've been through hell with Biggy in the name of love. I want to keep this baby for all good reasons. I want to be a mother... a good mother. I want some decency in my life. It's my choice.'

Some choice!

9.

I had taken Pam to Dunga beach to buy some fresh tilapia and we eventually sat down to talk business. Pam always had hard questions for me. You know the way *wazungus* have too many questions. Pam, being one of them, was no different. Today it

was no different, only it was a harder question: *what was I worth?*
Truth is I wasn't really a rich man. Comfort, yes I had. I had a
home in the Nandi Escarpment with a breathtaking view of
Kisumu. I was in the league of Zaïrean soukous stars like Aurlus
Mabele and I was driving a Volvo and a Mercedes. I had some
land and rental houses. I had a fishing business and had recently
ventured into export of *omena*. But I wasn't really rich; I was
constantly working for the next day like an average African.

We African musicians, even the most successful ones are not
rich in the mega-rich class of rock stars and I don't know why.
Even Franco at the highest point of his career with *Mario*
in '85, '86 was just another normal African. Before I entered into
active music I used to think the answer was in the purchasing
power and bad records. But now I knew the real reason. True,
people never really bought our records. But we had made so many
records and sold enough to make us live fairly comfortable lives
by Kenyan standards. The reason I was so famous yet I and my
musicians were struggling was because my records had been
massively pirated and the pirates were still in business. Last year a
young man wrote me from UK saying he had all my records yet I
had no licensing or distribution deals with anyone there. Neither
did Attamaxx know about this.

In order to re-enter that market through the African Dawn
contract, we needed to re-issue all our previous albums. The
album sleeves were going to be re-designed. Every effort was
being made to make Victoria big and bigger in the market and in
the minds of people.

Thanks to Pam's efforts, all our records had this year become
available in all the major European cities. I went further and
bought her idea to sell the masters to 'pirates' and other
producers. I had ready-mixed master tapes of all our previous
best-selling albums including our European tour collections, *Lake
Victoria Breeze, Golden Horizon, Wend Osote, Tiacha!, There's No
Mathematics In Love, Chris Tetemeko,* Agwenge's *You Came Too
Soon, Luopean* and *8th Anniversary* albums available for out-and-

out sale at an asking price of 2 million Kenya Shillings!

If this worked I was going to be a real millionaire!

But members of my marketing team were confident. My albums were selling a minimum 15,000 copies per month in Africa with the bestsellers *There's No Mathematics In Love* and *Luopean* topping about 60,000 each. As we were releasing at least two albums a year, the totals were building up steadily.

In the midst of it all, I was determined to succeed more as an artist. I wanted this. It's difficult to want something, not knowing what it'll mean to you to have it until you do, than internalize that old adage of loving things and being willing to let them go. When I formed Victoria, it was as an outlet for my artistic output. My dream was to create decent music and make a name. I never dreamt of being rich, mine was to record some good music, play some club shows and go home. But now it appeared like there was some really big money to be made using music and African Dawn was awakening me to this reality. I could feel the smell of money. I could feel the itch of it in my palms. Money was coming and for once I was going to be rich. But I didn't know how to respond to that whiff of money. I was so in love with my music, so much in obsessed with the desire to succeed in creating a musical enterprise; at the Urban Benga style I had created.

Pam was busy pushing African Dawn's next agenda. Pam knew she would sell it to me. She knew I would buy it, and I did. The plan was simple but well thought-through. Also in the deal which African Dawn, no doubt, were assiduously crafting for their own long term benefit, they were to purchase Lakeshore Studios from Uncle and make it into a 48-track. But in the event Uncle turned down their offer, they were ready to build or buy us a building in Kisumu and turn it into a recording studio, stuff it with state-of-the-art musical instruments. I would get fifty percent ownership to the facility that would also have rehearsal rooms, a club, offices and instruments for hire. I was to act as producer and bring in many fine new bands to record there, not only Victoria.

This was heart-jeeringly good. The thing standing between me and total accomplishment of my vision was a good studio. Without a studio, what you were finding out about my artistic output was inadequate; it was mostly masturbation. With a studio I was going to take full control of my product.

Pam understood this very well. I knew she was pushing in the Trojan Horse and His Excellency Ambassador Okoth Ochot cautioned me about it. Whatever the risk was, I was ready to take it. We were to use it to rehearse and record for free. They would handle marketing and distribution of all records. And they were to bring their engineers to work in the studio and arrange and direct recordings and create marvelous sound.

Pam and I were buried in the thick of reforming Victoria. By the end of one month of meetings and phone calls and chit-chatting with mucky-mucks, we got everything worked out.

For the band, Pam said, 'You guys need smart uniform.' And she personally made the choices of the fabric and separated the designs and colours of the singers from those of the instrumentalists. She directed these developments in a fair and constructive fashion, balancing the group's shortcomings with a reassessment of Victoria's many strengths.

10.

September rolled around and we rode the plaintive wails of new front man, 'Power Voice' Poli Poposso to a string of heart-jeering shows here in Kisumu. And I tell you things could get very messy whenever Poposso hit the dance floor at Kondele.

Fans loved Poposso, he had succeeded in duplicating Mawazo's emotive falsetto. With his distinct voice, he was poised to be another Mawazo. I was pushing him to the front rank and a new album was in the works. The other replacement vocalist, Okach Biggy, was also succeeding fast in curving an identity.

People thought I was responsible for this but, no. It was the fans. I was always sensitive to what the fans wanted. The significant foundation of the band had been Mawazo and Biggy Tembo, whom the two new singers now represented. It was natural.

My only disappointment was that the Five Bosses vocal squad appeared not to be working. Poposso now stuck on his own and the band was a good vehicle for him. The remaining four bosses tried to keep the journey brand viable as we approached the end of the year, but their vocals were all stiff. The idea of Five Bosses, it appeared, had only lasted as long as the double album *8th Anniversary*. I had become a little aloof on the artistic side of things and was more concerned about the business side. I was away in Nairobi to negotiate with Attamaxx over our master tapes and crack yet another piracy racket. Victoria was coughing badly. Aseela was making mutinous noises in the press. Roki Fela was looking for a way out and 'The Poet' Opiyo Willy had secretly recorded a single with Academy. Pajos was performing with a Zaïrean band. The grand old men, Mzee Frank and Mifupa Ya Zamani were talking to people about retiring from music.

I returned to Nairobi later in the month and was in a position to pay salaries. The band regrouped and the voices of dissension died.

His Excellency Ambassador Okoth Ochot came to DreamScape one bright morning with a new deal. It was something we hadn't done before and it was politics, stupid. Forum For Restoration of Democracy—FORD—wanted a song to drum up support to remove Kanu from power. It was not the first time political proposals of such nature had been given to me during general election times. But this one I had to consider. For very good reasons. Kenya was feverish, sick with burning hunger of removing Kanu from power. Well, Kenyans were sick and tired and FORD was beginning to fill Kanu's warm bed with burning charcoal.

In the deal, FORD's operatives wanted me to compose and record a song denouncing Moi and Kanu. More people put pressure on me to do the song, one was a woman who was a prominent member of Kisumu urban politics. Others were a lawyer, an activist, a nosey no-gooder typical Kisumu heckler and big mouth, an aspiring councilor and an all-around in-your-face opinionated University lecturer.

It was a doable thing, though. As an artist, I didn't compose to order. But, well... money, oh, money. I needed to finish my flat in Wigot and I could also do with some free money politicians were spending. It was my money, anyway: I was a taxpayer. Nobody in the band questioned my decision... I was the bandleader, wasn't I. I guess deep down I was as corrupt and as greedy as any average Kenyan. I took the money and asked 'The Poet' Opiyo Willy to write the song of all songs; an anthem.

The artistic direction during the rehearsals saw Victoria turning away from the loveless introspection of previous releases and approaching a more radical, political world view—as signposted by 'The Poet' Opiyo Willy in his driving song 'Yawa Kanu Tho.' No Nairobi producer wanted to do this LP, but Uncle, who was planning to contest the Kisumu Town parliamentary seat and was one of the top financiers of FORD, agreed to produce it. So we recorded it at Lakeshore Studio. The LP was an immediate critical and commercial smash. It was another product of my talent and genius, so I think I made a hearty contribution to Oginga's propaganda machine to remove Moi from power.

In the album 'The Poet' Opiyo Willy discussed several issues close to our hearts and maybe said things he shouldn't have said but said them, nonetheless. It captured the general Luo feeling about bad politics that had pushed us to the dangerous edge. Kisumu was colossally lost to Moi's idea of *maendeleo* (read civilization). We Kisumuans were used to being shunned and neglected and made to eat dregs. For decades, the Government turned its back on us and made Nyanza a wasteland. We were used to being sidelined and made to put up with under-every-word-you-can-think-of due to our unyielding radical political stand and our unwavering loyalty to Jaramogi Oginga Odinga. All Luos were fed up... but again we were used to it. Ours was a generation that was never going to see power. We perpetually stood outside watching Oginga struggling to undo the grave mistake he made in 1958. I put this in another unrecorded song. We lived in what the Nairobians considered the cemetery, which was a vast wasteland which we could only use productively to bury our dead in. If you are a Luo in Kenya you stand cursed. You don't need to be told you are in trouble; you are reminded time and again you are clever for nothing, you are all talk, and you are acting like an unskilled fisherman. If you are a Luo, don't be fooled there is any other way out of this: we all have the curse of Sisyphus. We naturally need to be in politics and fight from within before it swallows us. With Oginga and the FORD party, we were, once again, at the brink of populist-infested democracy killing Kanu to the last man, woman and child.

We could say all these things as artists and make our people feel angry or bad and put our destiny to hopelessness and ask hard questions but to me, I knew all this was a waste of time and money. With Moi's awesome political-gladiator system, we stood no chance. He was the president and the grandmaster, and he had everything in his bag: money, the media, the dogs, the knuckle dusters, the police, the GSU, the army, the navy, the air force, foreign powers that wanted to do business with him plus a battery of Kanu sycophant hyenas who still needed to eat.

Just because Kisumu wasn't portrayed as a slobbering, panting, salivating hotbed of anticipation and drooling expectancy didn't mean there was anything abnormal about the town and about our lives. Kisumu is as much a town of problems as it is a town of drama, subdivision of fantasy. Drama? This incongruous viewpoint spills over to my inadequate efforts at describing my pursuit as a human being. I served Kisumu (musically) and I did it well; and *really* not unwillingly. Kisumu never got tired of hearing us and dancing to our beats. But in matters politics, spare me. I was always a conservative soul. Conservative ever since I nearly died in the Russia massacre in 1969. I *hated* the monster called politics. Did you not see or read about the nasty things that happened to our people in more-or-less rapid fire order? Ofafa in 1953, Agwenge (read Argwings Kodhek) in 1969, Mboya in 1969 and Ouko last year.

October 25th, 1969 is a day I nearly died as a kid during the Russia massacre. Oh Pandpieri, my cradle, I sure lived, then, as a boy and grew up observing things. Now, as an adult, I could commit the memories to music in a lively and extensive fashion. How could I fail Kisumu? How had I failed Kisumu? You might understandably ask. That's not the issue. The issue is for all my efforts, then and now, what so far constituted my rendezvous in Kisumu will amount to a prequel.

Problems persist. Point of fact? I might as well not have bothered with all this stupid politics: I was not a political animal and I had bigger problems here in Kisumu.

The tapes were ready for mixing and ripping. I was leaving for Nairobi in a week to have the tracks mixed at Attamaxx and have production completed.

Pam suggested that we do a double album. She knew the hit potential in the album.

I wanted a maxi single.

11.

When Victoria Academy folded a scant towards the end of the year, Aseela prevailed upon me to welcome Ojua Kali Man back to his old position. Roki Fela said no.

On the eve of the launch of *Yawa Kanu Tho*, I spent a good evening with our manager His Excellency Ambassador Okoth Ochot, 'The Poet' Opiyo Willy, Biggy Tembo and Aseela at Koch Koch getting drunk. Another guy was with us. Pally Ouko was his name and he was the owner of Club Swagore Aswaga down by the lake along Marine Lane. The Ambasador had worked out a contract with him and we were to play VIP shows there every weekend for the next six months.

Ong'any the barman told me I had a call. It was Riana. She wanted to see me. I knew what she wanted. My mood was fouled, I battled conscience versus misgivings, but I knew I was game for a good hump. I finally stole away to be by himself. The day was uneventful as ever, and it passed far too quickly. For a while, I imagined how I might resist Riana, and ponder how much guilt I could endure. I really wasn't in the habit of being double-minded and I respected Pam. But Riana was someone I respected even more. The choices remaining were thin. I cruised restaurant rows, then got lost in the mid-town area before winding up on a small street artery and there I was at Agina's Kitchen next to Mama Tom's.

Pam liked Agina's food. They were old fashioned and of a time I cherished. They even had the real *aliya*. I was undecided as I bought takeaway of chicken and brown *ugali* known as *kuon bel*. Pam and Daudi loved Luo traditional vegetables laced with sour milk and *mor dhiang*.

Then I got in the Chevy and drove towards Kondele. I was almost home, and now I was starting to feel a little sad. I was not fully sure why. I wondered if Pam and Daudi were still up. Even if it wasn't the answer, I would have liked to see Riana tonight. We had brought a new life into the world and I, at least, wanted to bargain for my rights. Riana was the only woman who had given me something very special and something no other woman had given me: a daughter. A daughter that she didn't seem very thrilled about.

For reasons best known to her, she had chosen to cut me away from my daughter's life completely. I had only been shown photos. It was not blackmail, it was Riana's obscure principles which I respected still. She was not a demanding person, she had her priorities and she had her needs and she knew how to rationalize her demands. She only looked for me when she wanted essential needs fulfilled. Maybe that was why I was feeling different about her now—because I knew the consequences of our meetings: coupling. In her twenty-nine years, she could trust only me, not any other man. I could handle it, even if I didn't have much (if any) say in my future role as the father to her daughter. To me, it looked like we had a legal relationship now: we both had rights—her as the mother of my daughter and me the father. She was a bigger beneficiary.

Cars passed me, some honking. I was going at about forty kilometers per hour below the speed limit. As I passed Kong'er Shopping Centre and my neighborhood came into sight, I started to feel sick in my stomach, as if my guts were a loose mass of fish insides and ice being crunched by a large, cold hand. I branched on the rutted murrum road leading to DreamScape and as I neared, the dogs started barking even before my truck's headlights touched the wooden gate.

The dogs were barking furiously, a bizarre welcome routine. I brought the car to a stop and shut off the engine for a moment to collect myself. It was the barking that must have woken Pam up. Suddenly the lights of the bedroom went on. I saw the naked shape my *mzungu* woman silhouetted against the blind.

Heartfelt Thanks and Appreciation

It wasn't an easy thing writing a book about African music in the 1980s. It was even harder linking that with writing about my hometown. I had to wrack my brain doing research. Let's face it, if you're a Kenyan writer, the late seventies sucked. You couldn't have had more harder work spining the thin and scanty information available about Kenyan music into a book and I didn't want to do that. So I had to come up with a better idea if wanted to stick to the seventies and eighties, but I didn't want to write a complete oldies book, either. So I started talking to people who believed in me.

The mostly part had to do with the painter Patrick Adoyo, my art mentor. He suggested that I broaden my scope and write a book about Kisumu. Well, Patrick Adoyo told me great stories of the old Kisumu which shaped my story a great deal.

I would like to thank Tabu Osusa of Ketebul Music in Nairobi, for information on the Nairobi music scene in the 1980s. The same goes to Kabila Kabanze Evany of Orchestre Mangelepa, Mwalimu James Onyango Joel, Jerome Ogolla, Tabu Ngongo and Sammy Kasule. Akech Obat Masira of Ramogi Ensemble provided a background on the Kisumu art scene of the '80s; the staff at Department of Literature, Maseno University were also helpful in many ways. The singer and guitarist Musa Juma and his band Limpopo provided me with perfect model for fiction and I sat in with the band for many hours in Kisumu during the December holidays of 2007, later accompanying them on tour of Mombasa.

I am further indebted to Margaret Masbayi, of Nairobi, for her initial interest in this book and ispiring my shift into writing career in general; of course I cannot forget my buddy, Patrick Muraguri. Linguist and translator Alain Mpetsy of DRC graciously offered a lot of information about Congolese music and provided Lingala translations; Janet Adhiambo, George Nyabilla, Leo Ooro, Loise Karanja and many other Nairobians whose helpful friendships through very difficult times in Gill House were crucial to the inspiration of this book.

Other Books by Okang'a Ooko

Okang'a Ooko
Tandawuoya

He was a zealous man and his idea of Christianity was his own.

When Tandawuoya finds religion and accepts Jesus as his Saviour, he is convicted of all his sins and he takes matters into his own hands.

He lives a life of salvation as an eccentric Christian, trying to force all around him to accept Jesus, trying to enforce his teaching of End Time. His beliefs have evolved in some pretty radical ways and he is convinced the world is in the Apocalype. He fails miserably when he tries street preaching, casting out devils, speaking in tongues, and laying hands on the sick. *All the trappings of Christian divinity fail.*

He is in a severe battle of conscience against his personal demons; his old life continues to follow him and he can't shake off the lusts of the flesh and it drives him insane. After many Christians rip him off his money and a pastor's wife seduces him, he is forced to examine every interaction, and is confounded with the way in which his notions of reality become suddenly – irrevocably – stripped bare.

Tandawuoya is a story of loss, a story of destruction, a story of disappointment, a story of renewal. It's the story of dark extremes of an eccentric faith. It's a story that might not have been written. It's a story of dark dark evil in the hearts of men. In combining fantasy and allegory with minutely located naturalistic narrative this book turns out to be another of Okang'a Ooko's tour-de-force gems with twists and turns.

oba kunta octopus

OKANG'A OOKO
When You Sing To The Fishes

**He is back for some unfinished business in the town,
the city that made him. Kisumu.**

Guitarist Otis Dundos is back in Kisumu, the addictive and possessive
lakeside town. Back in the '80s, he was the Urban Benga guitar
legend. His commercially potent mix of hard benga and lofty rumba
was loud with a culture surrounding it, and a cult-like following. It
ignited an entire generation of music fans. It made him rich and
famous.

When he left Kisumu twenty years ago, it was a sudden unpleasant
event. Everything ended in tragedy. He was twenty-nine years and at
his peak . Today he still is the artsy man: the musician, the guitarist.
People have died fast; the men and women who helped him make
music... they have all died or wasted away. Is he about ready to follow
suit? What is left? The past has unfulfilled dreams, good life, nice cars,
easy money, expensive perfumes, glamourous women, living on the
road and in the studio. And conniving band mates, thieving
promoters and clever pirates.

The present is bearable but holds no promise: he is forty-seven. If he
has to accept his forced retirement, he has to learn to be a local
Kisumuan, not the famous name. He reminisces about the romantic
encounters of '70s. The future is uncertain. He is searching for sanity
and happiness. Happiness? In Kisumu lives the woman whose
unfulfilled love still dwells his heart. But his mind is too bamboozled
to even think.

oba kunta octopus

OKANG'A OOKO
Businesswoman's Fault

Thoth has a reputation.

He has a reputation as an organiser of grand schemes for the cartel-run Government. And in Nairobi, Kenya, corruption is King. His email marketing monitoring company is a side-show. *He has a plan.* He wants to expand his business into a full marketing force and he wants an existing advertising agency to take over. But in his grand scheme, he picks on the wrong turkey.

Atieno Mary, too, has a reputation.

She is ruthless, strong-willed never-say-die woman who has built her advertising agency from nothing into a million-shilling-making brand. Deep within this desirable woman burns the violent fires that could destroy a man.

Thoth had swindled his way to success. He thought he knew the ropes; and women. Maybe he did. But he didn't know Atieno, otherwise he'd have realised that he was just another fly stumbling into the deadly web of a woman who was beautiful to look at; but lethal to mess with.

Businesswoman's Fault is a collection of seven stories that zip along at a breakneck speed and points to the reason why Okang'a Ooko has gained such reputation for explosive and non-stop action. He is Kenya's new master storyteller and his debut thriller hits his peak, must be read at a sitting.

oba kuñfa octopus

Printed in Great Britain
by Amazon